BOOK TWO

BRIAN K. VAUGHAN

WRITER

FIONA STAPLES

ARTIST

FONOGRAFIKS

LETTERING + DESIGN

ERIC STEPHENSON

COORDINATOR

IMAGE COMICS, INC.

ROBERT KIRKMAN CHIEF OPERATING OFFICER | ERIK LARSEN CHIEF FINANCIAL OFFICER | TODD MCFARLANE PRESIDENT | MARC SILVESTRI CHIEF EXECUTIVE OFFICER | JIM VALENTINO VICE-PRESIDENT
ERIC STEPHENSON PUBLISHER | COREY MURPHY DIRECTOR OF SALES | JEFF BOISON DIRECTOR OF PUBLISHING PLANNING & BOOK TRADE SALES | CHRIS ROSS DIRECTOR OF DIGITAL
SALES | KAT SALAZAR DIRECTOR OF PR & MARKETING | BRANWYN BIGGLESTONE CONTROLLER | SUSAN KORPELA ACCOUNTS MANAGER | DREW GILL ART DIRECTOR
BRETT WARNOCK PRODUCTION MANAGER | MEREDITH WALLACE PRINT MANAGER | BRIAH SKELLY PUBLICIST | ALY HOFFMAN CONVENTIONS & EVENTS COORDINATOR
SASHA HEAD SALES & MARKETING PRODUCTION DESIGNER | DAVID BROTHERS BRANDING MANAGER | MELISSA GIFFORD CONTENT MANAGER | ERIKA SCHNATZ PRODUCTION ARTIST
RYAN BREWER PRODUCTION ARTIST | SHANNA MATUSZAK PRODUCTION ARTIST | TRICIA RAMOS PRODUCTION ARTIST | VINCENT KUKUA PRODUCTION ARTIST | JEFF STANG DIRECT MARKET
SALES REPRESENTATIVE | EMILIO BAUTISTA DIGITAL SALES ASSOCIATE | LEANNA CAUNTER ACCOUNTING ASSISTANT | CHLOE RAMOS-PETERSON LIBRARY MARKET SALES REPRESENTATIVE

WWW.IMAGECOMICS.COM

ga™

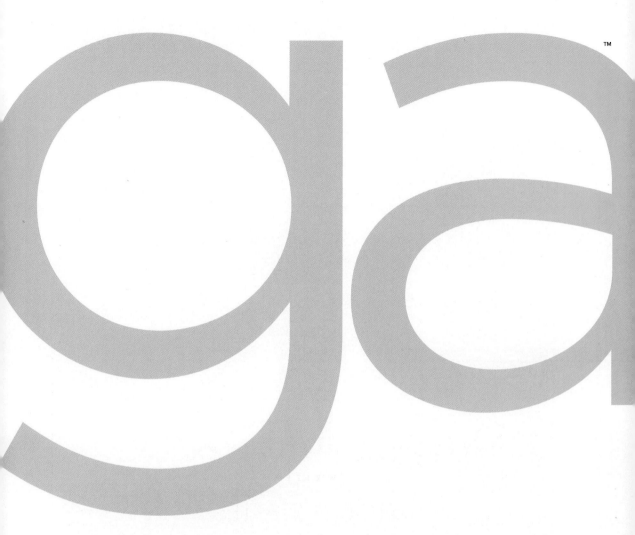

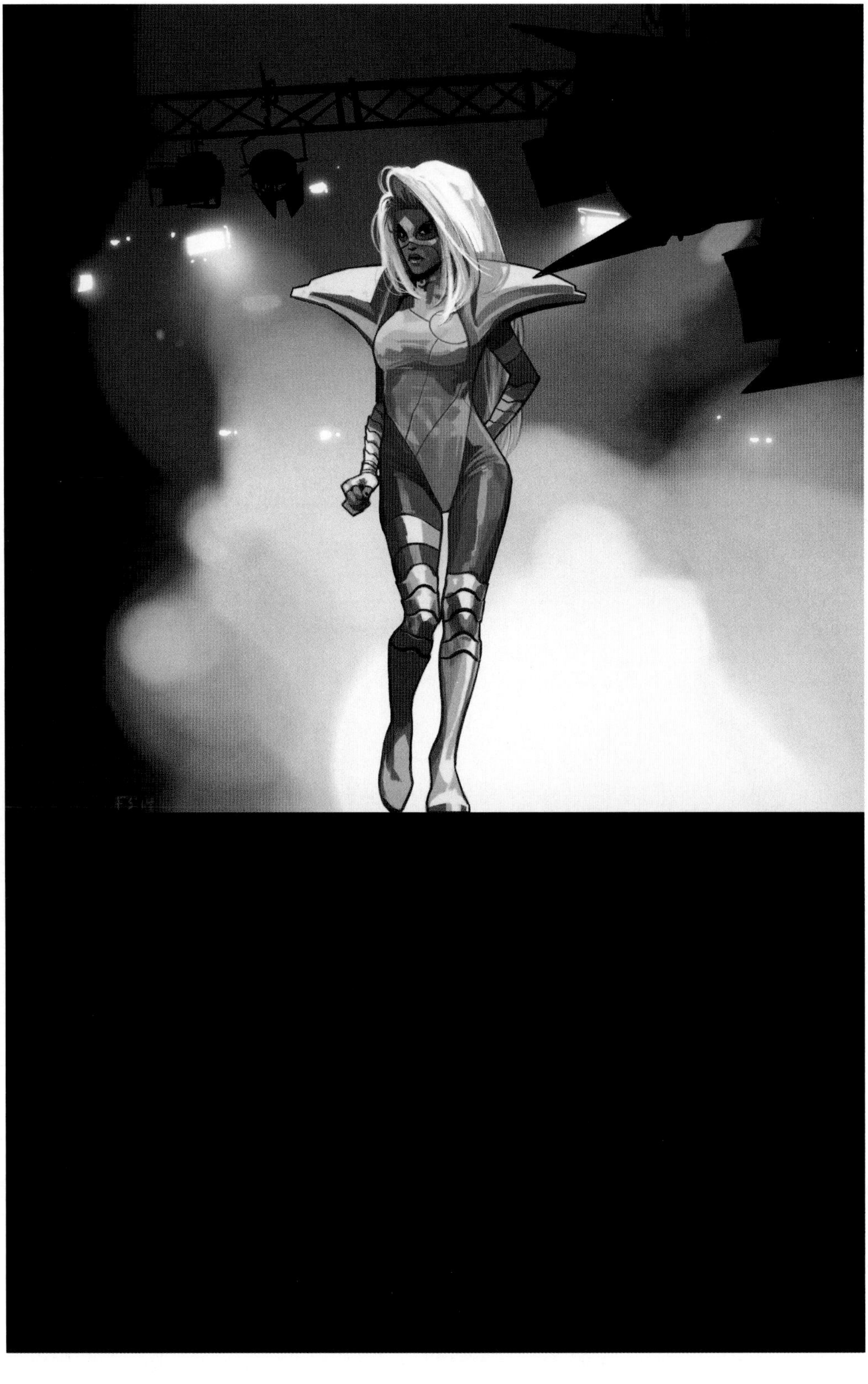

CHAPTER

NINETEEN

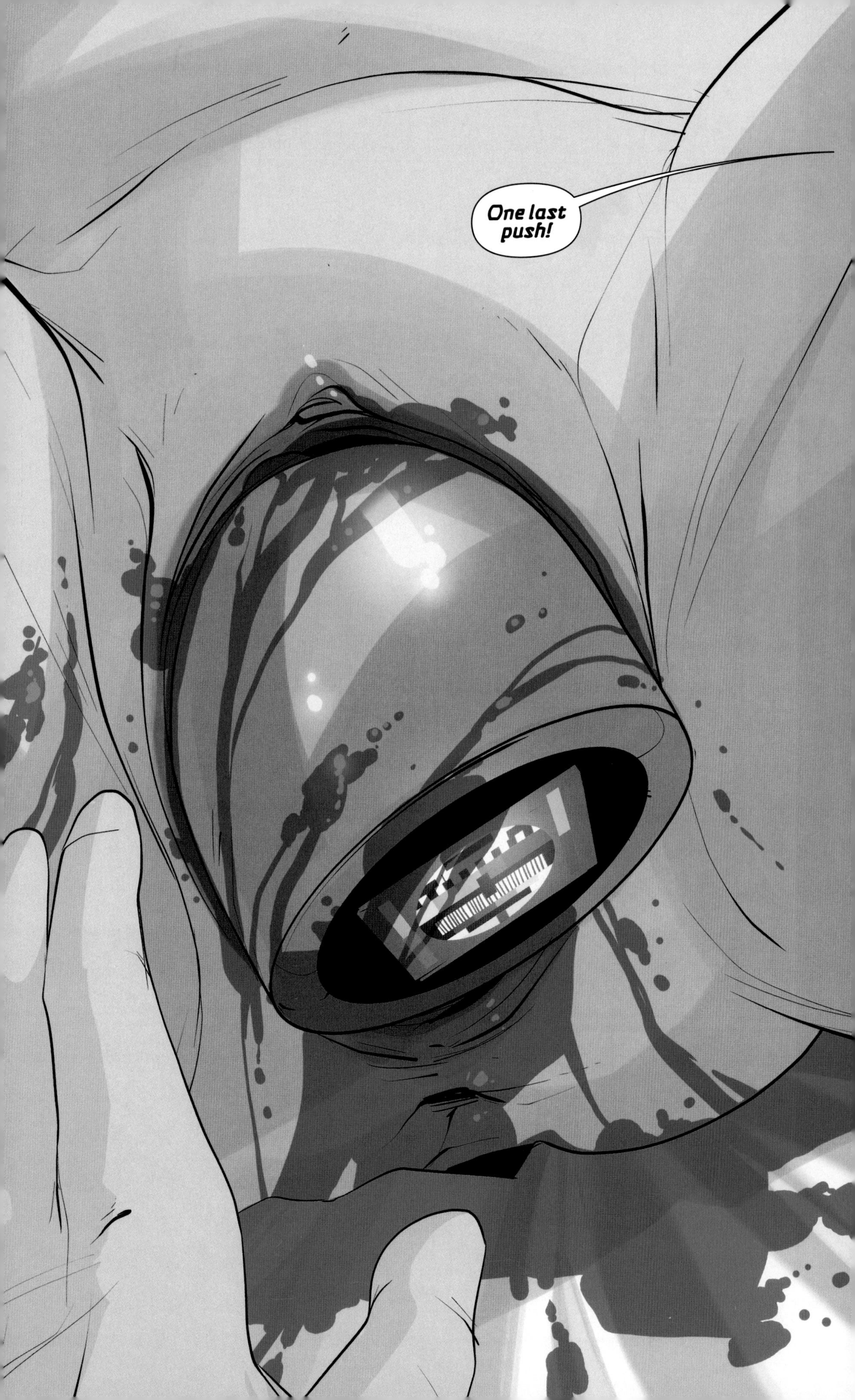
One last push!

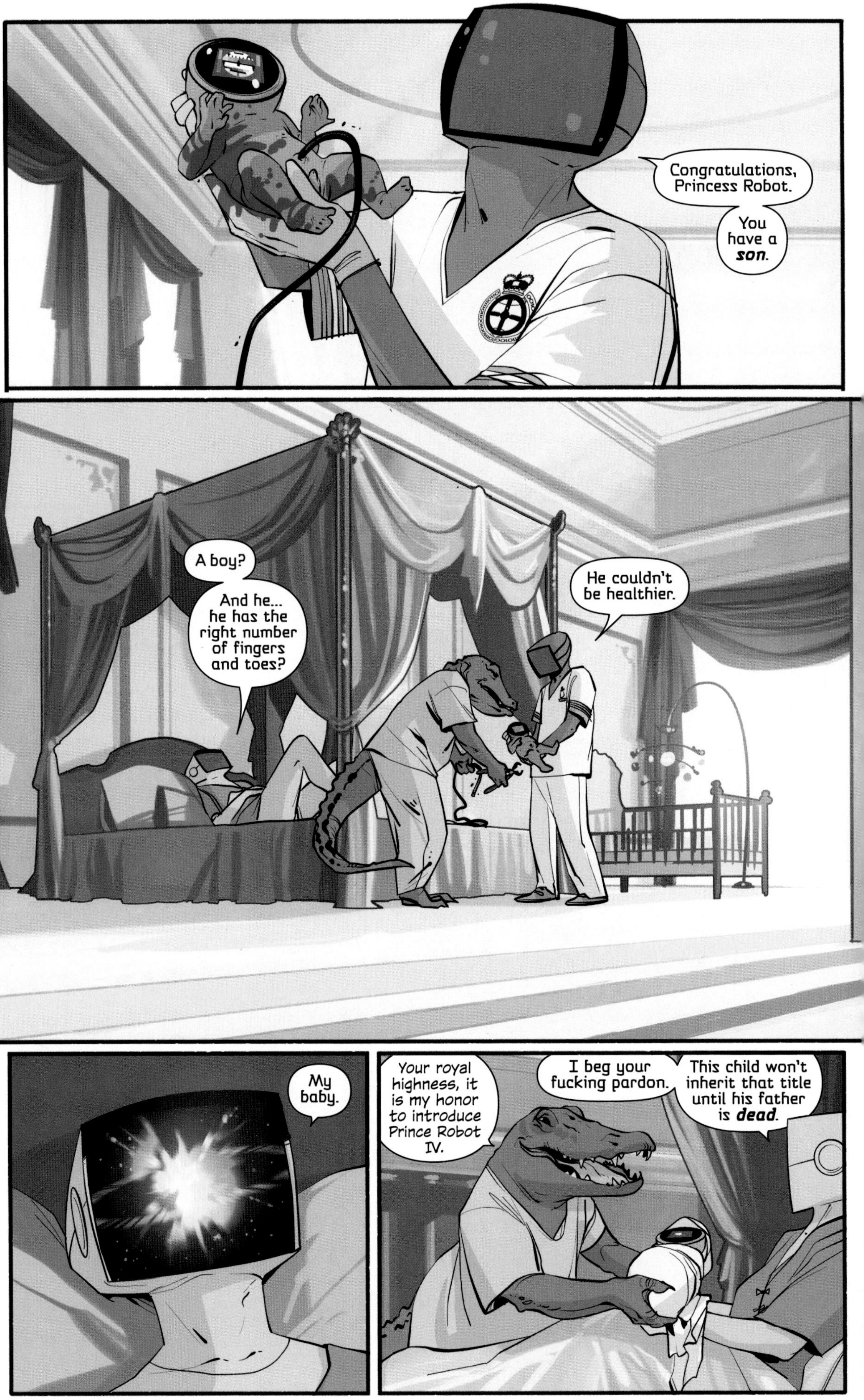
Congratulations, Princess Robot.
You have a ***son***.
A boy?
And he... he has the right number of fingers and toes?
He couldn't be healthier.
My baby.
Your royal highness, it is my honor to introduce Prince Robot IV.
I beg your fucking pardon.
This child won't inherit that title until his father is ***dead***.

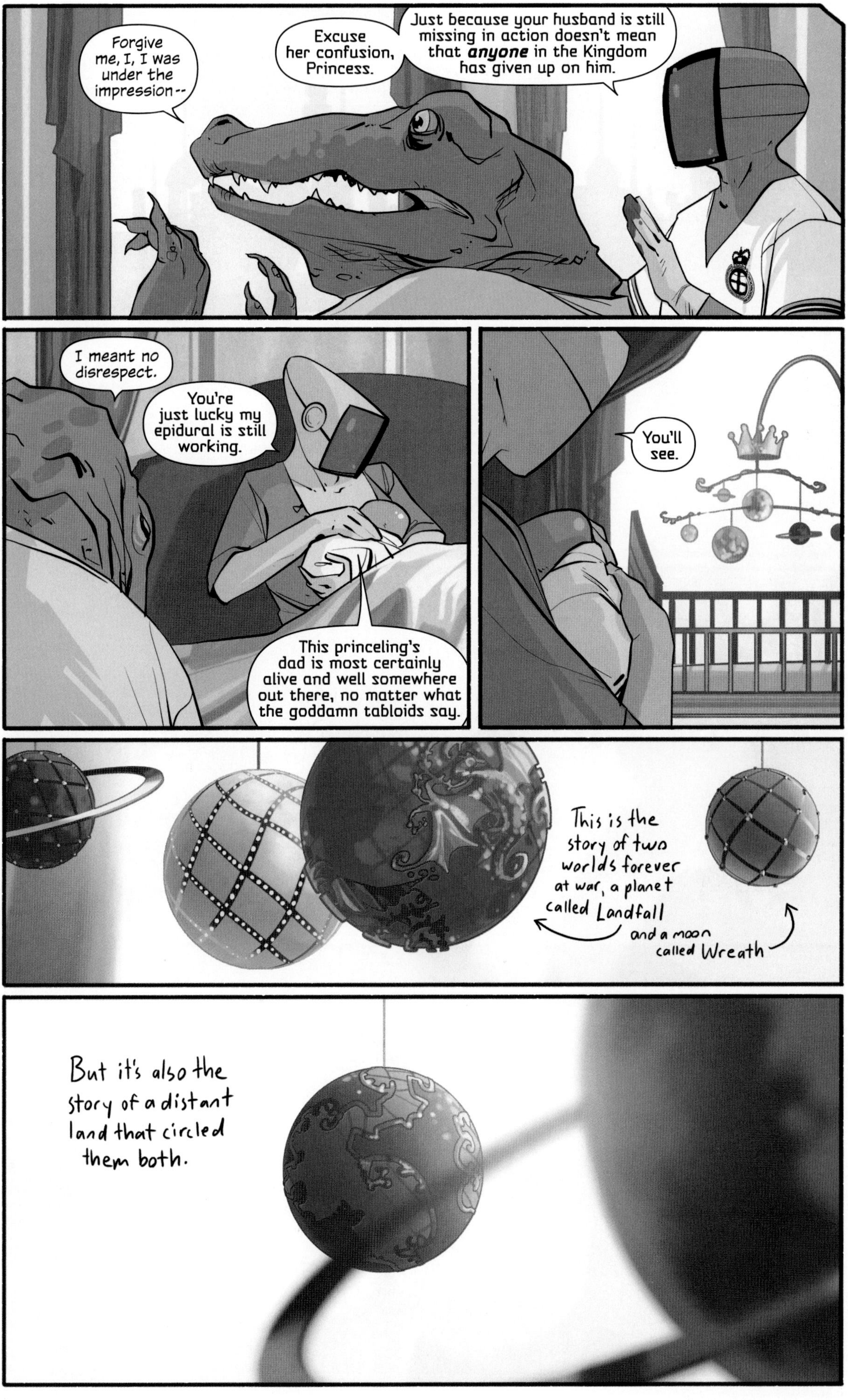
Forgive me, I, I was under the impression--
Excuse her confusion, Princess.
Just because your husband is still missing in action doesn't mean that **anyone** in the Kingdom has given up on him.
I meant no disrespect.
You're just lucky my epidural is still working.
This princeling's dad is most certainly alive and well somewhere out there, no matter what the goddamn tabloids say.
You'll see.
This is the story of two worlds forever at war, a planet called Landfall
and a moon called Wreath
But it's also the story of a distant land that circled them both.

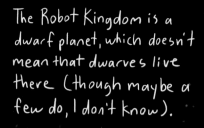
The Robot Kingdom is a dwarf planet, which doesn't mean that dwarves live there (though maybe a few do, I don't know).

It just means the place is too big to be considered a moon and too small to be considered a real planet.

So like all middle children, the Kingdom picked sides carefully.

For their many contributions to the Coalition of Landfall over the years, the Robots prospered handsomely.

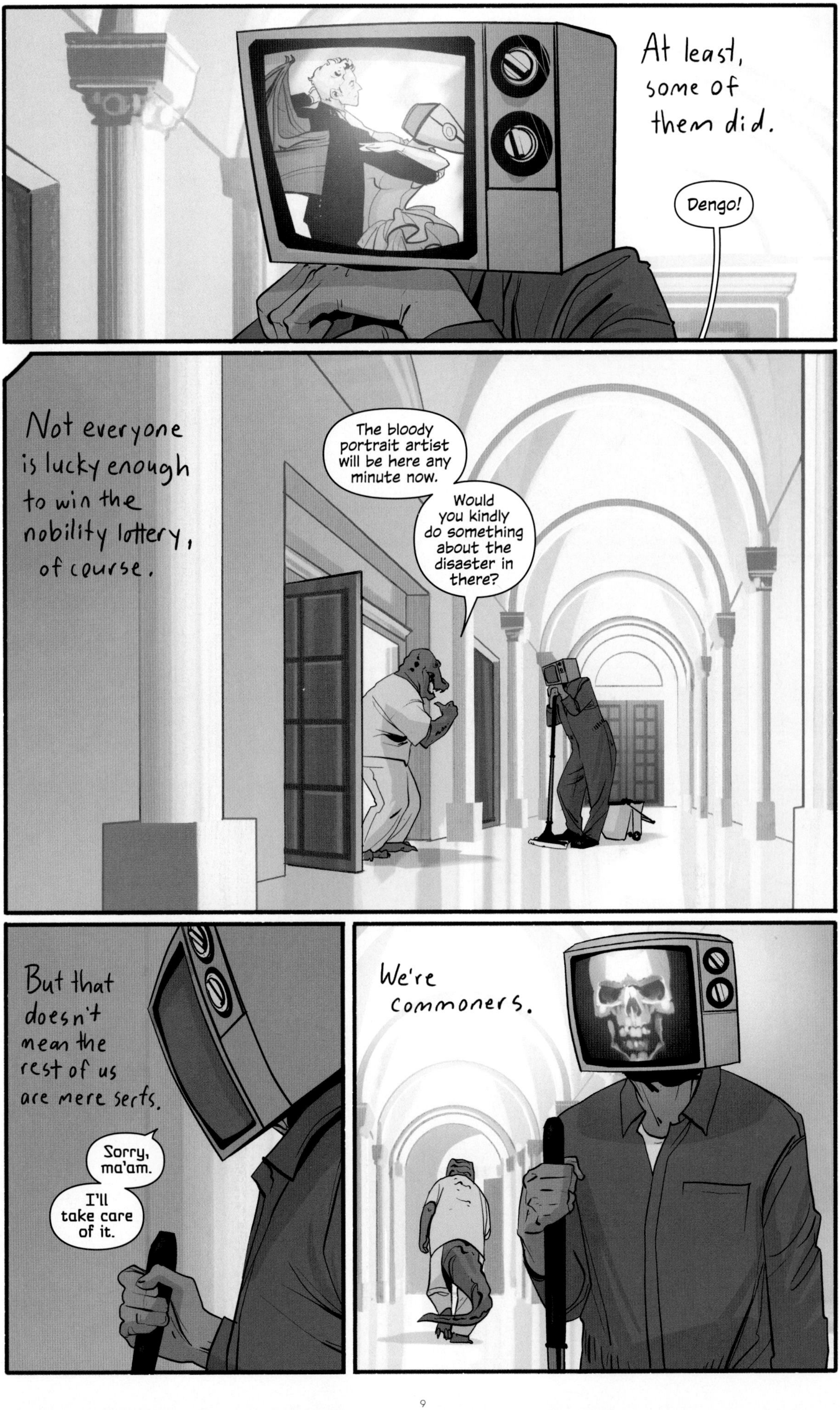
At least, some of them did.
Dengo!
Not everyone is lucky enough to win the nobility lottery, of course.
The bloody portrait artist will be here any minute now.
Would you kindly do something about the disaster in there?
But that doesn't mean the rest of us are mere serfs.
Sorry, ma'am.
I'll take care of it.
We're commoners.

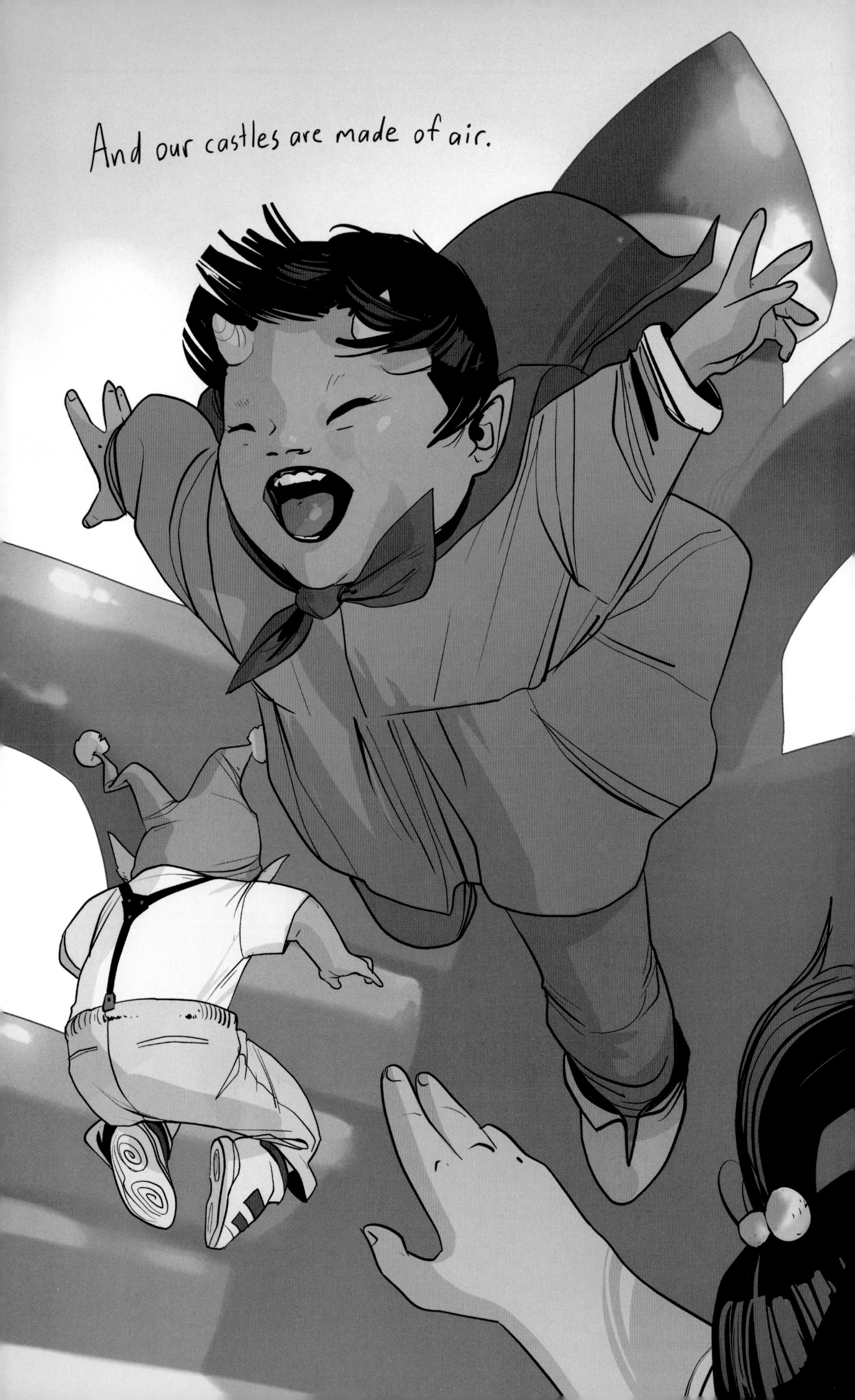
And our castles are made of air.

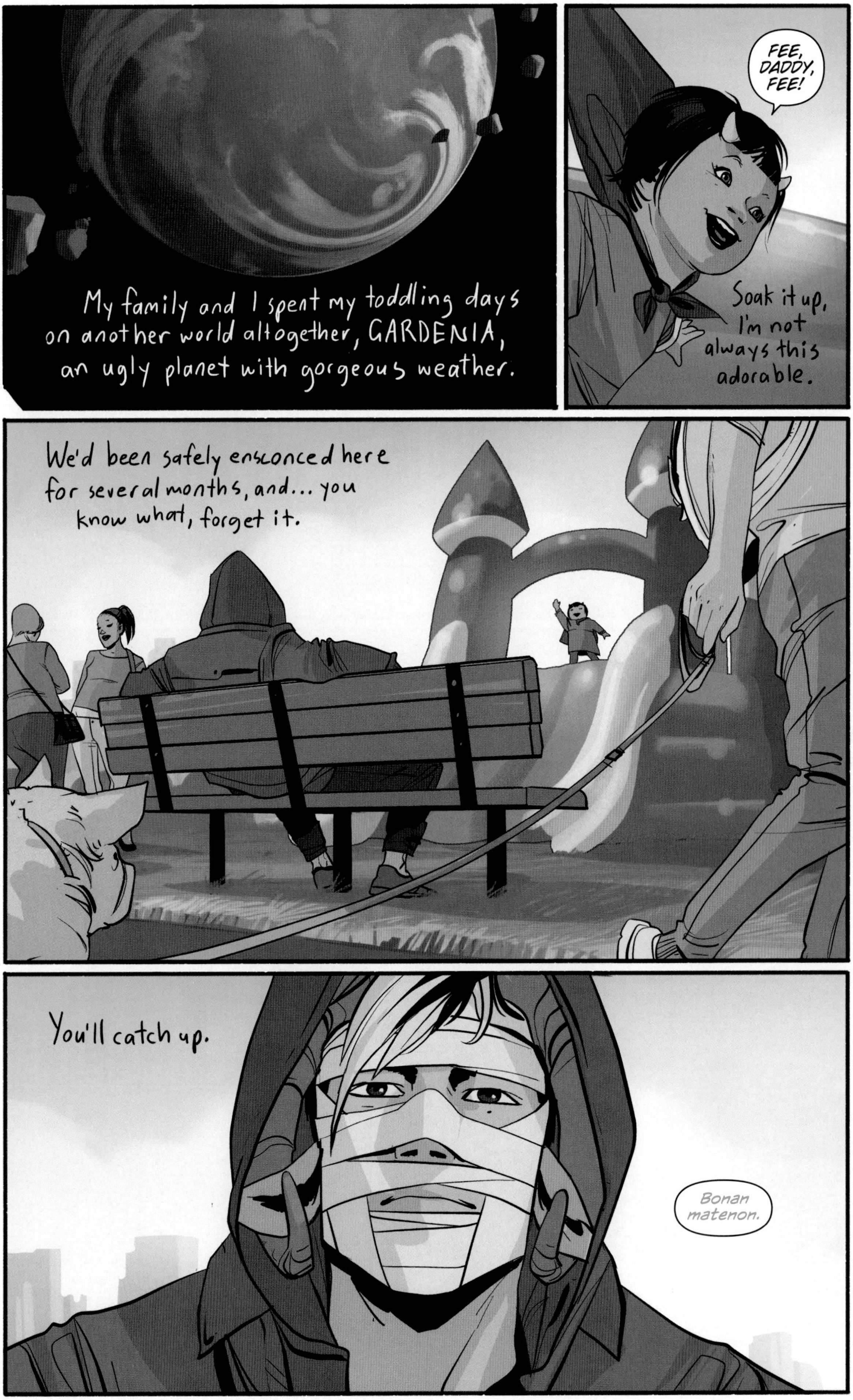
My family and I spent my toddling days on another world altogether, GARDENIA, an ugly planet with gorgeous weather.
FEE, DADDY, FEE!
Soak it up, I'm not always this adorable.
We'd been safely ensconced here for several months, and... you know what, forget it.
You'll catch up.
Bonan matenon.

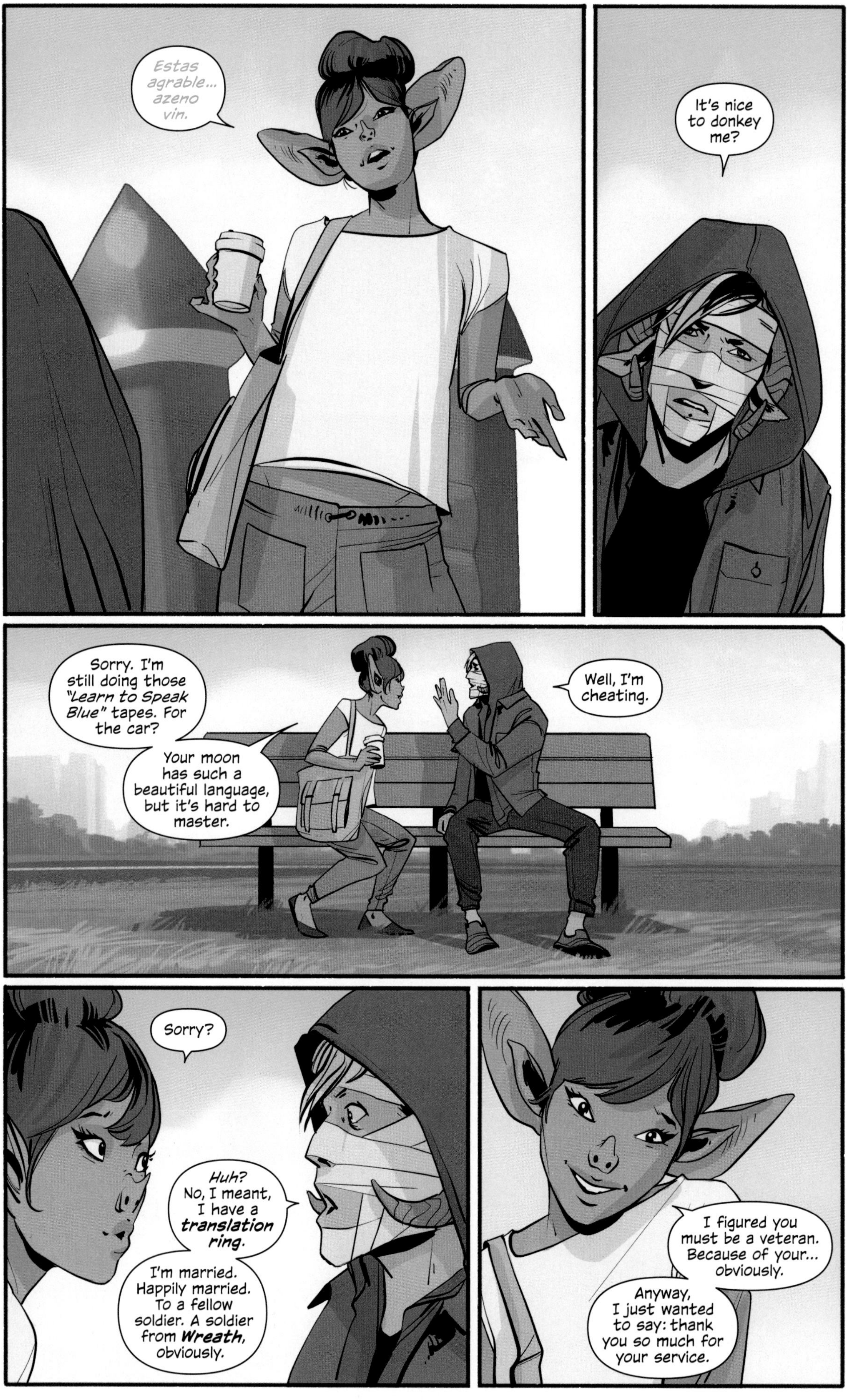
Estas agrable... azeno vin.
It's nice to donkey me?
Sorry. I'm still doing those "Learn to Speak Blue" tapes. For the car?
Your moon has such a beautiful language, but it's hard to master.
Well, I'm cheating.
Sorry?
Huh? No, I meant, I have a **translation ring**.
I'm married. Happily married. To a fellow soldier. A soldier from **Wreath**, obviously.
I figured you must be a veteran. Because of your... obviously.
Anyway, I just wanted to say: thank you so much for your service.

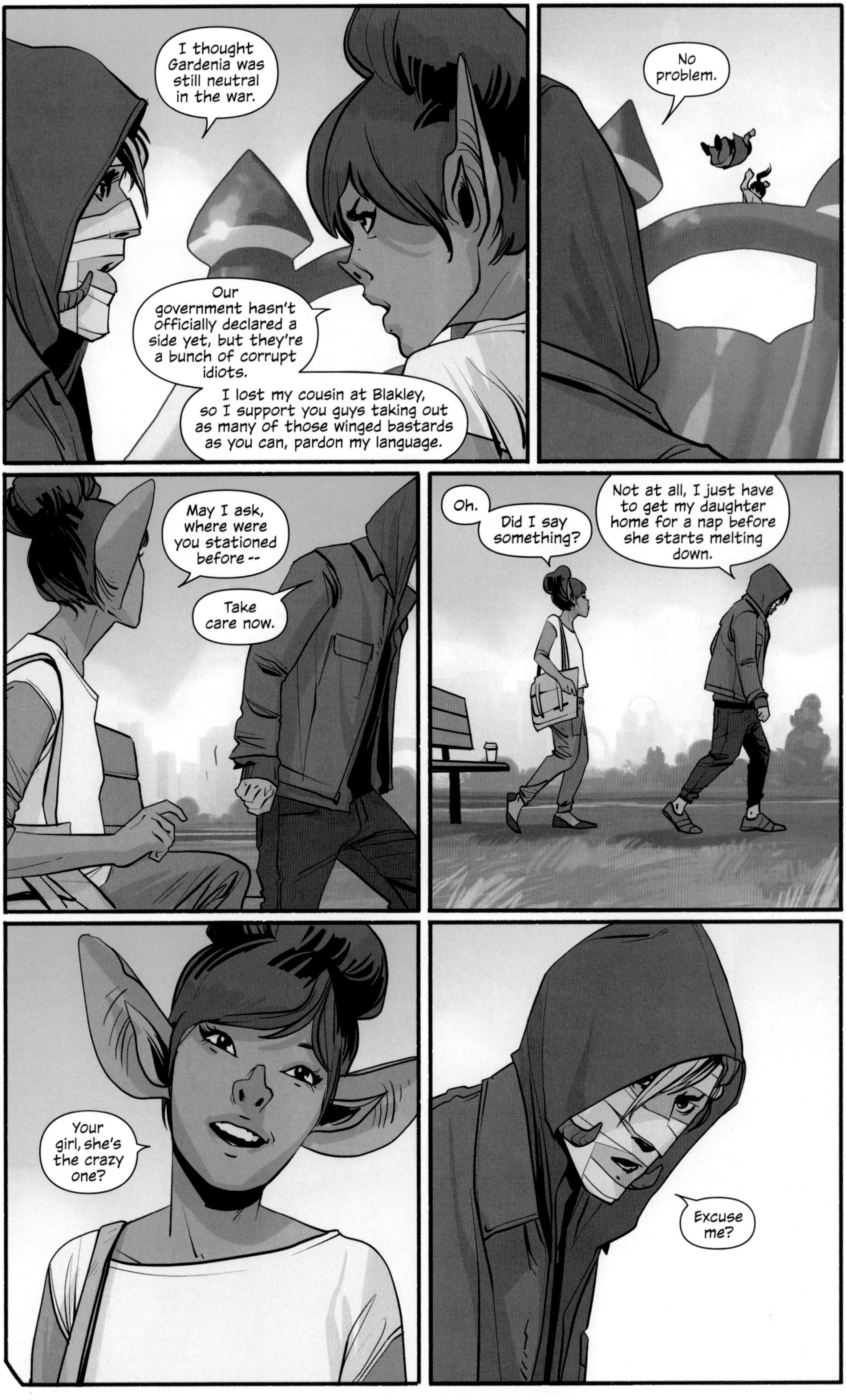
I thought Gardenia was still neutral in the war.
Our government hasn't officially declared a side yet, but they're a bunch of corrupt idiots.
I lost my cousin at Blakley, so I support you guys taking out as many of those winged bastards as you can, pardon my language.
No problem.
May I ask, where were you stationed before --
Take care now.
Oh.
Did I say something?
Not at all, I just have to get my daughter home for a nap before she starts melting down.
Your girl, she's the crazy one?
Excuse me?

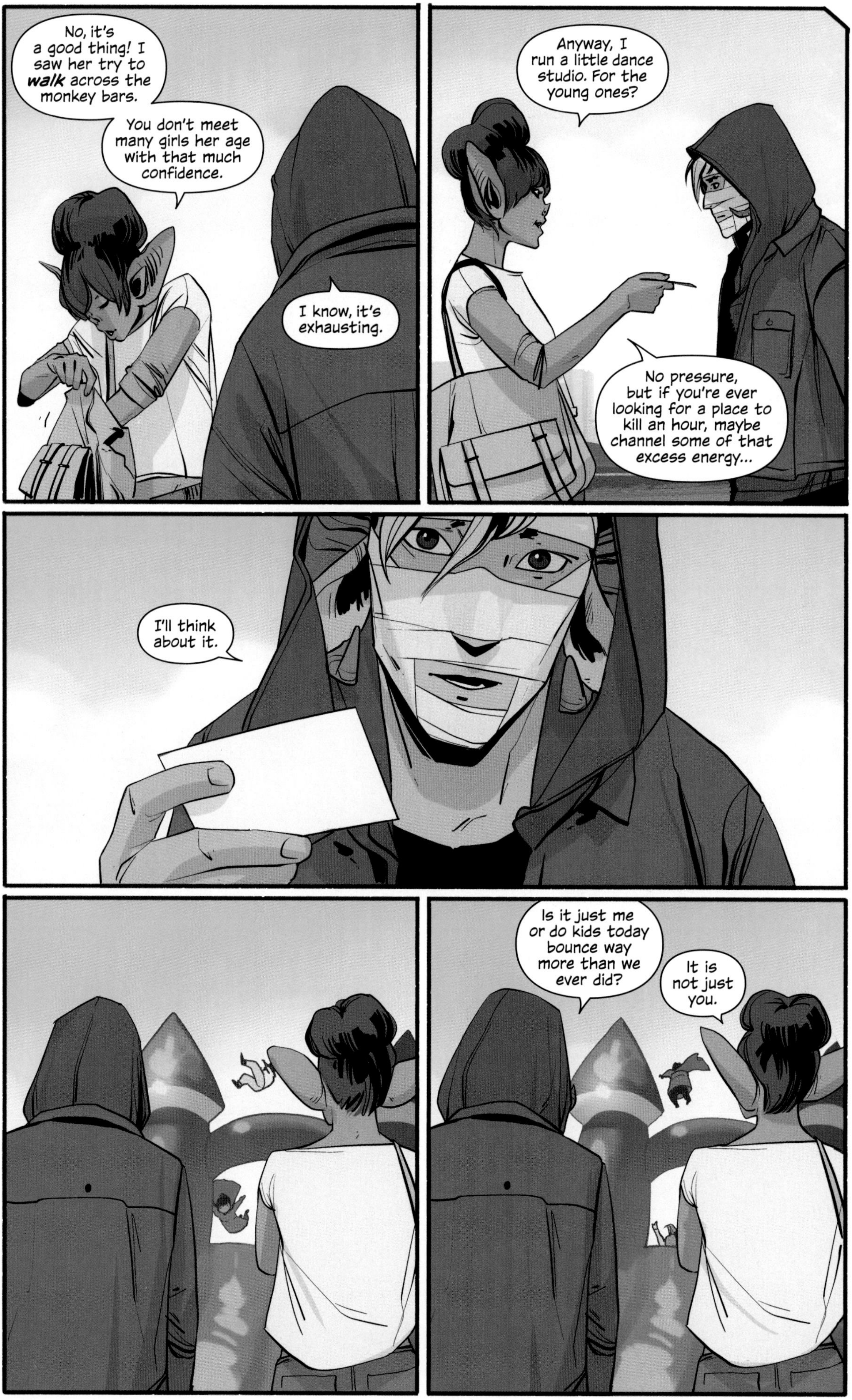
No, it's a good thing! I saw her try to **walk** across the monkey bars.
You don't meet many girls her age with that much confidence.
I know, it's exhausting.
Anyway, I run a little dance studio. For the young ones?
No pressure, but if you're ever looking for a place to kill an hour, maybe channel some of that excess energy...
I'll think about it.
Is it just me or do kids today bounce way more than we ever did?
It is not just you.

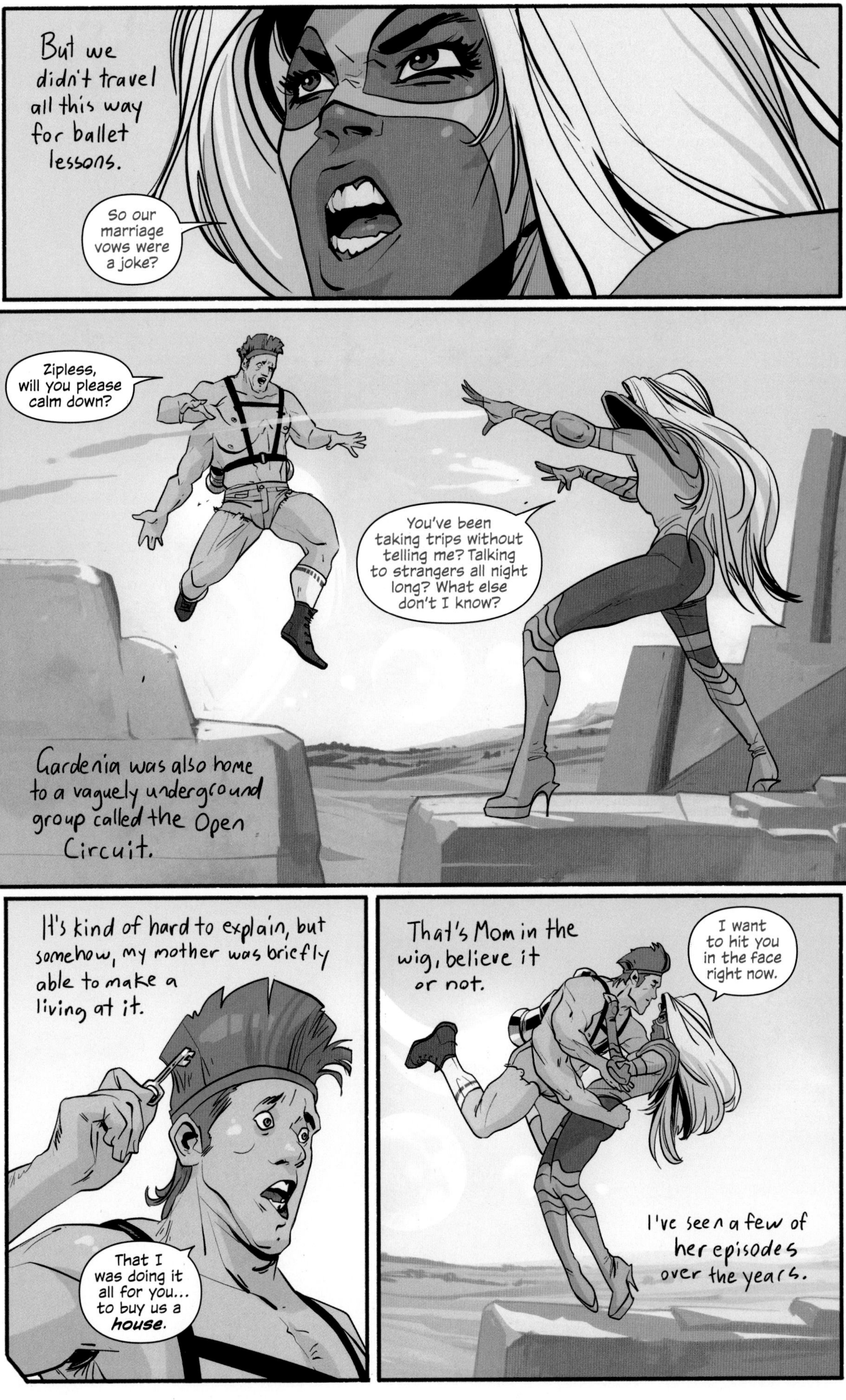
But we didn't travel all this way for ballet lessons.
So our marriage vows were a joke?
Zipless, will you please calm down?
You've been taking trips without telling me? Talking to strangers all night long? What else don't I know?
Gardenia was also home to a vaguely underground group called the Open Circuit.
It's kind of hard to explain, but somehow, my mother was briefly able to make a living at it.
That I was doing it all for you... to buy us a ***house***.
That's Mom in the wig, believe it or not.
I want to hit you in the face right now.
I've seen a few of her episodes over the years.

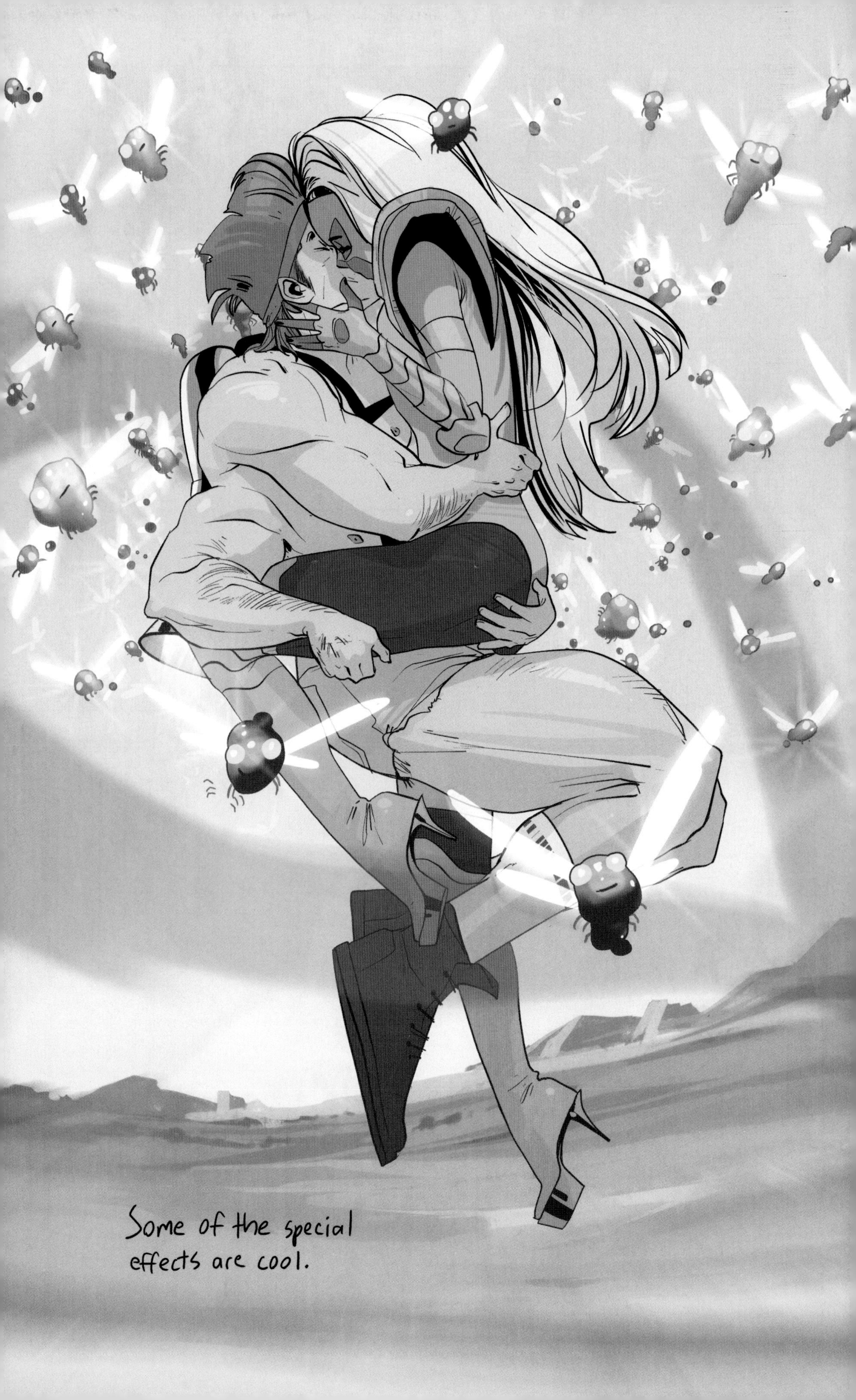
Some of the special
effects are cool.

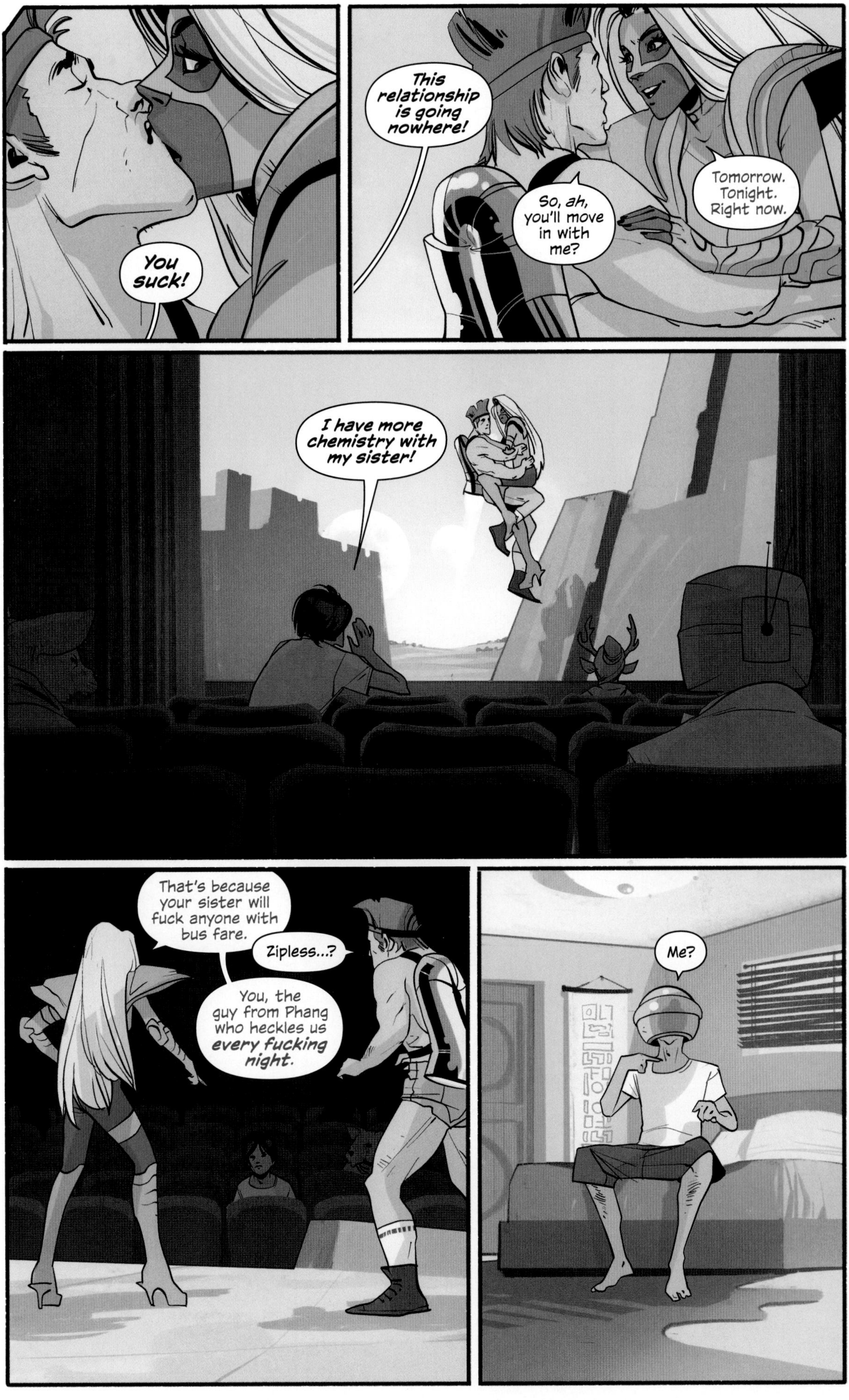
You suck!
This relationship is going nowhere!
So, ah, you'll move in with me?
Tomorrow. Tonight. Right now.
I have more chemistry with my sister!
That's because your sister will fuck anyone with bus fare.
Zipless...?
You, the guy from Phang who heckles us every fucking night.
Me?

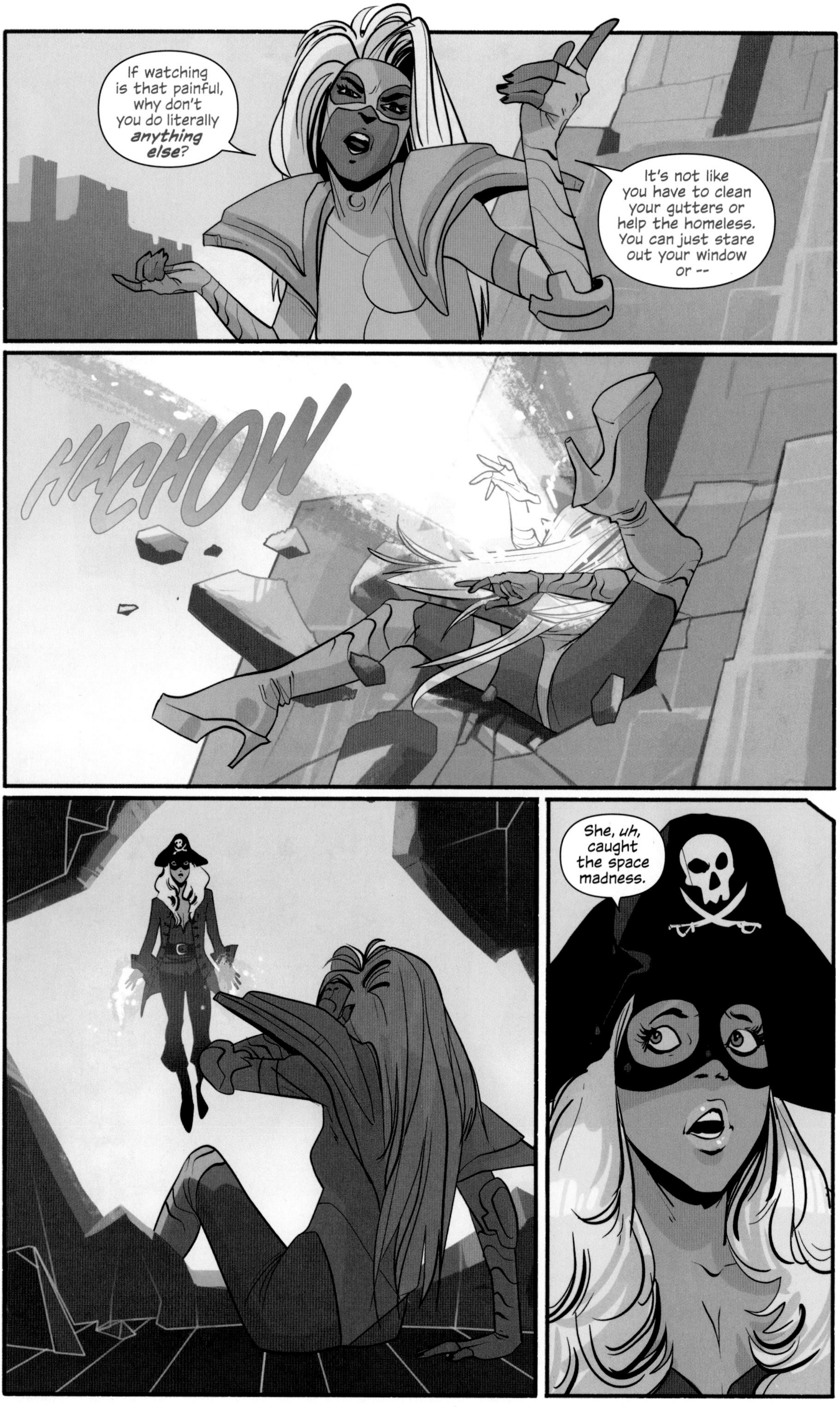
If watching is that painful, why don't you do literally ***anything else***?
It's not like you have to clean your gutters or help the homeless. You can just stare out your window or --
HACHOW
She, *uh*, caught the space madness.

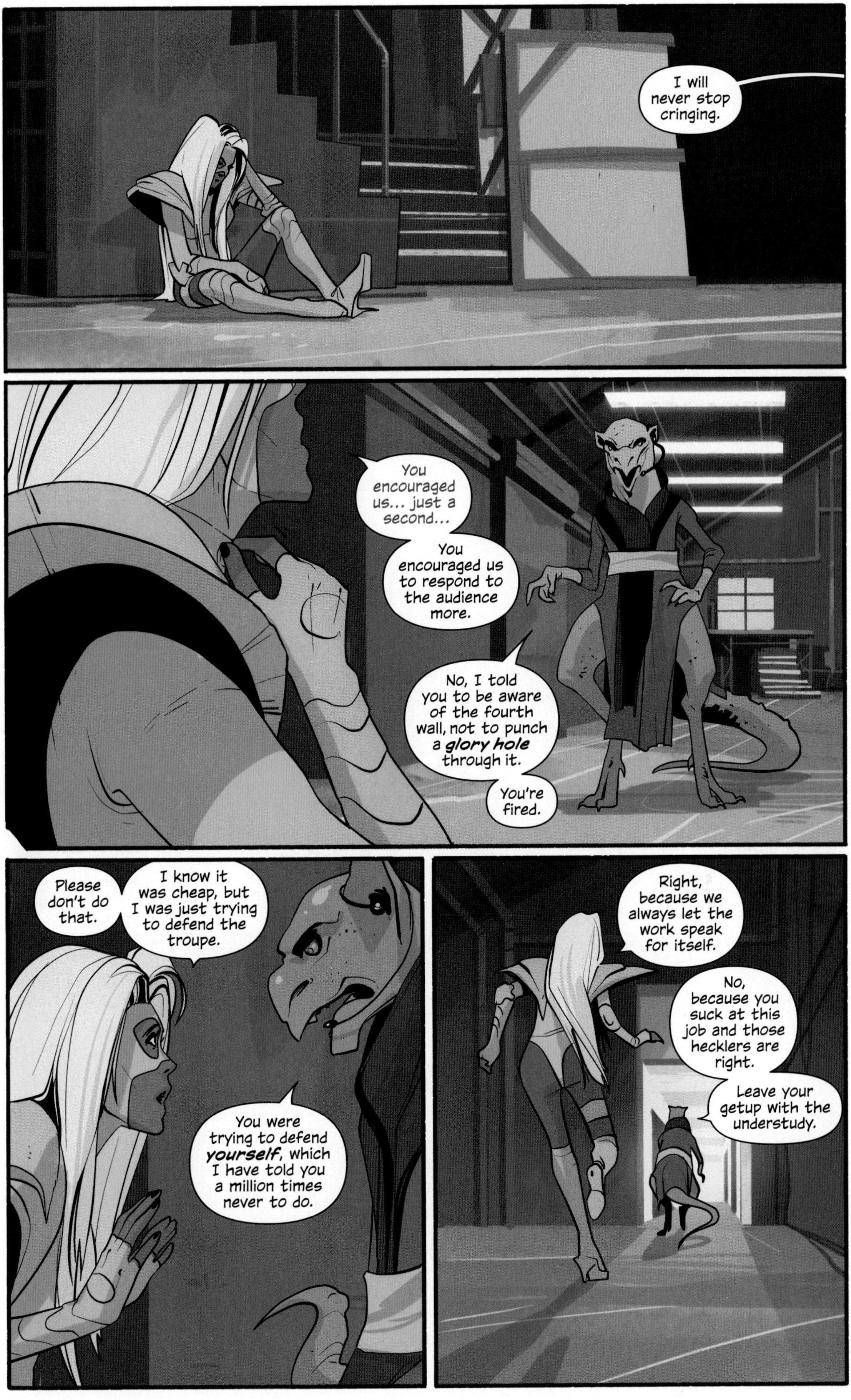
I will never stop cringing.
You encouraged us... just a second...
You encouraged us to respond to the audience more.
No, I told you to be aware of the fourth wall, not to punch a ***glory hole*** through it.
You're fired.
Please don't do that.
I know it was cheap, but I was just trying to defend the troupe.
You were trying to defend ***yourself***, which I have told you a million times never to do.
Right, because we always let the work speak for itself.
No, because you suck at this job and those hecklers are right.
Leave your getup with the understudy.

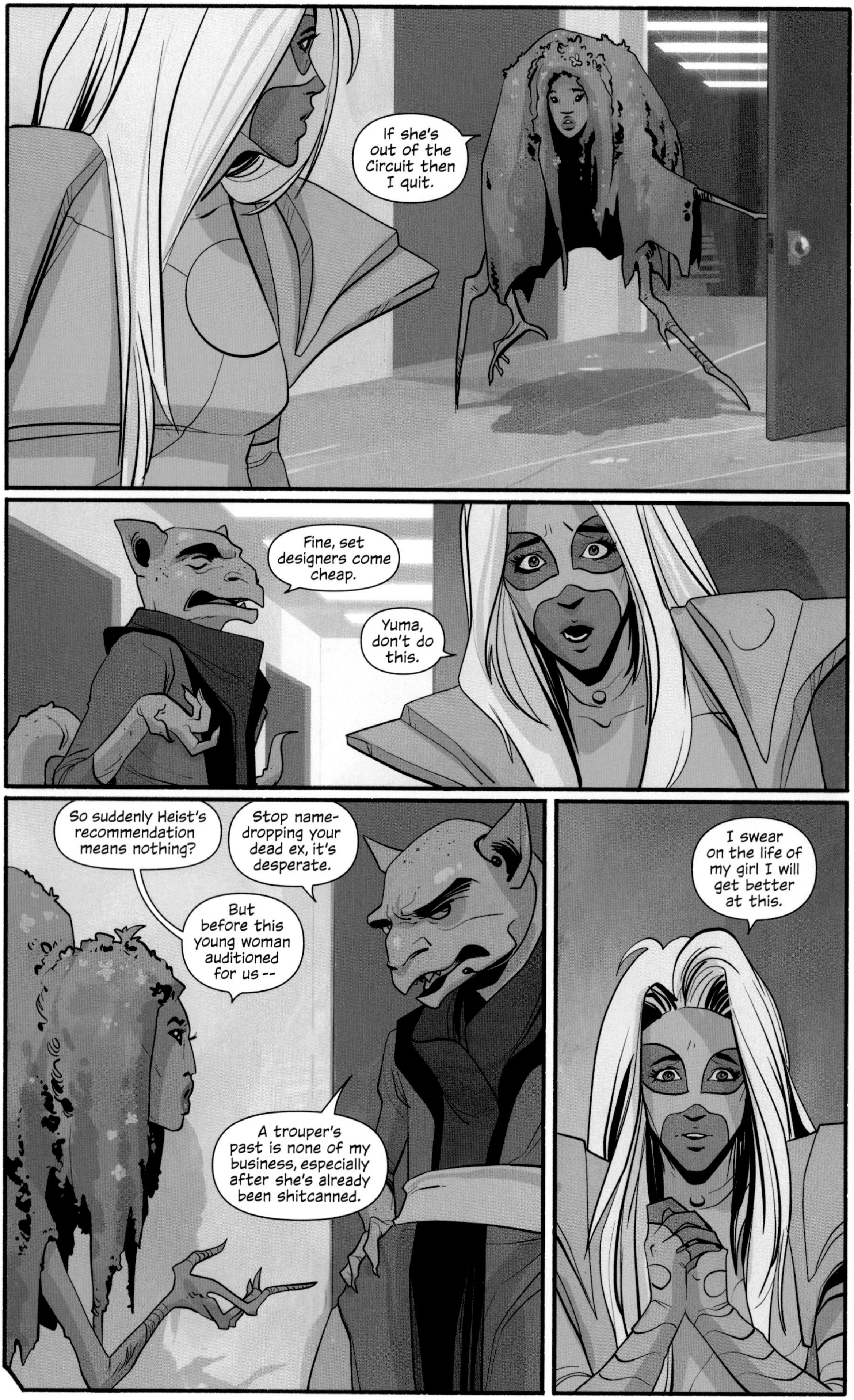
If she's out of the Circuit then I quit.
Fine, set designers come cheap.
Yuma, don't do this.
So suddenly Heist's recommendation means nothing?
Stop name-dropping your dead ex, it's desperate.
But before this young woman auditioned for us --
A trouper's past is none of my business, especially after she's already been shitcanned.
I swear on the life of my girl I will get better at this.

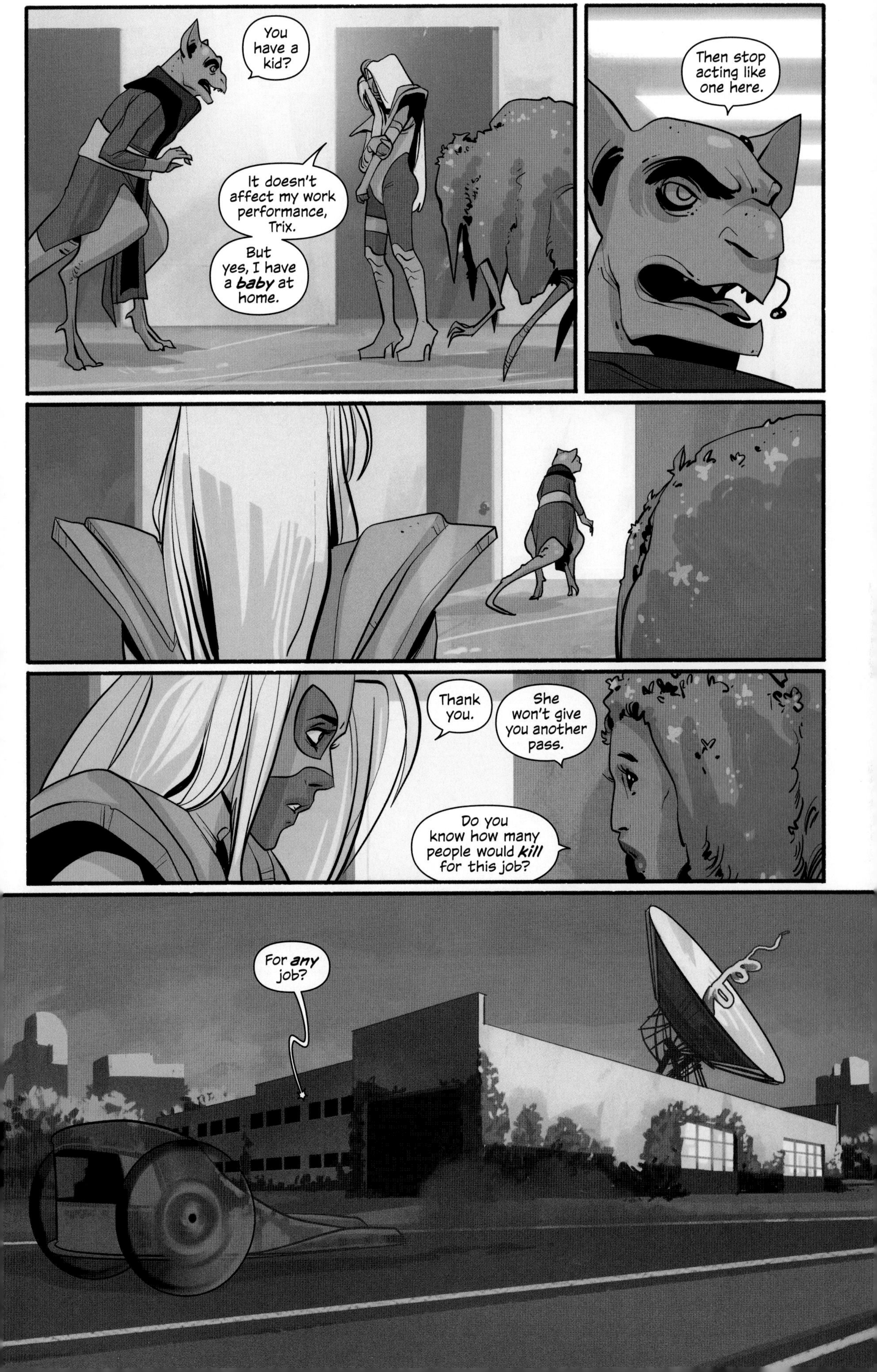
You have a kid?
It doesn't affect my work performance, Trix.
But yes, I have a *baby* at home.
Then stop acting like one here.
Thank you.
She won't give you another pass.
Do you know how many people would *kill* for this job?
For *any* job?

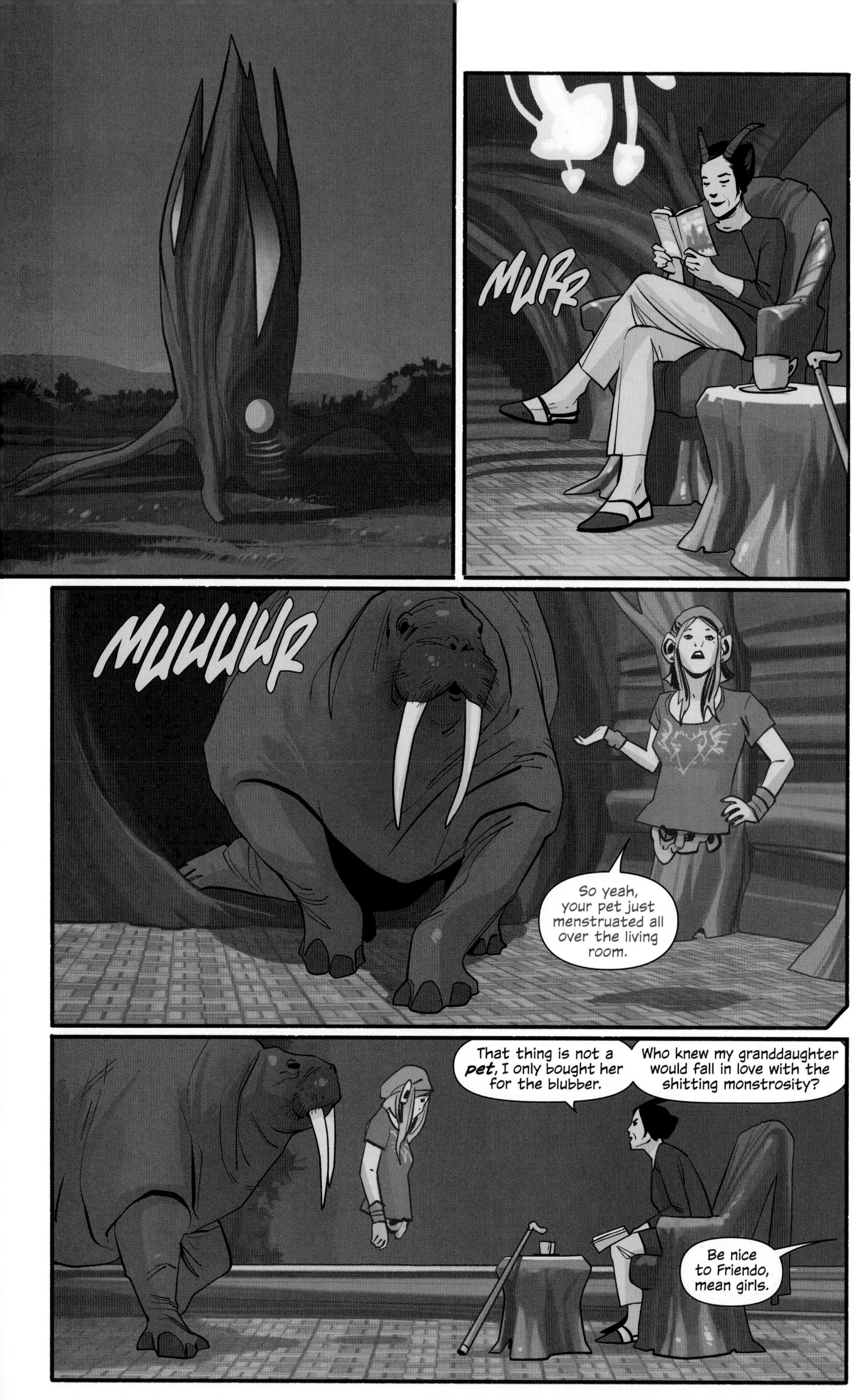
MURR
MUUUUR
So yeah, your pet just menstruated all over the living room.
That thing is not a **pet**, I only bought her for the blubber.
Who knew my granddaughter would fall in love with the shitting monstrosity?
Be nice to Friendo, mean girls.

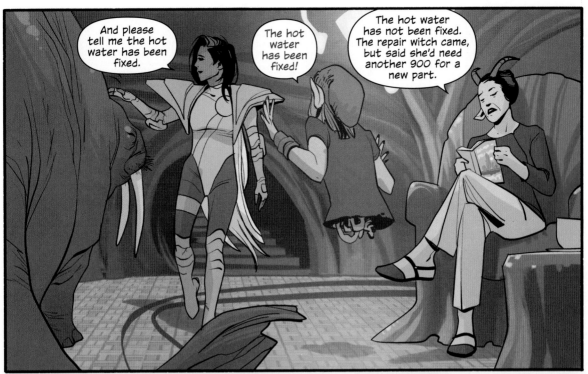

And please tell me the hot water has been fixed.

The hot water has been fixed!

The hot water has not been fixed. The repair witch came, but said she'd need another 900 for a new part.

900?! That's triple her estimate!

Something about the cost of petrified wood.

Is my child at least alive?

Sound asleep, boss.

I already missed her?

Blame the so-called man of the house.

He ran her ragged at the playground today.

He what.

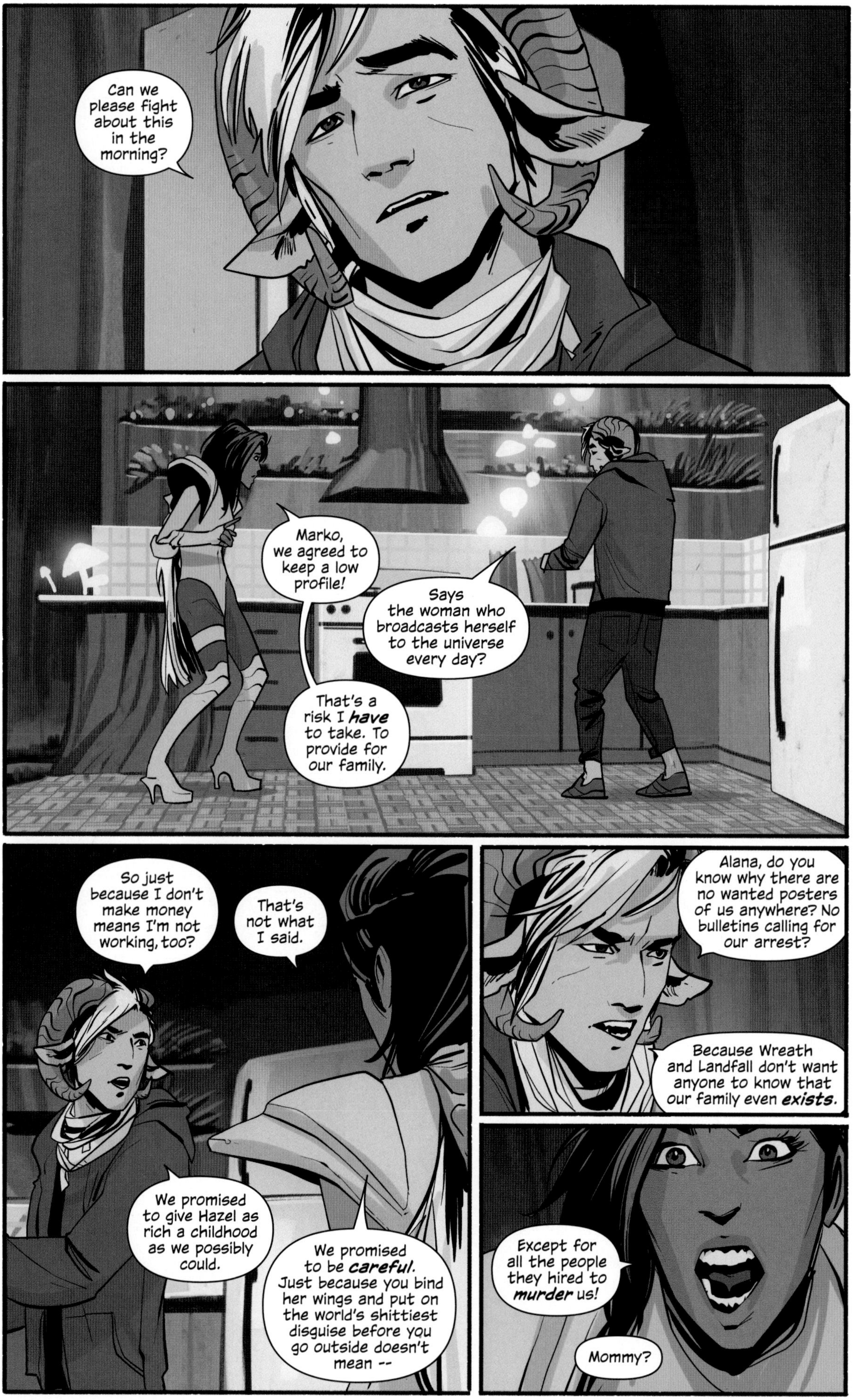

Can we please fight about this in the morning?
Marko, we agreed to keep a low profile!
Says the woman who broadcasts herself to the universe every day?
That's a risk I ***have*** to take. To provide for our family.
So just because I don't make money means I'm not working, too?
That's not what I said.
We promised to give Hazel as rich a childhood as we possibly could.
We promised to be ***careful***. Just because you bind her wings and put on the world's shittiest disguise before you go outside doesn't mean --
Alana, do you know why there are no wanted posters of us anywhere? No bulletins calling for our arrest?
Because Wreath and Landfall don't want anyone to know that our family even ***exists***.
Except for all the people they hired to ***murder*** us!
Mommy?

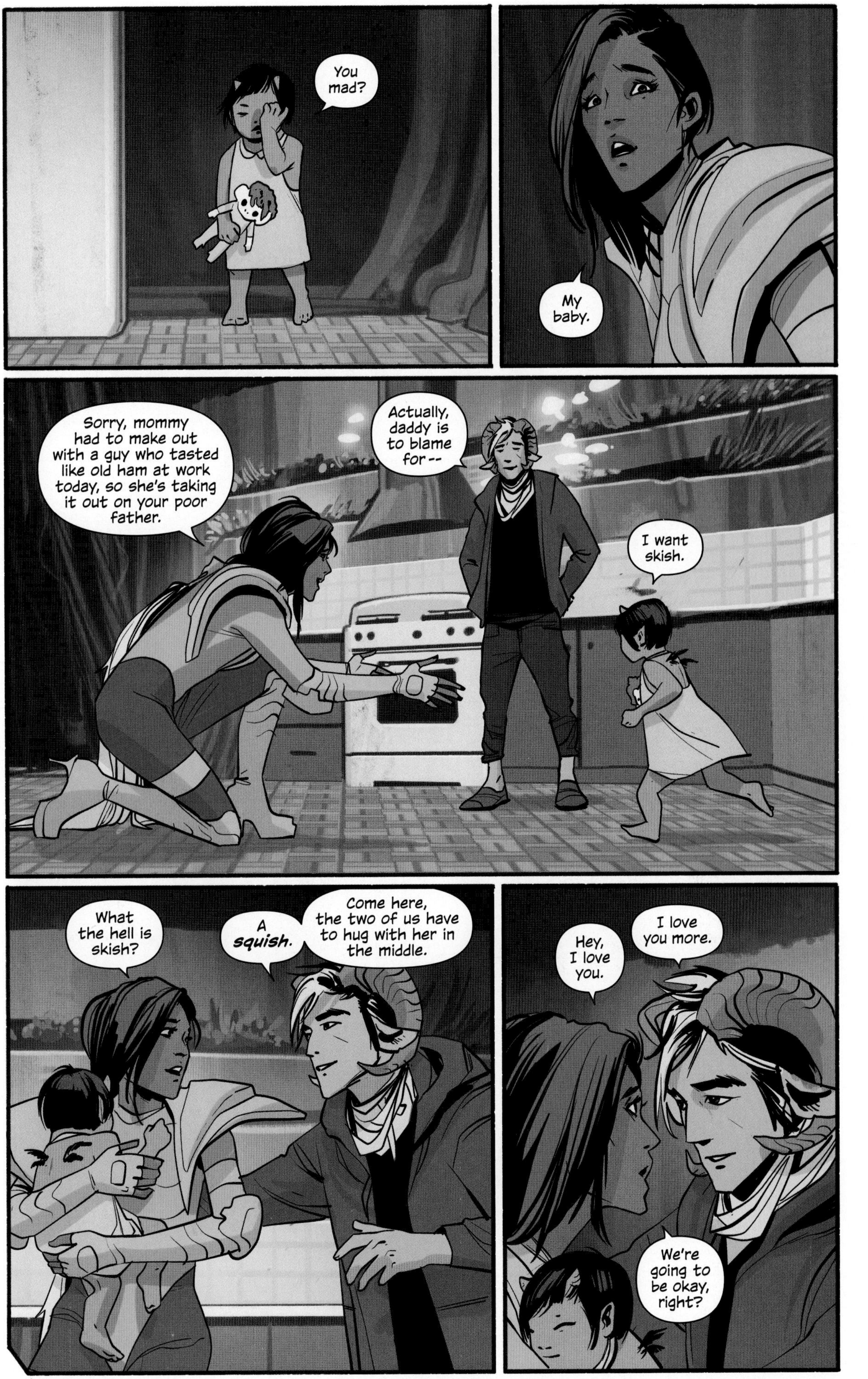

You mad?
My baby.
Sorry, mommy had to make out with a guy who tasted like old ham at work today, so she's taking it out on your poor father.
Actually, daddy is to blame for--
I want skish.
What the hell is skish?
A *squish*.
Come here, the two of us have to hug with her in the middle.
Hey, I love you.
I love you more.
We're going to be okay, right?

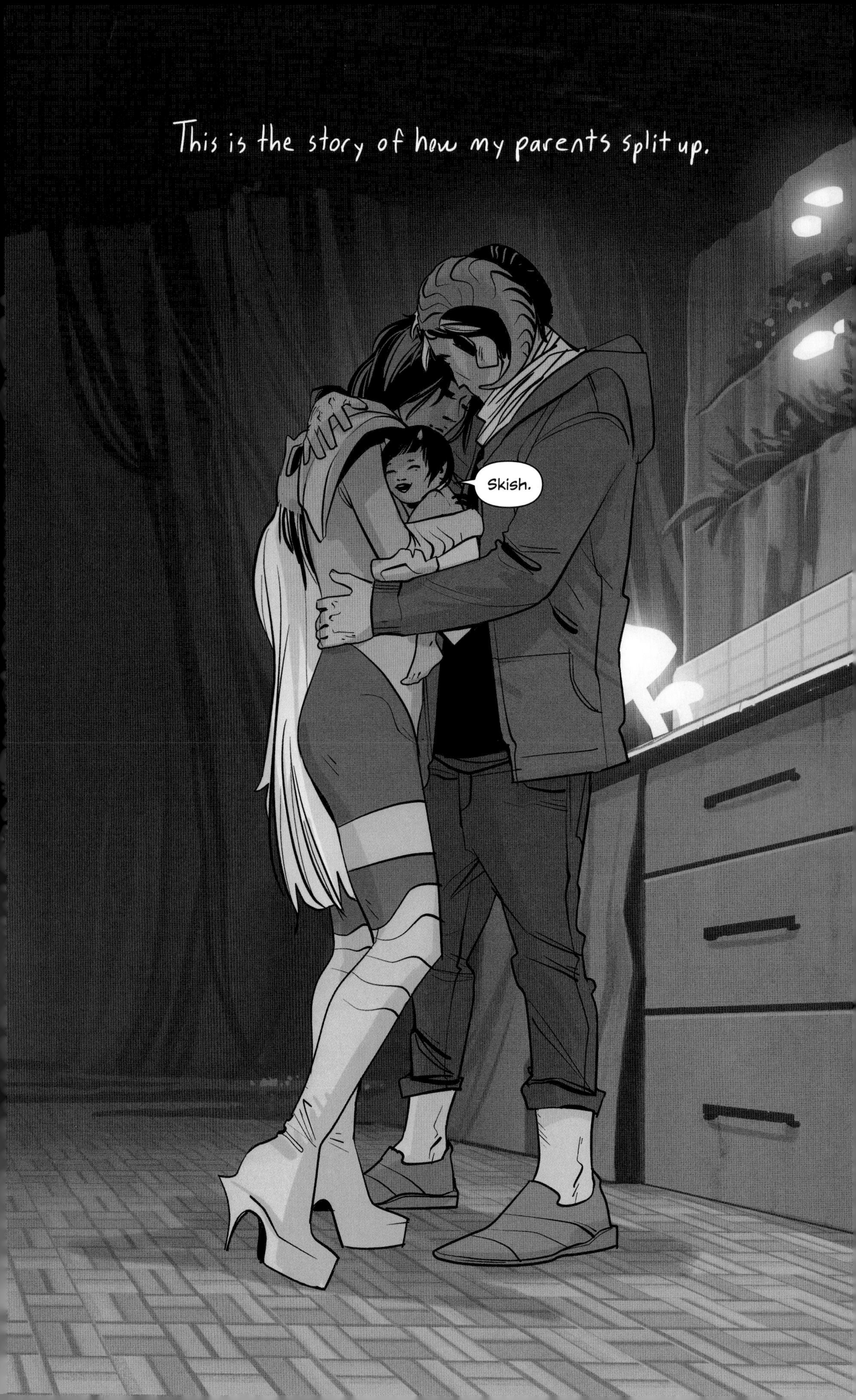
This is the story of how my parents split up.
Skish.

end chapter nineteen

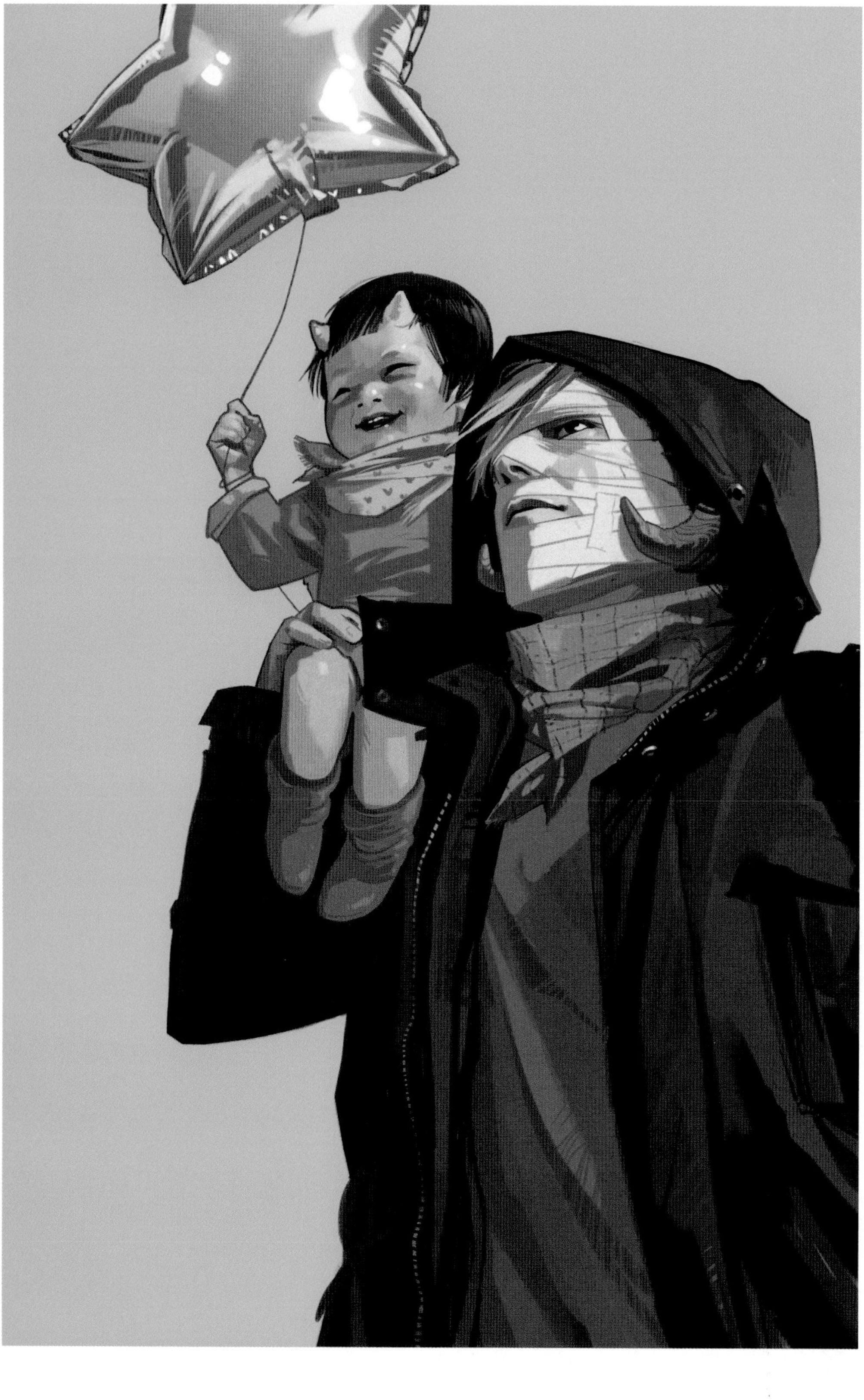

CHAPTER

TWENTY

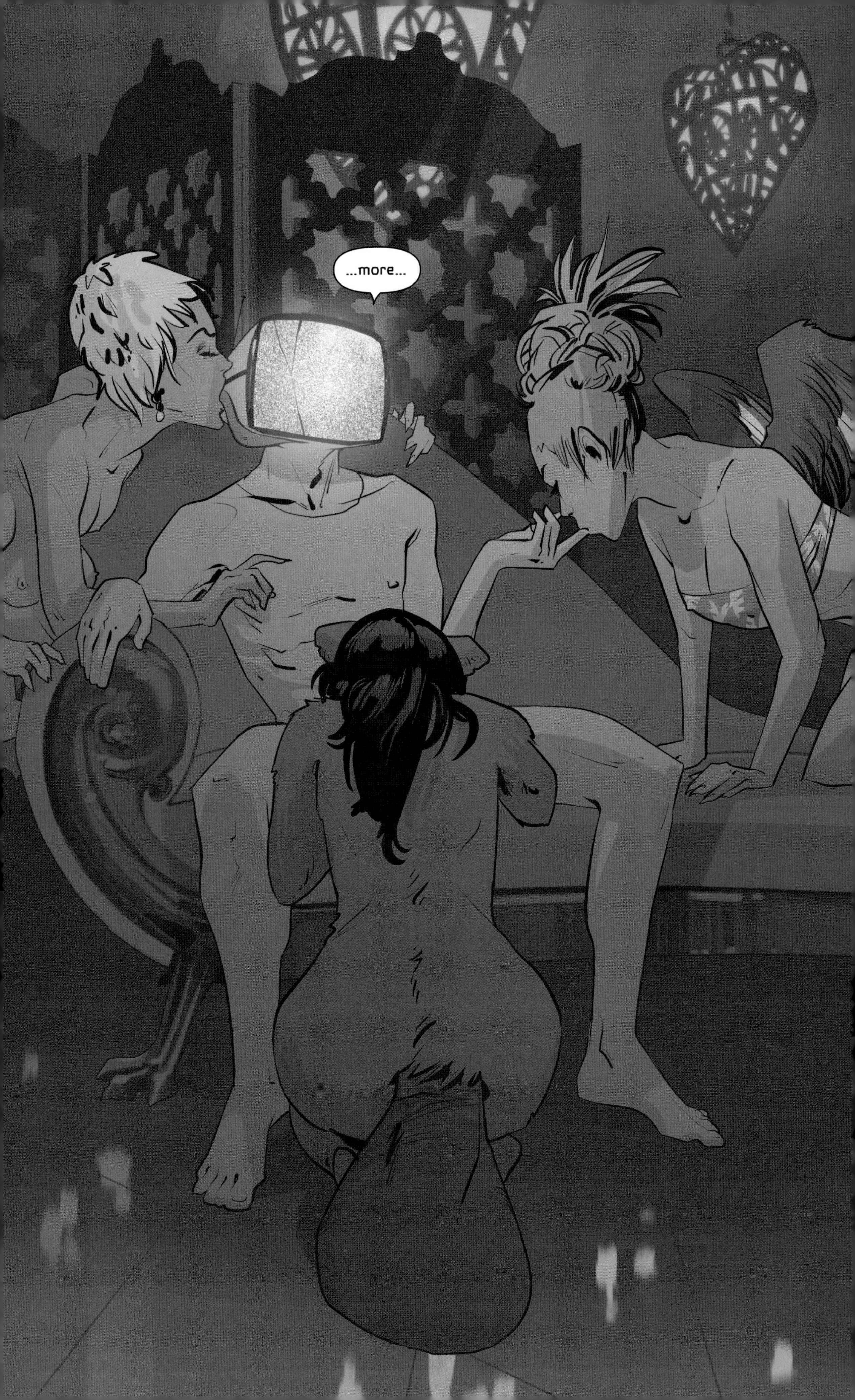
...more...

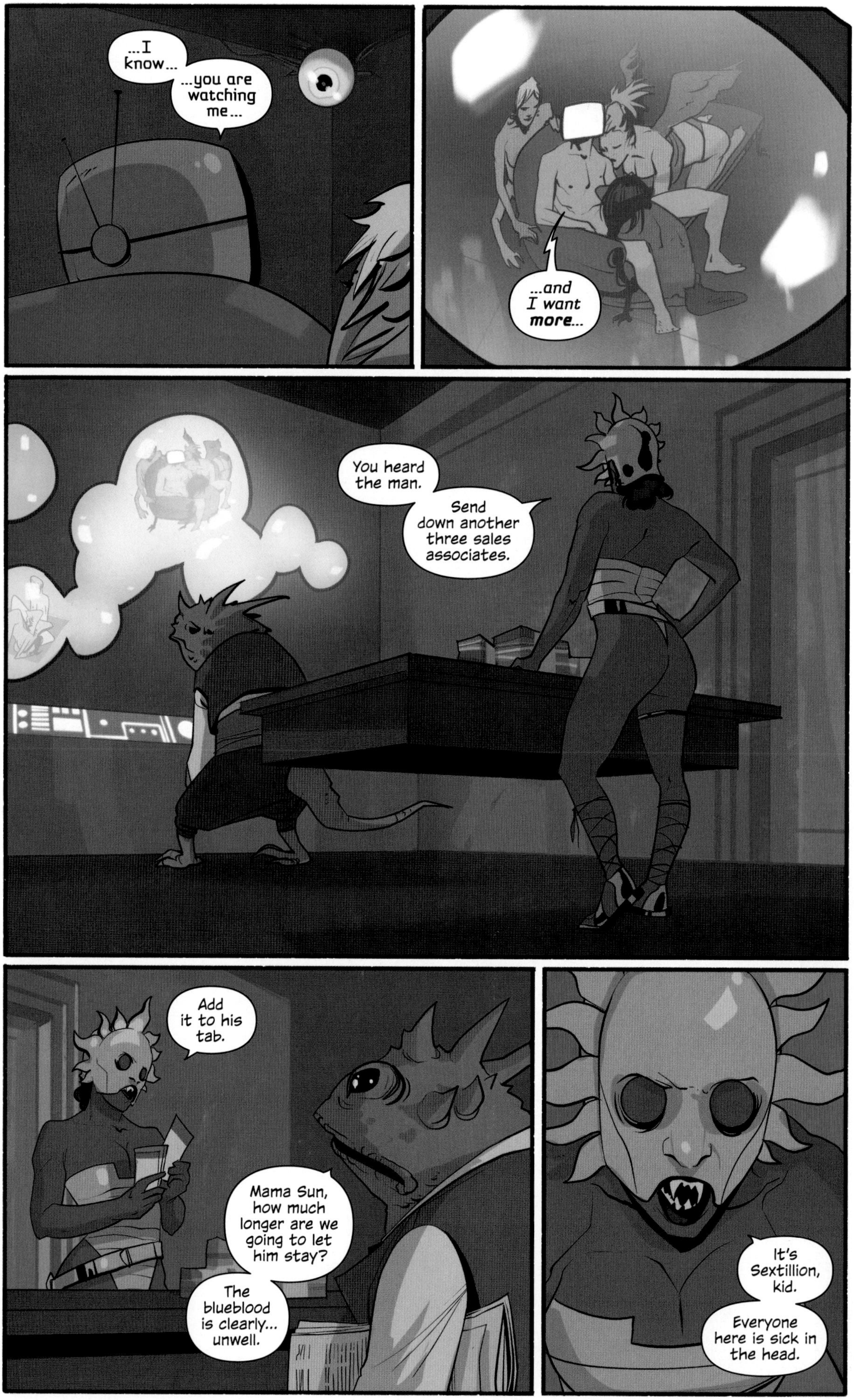
...I know...
...you are watching me...
...and I want more...
You heard the man.
Send down another three sales associates.
Add it to his tab.
Mama Sun, how much longer are we going to let him stay?
The blueblood is clearly... unwell.
It's Sextillion, kid.
Everyone here is sick in the head.

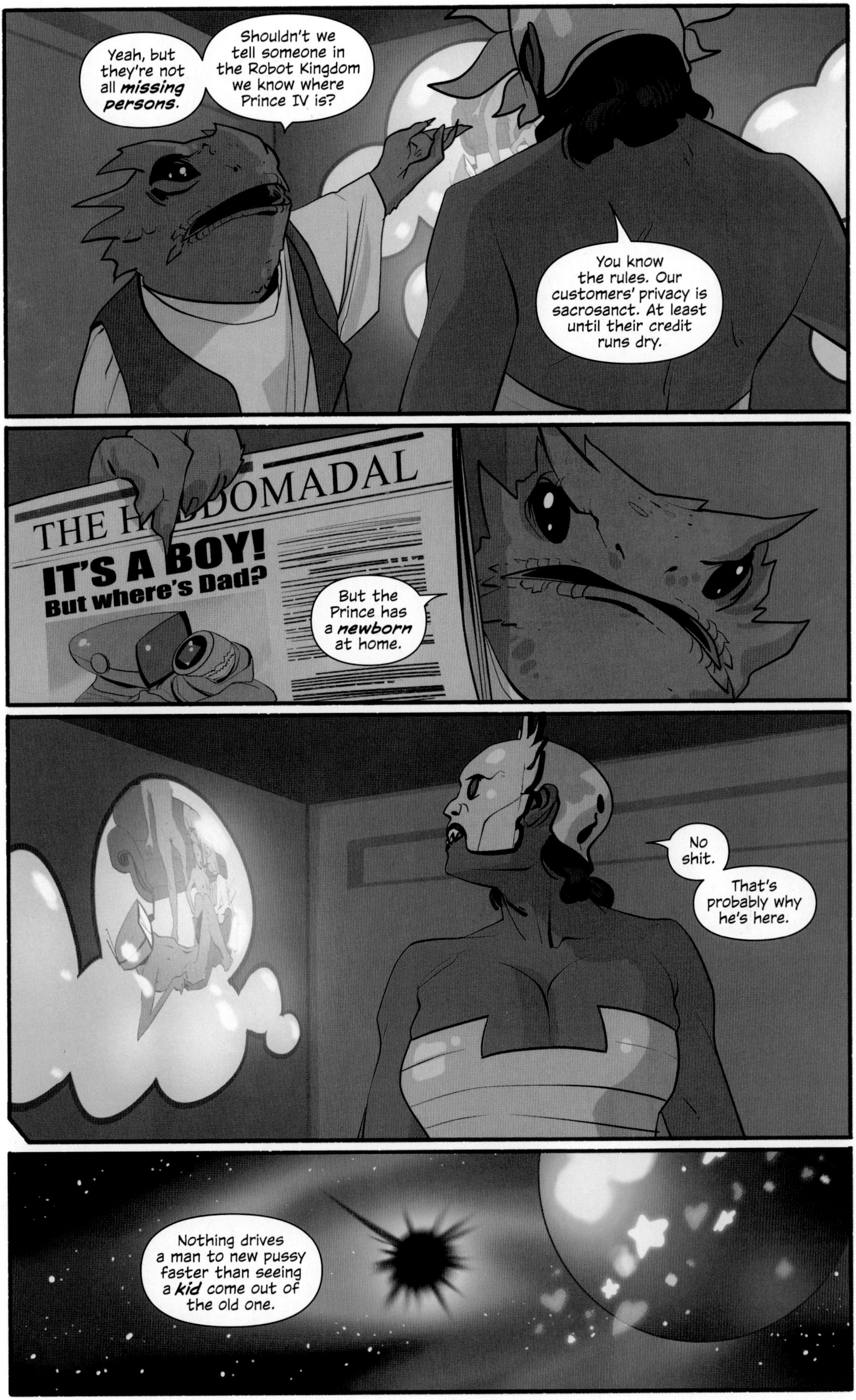

Yeah, but they're not all ***missing persons***.
Shouldn't we tell someone in the Robot Kingdom we know where Prince IV is?
You know the rules. Our customers' privacy is sacrosanct. At least until their credit runs dry.
THE H DOMADAL
IT'S A BOY!
But where's Dad?
But the Prince has a ***newborn*** at home.
No shit.
That's probably why he's here.
Nothing drives a man to new pussy faster than seeing a ***kid*** come out of the old one.

REHHHH!

Hazel?

What's the matter, bean?

REHHHH!

Crap, sorry, Marko.

I have no idea how she gets out of that crib.

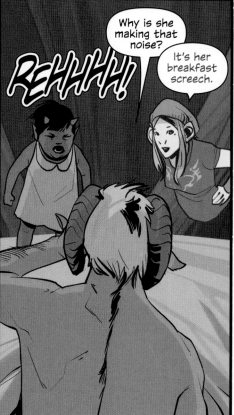

Why is she making that noise?

It's her breakfast screech.

REHHHH!

REHHHH!

Breakfast? What *time* is it?

And where the hell is my wife?

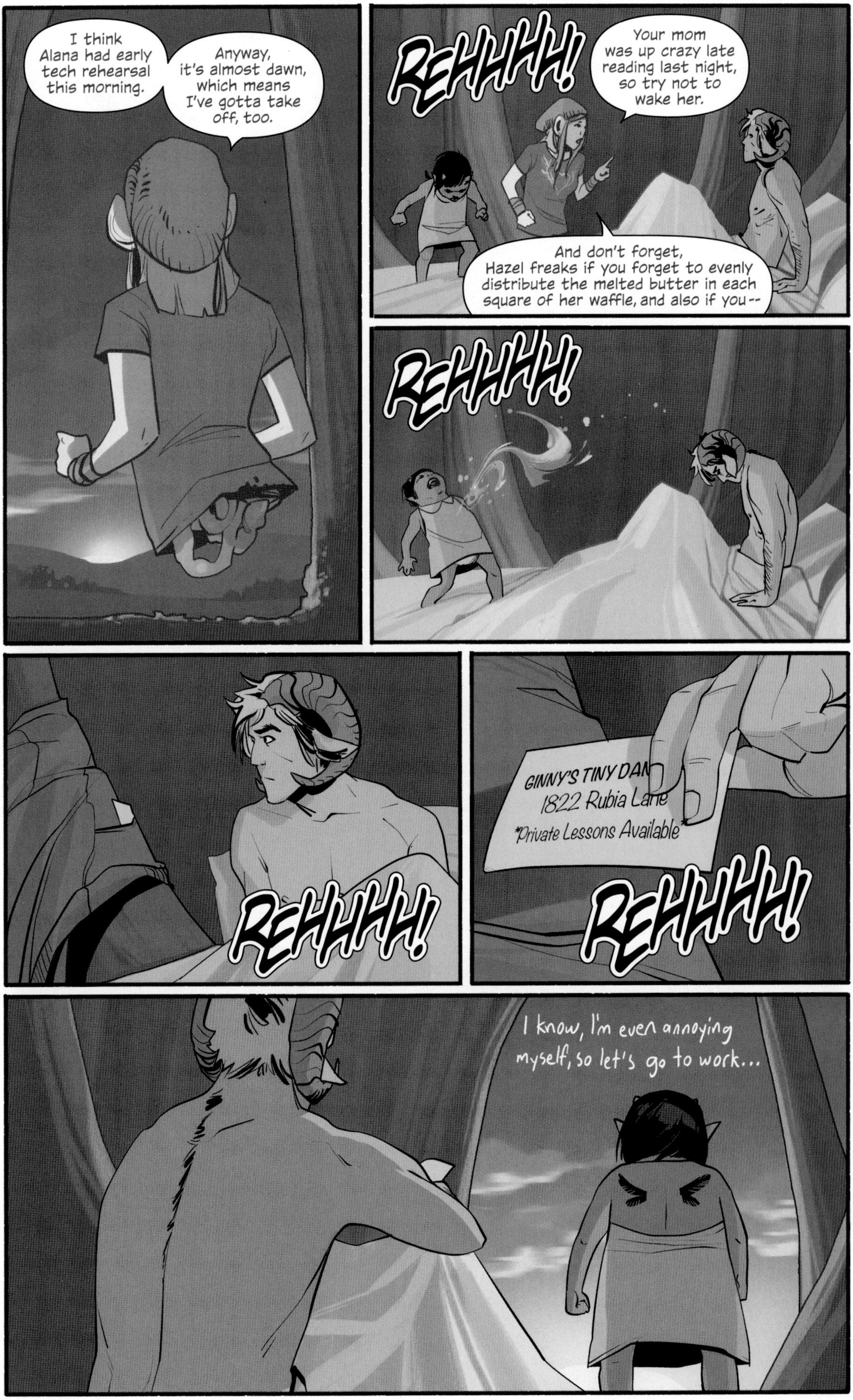
I think Alana had early tech rehearsal this morning.
Anyway, it's almost dawn, which means I've gotta take off, too.
REHHHH!
Your mom was up crazy late reading last night, so try not to wake her.
And don't forget, Hazel freaks if you forget to evenly distribute the melted butter in each square of her waffle, and also if you--
REHHHH!
REHHHH!
GINNY'S TINY DAN
1822 Rubia Lane
Private Lessons Available
REHHHH!
I know, I'm even annoying myself, so let's go to work...

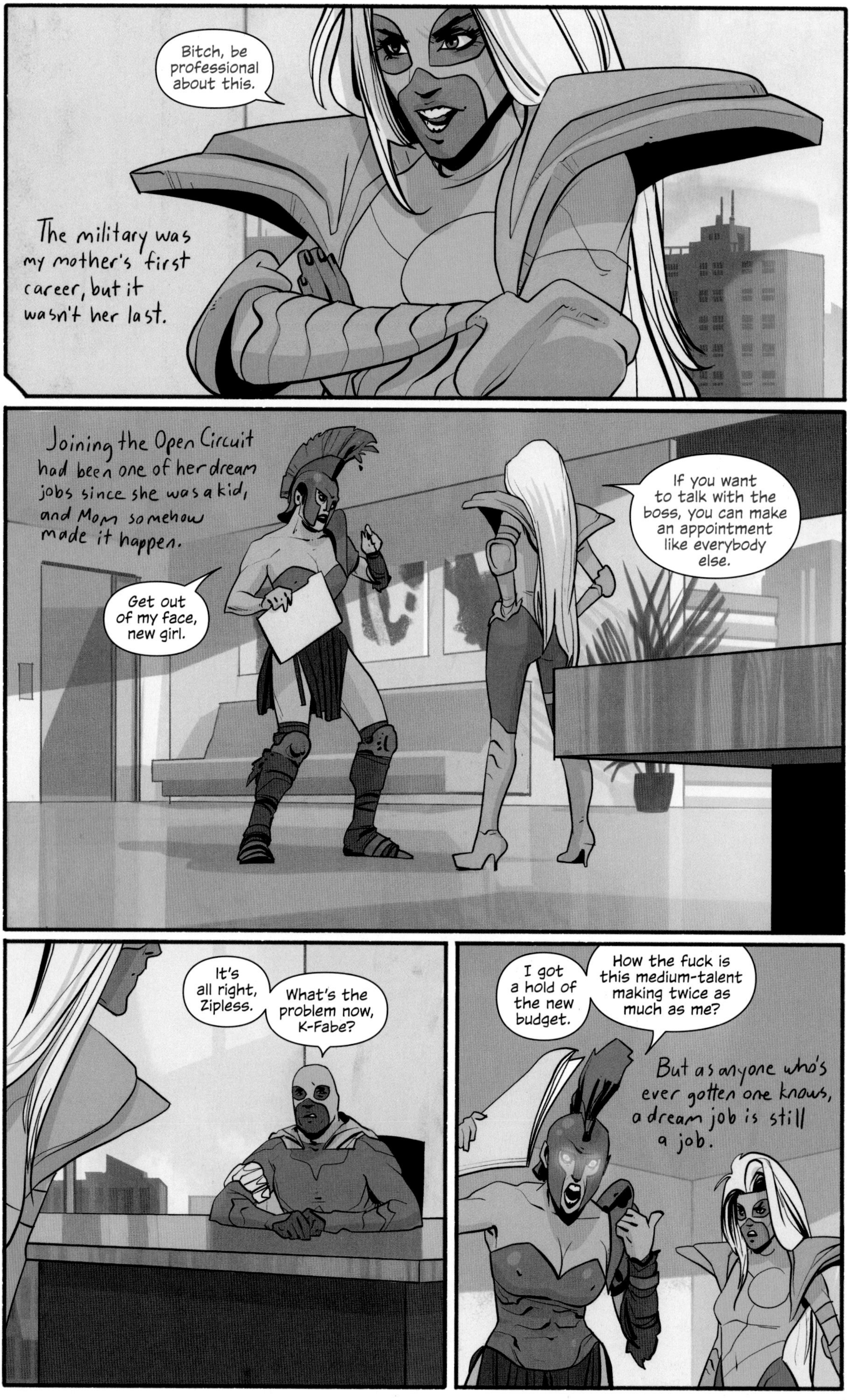

Bitch, be professional about this.
The military was my mother's first career, but it wasn't her last.
Joining the Open Circuit had been one of her dream jobs since she was a kid, and Mom somehow made it happen.
If you want to talk with the boss, you can make an appointment like everybody else.
Get out of my face, new girl.
It's all right, Zipless.
What's the problem now, K-Fabe?
I got a hold of the new budget.
How the fuck is this medium-talent making twice as much as me?
But as anyone who's ever gotten one knows, a dream job is still a job.

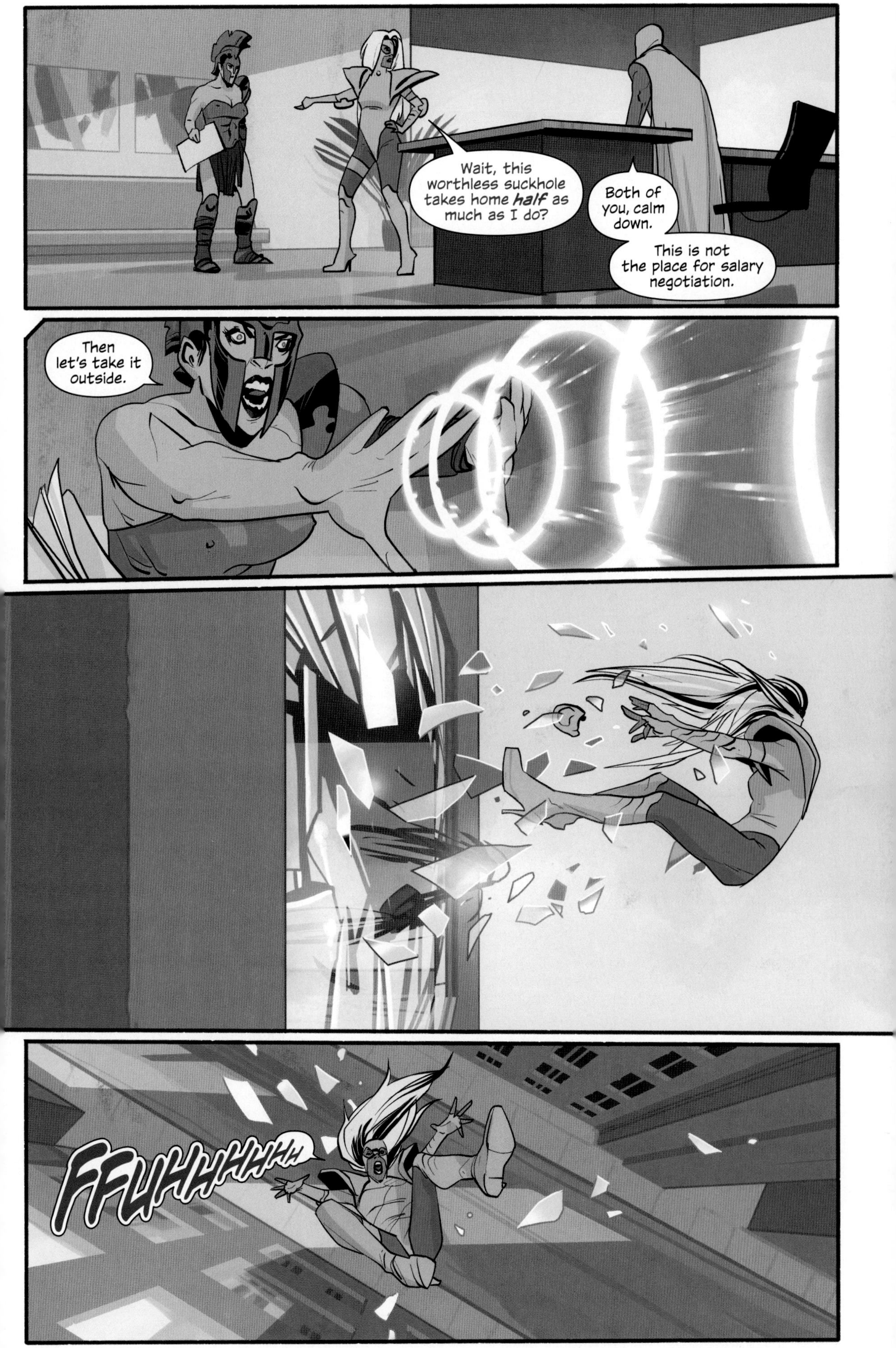

Wait, this worthless suckhole takes home *half* as much as I do?
Both of you, calm down.
This is not the place for salary negotiation.
Then let's take it outside.
FFUHHHHHHH

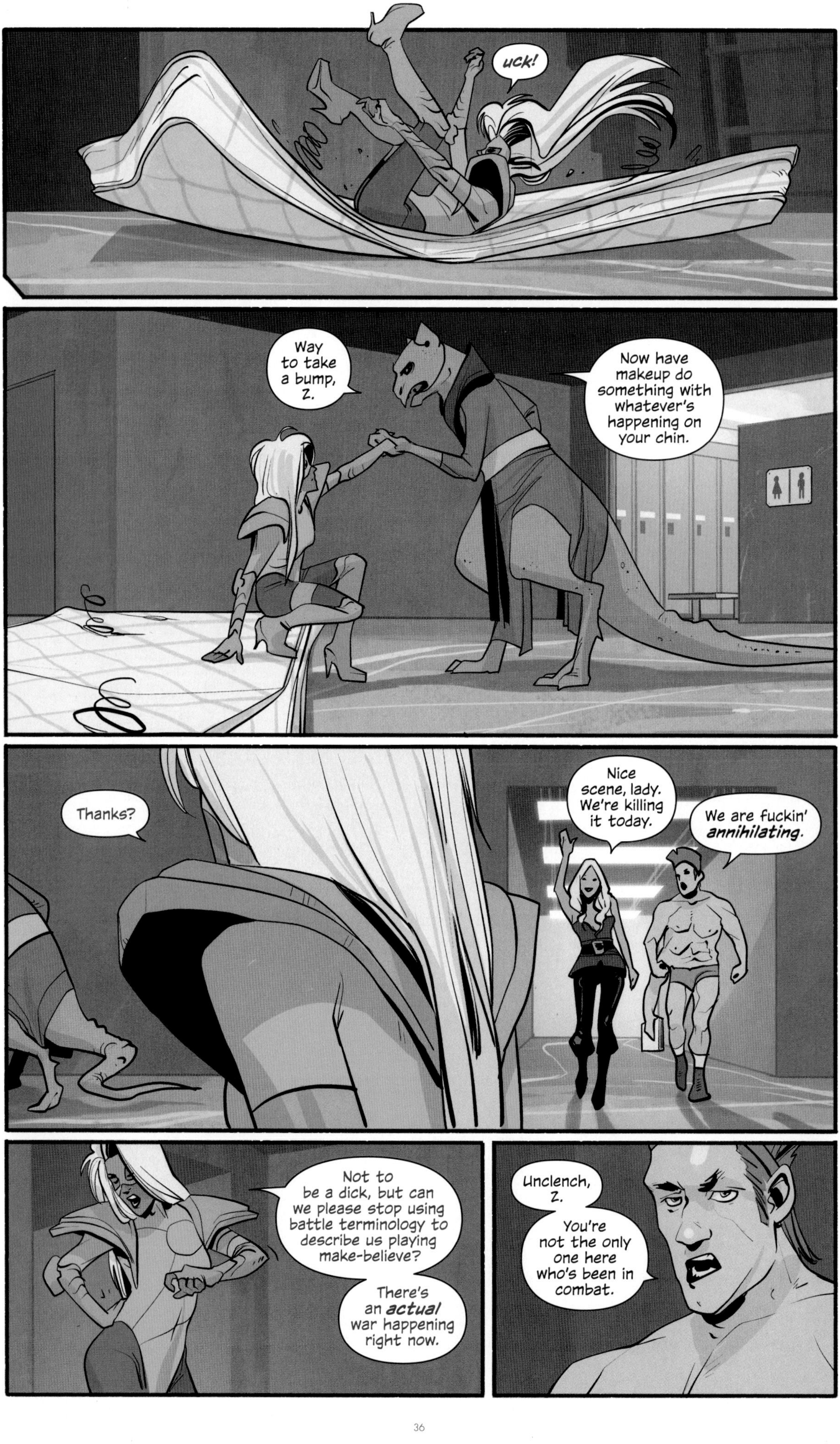
uck!
Way to take a bump, Z.
Now have makeup do something with whatever's happening on your chin.
Thanks?
Nice scene, lady. We're killing it today.
We are fuckin' *annihilating*.
Not to be a dick, but can we please stop using battle terminology to describe us playing make-believe?
There's an *actual* war happening right now.
Unclench, Z.
You're not the only one here who's been in combat.

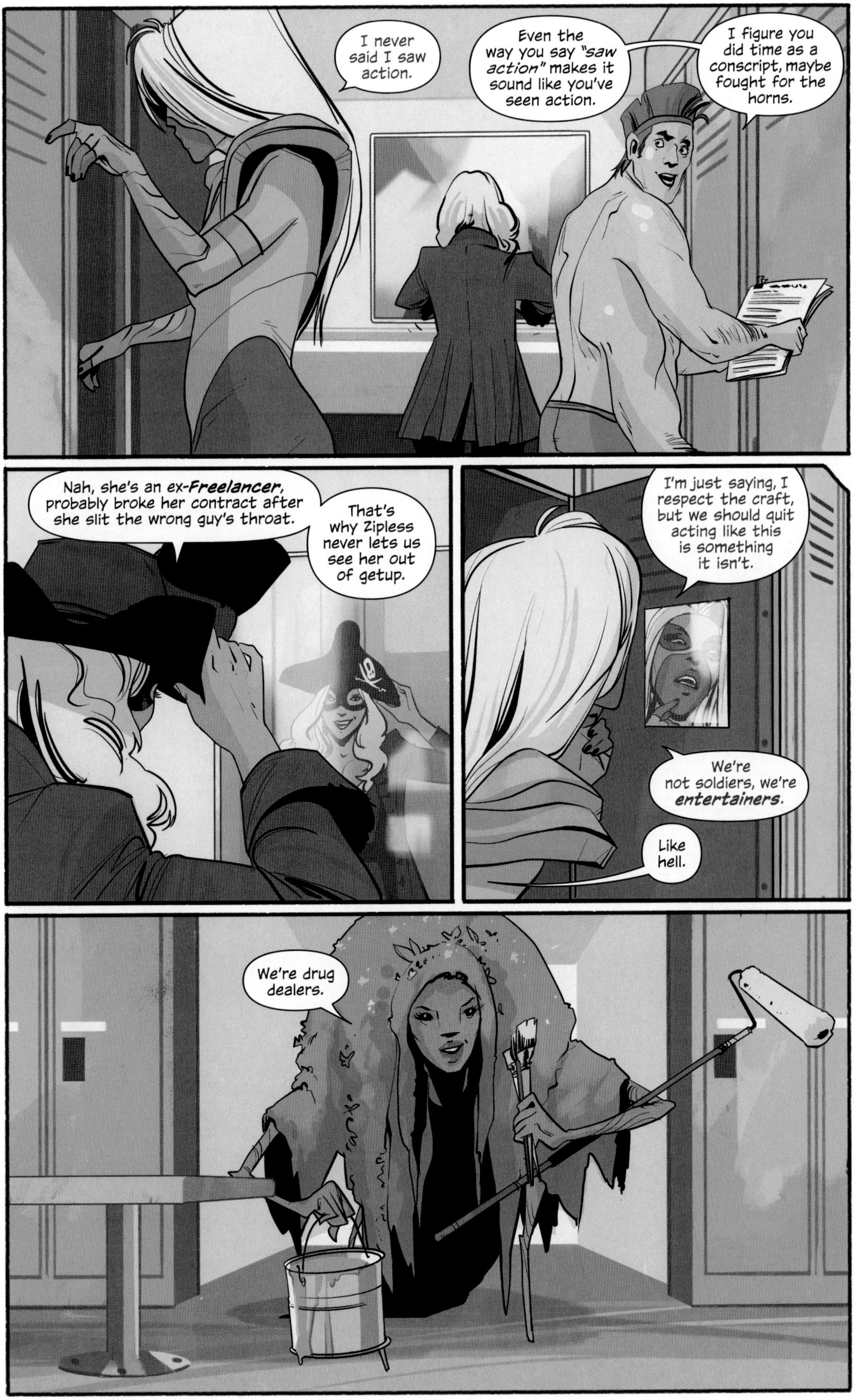
I never said I saw action.
Even the way you say "saw action" makes it sound like you've seen action.
I figure you did time as a conscript, maybe fought for the horns.
Nah, she's an ex-Freelancer, probably broke her contract after she slit the wrong guy's throat.
That's why Zipless never lets us see her out of getup.
I'm just saying, I respect the craft, but we should quit acting like this is something it isn't.
We're not soldiers, we're entertainers.
Like hell.
We're drug dealers.

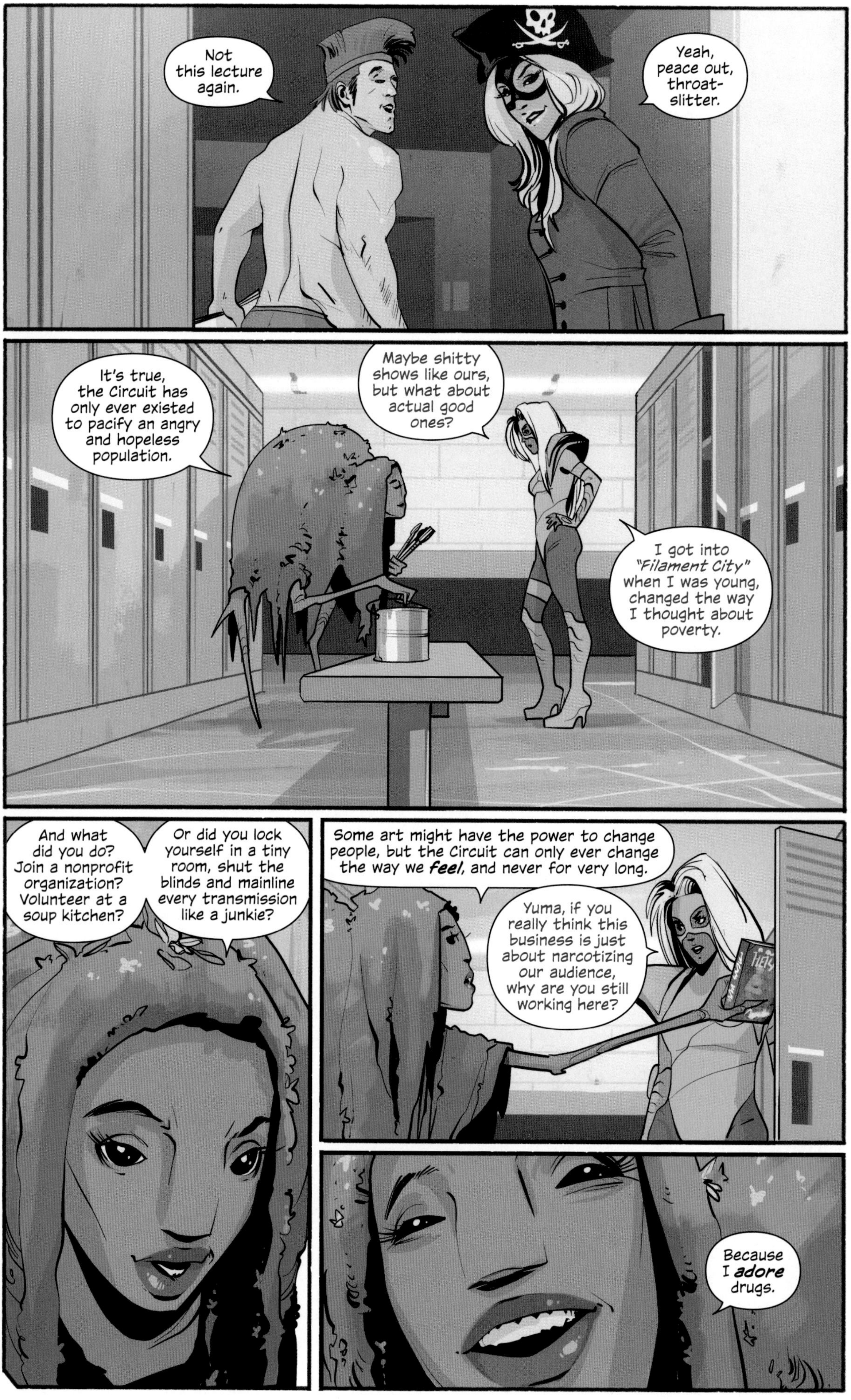
Not this lecture again.
Yeah, peace out, throat-slitter.
It's true, the Circuit has only ever existed to pacify an angry and hopeless population.
Maybe shitty shows like ours, but what about actual good ones?
I got into "Filament City" when I was young, changed the way I thought about poverty.
And what did you do? Join a nonprofit organization? Volunteer at a soup kitchen?
Or did you lock yourself in a tiny room, shut the blinds and mainline every transmission like a junkie?
Some art might have the power to change people, but the Circuit can only ever change the way we *feel*, and never for very long.
Yuma, if you really think this business is just about narcotizing our audience, why are you still working here?
Because I ***adore*** drugs.

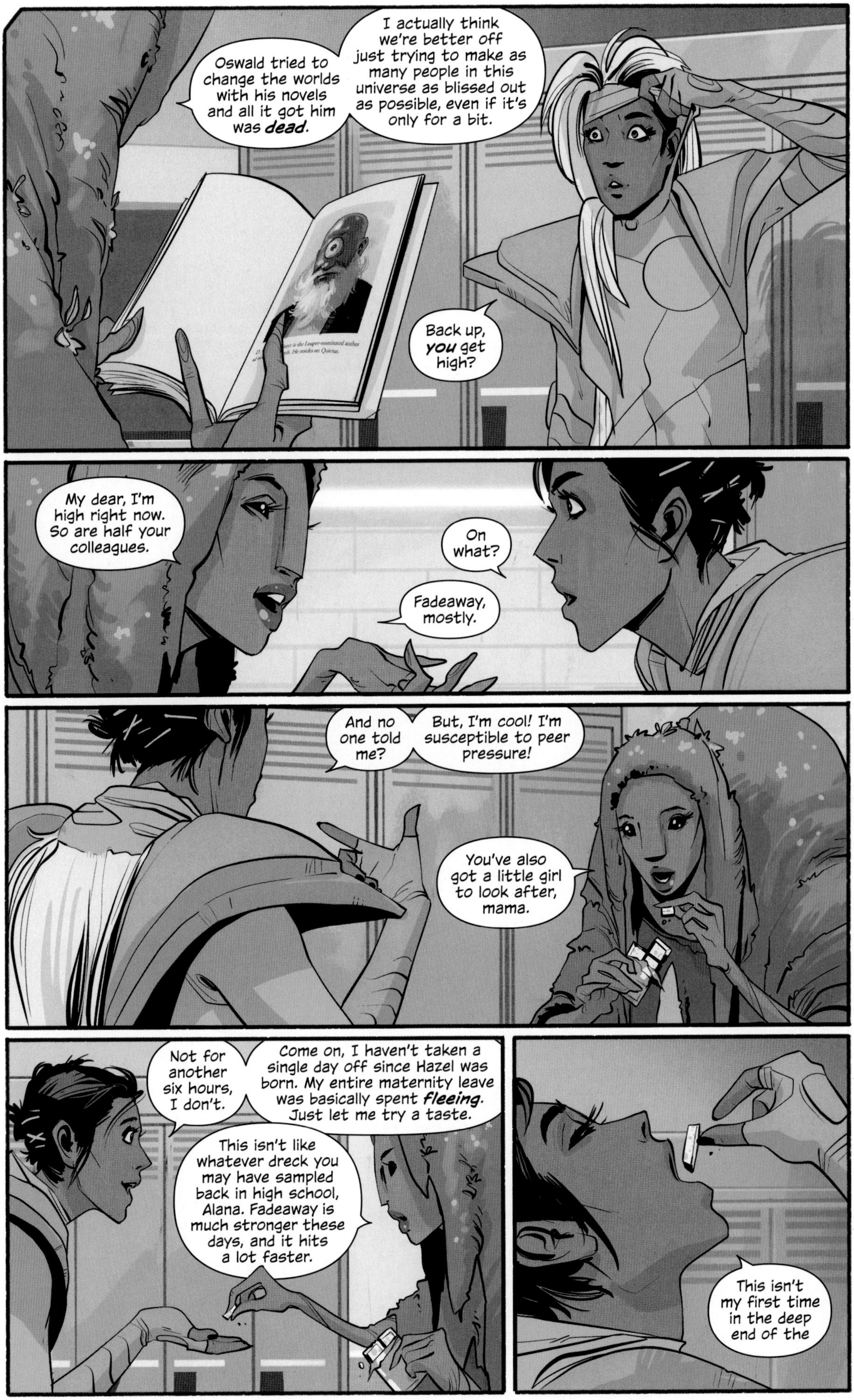
Oswald tried to change the worlds with his novels and all it got him was *dead.*
I actually think we're better off just trying to make as many people in this universe as blissed out as possible, even if it's only for a bit.
Back up, *you* get high?
My dear, I'm high right now. So are half your colleagues.
On what?
Fadeaway, mostly.
And no one told me?
But, I'm cool! I'm susceptible to peer pressure!
You've also got a little girl to look after, mama.
Not for another six hours, I don't.
Come on, I haven't taken a single day off since Hazel was born. My entire maternity leave was basically spent *fleeing.* Just let me try a taste.
This isn't like whatever dreck you may have sampled back in high school, Alana. Fadeaway is much stronger these days, and it hits a lot faster.
This isn't my first time in the deep end of the

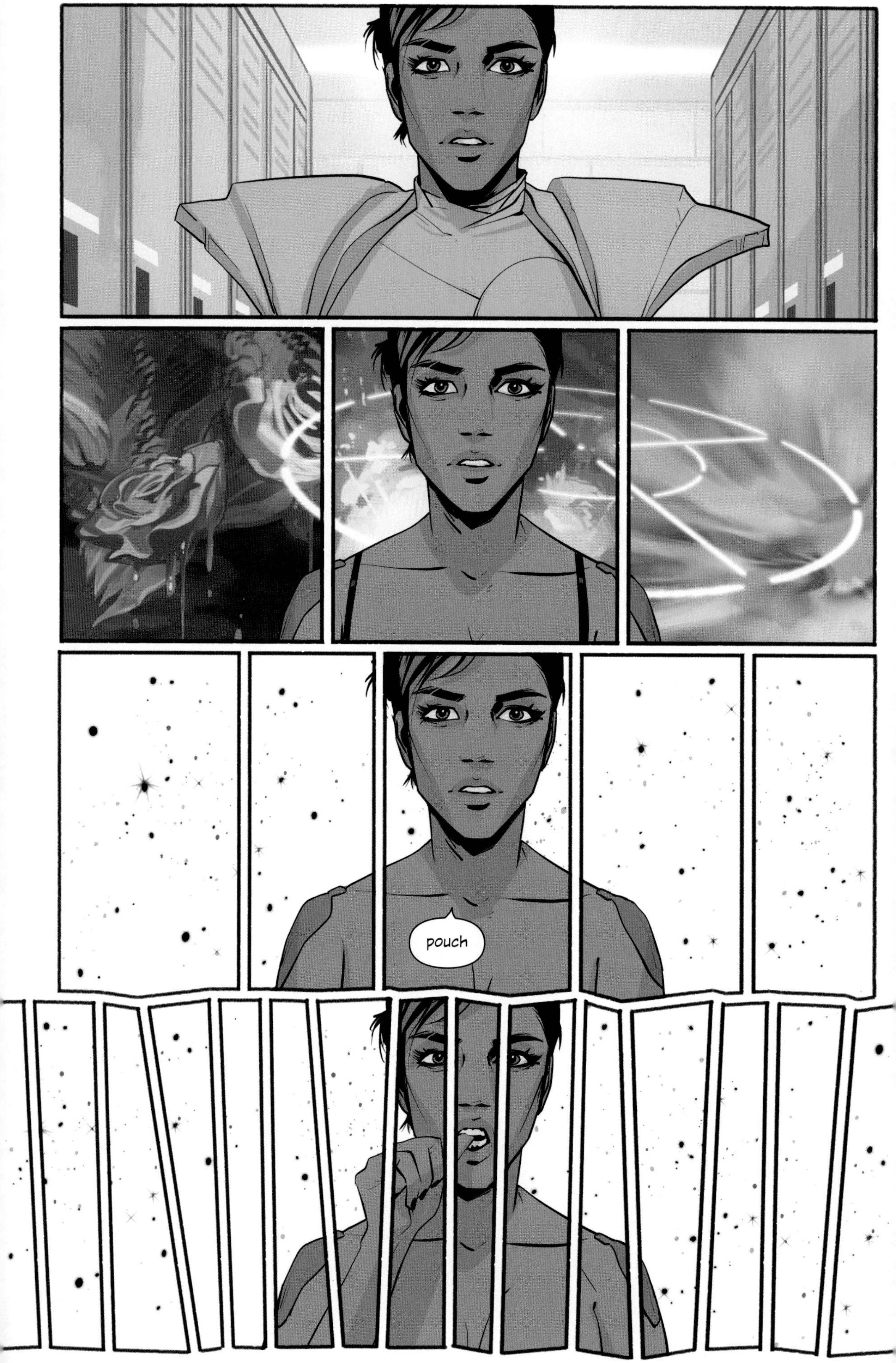
pouch

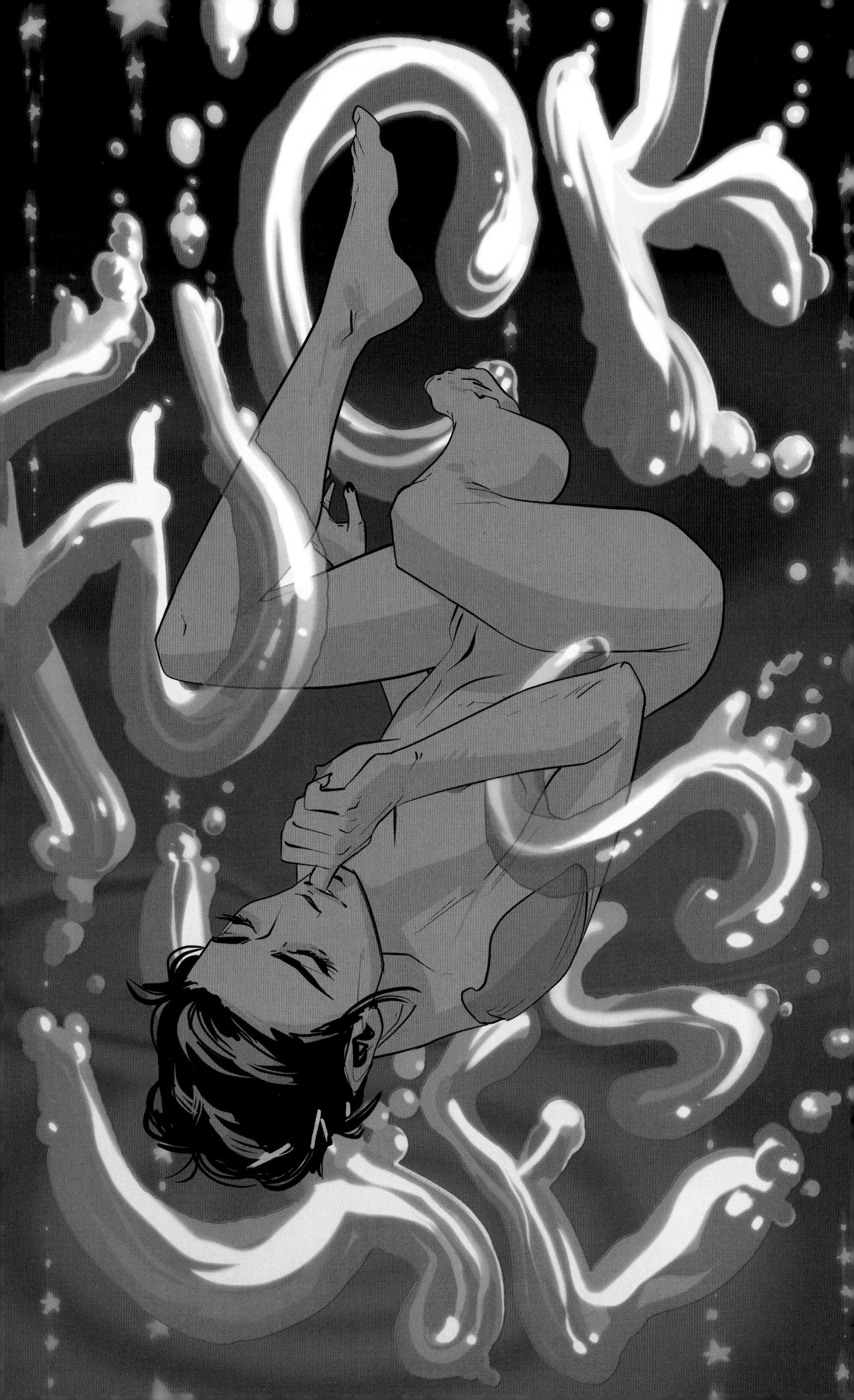

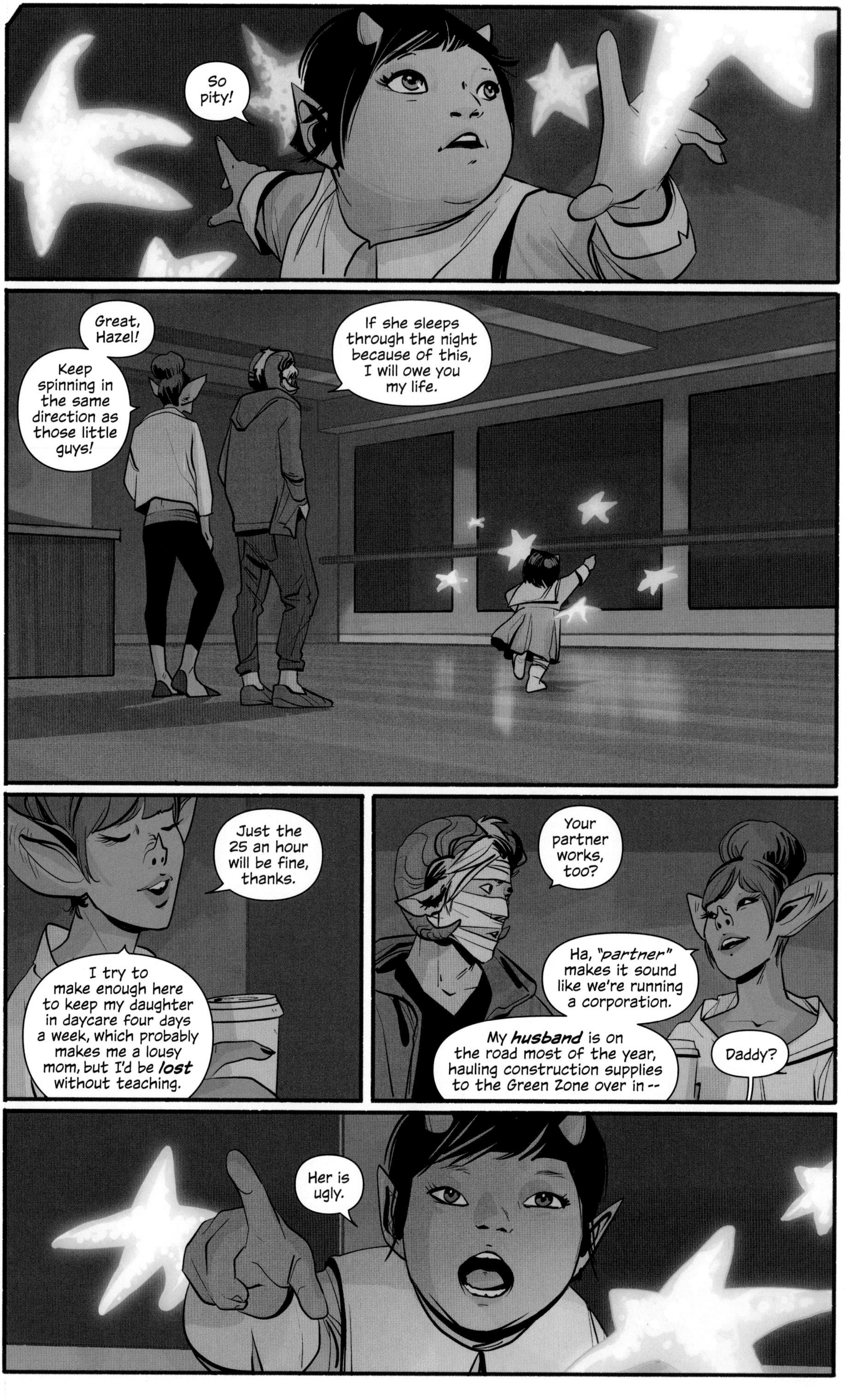
So pity!
Great, Hazel!
Keep spinning in the same direction as those little guys!
If she sleeps through the night because of this, I will owe you my life.
Just the 25 an hour will be fine, thanks.
I try to make enough here to keep my daughter in daycare four days a week, which probably makes me a lousy mom, but I'd be *lost* without teaching.
Your partner works, too?
Ha, *"partner"* makes it sound like we're running a corporation.
My **husband** is on the road most of the year, hauling construction supplies to the Green Zone over in --
Daddy?
Her is ugly.

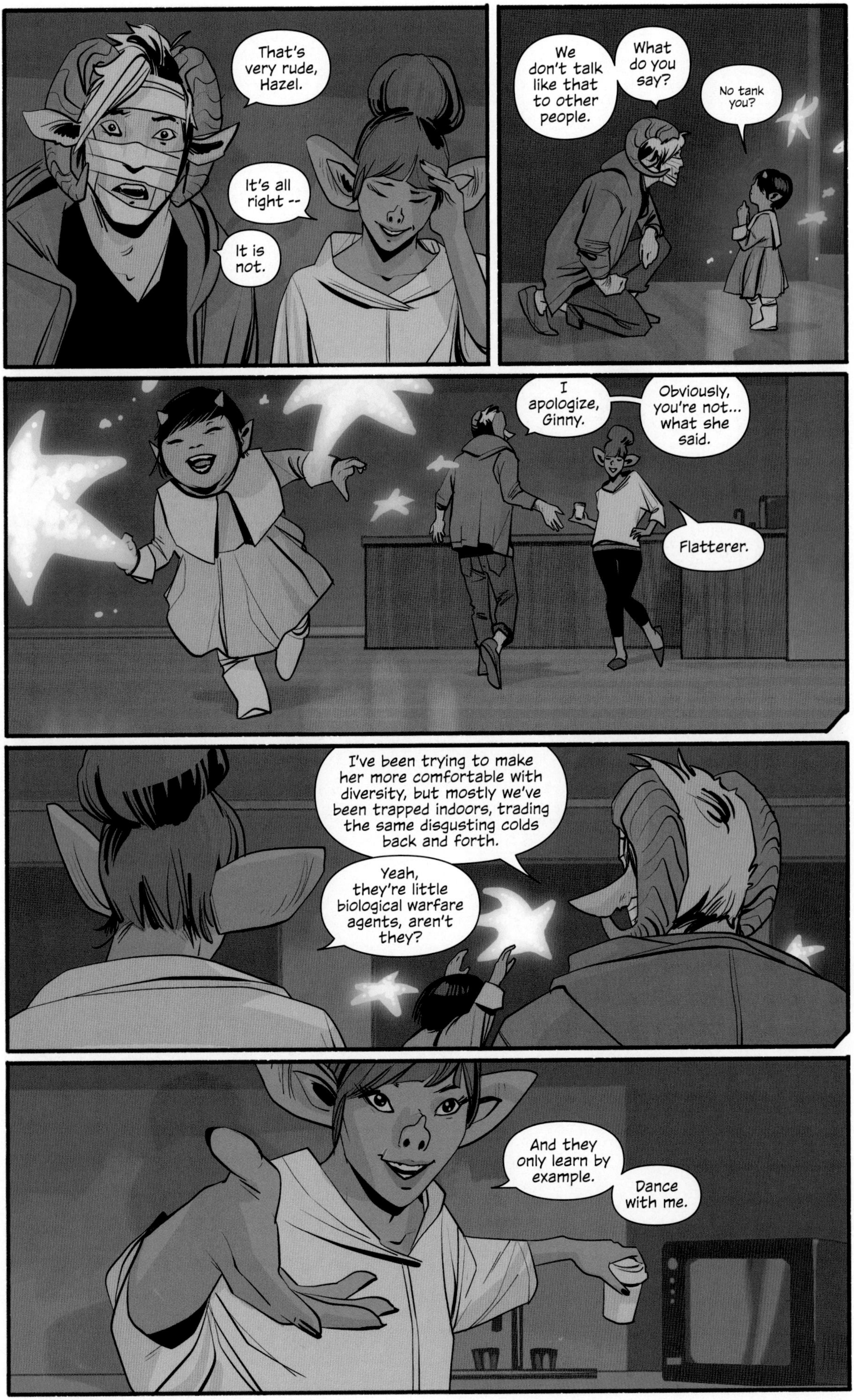

That's very rude, Hazel.
It's all right --
It is not.
We don't talk like that to other people.
What do you say?
No tank you?
I apologize, Ginny.
Obviously, you're not... what she said.
Flatterer.
I've been trying to make her more comfortable with diversity, but mostly we've been trapped indoors, trading the same disgusting colds back and forth.
Yeah, they're little biological warfare agents, aren't they?
And they only learn by example.
Dance with me.

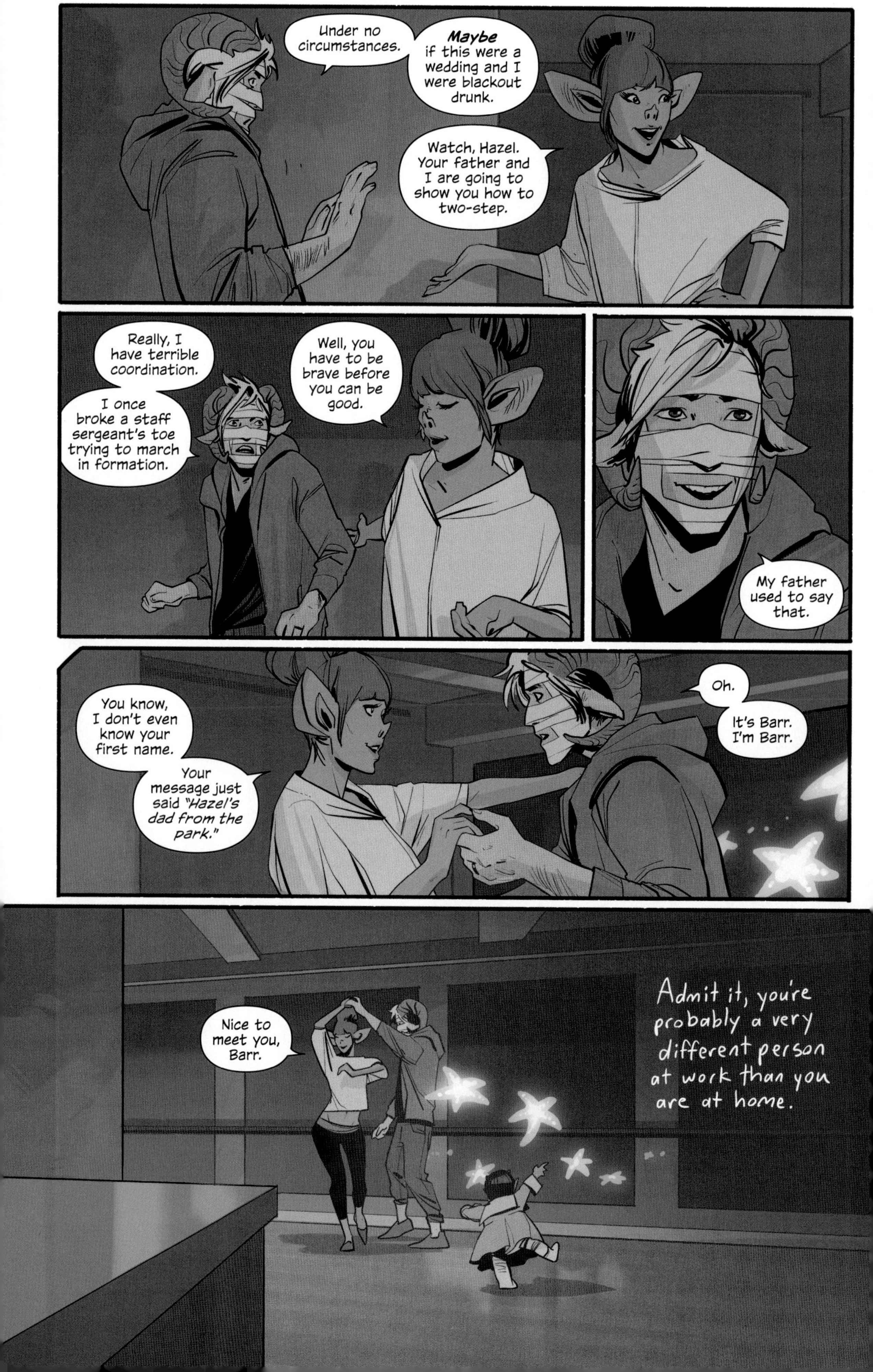

Under no circumstances.
Maybe if this were a wedding and I were blackout drunk.
Watch, Hazel. Your father and I are going to show you how to two-step.
Really, I have terrible coordination.
I once broke a staff sergeant's toe trying to march in formation.
Well, you have to be brave before you can be good.
My father used to say that.
You know, I don't even know your first name.
Your message just said *"Hazel's dad from the park."*
Oh.
It's Barr. I'm Barr.
Nice to meet you, Barr.
Admit it, you're probably a very different person at work than you are at home.

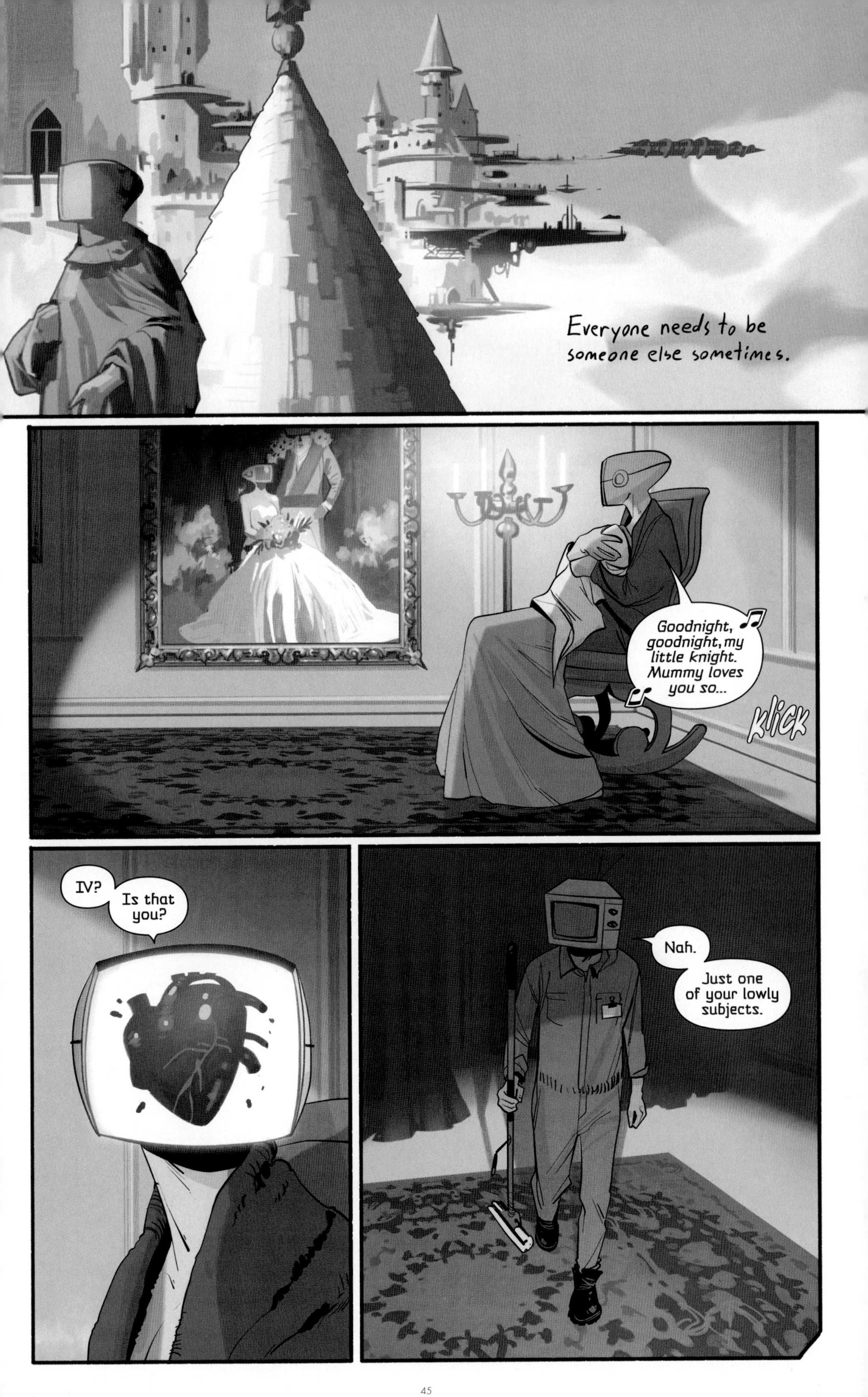
Everyone needs to be someone else sometimes.
Goodnight, goodnight, my little knight. Mummy loves you so...
KLICK
IV?
Is that you?
Nah.
Just one of your lowly subjects.

Who the fuck...?
I've been your custodian for nearly two years, and you don't even know my name?
HELP!
No need to wake the baby, Princess.
I gave your palace guards the night off.
Please.
I don't care what you do to me, but please don't hurt my boy.
I would never harm a child. I'm a father myself.
At least, I was for a time.

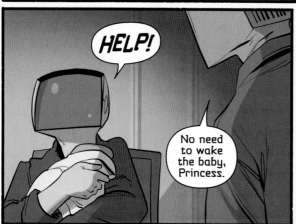

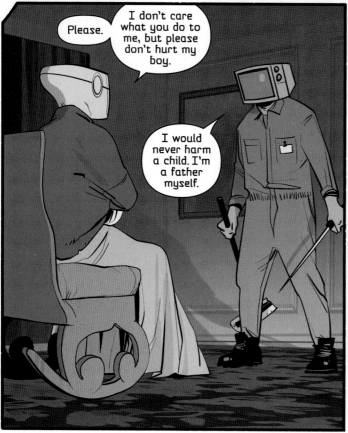

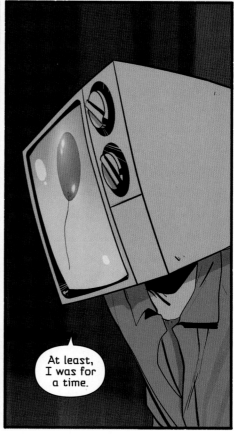

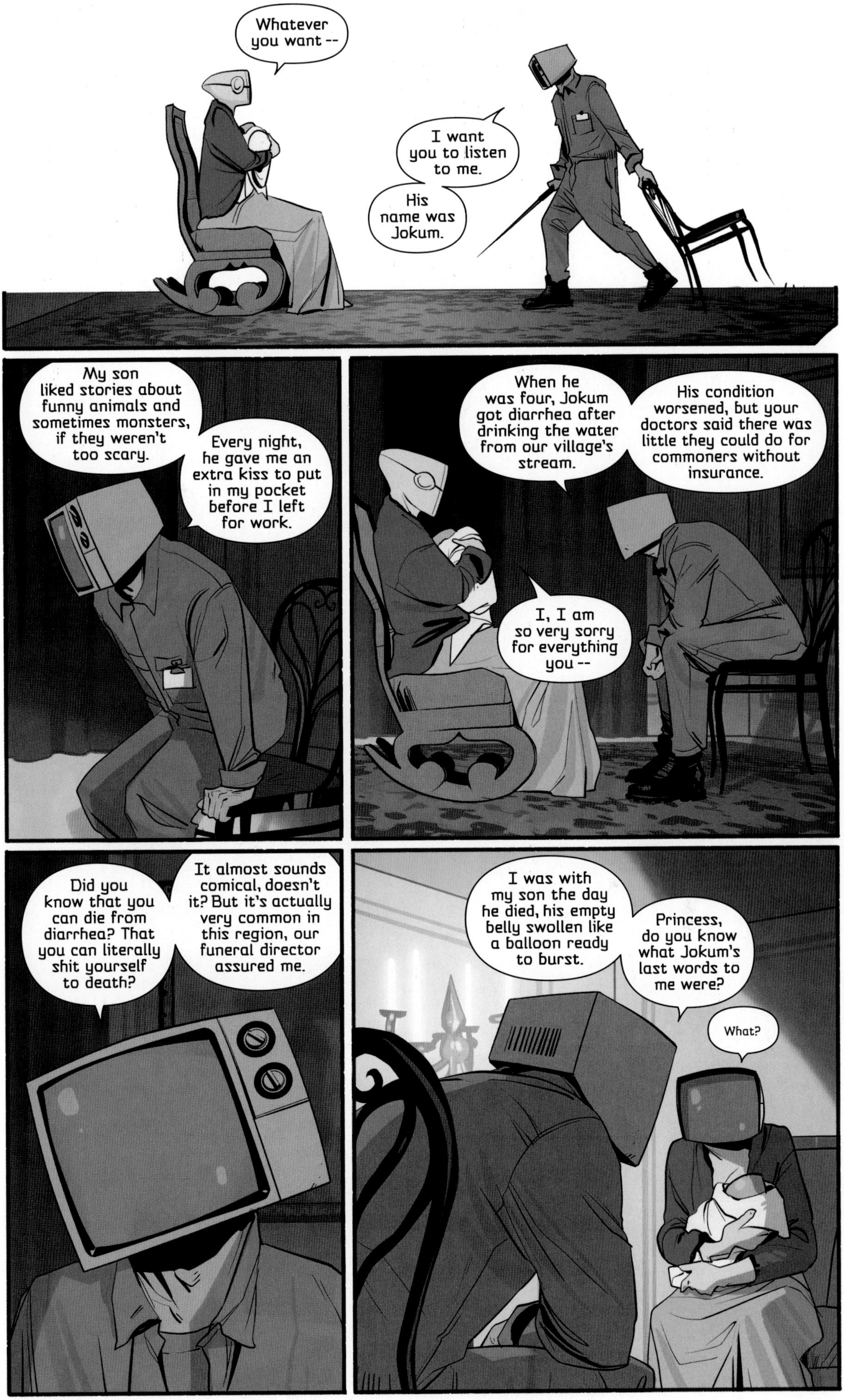
Whatever you want --
I want you to listen to me.
His name was Jokum.
My son liked stories about funny animals and sometimes monsters, if they weren't too scary.
Every night, he gave me an extra kiss to put in my pocket before I left for work.
When he was four, Jokum got diarrhea after drinking the water from our village's stream.
His condition worsened, but your doctors said there was little they could do for commoners without insurance.
I, I am so very sorry for everything you --
Did you know that you can die from diarrhea? That you can literally shit yourself to death?
It almost sounds comical, doesn't it? But it's actually very common in this region, our funeral director assured me.
I was with my son the day he died, his empty belly swollen like a balloon ready to burst.
Princess, do you know what Jokum's last words to me were?
What?

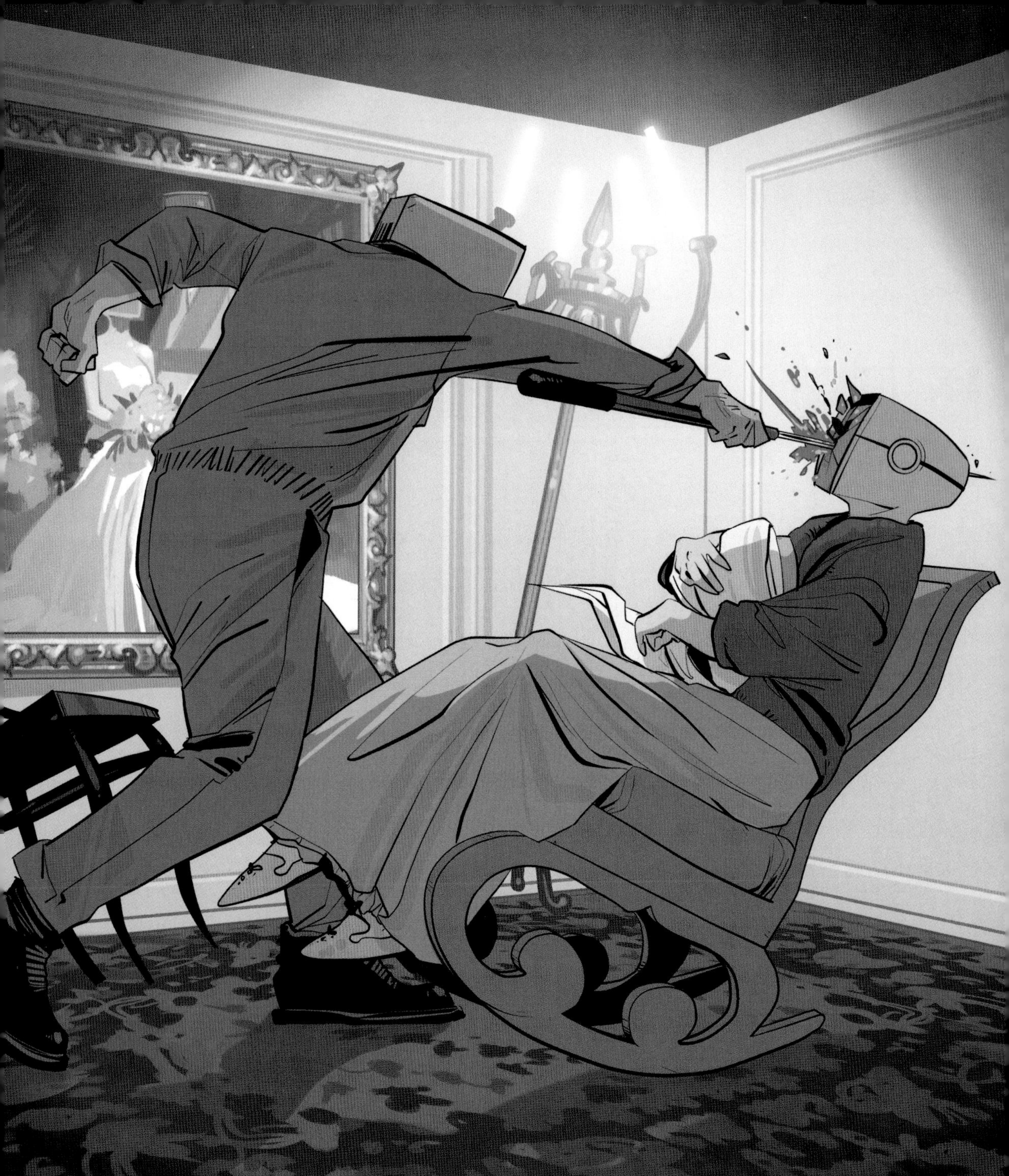

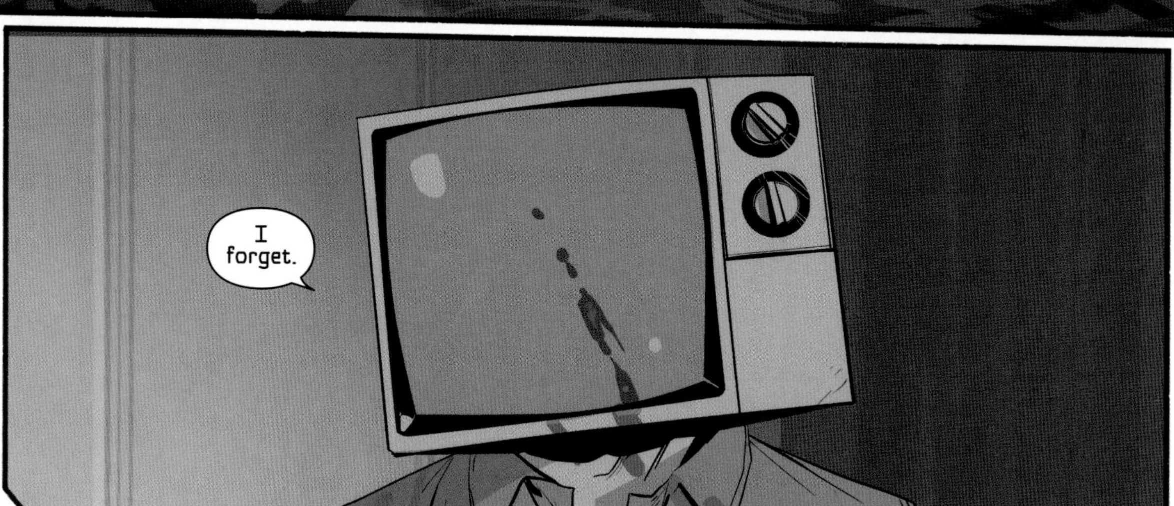
I forget.

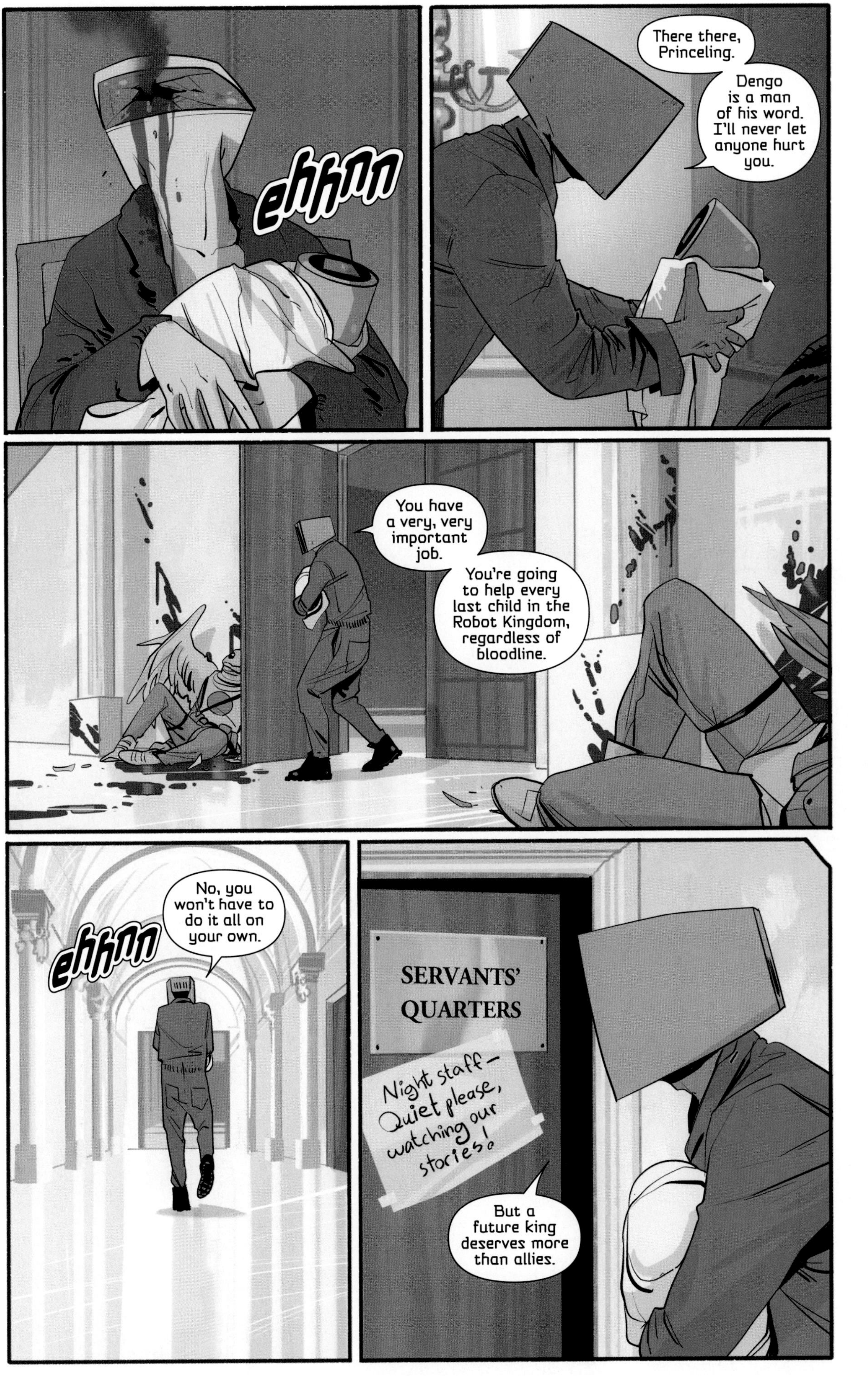
ehhnn
There there, Princeling.
Dengo is a man of his word. I'll never let anyone hurt you.
You have a very, very important job.
You're going to help every last child in the Robot Kingdom, regardless of bloodline.
ehhnn
No, you won't have to do it all on your own.
SERVANTS' QUARTERS
Night staff— Quiet please, watching our stories!
But a future king deserves more than allies.

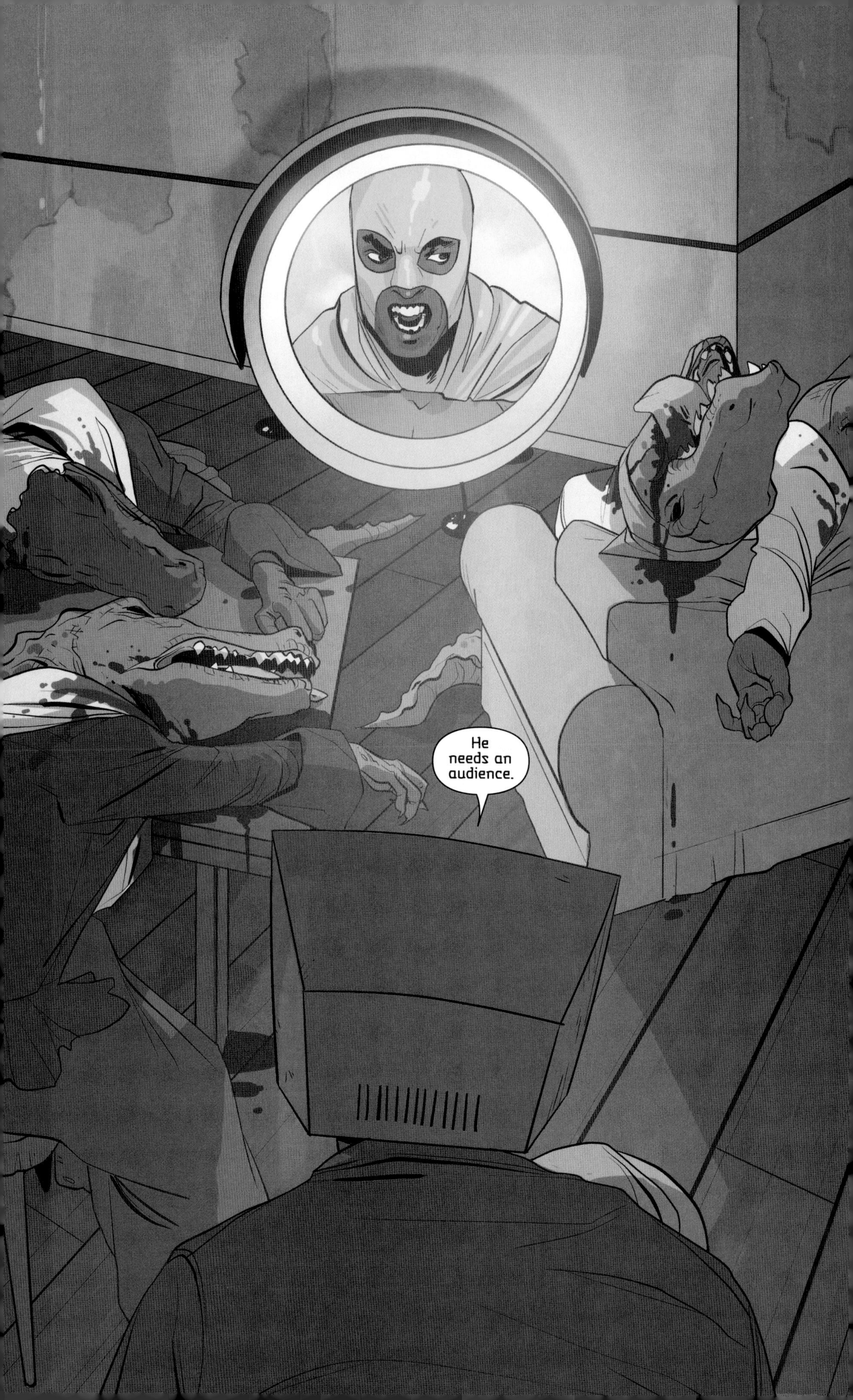
He needs an audience.

end chapter twenty

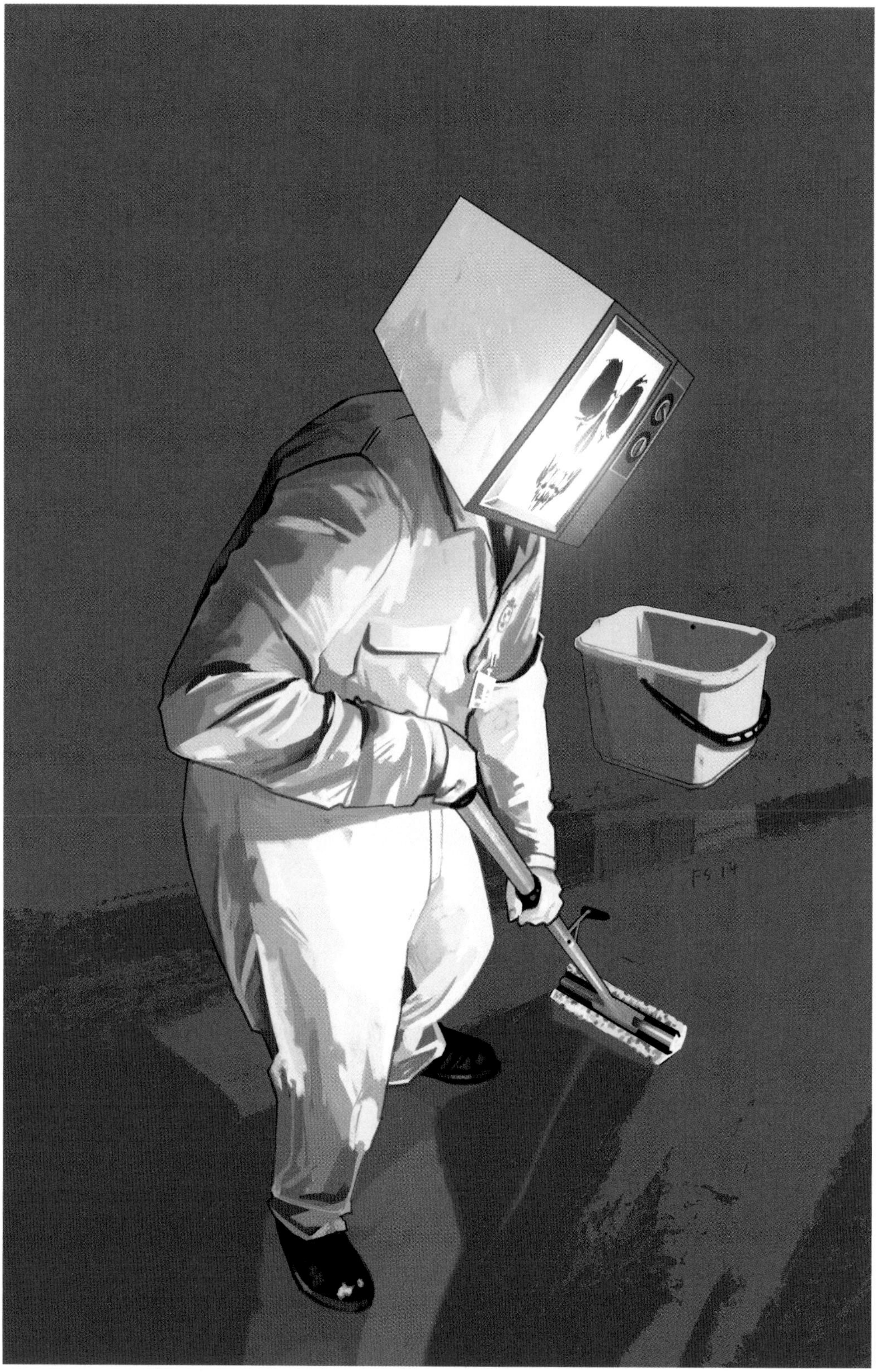

CHAPTER

TWENTY-ONE

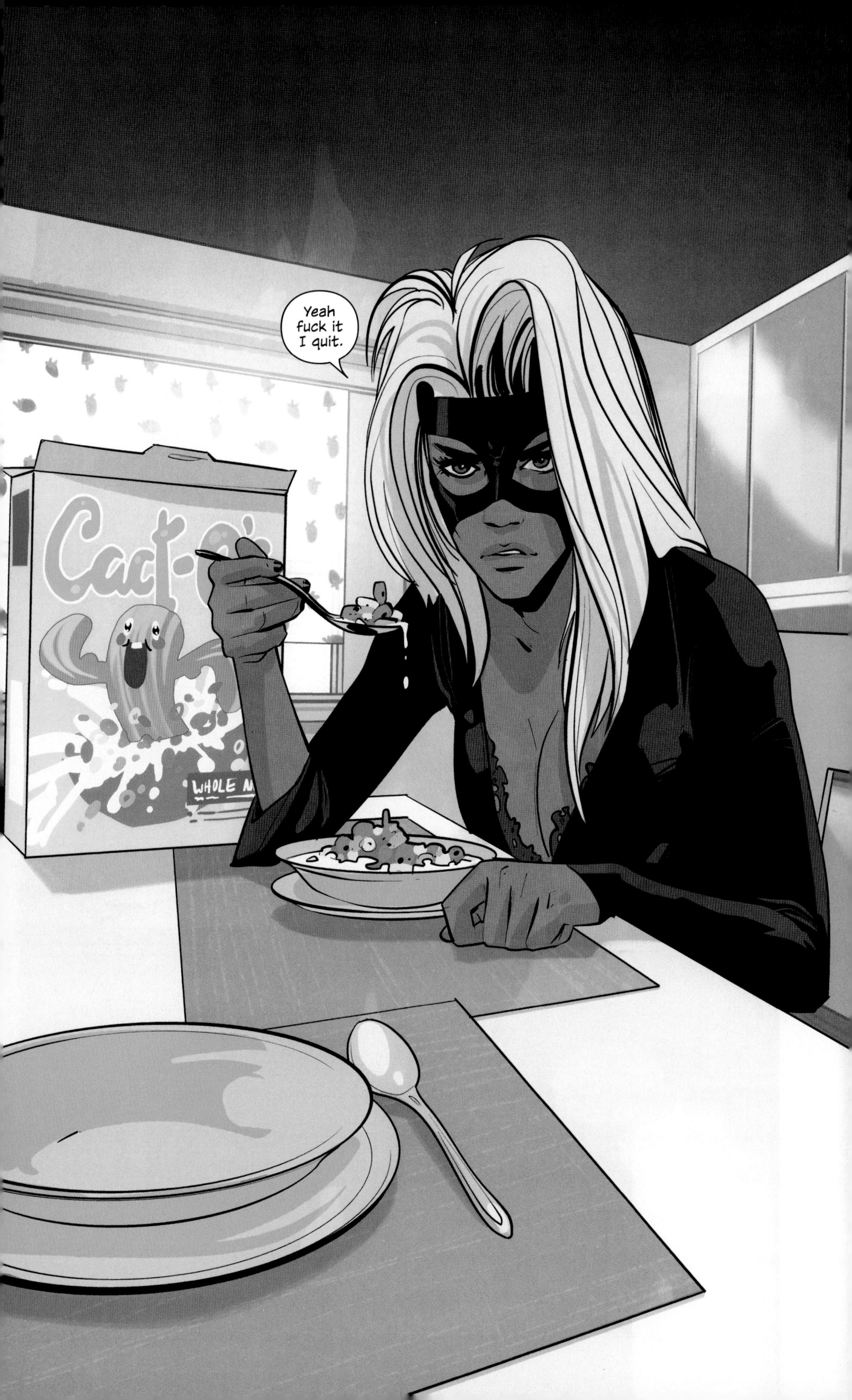
Yeah fuck it I quit.
Cact-O's
WHOLE

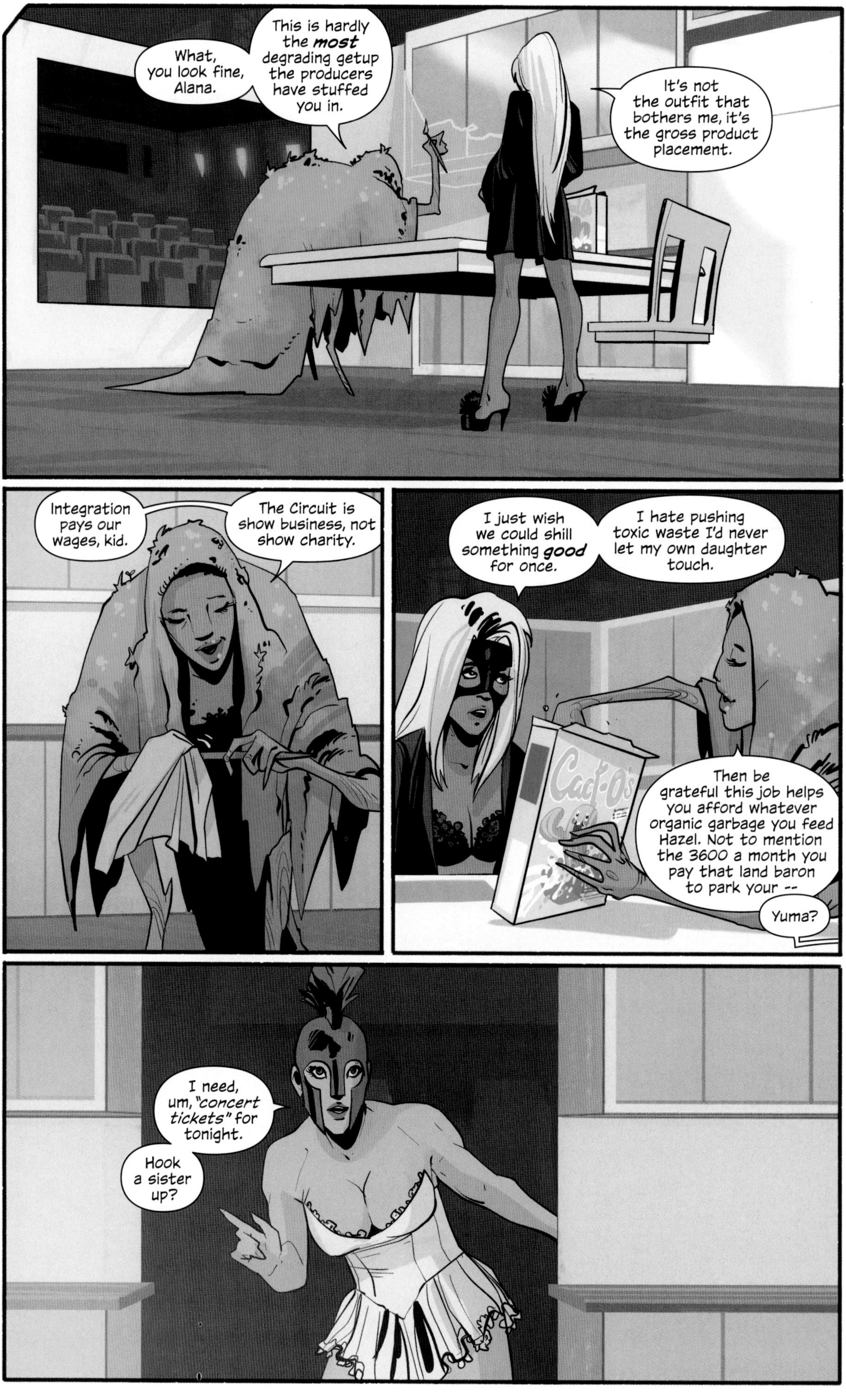

What, you look fine, Alana.
This is hardly the *most* degrading getup the producers have stuffed you in.
It's not the outfit that bothers me, it's the gross product placement.
Integration pays our wages, kid.
The Circuit is show business, not show charity.
I just wish we could shill something *good* for once.
I hate pushing toxic waste I'd never let my own daughter touch.
Cact-O's
Then be grateful this job helps you afford whatever organic garbage you feed Hazel. Not to mention the 3600 a month you pay that land baron to park your --
Yuma?
I need, um, *"concert tickets"* for tonight.
Hook a sister up?

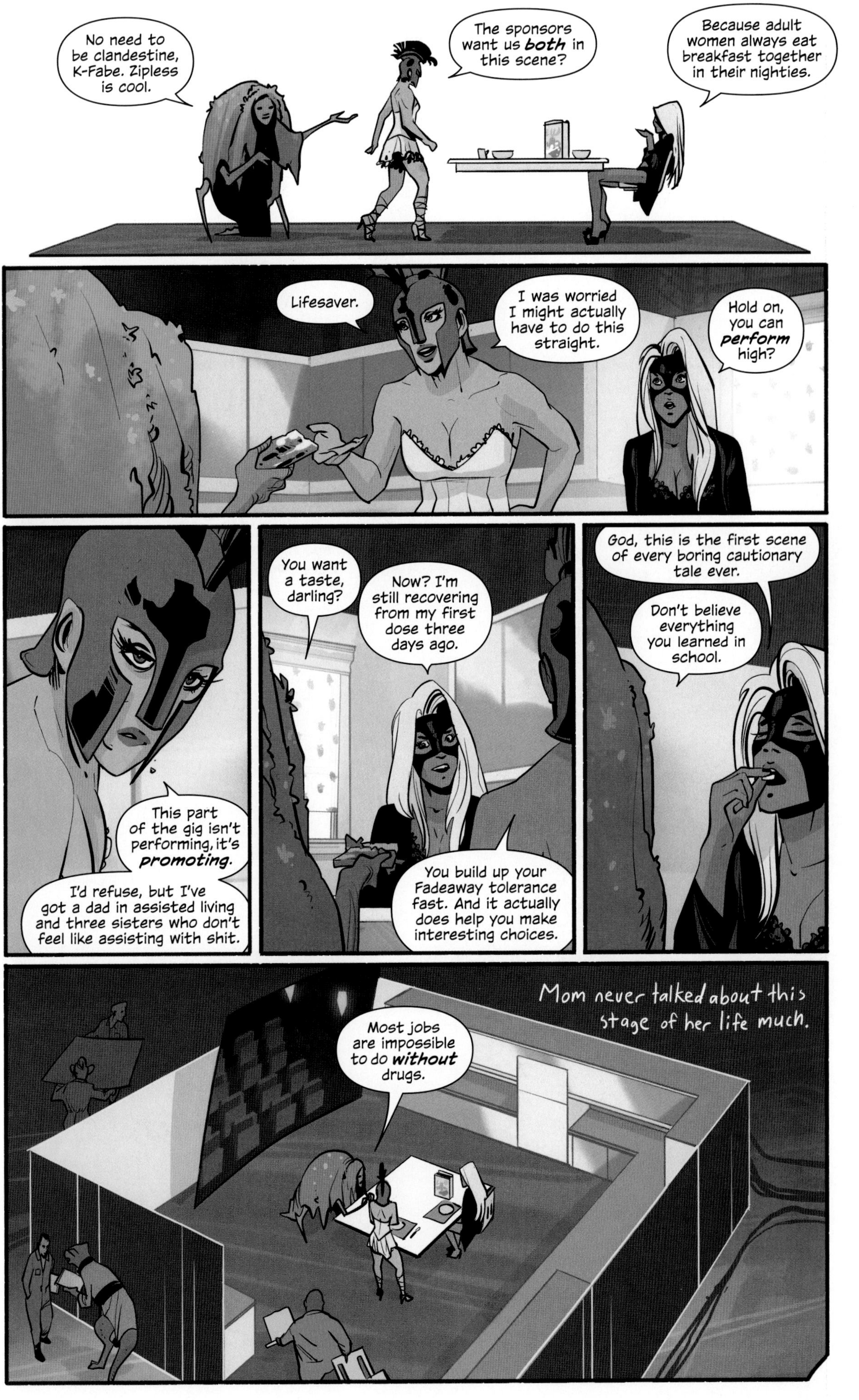
No need to be clandestine, K-Fabe. Zipless is cool.
The sponsors want us *both* in this scene?
Because adult women always eat breakfast together in their nighties.
Lifesaver.
I was worried I might actually have to do this straight.
Hold on, you can *perform* high?
This part of the gig isn't performing, it's *promoting*.
I'd refuse, but I've got a dad in assisted living and three sisters who don't feel like assisting with shit.
You want a taste, darling?
Now? I'm still recovering from my first dose three days ago.
You build up your Fadeaway tolerance fast. And it actually does help you make interesting choices.
God, this is the first scene of every boring cautionary tale ever.
Don't believe everything you learned in school.
Mom never talked about this stage of her life much.
Most jobs are impossible to do *without* drugs.

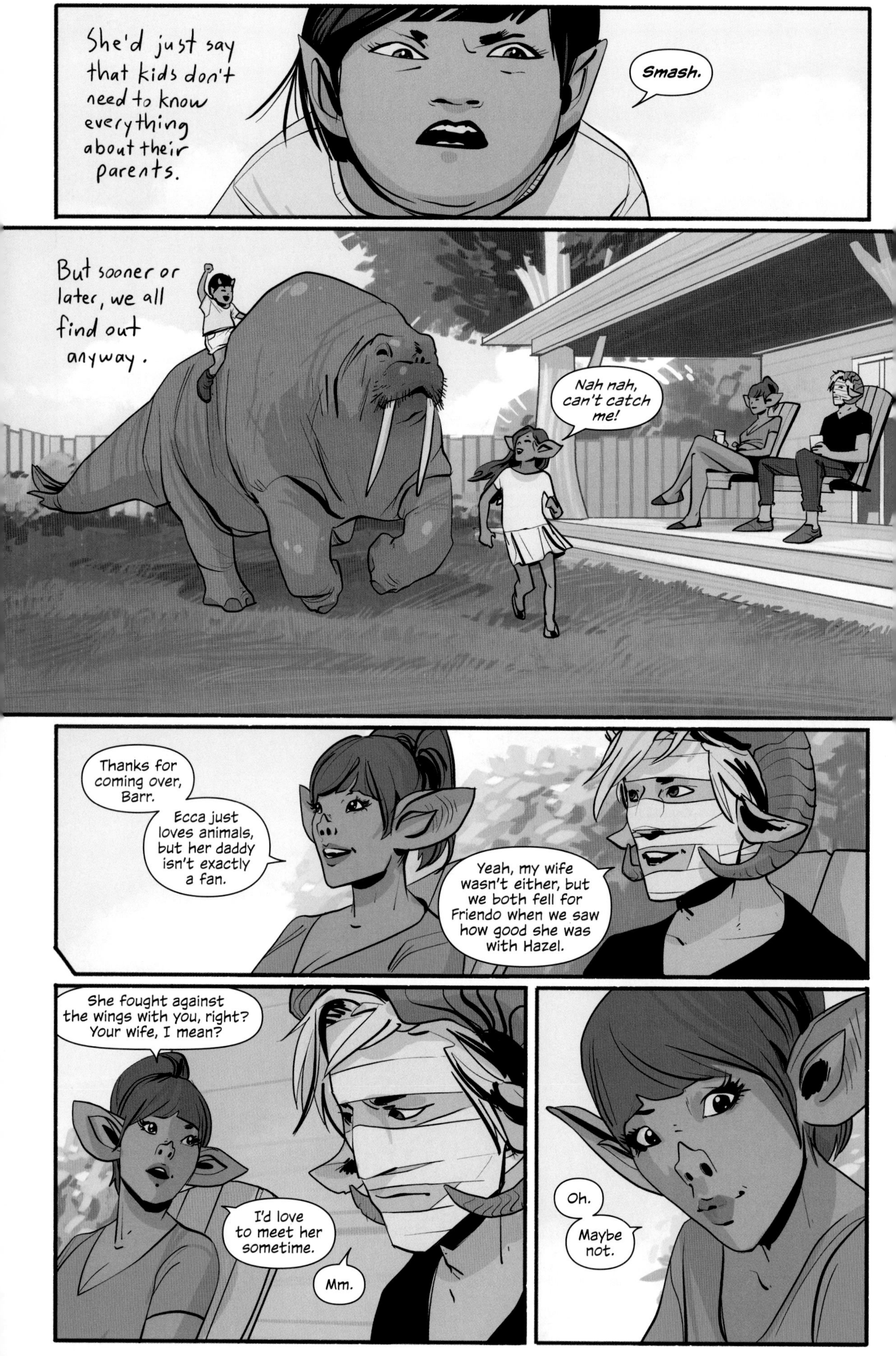
She'd just say that kids don't need to know everything about their parents.
Smash.
But sooner or later, we all find out anyway.
Nah nah, can't catch me!
Thanks for coming over, Barr.
Ecca just loves animals, but her daddy isn't exactly a fan.
Yeah, my wife wasn't either, but we both fell for Friendo when we saw how good she was with Hazel.
She fought against the wings with you, right? Your wife, I mean?
I'd love to meet her sometime.
Mm.
Oh.
Maybe not.

It's not like that, Ginny.

I just don't see much of her myself these days. She's been putting in crazy hours all month.

What line of work, if you don't mind me prying?

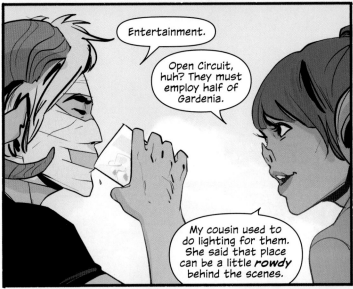

Entertainment.

Open Circuit, huh? They must employ half of Gardenia.

My cousin used to do lighting for them. She said that place can be a little *rowdy* behind the scenes.

I wouldn't know.

Ala... Alexis doesn't really like to talk shop with what little time off she has, so I try not to ask.

Sounds like Henri and me.

When we're together, we're *together*, but when he's on the road... we trust each other to live our lives.

A healthy marriage needs a few secrets, right?

Mom!

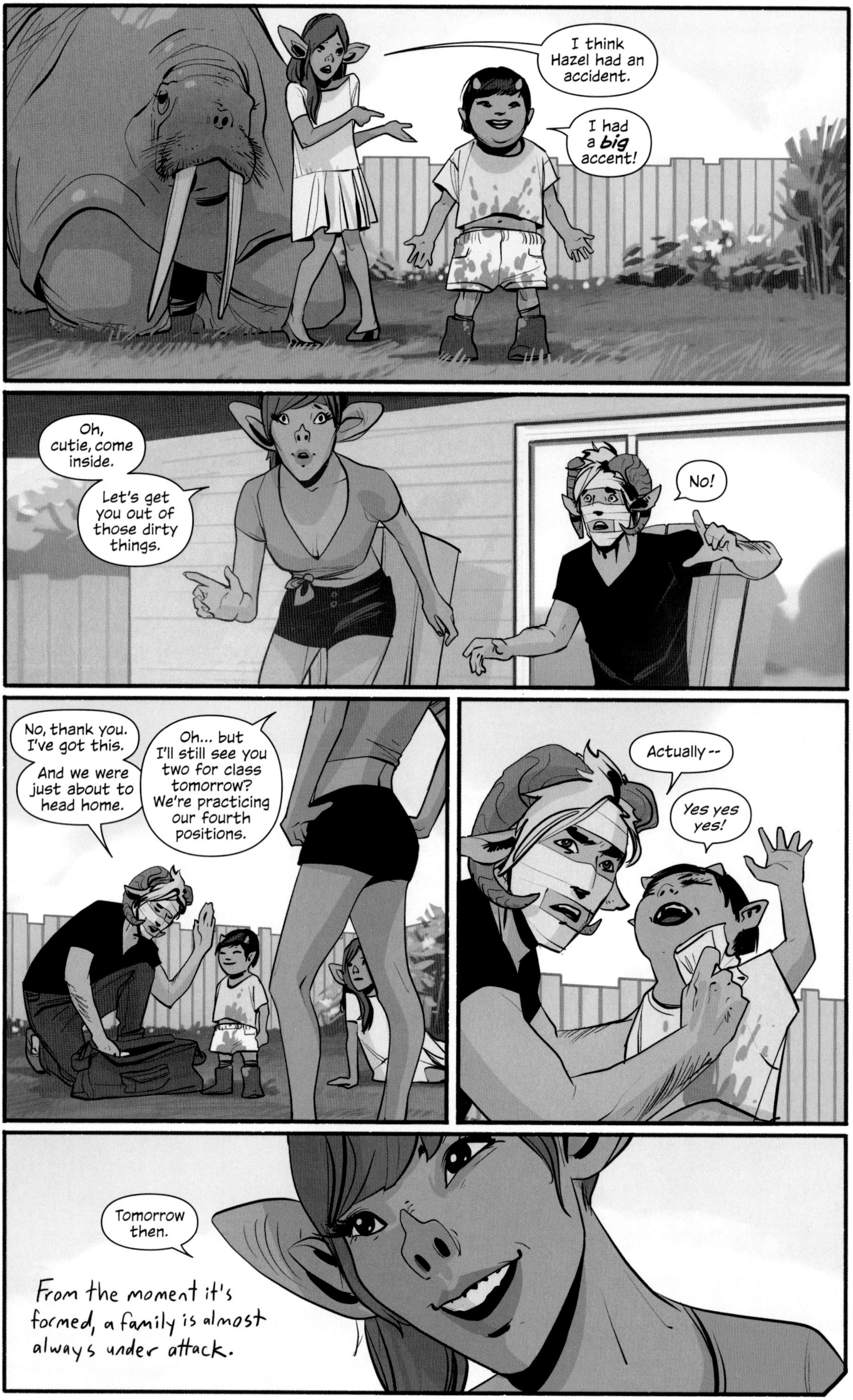
I think Hazel had an accident.
I had a **big** accent!
Oh, cutie, come inside.
Let's get you out of those dirty things.
No!
No, thank you. I've got this.
And we were just about to head home.
Oh... but I'll still see you two for class tomorrow? We're practicing our fourth positions.
Actually --
Yes yes yes!
Tomorrow then.
From the moment it's formed, a family is almost always under attack.

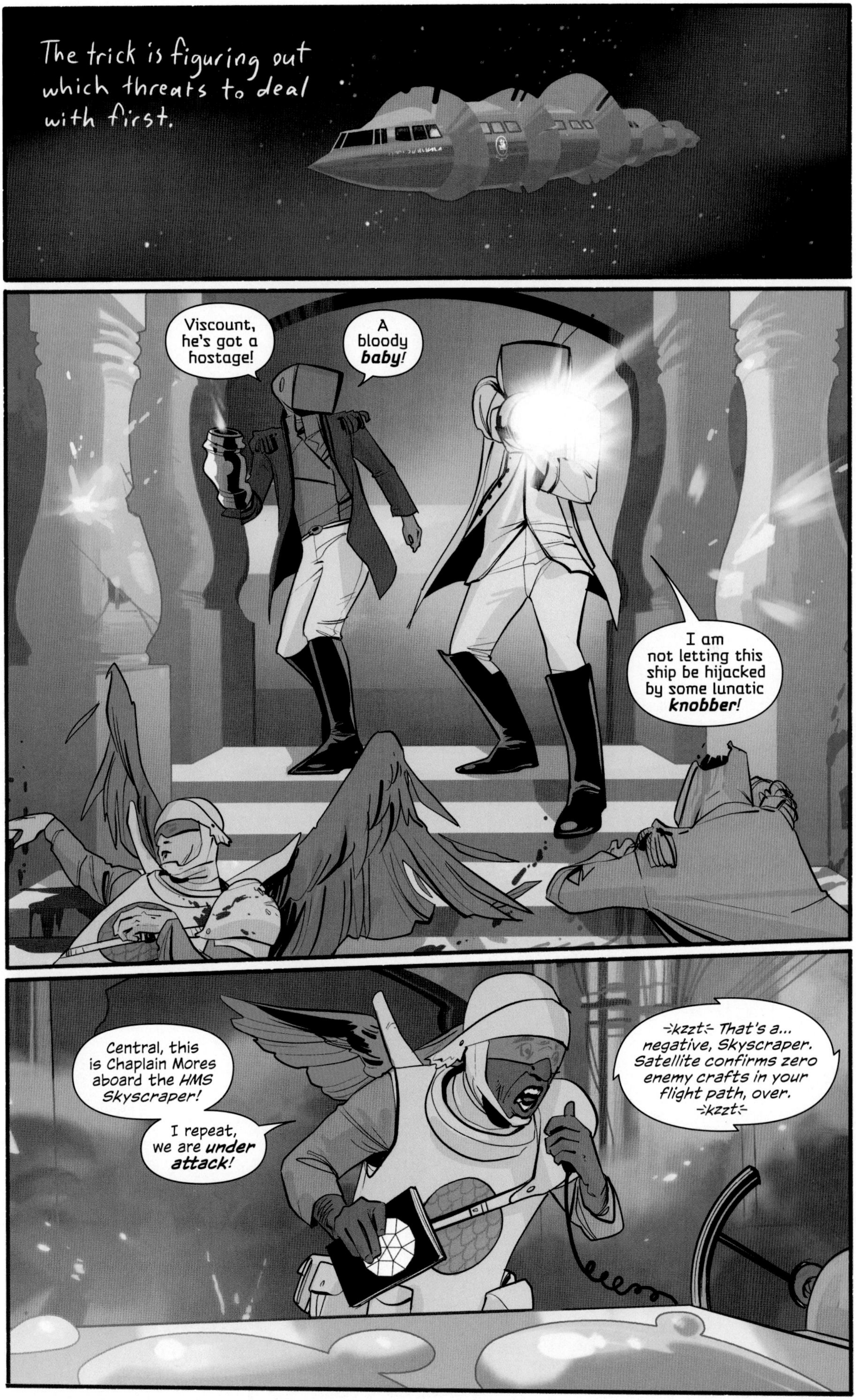
The trick is figuring out which threats to deal with first.
Viscount, he's got a hostage!
A bloody *baby*!
I am not letting this ship be hijacked by some lunatic **knobber**!
Central, this is Chaplain Mores aboard the *HMS Skyscraper*!
I repeat, we are ***under attack***!
-kzzt- That's a... negative, Skyscraper. Satellite confirms zero enemy crafts in your flight path, over. -kzzt-

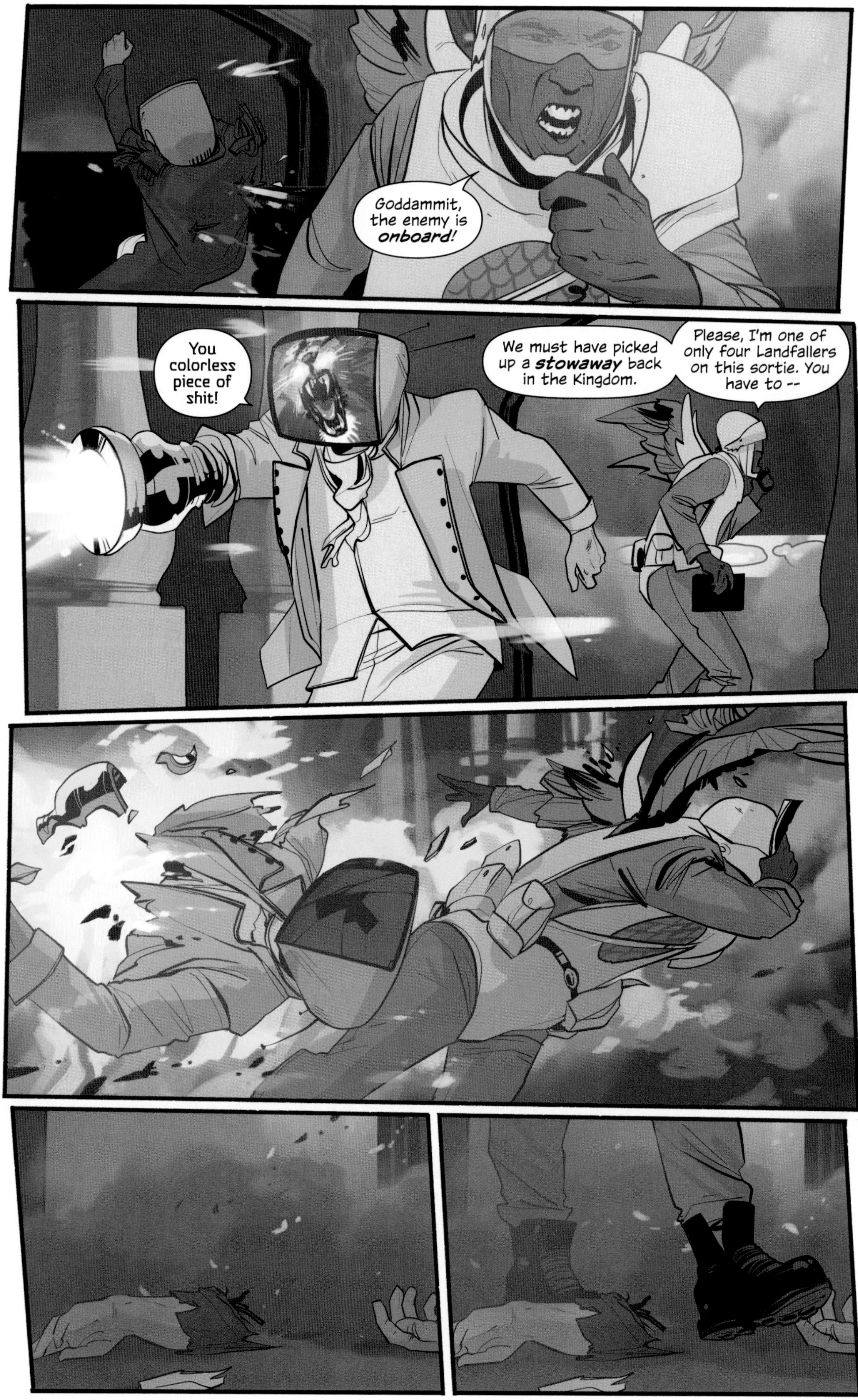
Goddammit, the enemy is *onboard!*
You colorless piece of shit!
We must have picked up a *stowaway* back in the Kingdom.
Please, I'm one of only four Landfallers on this sortie. You have to --

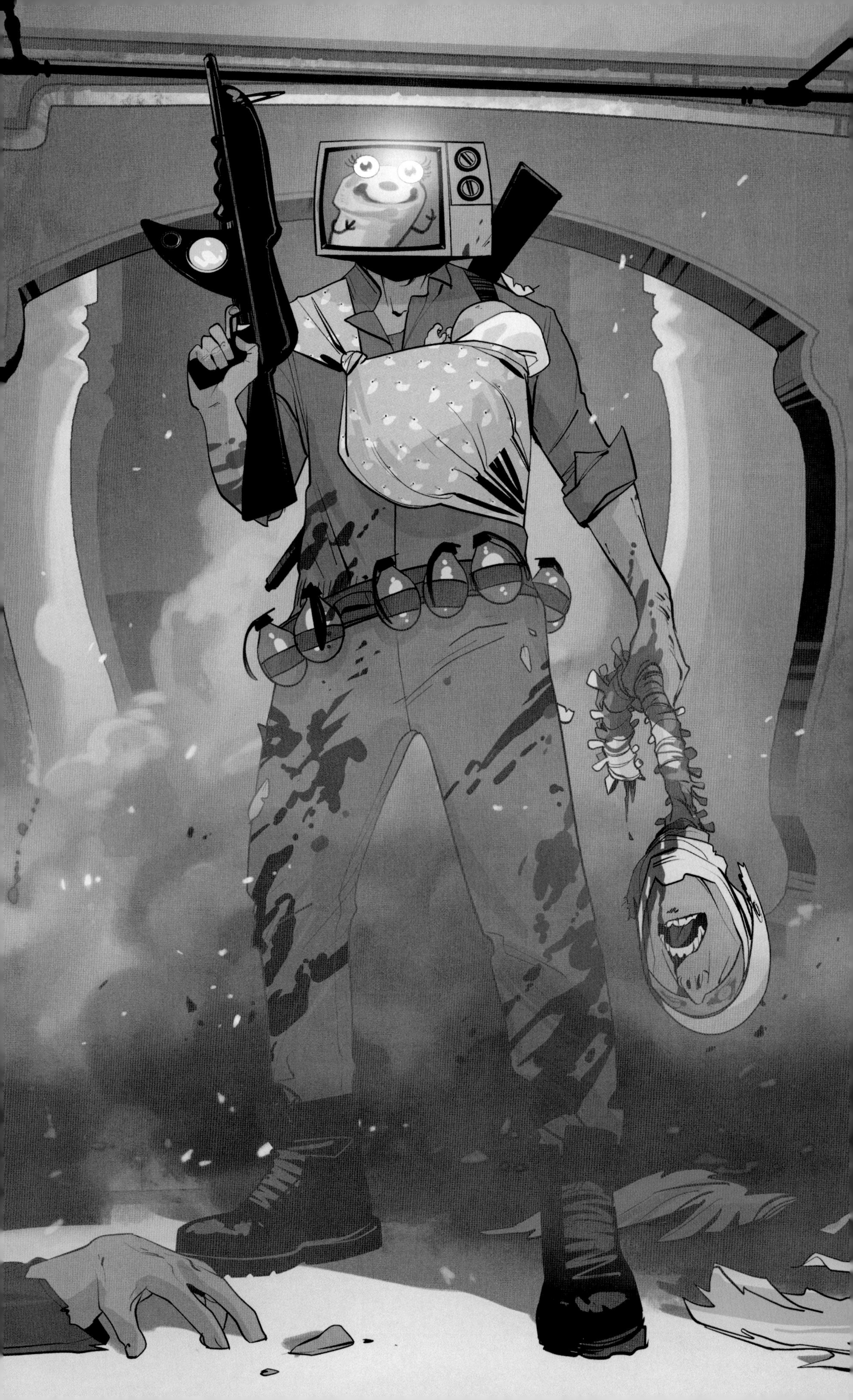

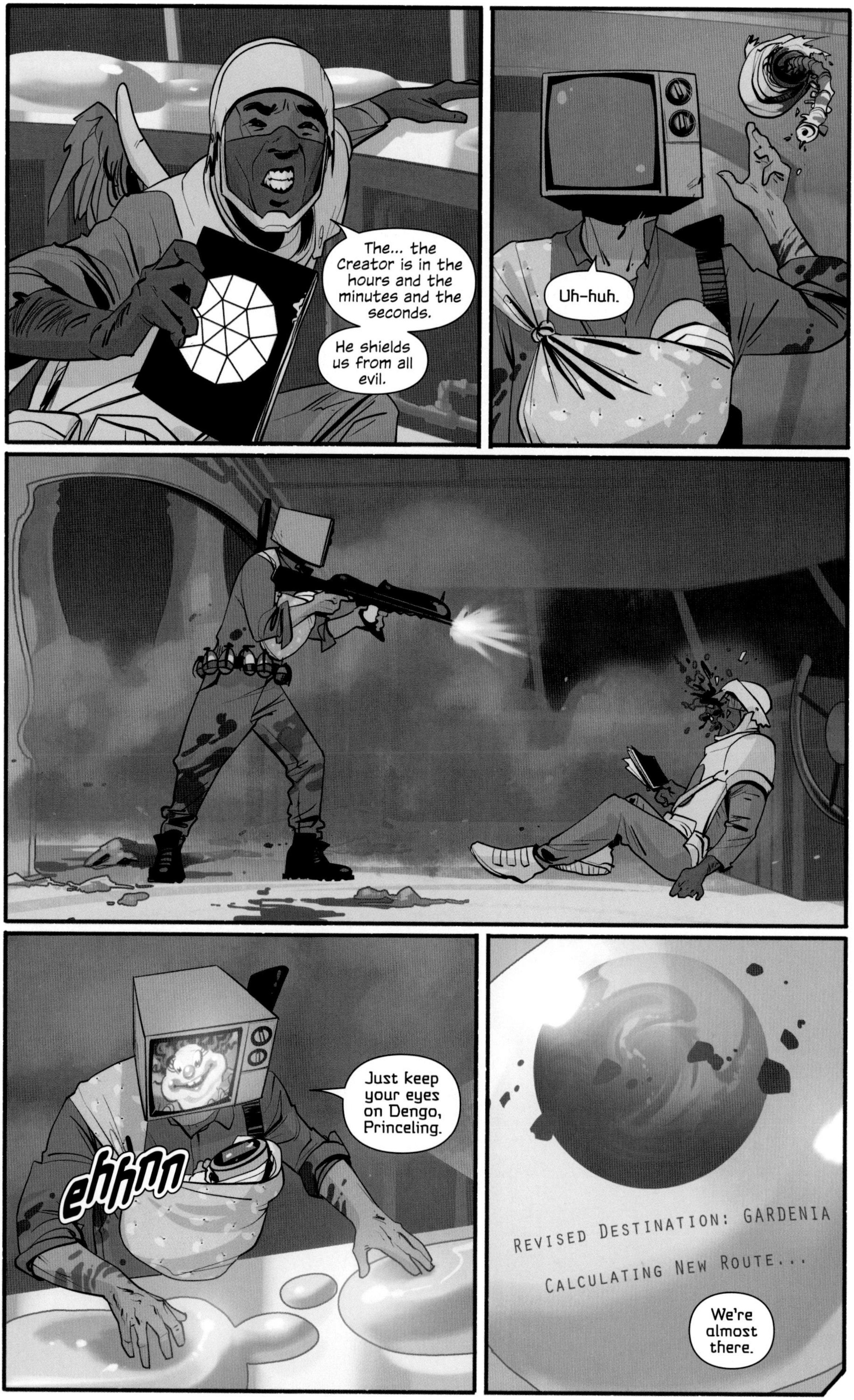
The... the Creator is in the hours and the minutes and the seconds.
He shields us from all evil.
Uh-huh.
Just keep your eyes on Dengo, Princeling.
ehhnn
REVISED DESTINATION: GARDENIA
CALCULATING NEW ROUTE...
We're almost there.

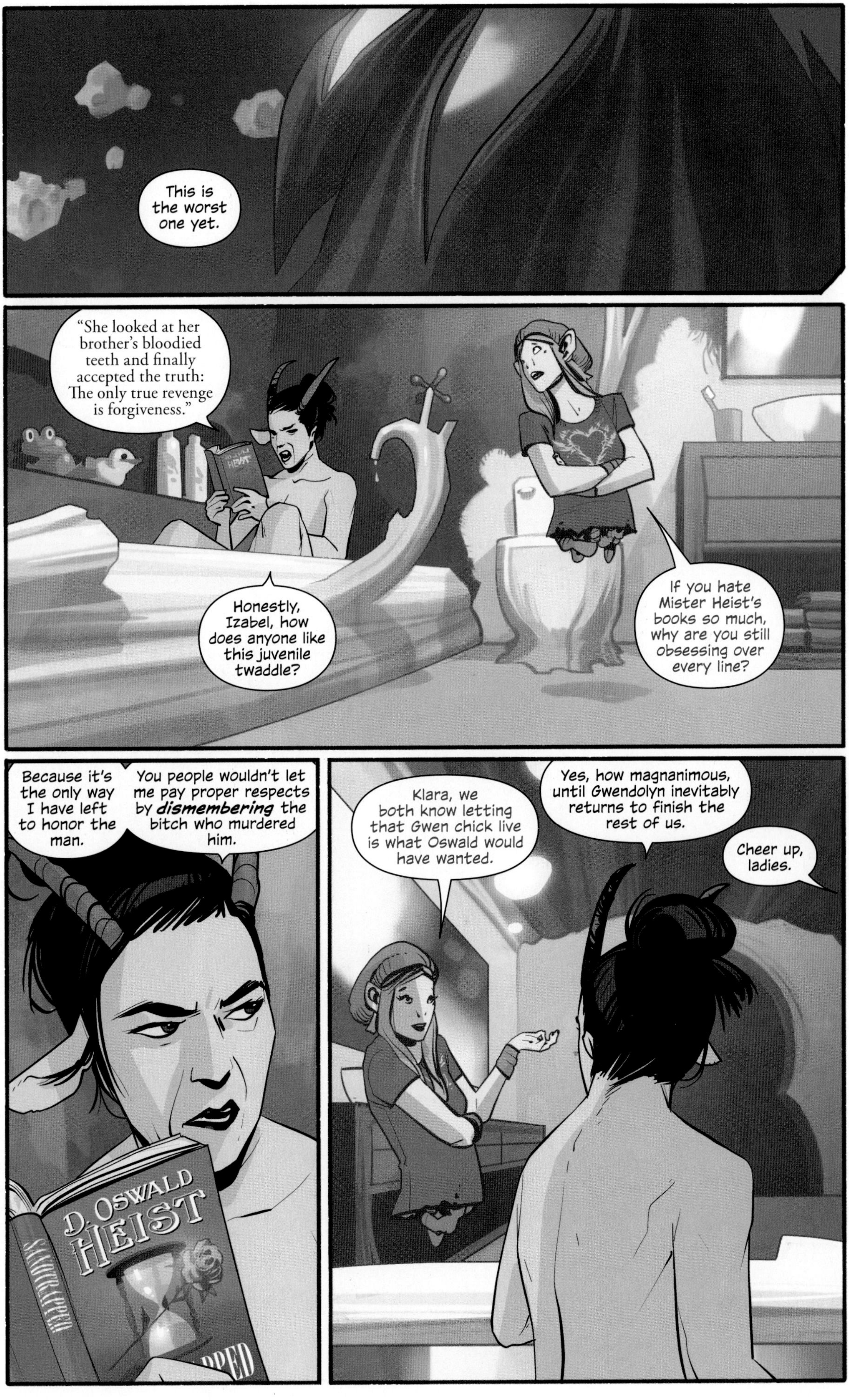
This is the worst one yet.
"She looked at her brother's bloodied teeth and finally accepted the truth: The only true revenge is forgiveness."
Honestly, Izabel, how does anyone like this juvenile twaddle?
If you hate Mister Heist's books so much, why are you still obsessing over every line?
Because it's the only way I have left to honor the man.
You people wouldn't let me pay proper respects by *dismembering* the bitch who murdered him.
D. OSWALD HEIST
Klara, we both know letting that Gwen chick live is what Oswald would have wanted.
Yes, how magnanimous, until Gwendolyn inevitably returns to finish the rest of us.
Cheer up, ladies.

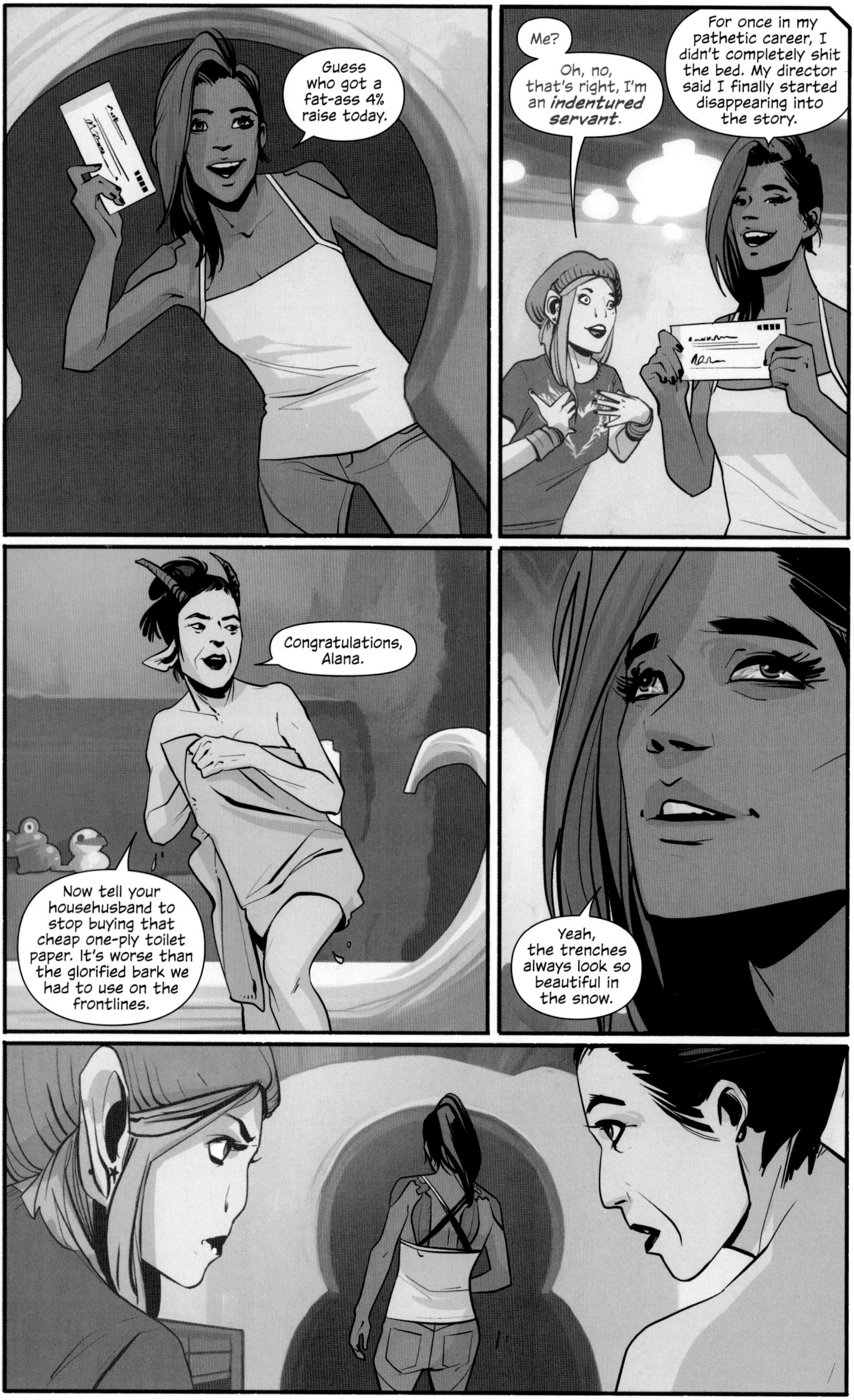
Guess who got a fat-ass 4% raise today.
Me?
Oh, no, that's right, I'm an *indentured servant*.
For once in my pathetic career, I didn't completely shit the bed. My director said I finally started disappearing into the story.
Congratulations, Alana.
Now tell your househusband to stop buying that cheap one-ply toilet paper. It's worse than the glorified bark we had to use on the frontlines.
Yeah, the trenches always look so beautiful in the snow.

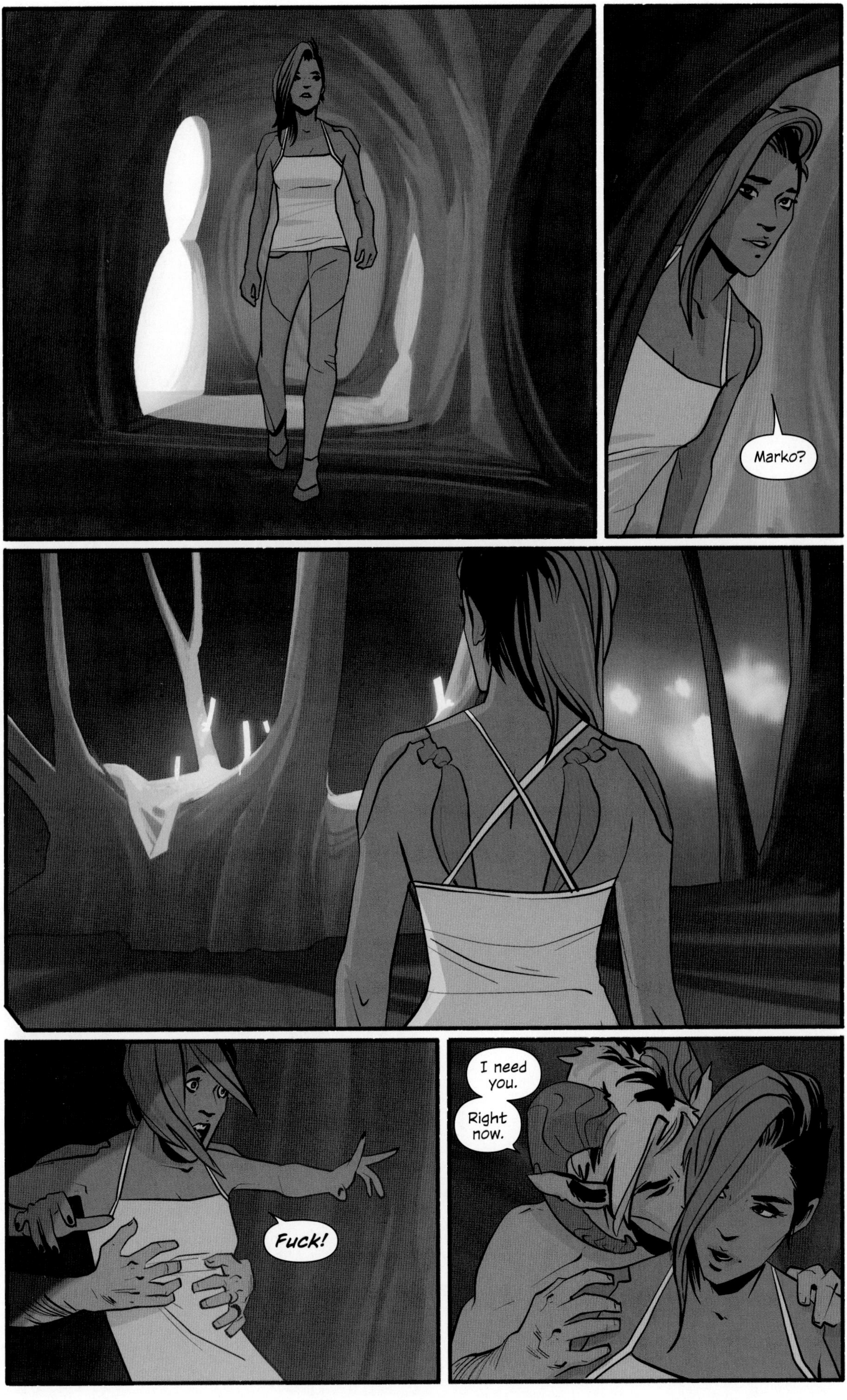
Marko?
Fuck!
I need you.
Right now.

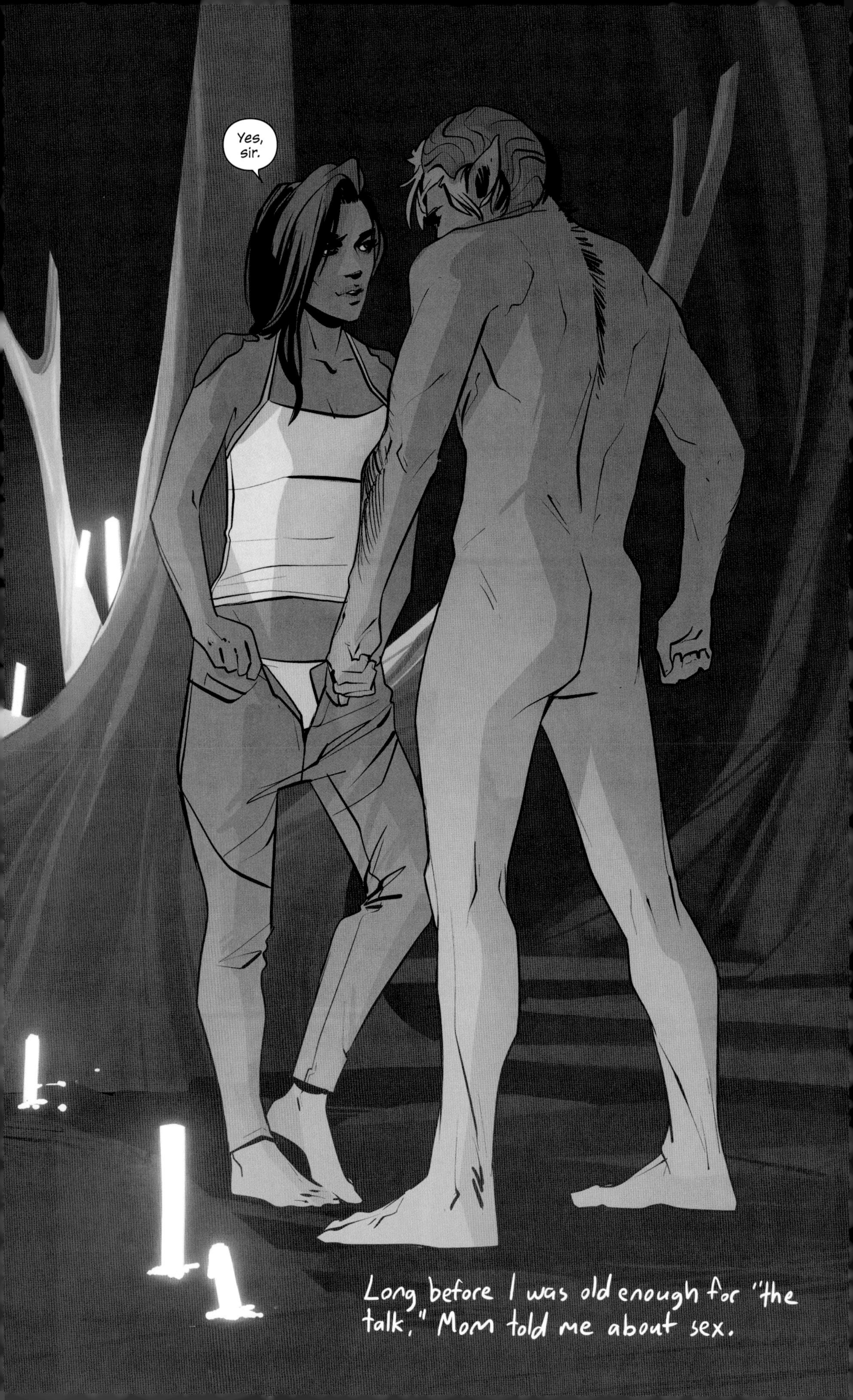
Yes, sir.
Long before I was old enough for "the talk," Mom told me about sex.

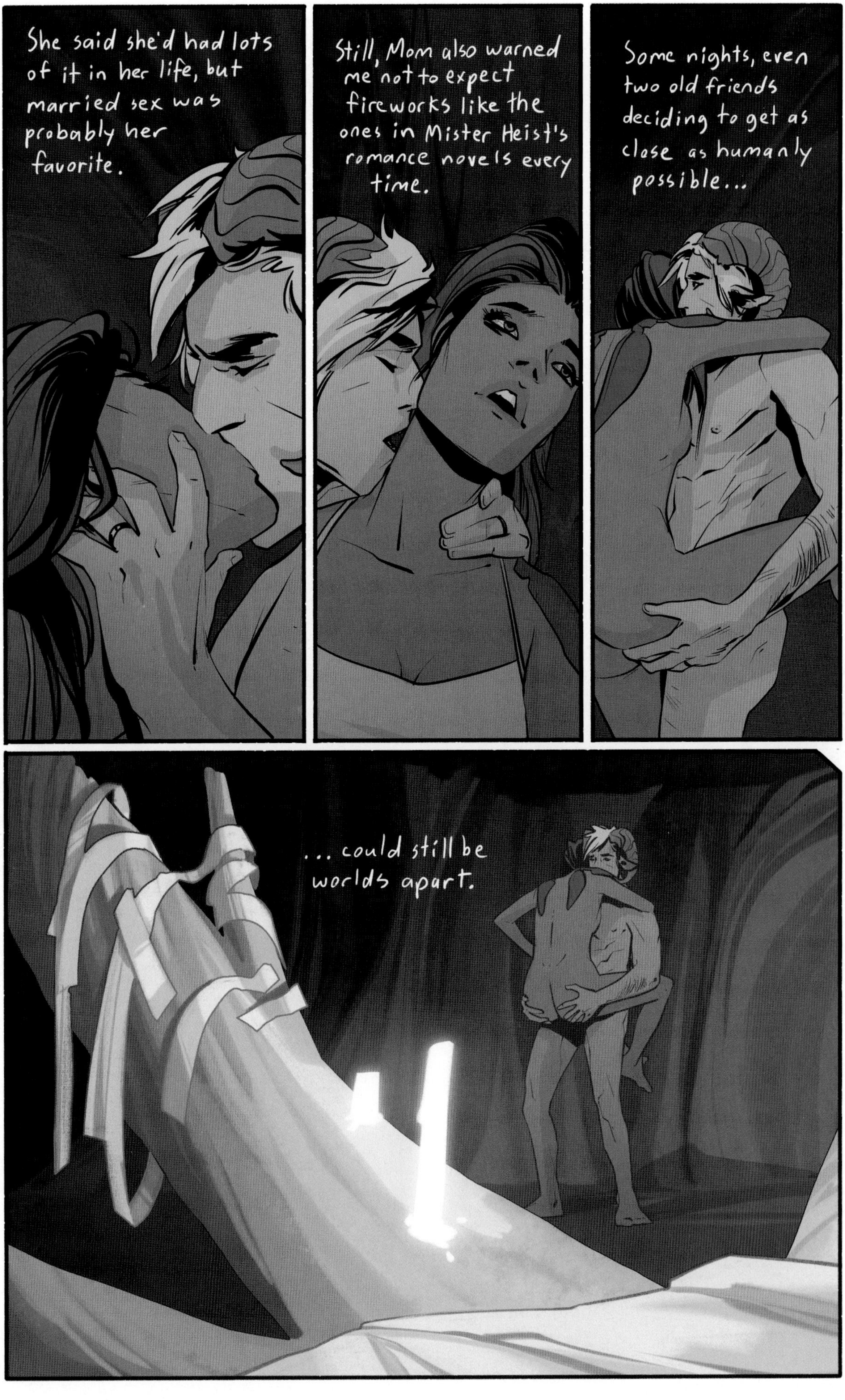
She said she'd had lots of it in her life, but married sex was probably her favorite.
Still, Mom also warned me not to expect fireworks like the ones in Mister Heist's romance novels every time.
Some nights, even two old friends deciding to get as close as humanly possible...
...could still be worlds apart.

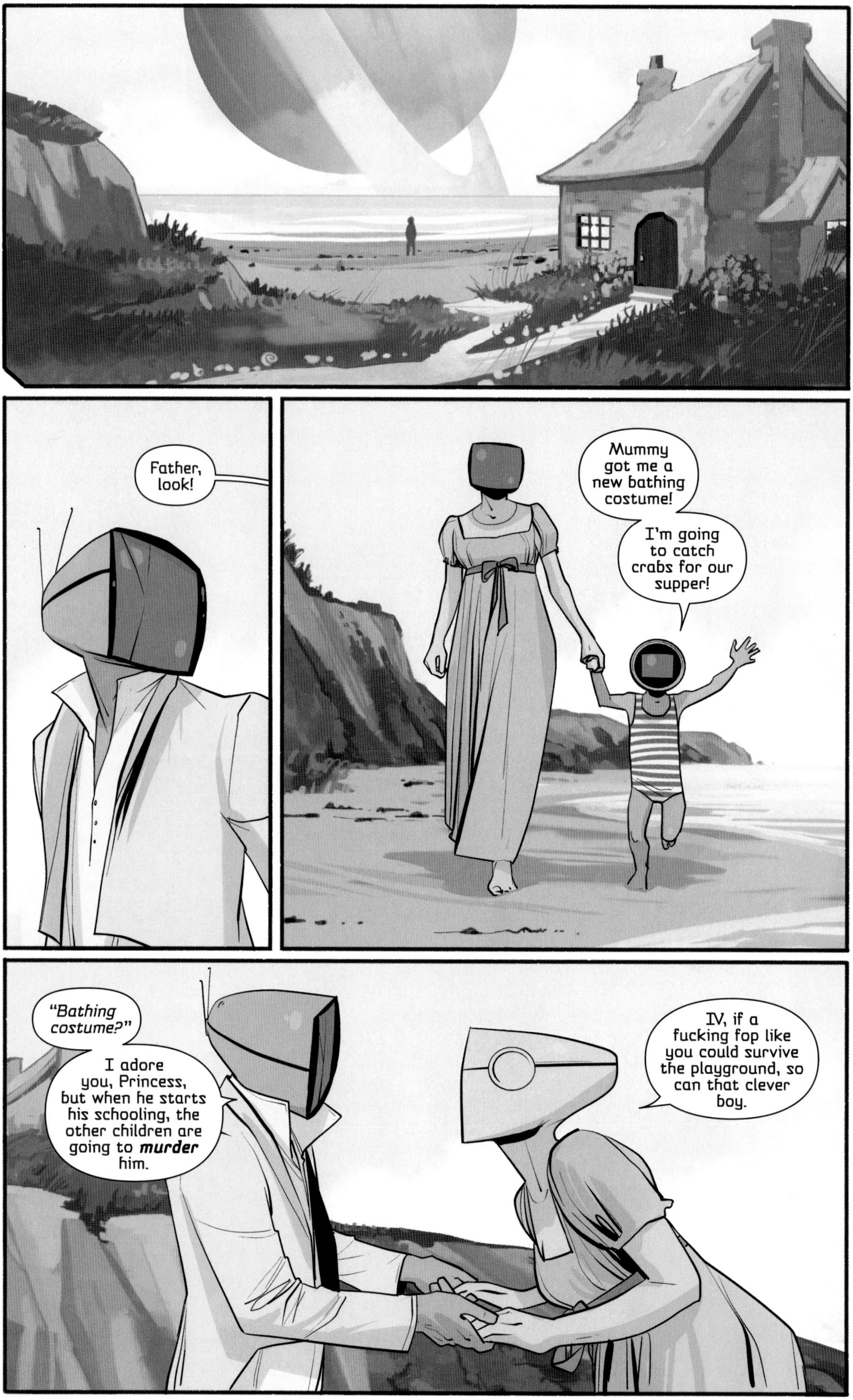
Father, look!
Mummy got me a new bathing costume!
I'm going to catch crabs for our supper!
"Bathing costume?"
I adore you, Princess, but when he starts his schooling, the other children are going to ***murder*** him.
IV, if a fucking fop like you could survive the playground, so can that clever boy.

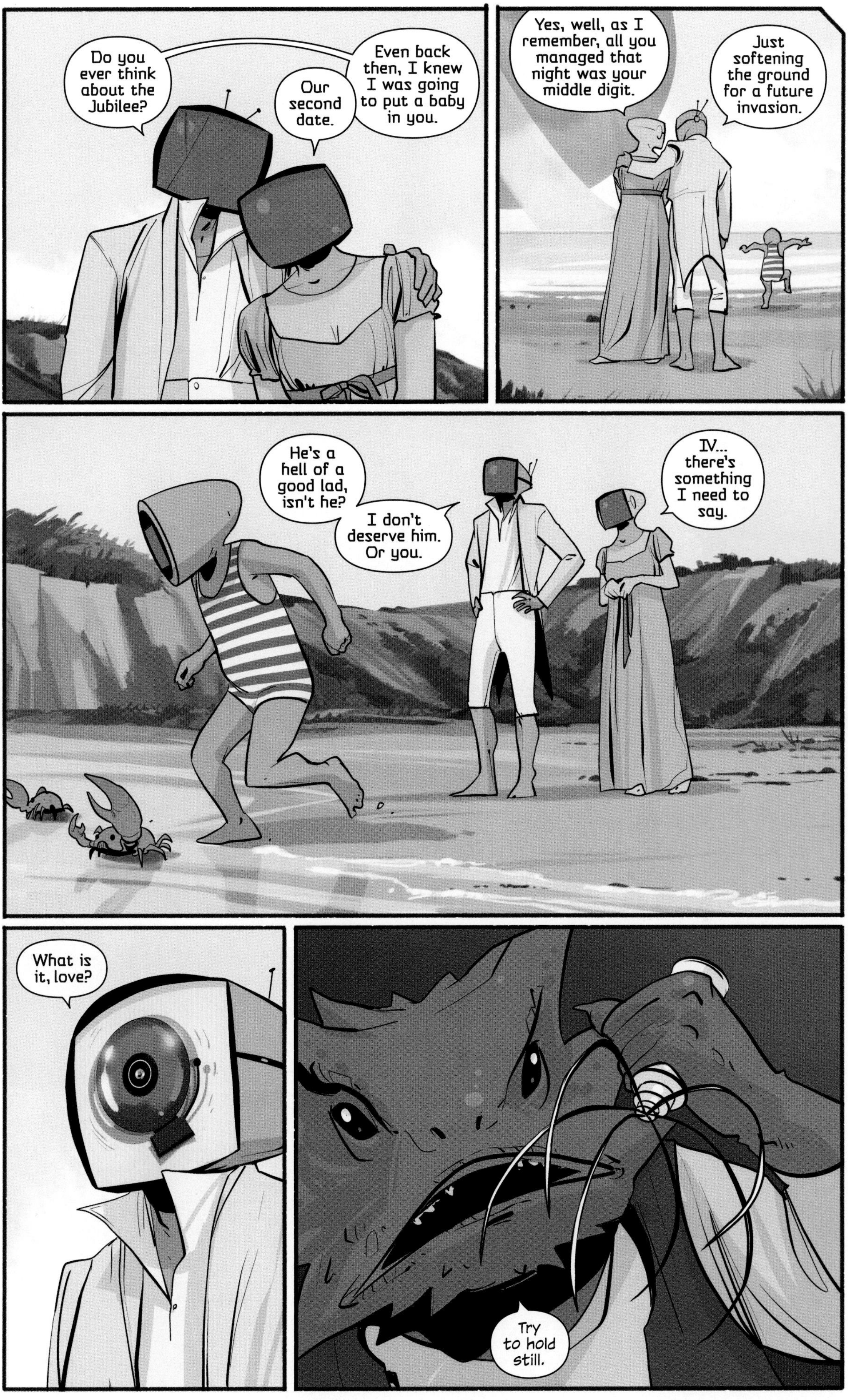
Do you ever think about the Jubilee?
Our second date.
Even back then, I knew I was going to put a baby in you.
Yes, well, as I remember, all you managed that night was your middle digit.
Just softening the ground for a future invasion.
He's a hell of a good lad, isn't he?
I don't deserve him. Or you.
IV... there's something I need to say.
What is it, love?
Try to hold still.

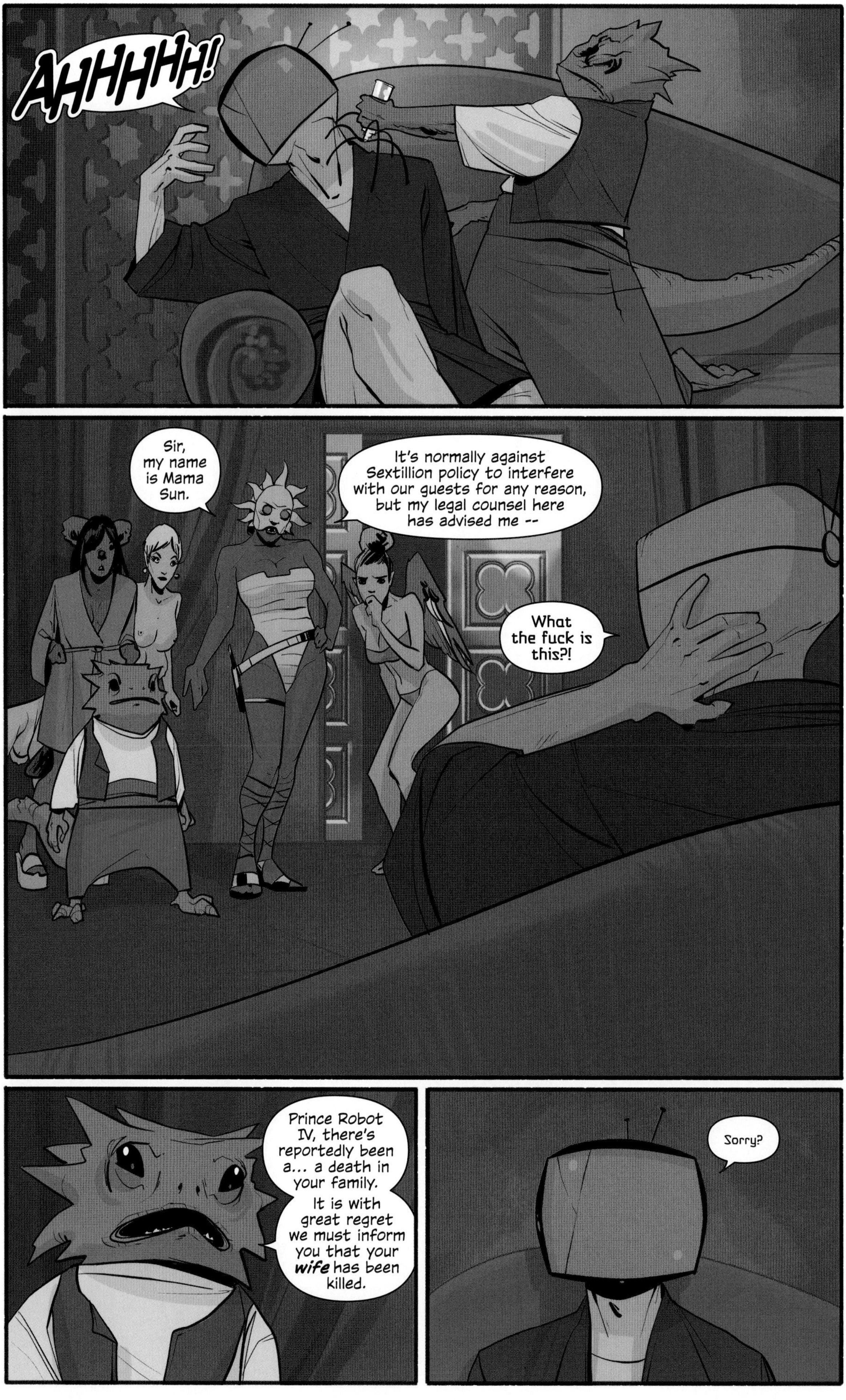
AHHHHH!
Sir, my name is Mama Sun.
It's normally against Sextillion policy to interfere with our guests for any reason, but my legal counsel here has advised me --
What the fuck is this?!
Prince Robot IV, there's reportedly been a... a death in your family.
It is with great regret we must inform you that your *wife* has been killed.
Sorry?

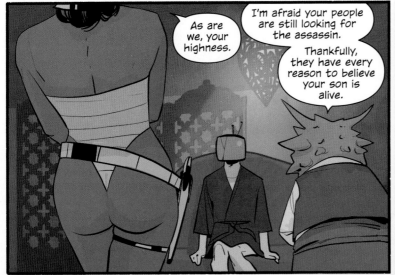

As are we, your highness.

I'm afraid your people are still looking for the assassin.

Thankfully, they have every reason to believe your son is alive.

I have a son?

A healthy male heir.

When?

When the hell was he born?

...twenty-one days ago.

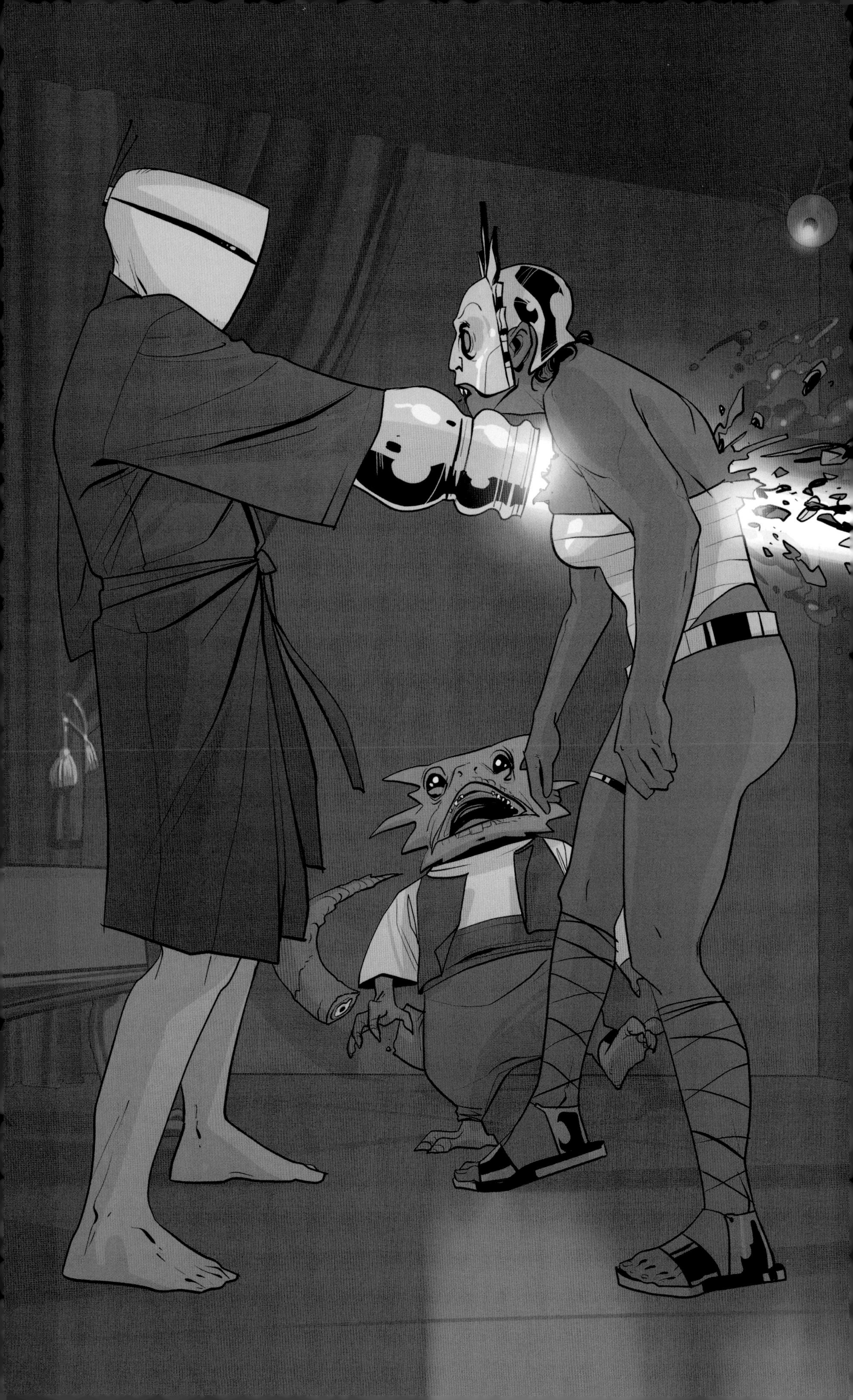

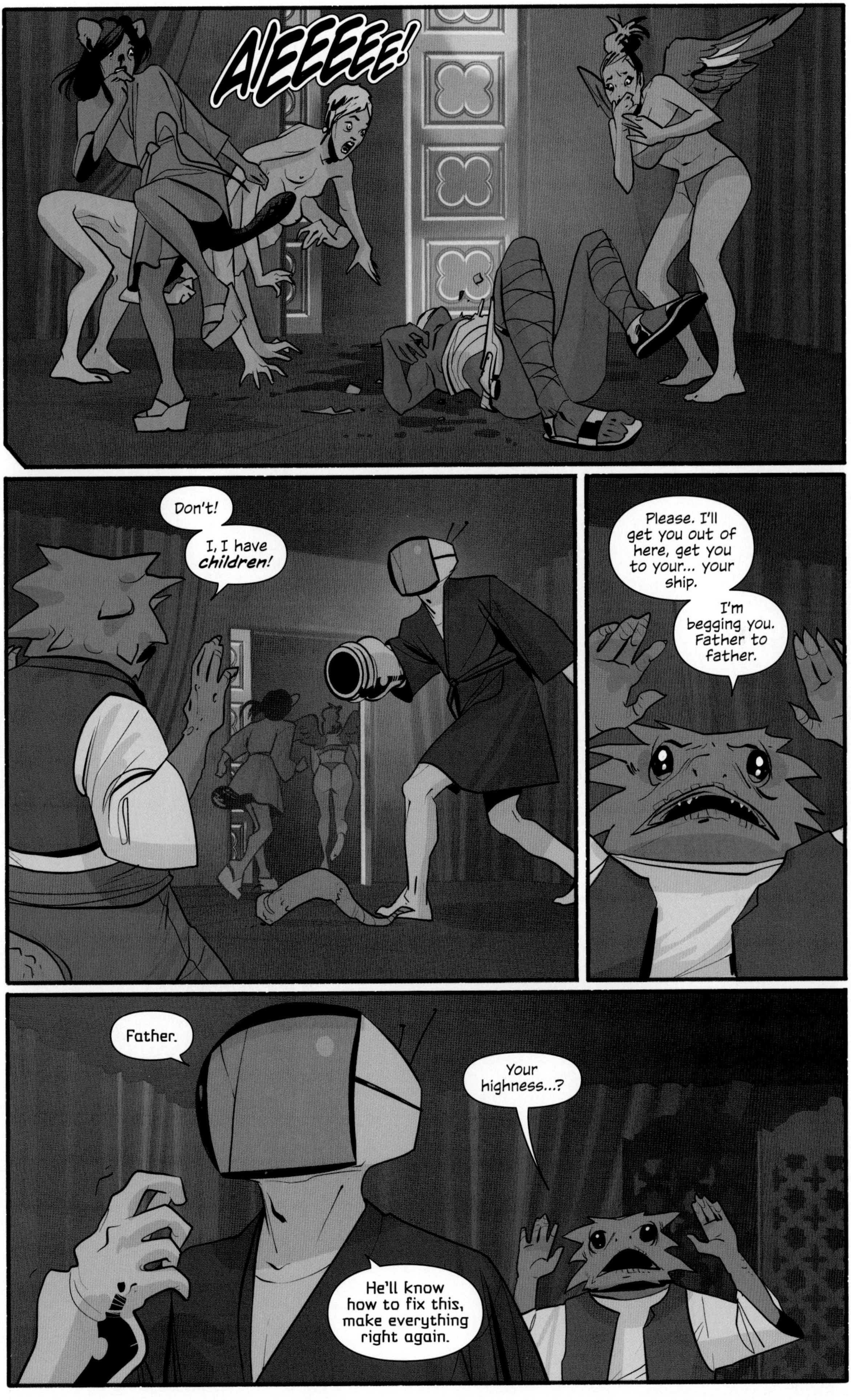
AIEEEEE!
Don't!
I, I have **children!**
Please. I'll get you out of here, get you to your... your ship.
I'm begging you. Father to father.
Father.
Your highness...?
He'll know how to fix this, make everything right again.

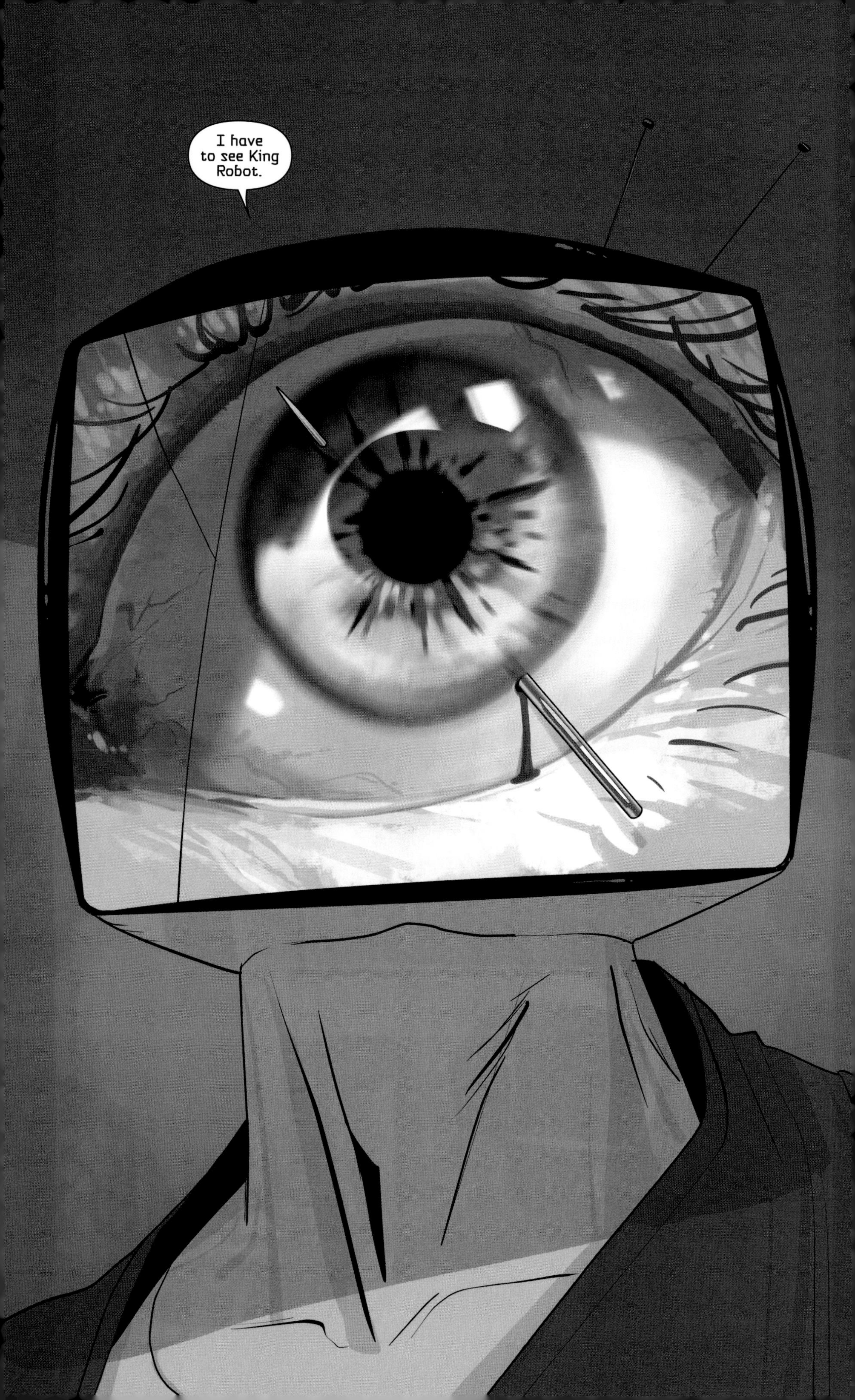
I have to see King Robot.

end chapter twenty-one

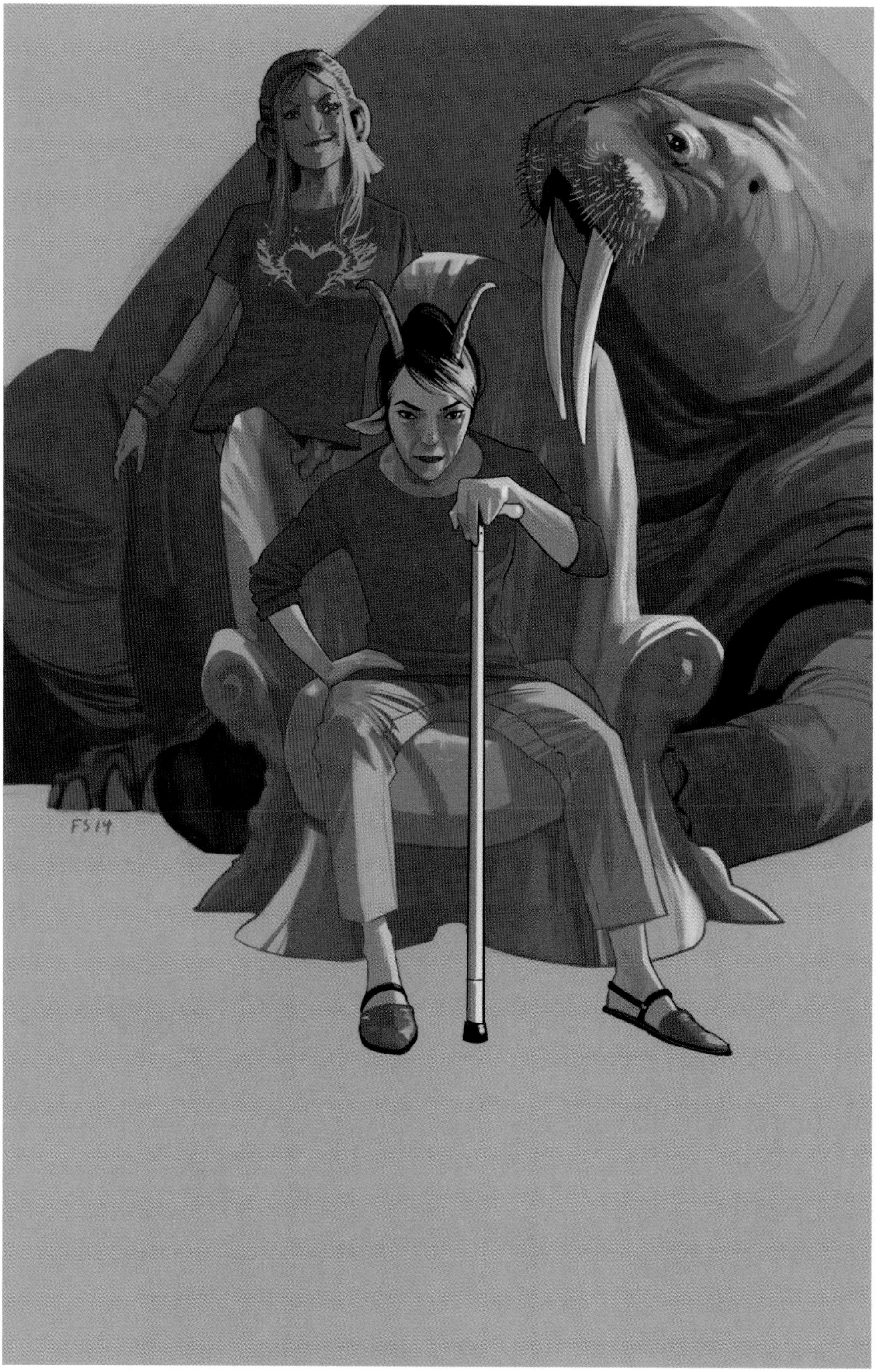
FS14

CHAPTER

TWENTY-TWO

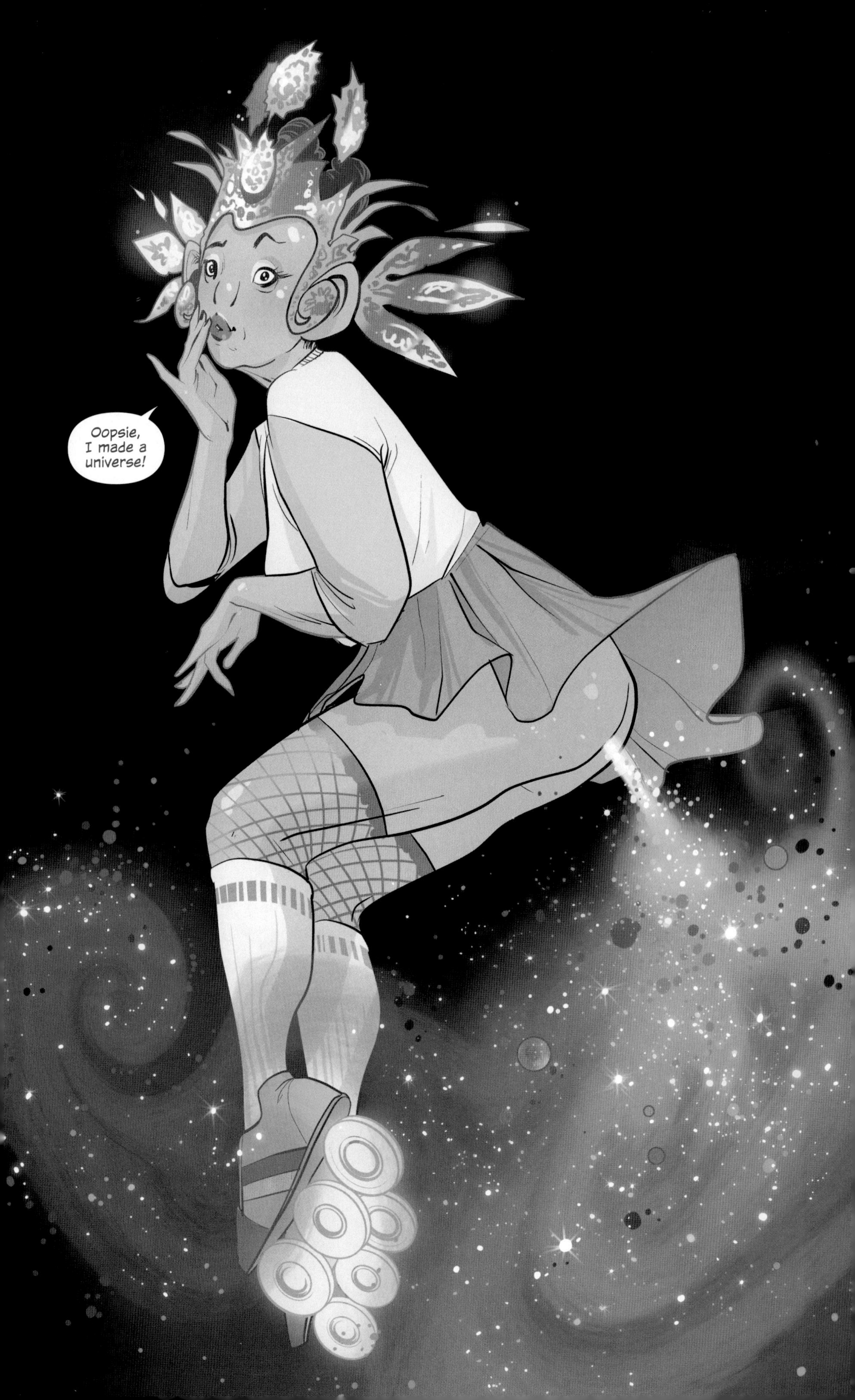
Oopsie, I made a universe!

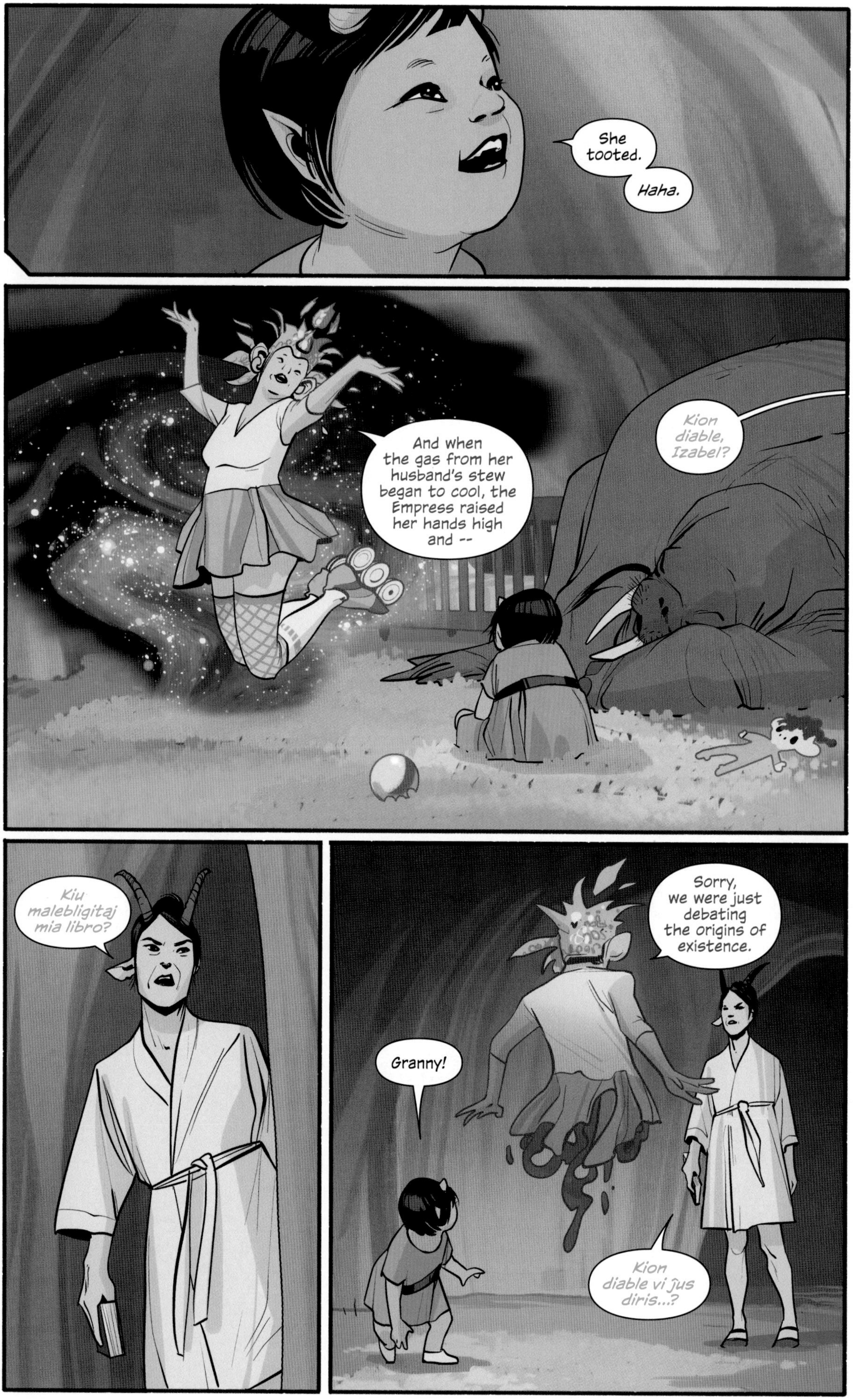
She tooted.
Haha.
And when the gas from her husband's stew began to cool, the Empress raised her hands high and --
Kion diable, Izabel?
Kiu malebligitaj mia libro?
Sorry, we were just debating the origins of existence.
Granny!
Kion diable vi ĵus diris...?

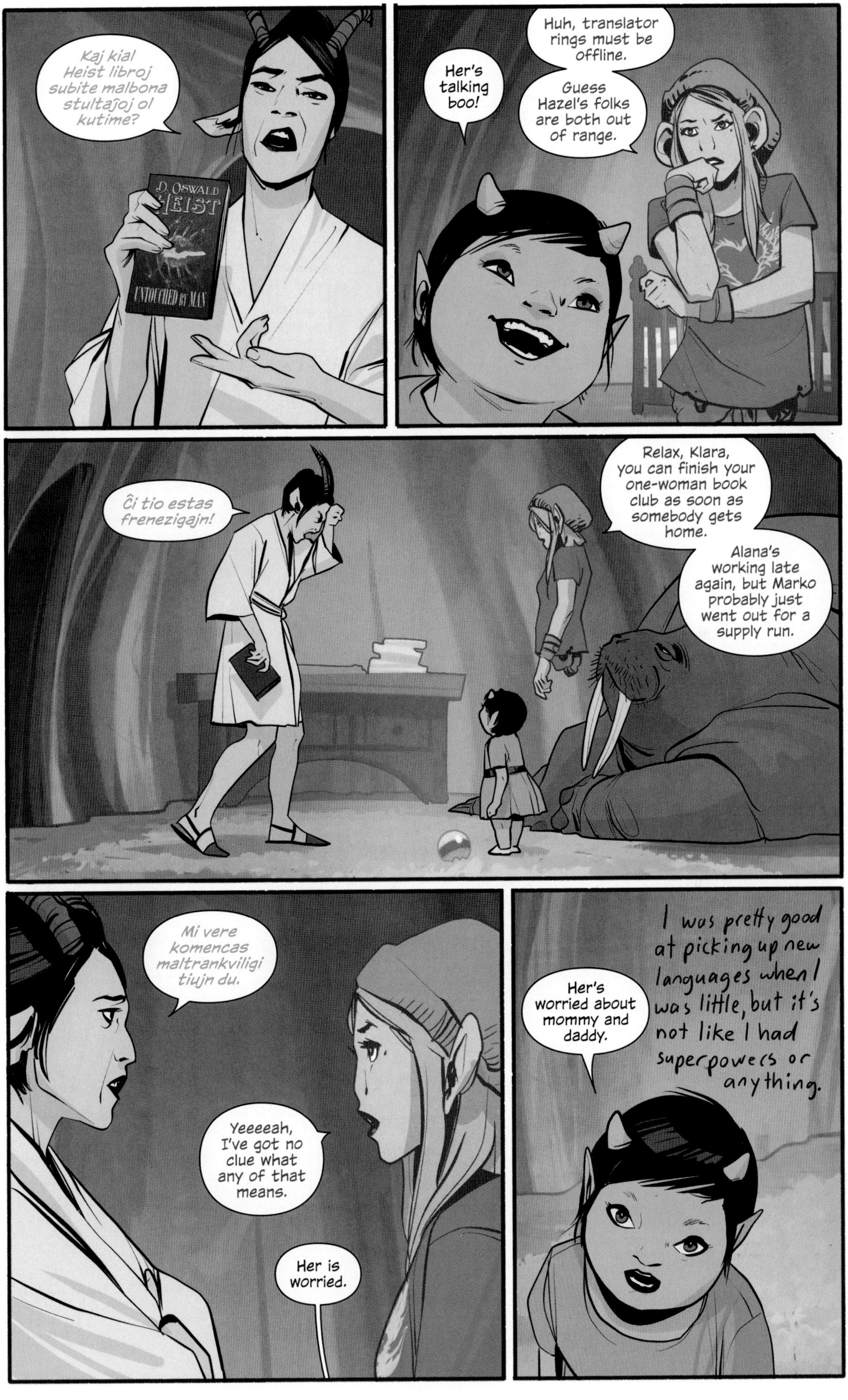
Kaj kial Heist libroj subite malbona stultaĵoj ol kutime?
Her's talking boo!
Huh, translator rings must be offline.
Guess Hazel's folks are both out of range.
D. OSWALD HEIST
UNTOUCHED BY MAN
Ĉi tio estas frenezigajn!
Relax, Klara, you can finish your one-woman book club as soon as somebody gets home.
Alana's working late again, but Marko probably just went out for a supply run.
Mi vere komencas maltrankviligi tiujn du.
Yeeeeah, I've got no clue what any of that means.
Her is worried.
I was pretty good at picking up new languages when I was little, but it's not like I had superpowers or anything.
Her's worried about mommy and daddy.

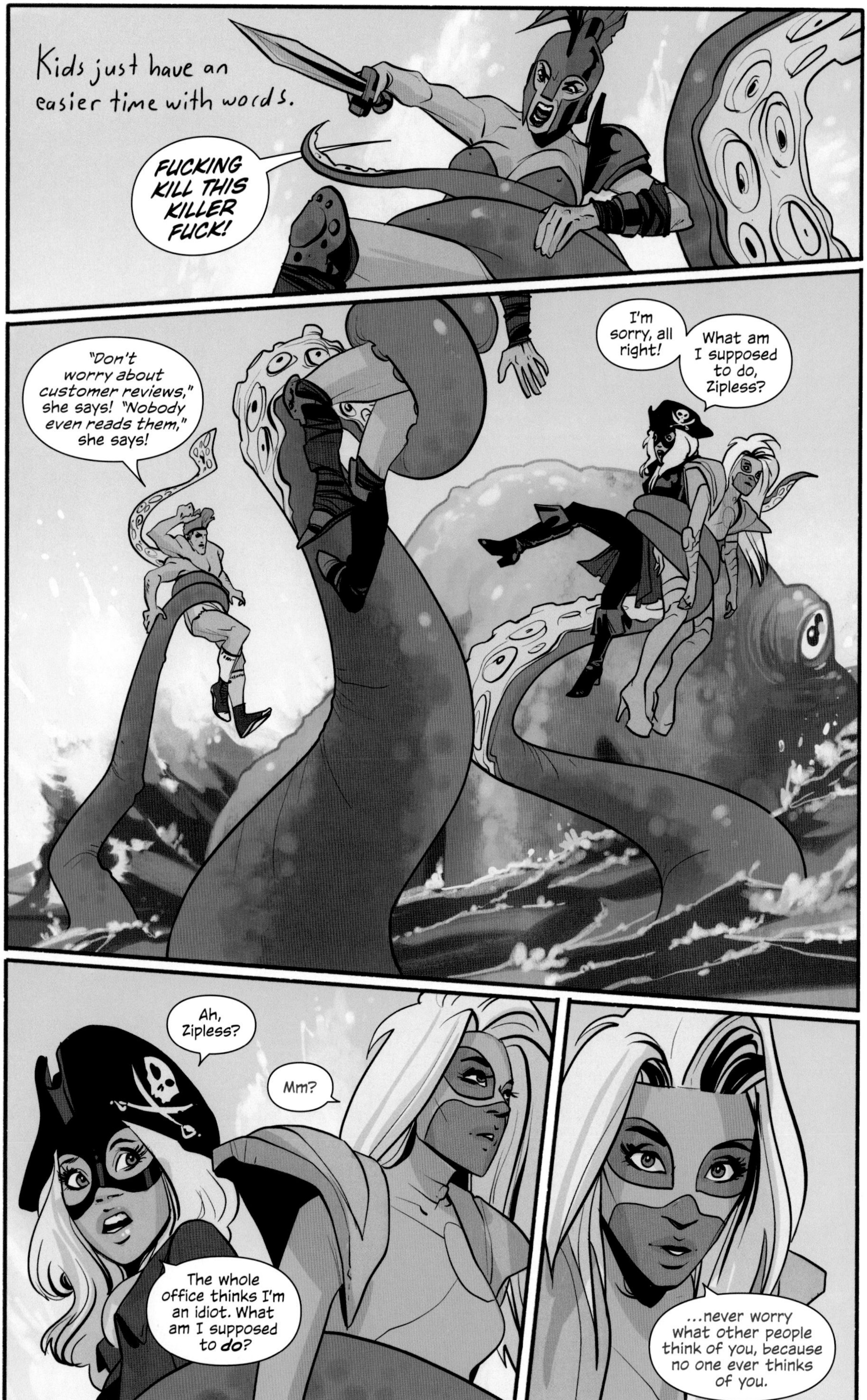
Kids just have an easier time with words.
FUCKING KILL THIS KILLER FUCK!
"Don't worry about customer reviews," she says! "Nobody even reads them," she says!
I'm sorry, all right!
What am I supposed to do, Zipless?
Ah, Zipless?
Mm?
The whole office thinks I'm an idiot. What am I supposed to do?
...never worry what other people think of you, because no one ever thinks of you.

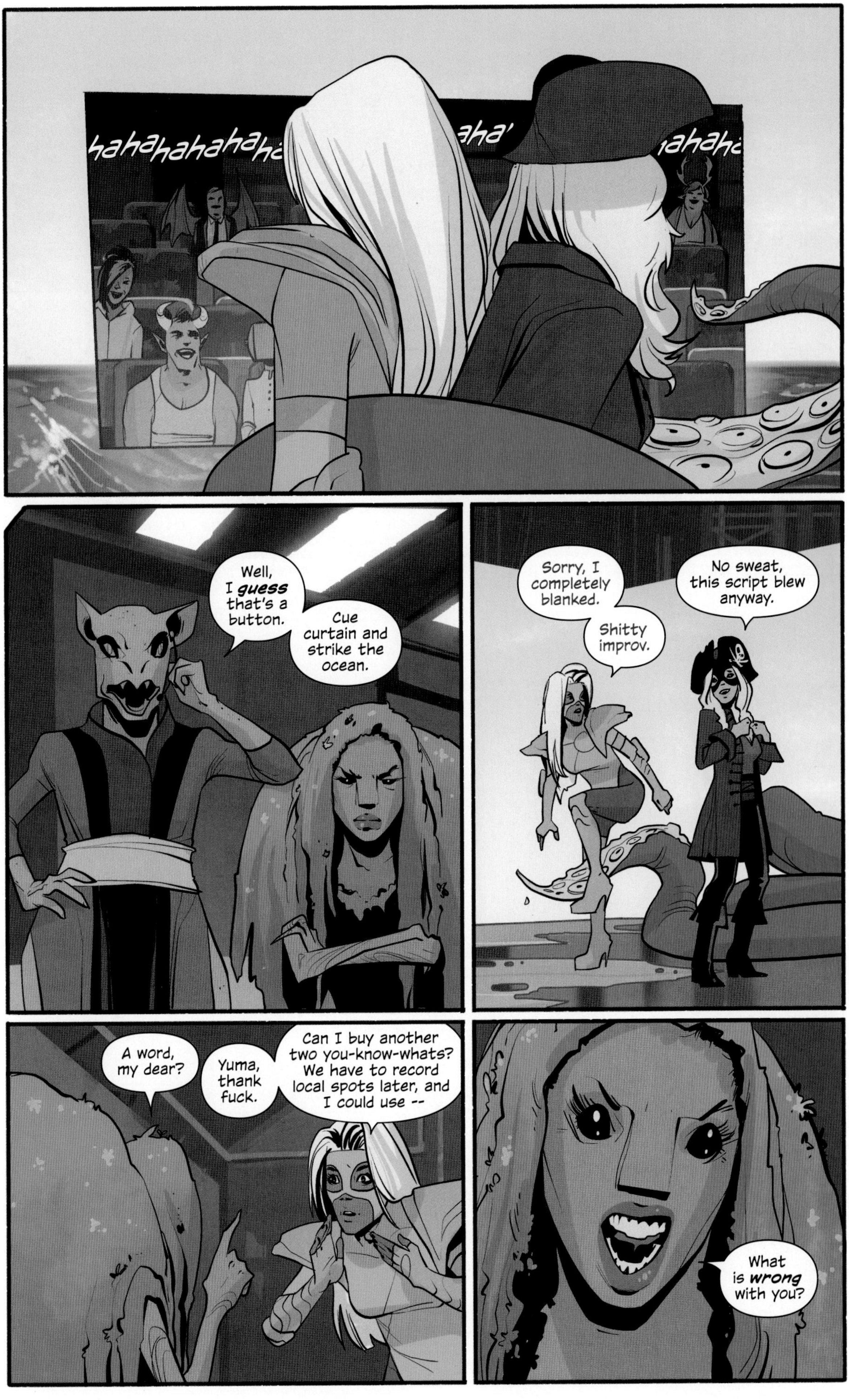
hahahahahaha
haha
hahaha
Well, I guess that's a button.
Cue curtain and strike the ocean.
Sorry, I completely blanked.
Shitty improv.
No sweat, this script blew anyway.
A word, my dear?
Yuma, thank fuck.
Can I buy another two you-know-whats? We have to record local spots later, and I could use --
What is wrong with you?

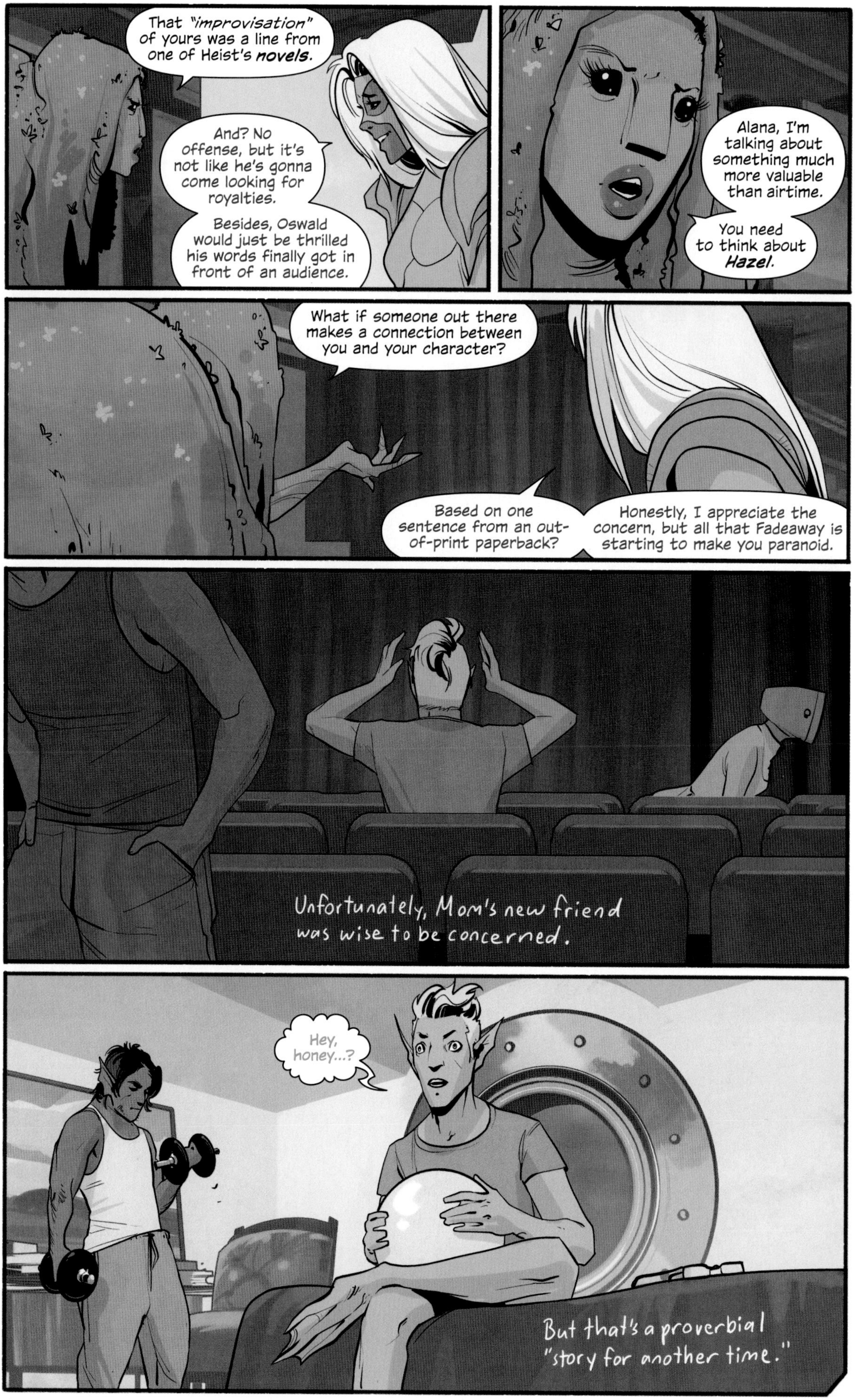
That "improvisation" of yours was a line from one of Heist's novels.
And? No offense, but it's not like he's gonna come looking for royalties.
Besides, Oswald would just be thrilled his words finally got in front of an audience.
Alana, I'm talking about something much more valuable than airtime.
You need to think about Hazel.
What if someone out there makes a connection between you and your character?
Based on one sentence from an out-of-print paperback?
Honestly, I appreciate the concern, but all that Fadeaway is starting to make you paranoid.
Unfortunately, Mom's new friend was wise to be concerned.
Hey, honey...?
But that's a proverbial "story for another time."

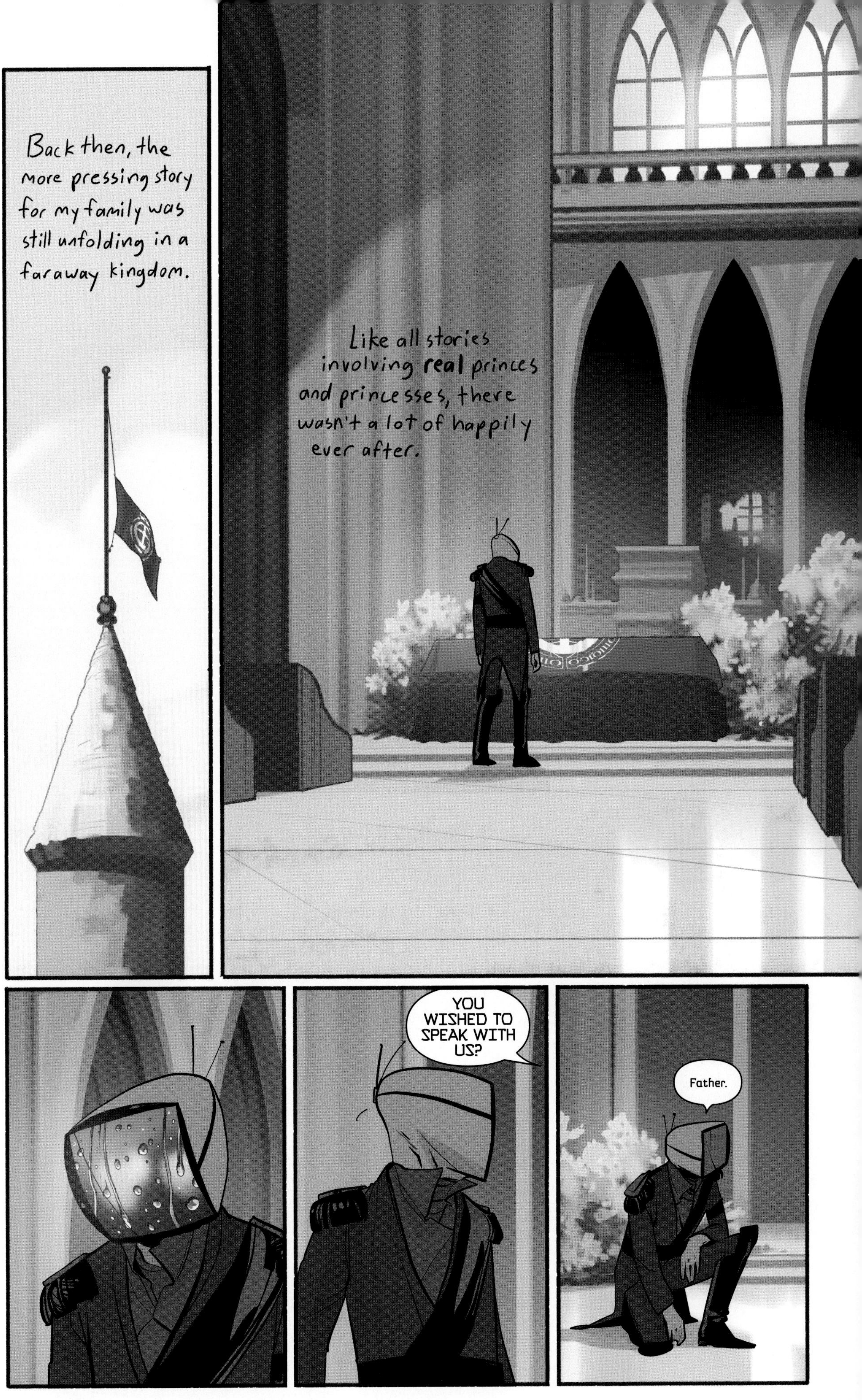
Back then, the more pressing story for my family was still unfolding in a faraway kingdom.
Like all stories involving **real** princes and princesses, there wasn't a lot of happily ever after.
YOU WISHED TO SPEAK WITH US?
Father.

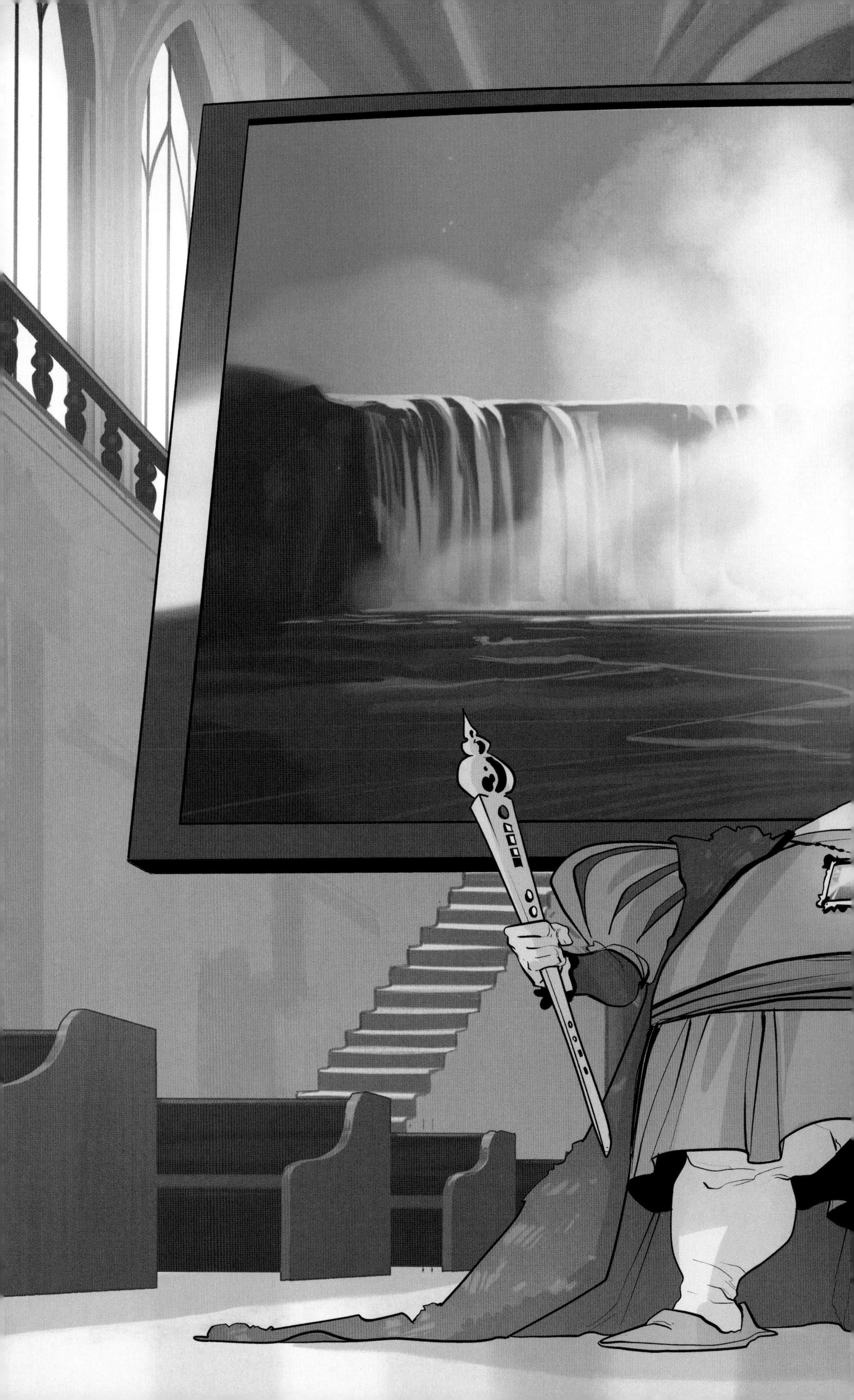

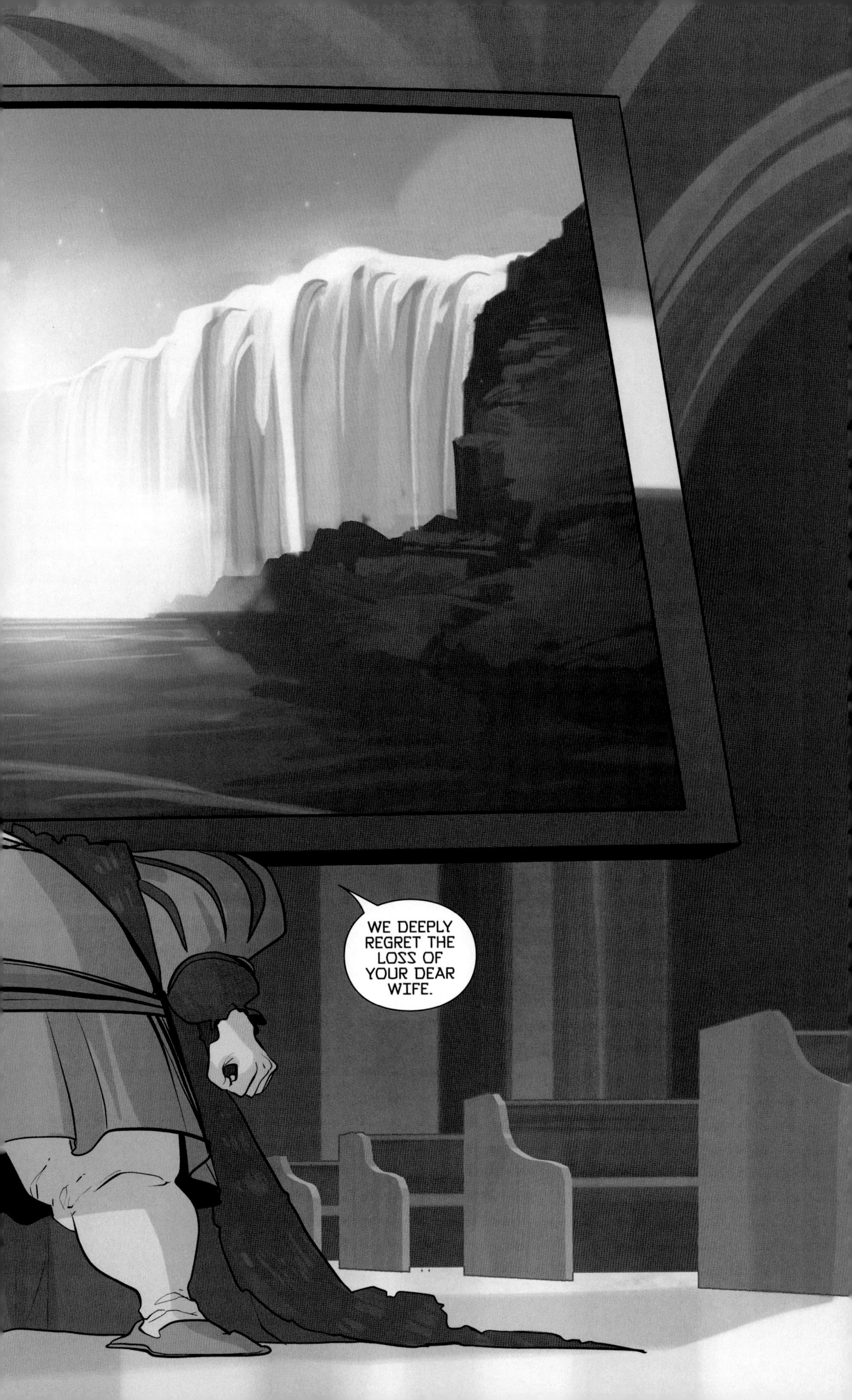
WE DEEPLY REGRET THE LOSS OF YOUR DEAR WIFE.

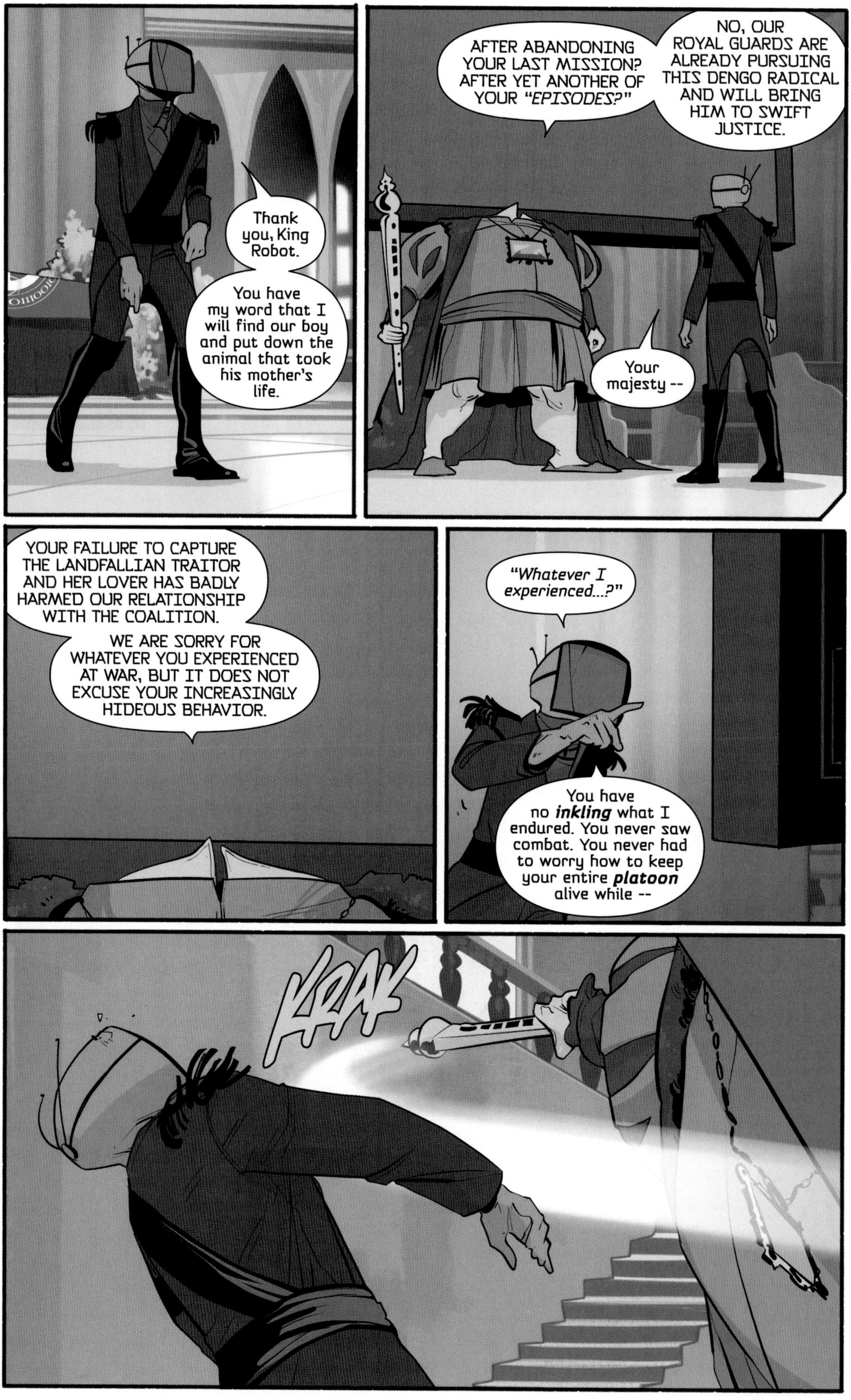
Thank you, King Robot.
You have my word that I will find our boy and put down the animal that took his mother's life.
AFTER ABANDONING YOUR LAST MISSION? AFTER YET ANOTHER OF YOUR "EPISODES?"
NO, OUR ROYAL GUARDS ARE ALREADY PURSUING THIS DENGO RADICAL AND WILL BRING HIM TO SWIFT JUSTICE.
Your majesty --
YOUR FAILURE TO CAPTURE THE LANDFALLIAN TRAITOR AND HER LOVER HAS BADLY HARMED OUR RELATIONSHIP WITH THE COALITION.
WE ARE SORRY FOR WHATEVER YOU EXPERIENCED AT WAR, BUT IT DOES NOT EXCUSE YOUR INCREASINGLY HIDEOUS BEHAVIOR.
"Whatever I experienced...?"
You have no inkling what I endured. You never saw combat. You never had to worry how to keep your entire platoon alive while --
KRAK

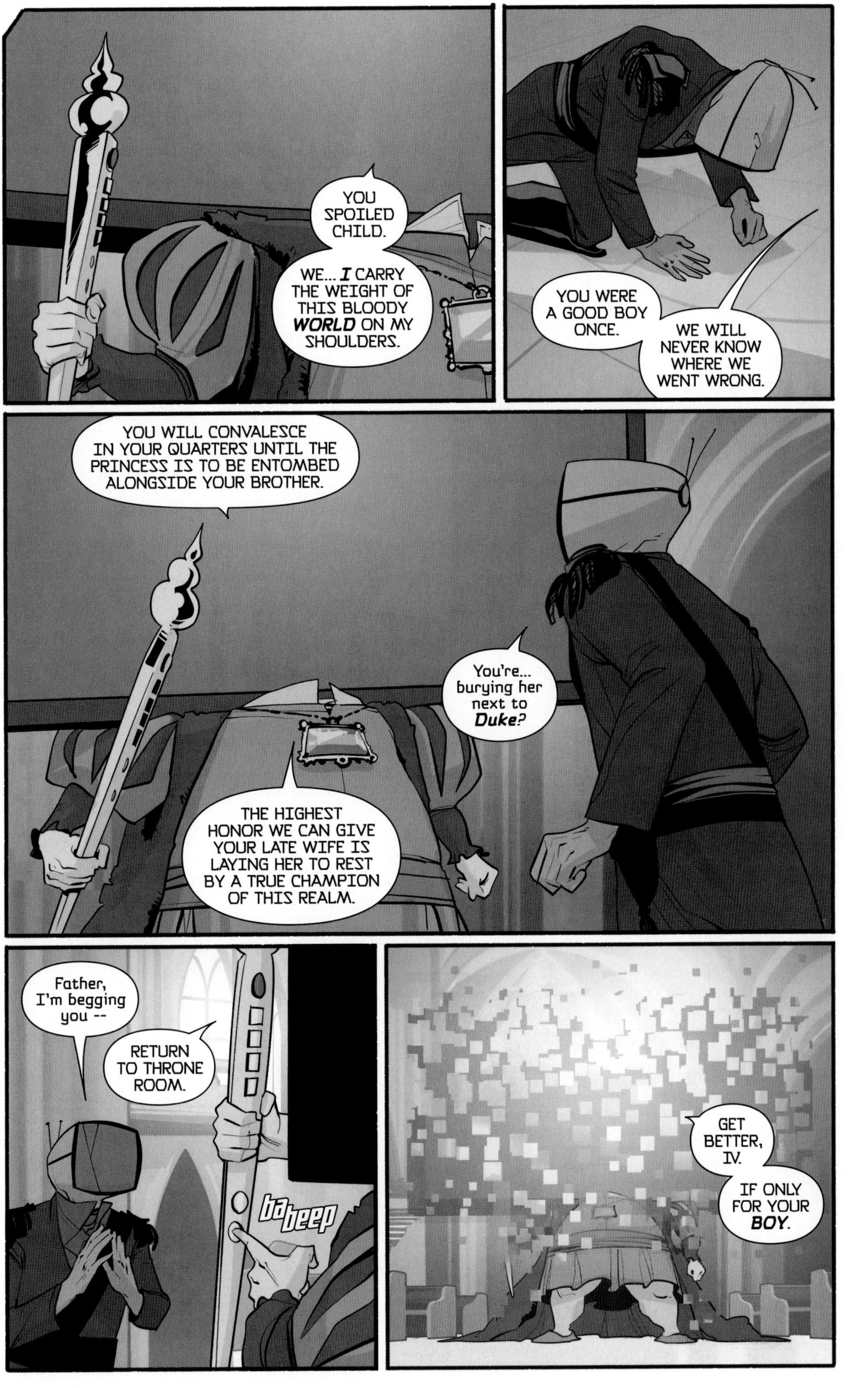
YOU SPOILED CHILD.
WE... I CARRY THE WEIGHT OF THIS BLOODY WORLD ON MY SHOULDERS.
YOU WERE A GOOD BOY ONCE.
WE WILL NEVER KNOW WHERE WE WENT WRONG.
YOU WILL CONVALESCE IN YOUR QUARTERS UNTIL THE PRINCESS IS TO BE ENTOMBED ALONGSIDE YOUR BROTHER.
You're... burying her next to Duke?
THE HIGHEST HONOR WE CAN GIVE YOUR LATE WIFE IS LAYING HER TO REST BY A TRUE CHAMPION OF THIS REALM.
Father, I'm begging you --
RETURN TO THRONE ROOM.
ba beep
GET BETTER, IV.
IF ONLY FOR YOUR BOY.

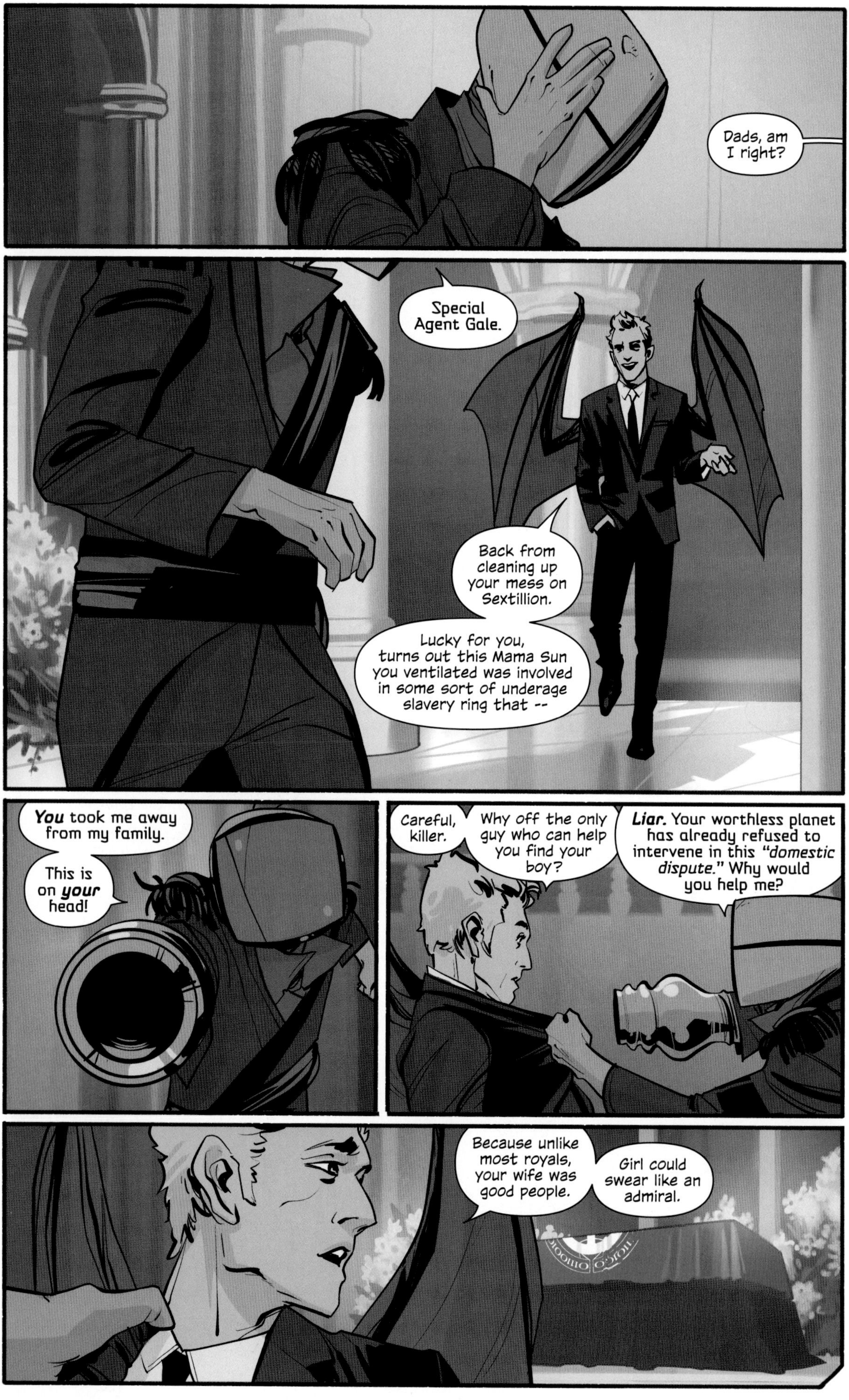
Dads, am I right?
Special Agent Gale.
Back from cleaning up your mess on Sextillion.
Lucky for you, turns out this Mama Sun you ventilated was involved in some sort of underage slavery ring that --
You took me away from my family.
This is on *your* head!
Careful, killer.
Why off the only guy who can help you find your boy?
Liar. Your worthless planet has already refused to intervene in this *"domestic dispute."* Why would you help me?
Because unlike most royals, your wife was good people.
Girl could swear like an admiral.

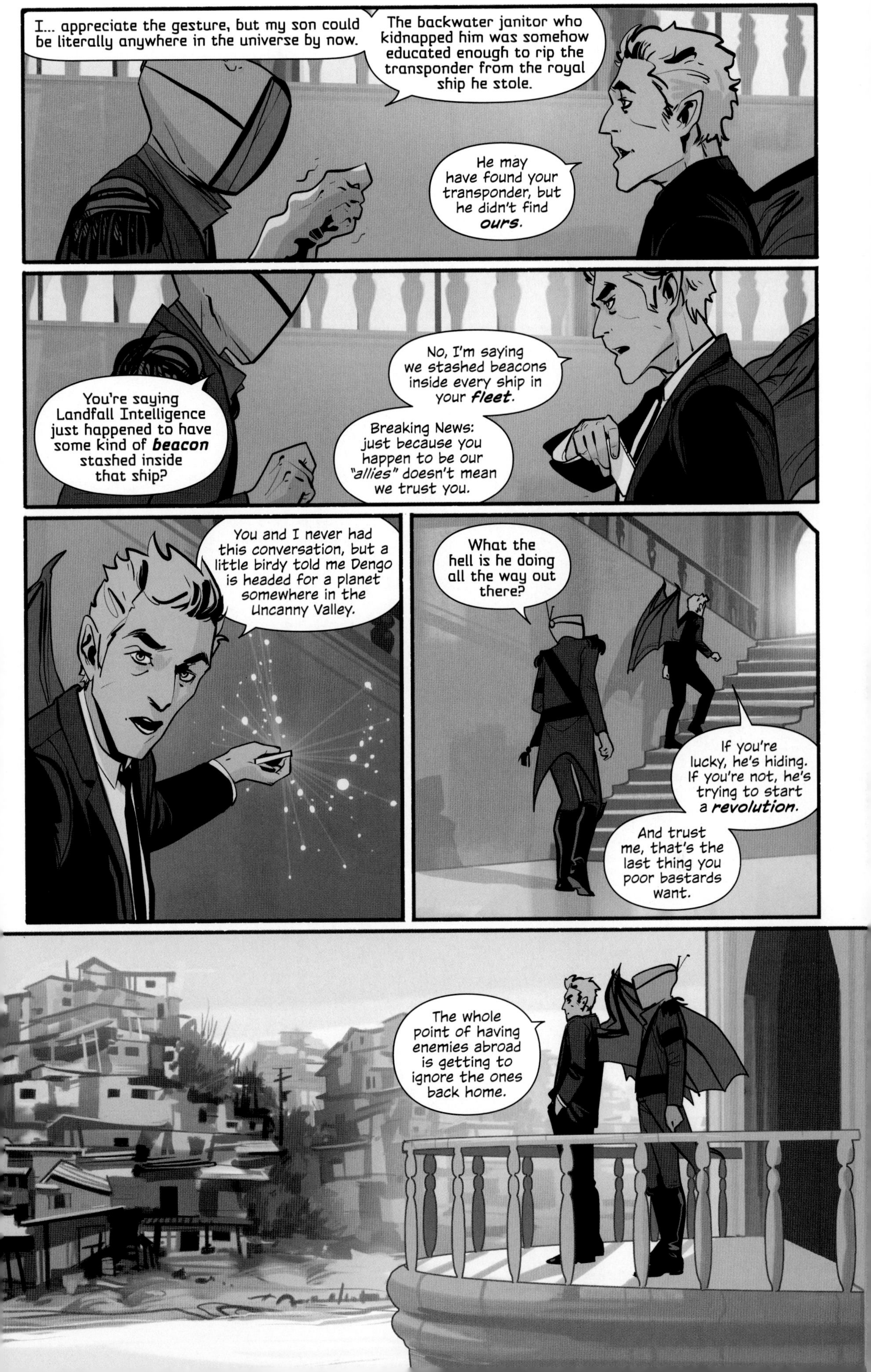
I... appreciate the gesture, but my son could be literally anywhere in the universe by now.
The backwater janitor who kidnapped him was somehow educated enough to rip the transponder from the royal ship he stole.
He may have found your transponder, but he didn't find ***ours***.
You're saying Landfall Intelligence just happened to have some kind of ***beacon*** stashed inside that ship?
No, I'm saying we stashed beacons inside every ship in your ***fleet***.
Breaking News: just because you happen to be our *"allies"* doesn't mean we trust you.
You and I never had this conversation, but a little birdy told me Dengo is headed for a planet somewhere in the Uncanny Valley.
What the hell is he doing all the way out there?
If you're lucky, he's hiding. If you're not, he's trying to start a ***revolution***.
And trust me, that's the last thing you poor bastards want.
The whole point of having enemies abroad is getting to ignore the ones back home.

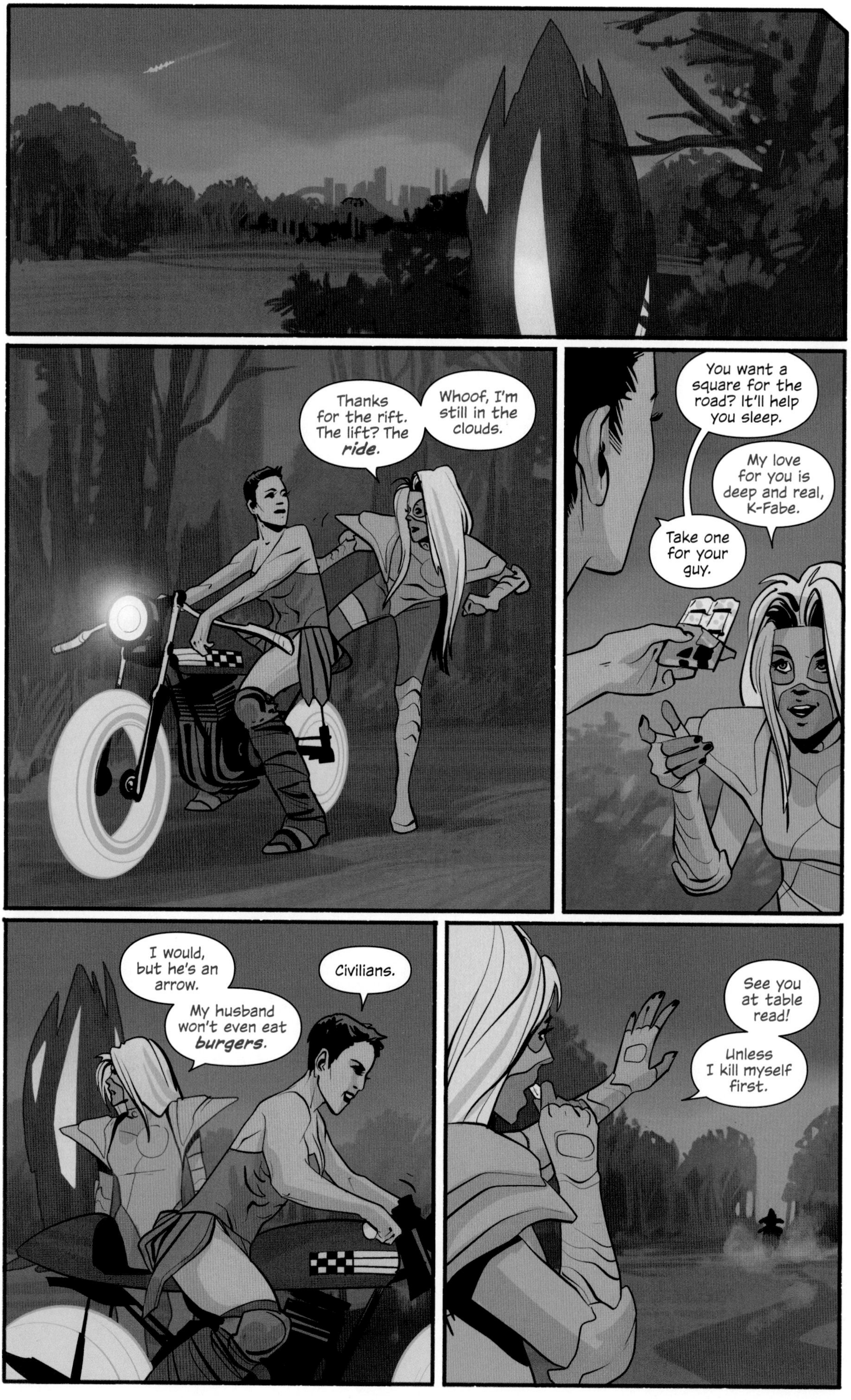
Thanks for the rift. The lift? The ride.
Whoof, I'm still in the clouds.
You want a square for the road? It'll help you sleep.
My love for you is deep and real, K-Fabe.
Take one for your guy.
I would, but he's an arrow.
My husband won't even eat burgers.
Civilians.
See you at table read!
Unless I kill myself first.

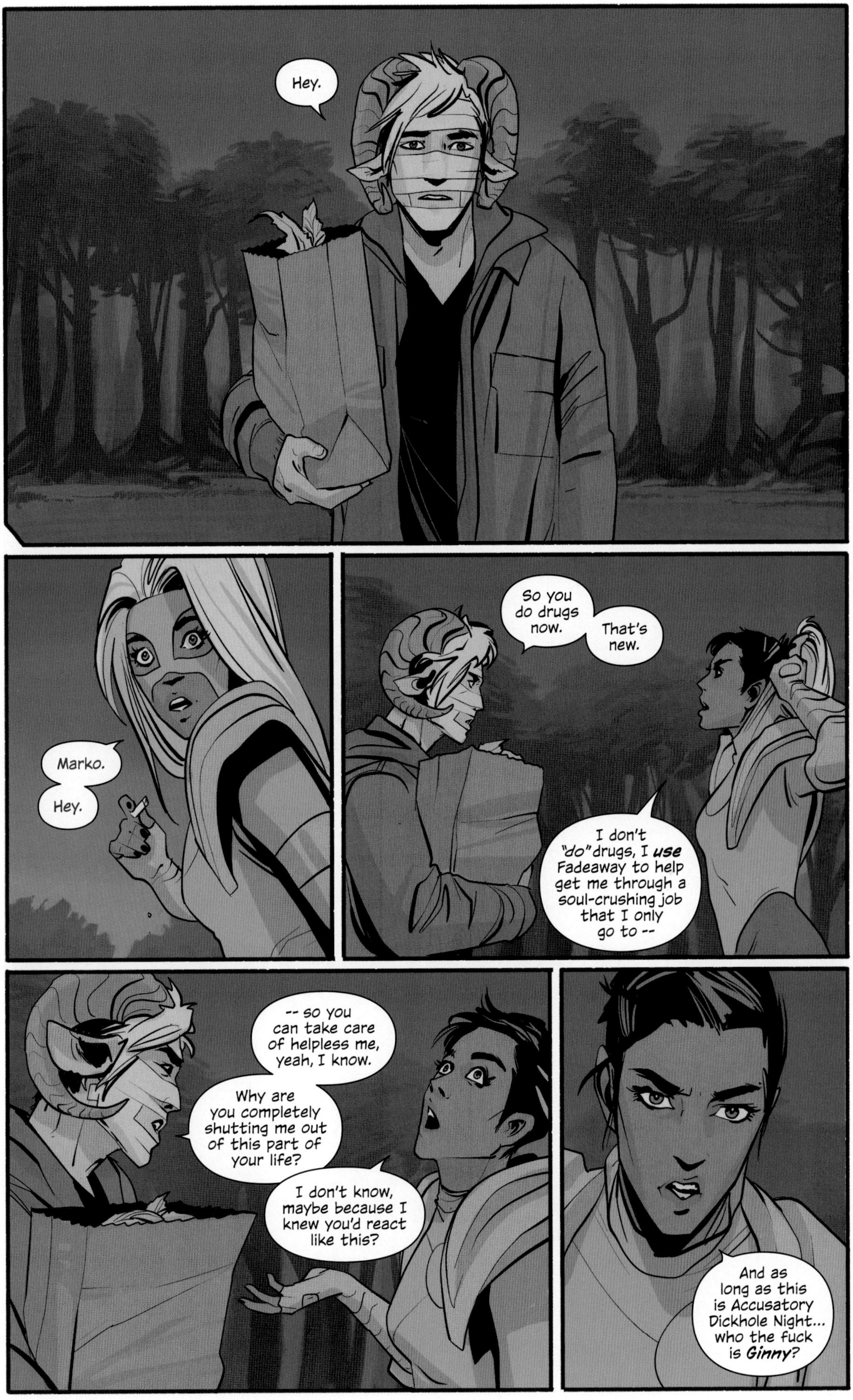
Hey.
Marko.
Hey.
So you do drugs now.
That's new.
I don't "do" drugs, I ***use*** Fadeaway to help get me through a soul-crushing job that I only go to --
-- so you can take care of helpless me, yeah, I know.
Why are you completely shutting me out of this part of your life?
I don't know, maybe because I knew you'd react like this?
And as long as this is Accusatory Dickhole Night... who the fuck is ***Ginny***?

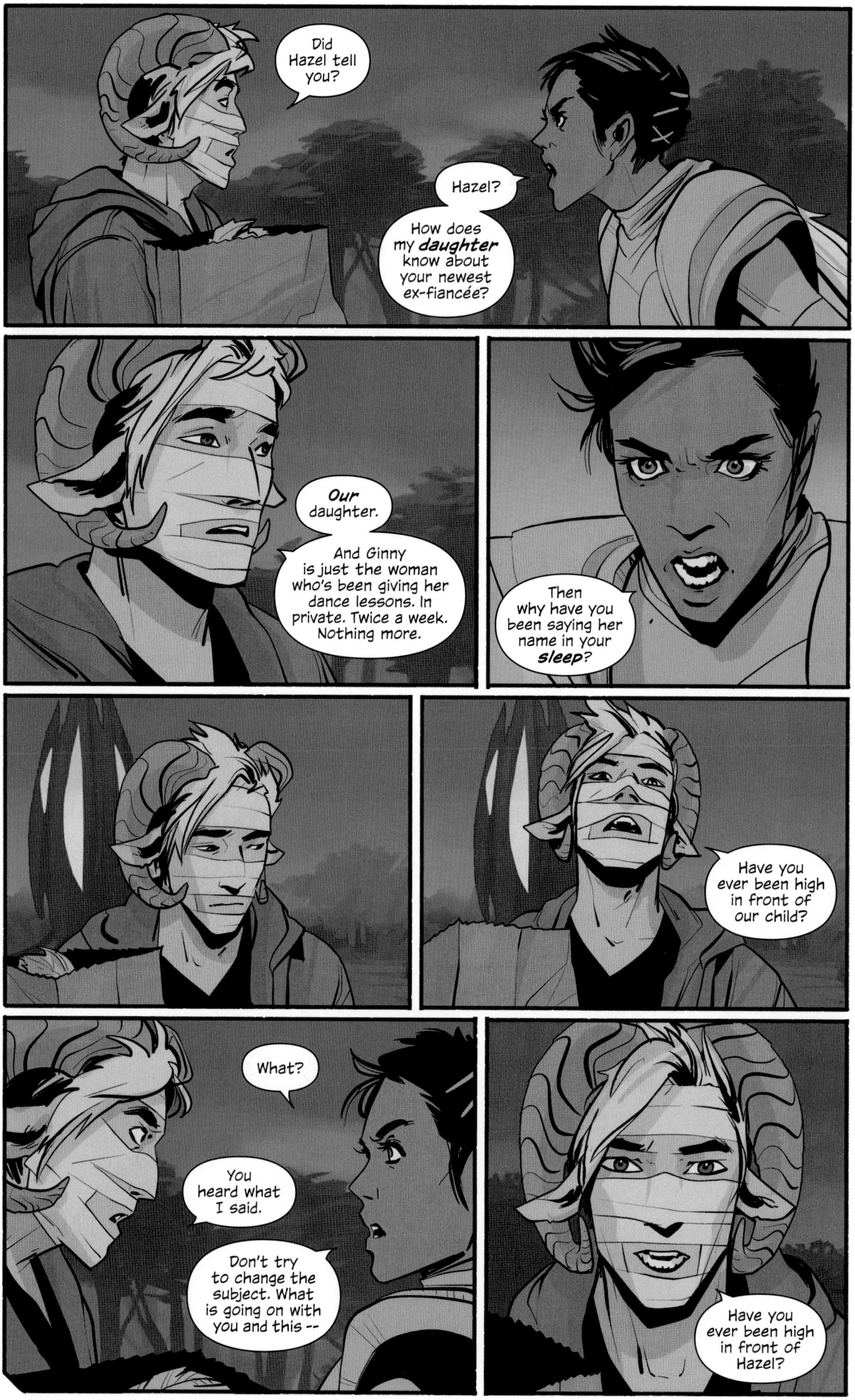

Did Hazel tell you?
Hazel?
How does my ***daughter*** know about your newest ex-fiancée?
Our daughter.
And Ginny is just the woman who's been giving her dance lessons. In private. Twice a week. Nothing more.
Then why have you been saying her name in your ***sleep***?
Have you ever been high in front of our child?
What?
You heard what I said.
Don't try to change the subject. What is going on with you and this --
Have you ever been high in front of Hazel?

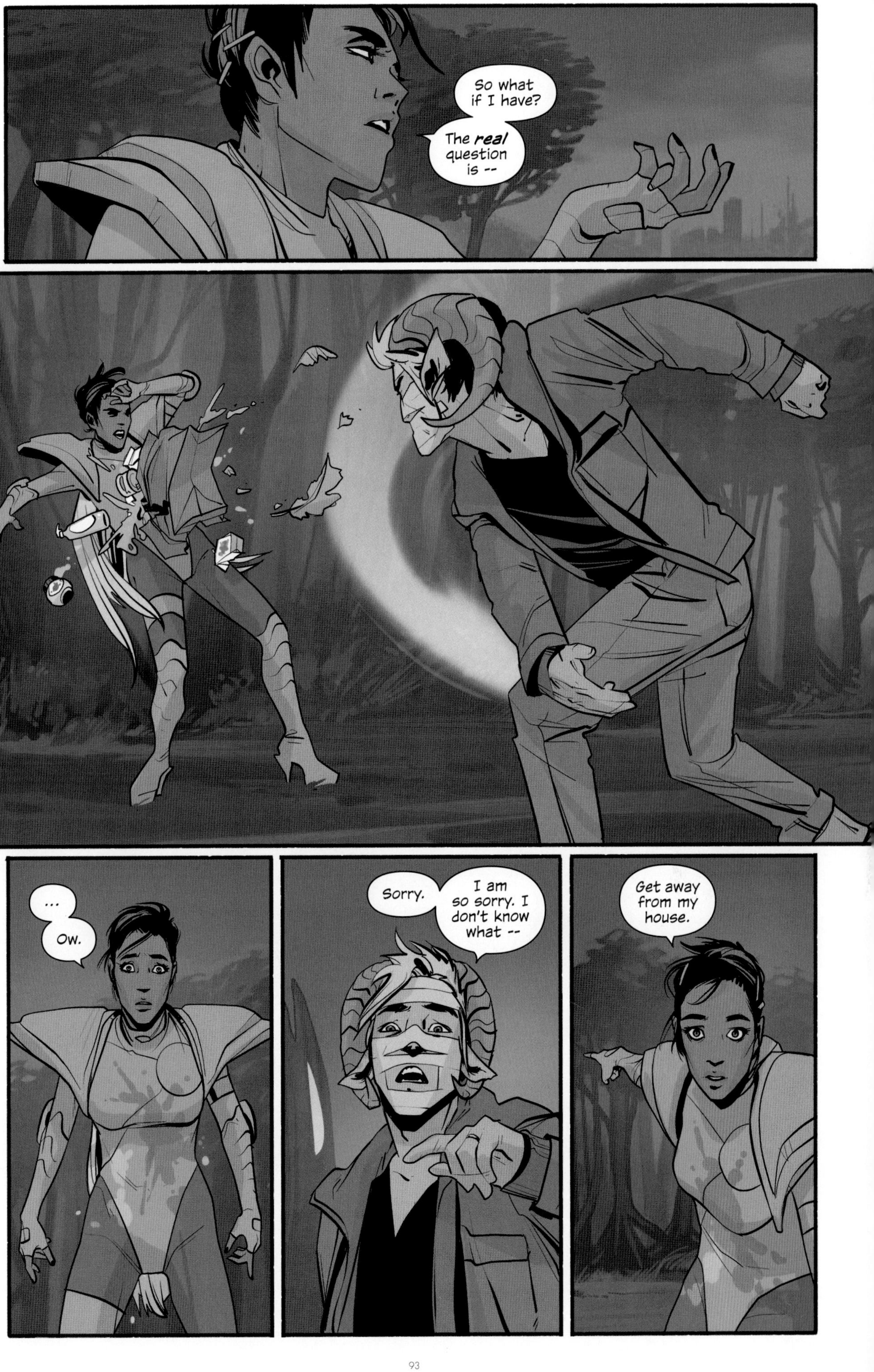
So what if I have?
The *real* question is --
...
Ow.
Sorry.
I am so sorry. I don't know what --
Get away from my house.

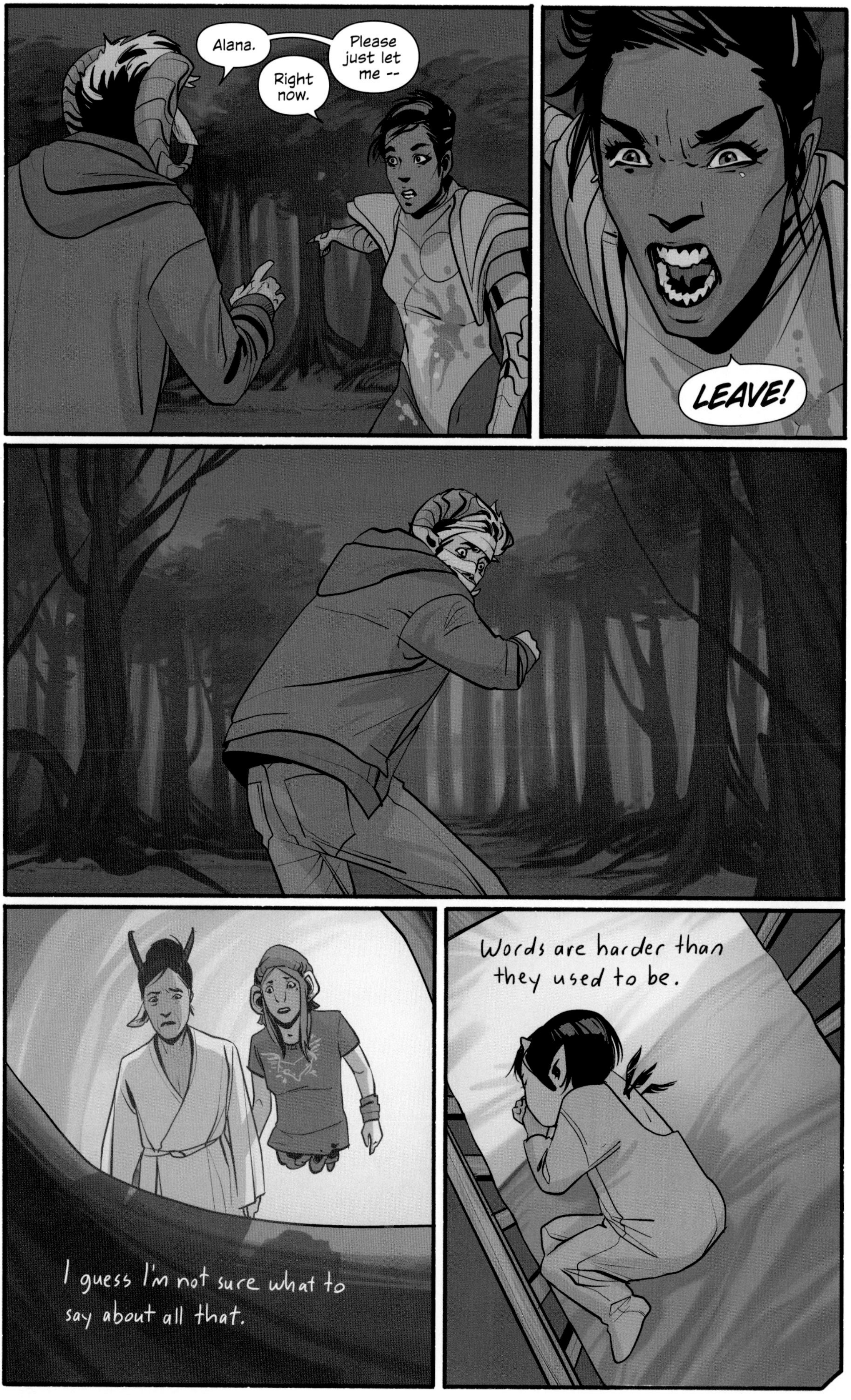
Alana.
Right now.
Please just let me --
LEAVE!
I guess I'm not sure what to say about all that.
Words are harder than they used to be.

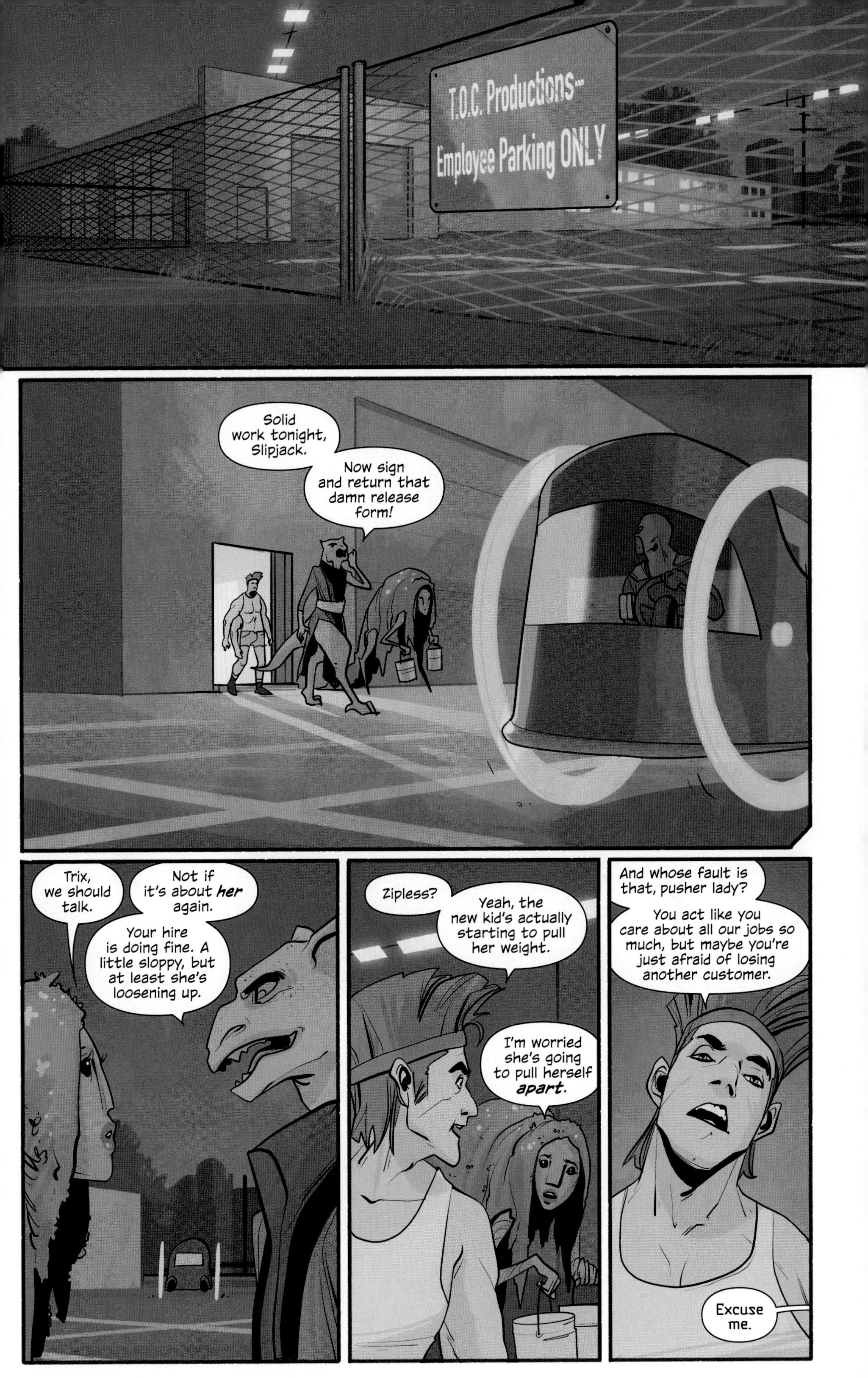
T.O.C. Productions—
Employee Parking ONLY
Solid work tonight, Slipjack.
Now sign and return that damn release form!
Trix, we should talk.
Not if it's about *her* again.
Your hire is doing fine. A little sloppy, but at least she's loosening up.
Zipless?
Yeah, the new kid's actually starting to pull her weight.
I'm worried she's going to pull herself *apart*.
And whose fault is that, pusher lady?
You act like you care about all our jobs so much, but maybe you're just afraid of losing another customer.
Excuse me.

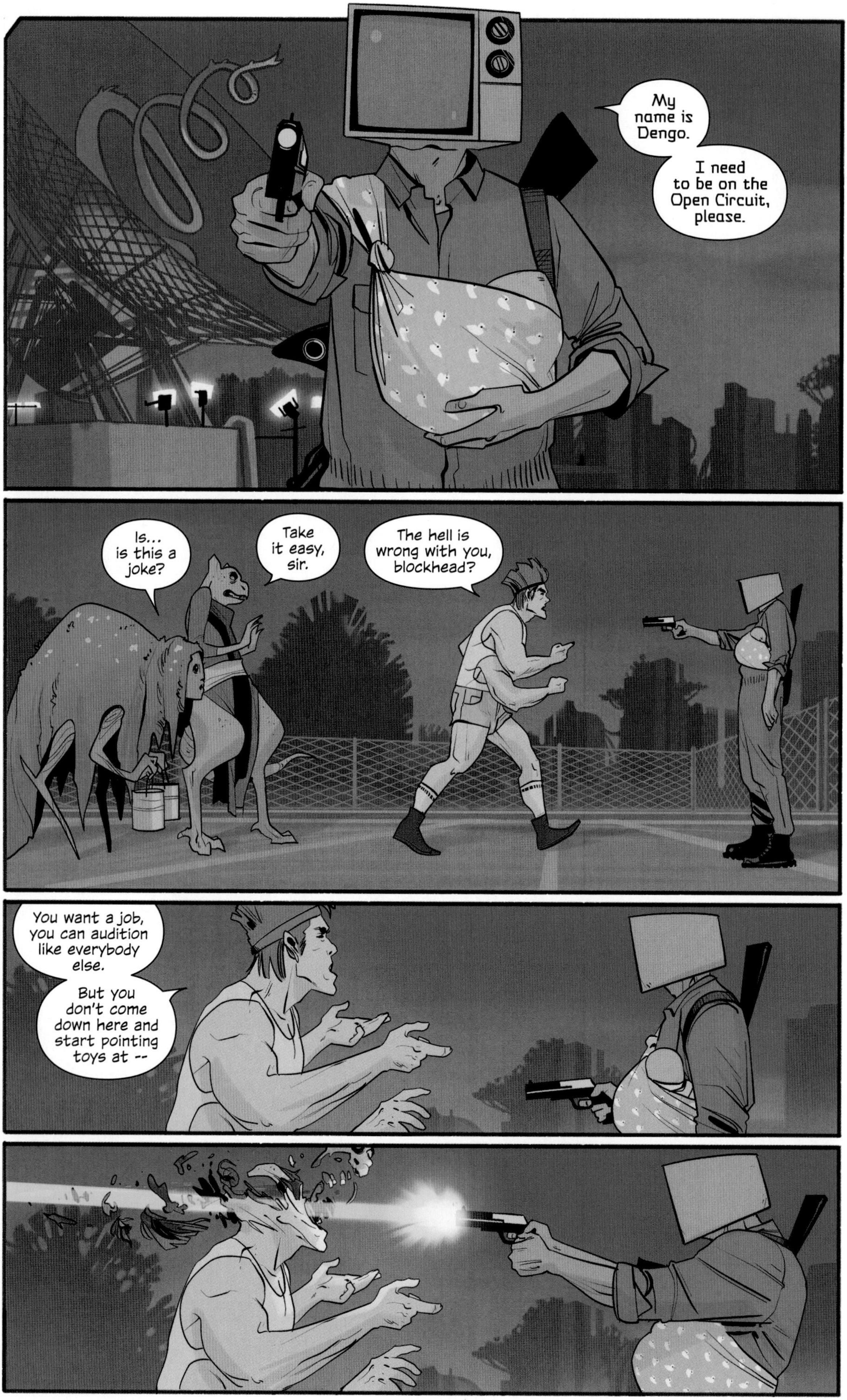
My name is Dengo.
I need to be on the Open Circuit, please.
Is... is this a joke?
Take it easy, sir.
The hell is wrong with you, blockhead?
You want a job, you can audition like everybody else.
But you don't come down here and start pointing toys at --

FUCK!

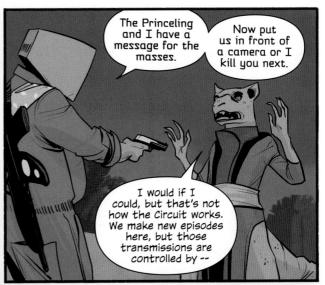

The Princeling and I have a message for the masses.

Now put us in front of a camera or I kill you next.

I would if I could, but that's not how the Circuit works. We make new episodes here, but those transmissions are controlled by --

God, please!

You, help me broadcast my speech to all stations right now or --

I can't! Nobody here can!

But if... if you let me *live*...

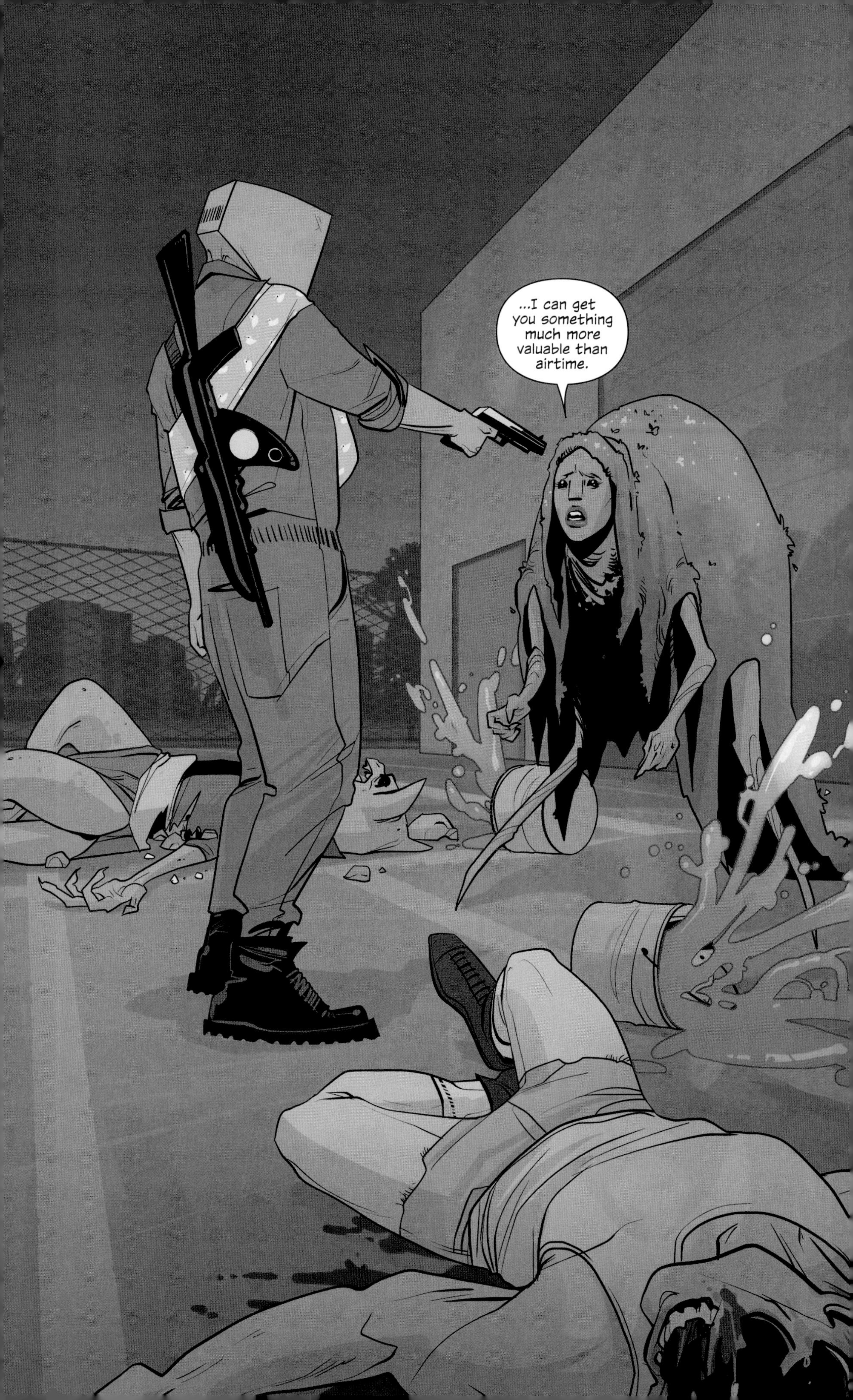
...I can get you something much more valuable than airtime.

end chapter twenty-two

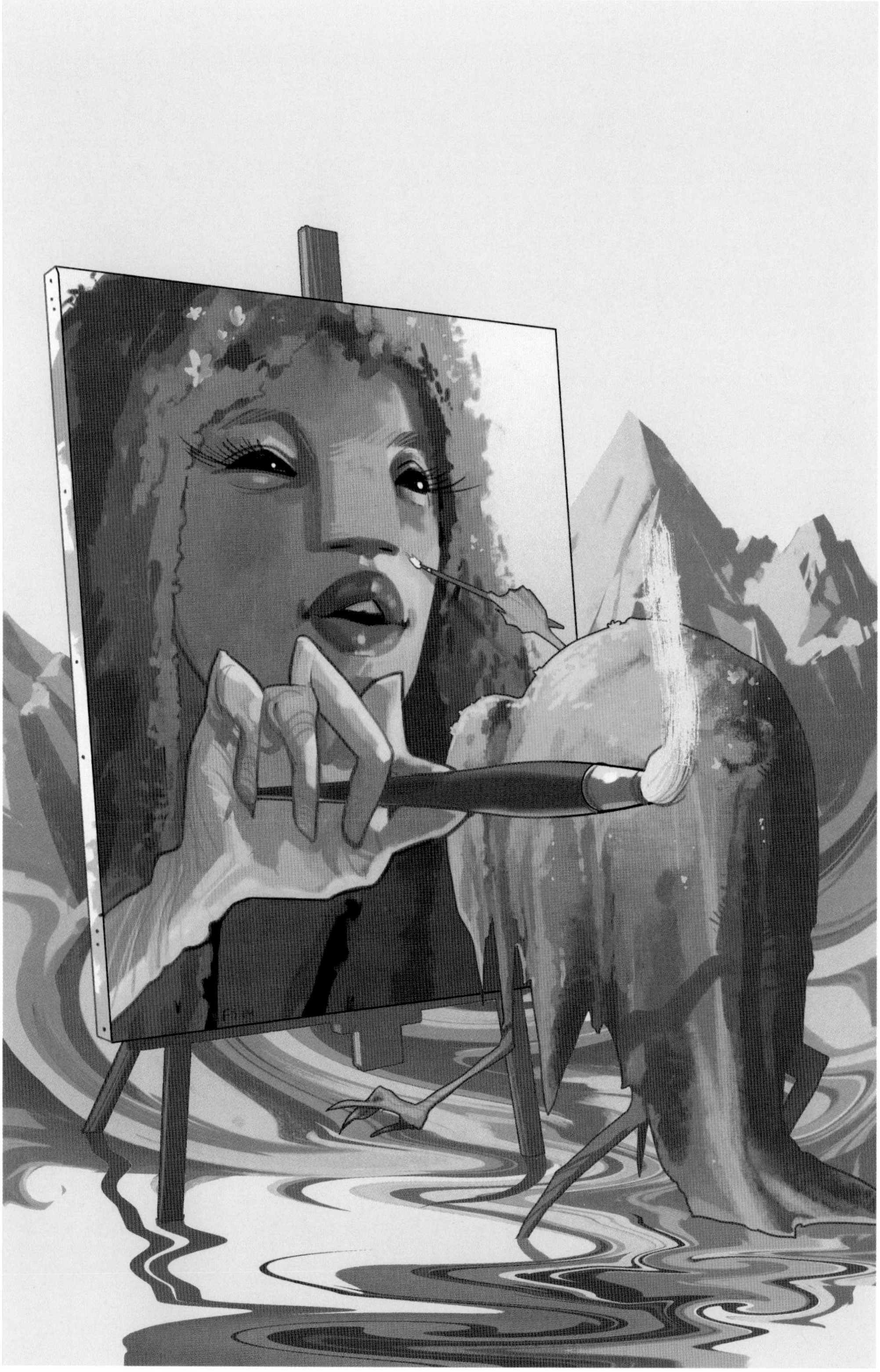

CHAPTER

TWENTY-THREE

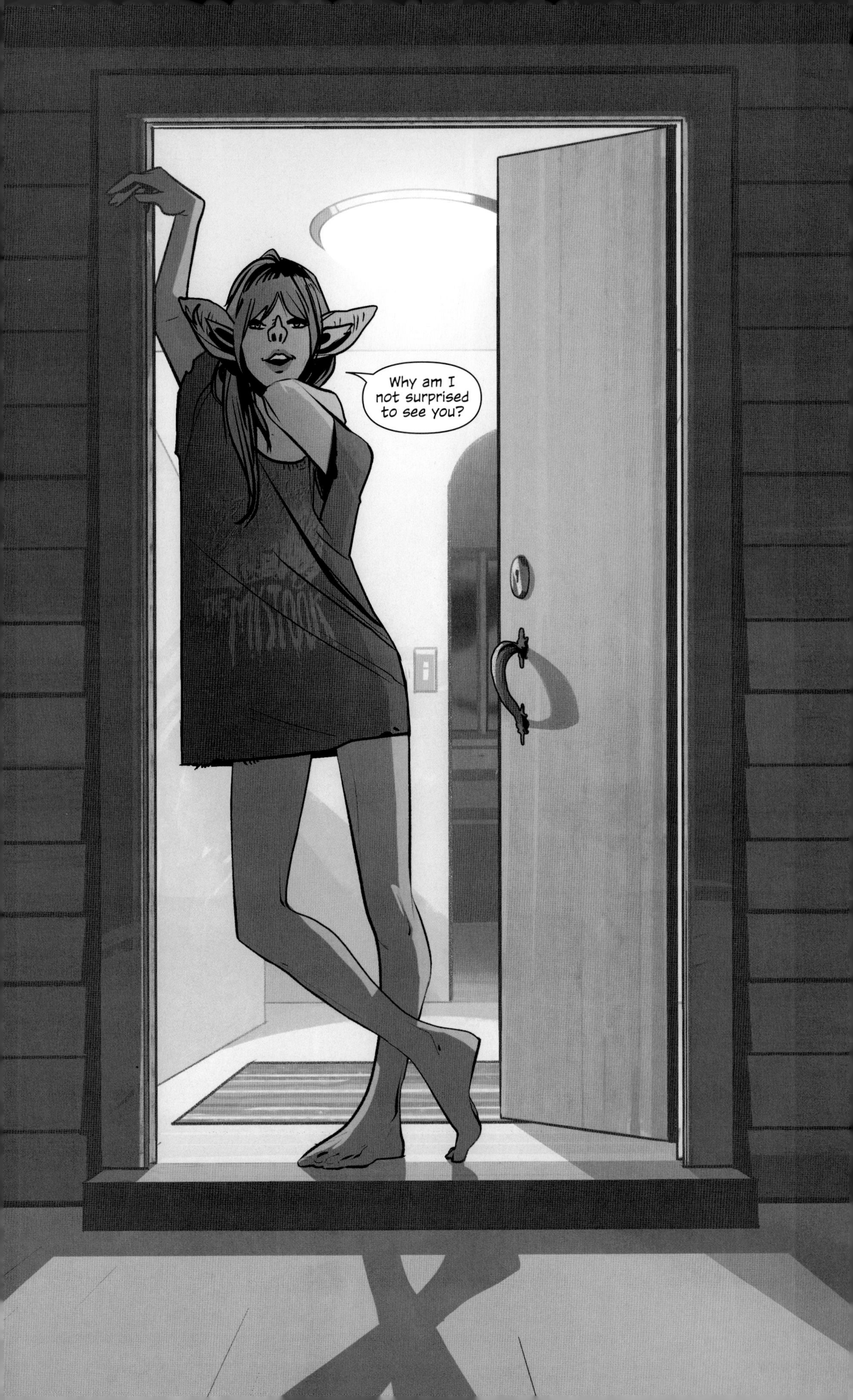
Why am I not surprised to see you?

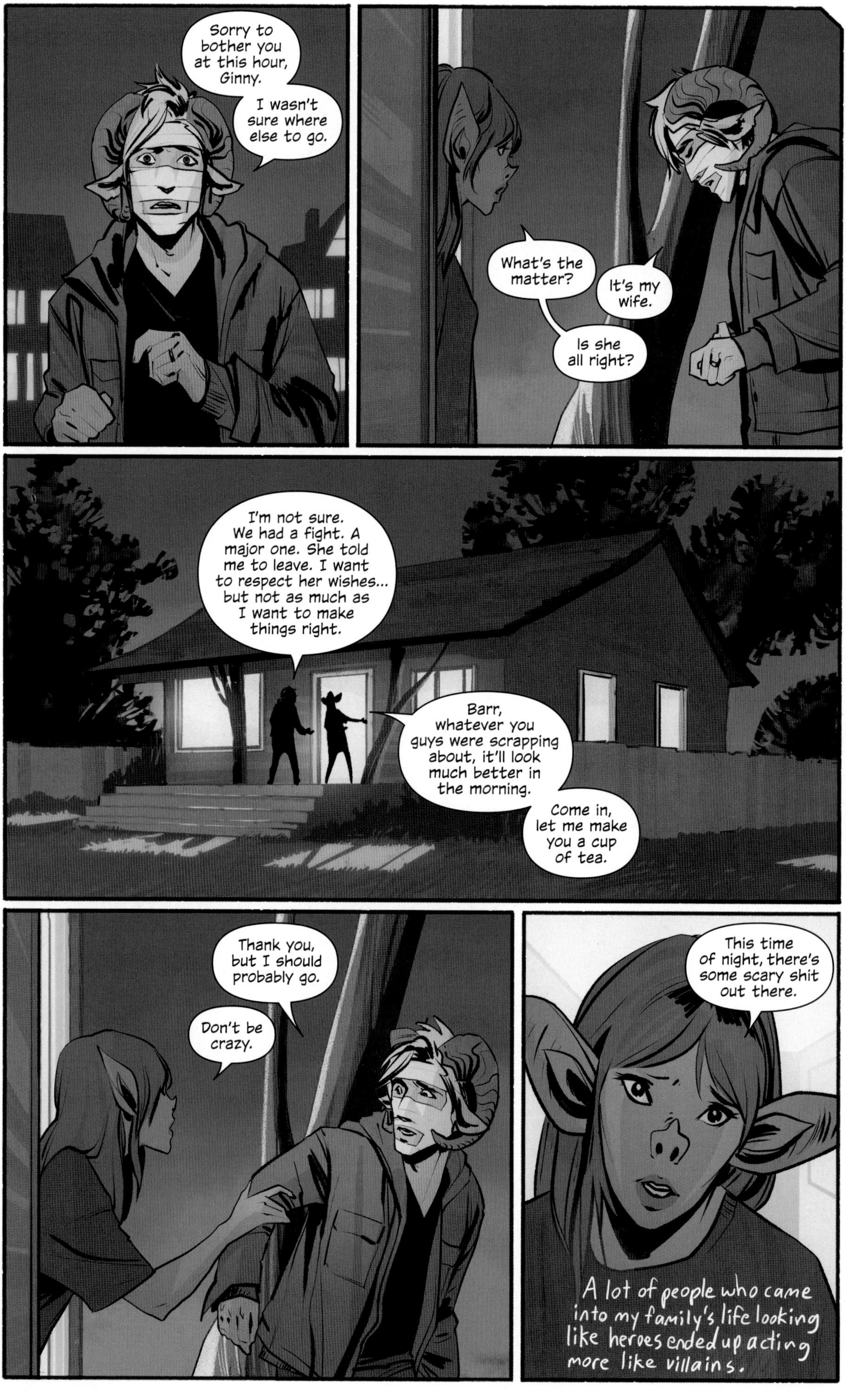
Sorry to bother you at this hour, Ginny.
I wasn't sure where else to go.
What's the matter?
It's my wife.
Is she all right?
I'm not sure. We had a fight. A major one. She told me to leave. I want to respect her wishes... but not as much as I want to make things right.
Barr, whatever you guys were scrapping about, it'll look much better in the morning.
Come in, let me make you a cup of tea.
Thank you, but I should probably go.
Don't be crazy.
This time of night, there's some scary shit out there.
A lot of people who came into my family's life looking like heroes ended up acting more like villains.

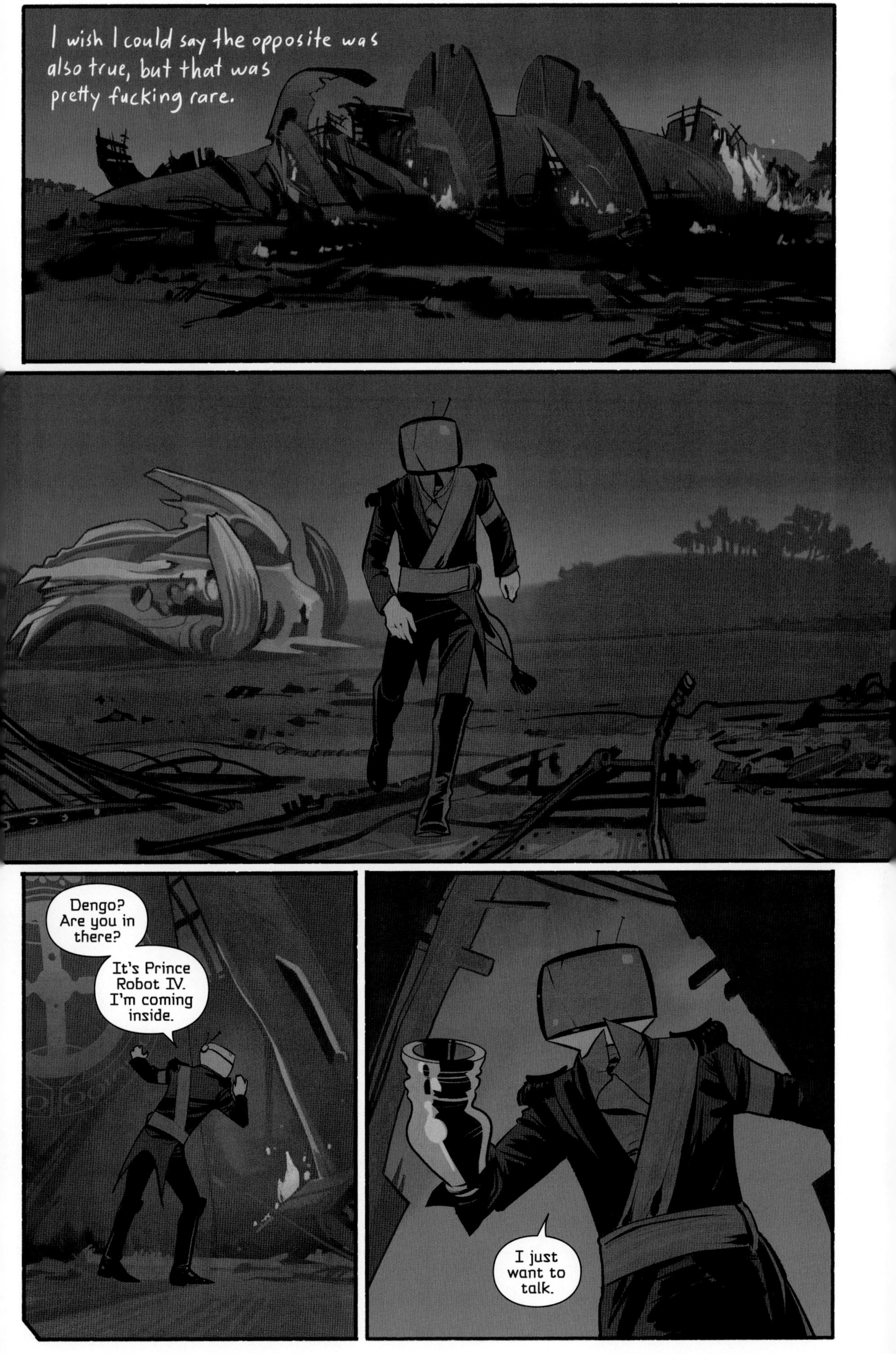
I wish I could say the opposite was also true, but that was pretty fucking rare.
Dengo? Are you in there?
It's Prince Robot IV. I'm coming inside.
I just want to talk.

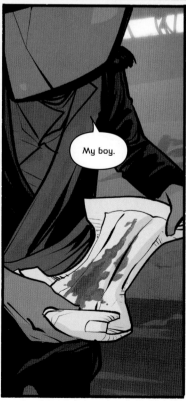

My boy.

He's alive.

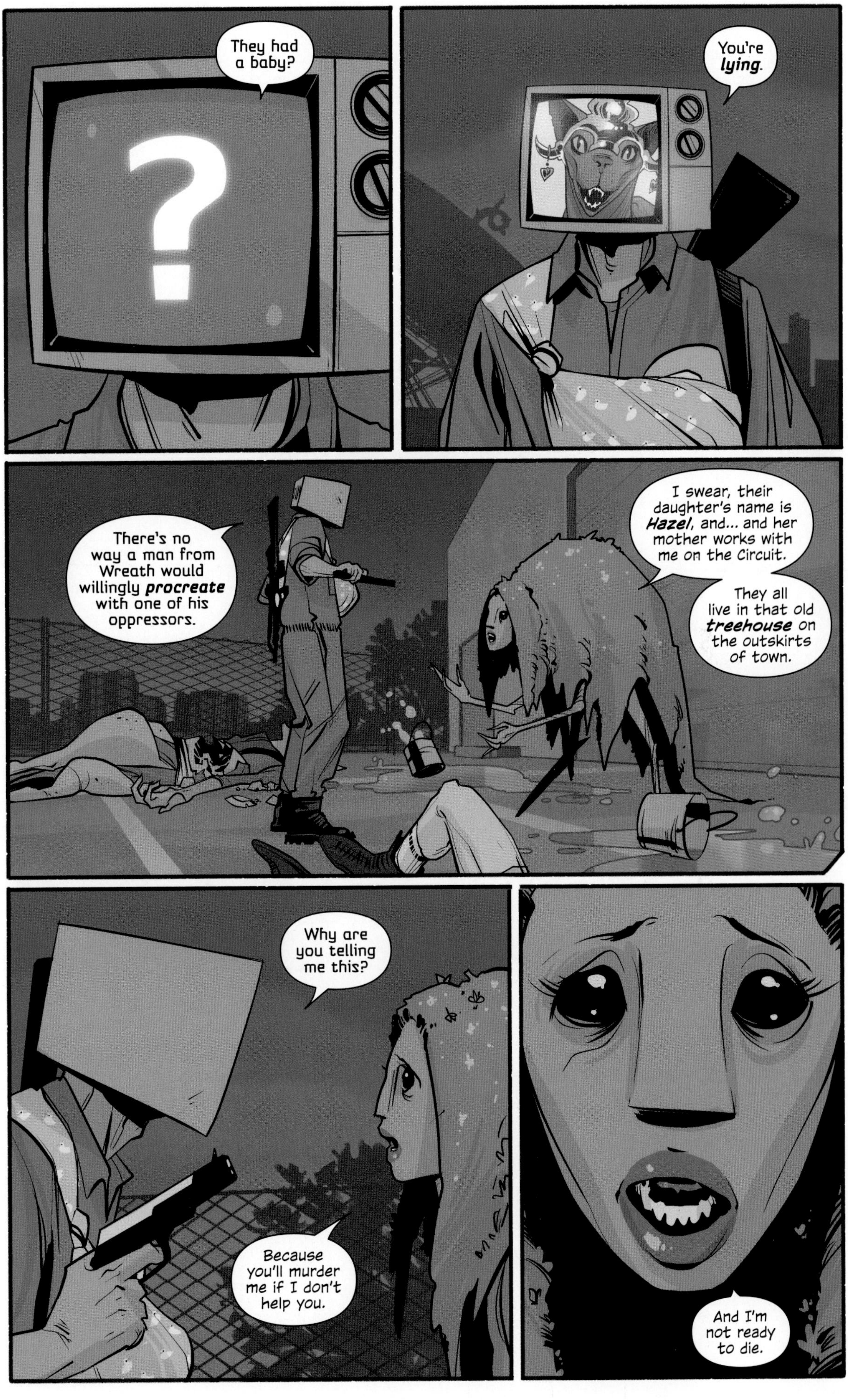
They had a baby?
You're *lying*.
There's no way a man from Wreath would willingly *procreate* with one of his oppressors.
I swear, their daughter's name is *Hazel*, and... and her mother works with me on the Circuit.
They all live in that old *treehouse* on the outskirts of town.
Why are you telling me this?
Because you'll murder me if I don't help you.
And I'm not ready to die.

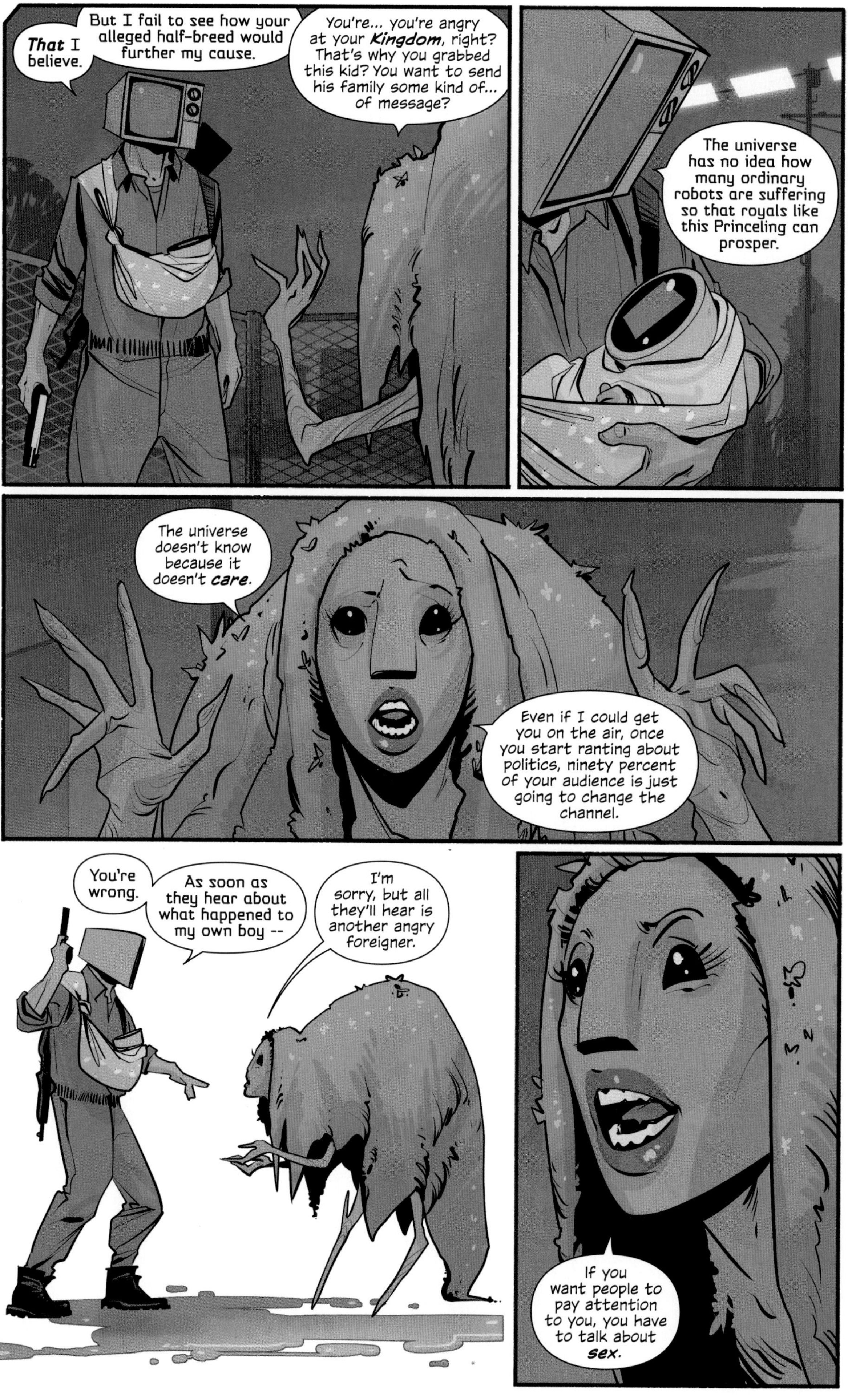

That I believe.
But I fail to see how your alleged half-breed would further my cause.
You're... you're angry at your Kingdom, right? That's why you grabbed this kid? You want to send his family some kind of... of message?
The universe has no idea how many ordinary robots are suffering so that royals like this Princeling can prosper.
The universe doesn't know because it doesn't care.
Even if I could get you on the air, once you start ranting about politics, ninety percent of your audience is just going to change the channel.
You're wrong.
As soon as they hear about what happened to my own boy --
I'm sorry, but all they'll hear is another angry foreigner.
If you want people to pay attention to you, you have to talk about sex.

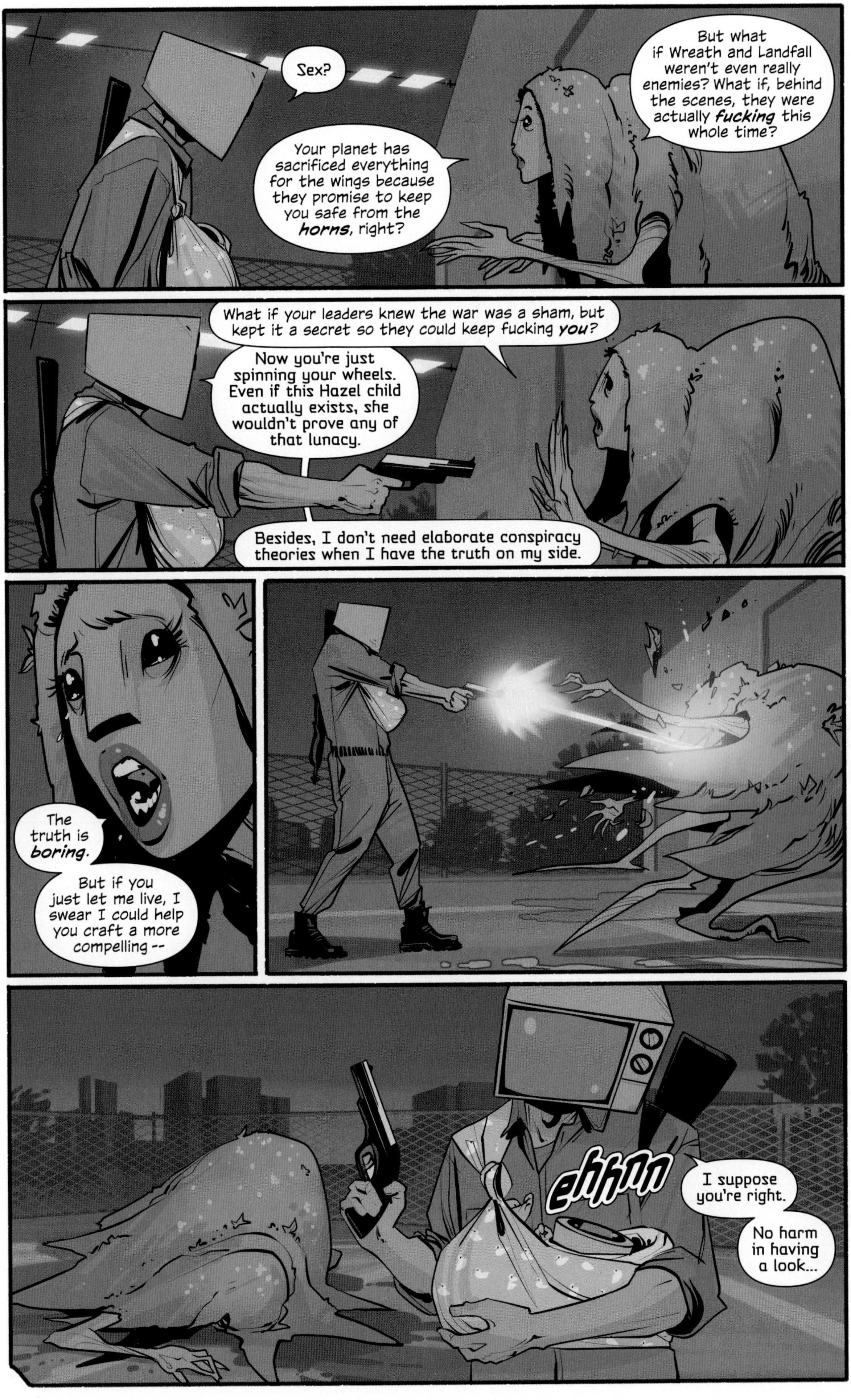

Sex?
Your planet has sacrificed everything for the wings because they promise to keep you safe from the **horns**, right?
But what if Wreath and Landfall weren't even really enemies? What if, behind the scenes, they were actually **fucking** this whole time?
What if your leaders knew the war was a sham, but kept it a secret so they could keep fucking **you**?
Now you're just spinning your wheels. Even if this Hazel child actually exists, she wouldn't prove any of that lunacy.
Besides, I don't need elaborate conspiracy theories when I have the truth on my side.
The truth is **boring**.
But if you just let me live, I swear I could help you craft a more compelling --
ehhnn
I suppose you're right.
No harm in having a look...

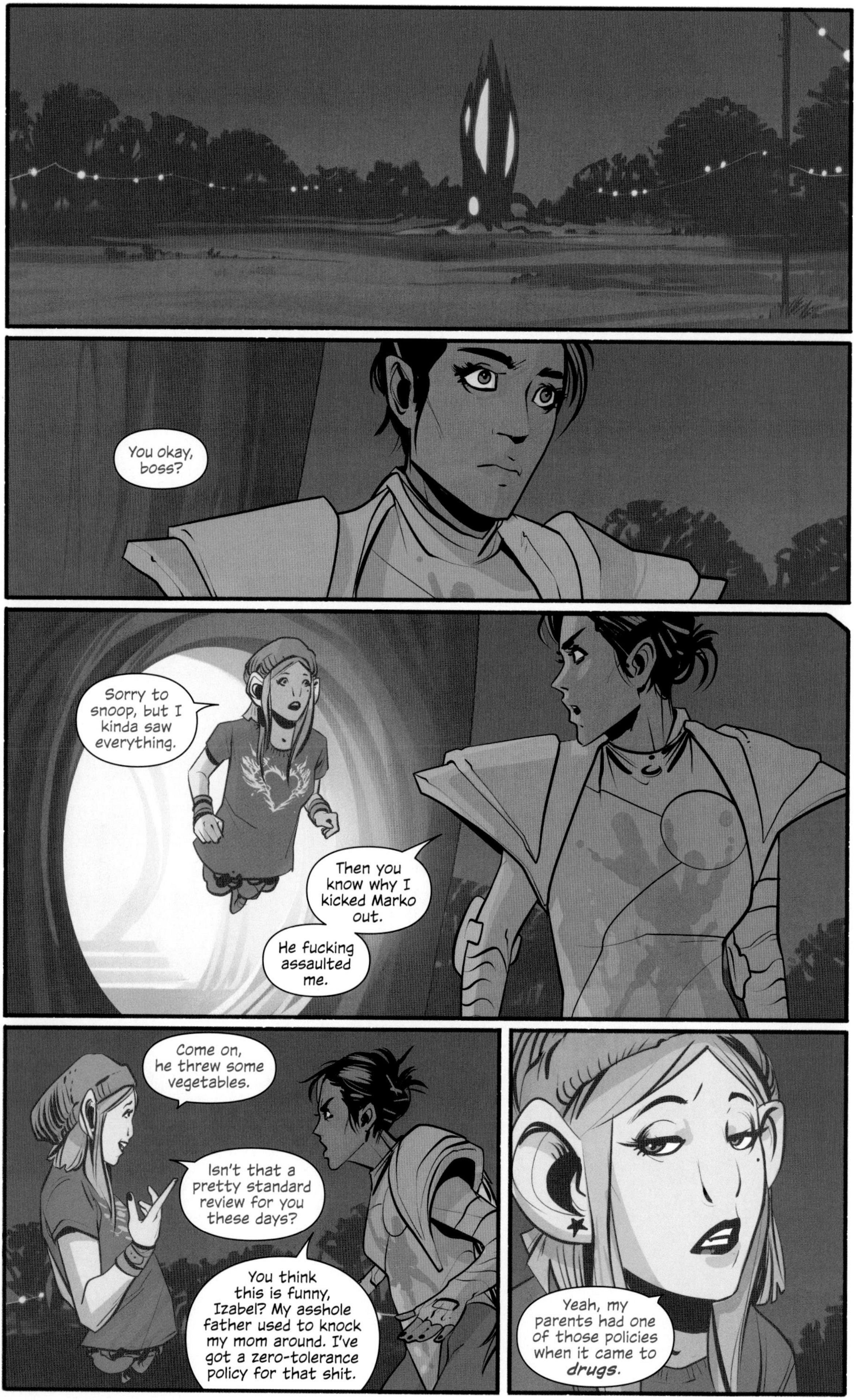
You okay, boss?
Sorry to snoop, but I kinda saw everything.
Then you know why I kicked Marko out.
He fucking assaulted me.
Come on, he threw some vegetables.
Isn't that a pretty standard review for you these days?
You think this is funny, Izabel? My asshole father used to knock my mom around. I've got a zero-tolerance policy for that shit.
Yeah, my parents had one of those policies when it came to *drugs*.

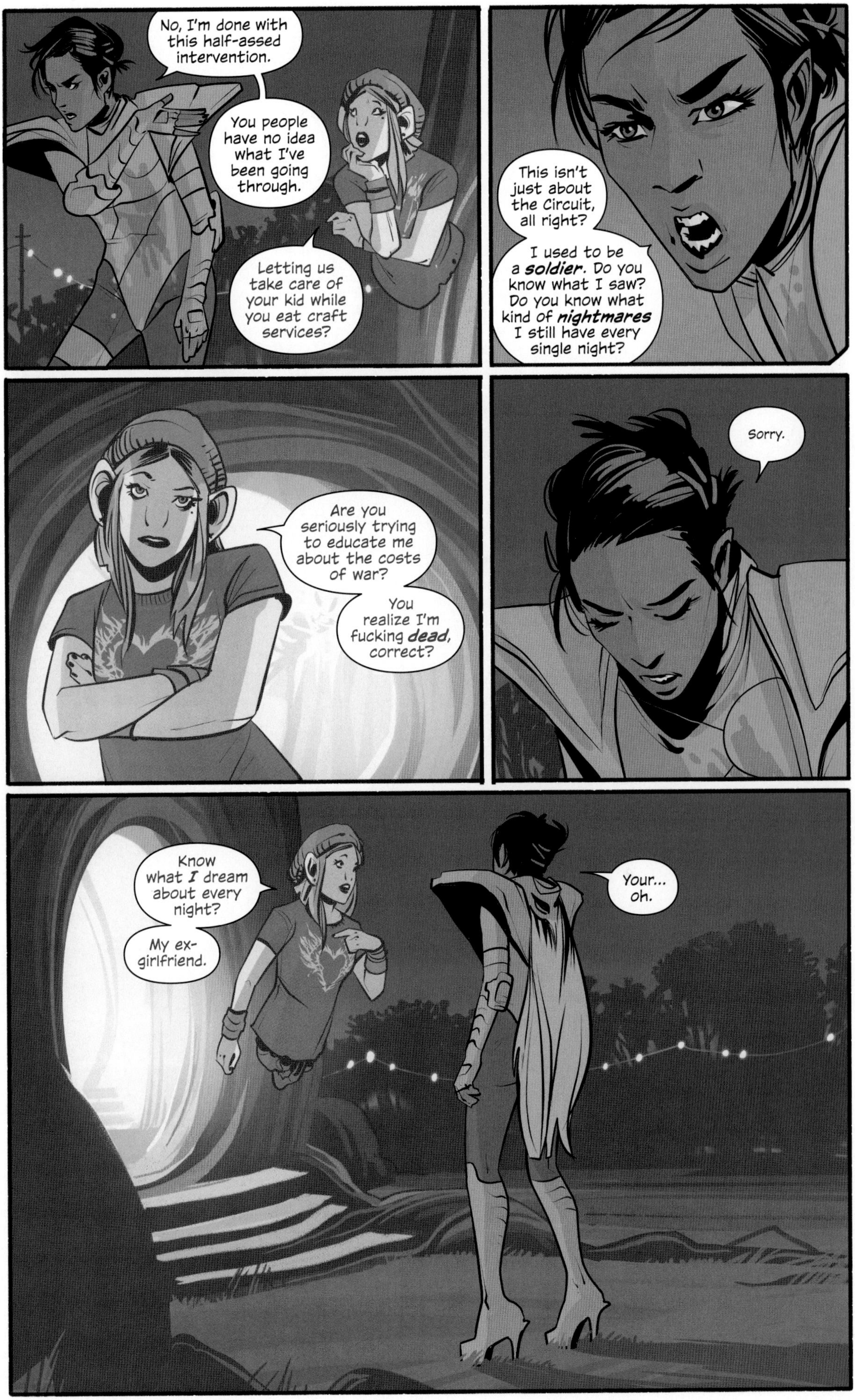
No, I'm done with this half-assed intervention.
You people have no idea what I've been going through.
Letting us take care of your kid while you eat craft services?
This isn't just about the Circuit, all right?
I used to be a **soldier**. Do you know what I saw? Do you know what kind of **nightmares** I still have every single night?
Are you seriously trying to educate me about the costs of war?
You realize I'm fucking **dead**, correct?
Sorry.
Know what *I* dream about every night?
My ex-girlfriend.
Your... oh.

Her name was Windy. We were just stupid kids.

She was smart and gorgeous and sweet to me, but she was also super into our planet's most judgy religion, so I eventually broke up with her.

Two days later, I stepped on whatever anti-personnel crap one of your sides buried in our backyard.

The whole time I was bleeding out, all I could think was, *"Damn, I will never feel her breath on my neck again."*

How pathetic is that? I need to get blown in half before I realize what a good thing I had?

I get what you're trying to say, but this is a completely different situation.

Yeah, life is complicated. But it's also very fucking short.

If you find someone who can forgive all your bullshit... the least you can do is try to forgive them.

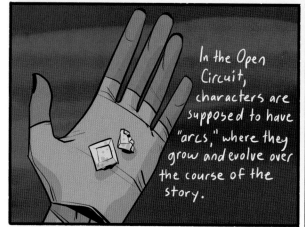

In the Open Circuit, characters are supposed to have "arcs," where they grow and evolve over the course of the story.

But Mom always thought that was nonsense.

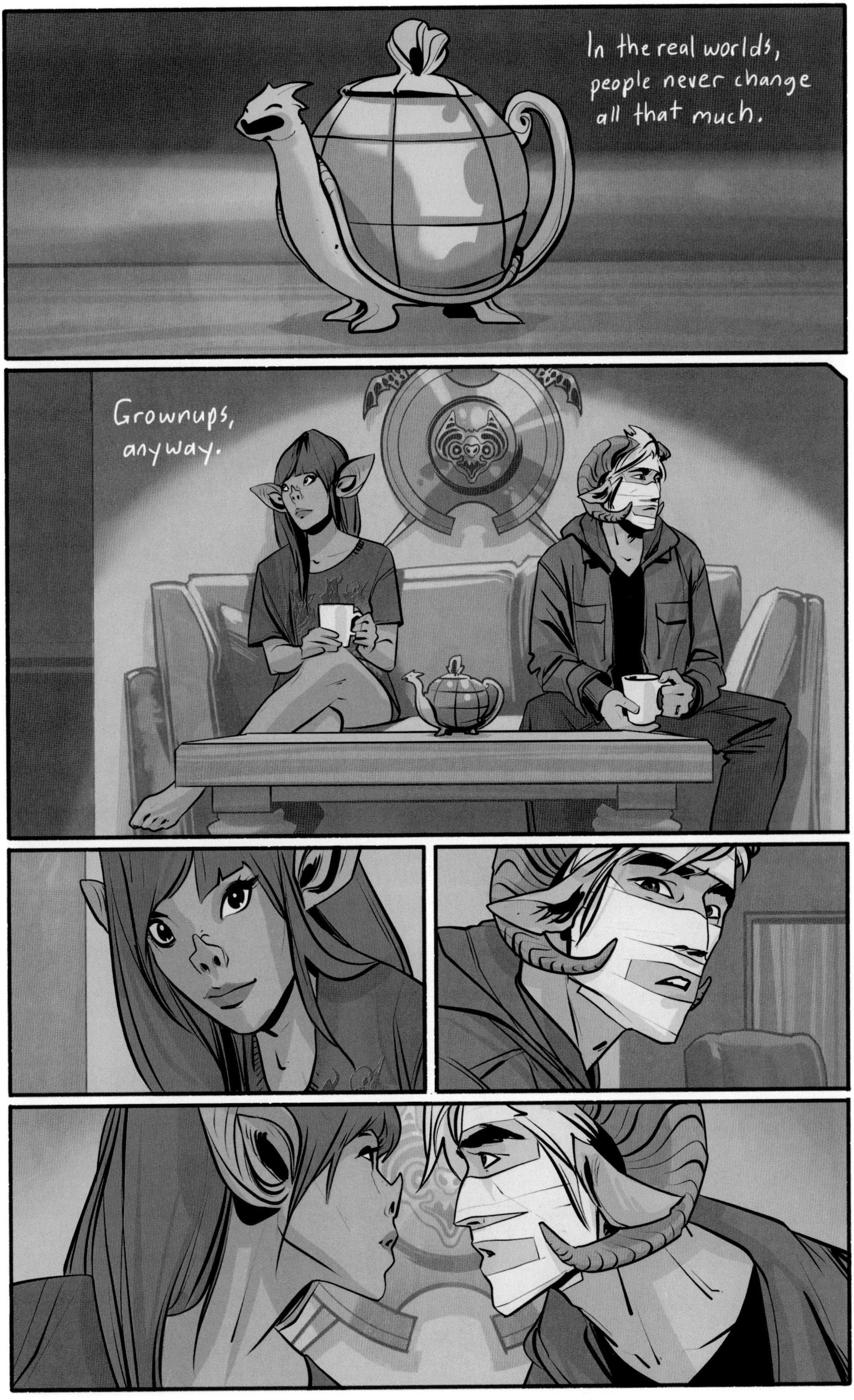
In the real worlds, people never change all that much.
Grownups, anyway.

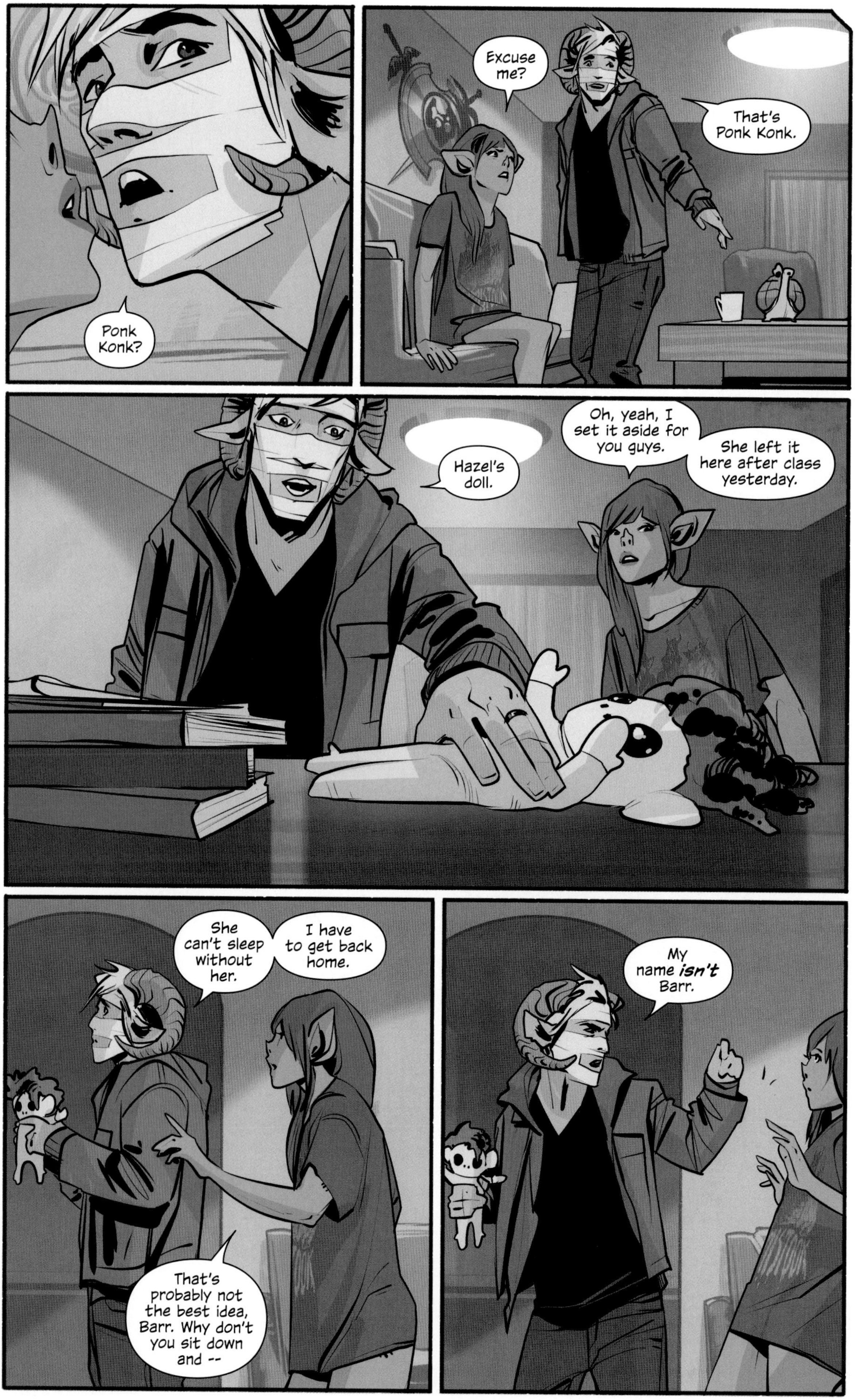
Ponk Konk?
Excuse me?
That's Ponk Konk.
Hazel's doll.
Oh, yeah, I set it aside for you guys.
She left it here after class yesterday.
She can't sleep without her.
I have to get back home.
That's probably not the best idea, Barr. Why don't you sit down and --
My name *isn't* Barr.

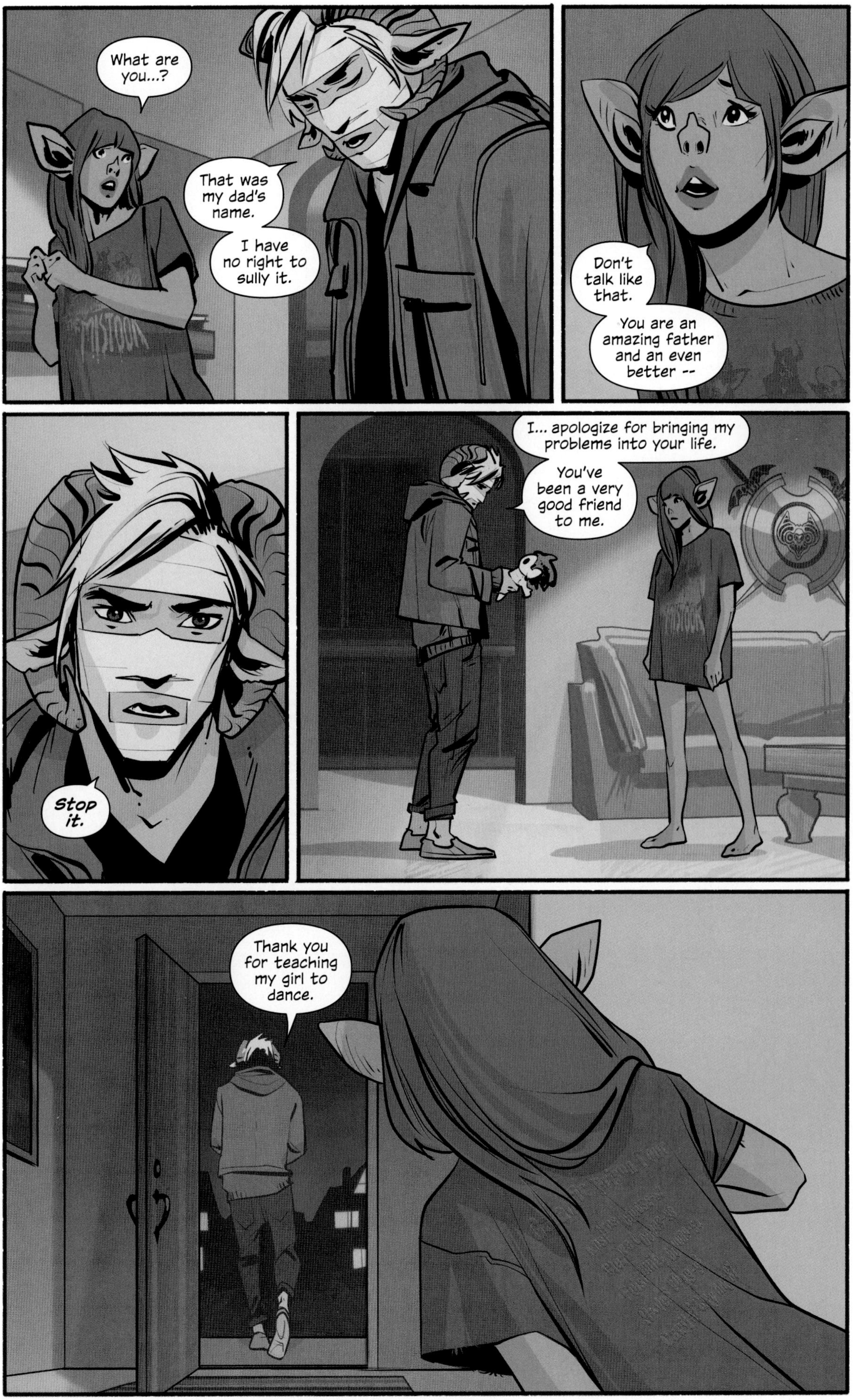
What are you...?
That was my dad's name.
I have no right to sully it.
Don't talk like that.
You are an amazing father and an even better --
Stop it.
I... apologize for bringing my problems into your life.
You've been a very good friend to me.
Thank you for teaching my girl to dance.

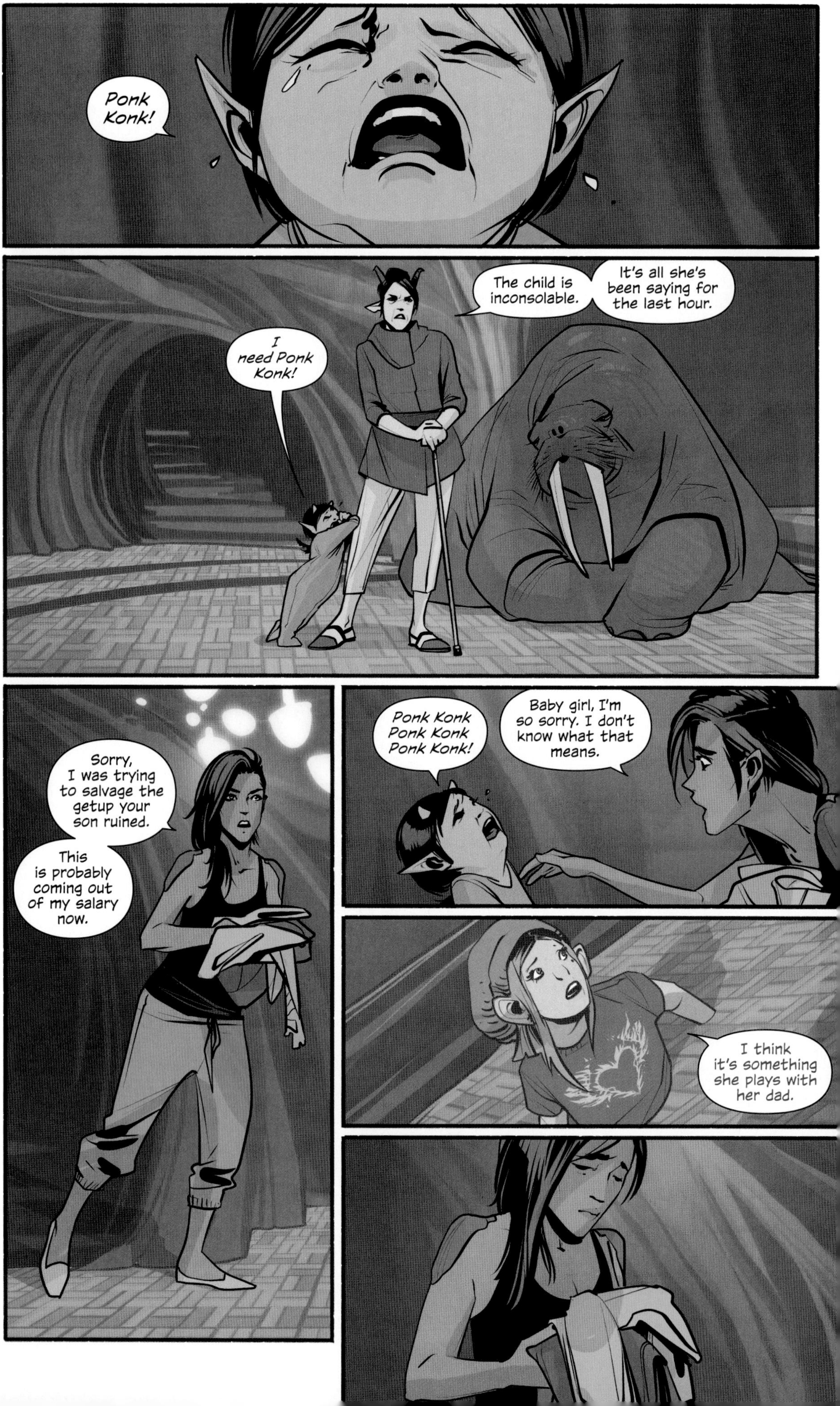
Ponk Konk!
The child is inconsolable.
It's all she's been saying for the last hour.
I need Ponk Konk!
Sorry, I was trying to salvage the getup your son ruined.
This is probably coming out of my salary now.
Ponk Konk Ponk Konk Ponk Konk!
Baby girl, I'm so sorry. I don't know what that means.
I think it's something she plays with her dad.

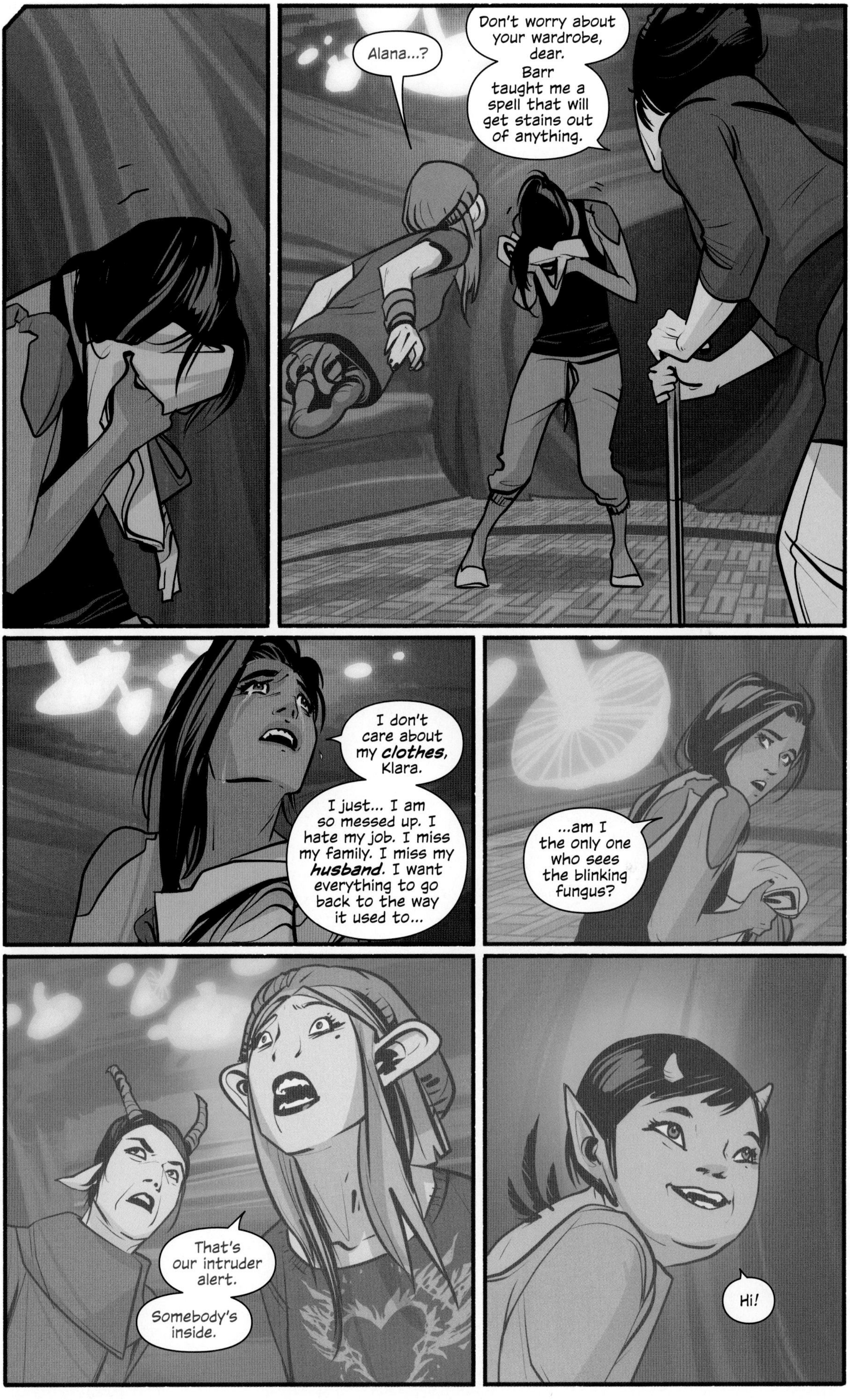
Alana...?
Don't worry about your wardrobe, dear.
Barr taught me a spell that will get stains out of anything.
I don't care about my *clothes*, Klara.
I just... I am so messed up. I hate my job. I miss my family. I miss my *husband*. I want everything to go back to the way it used to...
...am I the only one who sees the blinking fungus?
That's our intruder alert.
Somebody's inside.
Hi!

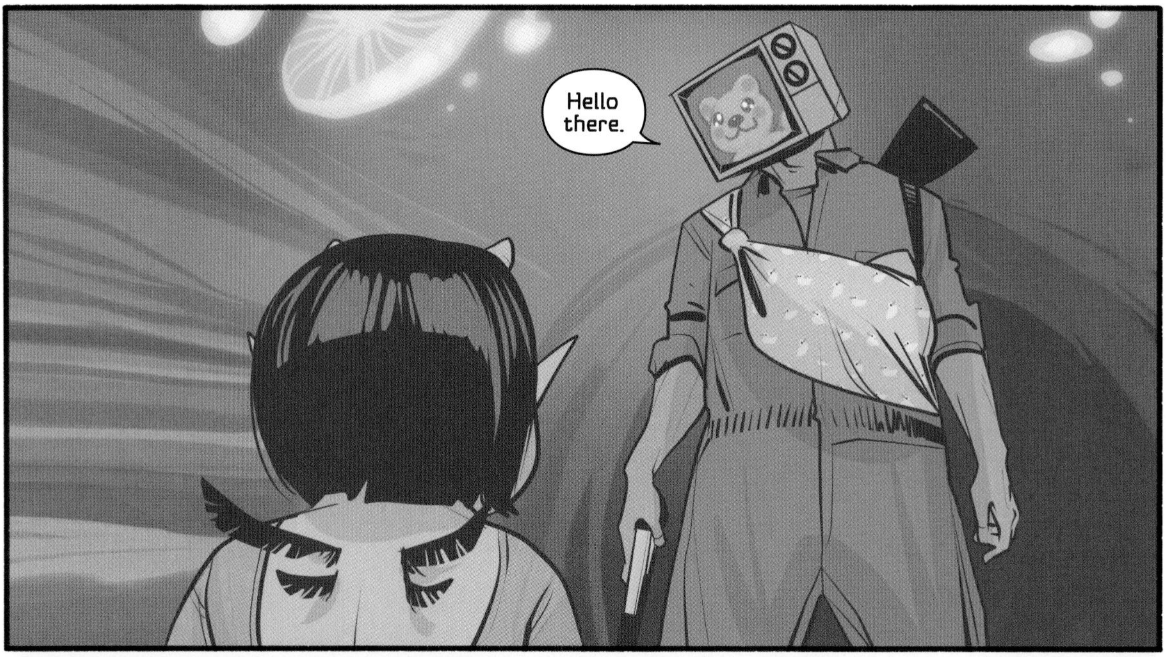
Hello there.

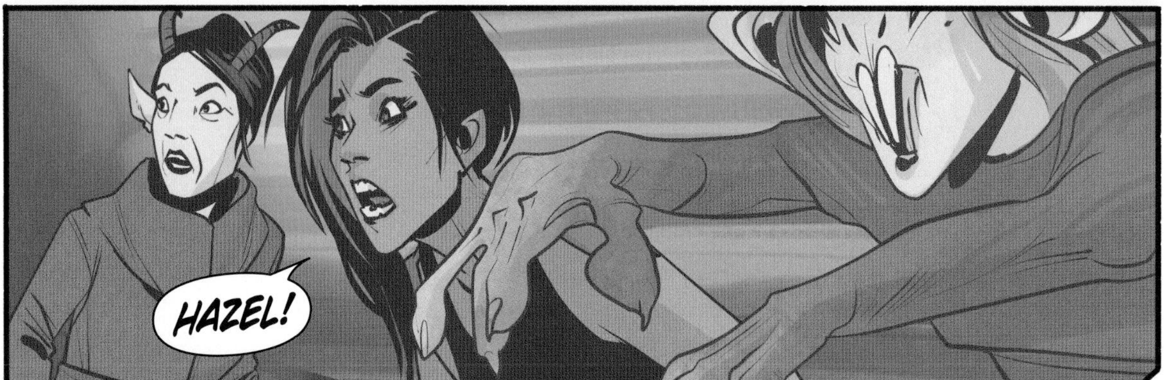
HAZEL!

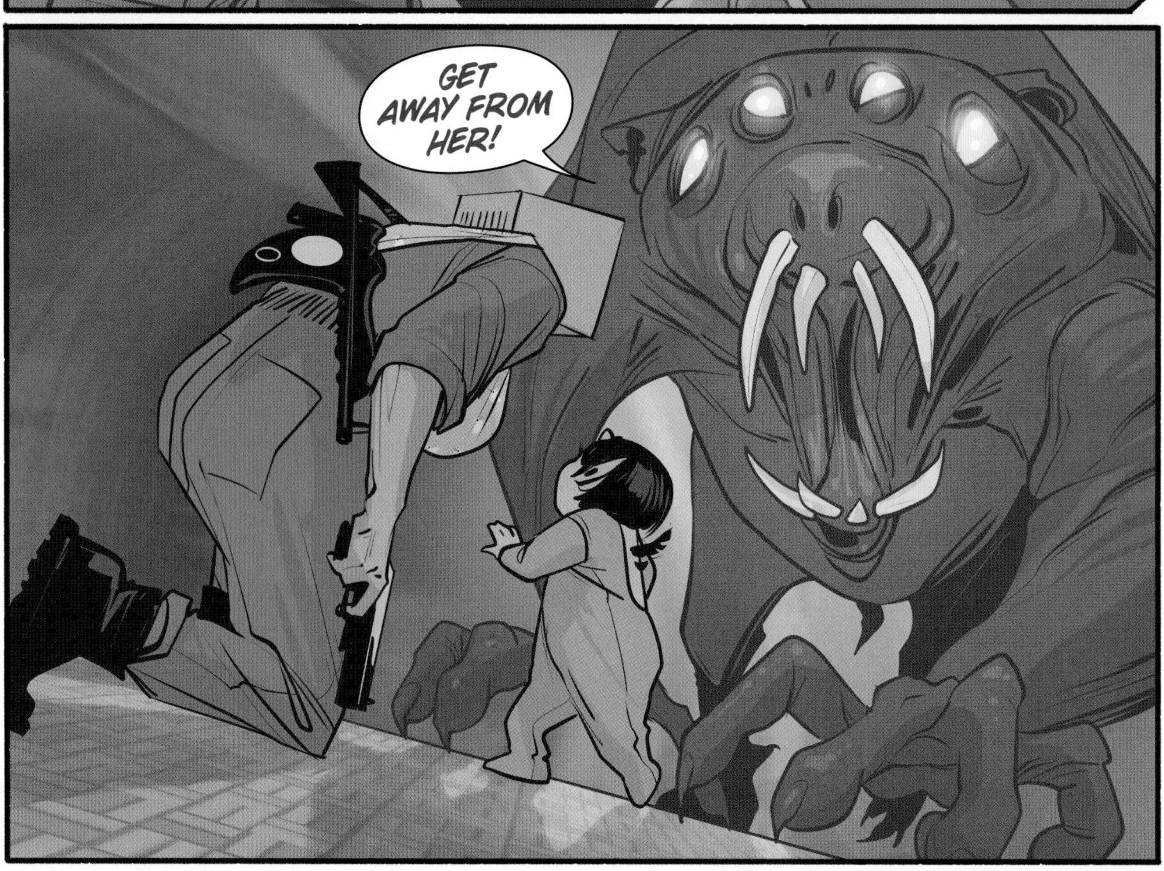
GET AWAY FROM HER!

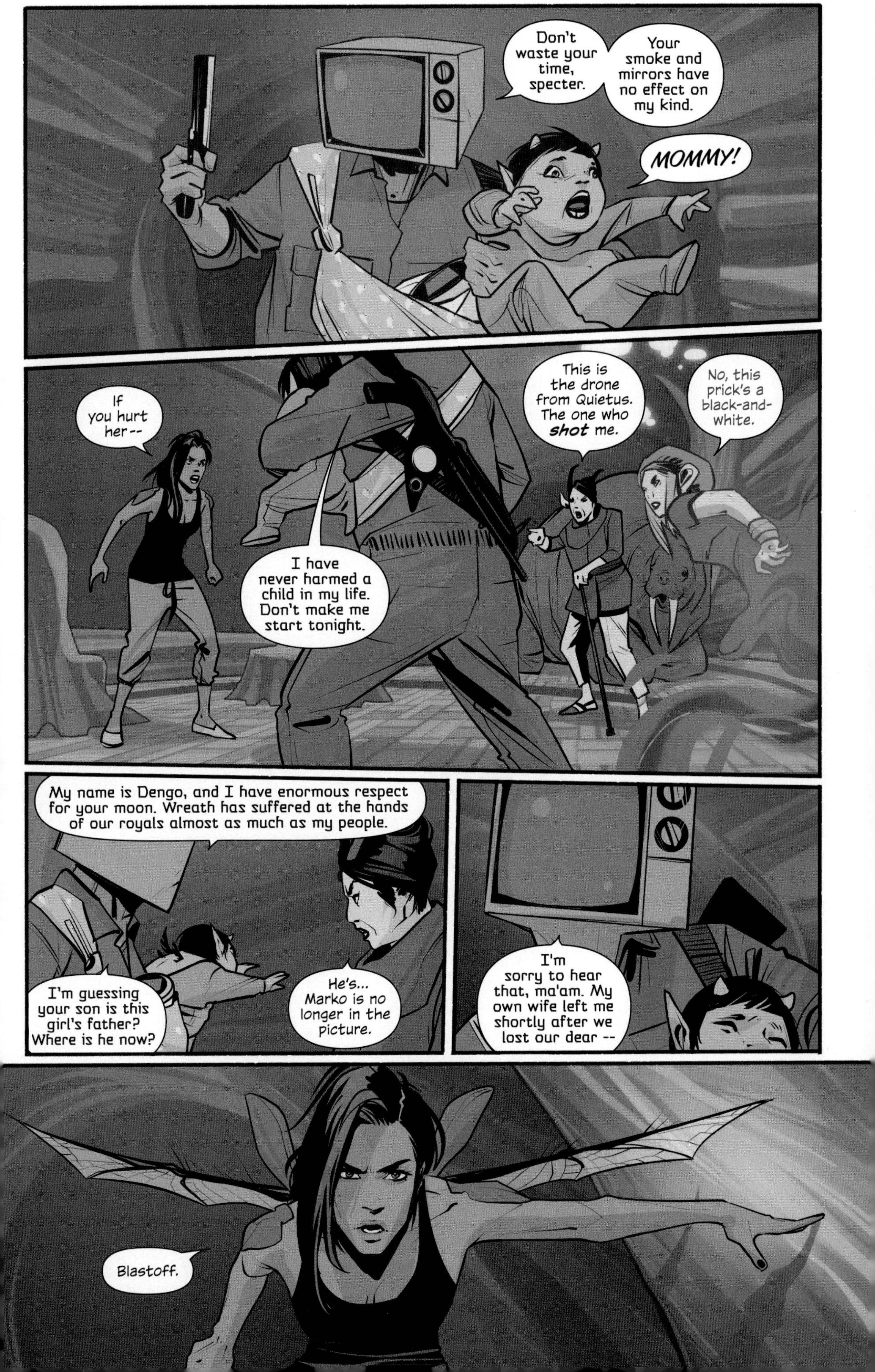
Don't waste your time, specter.
Your smoke and mirrors have no effect on my kind.
MOMMY!
If you hurt her --
This is the drone from Quietus. The one who **shot** me.
No, this prick's a black-and-white.
I have never harmed a child in my life. Don't make me start tonight.
My name is Dengo, and I have enormous respect for your moon. Wreath has suffered at the hands of our royals almost as much as my people.
I'm guessing your son is this girl's father? Where is he now?
He's... Marko is no longer in the picture.
I'm sorry to hear that, ma'am. My own wife left me shortly after we lost our dear --
Blastoff.

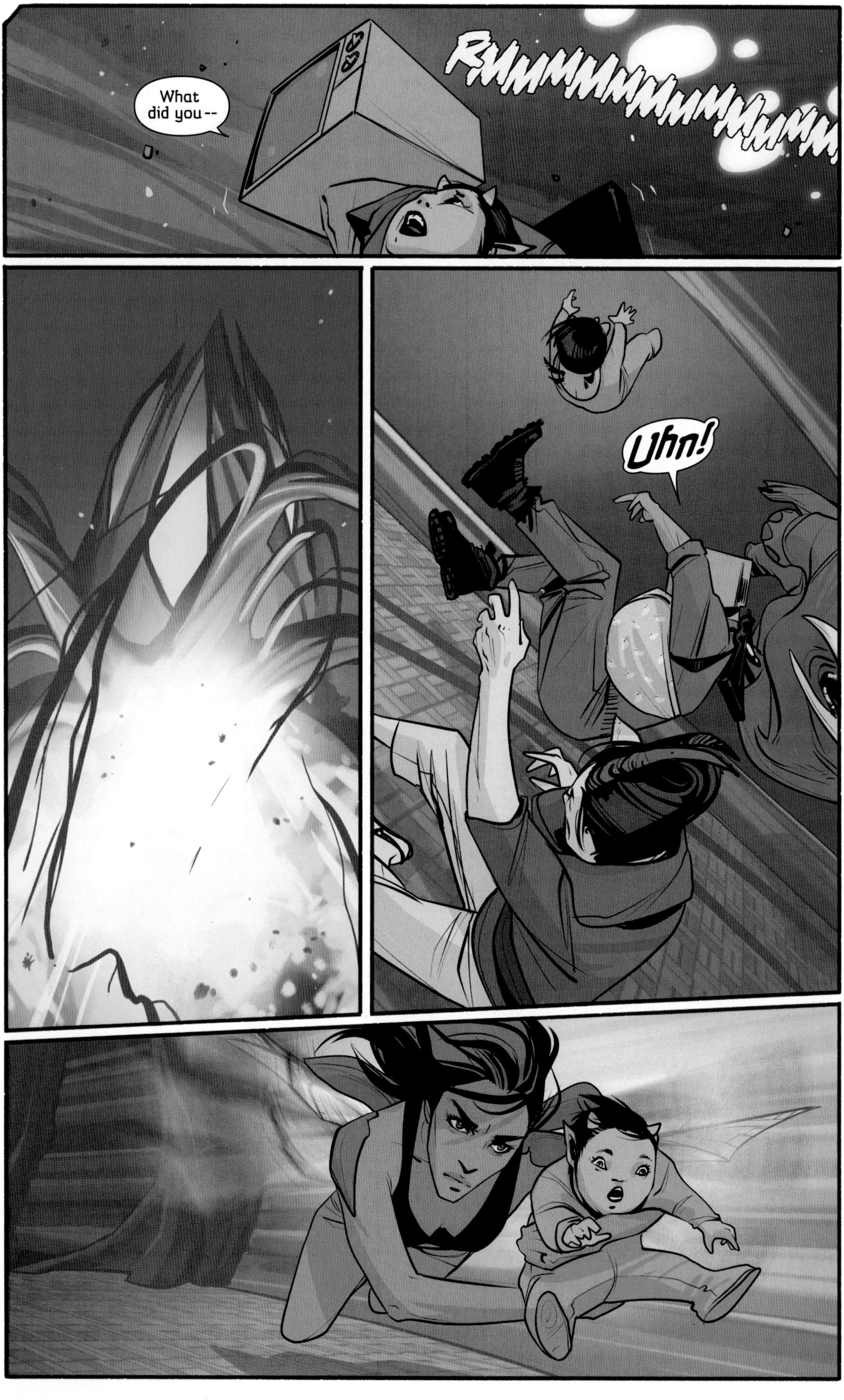
What did you --
RMMMMMMMMMMMMMM
Uhn!

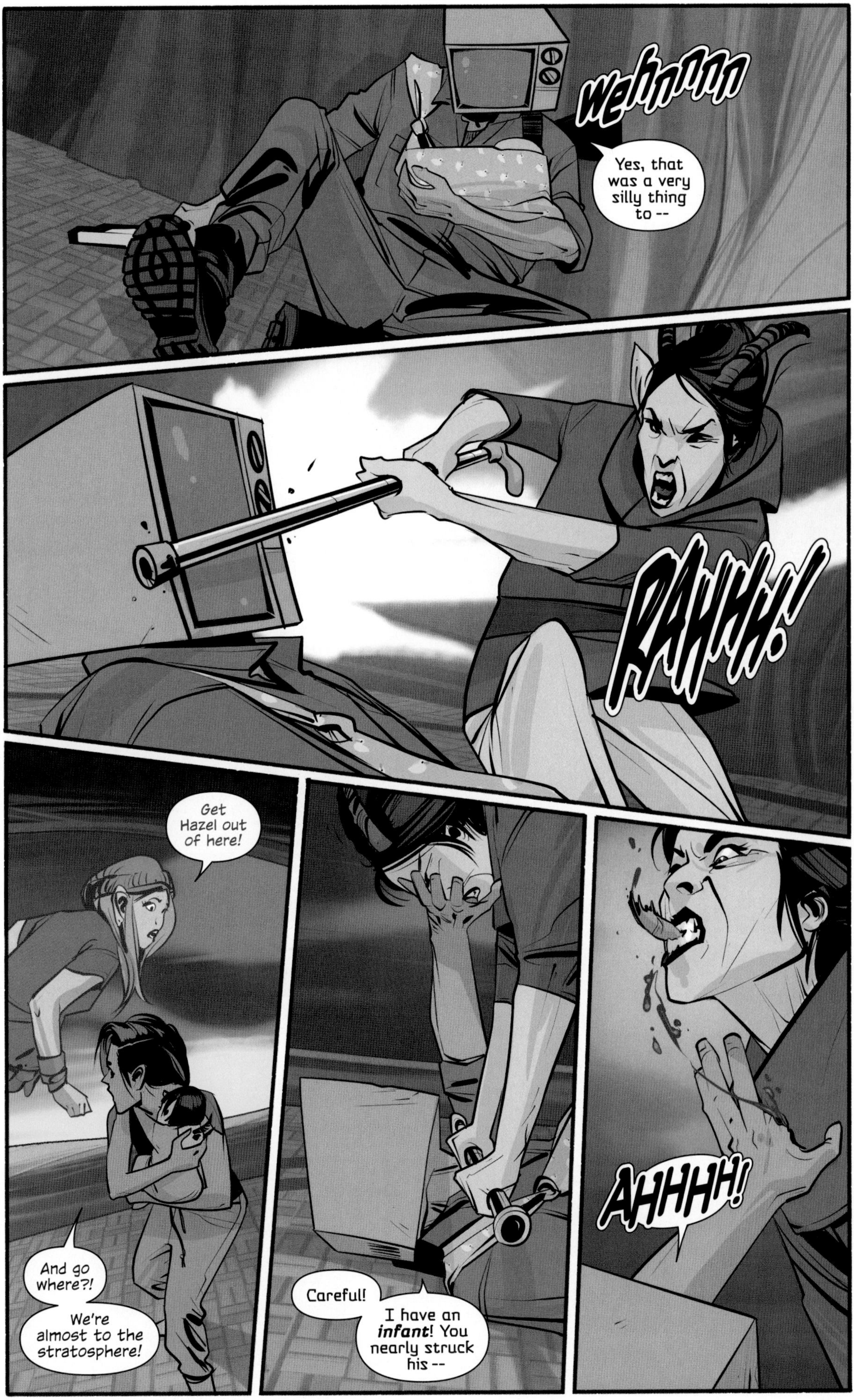
wehnnnn
Yes, that was a very silly thing to --
RAHHH!
Get Hazel out of here!
And go where?!
We're almost to the stratosphere!
Careful!
I have an **infant**! You nearly struck his --
AHHHH!

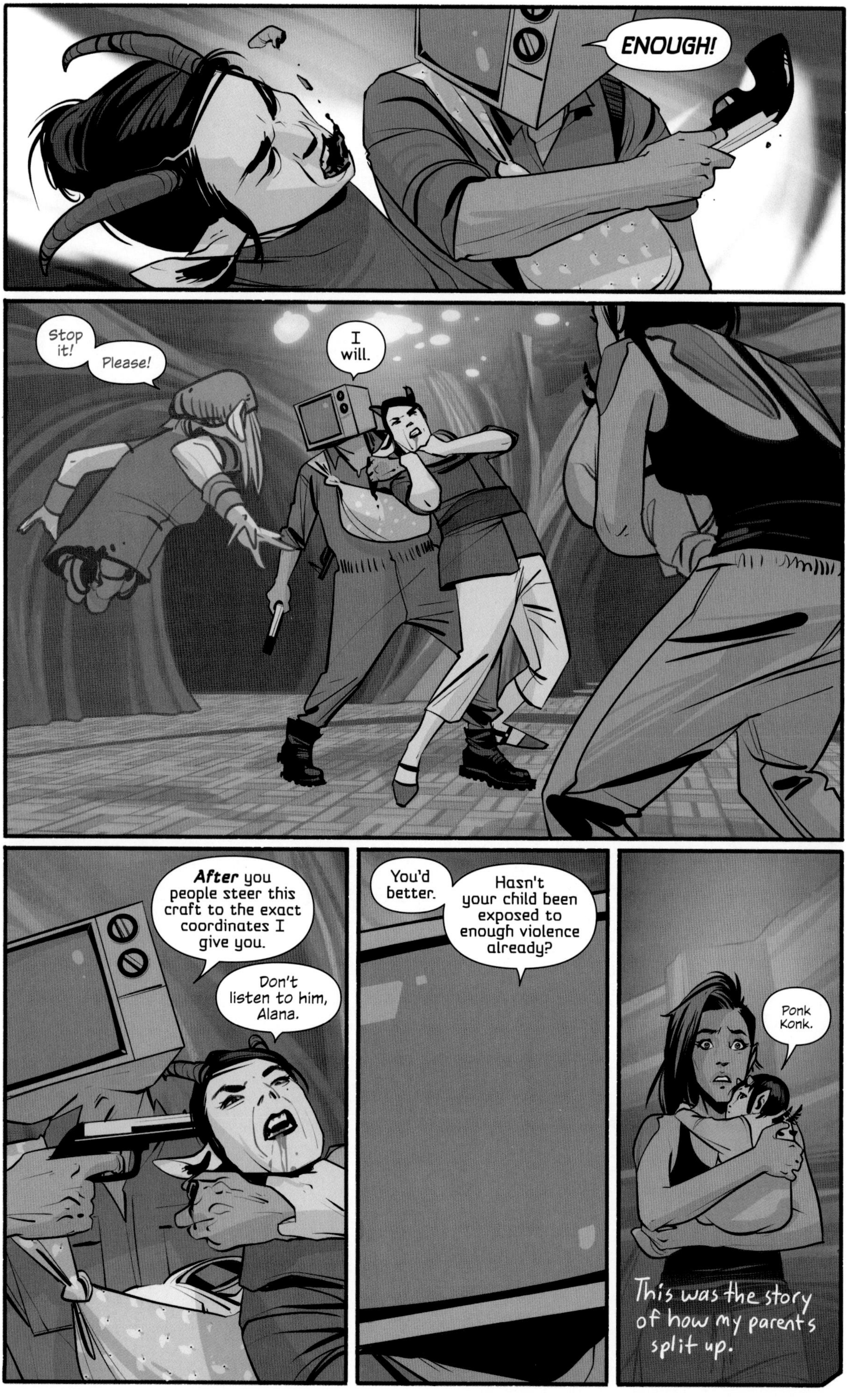
ENOUGH!
Stop it!
Please!
I will.
After you people steer this craft to the exact coordinates I give you.
Don't listen to him, Alana.
You'd better.
Hasn't your child been exposed to enough violence already?
Ponk Konk.
This was the story of how my parents split up.

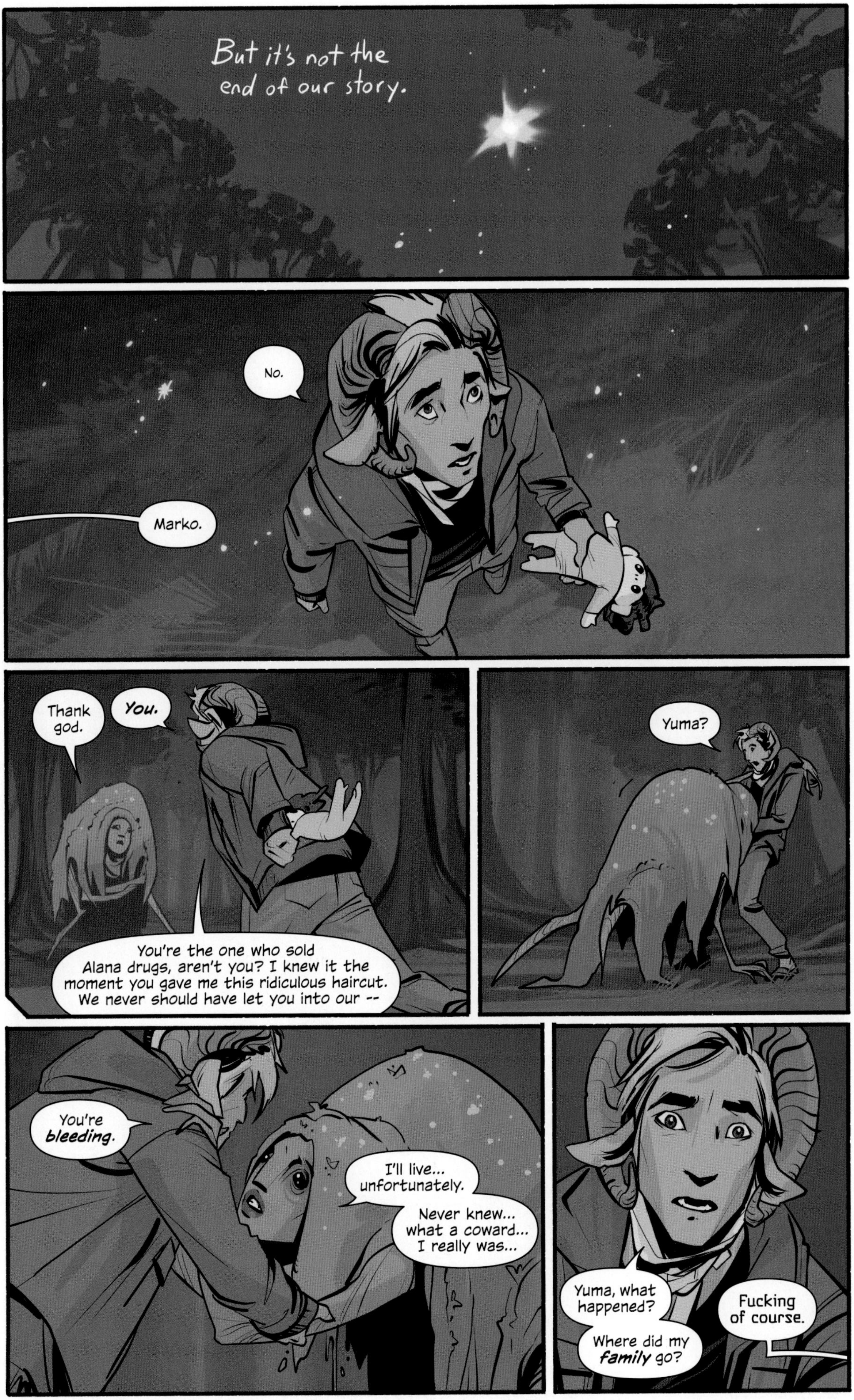

But it's not the end of our story.
No.
Marko.
Thank god.
You.
You're the one who sold Alana drugs, aren't you? I knew it the moment you gave me this ridiculous haircut. We never should have let you into our --
Yuma?
You're bleeding.
I'll live... unfortunately.
Never knew... what a coward... I really was...
Yuma, what happened?
Where did my family go?
Fucking of course.

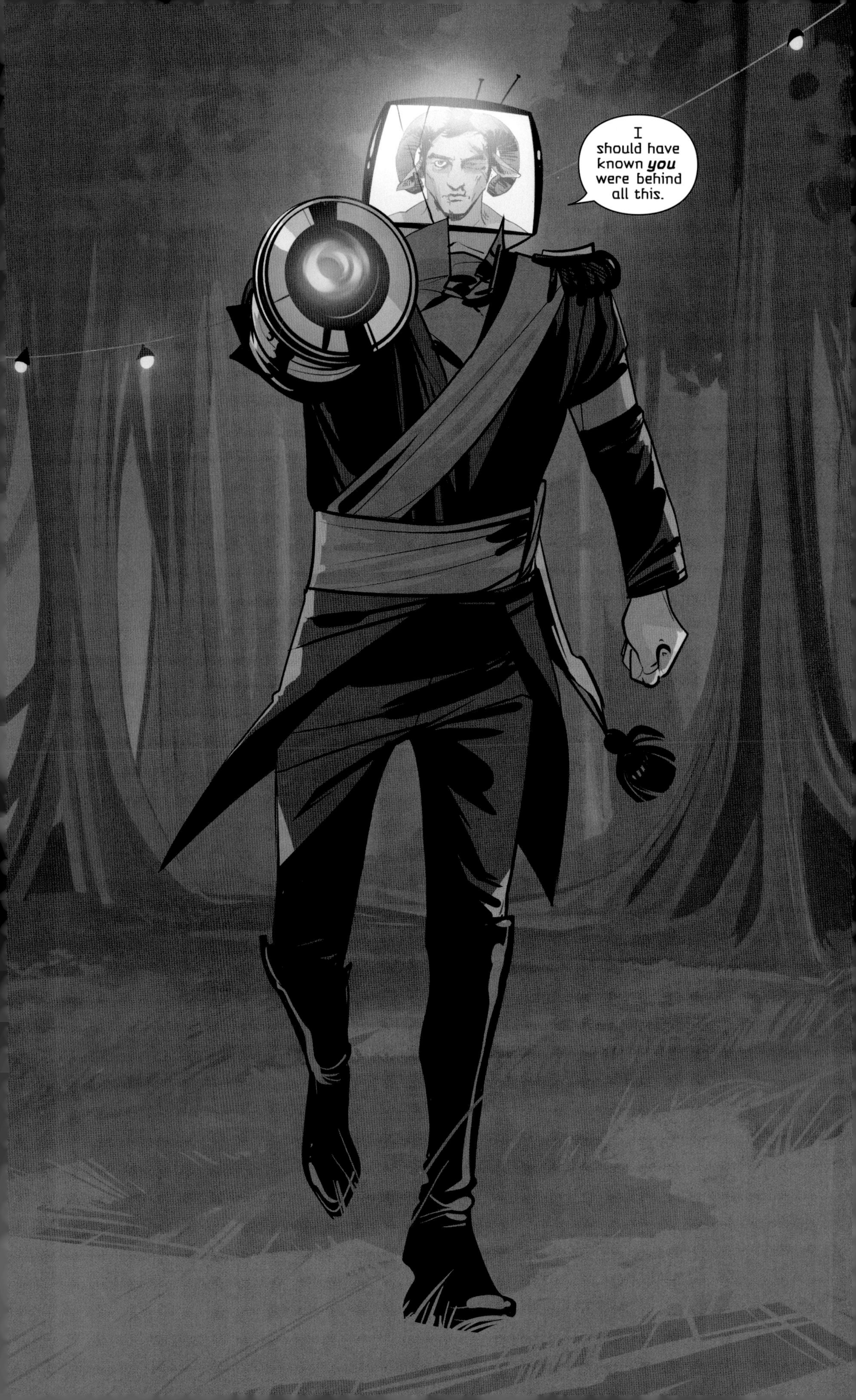
I should have known ***you*** were behind all this.

end chapter twenty-three

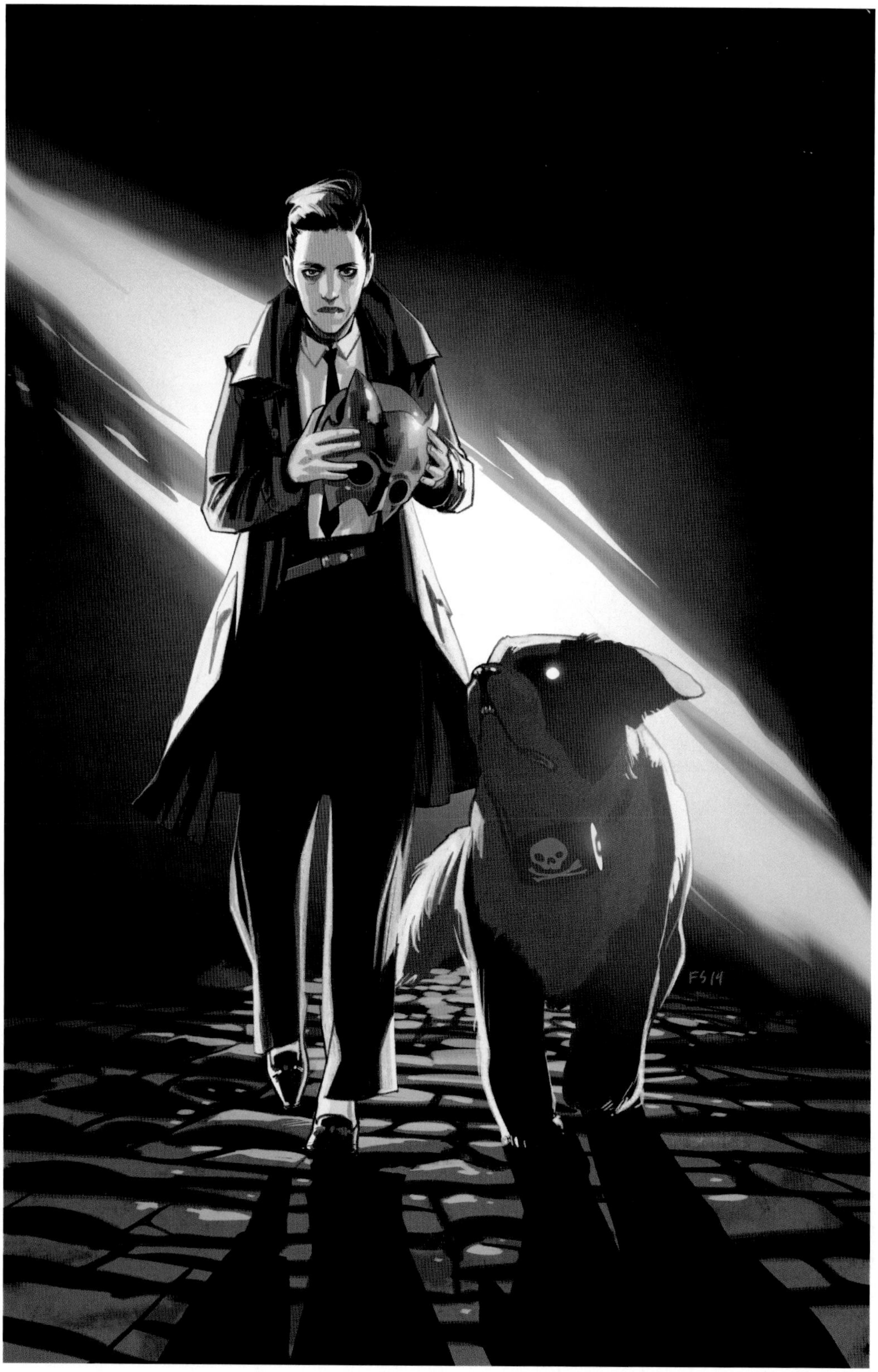

CHAPTER

TWENTY-FOUR

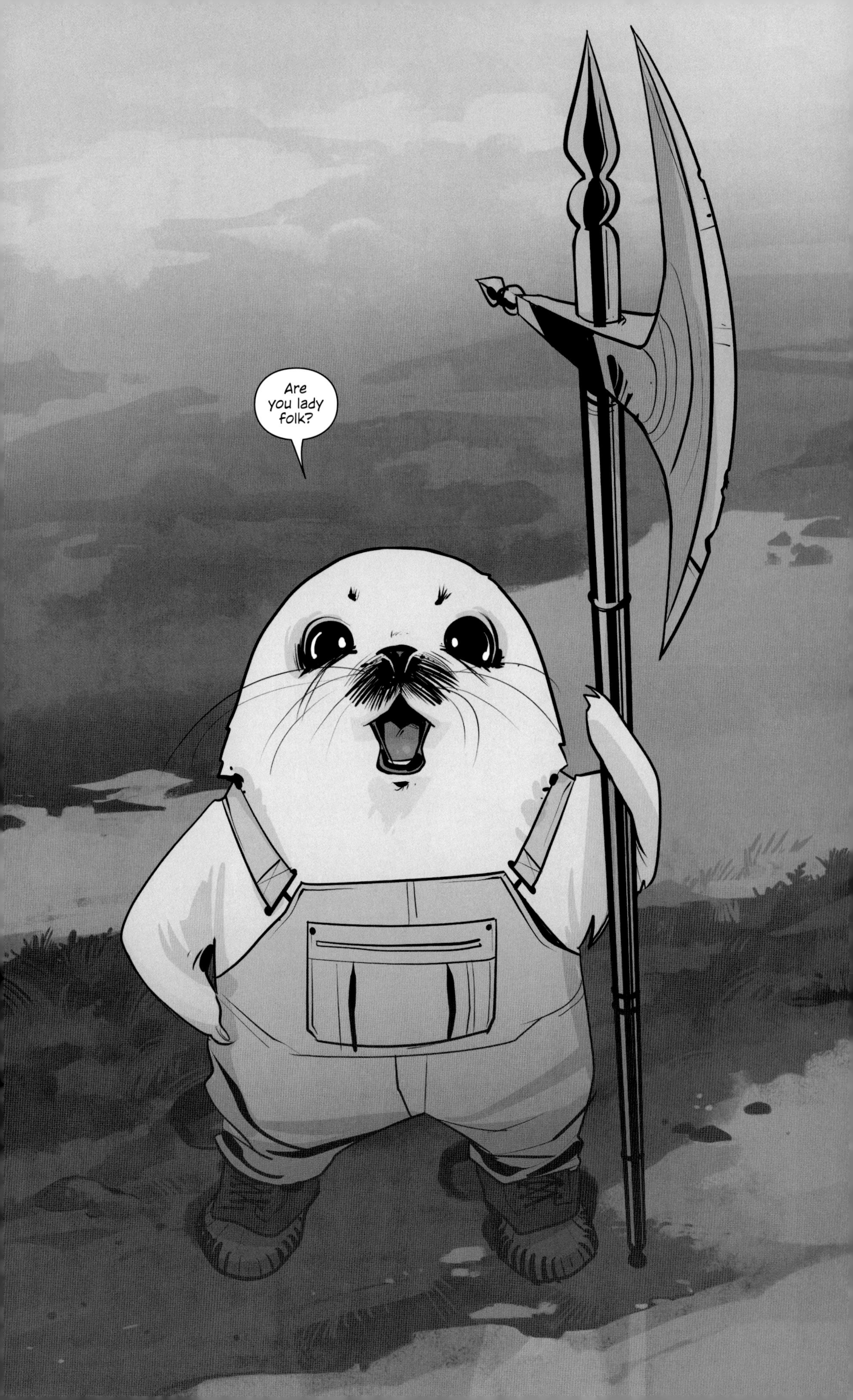
Are you lady folk?

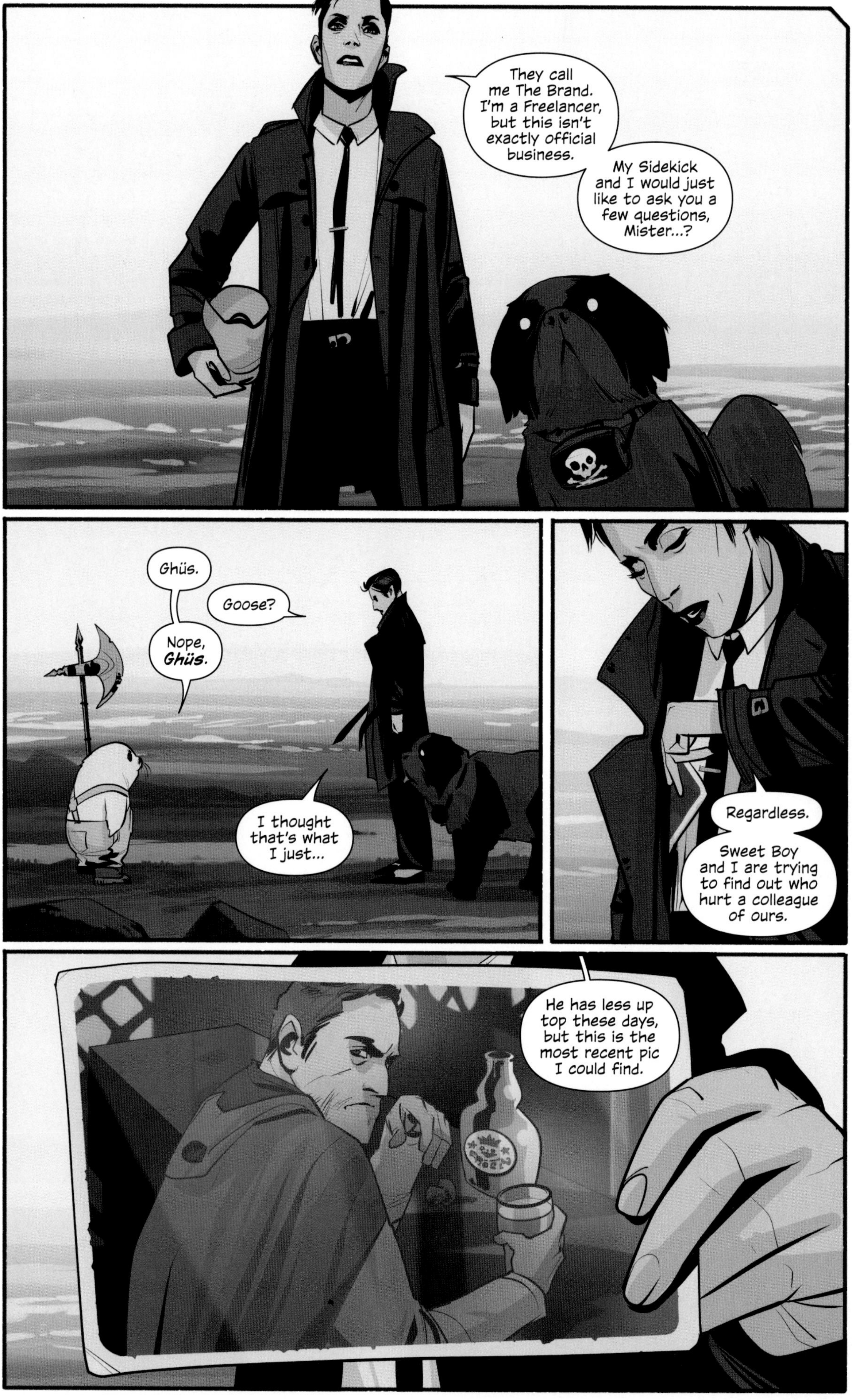
They call me The Brand. I'm a Freelancer, but this isn't exactly official business.
My Sidekick and I would just like to ask you a few questions, Mister...?
Ghüs.
Goose?
Nope, **Ghüs**.
I thought that's what I just...
Regardless.
Sweet Boy and I are trying to find out who hurt a colleague of ours.
He has less up top these days, but this is the most recent pic I could find.

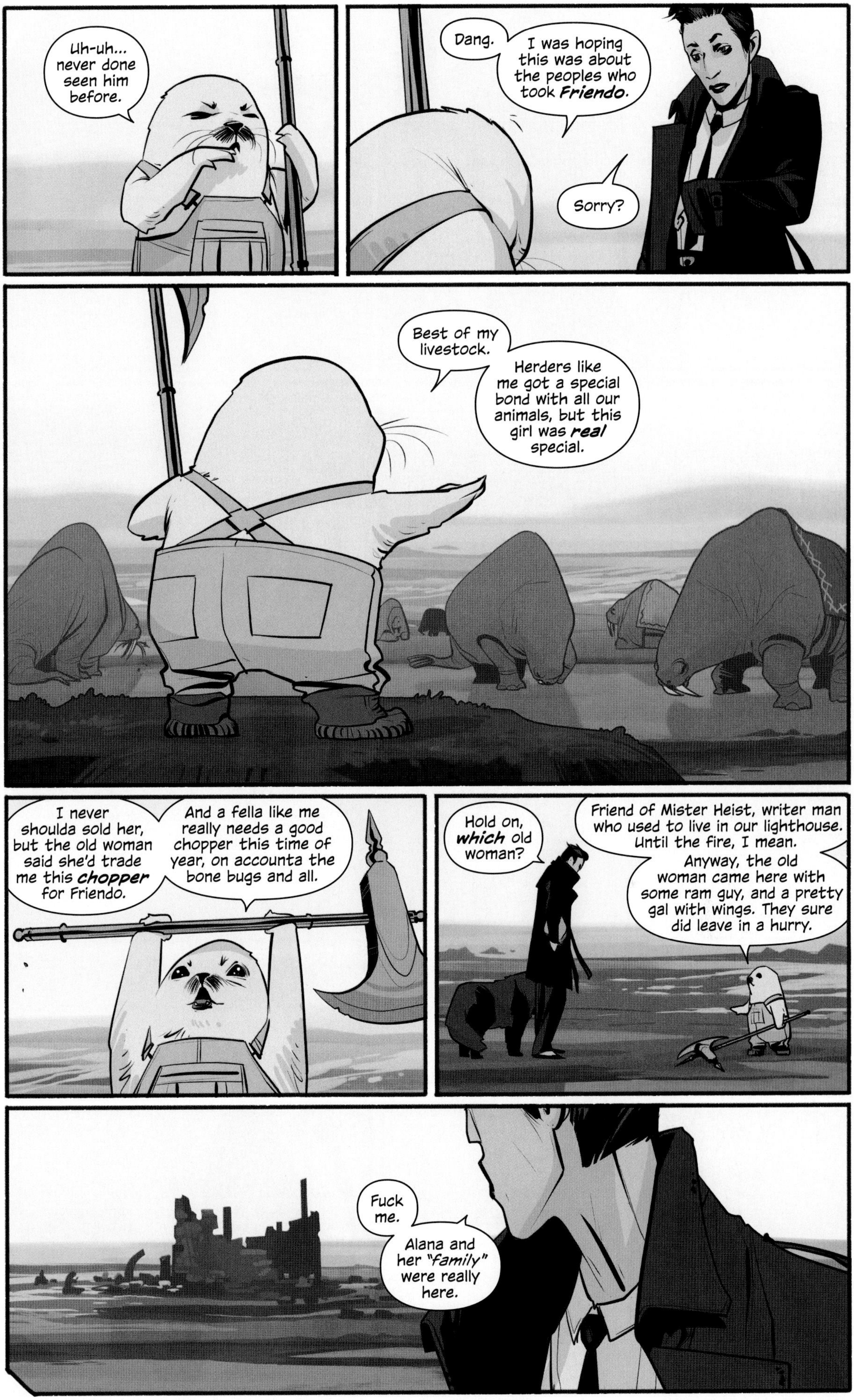

Uh-uh... never done seen him before.
Dang.
I was hoping this was about the peoples who took *Friendo*.
Sorry?
Best of my livestock.
Herders like me got a special bond with all our animals, but this girl was *real* special.
I never shoulda sold her, but the old woman said she'd trade me this *chopper* for Friendo.
And a fella like me really needs a good chopper this time of year, on accounta the bone bugs and all.
Hold on, *which* old woman?
Friend of Mister Heist, writer man who used to live in our lighthouse. Until the fire, I mean.
Anyway, the old woman came here with some ram guy, and a pretty gal with wings. They sure did leave in a hurry.
Fuck me.
Alana and her *"family"* were really here.

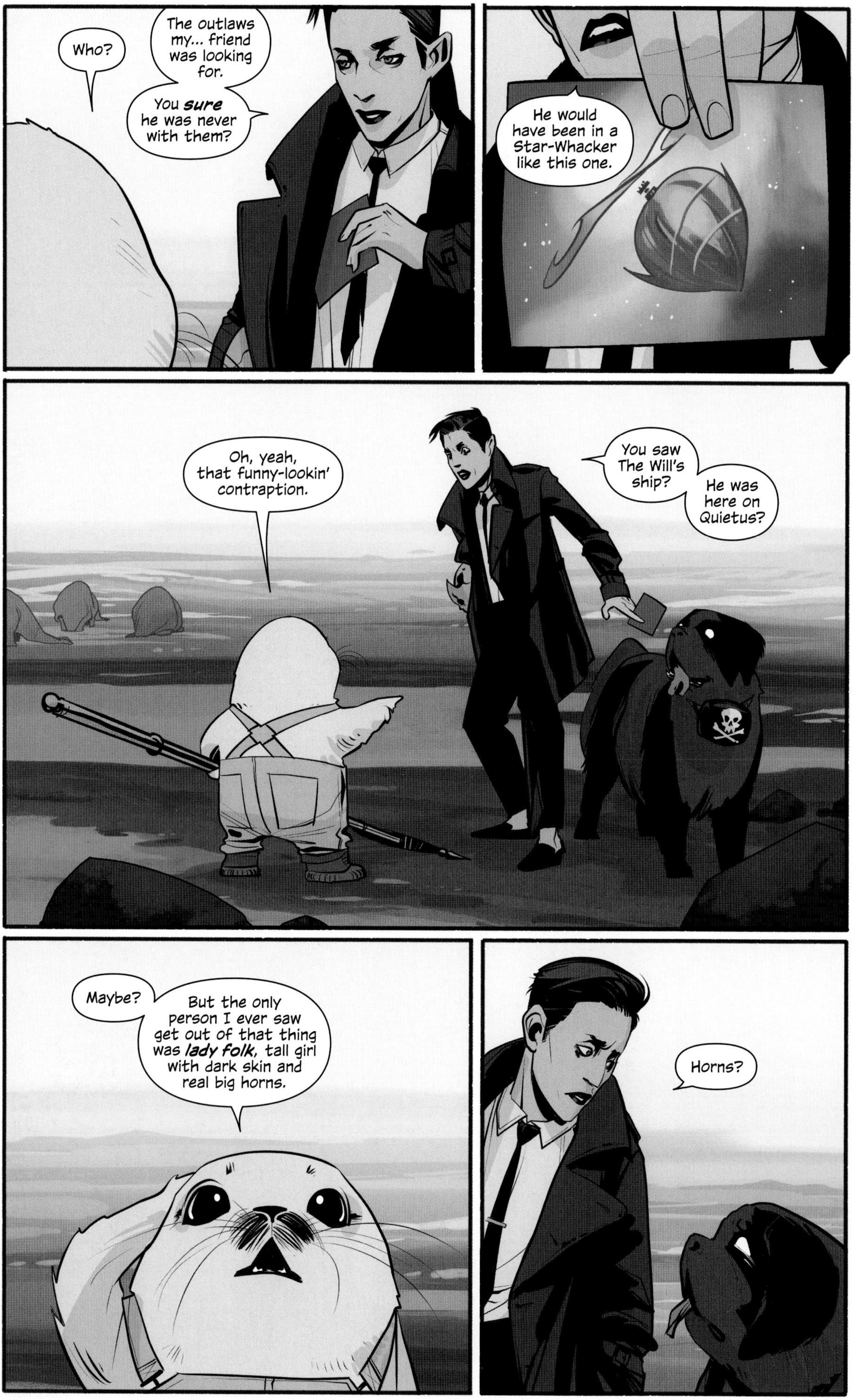
Who?
The outlaws my... friend was looking for.
You sure he was never with them?
He would have been in a Star-Whacker like this one.
Oh, yeah, that funny-lookin' contraption.
You saw The Will's ship?
He was here on Quietus?
Maybe?
But the only person I ever saw get out of that thing was lady folk, tall girl with dark skin and real big horns.
Horns?

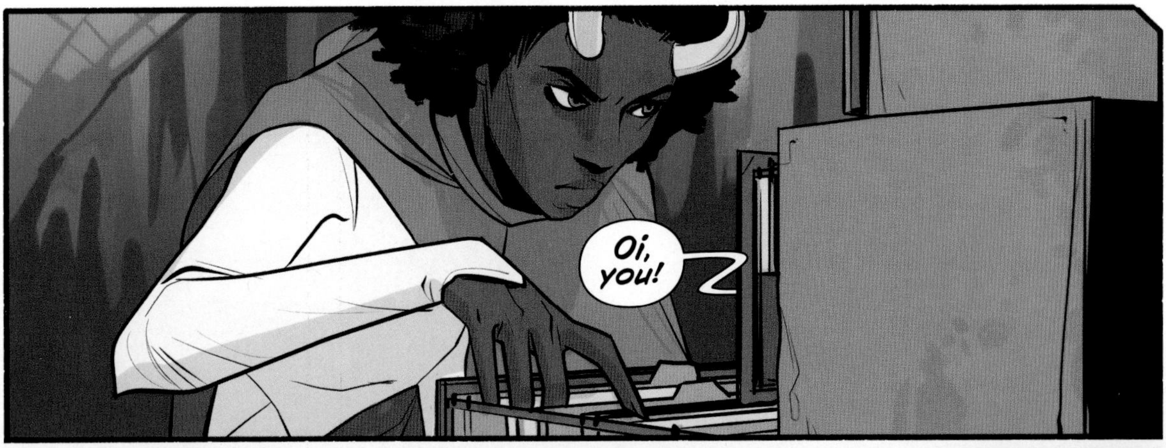
Oi, you!

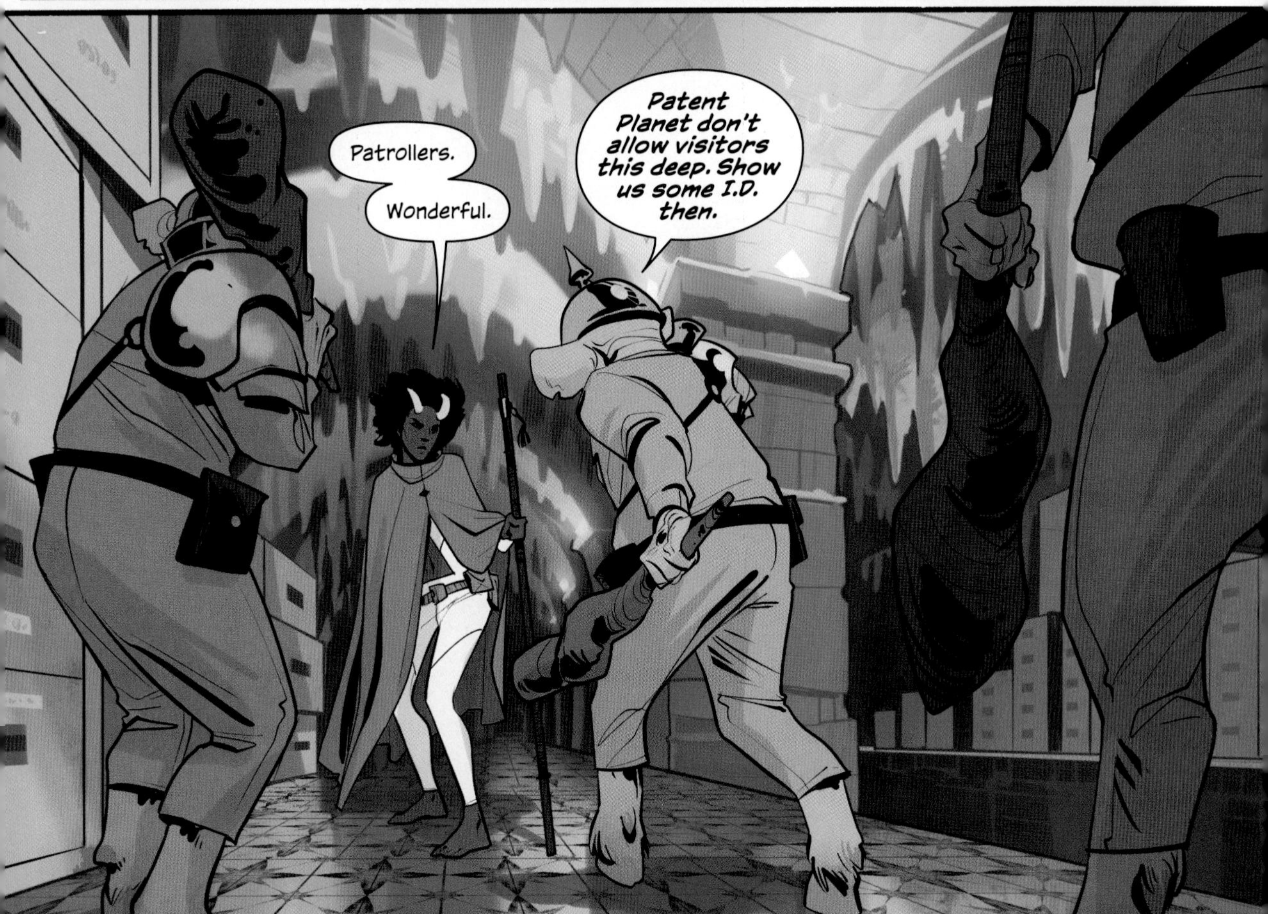
Patrollers.
Wonderful.
Patent Planet don't allow visitors this deep. Show us some I.D. then.

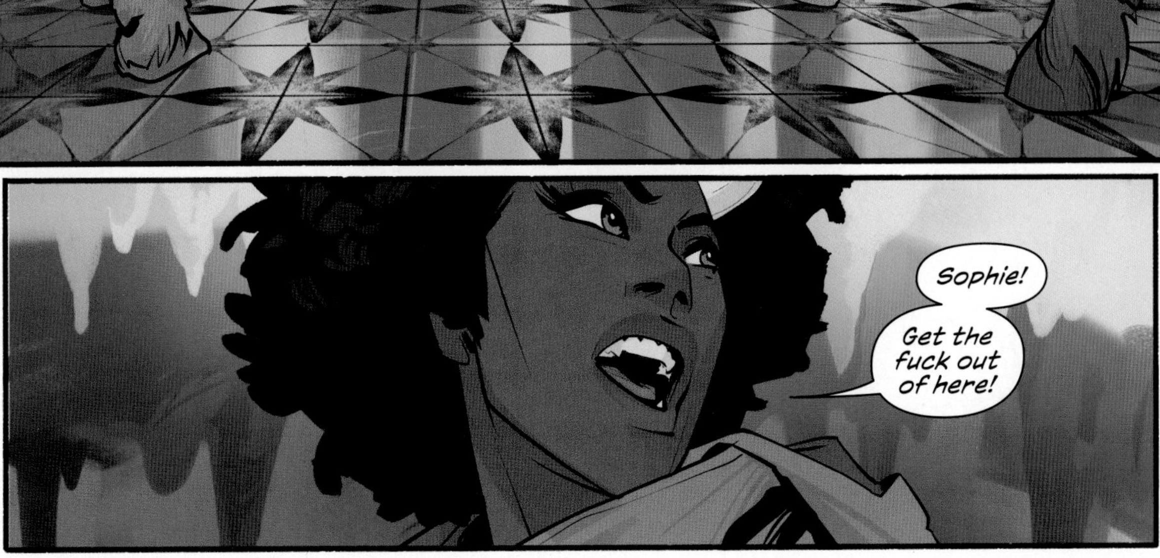
Sophie!
Get the fuck out of here!

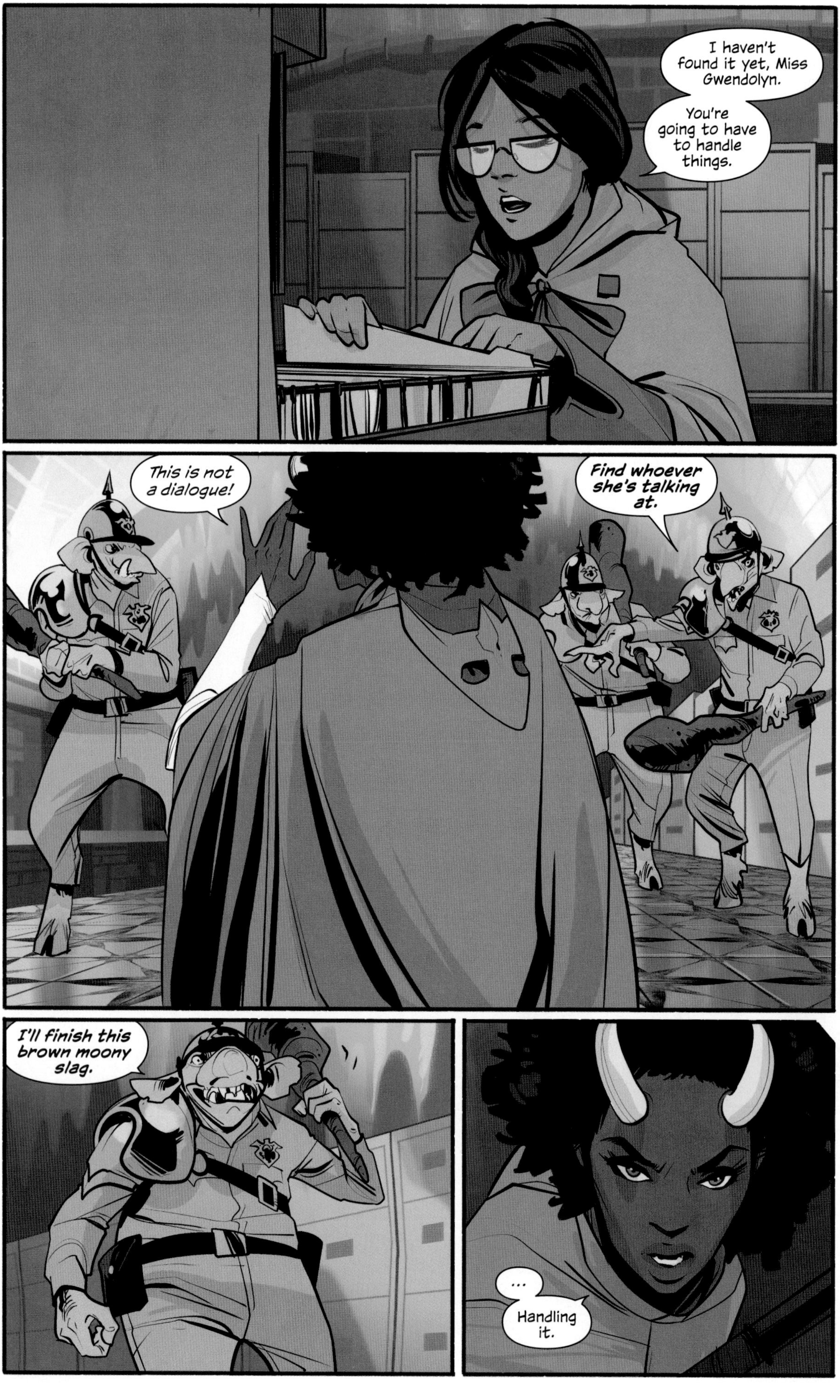

I haven't found it yet, Miss Gwendolyn.
You're going to have to handle things.
This is not a dialogue!
Find whoever she's talking at.
I'll finish this brown moony slag.
...
Handling it.

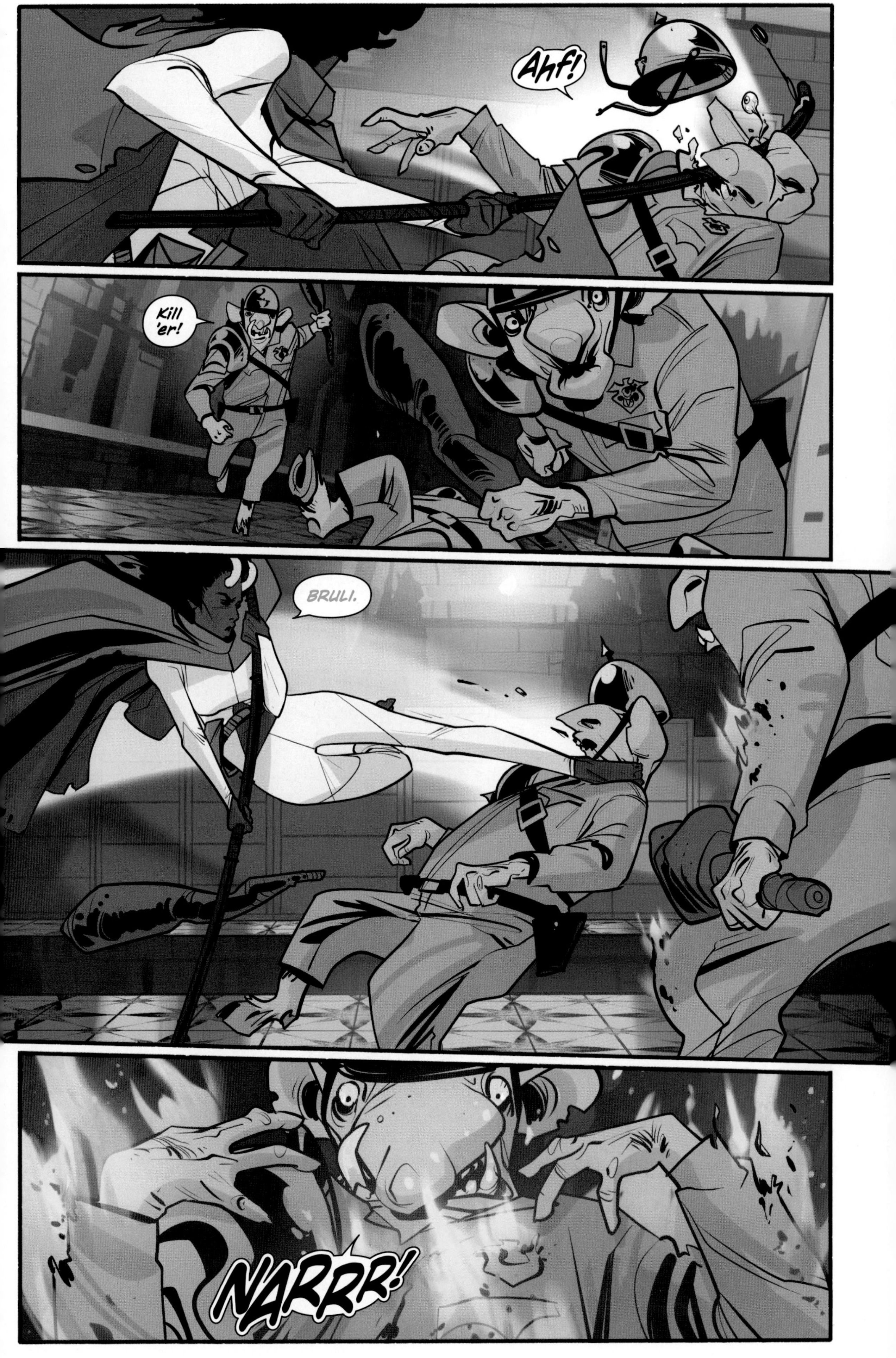

Ahf!
Kill 'er!
BRULI.
NARRR!

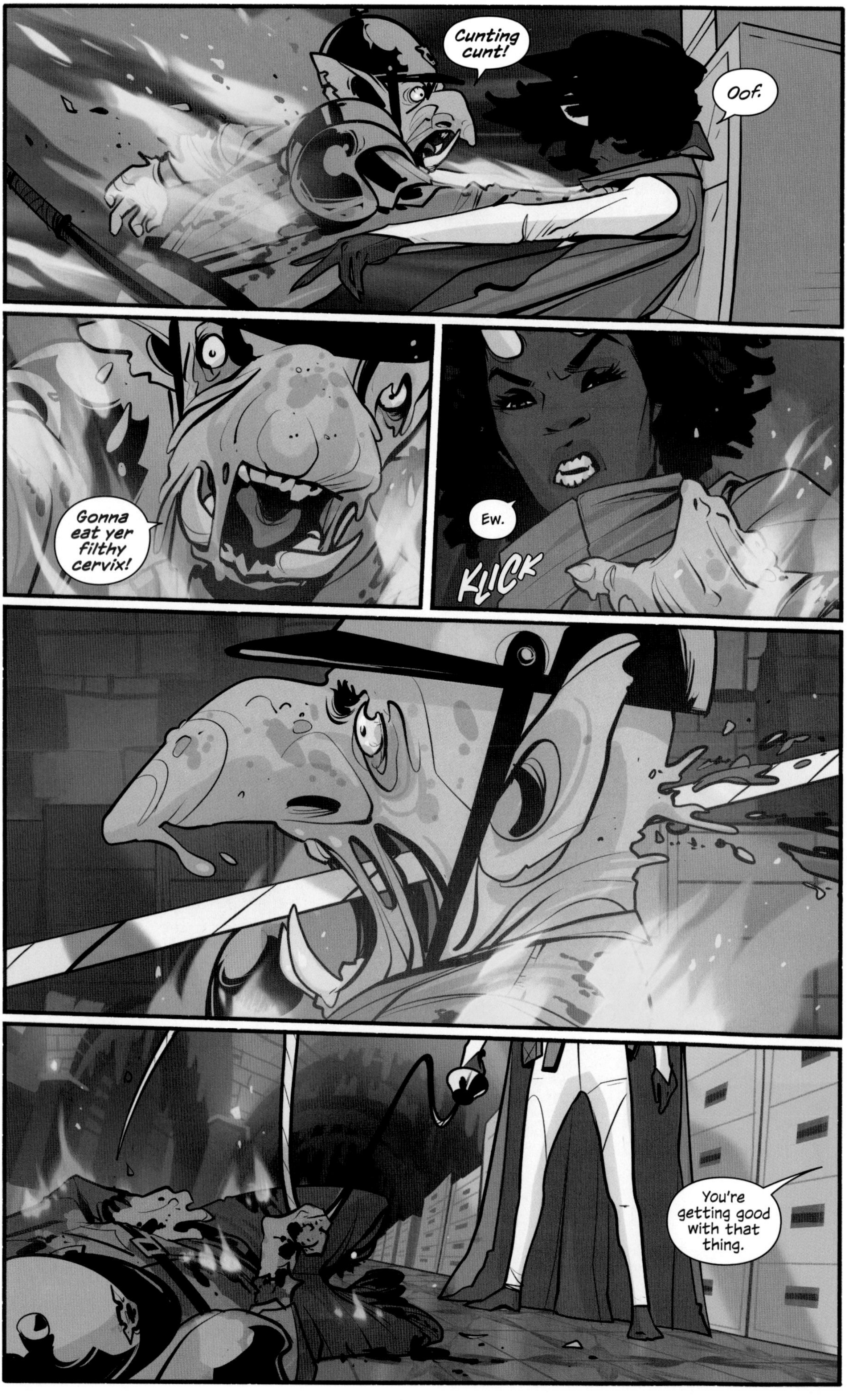
Cunting cunt!
Oof.
Gonna eat yer filthy cervix!
Ew.
KLICK
You're getting good with that thing.

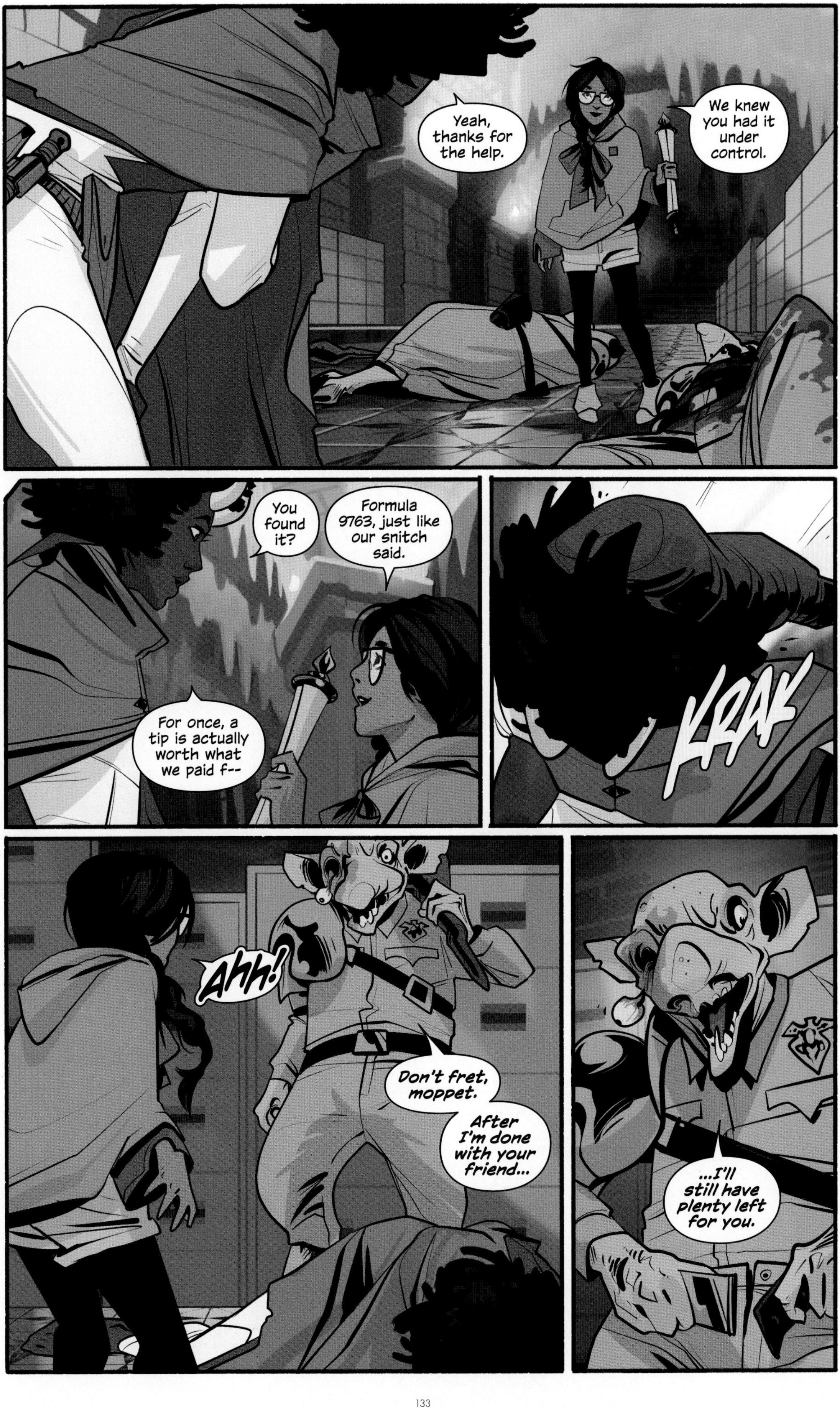
Yeah, thanks for the help.
We knew you had it under control.
You found it?
Formula 9763, just like our snitch said.
For once, a tip is actually worth what we paid f--
KRAK
Ahh!
Don't fret, moppet.
After I'm done with your friend...
...I'll still have plenty left for you.

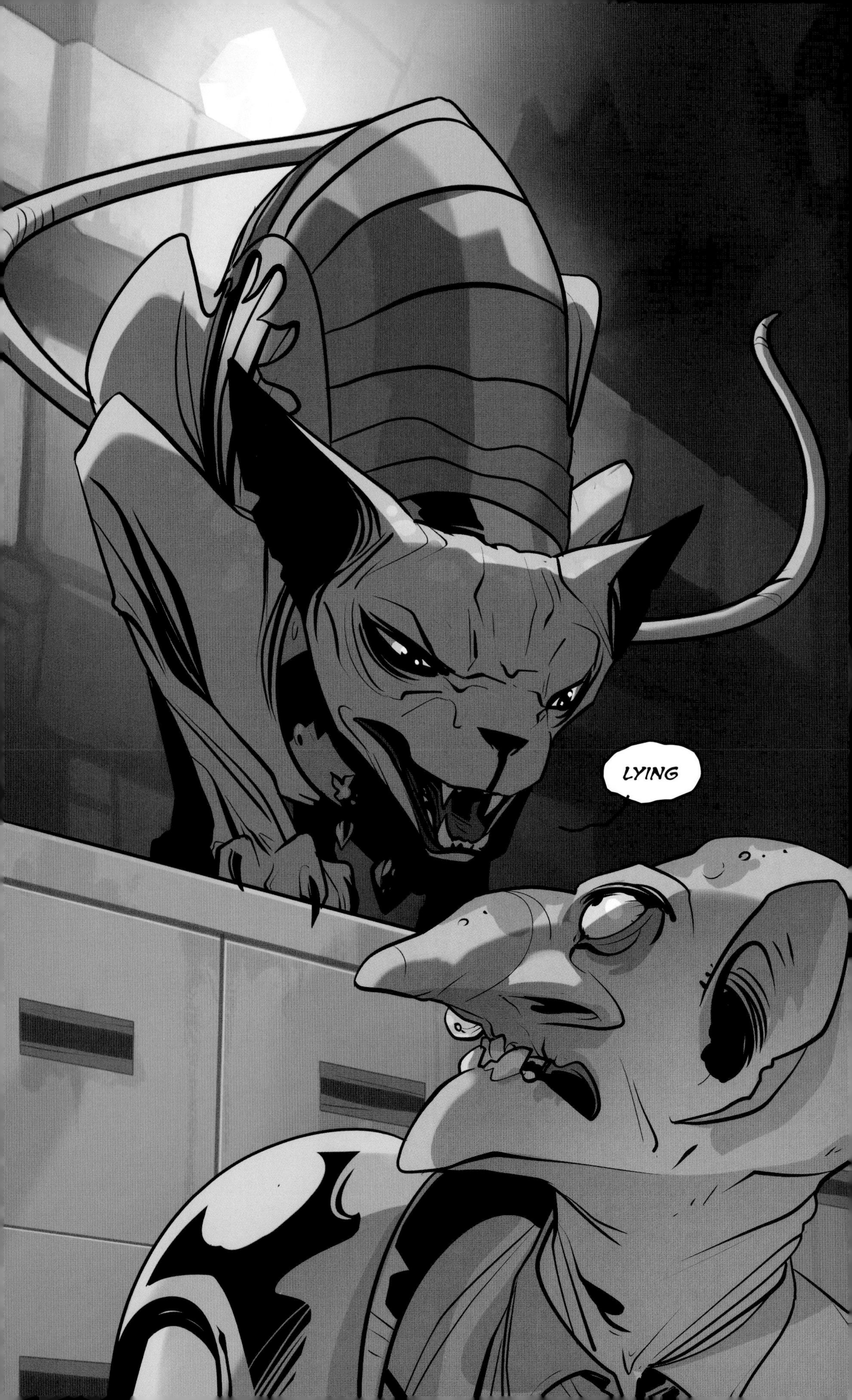
LYING

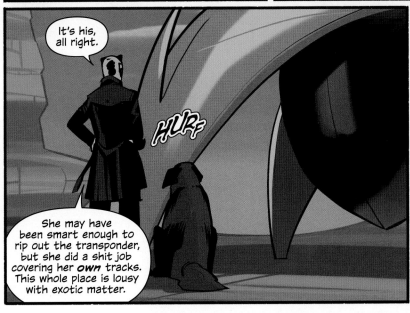

It's his, all right.

HURF

She may have been smart enough to rip out the transponder, but she did a shit job covering her *own* tracks. This whole place is lousy with exotic matter.

Billy, Billy, Billy... always getting mixed up with reckless broads.

It's unseemly!

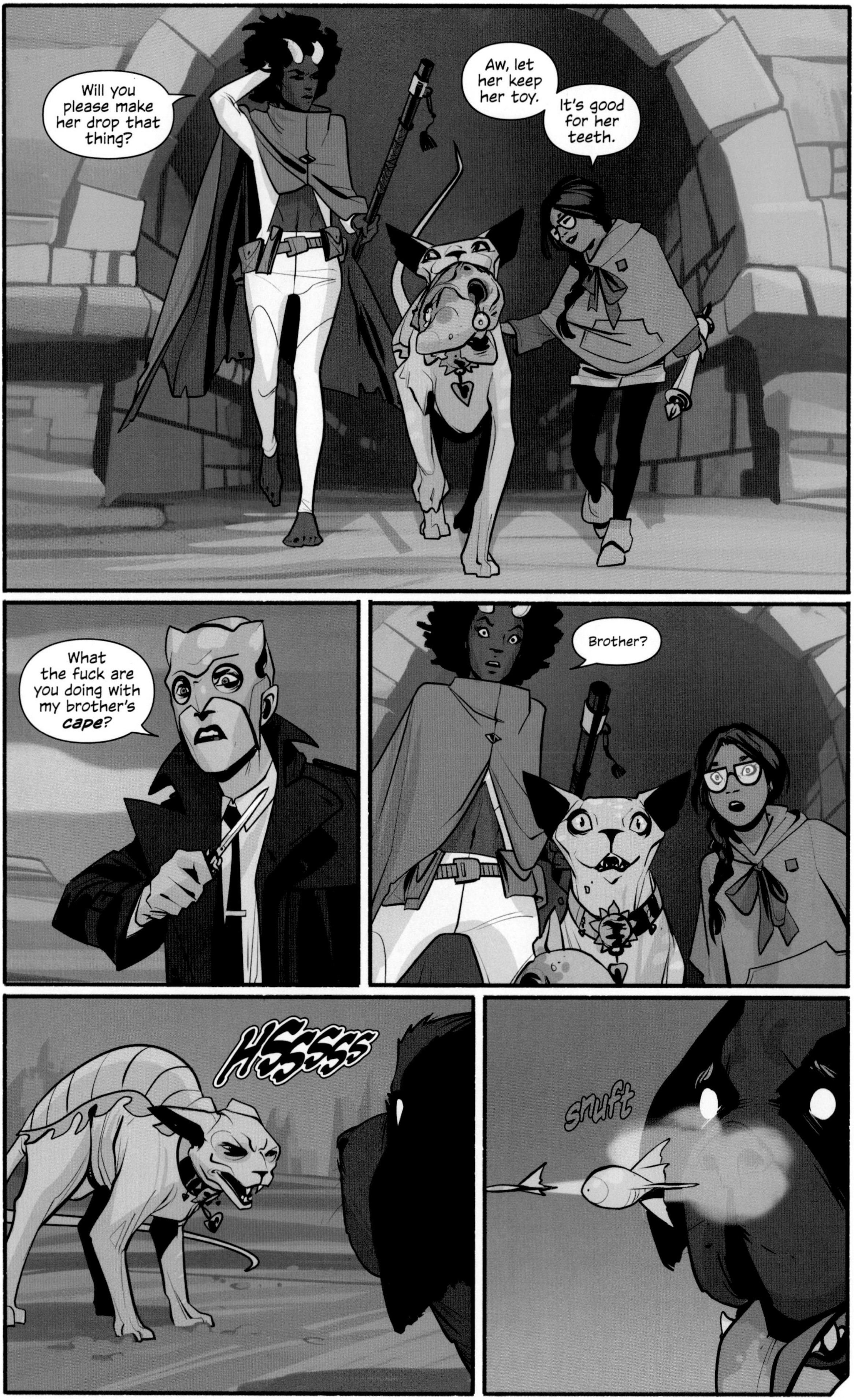
Will you please make her drop that thing?
Aw, let her keep her toy.
It's good for her teeth.
What the fuck are you doing with my brother's *cape*?
Brother?
HSSSSS
snuft

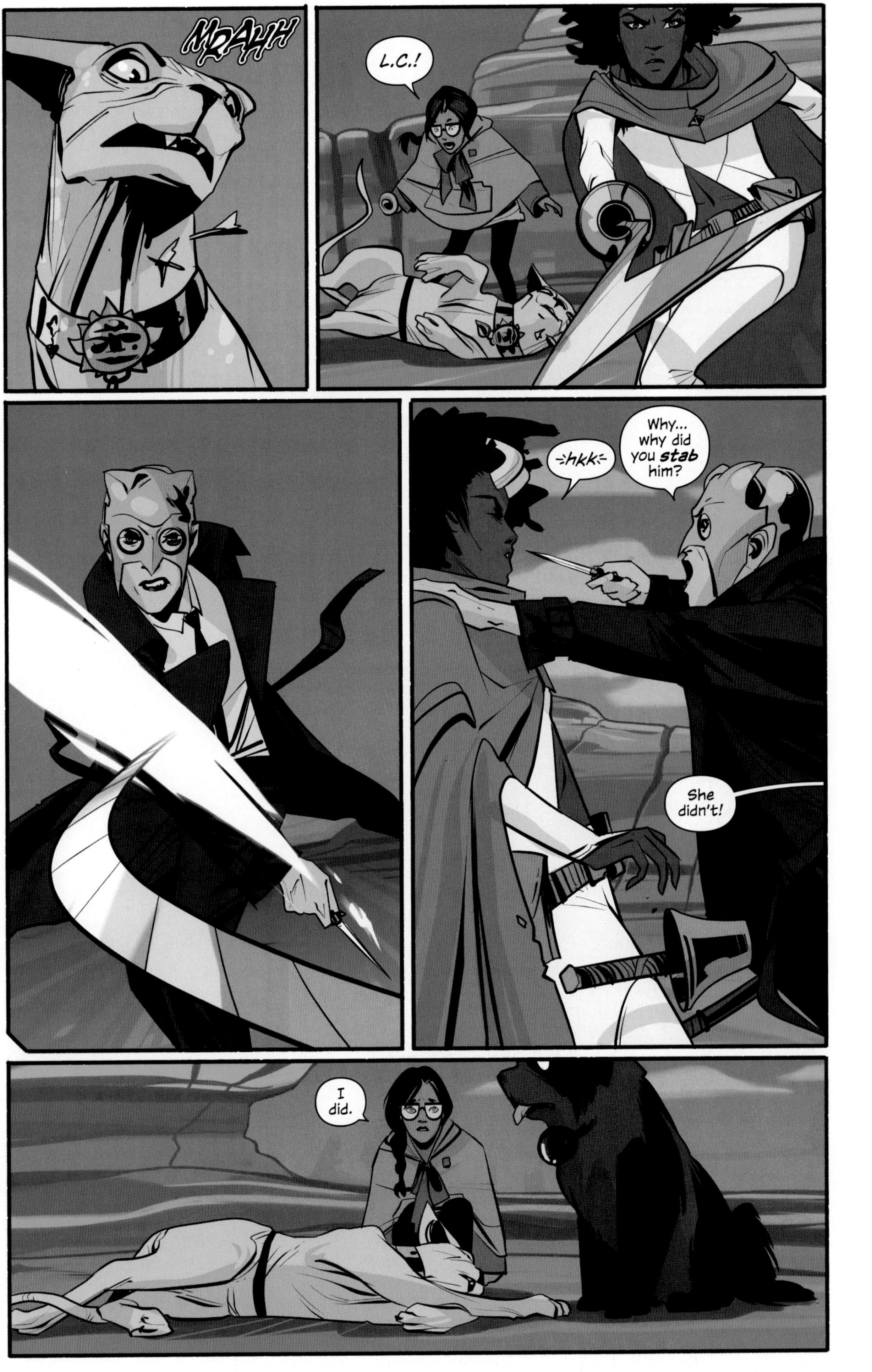
MRAHH
L.C.!
-hkk-
Why... why did you **stab** him?
She didn't!
I did.

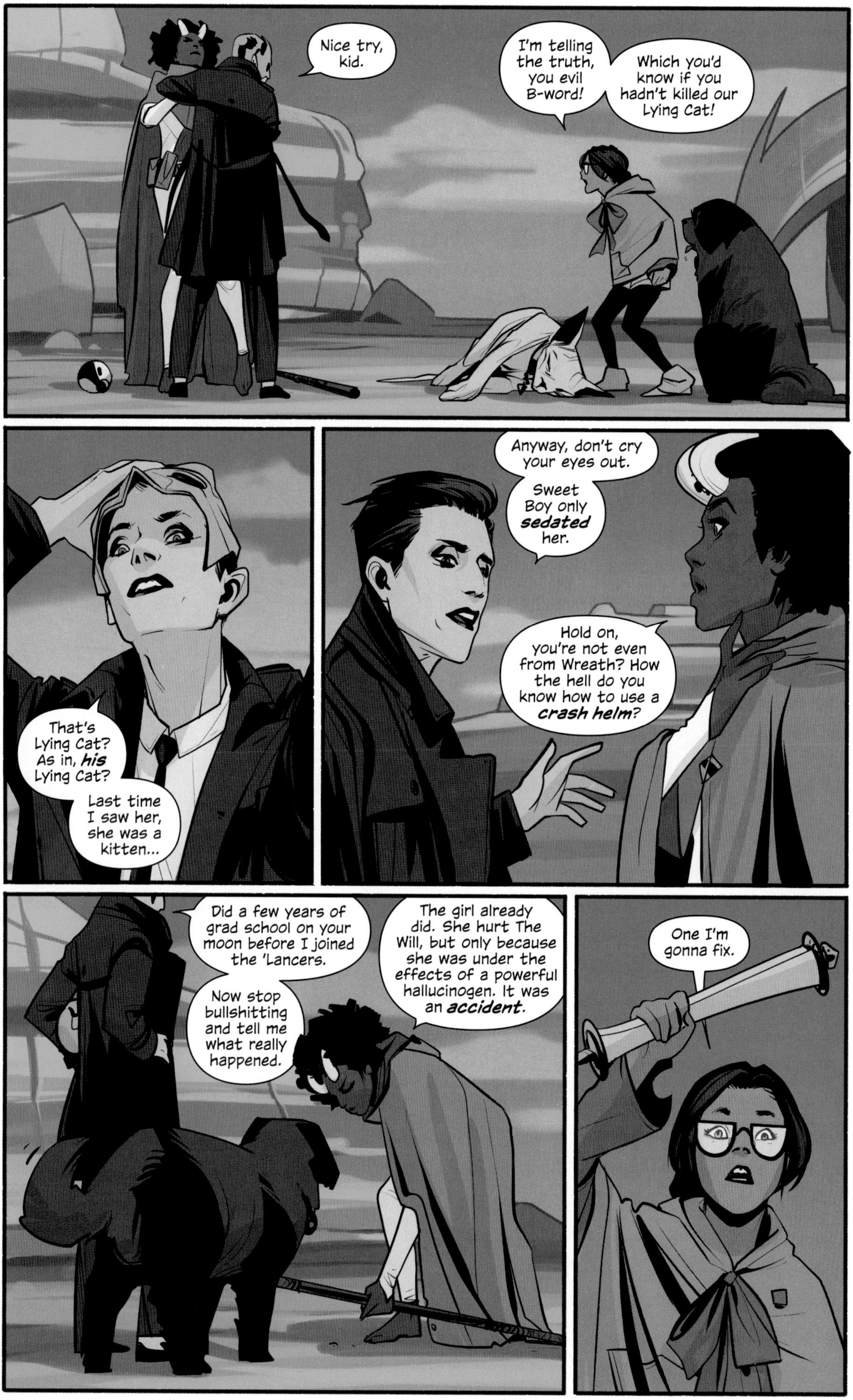
Nice try, kid.
I'm telling the truth, you evil B-word!
Which you'd know if you hadn't killed our Lying Cat!
That's Lying Cat? As in, ***his*** Lying Cat?
Last time I saw her, she was a kitten...
Anyway, don't cry your eyes out.
Sweet Boy only ***sedated*** her.
Hold on, you're not even from Wreath? How the hell do you know how to use a ***crash helm***?
Did a few years of grad school on your moon before I joined the 'Lancers.
Now stop bullshitting and tell me what really happened.
The girl already did. She hurt The Will, but only because she was under the effects of a powerful hallucinogen. It was an ***accident***.
One I'm gonna fix.

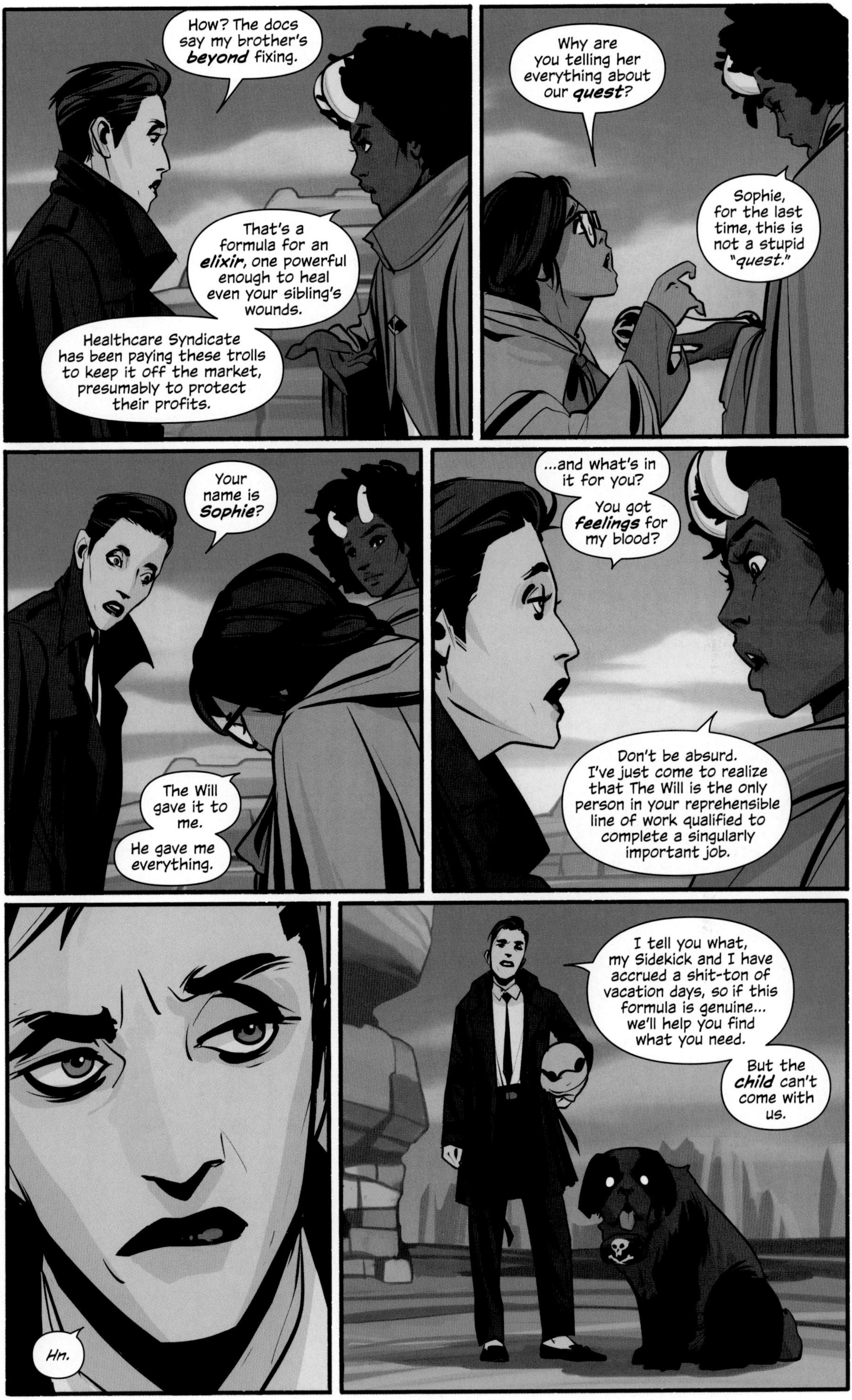
How? The docs say my brother's *beyond* fixing.
That's a formula for an *elixir*, one powerful enough to heal even your sibling's wounds.
Healthcare Syndicate has been paying these trolls to keep it off the market, presumably to protect their profits.
Why are you telling her everything about our *quest*?
Sophie, for the last time, this is not a stupid *"quest."*
Your name is *Sophie*?
The Will gave it to me.
He gave me everything.
...and what's in it for you?
You got *feelings* for my blood?
Don't be absurd. I've just come to realize that The Will is the only person in your reprehensible line of work qualified to complete a singularly important job.
Hn.
I tell you what, my Sidekick and I have accrued a shit-ton of vacation days, so if this formula is genuine... we'll help you find what you need.
But the *child* can't come with us.

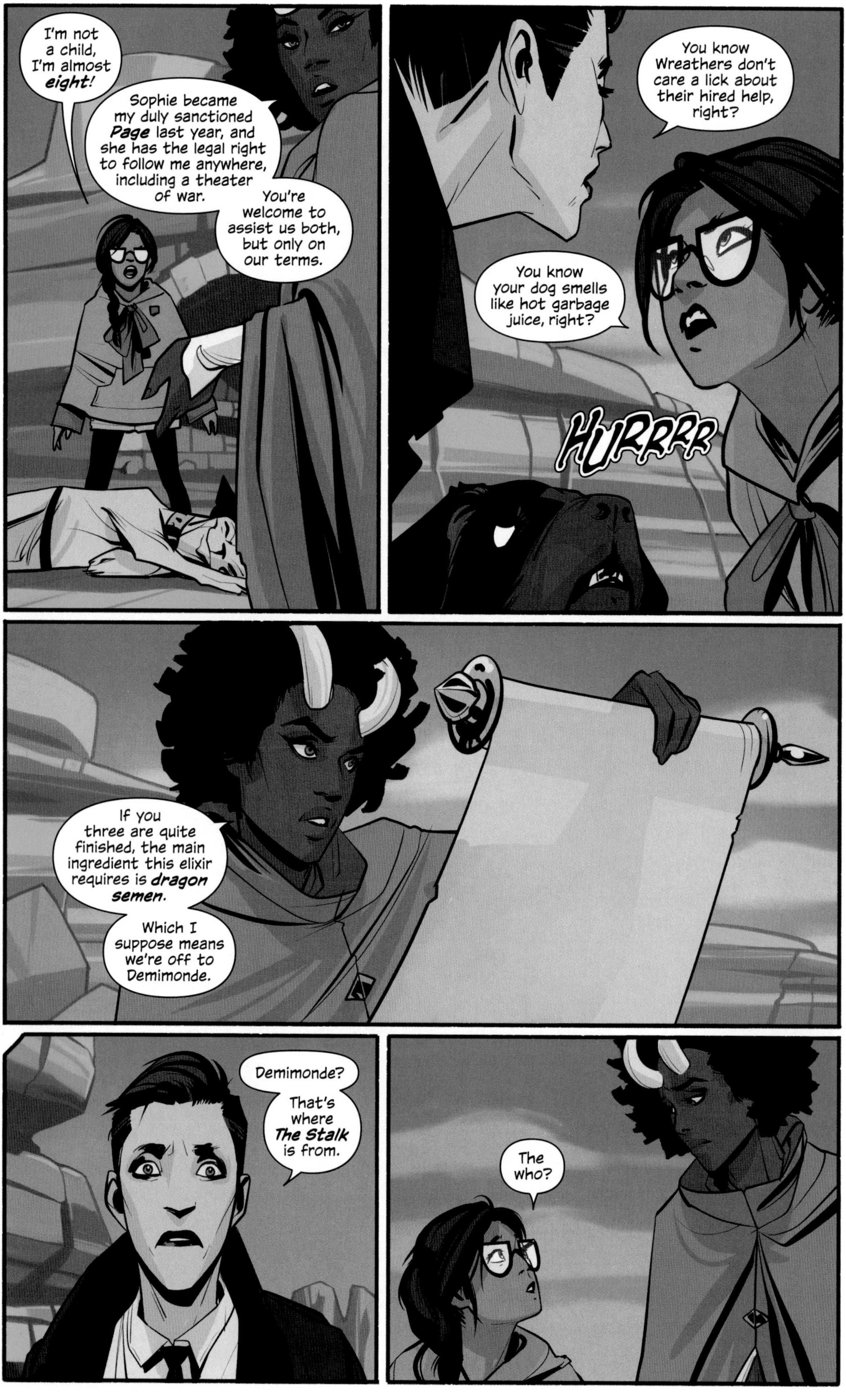
I'm not a child, I'm almost ***eight!***
Sophie became my duly sanctioned ***Page*** last year, and she has the legal right to follow me anywhere, including a theater of war.
You're welcome to assist us both, but only on our terms.
You know Wreathers don't care a lick about their hired help, right?
You know your dog smells like hot garbage juice, right?
HURRRR
If you three are quite finished, the main ingredient this elixir requires is ***dragon semen***.
Which I suppose means we're off to Demimonde.
Demimonde?
That's where ***The Stalk*** is from.
The who?

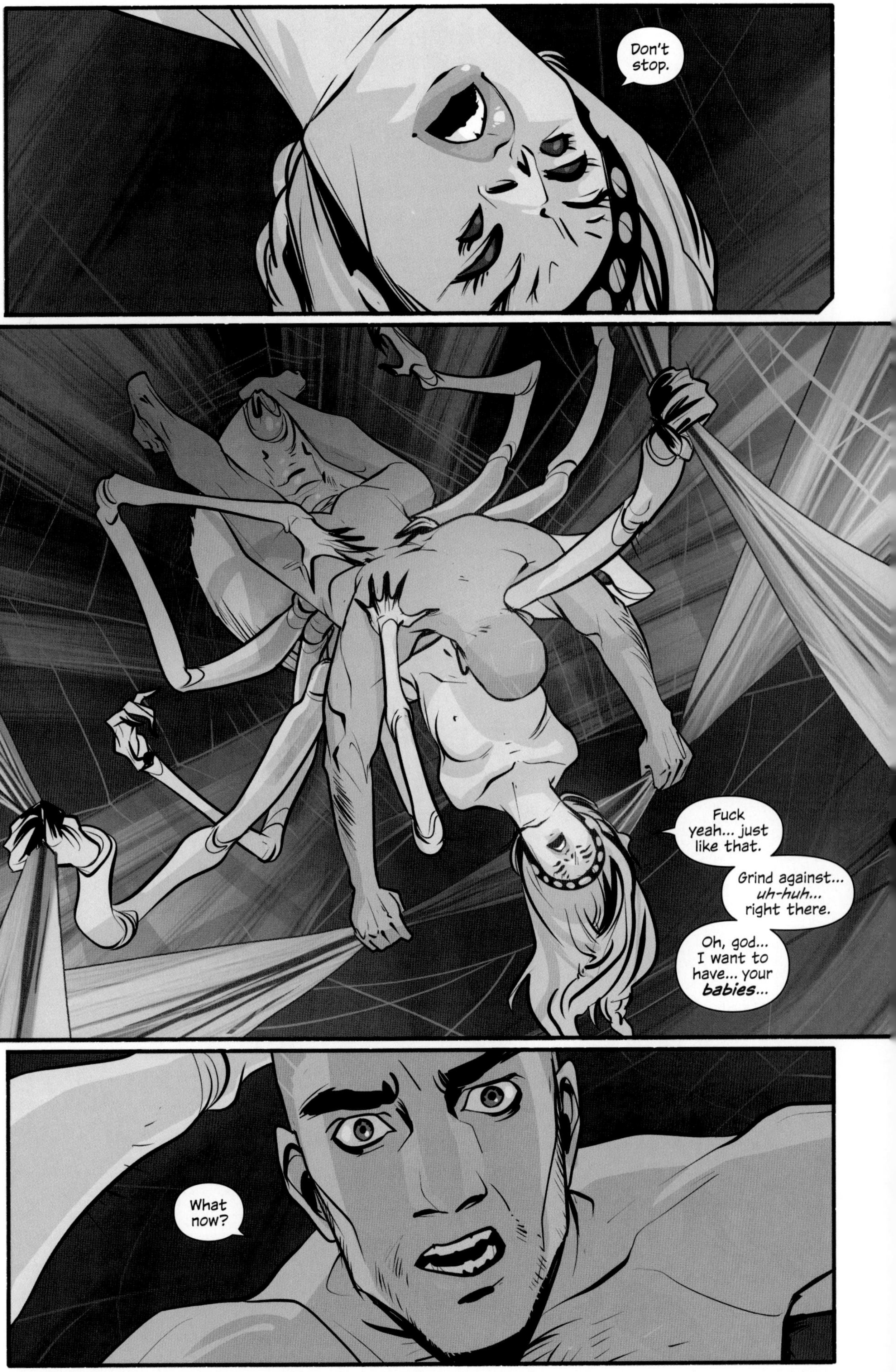
Don't stop.
Fuck yeah... just like that.
Grind against... *uh-huh...* right there.
Oh, god... I want to have... your ***babies***...
What now?

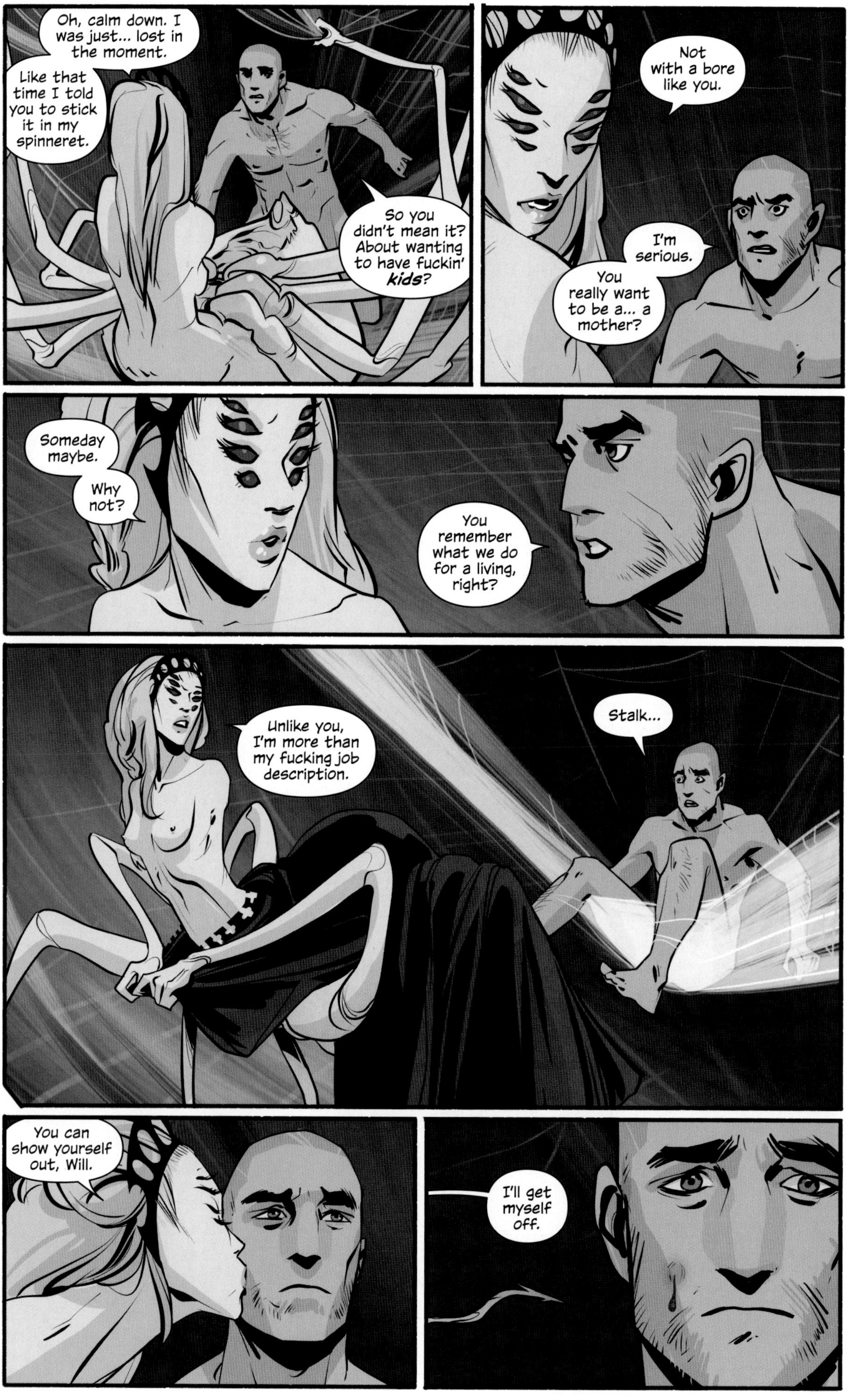

Oh, calm down. I was just... lost in the moment.
Like that time I told you to stick it in my spinneret.
So you didn't mean it? About wanting to have fuckin' *kids*?
Not with a bore like you.
I'm serious.
You really want to be a... a mother?
Someday maybe.
Why not?
You remember what we do for a living, right?
Unlike you, I'm more than my fucking job description.
Stalk...
You can show yourself out, Will.
I'll get myself off.

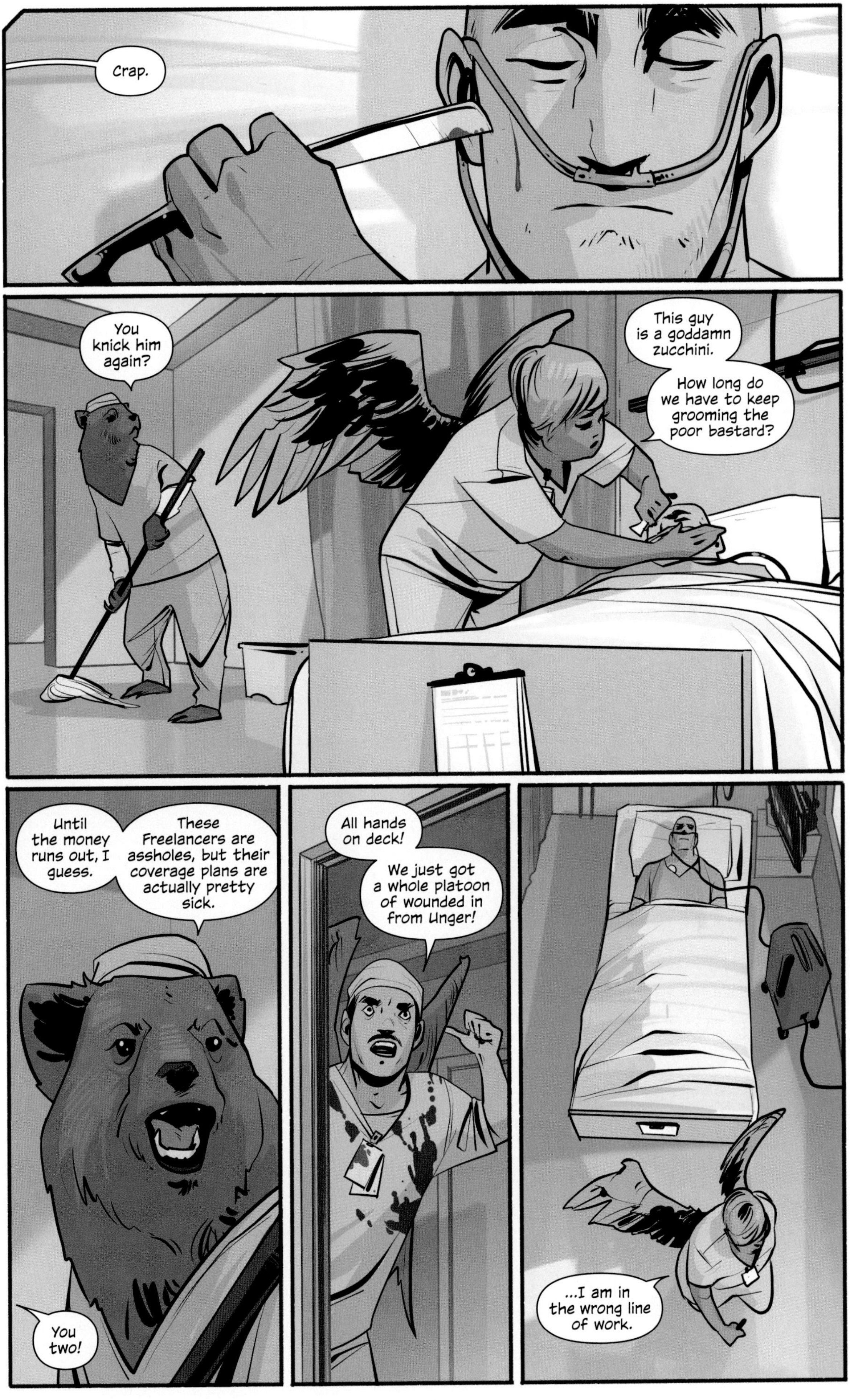
Crap.
You knick him again?
This guy is a goddamn zucchini.
How long do we have to keep grooming the poor bastard?
Until the money runs out, I guess.
These Freelancers are assholes, but their coverage plans are actually pretty sick.
You two!
All hands on deck!
We just got a whole platoon of wounded in from Unger!
...I am in the wrong line of work.

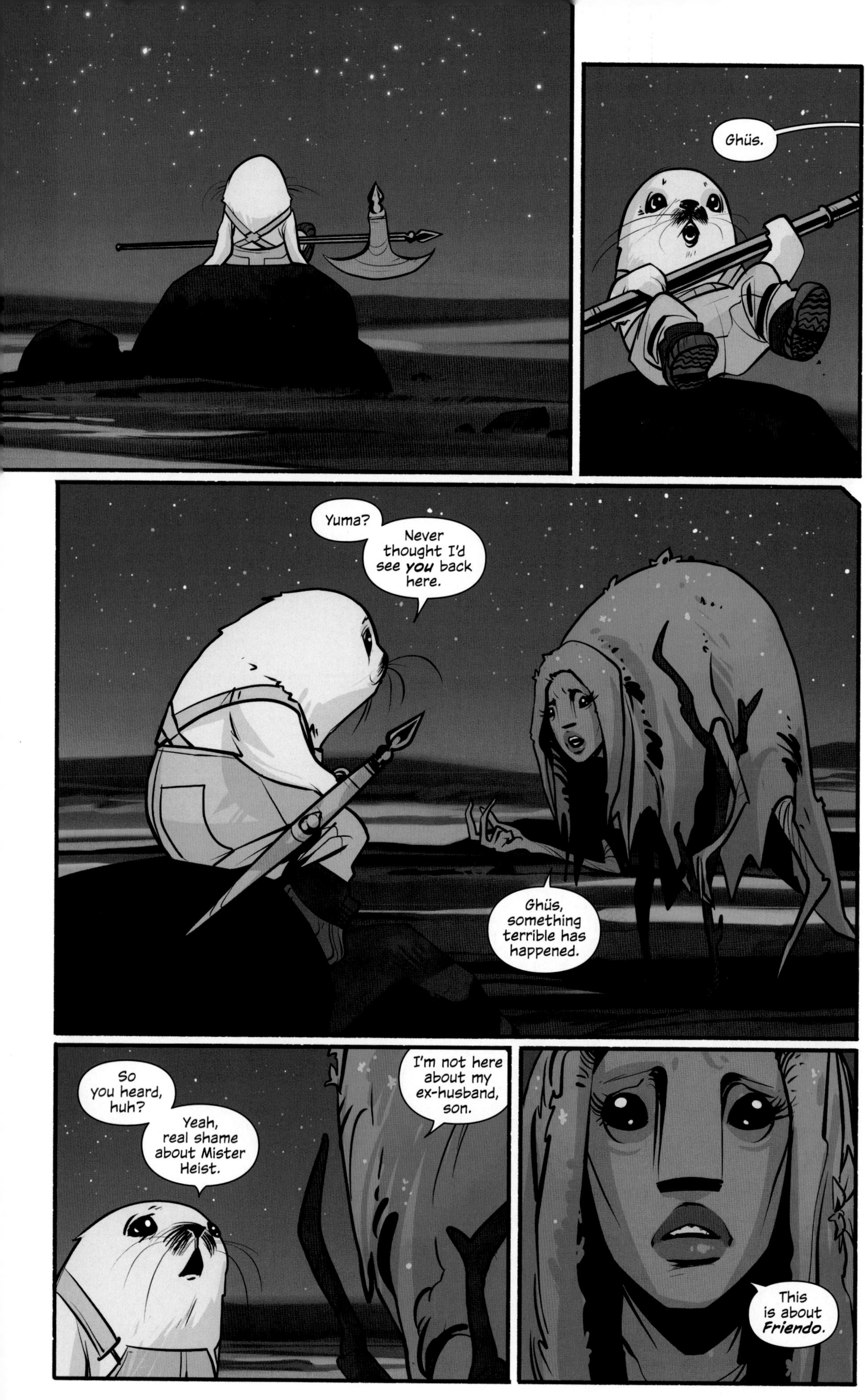
Ghüs.
Yuma?
Never thought I'd see ***you*** back here.
Ghüs, something terrible has happened.
So you heard, huh?
Yeah, real shame about Mister Heist.
I'm not here about my ex-husband, son.
This is about ***Friendo.***

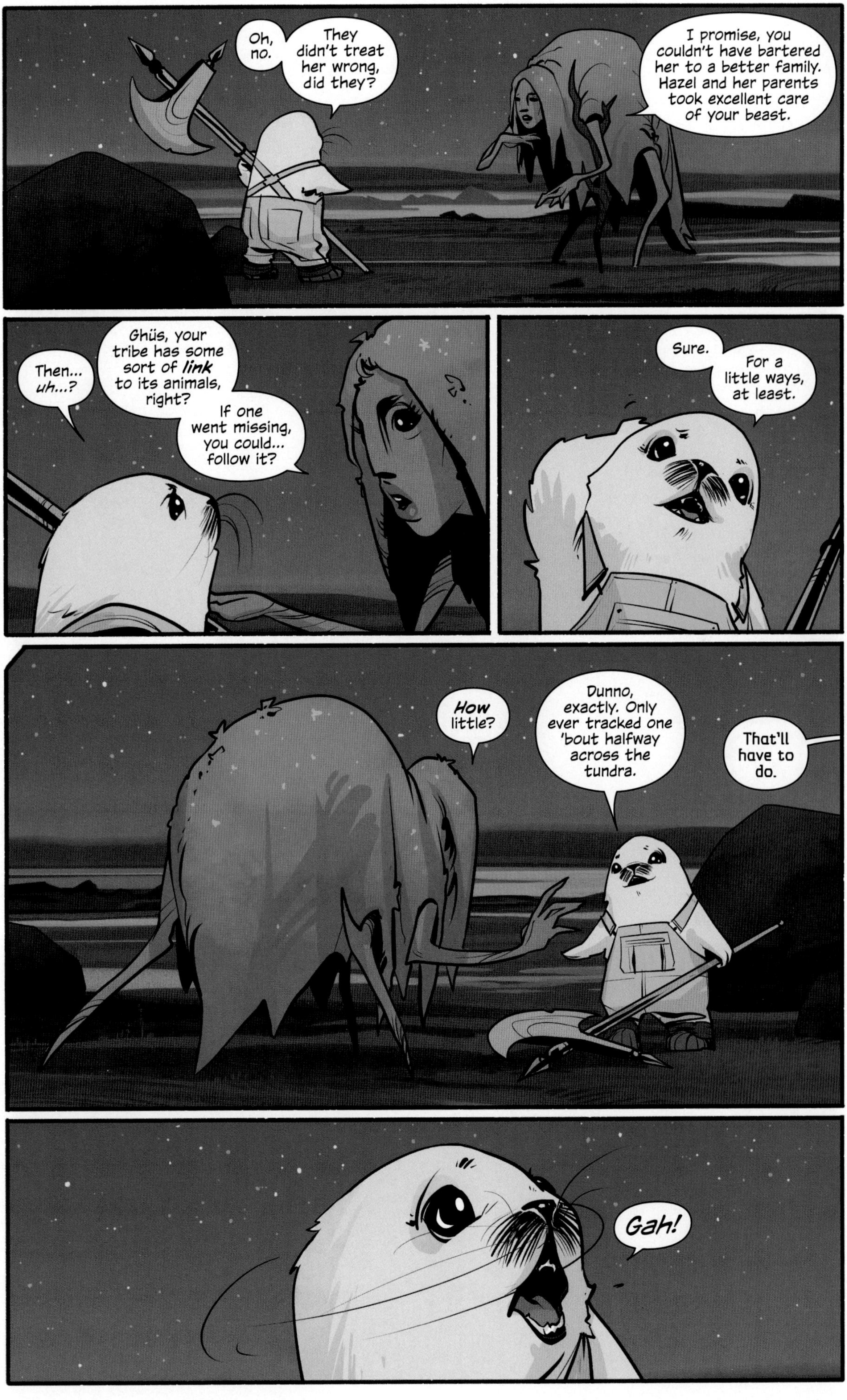
Oh, no.
They didn't treat her wrong, did they?
I promise, you couldn't have bartered her to a better family. Hazel and her parents took excellent care of your beast.
Then... uh...?
Ghüs, your tribe has some sort of *link* to its animals, right?
If one went missing, you could... follow it?
Sure.
For a little ways, at least.
How little?
Dunno, exactly. Only ever tracked one 'bout halfway across the tundra.
That'll have to do.
Gah!

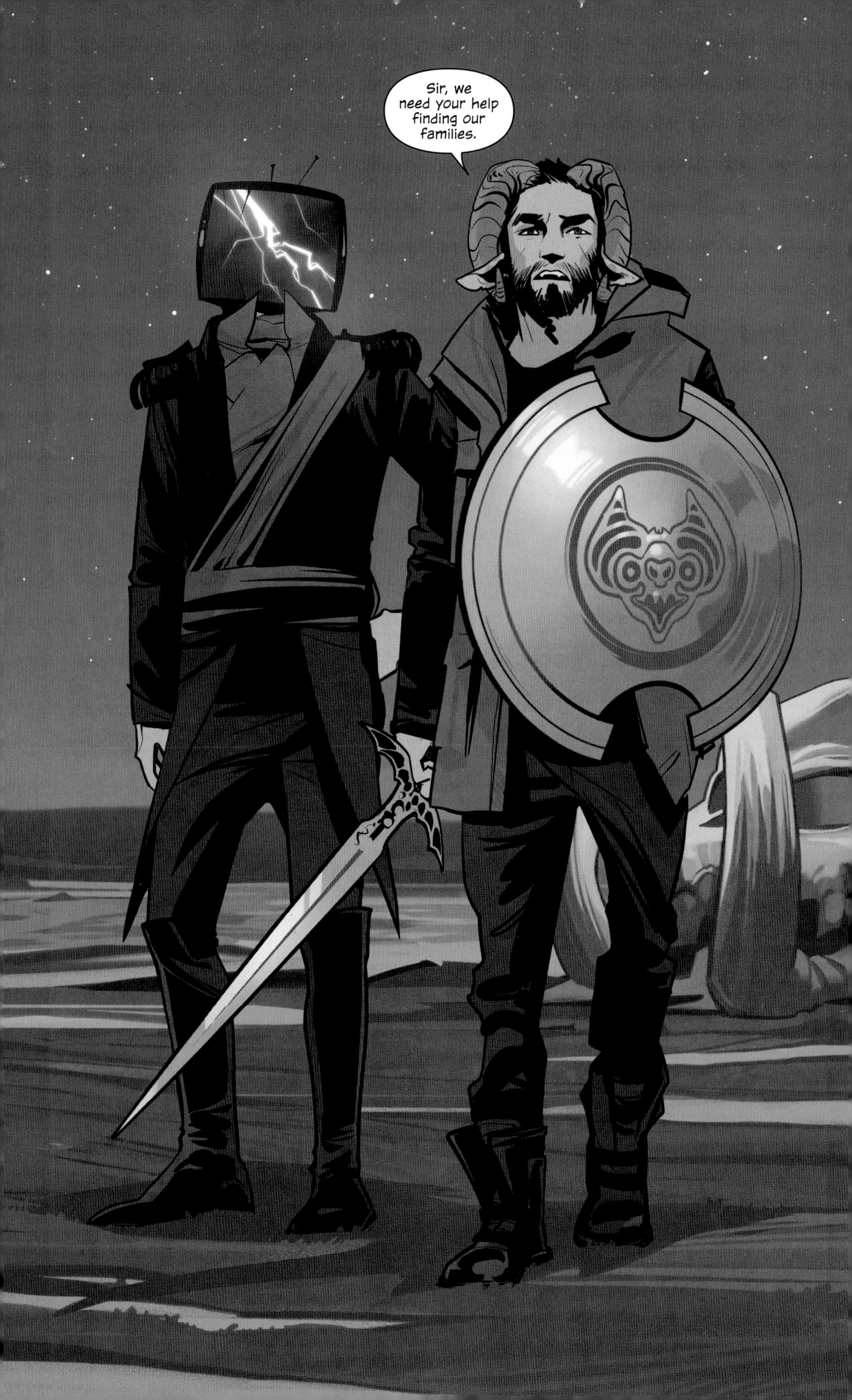
Sir, we need your help finding our families.

end chapter twenty-four

CHAPTER
TWENTY-FIVE

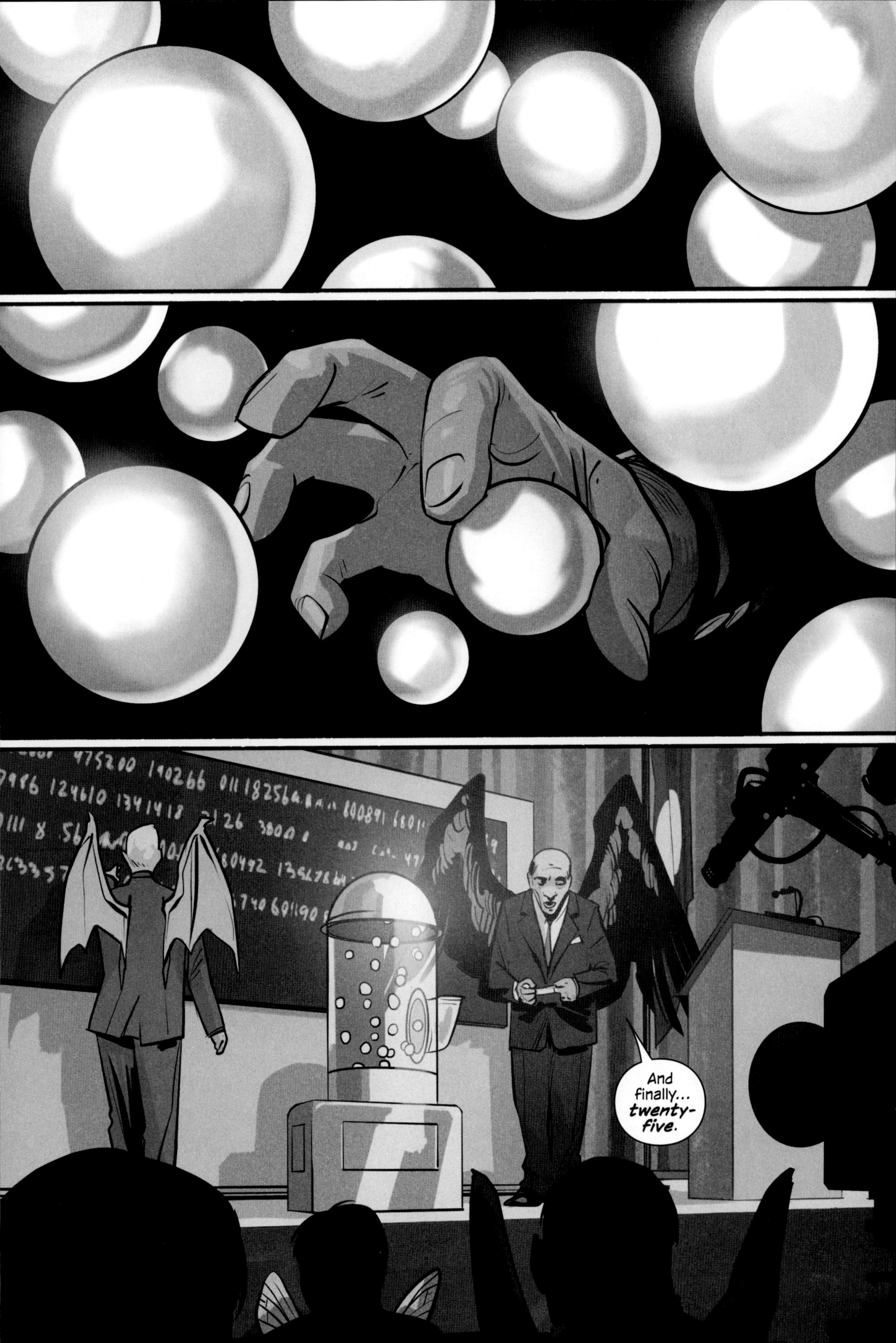
And finally... *twenty-five.*

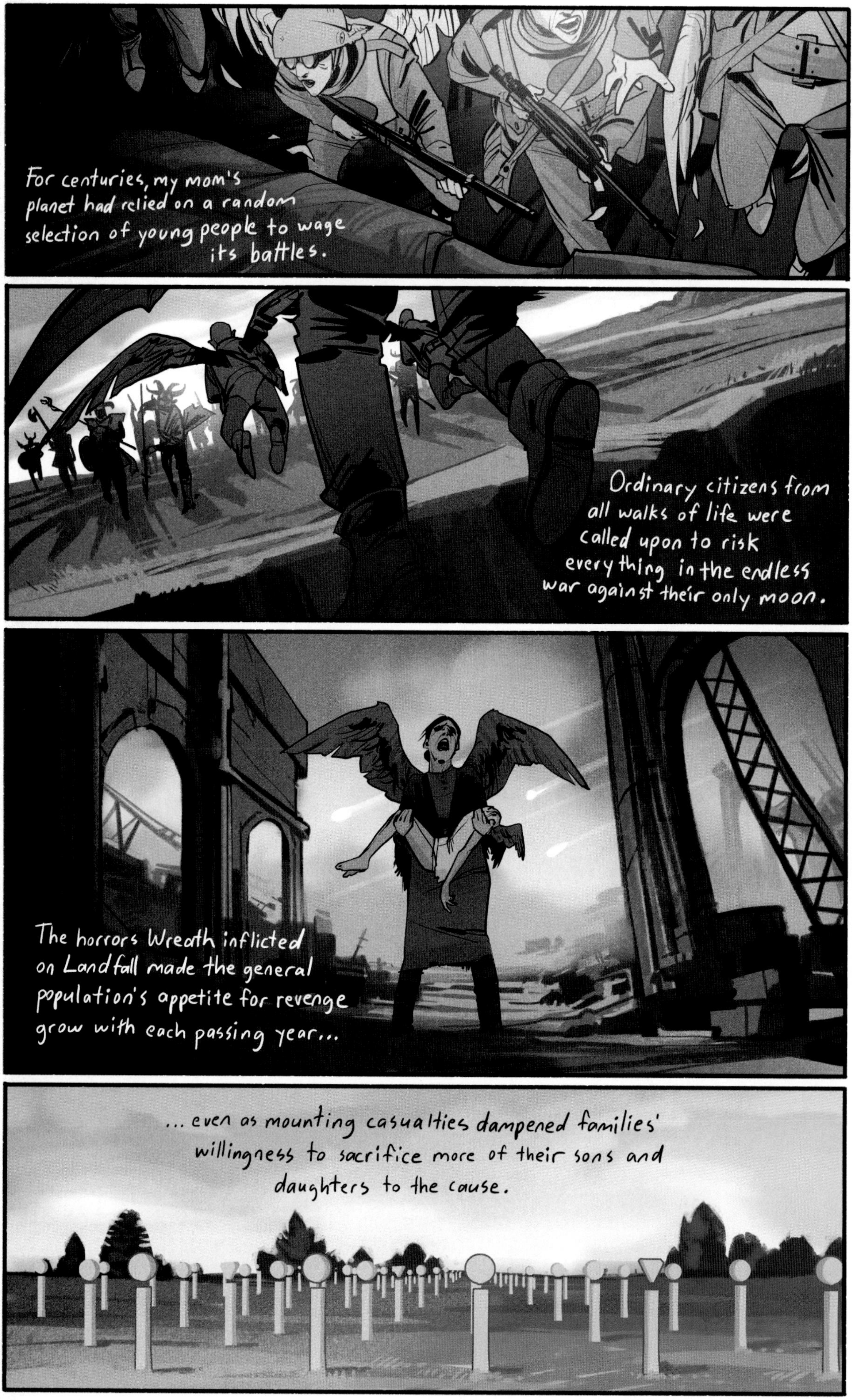

For centuries, my mom's planet had relied on a random selection of young people to wage its battles.
Ordinary citizens from all walks of life were called upon to risk everything in the endless war against their only moon.
The horrors Wreath inflicted on Landfall made the general population's appetite for revenge grow with each passing year...
...even as mounting casualties dampened families' willingness to sacrifice more of their sons and daughters to the cause.

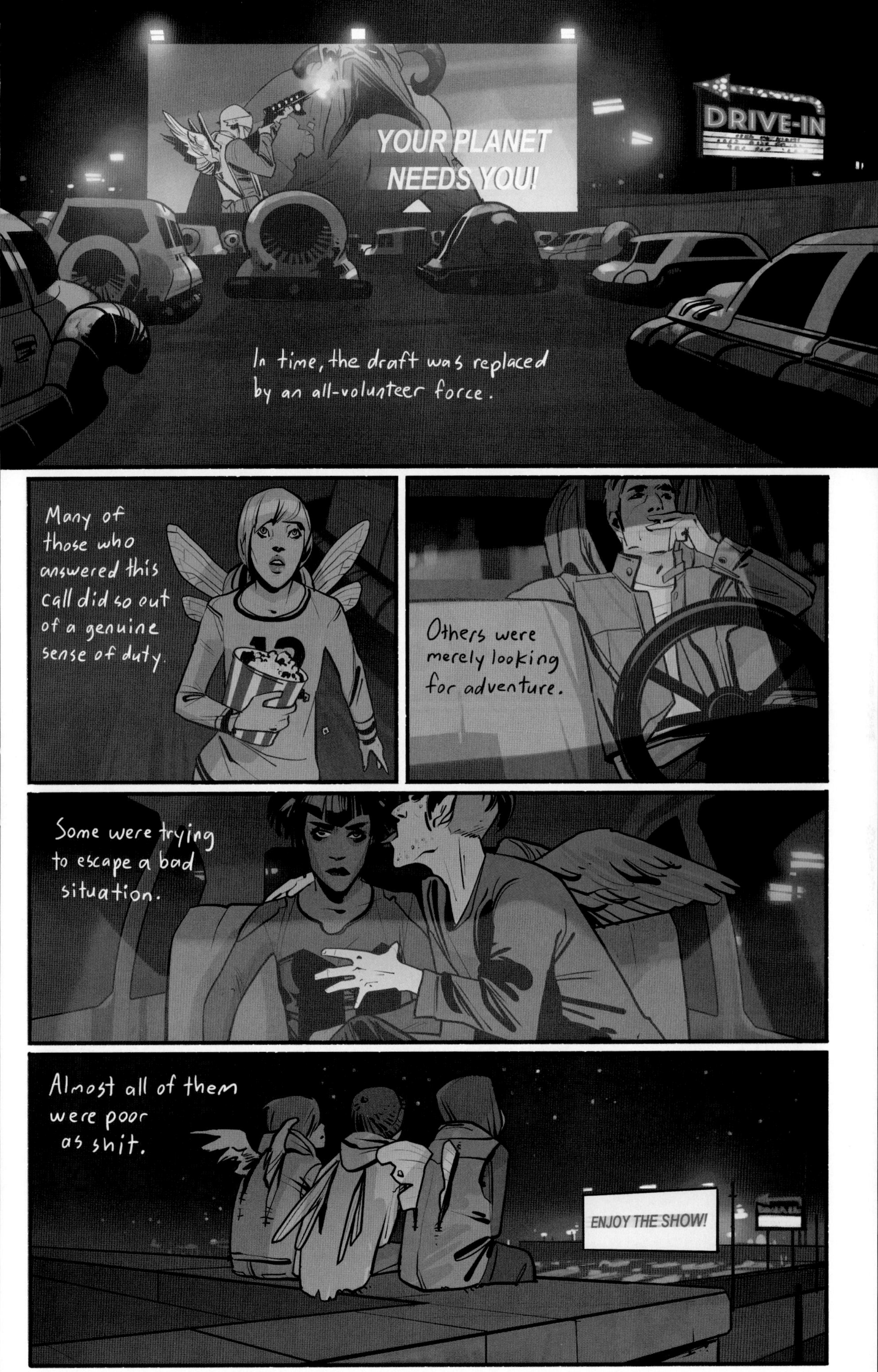
YOUR PLANET NEEDS YOU!
DRIVE-IN
In time, the draft was replaced by an all-volunteer force.
Many of those who answered this call did so out of a genuine sense of duty.
Others were merely looking for adventure.
Some were trying to escape a bad situation.
Almost all of them were poor as shit.
ENJOY THE SHOW!

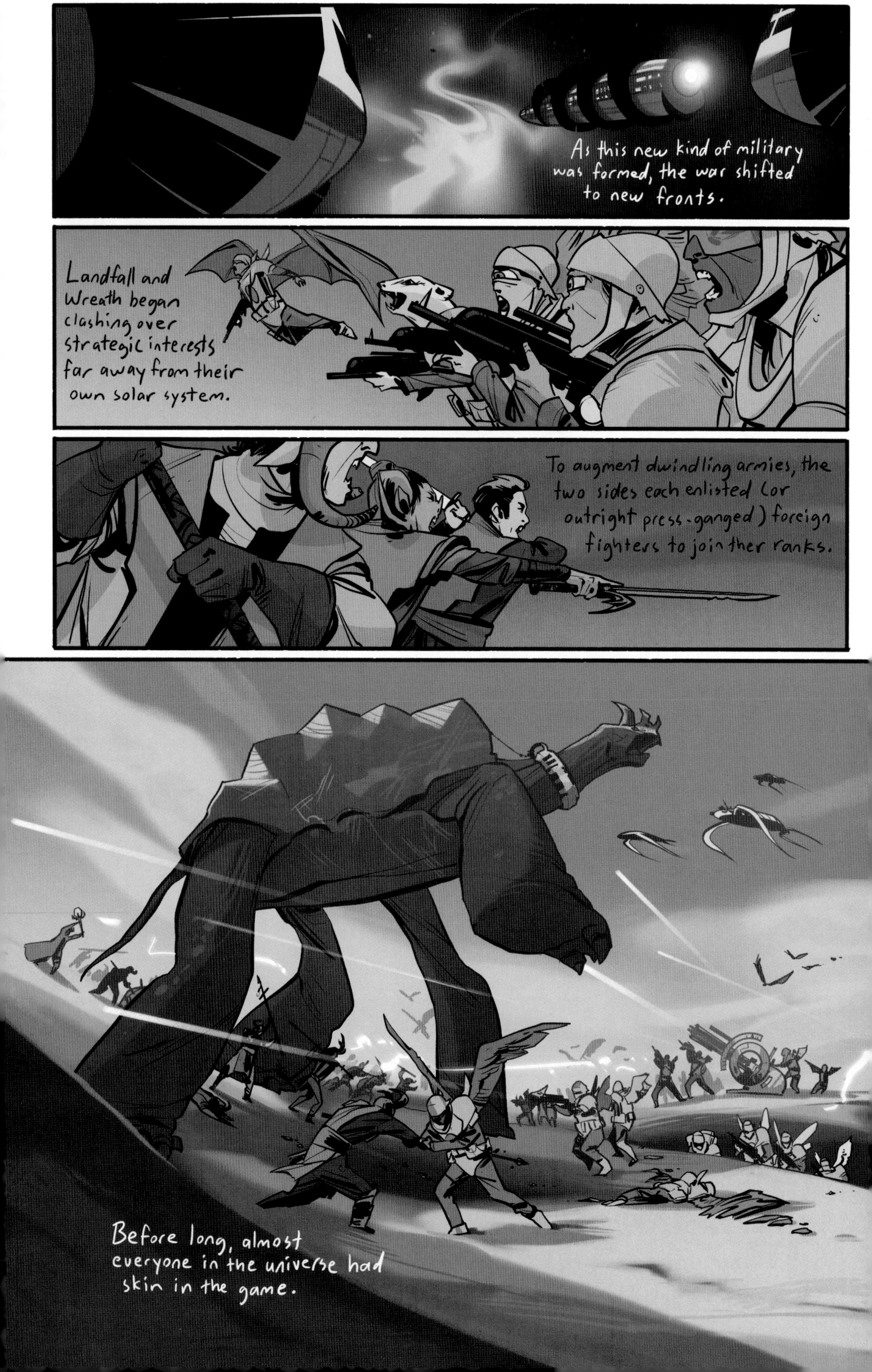

As this new kind of military was formed, the war shifted to new fronts.
Landfall and Wreath began clashing over strategic interests far away from their own solar system.
To augment dwindling armies, the two sides each enlisted (or outright press-ganged) foreign fighters to join ther ranks.
Before long, almost everyone in the universe had skin in the game.

But as the conflict moved further into the cosmos, an unfamiliar quiet fell over the two worlds that had given birth to this bloodshed.

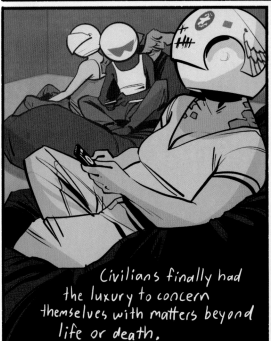

Civilians finally had the luxury to concern themselves with matters beyond life or death.

Everyone still supported the troops, of course, but in a more... abstract way than times past.

For most folks back on Landfall, war was something that would never directly impact their lives.

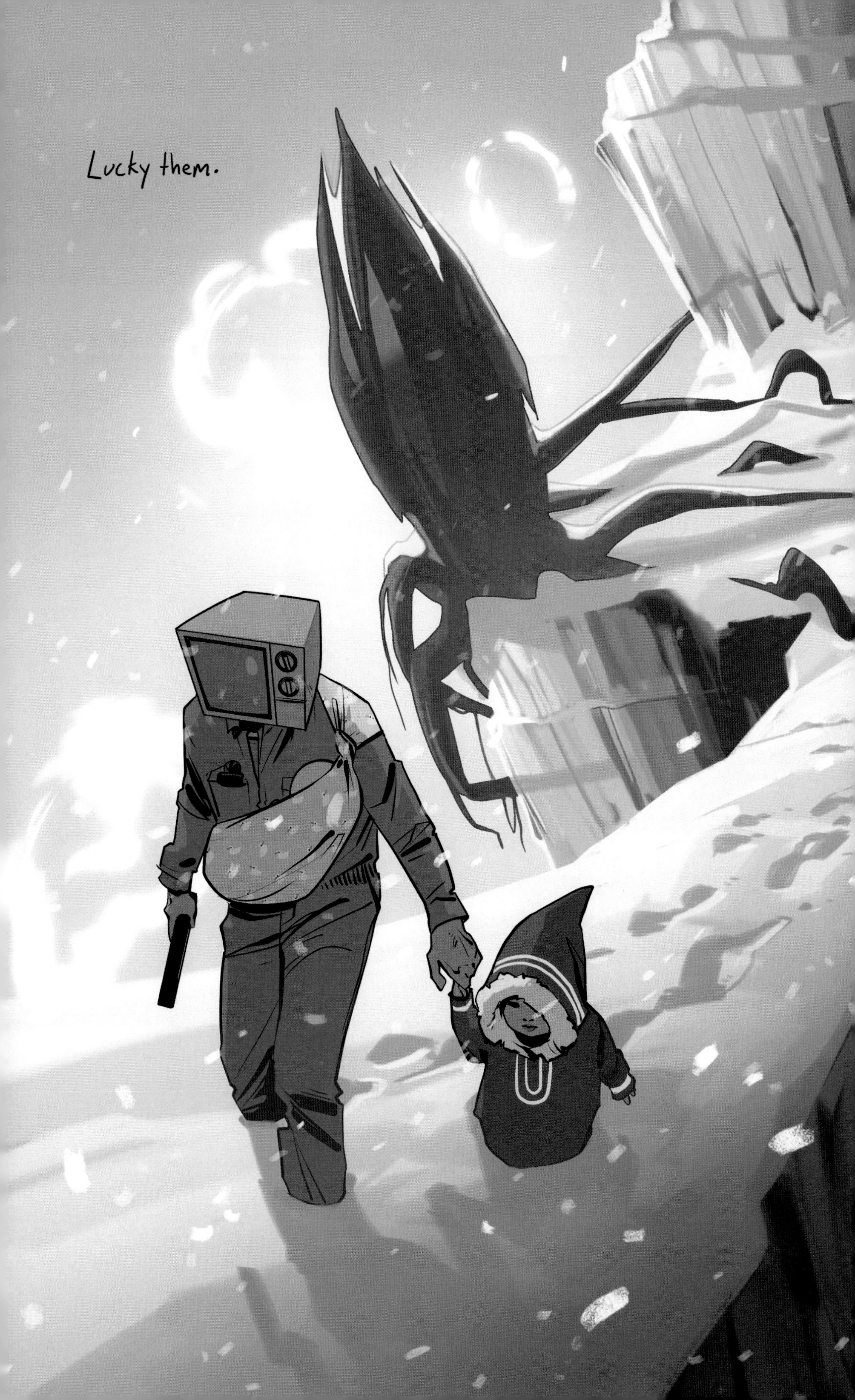
Lucky them.

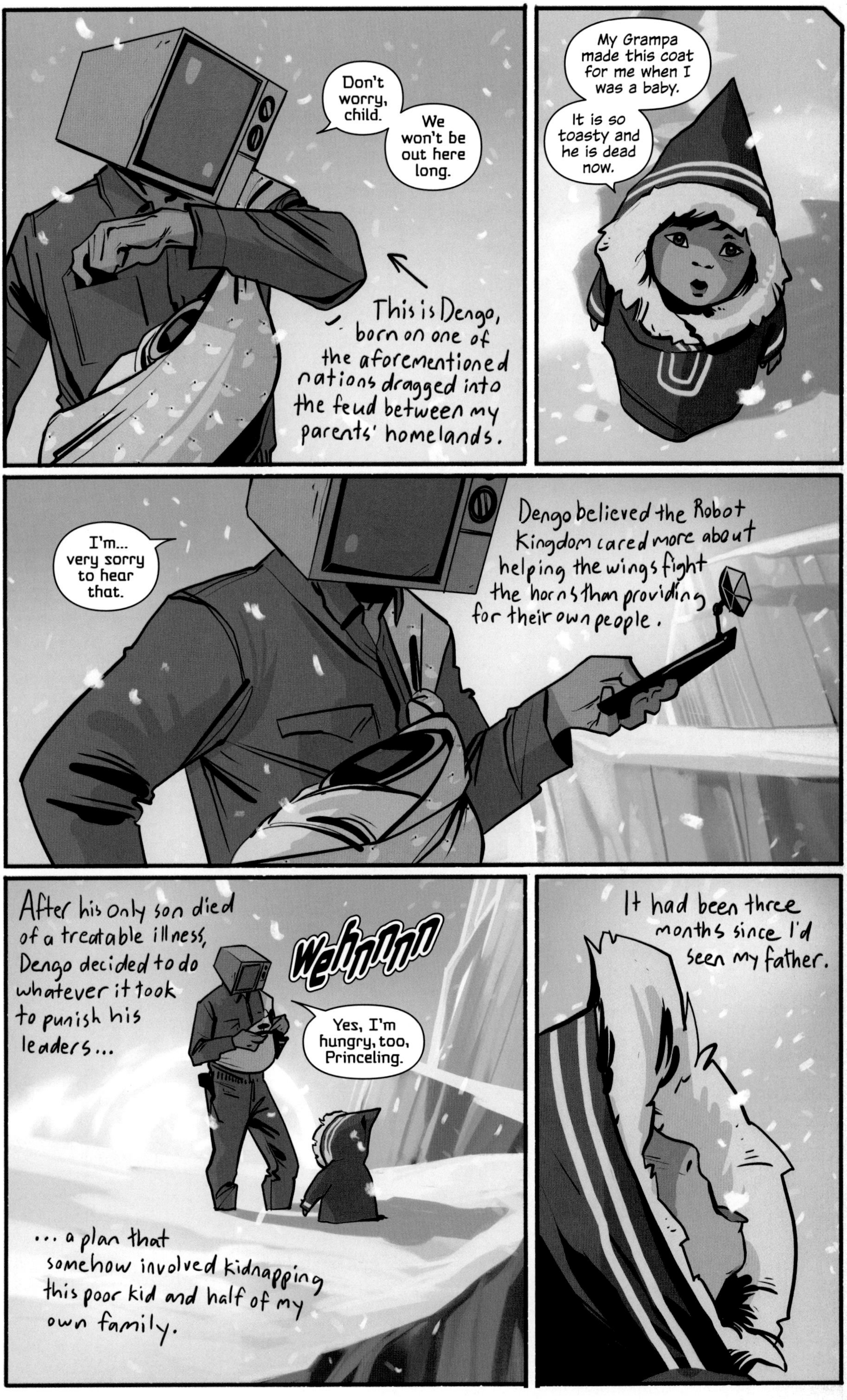

Don't worry, child.
We won't be out here long.
This is Dengo, born on one of the aforementioned nations dragged into the feud between my parents' homelands.
My Grampa made this coat for me when I was a baby.
It is so toasty and he is dead now.
I'm... very sorry to hear that.
Dengo believed the Robot Kingdom cared more about helping the wings fight the horns than providing for their own people.
After his only son died of a treatable illness, Dengo decided to do whatever it took to punish his leaders...
Wehnnnn
Yes, I'm hungry, too, Princeling.
... a plan that somehow involved kidnapping this poor kid and half of my own family.
It had been three months since I'd seen my father.

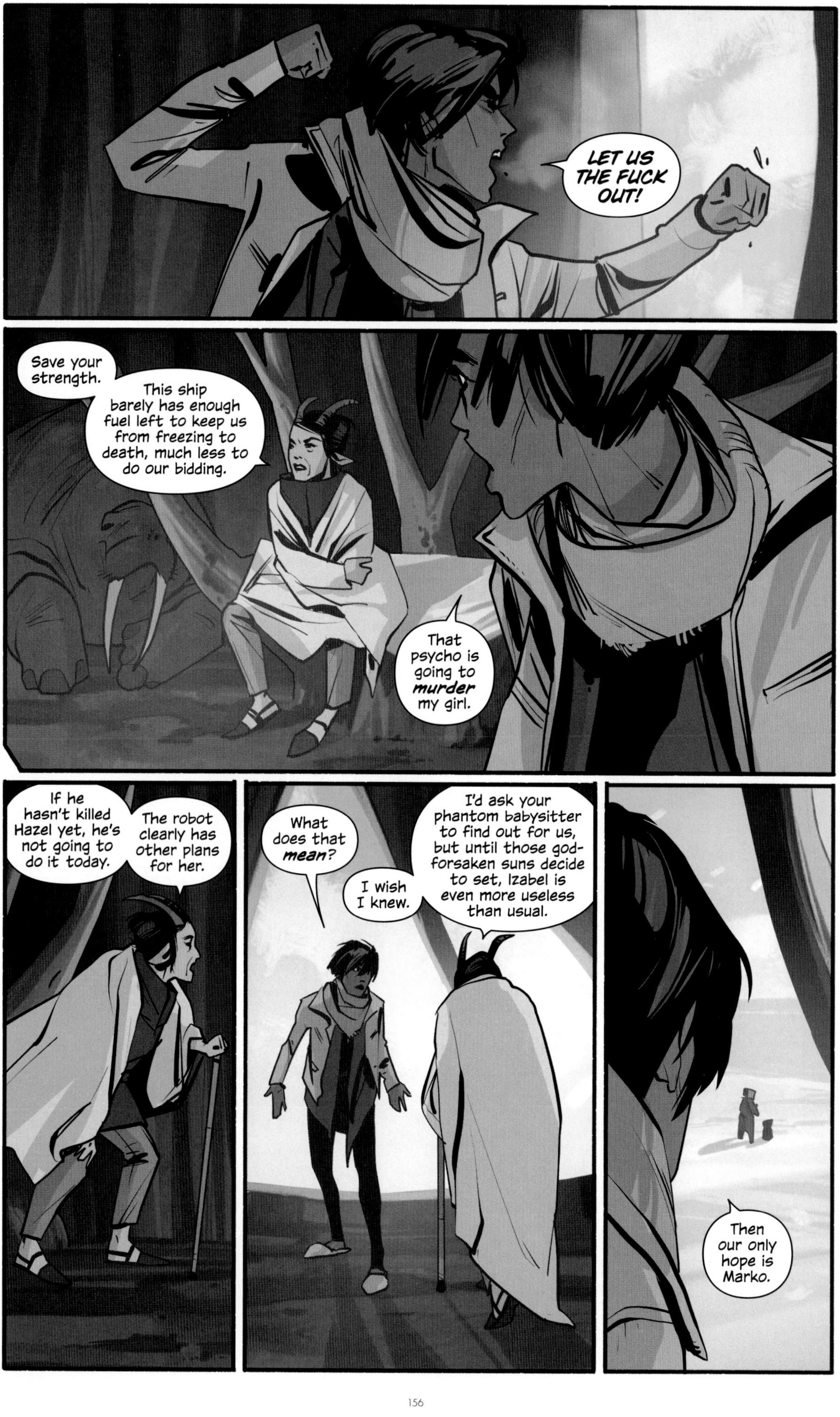
LET US THE FUCK OUT!
Save your strength.
This ship barely has enough fuel left to keep us from freezing to death, much less to do our bidding.
That psycho is going to *murder* my girl.
If he hasn't killed Hazel yet, he's not going to do it today.
The robot clearly has other plans for her.
What does that *mean*?
I wish I knew.
I'd ask your phantom babysitter to find out for us, but until those god-forsaken suns decide to set, Izabel is even more useless than usual.
Then our only hope is Marko.

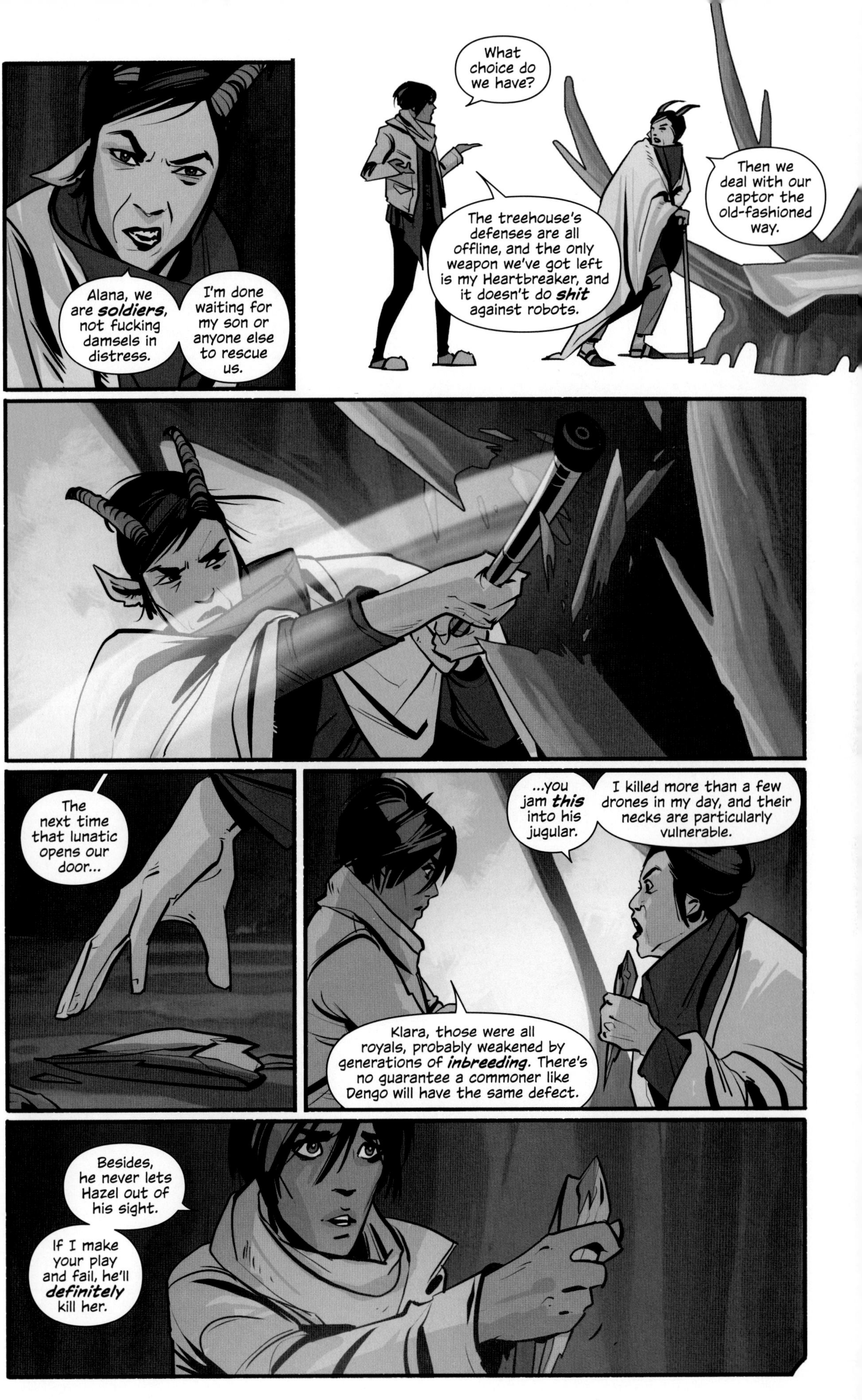
Alana, we are soldiers, not fucking damsels in distress.
I'm done waiting for my son or anyone else to rescue us.
What choice do we have?
The treehouse's defenses are all offline, and the only weapon we've got left is my Heartbreaker, and it doesn't do shit against robots.
Then we deal with our captor the old-fashioned way.
The next time that lunatic opens our door...
...you jam this into his jugular.
I killed more than a few drones in my day, and their necks are particularly vulnerable.
Klara, those were all royals, probably weakened by generations of inbreeding. There's no guarantee a commoner like Dengo will have the same defect.
Besides, he never lets Hazel out of his sight.
If I make your play and fail, he'll definitely kill her.

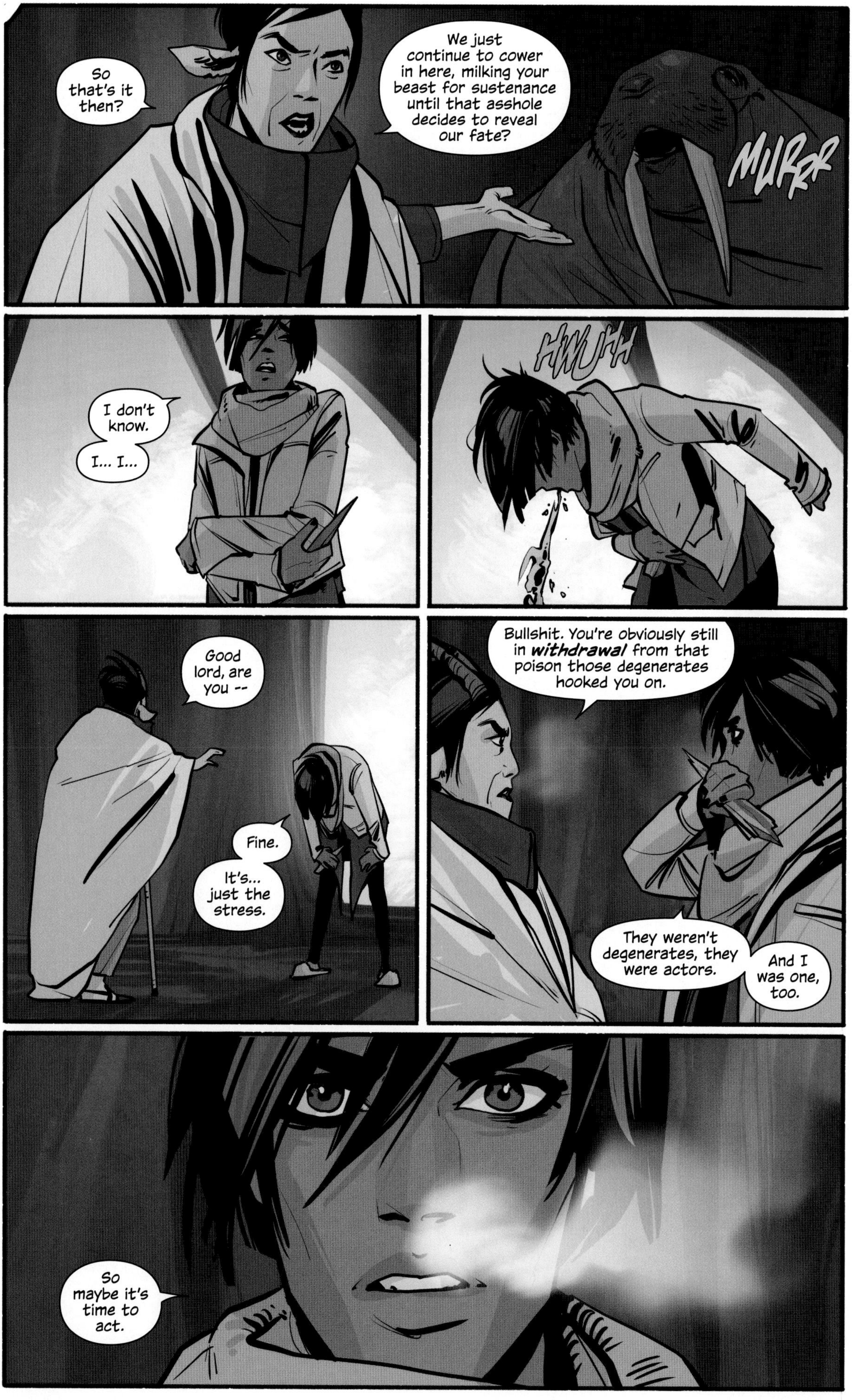

So that's it then?
We just continue to cower in here, milking your beast for sustenance until that asshole decides to reveal our fate?
MURRR
I don't know.
I... I...
HWUHH
Good lord, are you --
Fine.
It's... just the stress.
Bullshit. You're obviously still in *withdrawal* from that poison those degenerates hooked you on.
They weren't degenerates, they were actors.
And I was one, too.
So maybe it's time to act.

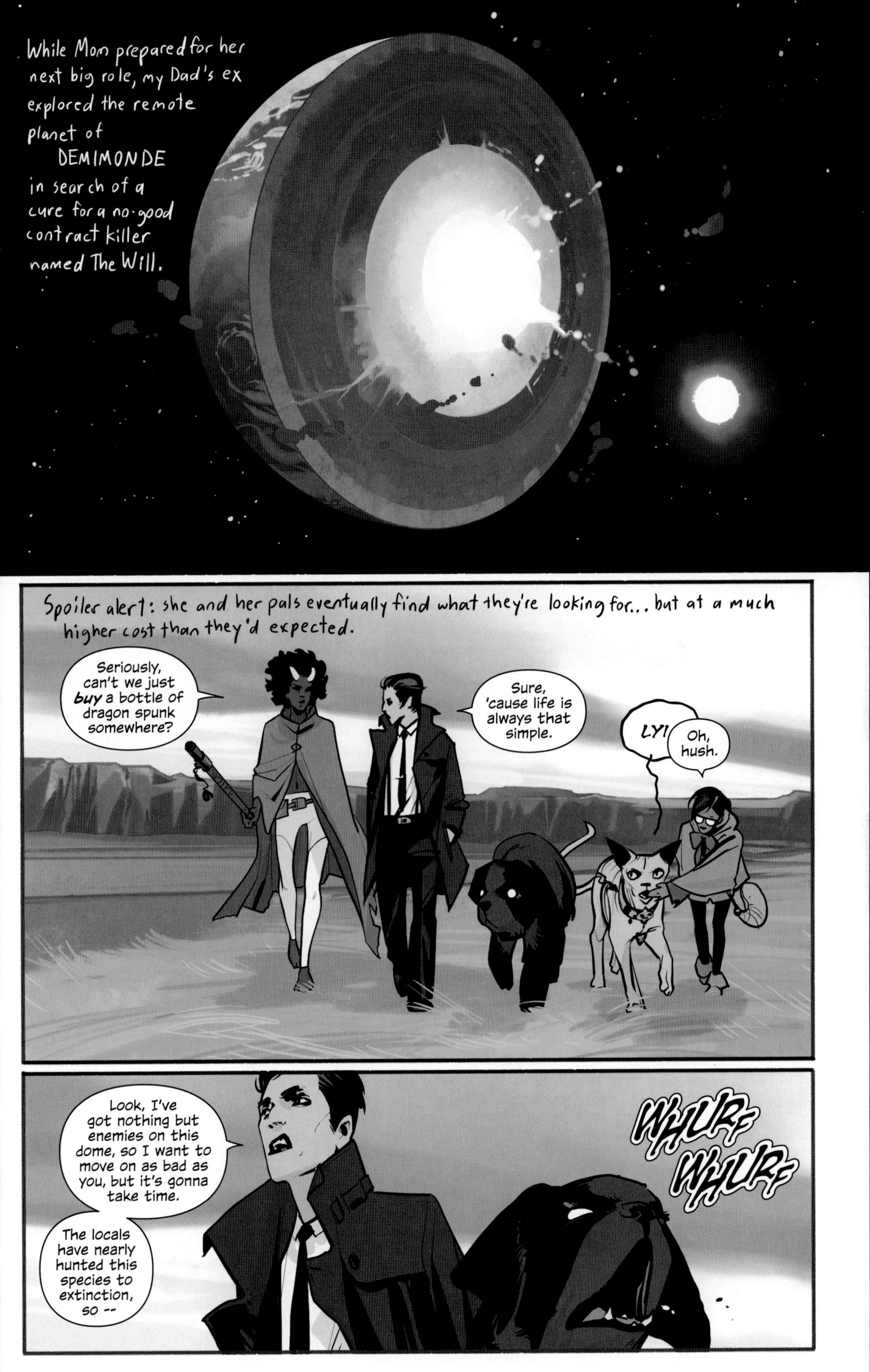
While Mom prepared for her next big role, my Dad's ex explored the remote planet of DEMIMONDE in search of a cure for a no-good contract killer named The Will.
Spoiler alert: she and her pals eventually find what they're looking for... but at a much higher cost than they'd expected.
Seriously, can't we just **buy** a bottle of dragon spunk somewhere?
Sure, 'cause life is always that simple.
LY!
Oh, hush.
Look, I've got nothing but enemies on this dome, so I want to move on as bad as you, but it's gonna take time.
The locals have nearly hunted this species to extinction, so --
WHURF
WHURF

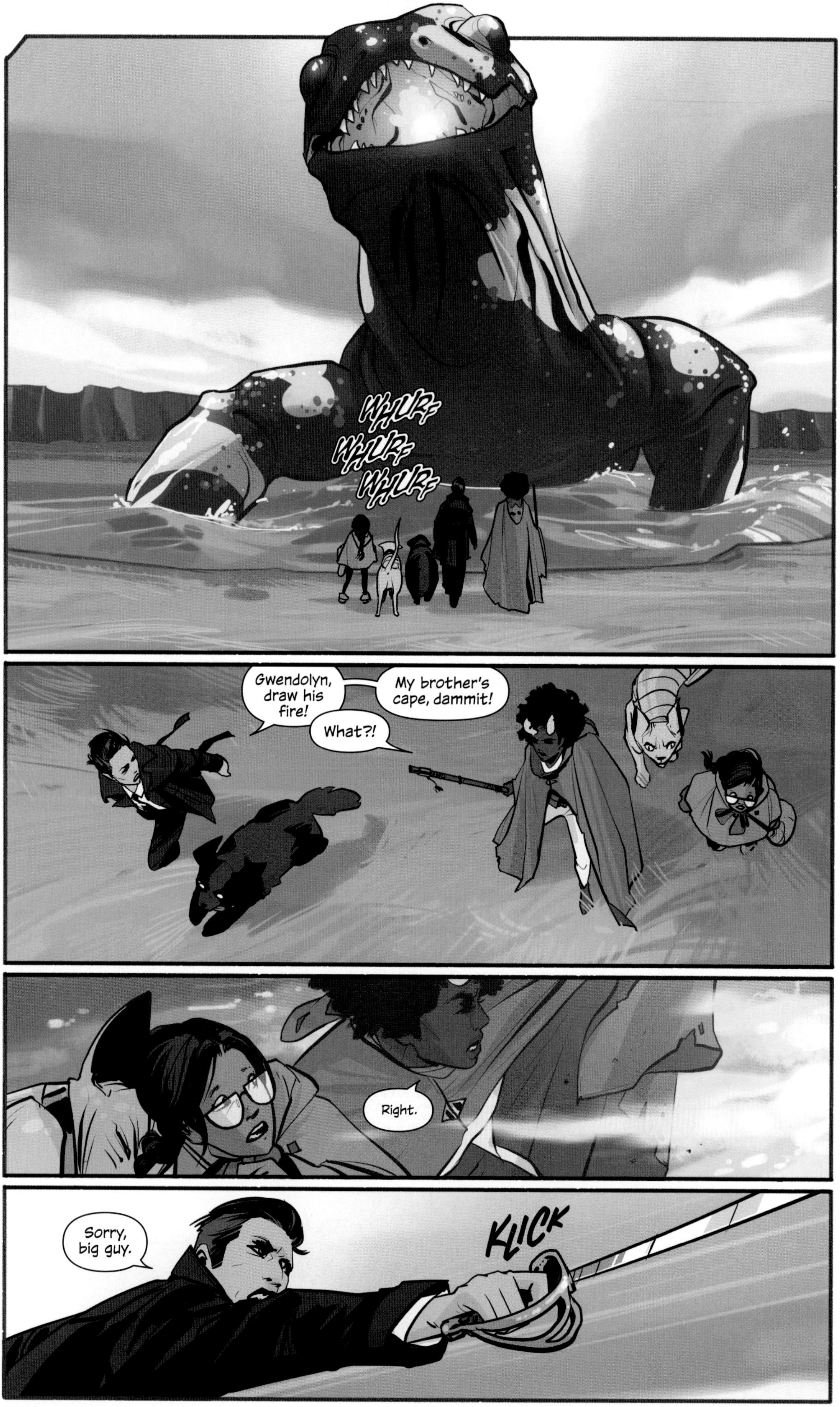
WHURF
WHURF
WHURF
Gwendolyn, draw his fire!
What?!
My brother's cape, dammit!
Right.
Sorry, big guy.
KLICK

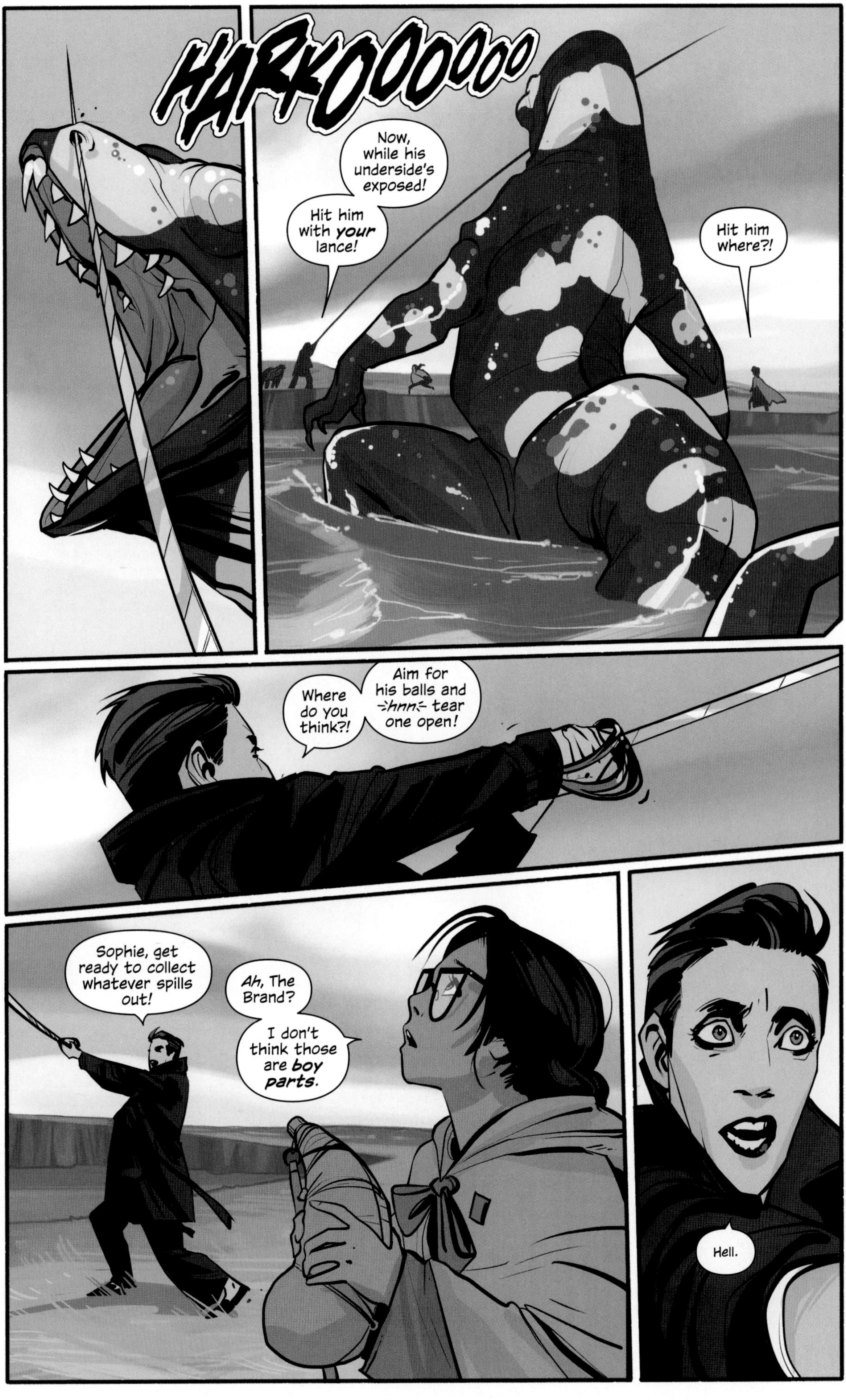
HARKOOOOOO
Now, while his underside's exposed!
Hit him with *your* lance!
Hit him where?!
Where do you think?!
Aim for his balls and -hnn- tear one open!
Sophie, get ready to collect whatever spills out!
Ah, The Brand?
I don't think those are ***boy parts***.
Hell.

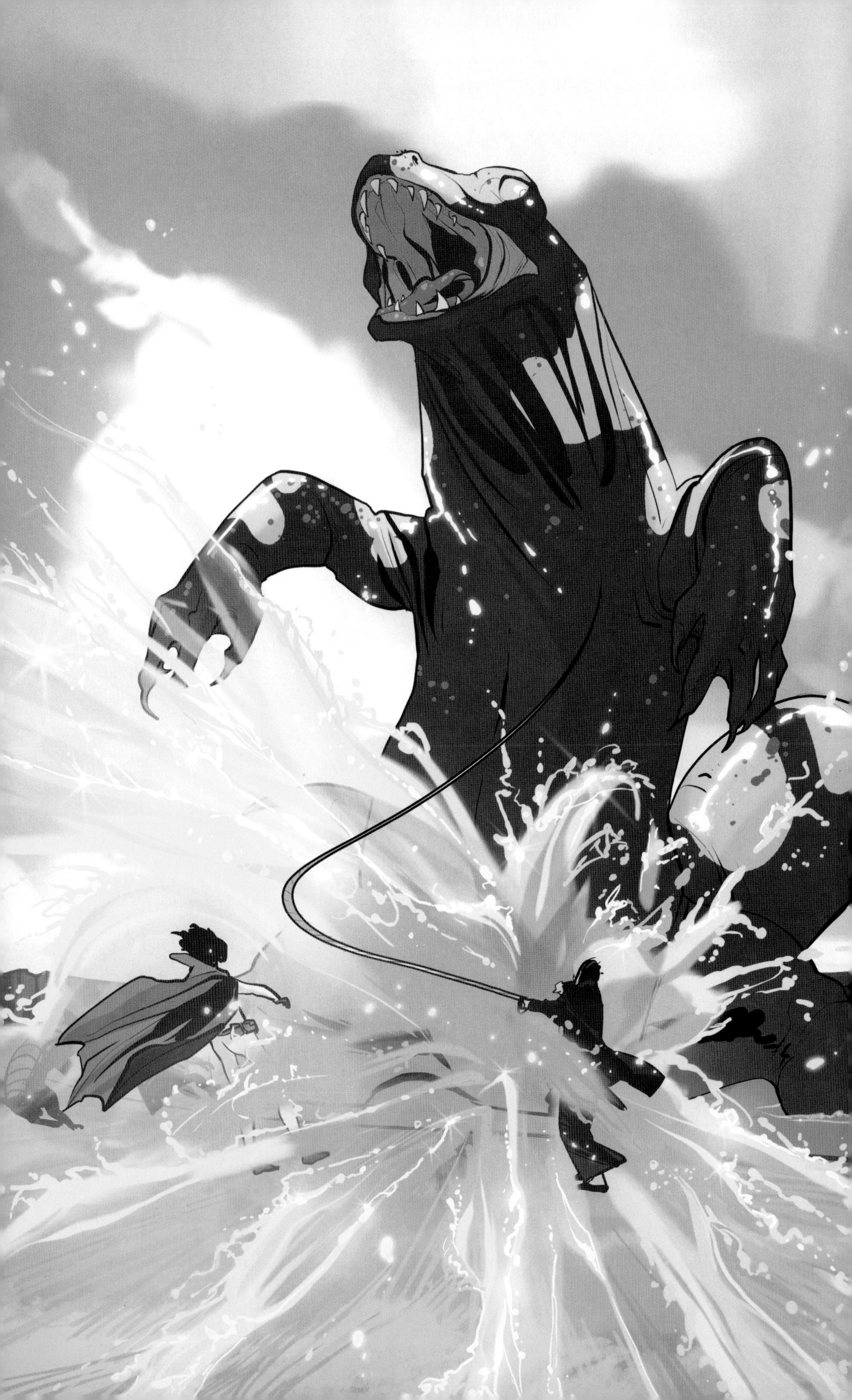

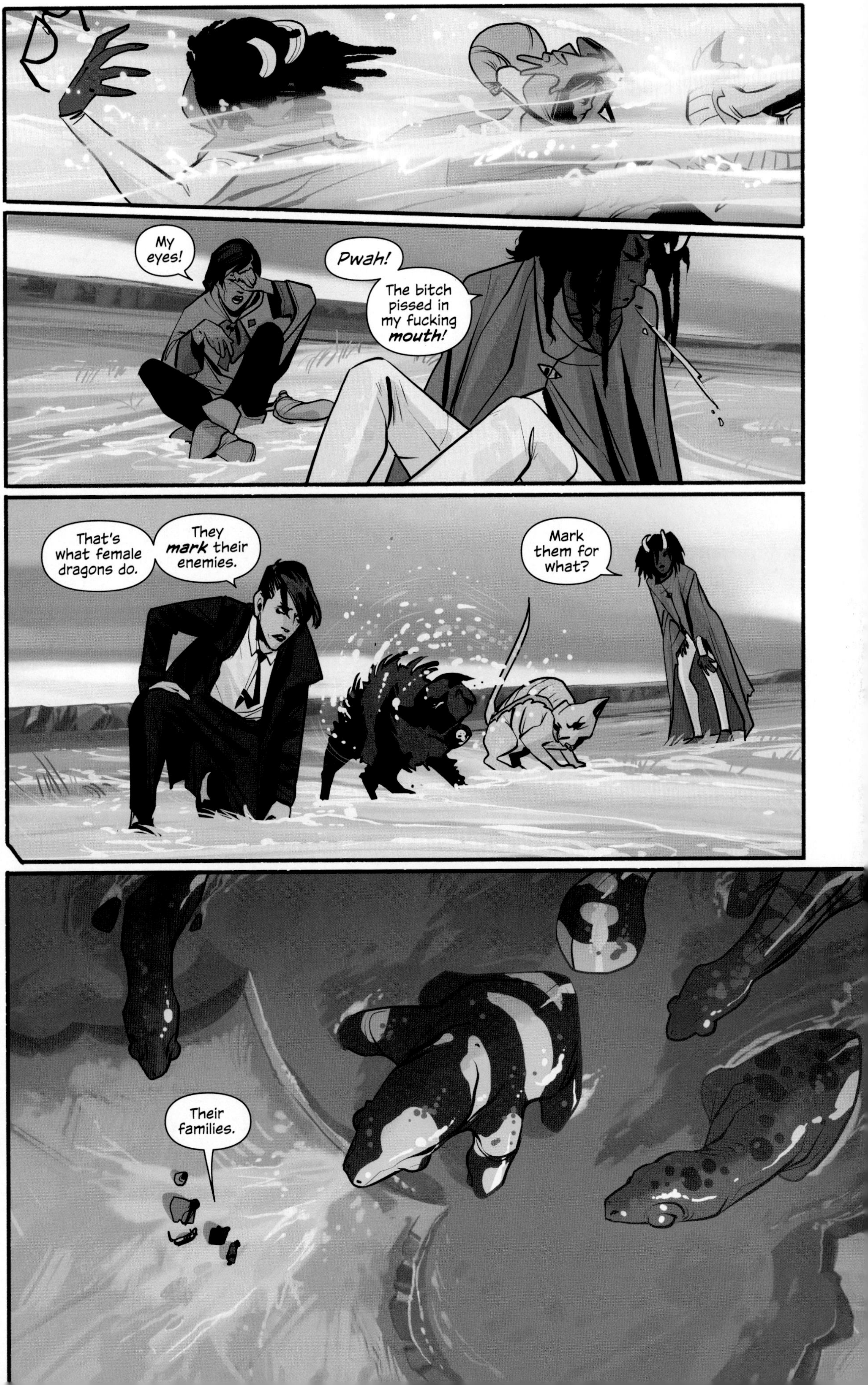

My eyes!
Pwah!
The bitch pissed in my fucking **mouth**!
That's what female dragons do.
They **mark** their enemies.
Mark them for what?
Their families.

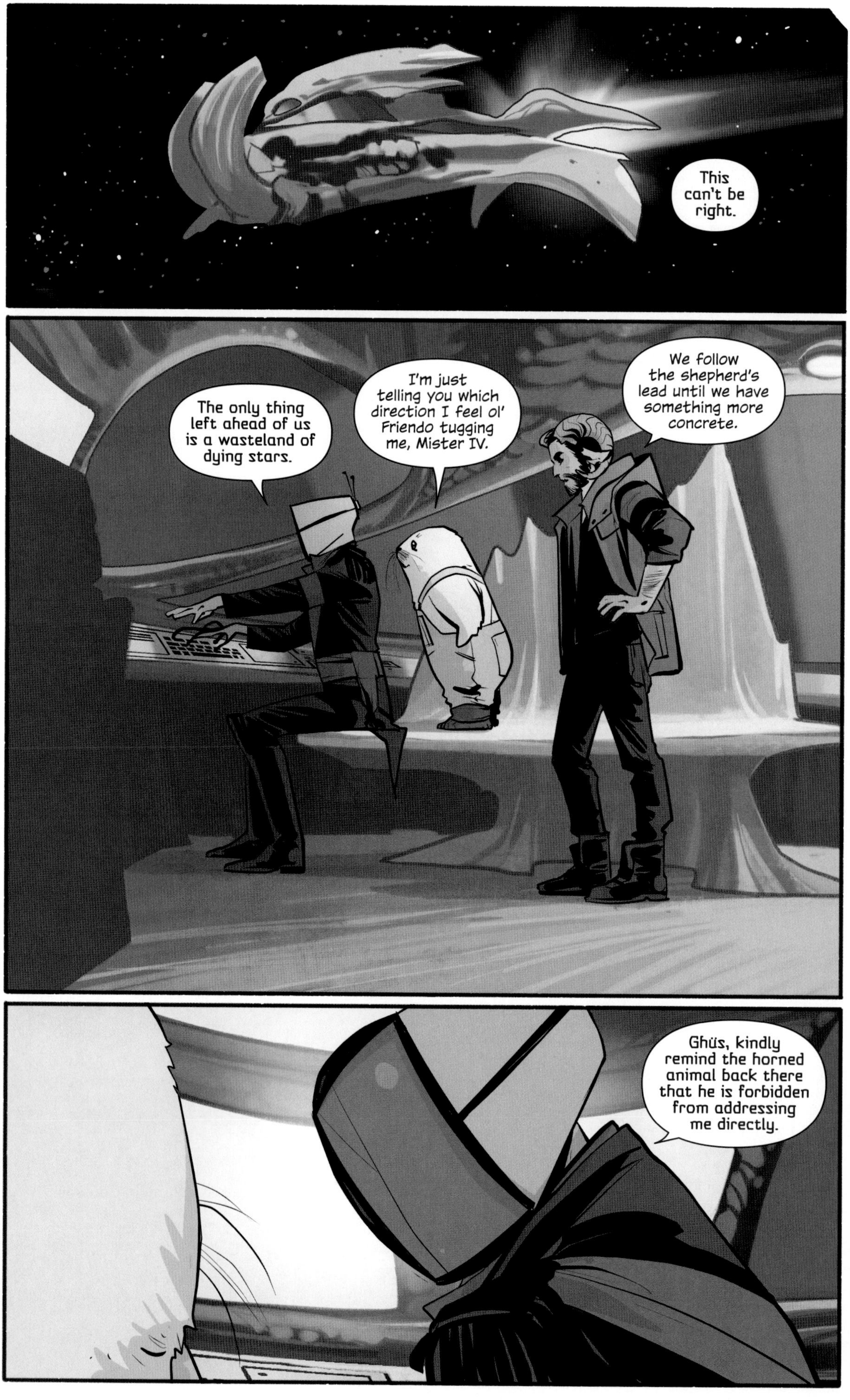
This can't be right.
The only thing left ahead of us is a wasteland of dying stars.
I'm just telling you which direction I feel ol' Friendo tugging me, Mister IV.
We follow the shepherd's lead until we have something more concrete.
Ghüs, kindly remind the horned animal back there that he is forbidden from addressing me directly.

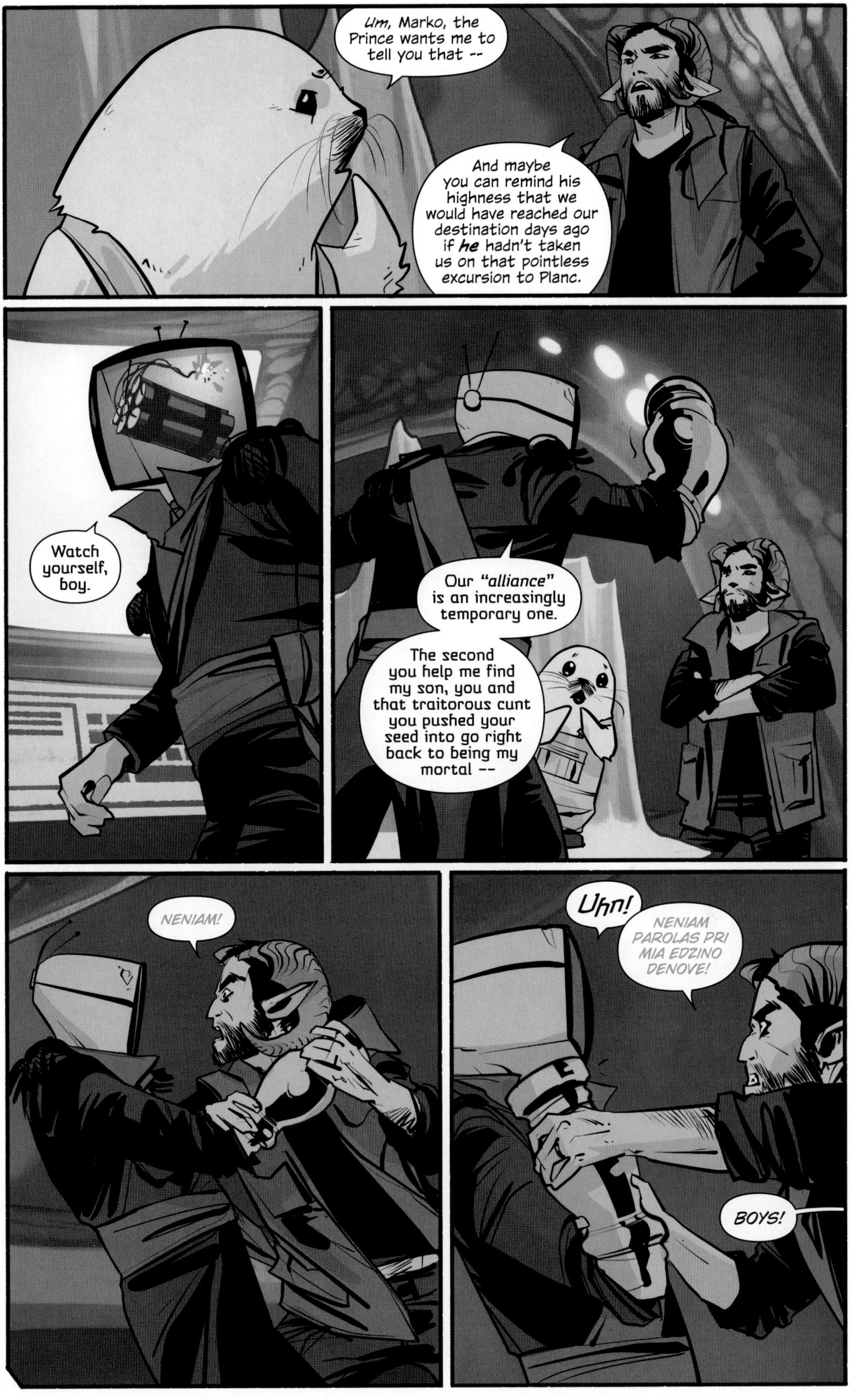
Um, Marko, the Prince wants me to tell you that --
And maybe you can remind his highness that we would have reached our destination days ago if he hadn't taken us on that pointless excursion to Planc.
Watch yourself, boy.
Our "alliance" is an increasingly temporary one.
The second you help me find my son, you and that traitorous cunt you pushed your seed into go right back to being my mortal --
NENIAM!
Uhn!
NENIAM PAROLAS PRI MIA EDZINO DENOVE!
BOYS!

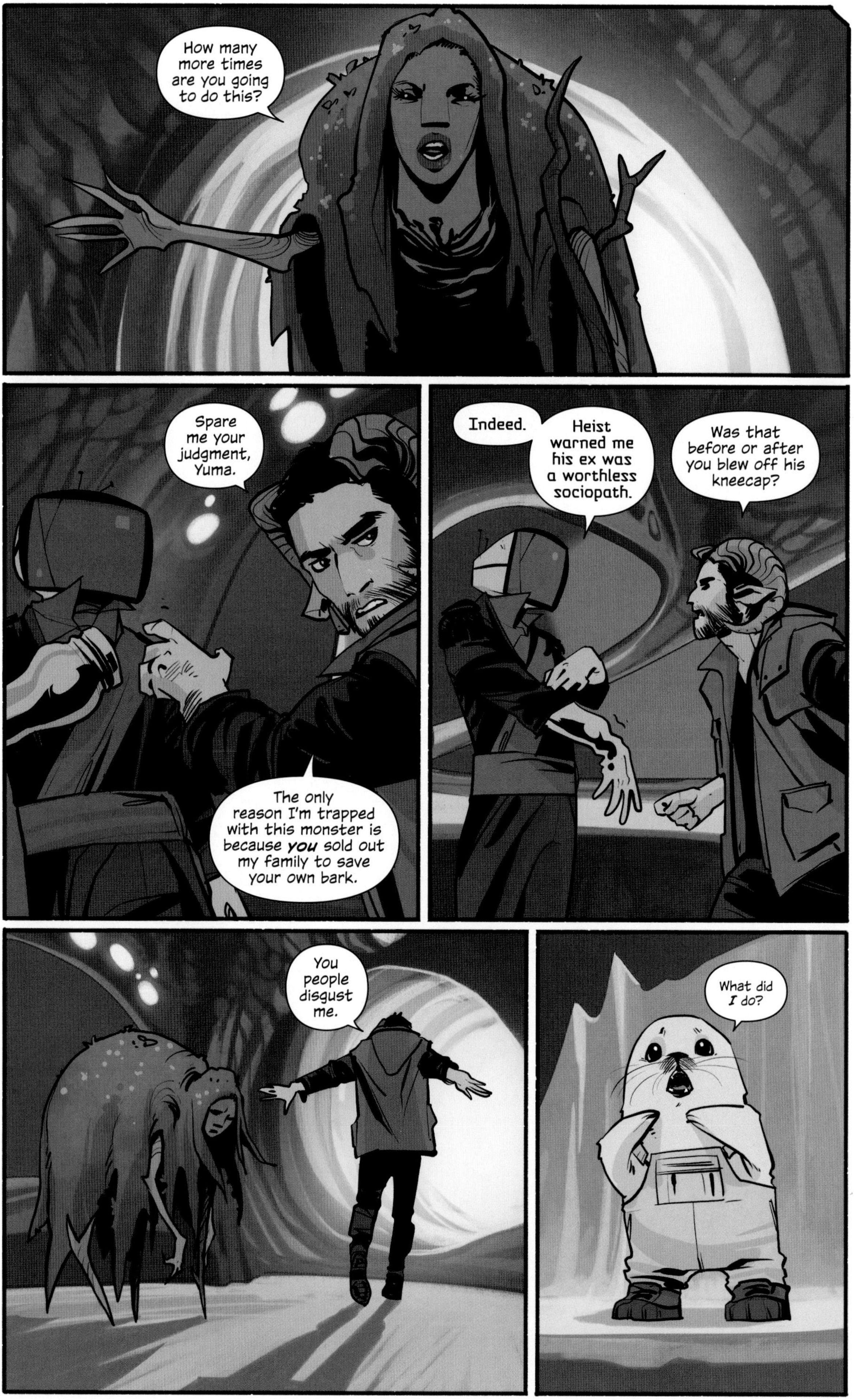
How many more times are you going to do this?
Spare me your judgment, Yuma.
The only reason I'm trapped with this monster is because ***you*** sold out my family to save your own bark.
Indeed.
Heist warned me his ex was a worthless sociopath.
Was that before or after you blew off his kneecap?
You people disgust me.
What did ***I*** do?

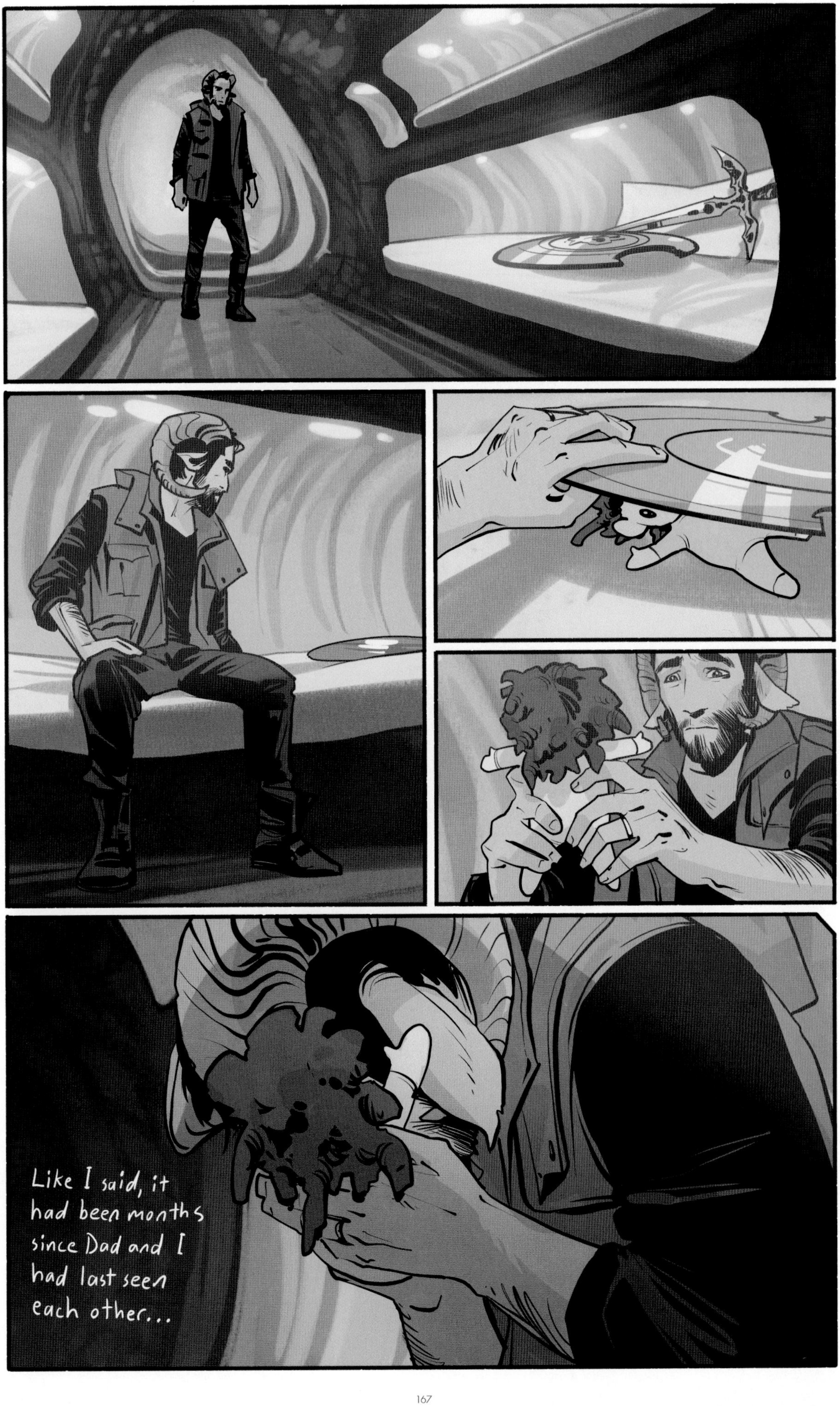

Like I said, it had been months since Dad and I had last seen each other...

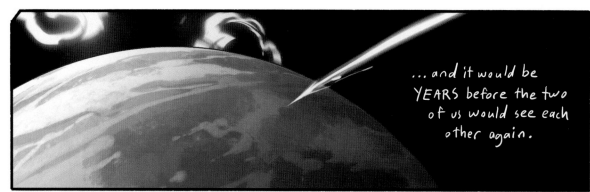

...and it would be YEARS before the two of us would see each other again.

What *is* that?

Looks like the hoof of an old *Astronomical*.

But Landfall decommissioned those things years ago.

If Dengo really summoned the wings... they'll slaughter Hazel the moment they see the nubs on her head.

NOK NOK

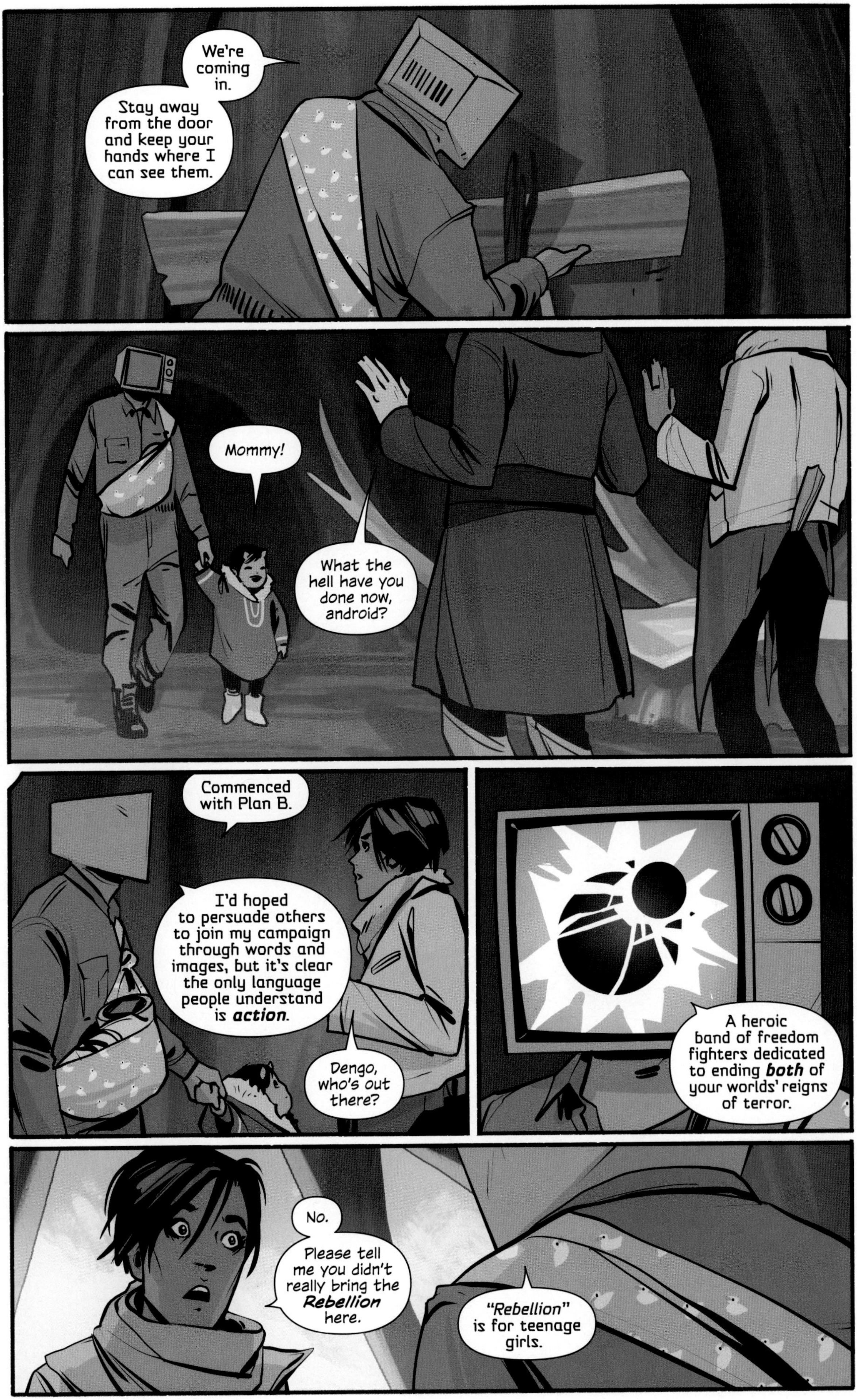
We're coming in.
Stay away from the door and keep your hands where I can see them.
Mommy!
What the hell have you done now, android?
Commenced with Plan B.
I'd hoped to persuade others to join my campaign through words and images, but it's clear the only language people understand is ***action***.
Dengo, who's out there?
A heroic band of freedom fighters dedicated to ending ***both*** of your worlds' reigns of terror.
No.
Please tell me you didn't really bring the ***Rebellion*** here.
"Rebellion" is for teenage girls.

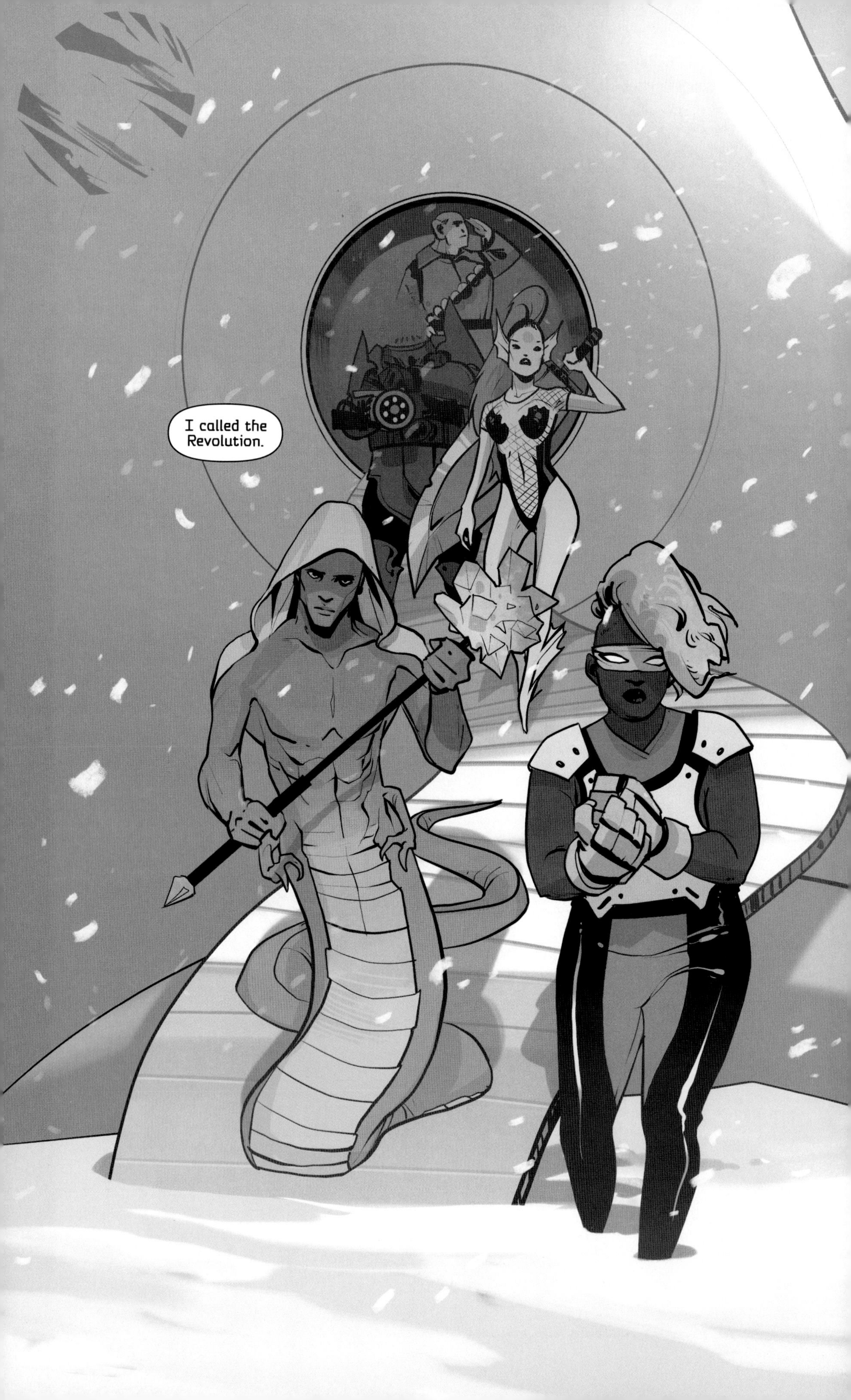
I called the Revolution.

end chapter twenty-five

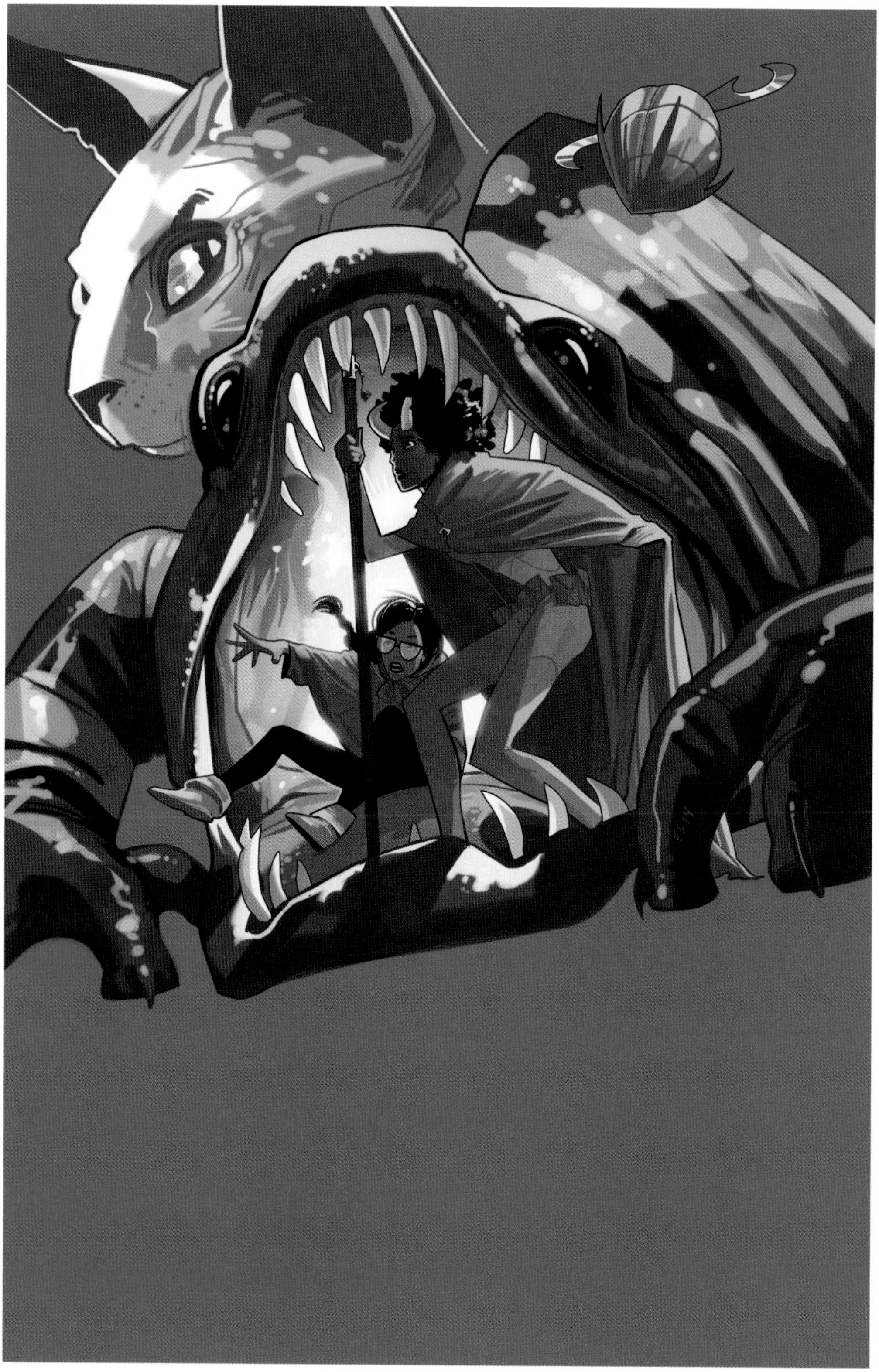

CHAPTER

TWENTY-SIX

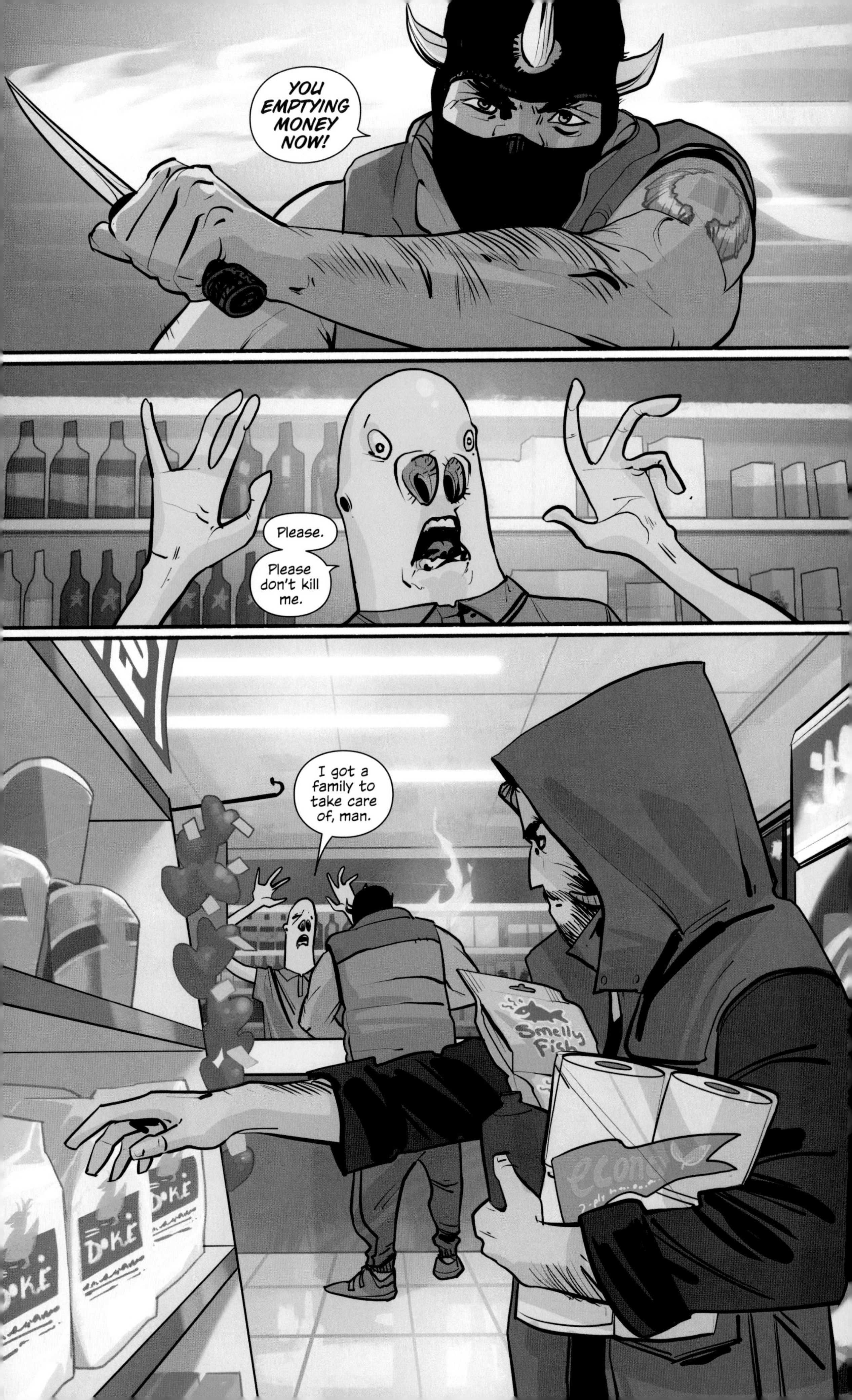
YOU EMPTYING MONEY NOW!
Please.
Please don't kill me.
I got a family to take care of, man.
Smelly Fish

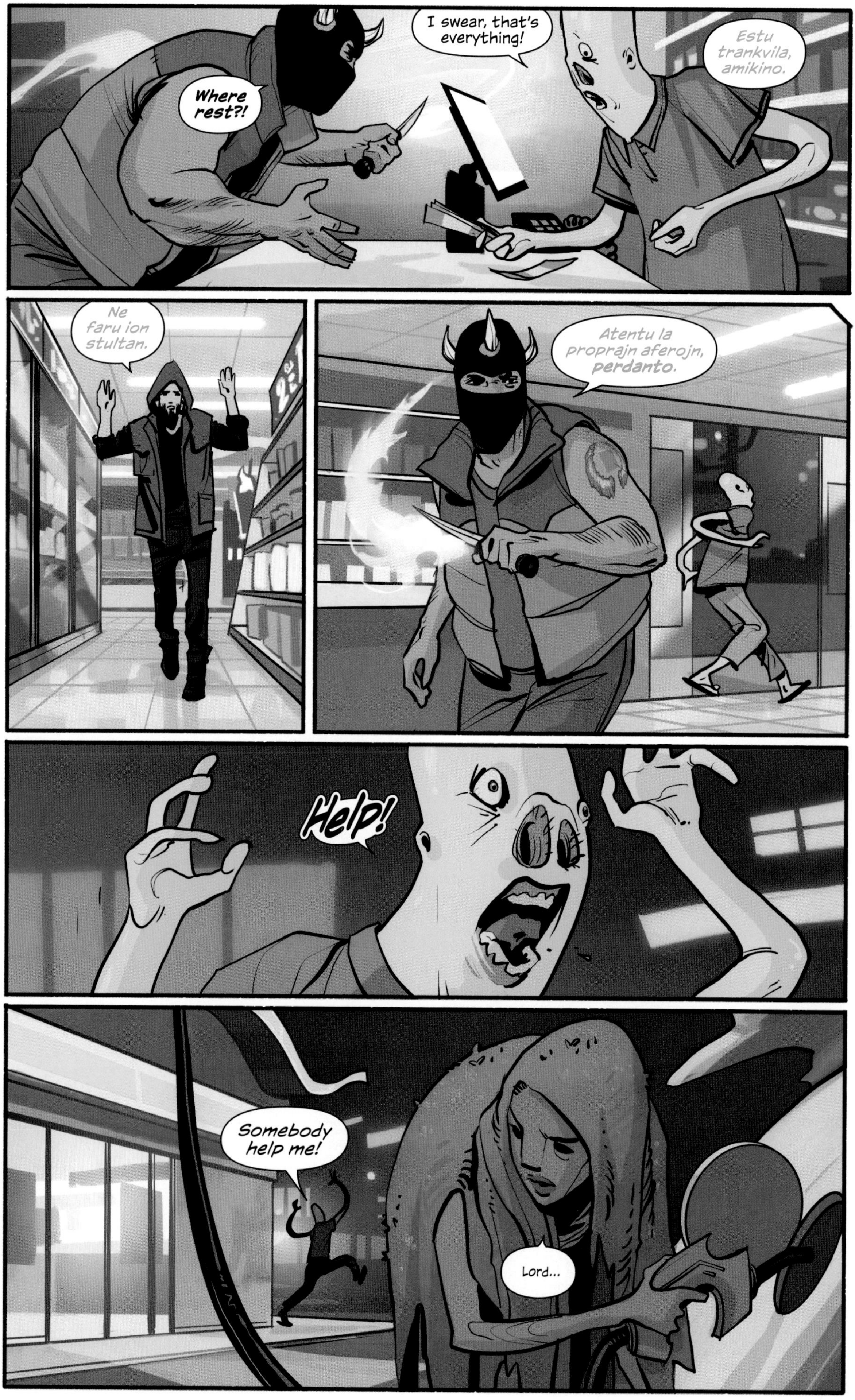
I swear, that's everything!
Where rest?!
Estu trankvila, amikino.
Ne faru ion stultan.
Atentu la proprajn aferojn, perdanto.
Help!
Somebody help me!
Lord...

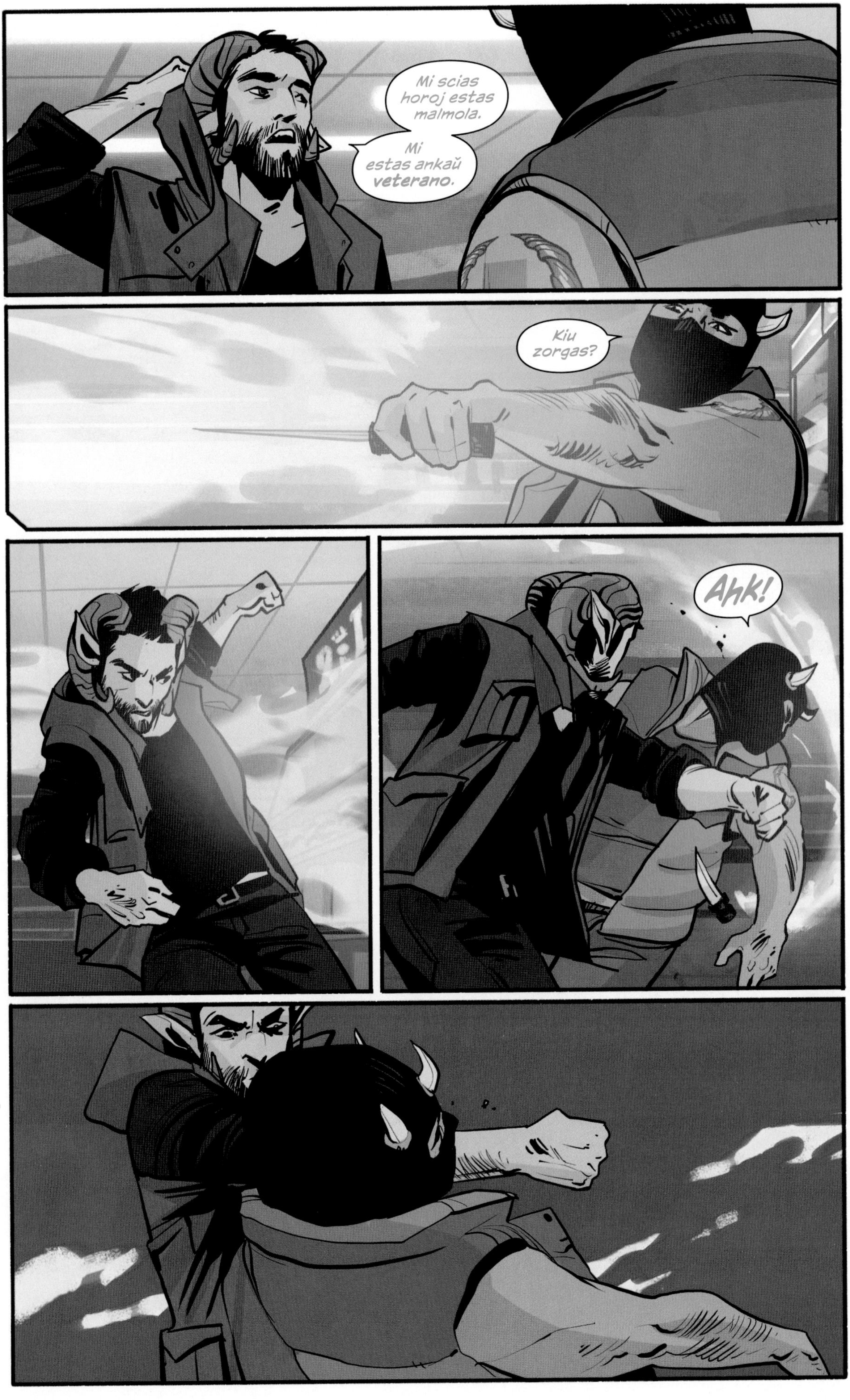
Mi scias horoj estas malmola.
Mi estas ankaŭ veterano.
Kiu zorgas?
Ahk!

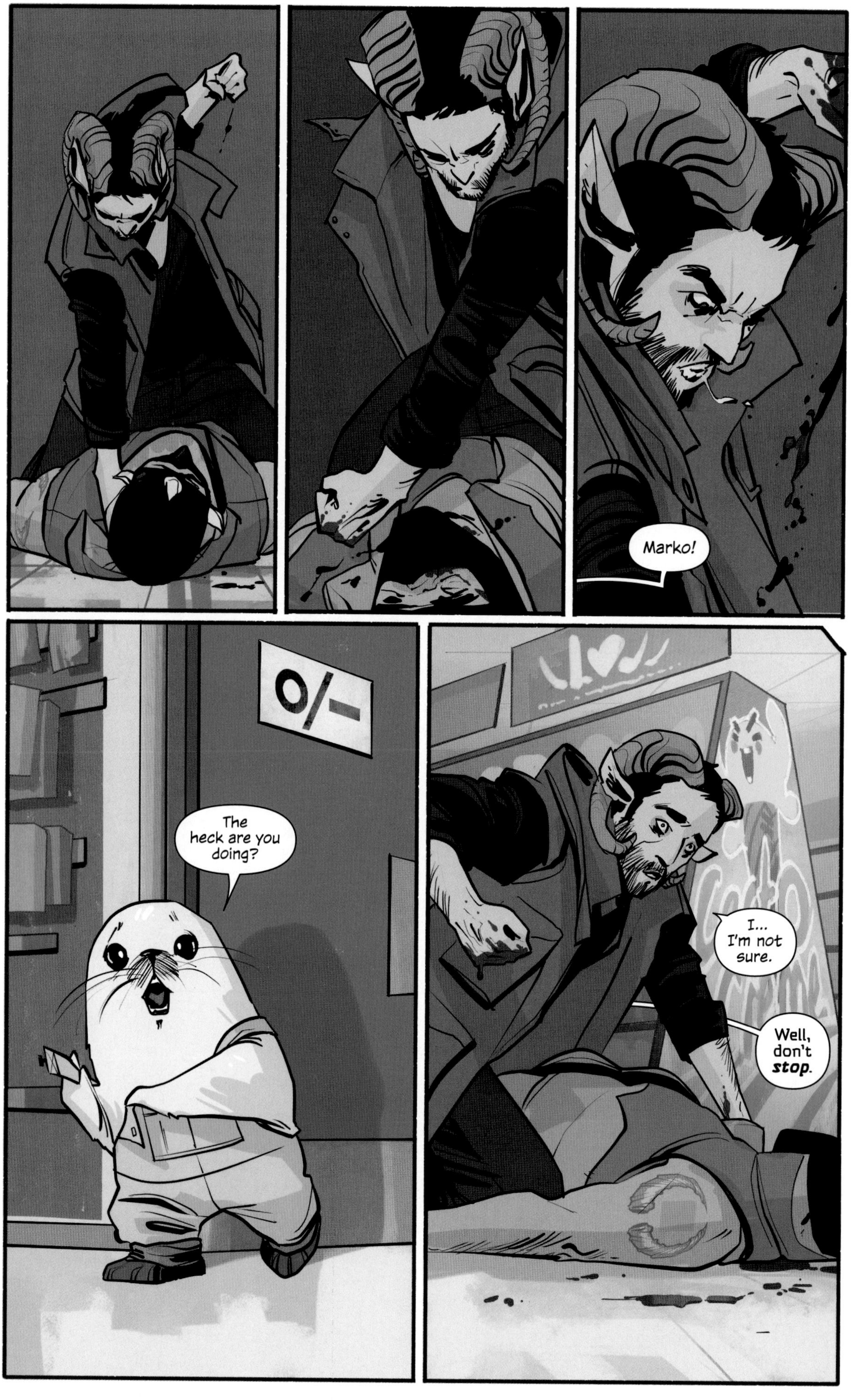
Marko!
0/-
The heck are you doing?
I... I'm not sure.
Well, don't *stop*.

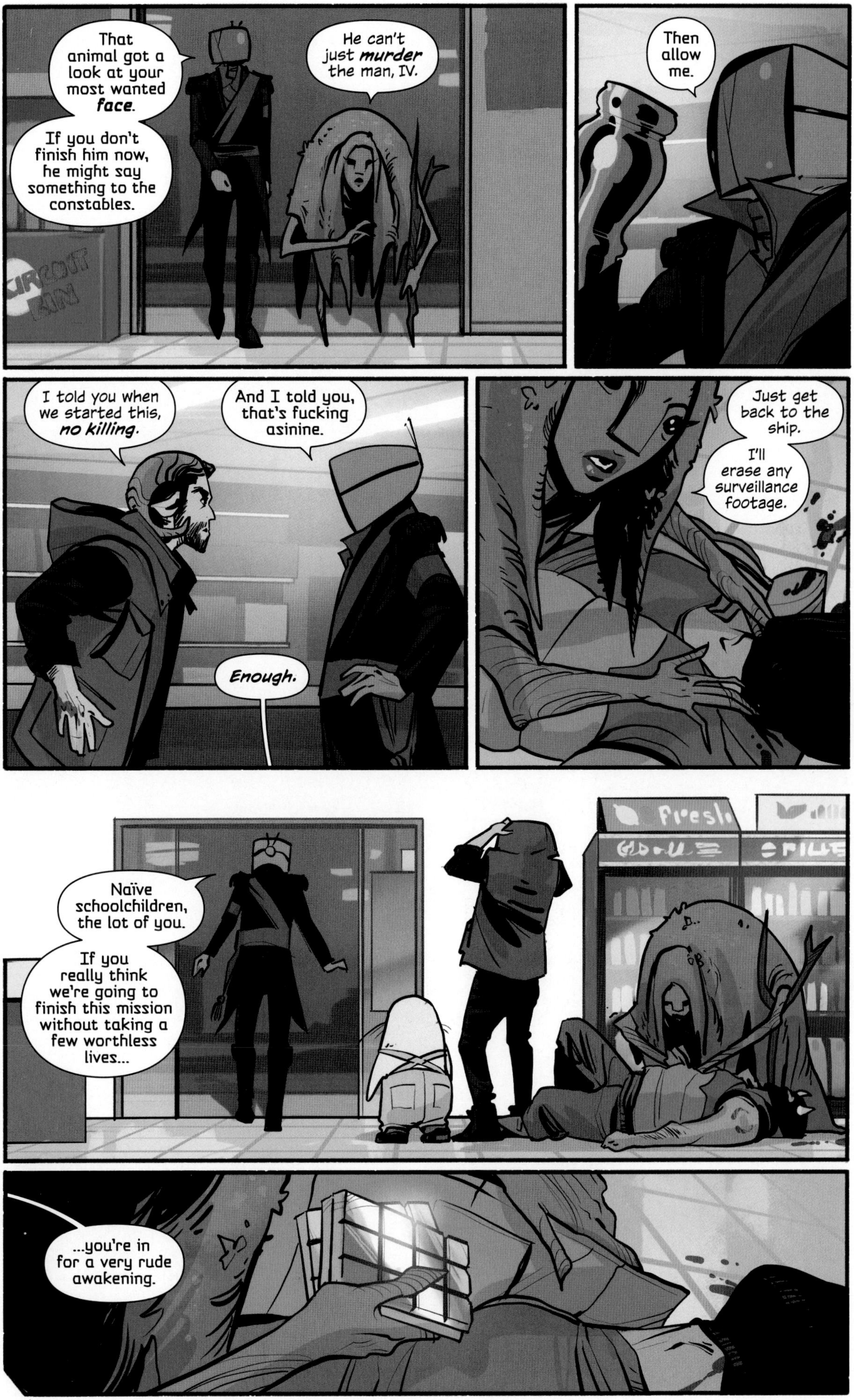
That animal got a look at your most wanted *face*.
If you don't finish him now, he might say something to the constables.
He can't just *murder* the man, IV.
Then allow me.
I told you when we started this, *no killing*.
And I told you, that's fucking asinine.
Enough.
Just get back to the ship.
I'll erase any surveillance footage.
Naïve schoolchildren, the lot of you.
If you really think we're going to finish this mission without taking a few worthless lives...
...you're in for a very rude awakening.

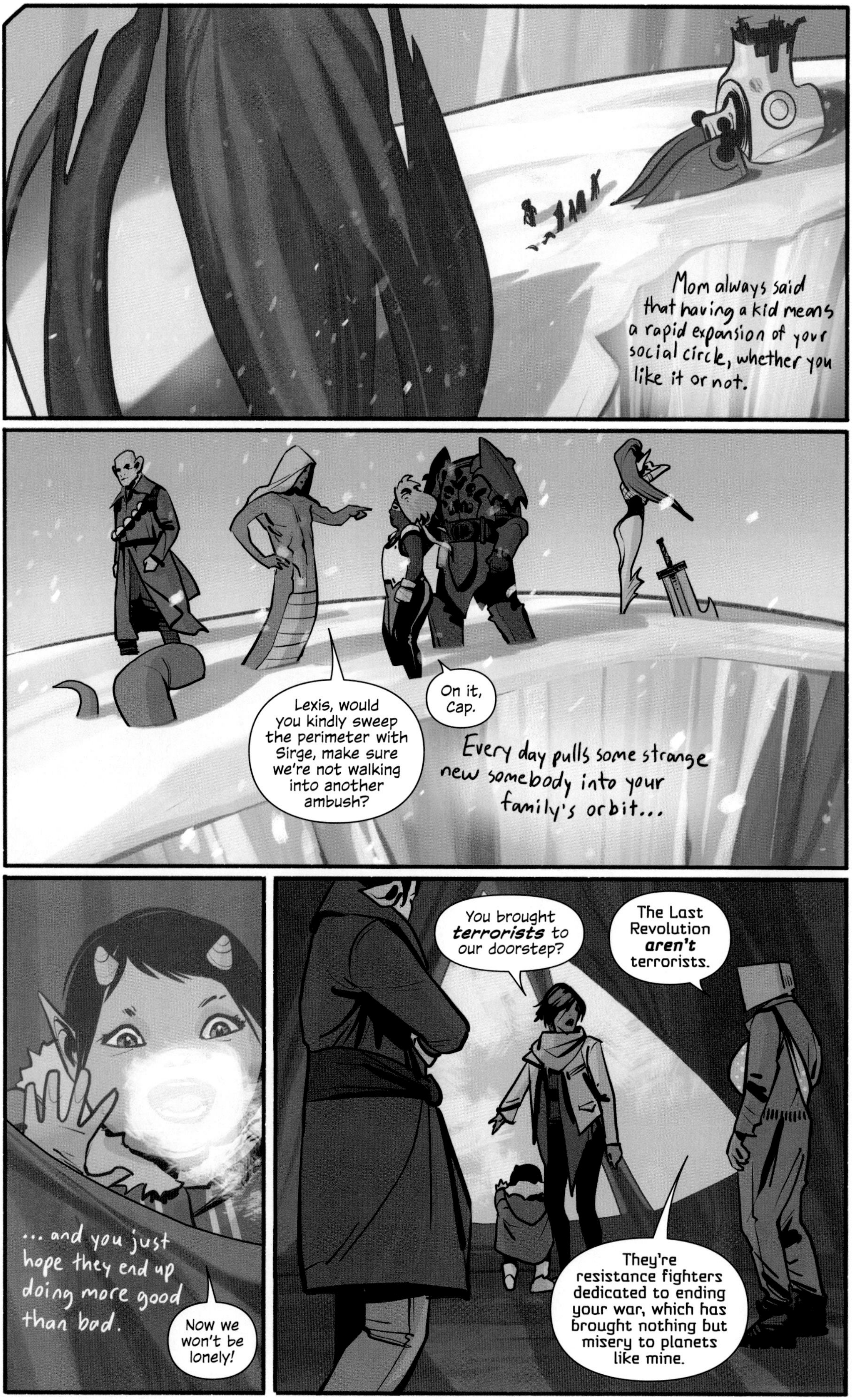
Mom always said that having a kid means a rapid expansion of your social circle, whether you like it or not.
Lexis, would you kindly sweep the perimeter with Sirge, make sure we're not walking into another ambush?
On it, Cap.
Every day pulls some strange new somebody into your family's orbit...
... and you just hope they end up doing more good than bad.
Now we won't be lonely!
You brought **terrorists** to our doorstep?
The Last Revolution **aren't** terrorists.
They're resistance fighters dedicated to ending your war, which has brought nothing but misery to planets like mine.

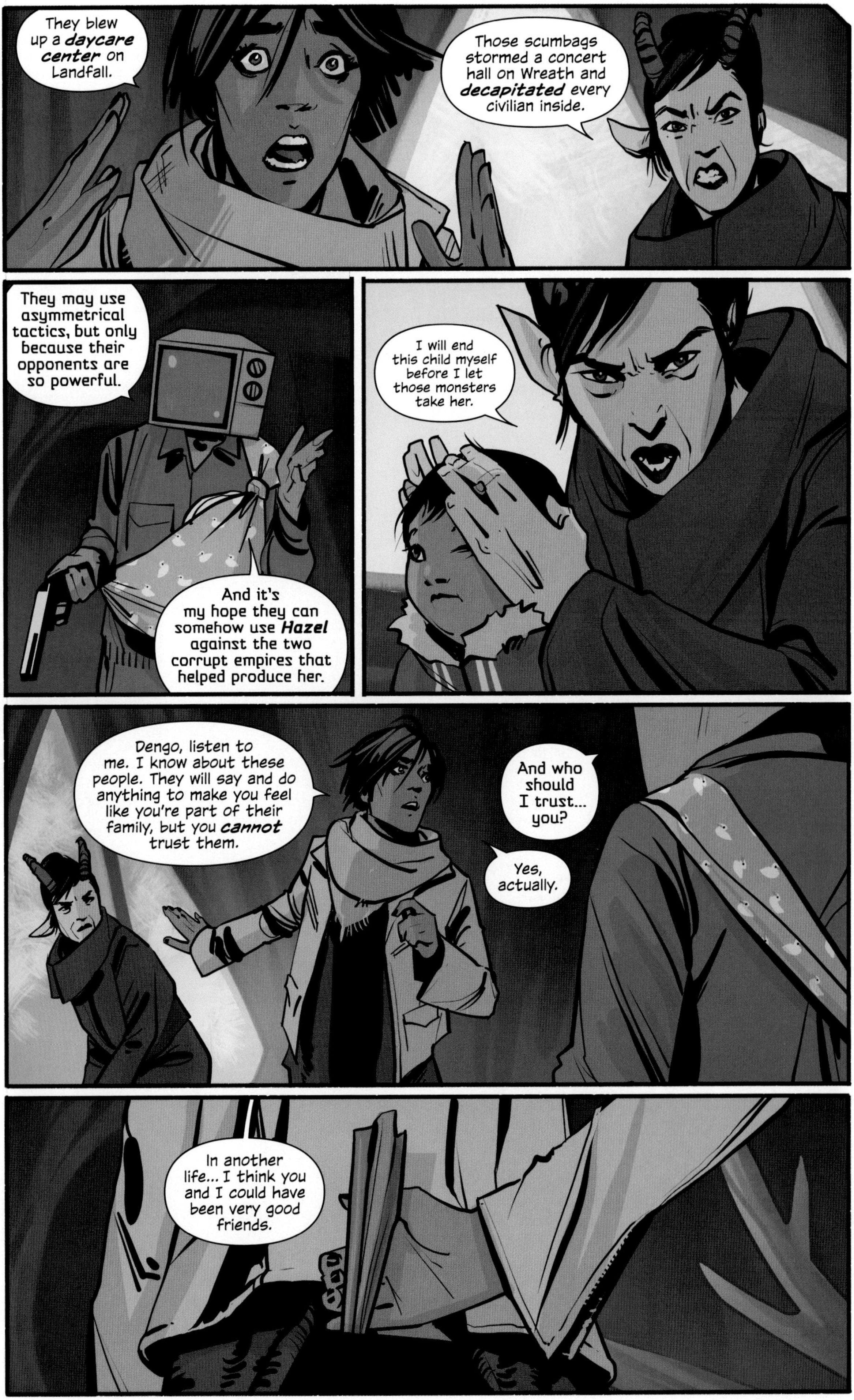
They blew up a daycare center on Landfall.
Those scumbags stormed a concert hall on Wreath and decapitated every civilian inside.
They may use asymmetrical tactics, but only because their opponents are so powerful.
And it's my hope they can somehow use Hazel against the two corrupt empires that helped produce her.
I will end this child myself before I let those monsters take her.
Dengo, listen to me. I know about these people. They will say and do anything to make you feel like you're part of their family, but you cannot trust them.
And who should I trust... you?
Yes, actually.
In another life... I think you and I could have been very good friends.

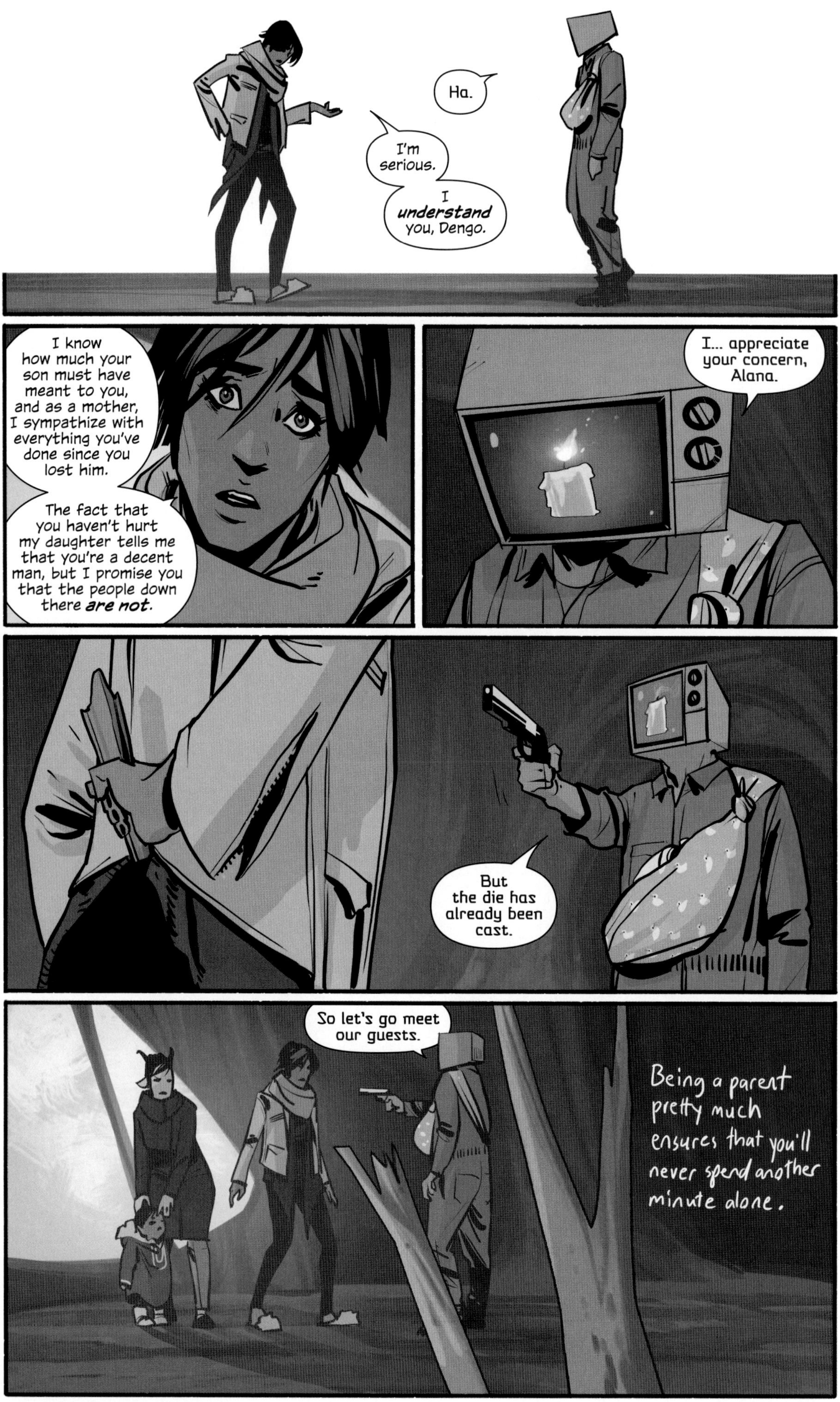
Ha.
I'm serious.
I *understand* you, Dengo.
I know how much your son must have meant to you, and as a mother, I sympathize with everything you've done since you lost him.
The fact that you haven't hurt my daughter tells me that you're a decent man, but I promise you that the people down there *are not*.
I... appreciate your concern, Alana.
But the die has already been cast.
So let's go meet our guests.
Being a parent pretty much ensures that you'll never spend another minute alone.

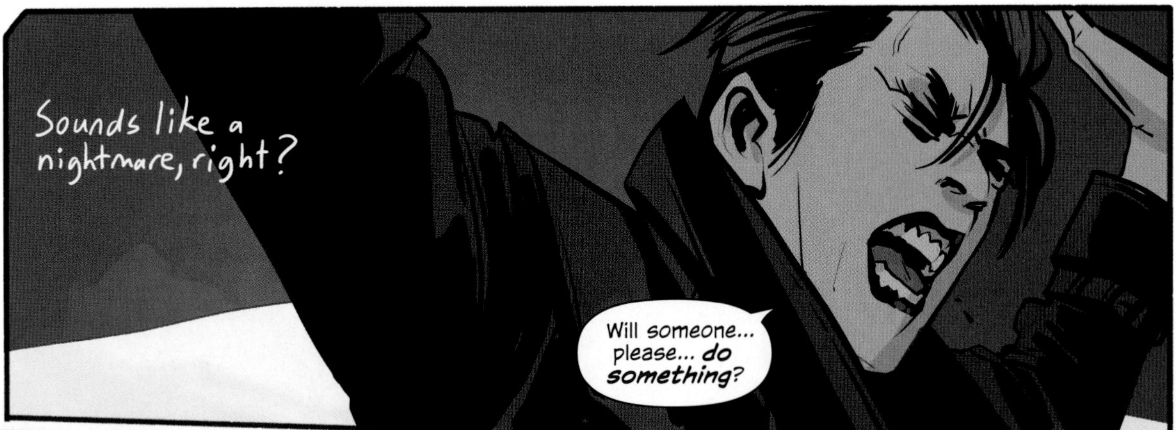
Sounds like a nightmare, right?
Will someone... please... **do *something***?

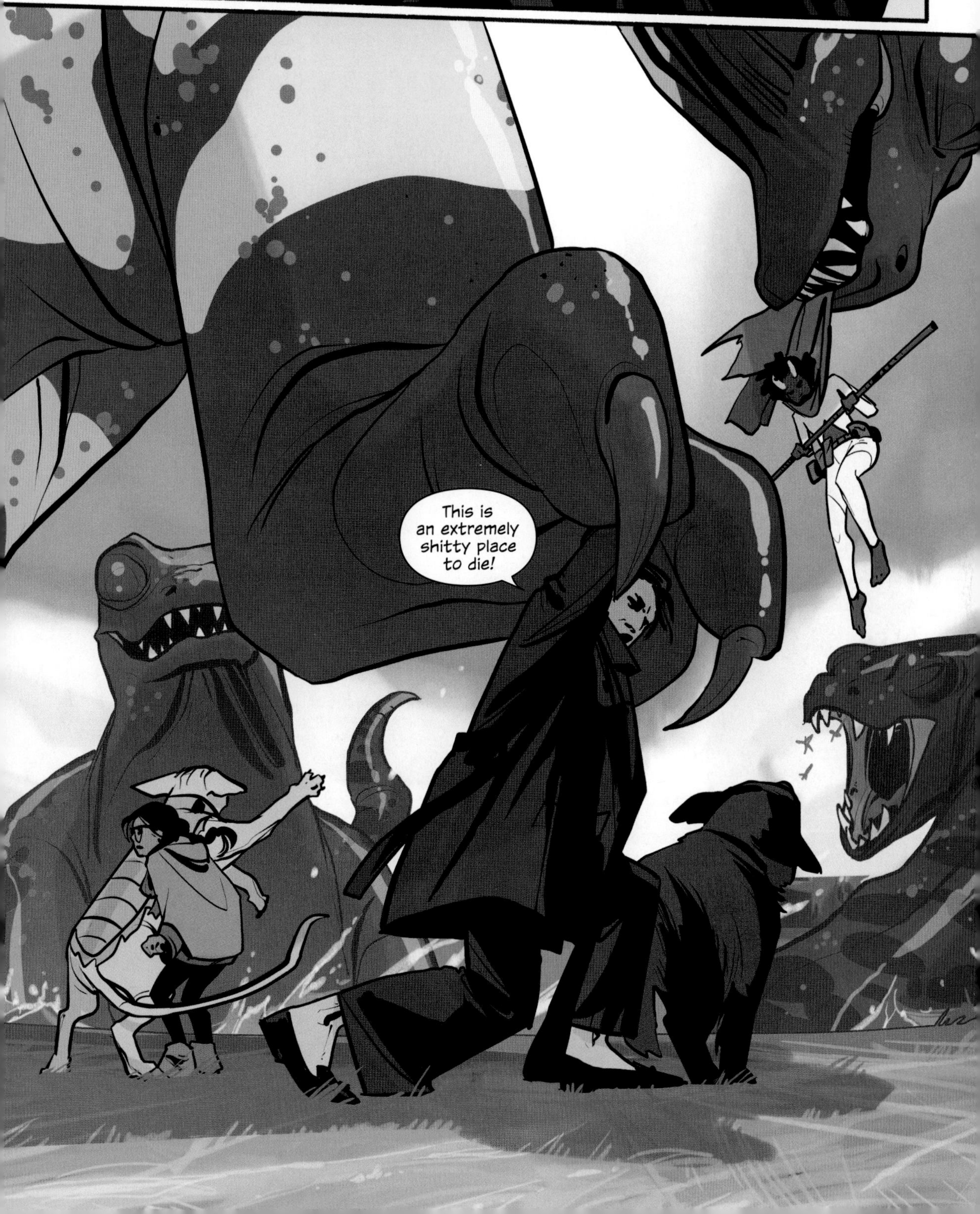
This is an extremely shitty place to die!

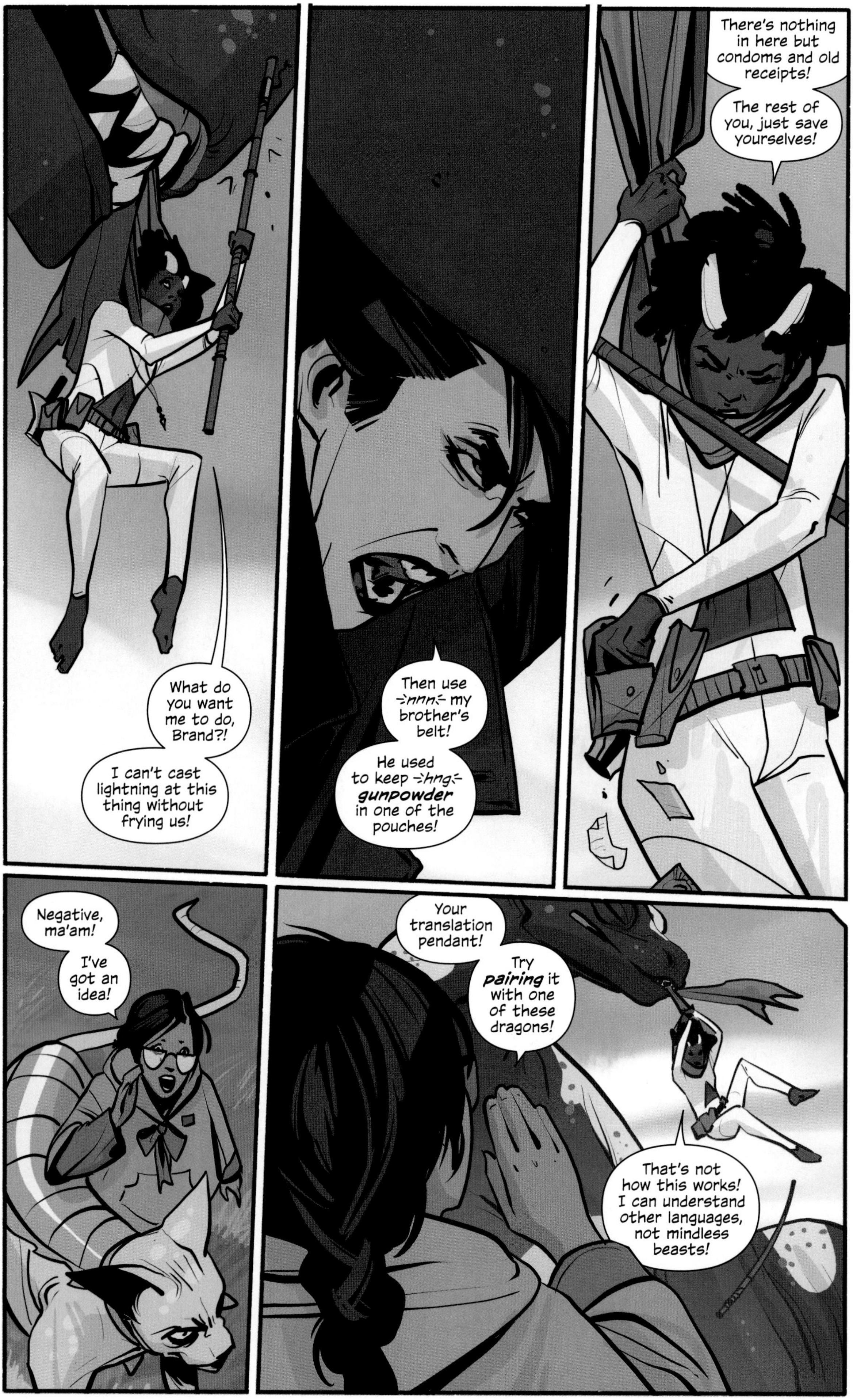
What do you want me to do, Brand?!
I can't cast lightning at this thing without frying us!
Then use -nnn- my brother's belt!
He used to keep -hng- ***gunpowder*** in one of the pouches!
There's nothing in here but condoms and old receipts!
The rest of you, just save yourselves!
Negative, ma'am!
I've got an idea!
Your translation pendant!
Try ***pairing*** it with one of these dragons!
That's not how this works! I can understand other languages, not mindless beasts!

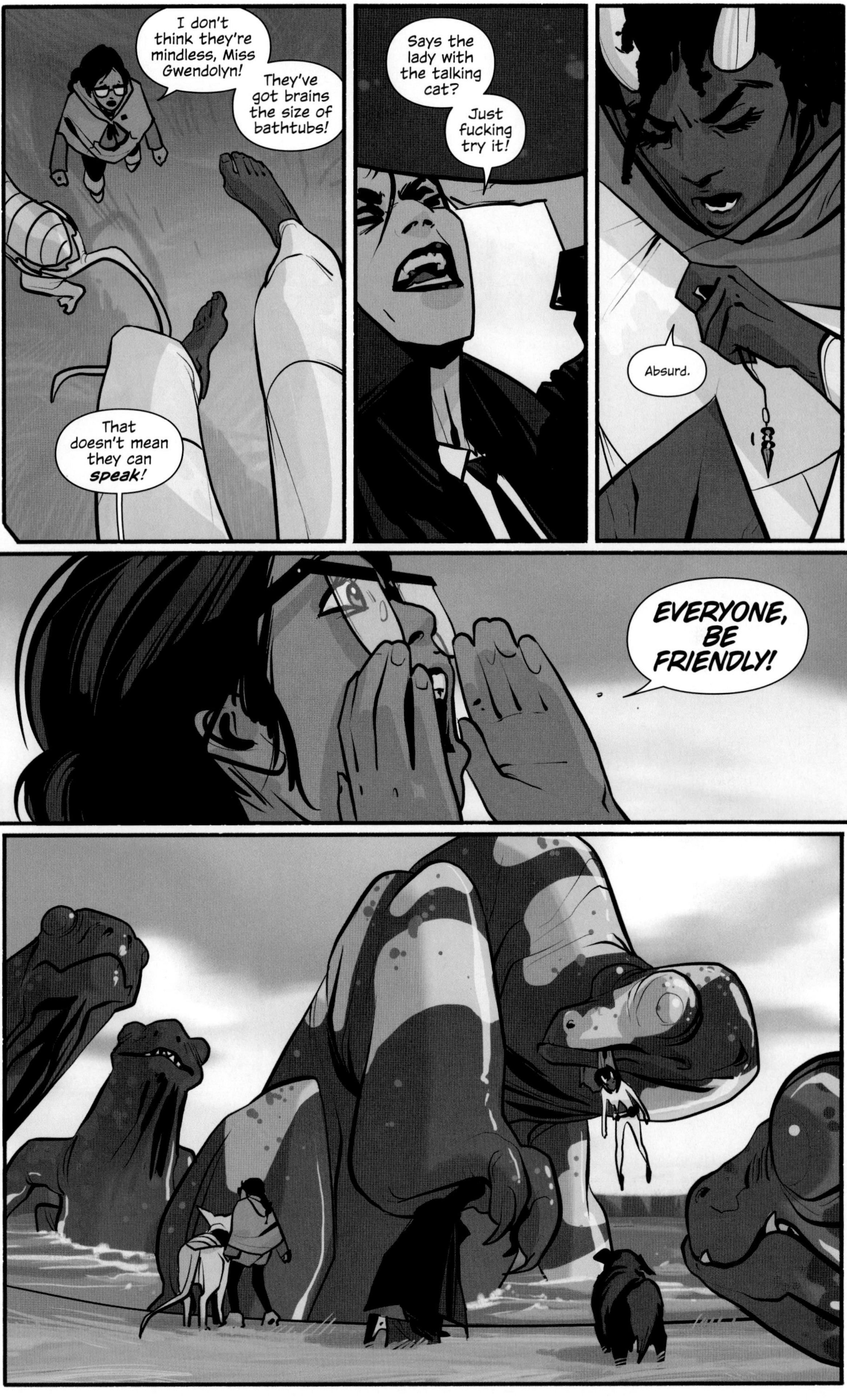
I don't think they're mindless, Miss Gwendolyn!
They've got brains the size of bathtubs!
That doesn't mean they can *speak*!
Says the lady with the talking cat?
Just fucking try it!
Absurd.
EVERYONE, BE FRIENDLY!

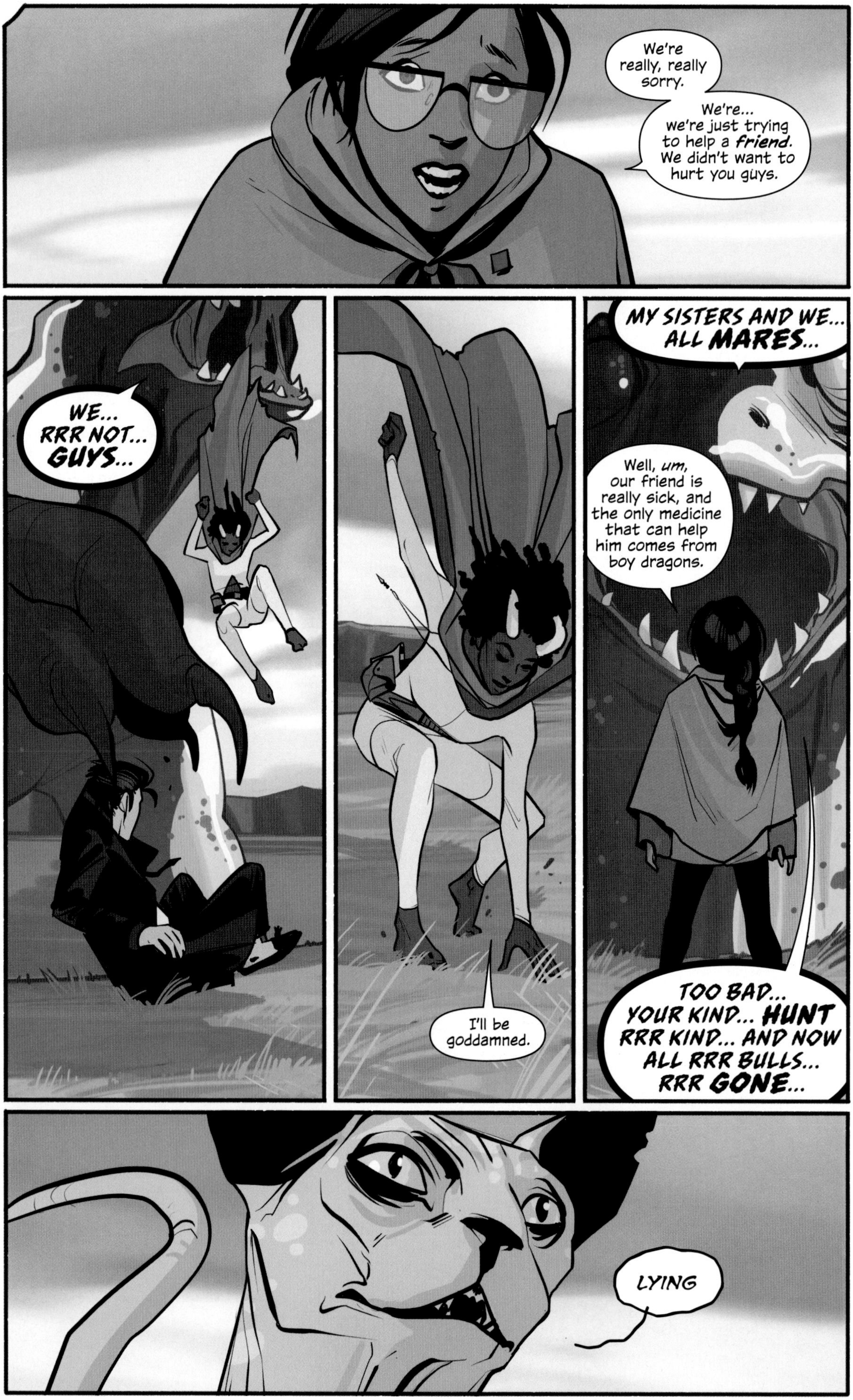
We're really, really sorry.
We're... we're just trying to help a *friend*. We didn't want to hurt you guys.
WE... RRR NOT... GUYS...
I'll be goddamned.
MY SISTERS AND WE... ALL MARES...
Well, *um*, our friend is really sick, and the only medicine that can help him comes from boy dragons.
TOO BAD... YOUR KIND... HUNT RRR KIND... AND NOW ALL RRR BULLS... RRR GONE...
LYING

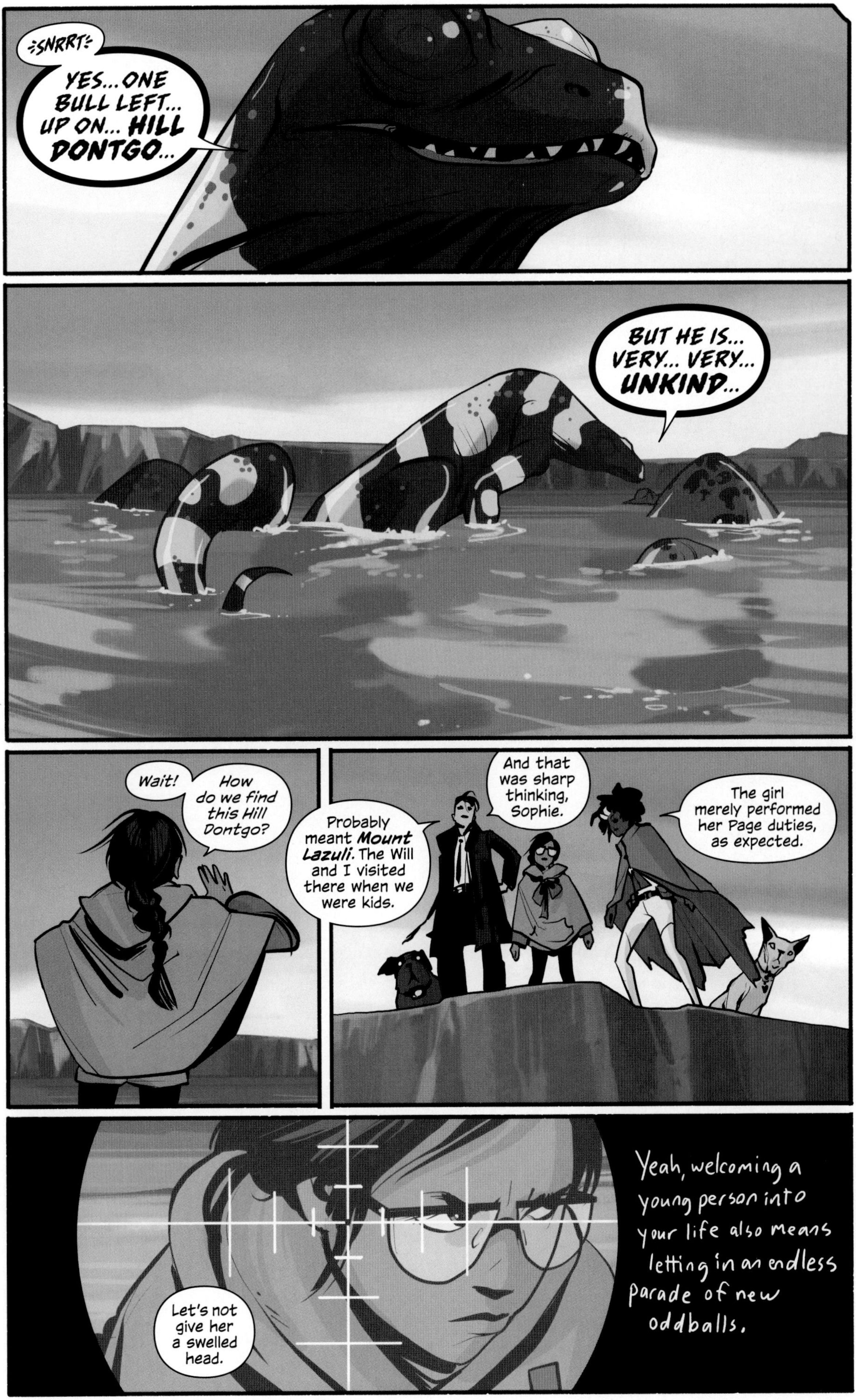

SNRRT
YES... ONE BULL LEFT... UP ON... HILL DONTGO...
BUT HE IS... VERY... VERY... UNKIND...
Wait!
How do we find this Hill Dontgo?
Probably meant Mount Lazuli. The Will and I visited there when we were kids.
And that was sharp thinking, Sophie.
The girl merely performed her Page duties, as expected.
Yeah, welcoming a young person into your life also means letting in an endless parade of new oddballs.
Let's not give her a swelled head.

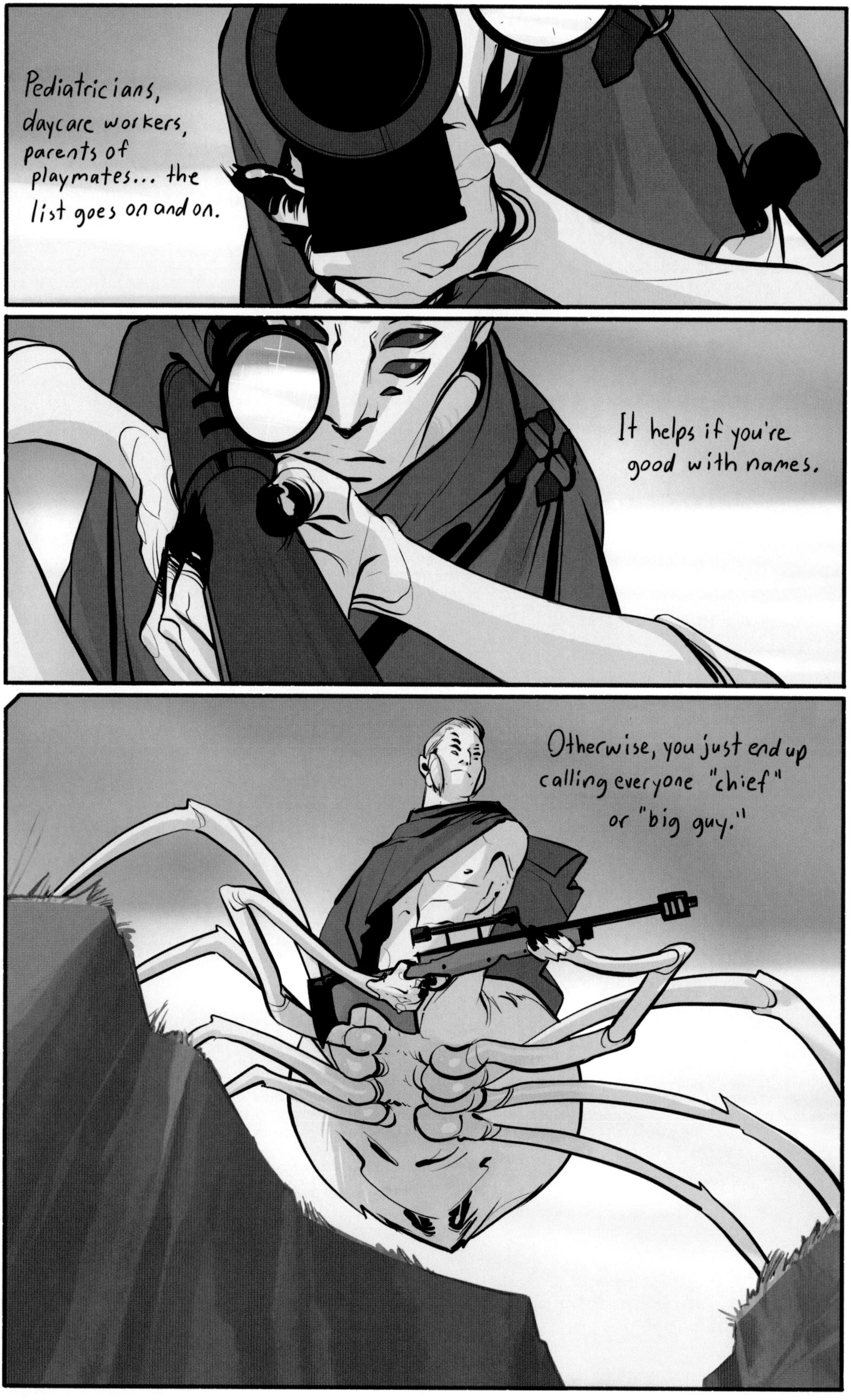

Pediatricians, daycare workers, parents of playmates... the list goes on and on.
It helps if you're good with names.
Otherwise, you just end up calling everyone "chief" or "big guy."

Cheer up, Beard of Sorrow.

We're going to get your family back.

All I care about is getting them to safety. I don't expect my wife and child to ever take *me* back.

What are you talking about?

I'm sick, Yuma. No matter how hard I try to quit, I'm obviously **addicted** to the very thing I've taken an oath against.

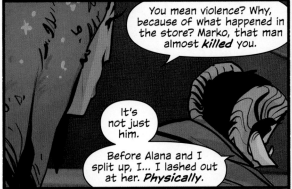

You mean violence? Why, because of what happened in the store? Marko, that man almost **killed** you.

It's not just him.

Before Alana and I split up, I... I lashed out at her. **Physically.**

It was horrific, **unforgivable**.

If I can't be trusted around the love of my life, why should I be allowed near Hazel again?

Whatever is inside of me is --

-- like the ink from some ancient sea creature. It's so perfectly black out there you can almost taste it.

Are you **high**?

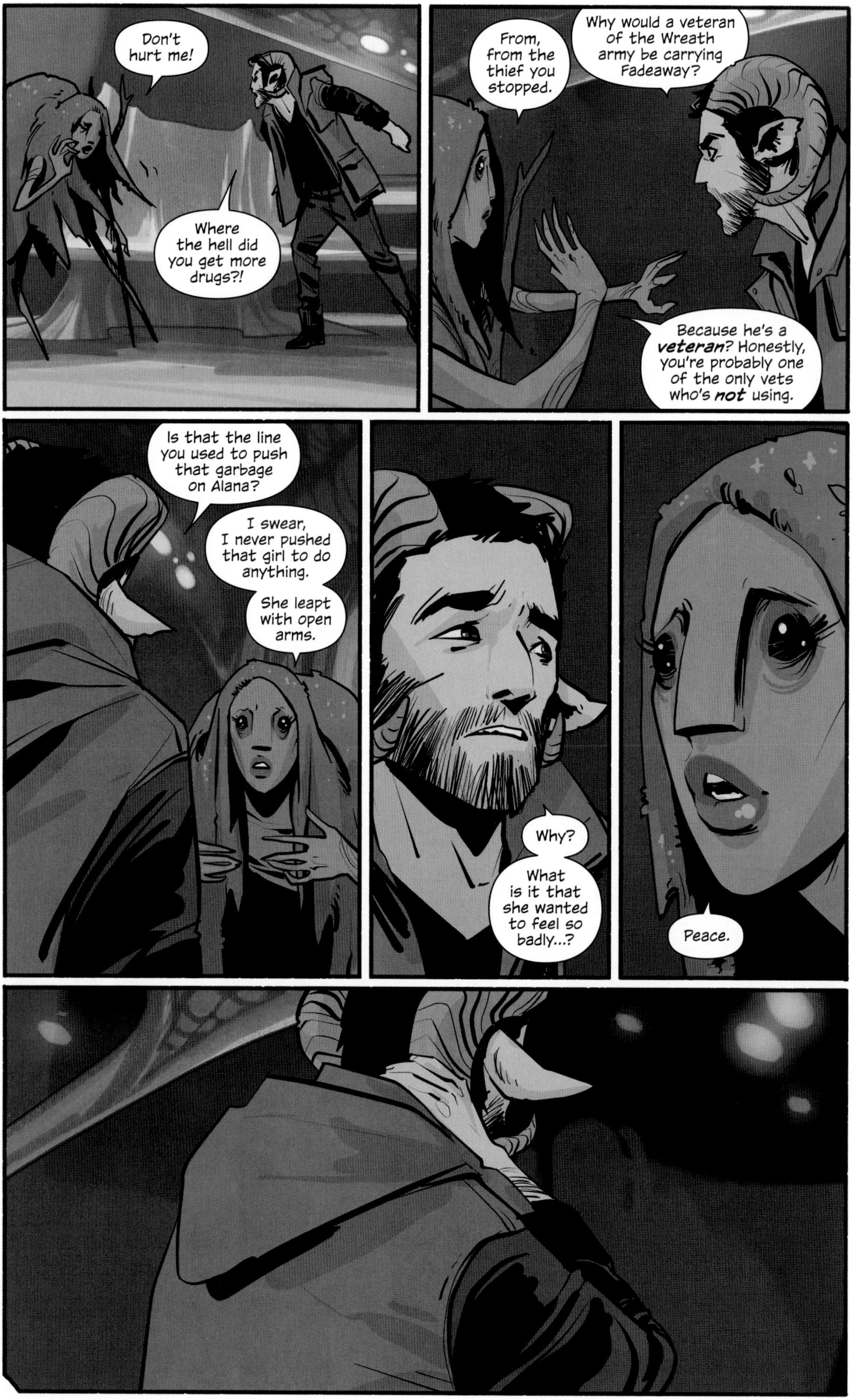
Don't hurt me!
Where the hell did you get more drugs?!
From, from the thief you stopped.
Why would a veteran of the Wreath army be carrying Fadeaway?
Because he's a *veteran*? Honestly, you're probably one of the only vets who's *not* using.
Is that the line you used to push that garbage on Alana?
I swear, I never pushed that girl to do anything.
She leapt with open arms.
Why?
What is it that she wanted to feel so badly...?
Peace.

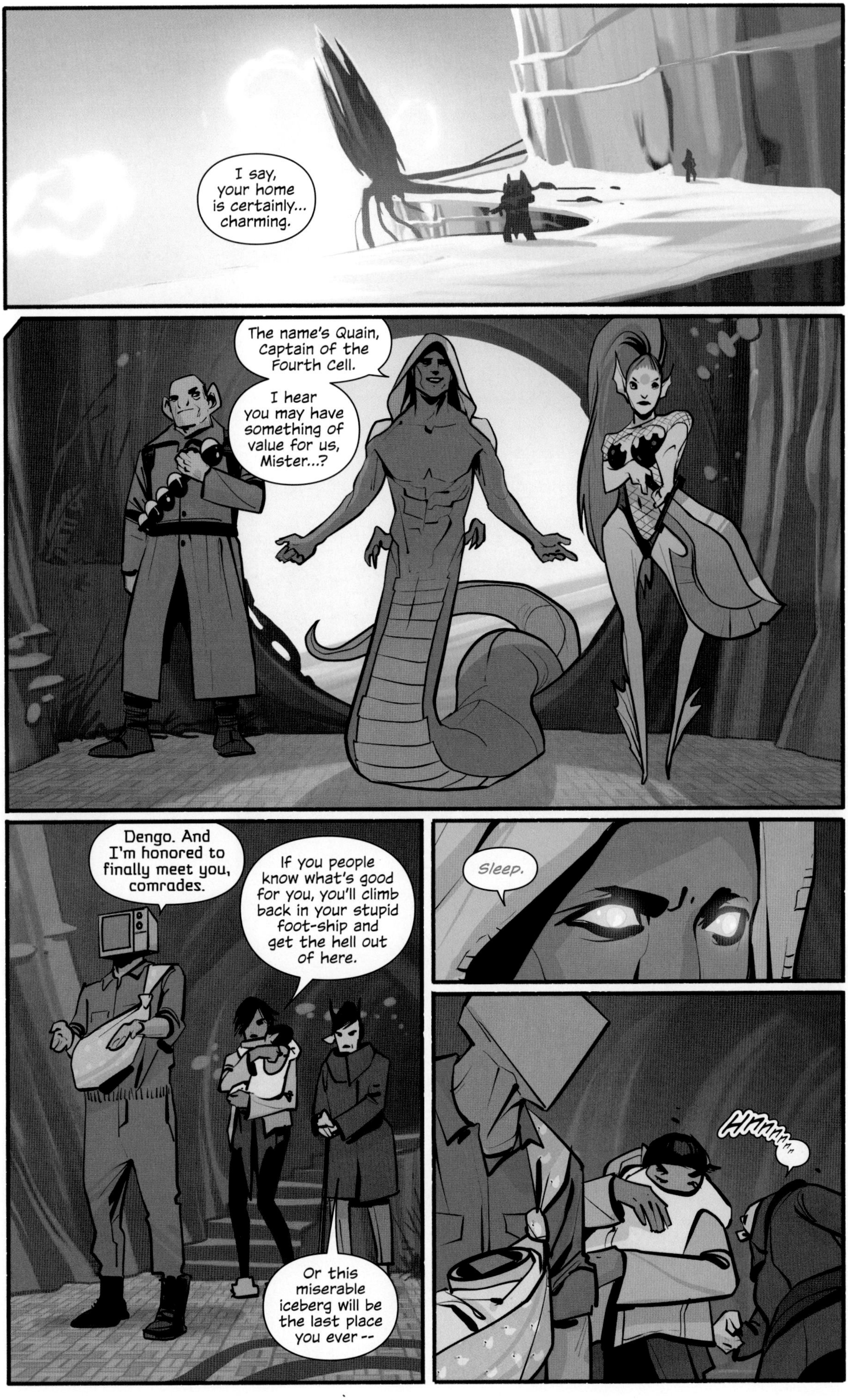
I say, your home is certainly... charming.
The name's Quain, Captain of the Fourth Cell.
I hear you may have something of value for us, Mister...?
Dengo. And I'm honored to finally meet you, comrades.
If you people know what's good for you, you'll climb back in your stupid foot-ship and get the hell out of here.
Or this miserable iceberg will be the last place you ever --
Sleep.

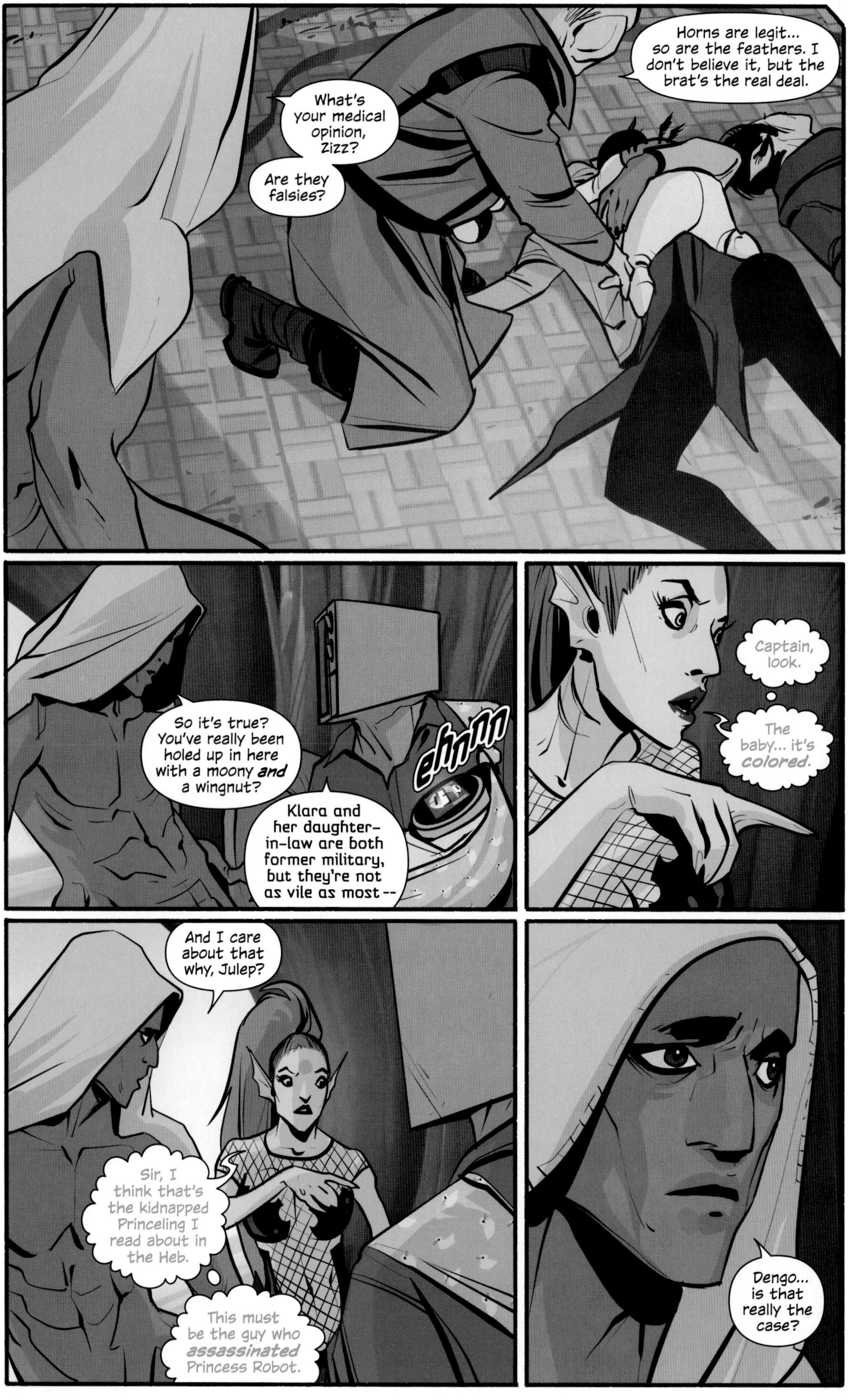
What's your medical opinion, Zizz?
Are they falsies?
Horns are legit... so are the feathers. I don't believe it, but the brat's the real deal.
So it's true? You've really been holed up in here with a moony *and* a wingnut?
ehnnn
Klara and her daughter-in-law are both former military, but they're not as vile as most --
Captain, look.
The baby... it's *colored*.
And I care about that why, Julep?
Sir, I think that's the kidnapped Princeling I read about in the Heb.
This must be the guy who *assassinated* Princess Robot.
Dengo... is that really the case?

I, I only wanted this meeting to concern the hybrid girl, not my actions on --

Come here, you magnificent bastard.

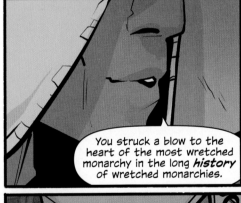

You struck a blow to the heart of the most wretched monarchy in the long *history* of wretched monarchies.

Brother, you and I are going to do wonderful things.

This is the moment when Denge began to suspect that my mom had been right.

How could he have forgotten everything he learned as a father?

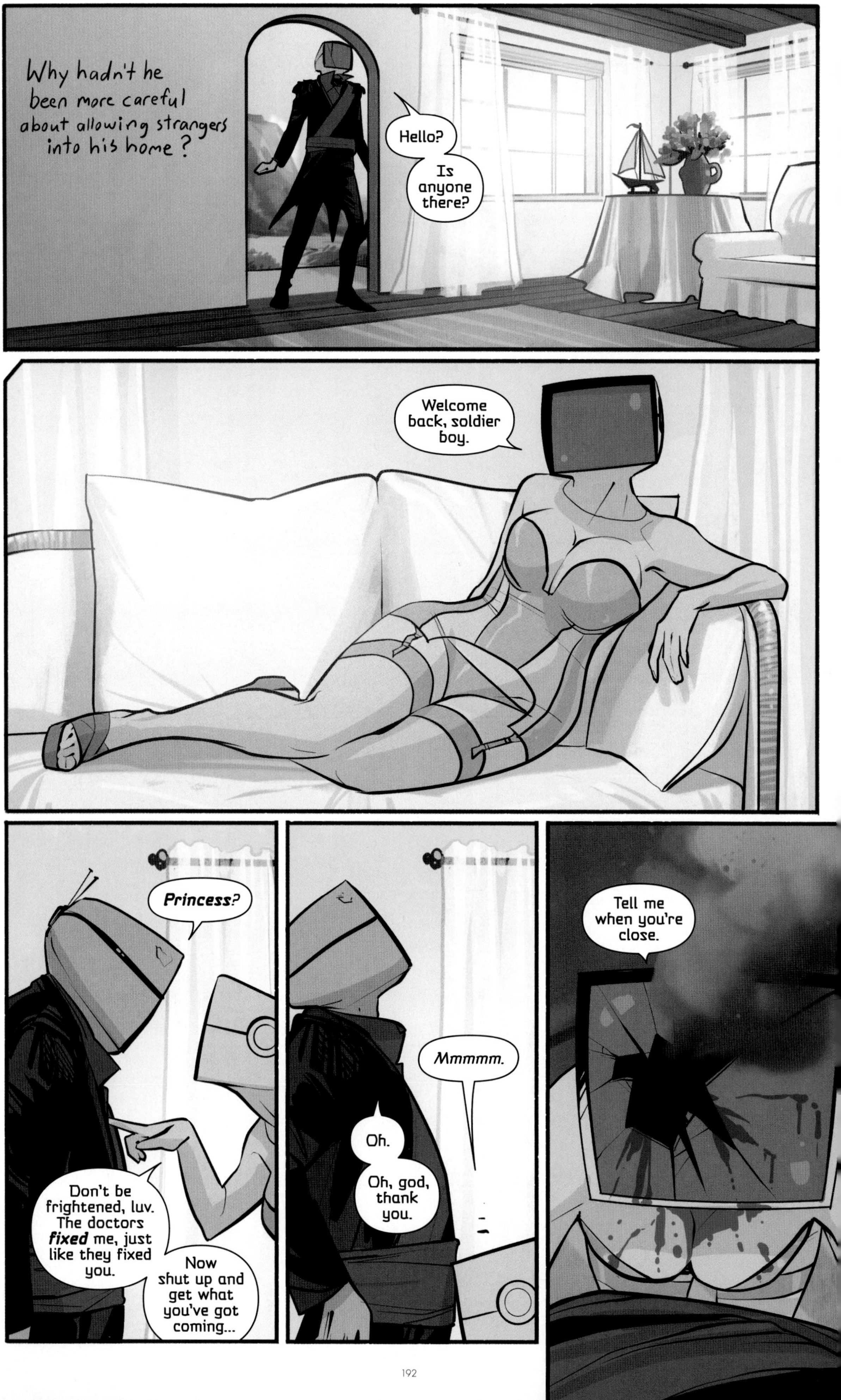
Why hadn't he been more careful about allowing strangers into his home?
Hello?
Is anyone there?
Welcome back, soldier boy.
Princess?
Don't be frightened, luv. The doctors fixed me, just like they fixed you.
Now shut up and get what you've got coming...
Mmmmm.
Oh.
Oh, god, thank you.
Tell me when you're close.

guh

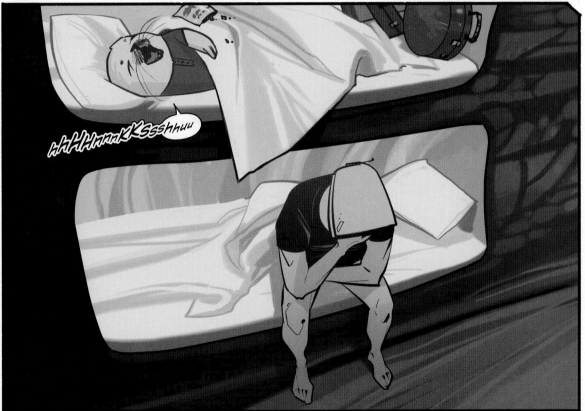

hhHhnnnKSsshhuu

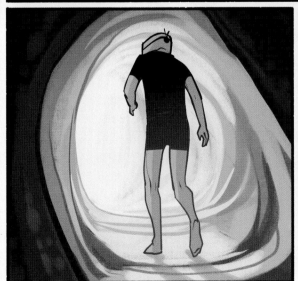

...bugger.

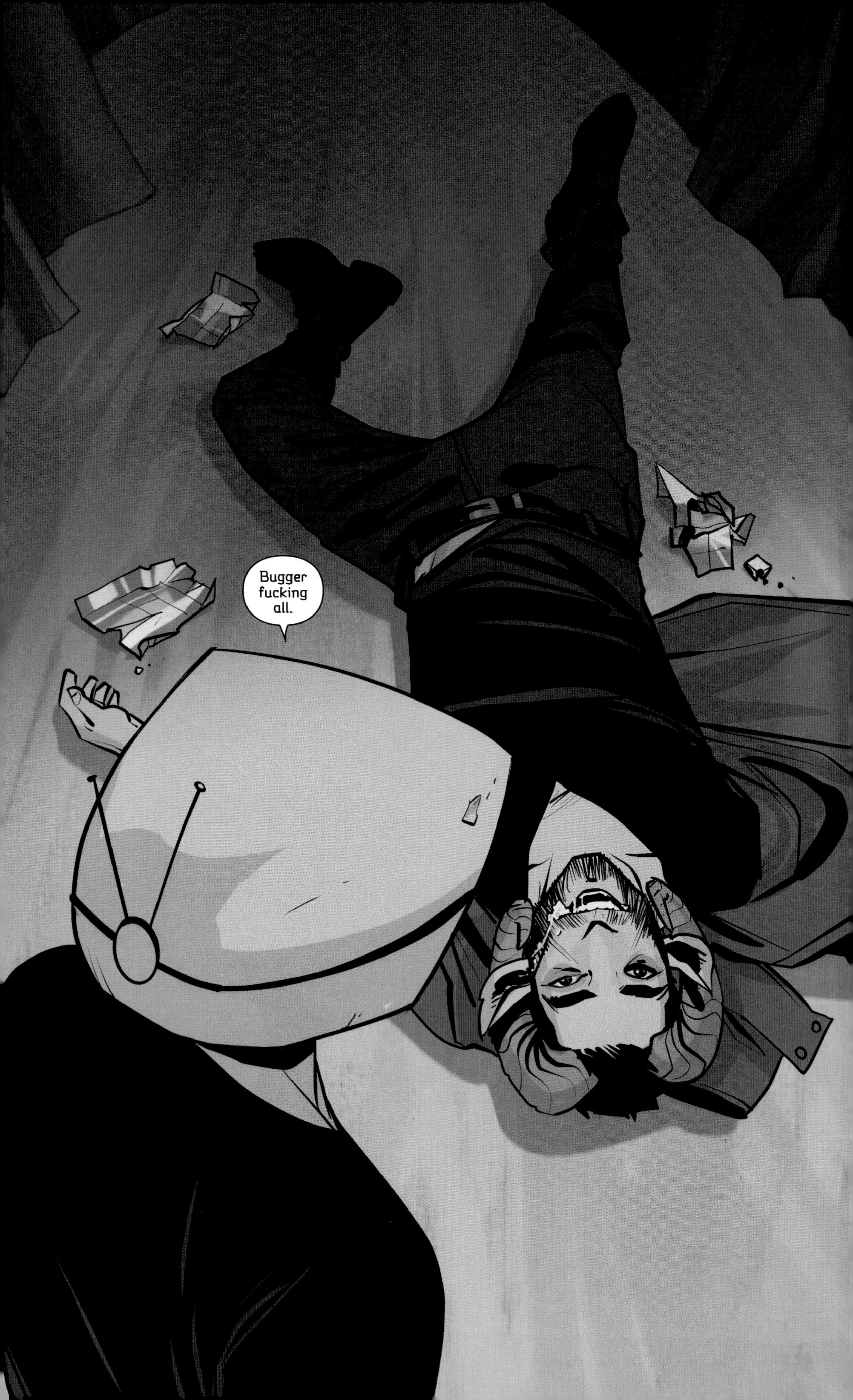
Bugger fucking all.

end chapter twenty-six

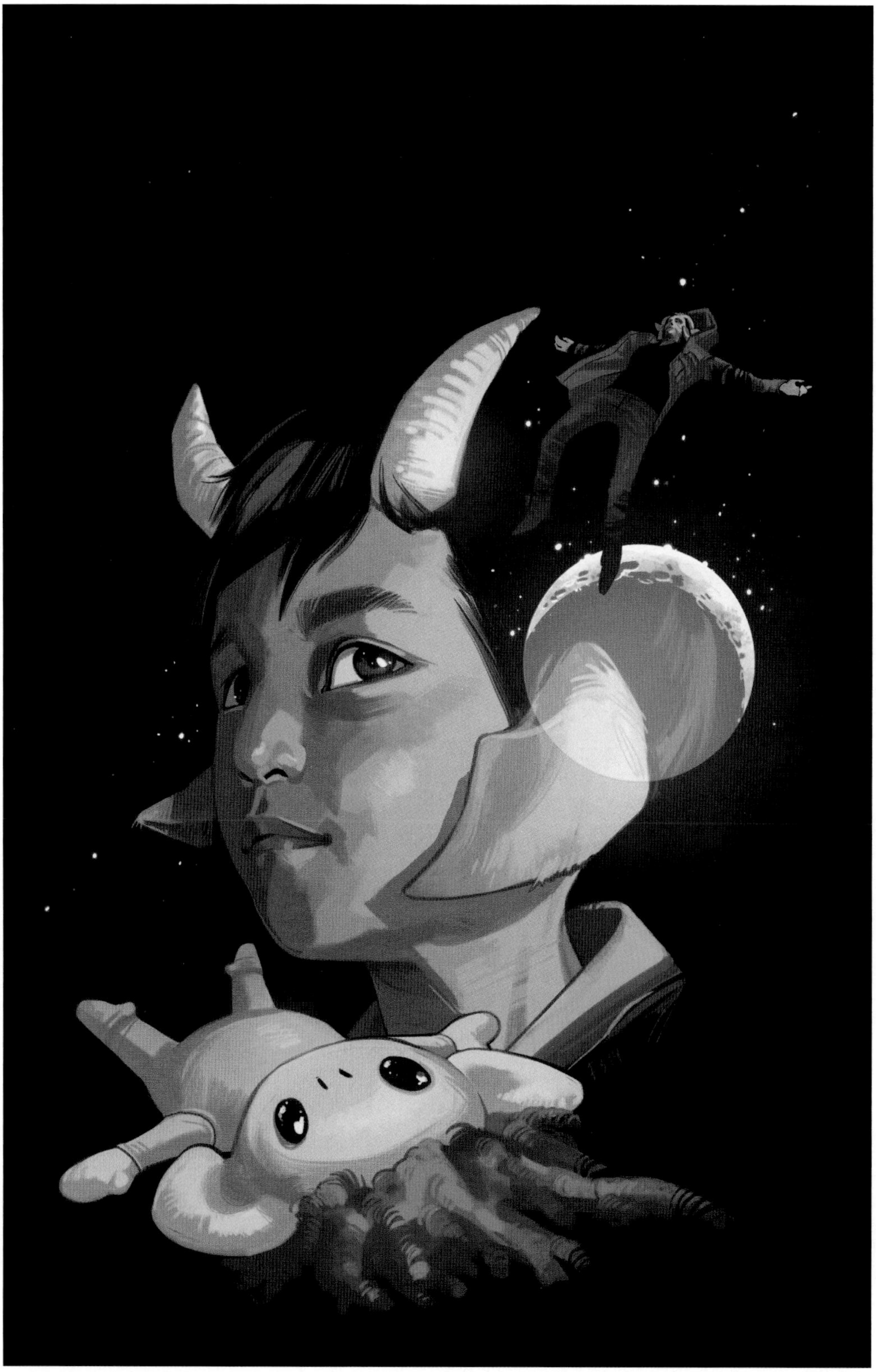

CHAPTER

TWENTY-SEVEN

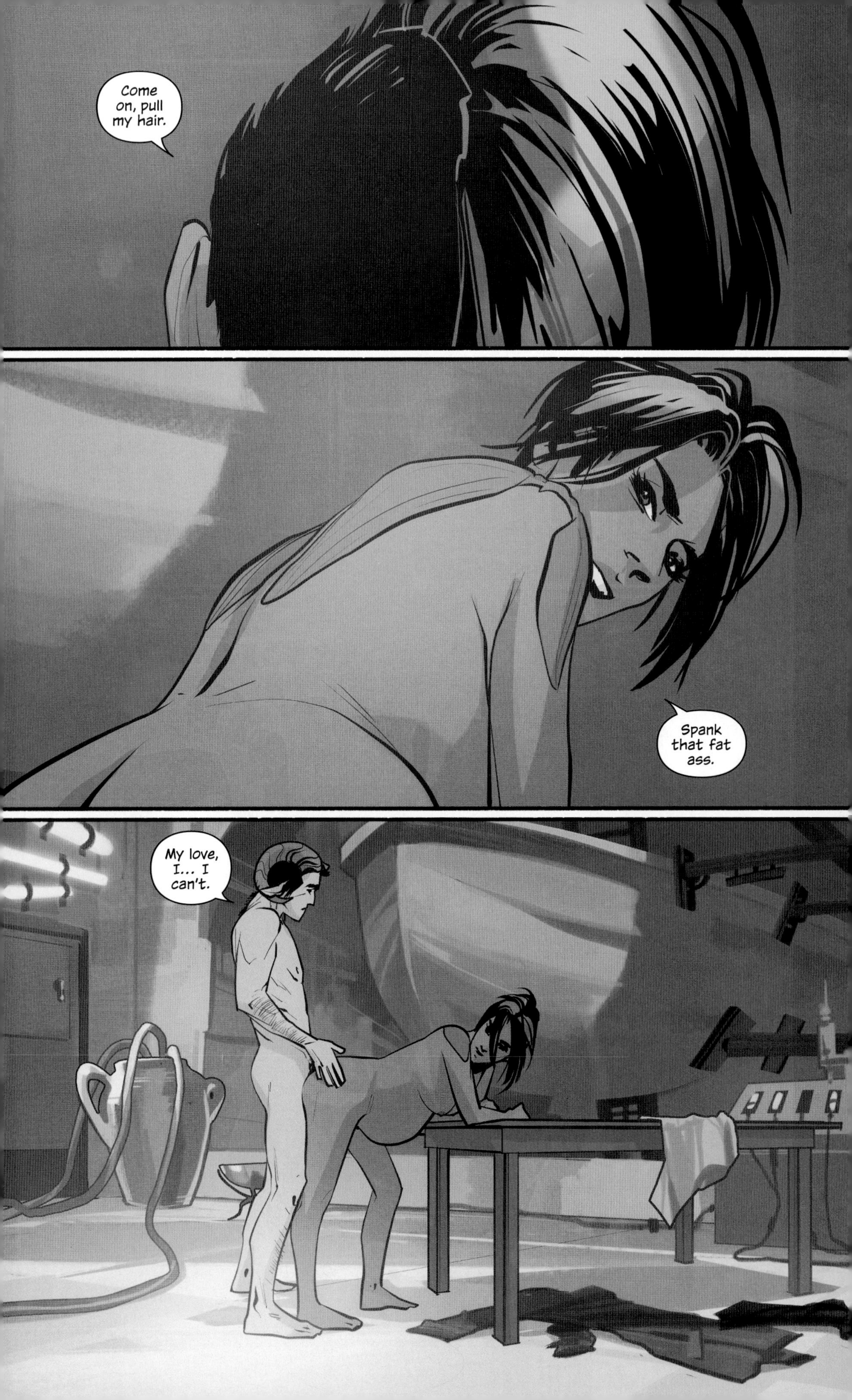
Come on, pull my hair.
Spank that fat ass.
My love, I... I can't.

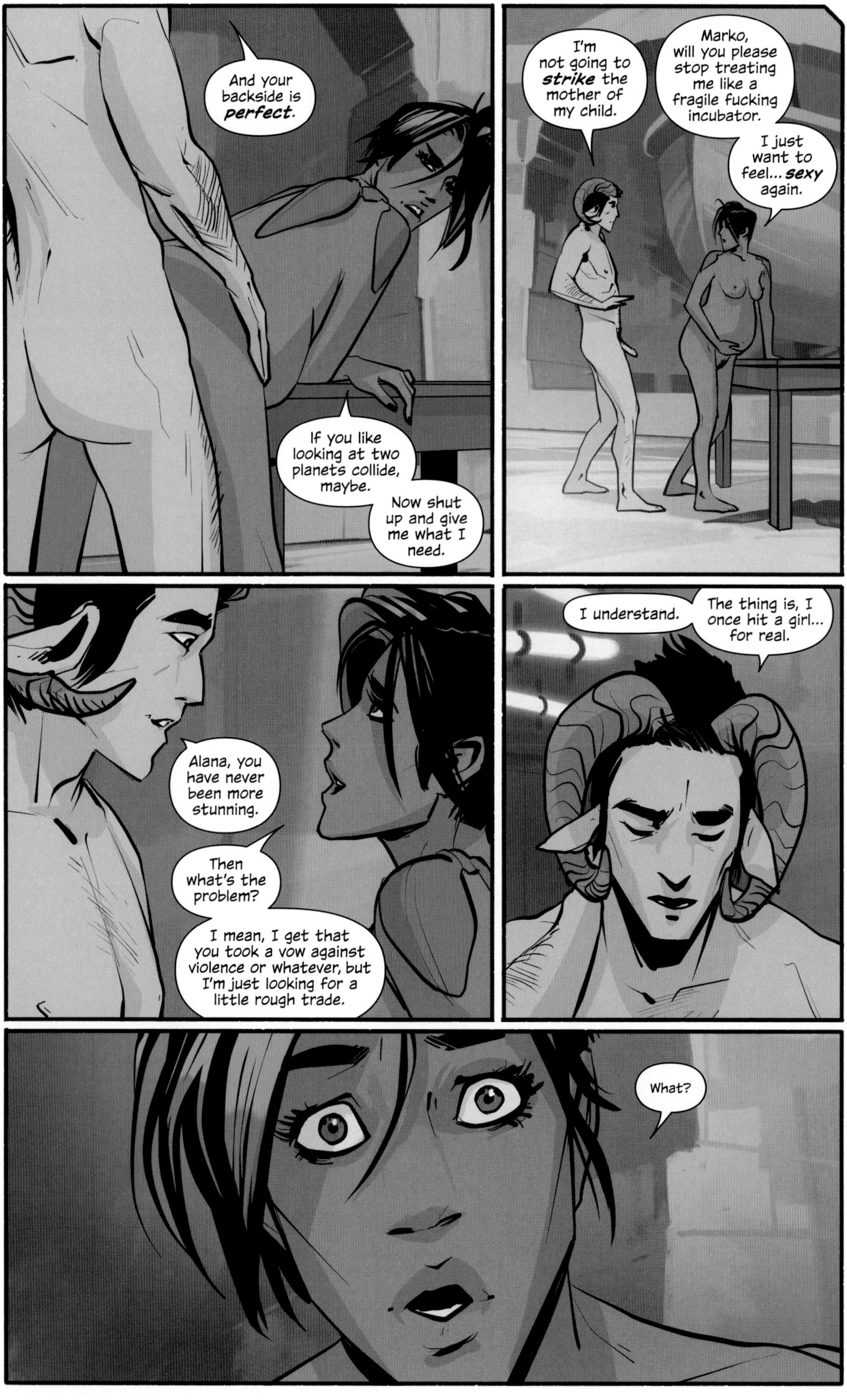

And your backside is *perfect*.
If you like looking at two planets collide, maybe.
Now shut up and give me what I need.
I'm not going to *strike* the mother of my child.
Marko, will you please stop treating me like a fragile fucking incubator.
I just want to feel... *sexy* again.
Alana, you have never been more stunning.
Then what's the problem?
I mean, I get that you took a vow against violence or whatever, but I'm just looking for a little rough trade.
I understand.
The thing is, I once hit a girl... for real.
What?

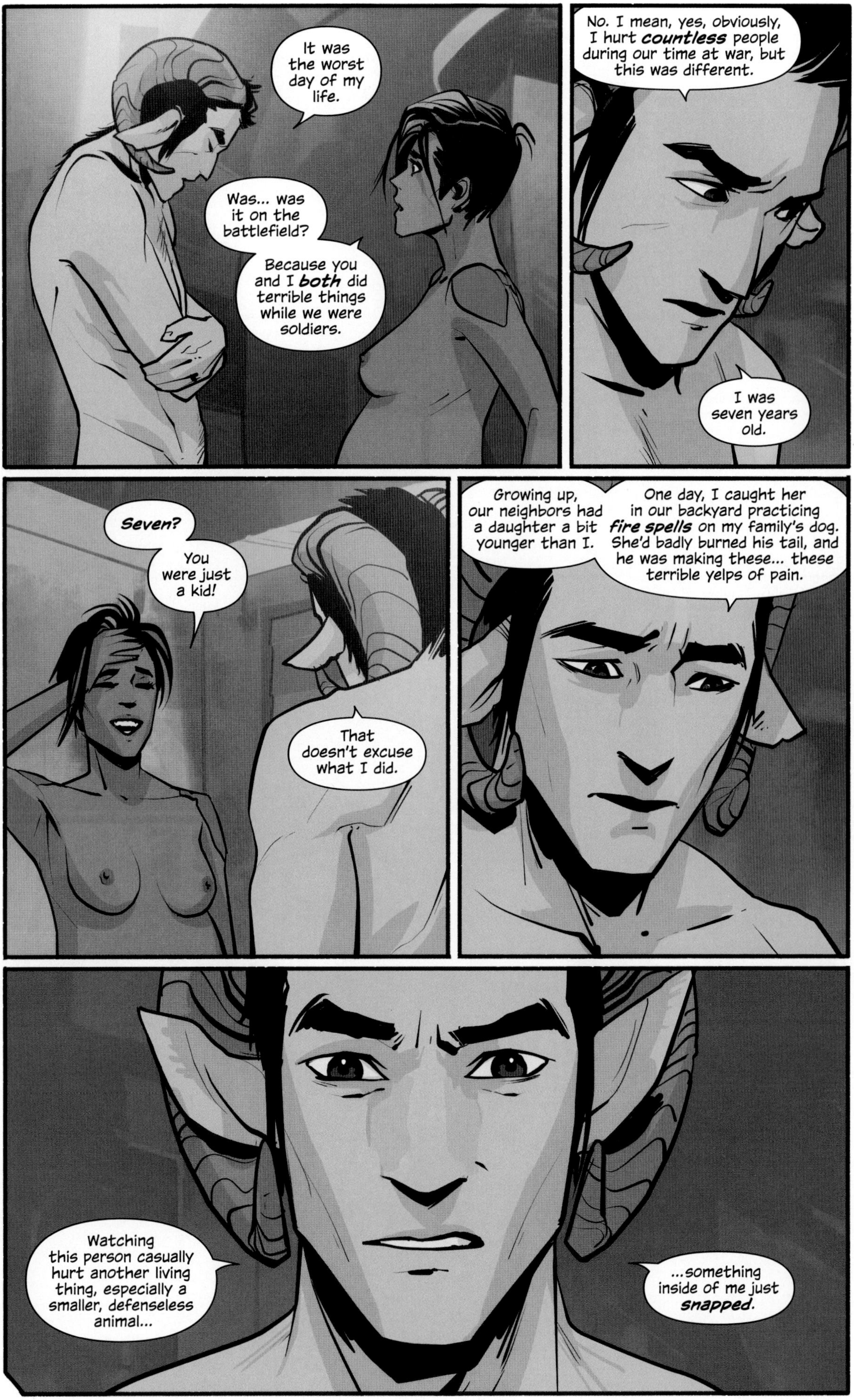
It was the worst day of my life.
Was... was it on the battlefield?
Because you and I **both** did terrible things while we were soldiers.
No. I mean, yes, obviously, I hurt **countless** people during our time at war, but this was different.
I was seven years old.
Seven?
You were just a kid!
That doesn't excuse what I did.
Growing up, our neighbors had a daughter a bit younger than I.
One day, I caught her in our backyard practicing **fire spells** on my family's dog. She'd badly burned his tail, and he was making these... these terrible yelps of pain.
Watching this person casually hurt another living thing, especially a smaller, defenseless animal...
...something inside of me just **snapped**.

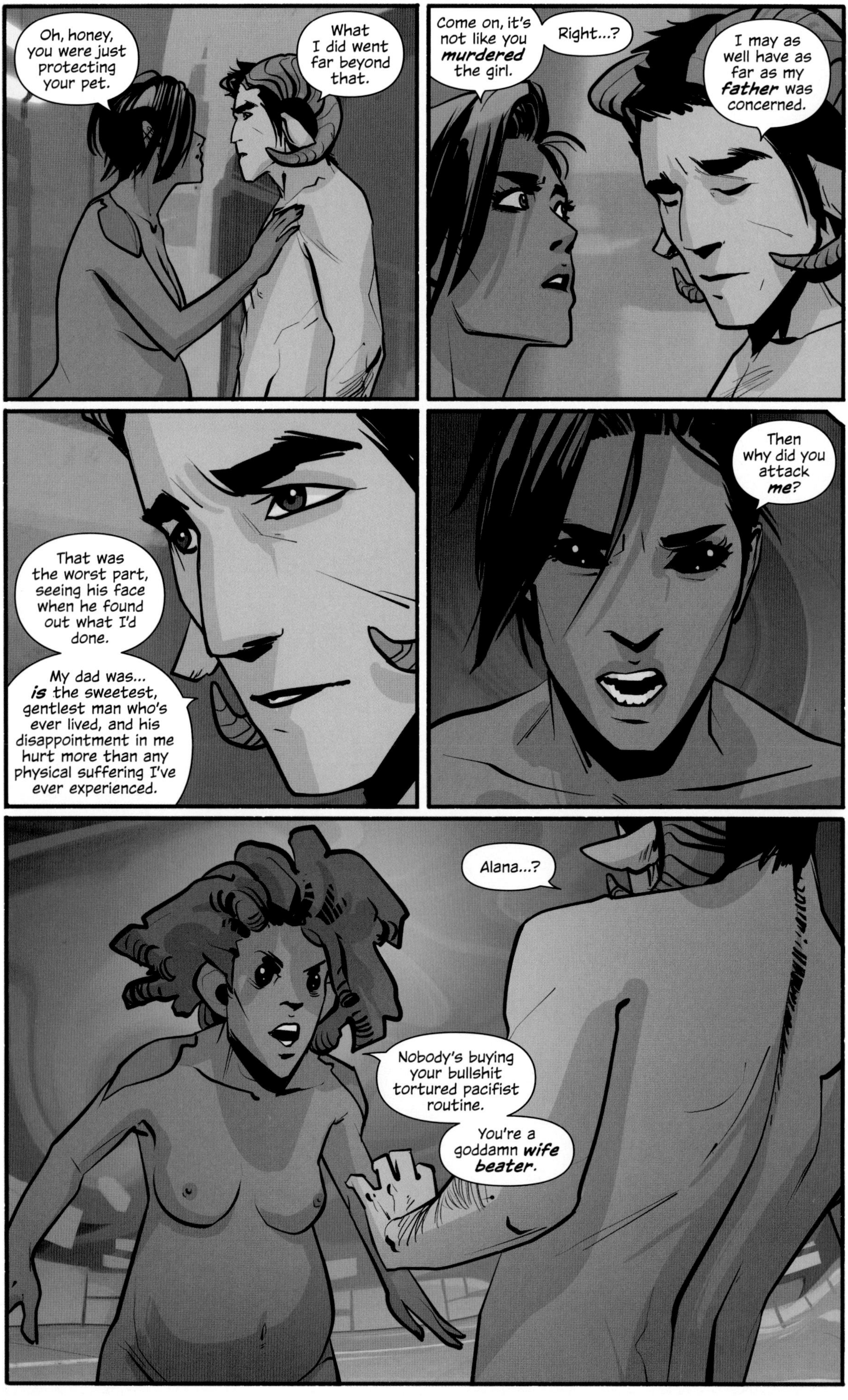
Oh, honey, you were just protecting your pet.
What I did went far beyond that.
Come on, it's not like you *murdered* the girl.
Right...?
I may as well have as far as my *father* was concerned.
That was the worst part, seeing his face when he found out what I'd done.
My dad was... *is* the sweetest, gentlest man who's ever lived, and his disappointment in me hurt more than any physical suffering I've ever experienced.
Then why did you attack *me*?
Alana...?
Nobody's buying your bullshit tortured pacifist routine.
You're a goddamn *wife beater*.

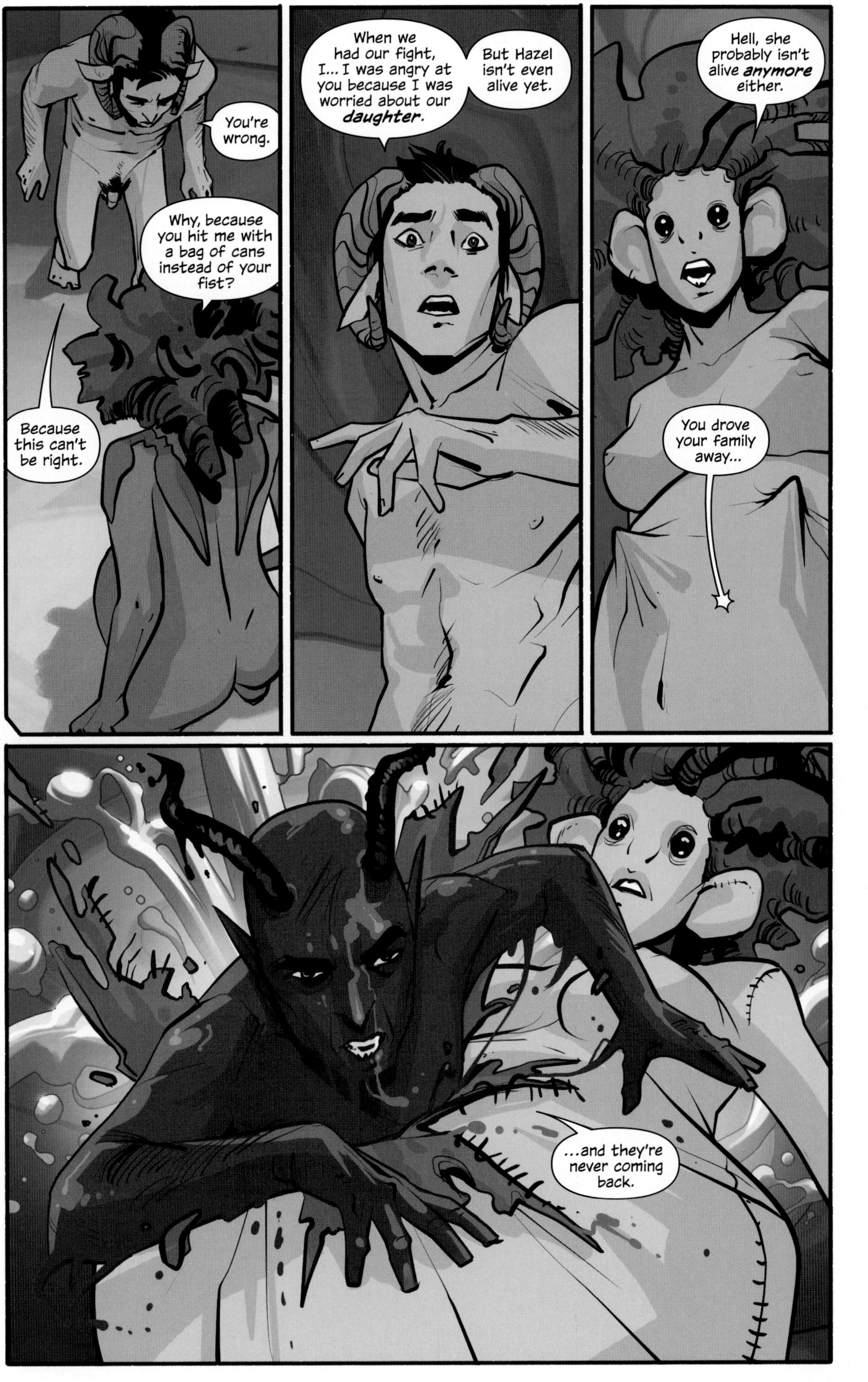
You're wrong.
Why, because you hit me with a bag of cans instead of your fist?
Because this can't be right.
When we had our fight, I... I was angry at you because I was worried about our **daughter**.
But Hazel isn't even alive yet.
Hell, she probably isn't alive **anymore** either.
You drove your family away...
...and they're never coming back.

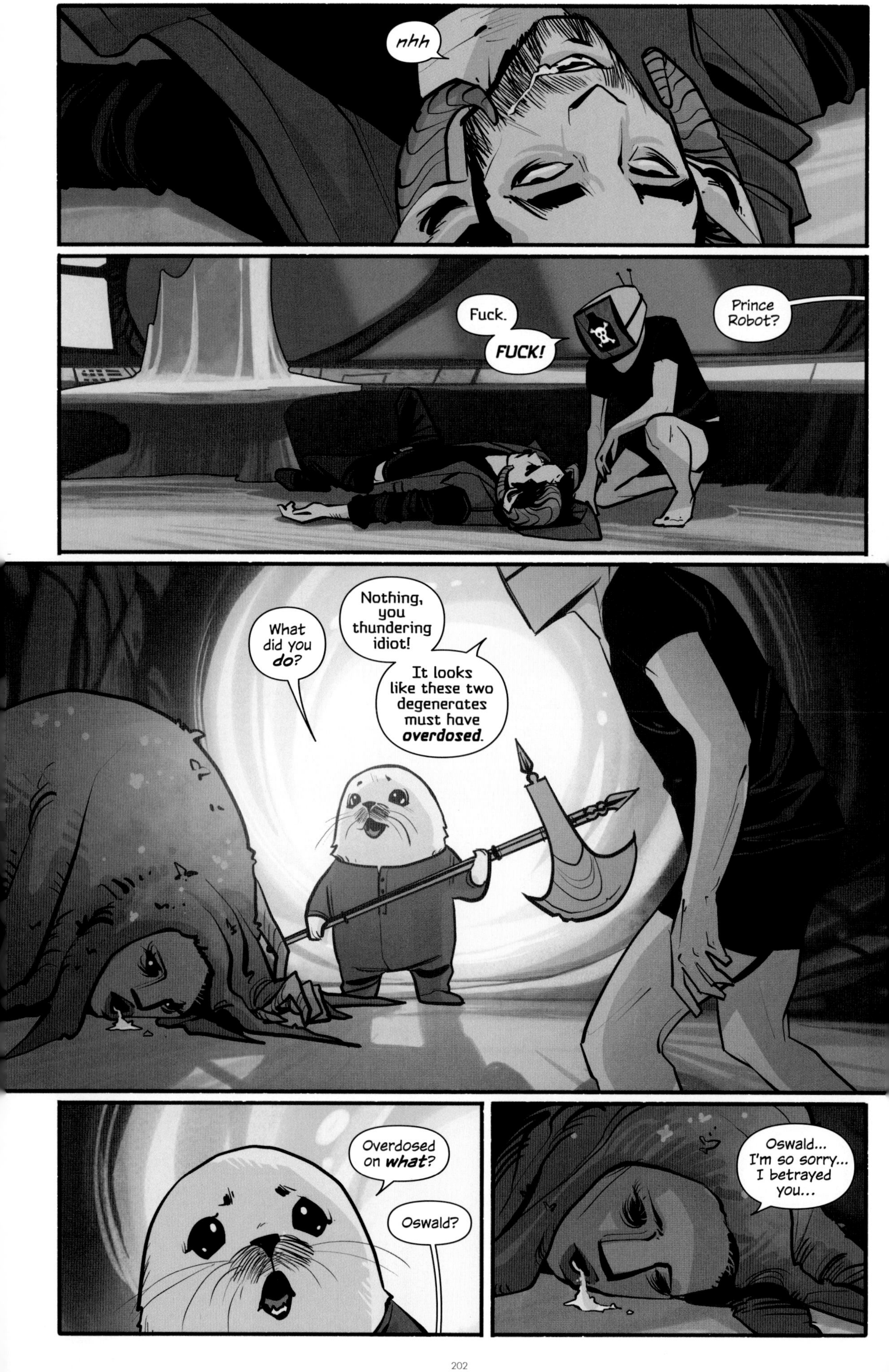
nhh
Fuck.
FUCK!
Prince Robot?
What did you do?
Nothing, you thundering idiot!
It looks like these two degenerates must have overdosed.
Overdosed on what?
Oswald?
Oswald... I'm so sorry... I betrayed you...

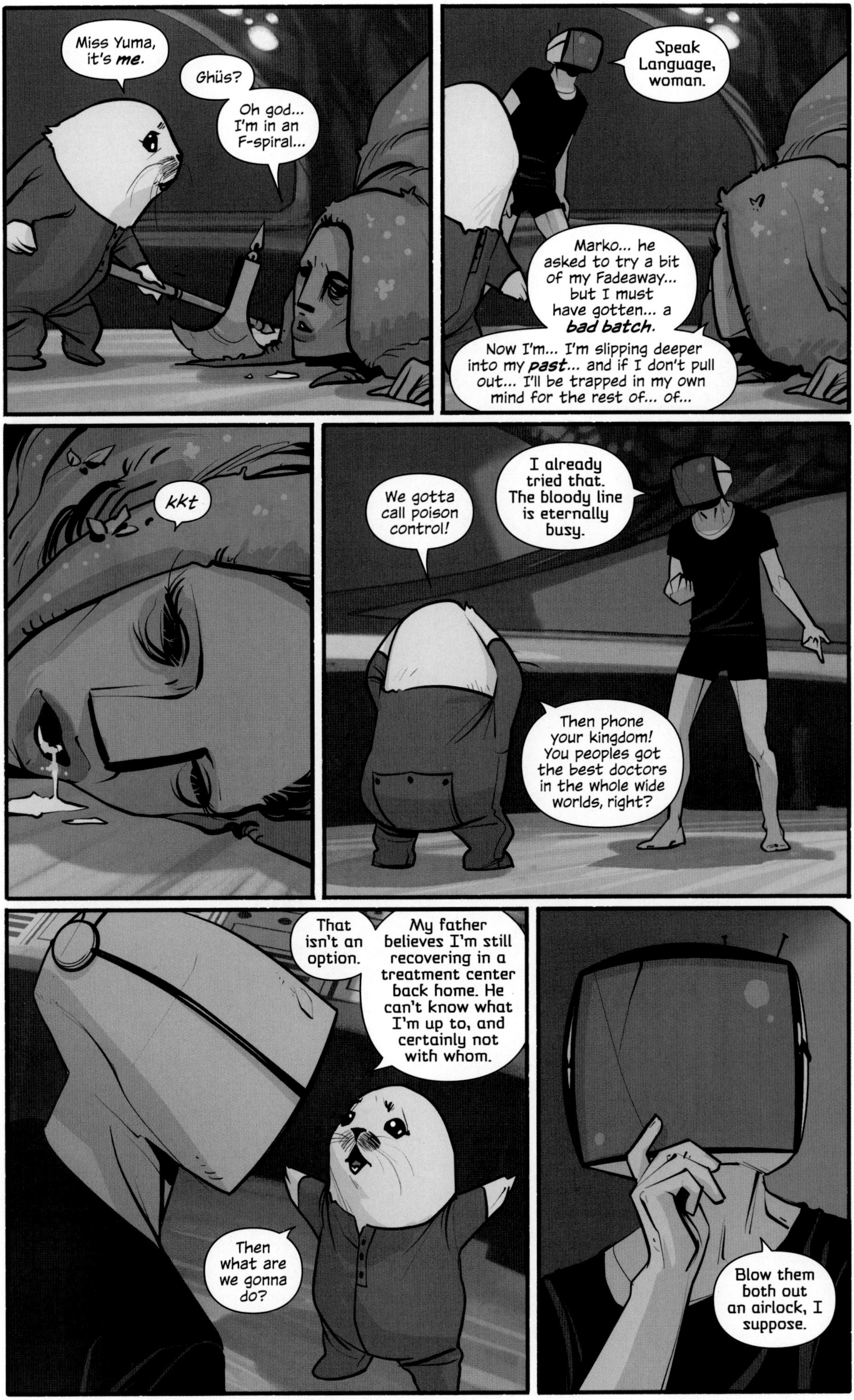
Miss Yuma, it's **me**.
Ghüs?
Oh god... I'm in an F-spiral...
Speak Language, woman.
Marko... he asked to try a bit of my Fadeaway... but I must have gotten... a **bad batch**.
Now I'm... I'm slipping deeper into my **past**... and if I don't pull out... I'll be trapped in my own mind for the rest of... of...
kkt
We gotta call poison control!
I already tried that. The bloody line is eternally busy.
Then phone your kingdom! You peoples got the best doctors in the whole wide worlds, right?
That isn't an option.
My father believes I'm still recovering in a treatment center back home. He can't know what I'm up to, and certainly not with whom.
Then what are we gonna do?
Blow them both out an airlock, I suppose.

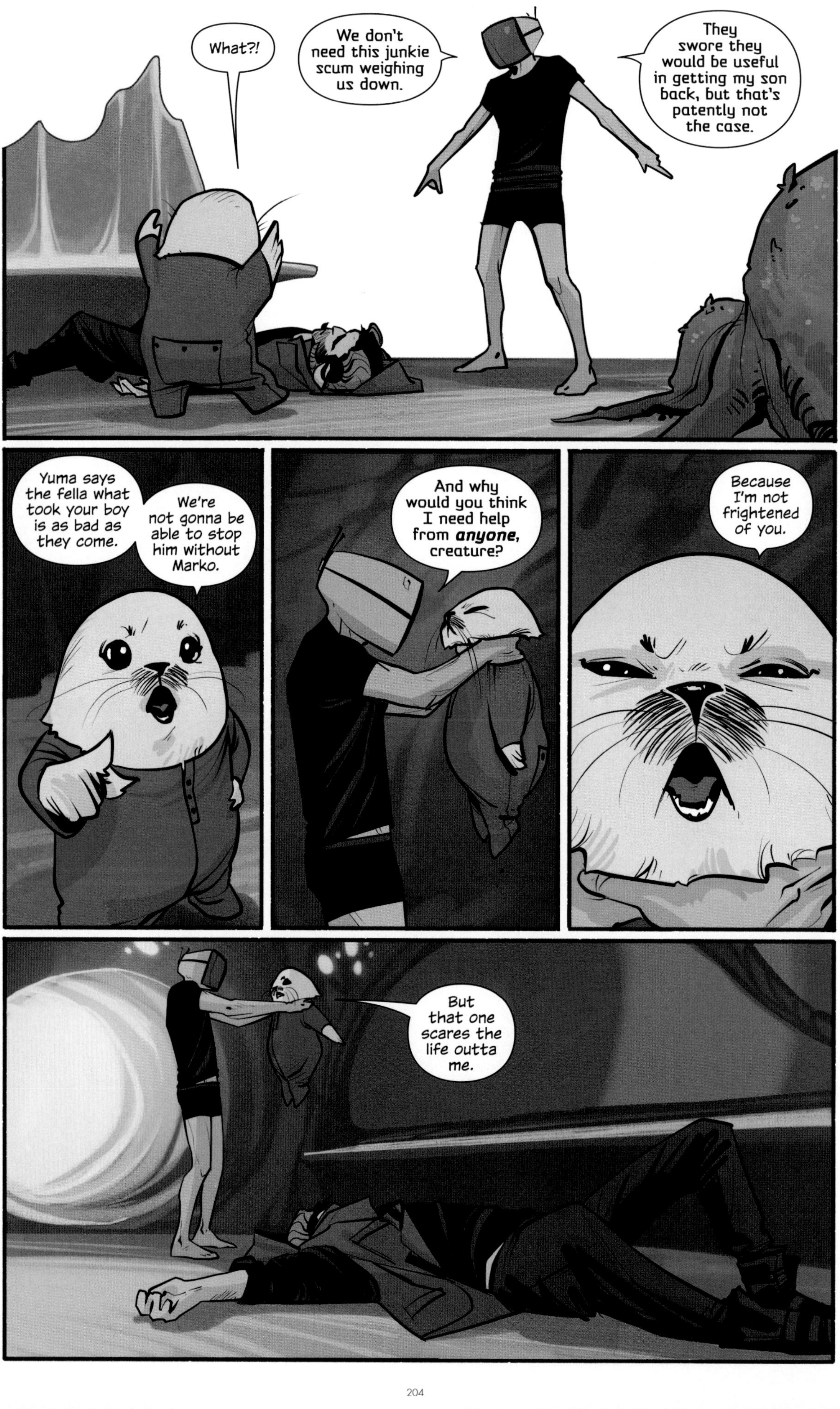
What?!
We don't need this junkie scum weighing us down.
They swore they would be useful in getting my son back, but that's patently not the case.
Yuma says the fella what took your boy is as bad as they come.
We're not gonna be able to stop him without Marko.
And why would you think I need help from ***anyone,*** creature?
Because I'm not frightened of you.
But that one scares the life outta me.

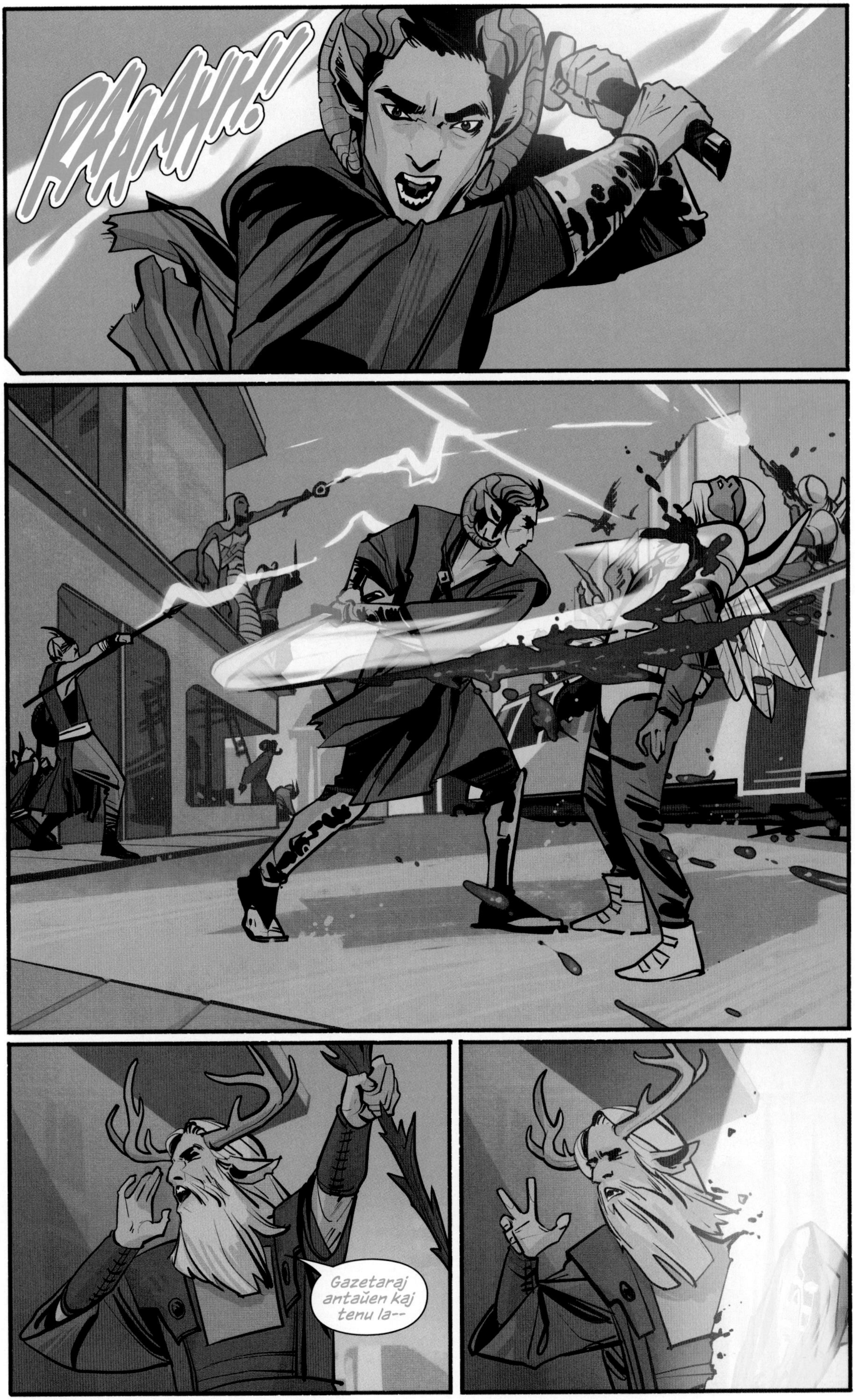
RAAAHH!!
Gazetaraj antaŭen kaj tenu la--

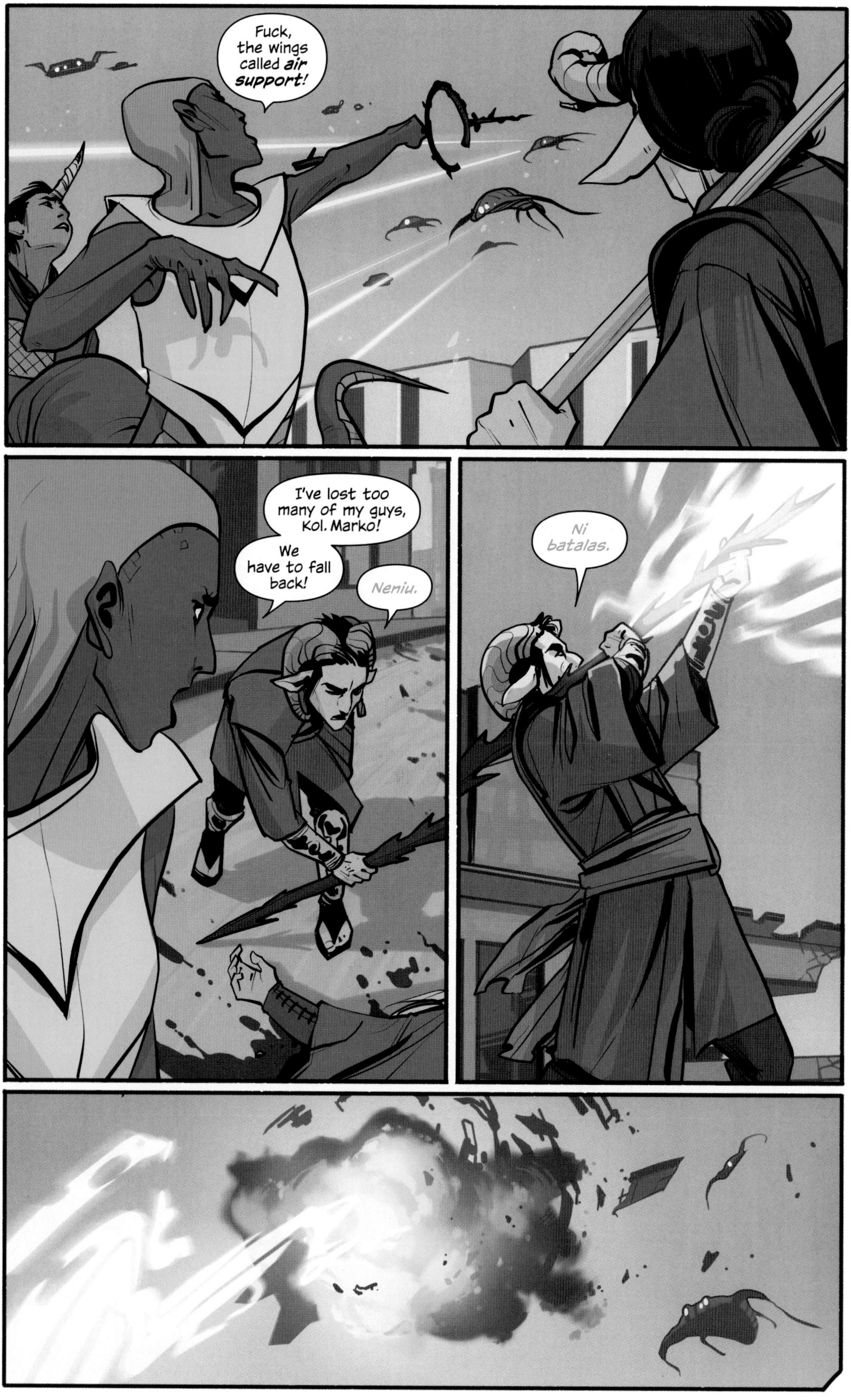
Fuck, the wings called air support!
I've lost too many of my guys, Kol. Marko!
We have to fall back!
Neniu.
Ni batalas.

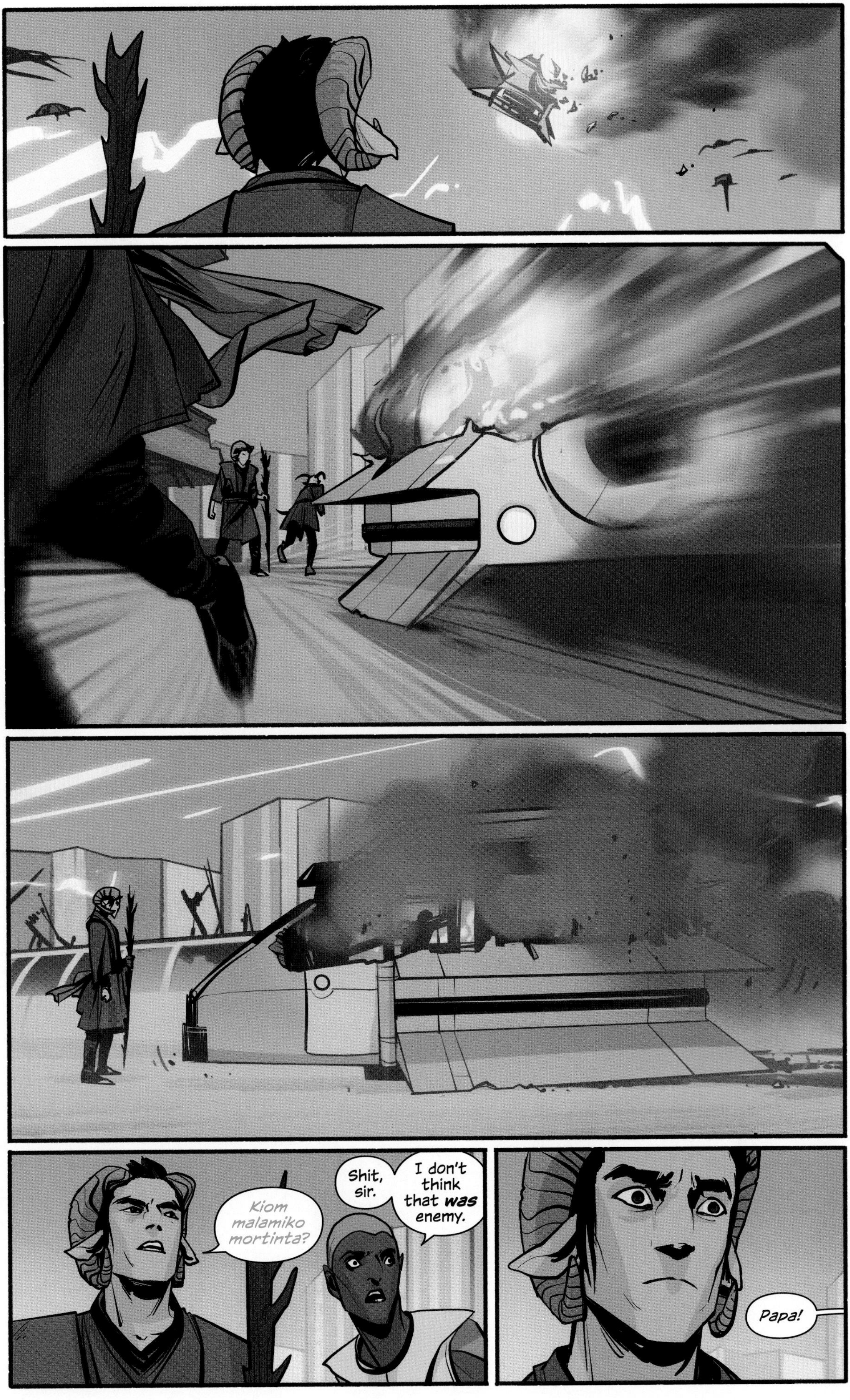

Kiom malamiko mortinta?
Shit, sir.
I don't think that **was** enemy.
Papa!

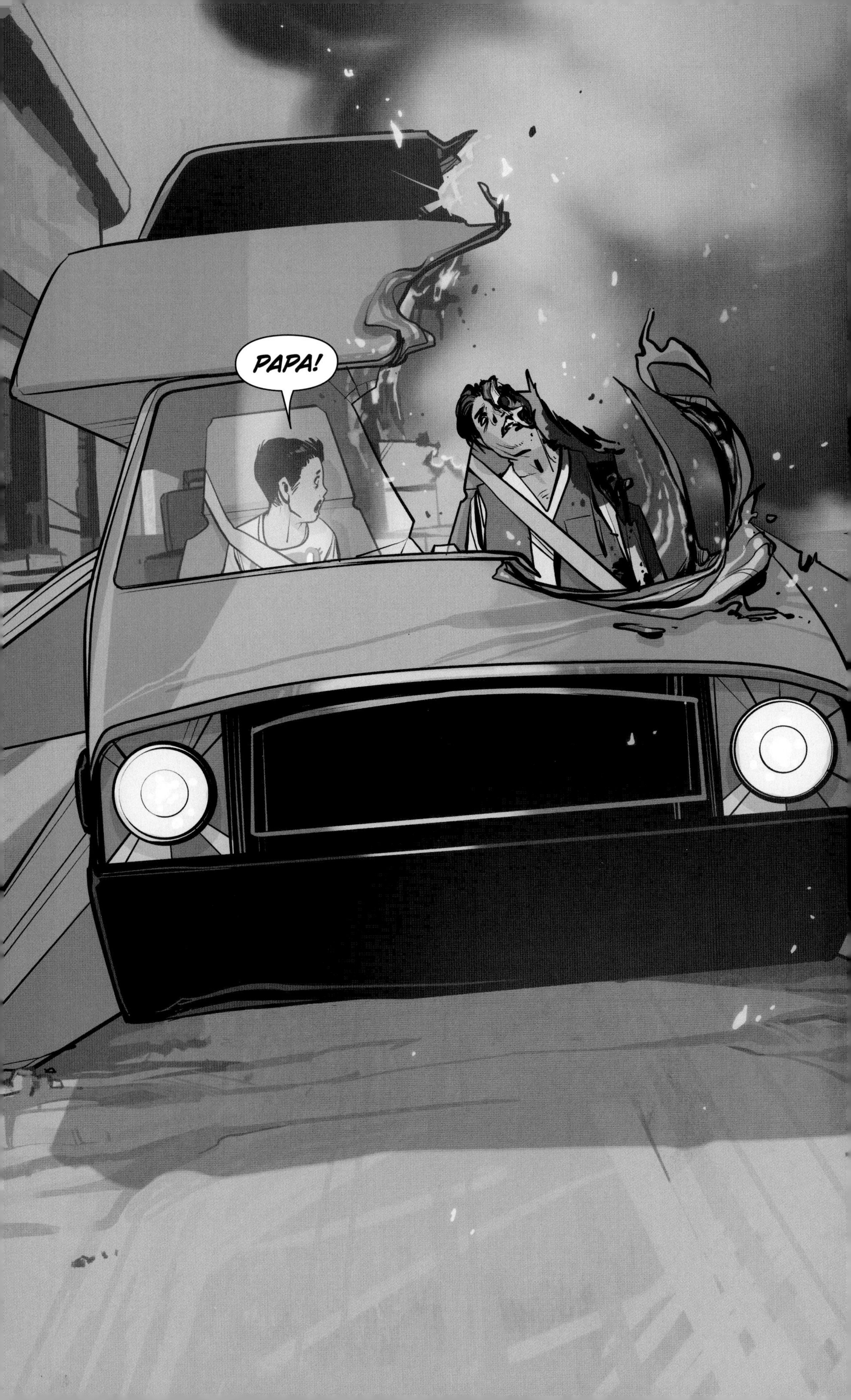
PAPA!

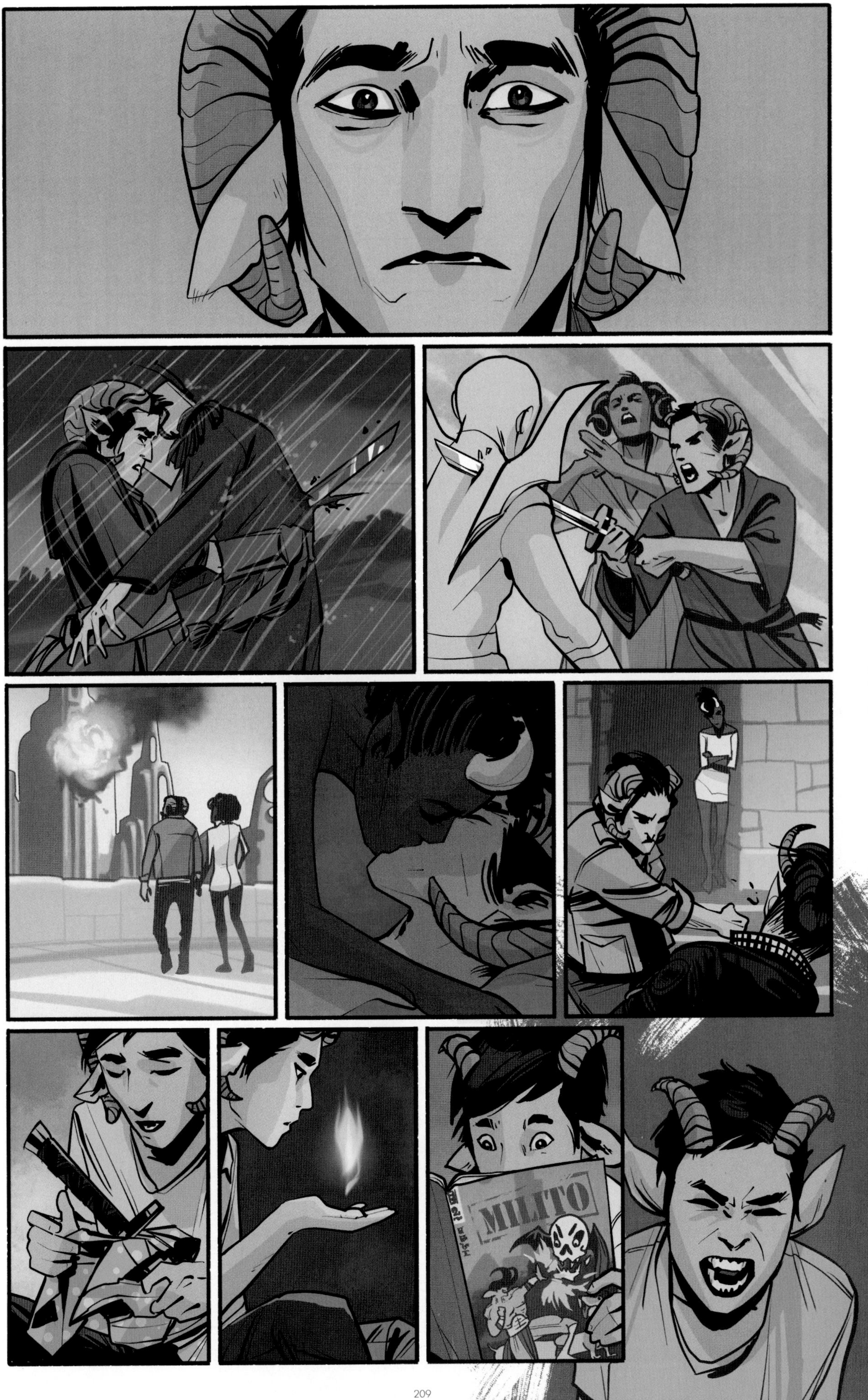
MILITO

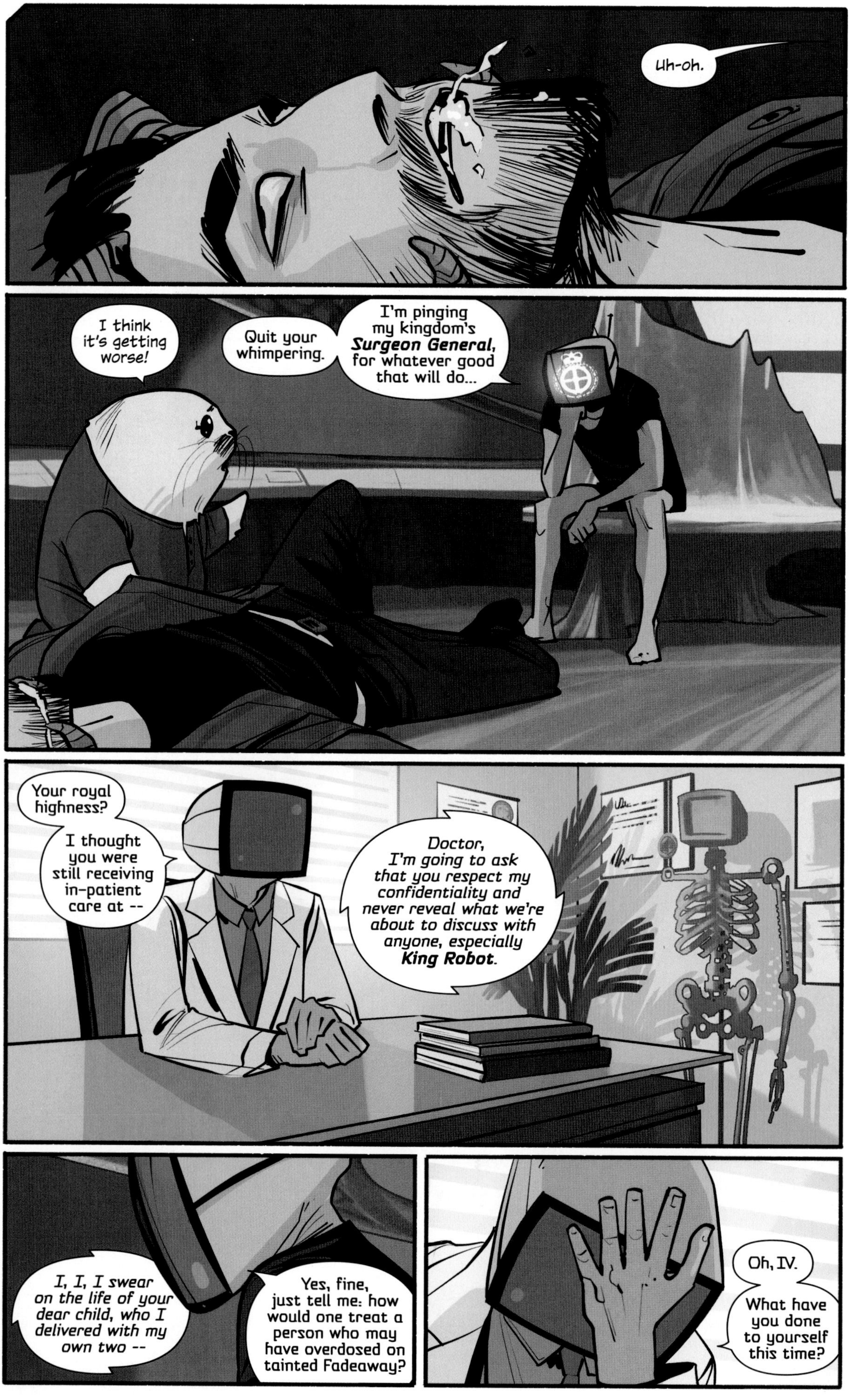

Uh-oh.
I think it's getting worse!
Quit your whimpering.
I'm pinging my kingdom's **Surgeon General**, for whatever good that will do...
Your royal highness?
I thought you were still receiving in-patient care at --
Doctor, I'm going to ask that you respect my confidentiality and never reveal what we're about to discuss with anyone, especially ***King Robot****.*
I, I, I swear on the life of your dear child, who I delivered with my own two --
Yes, fine, just tell me: how would one treat a person who may have overdosed on tainted Fadeaway?
Oh, IV.
What have you done to yourself this time?

This isn't about me, it's for two... acquaintances.

Fellow robots?

Quite the opposite, I would say.

You're not back on **Sextillion**, are you?

Son, I've seen men come back from that place with some of the most virulent anal warts in the --

Doctor, for the love of fuck, just tell me what I'm supposed to do.

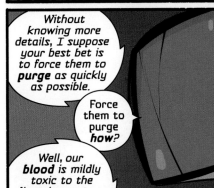

Without knowing more details, I suppose your best bet is to force them to **purge** as quickly as possible.

Force them to purge **how**?

Well, our **blood** is mildly toxic to the digestive systems of most lesser species.

Huh.

You don't say.

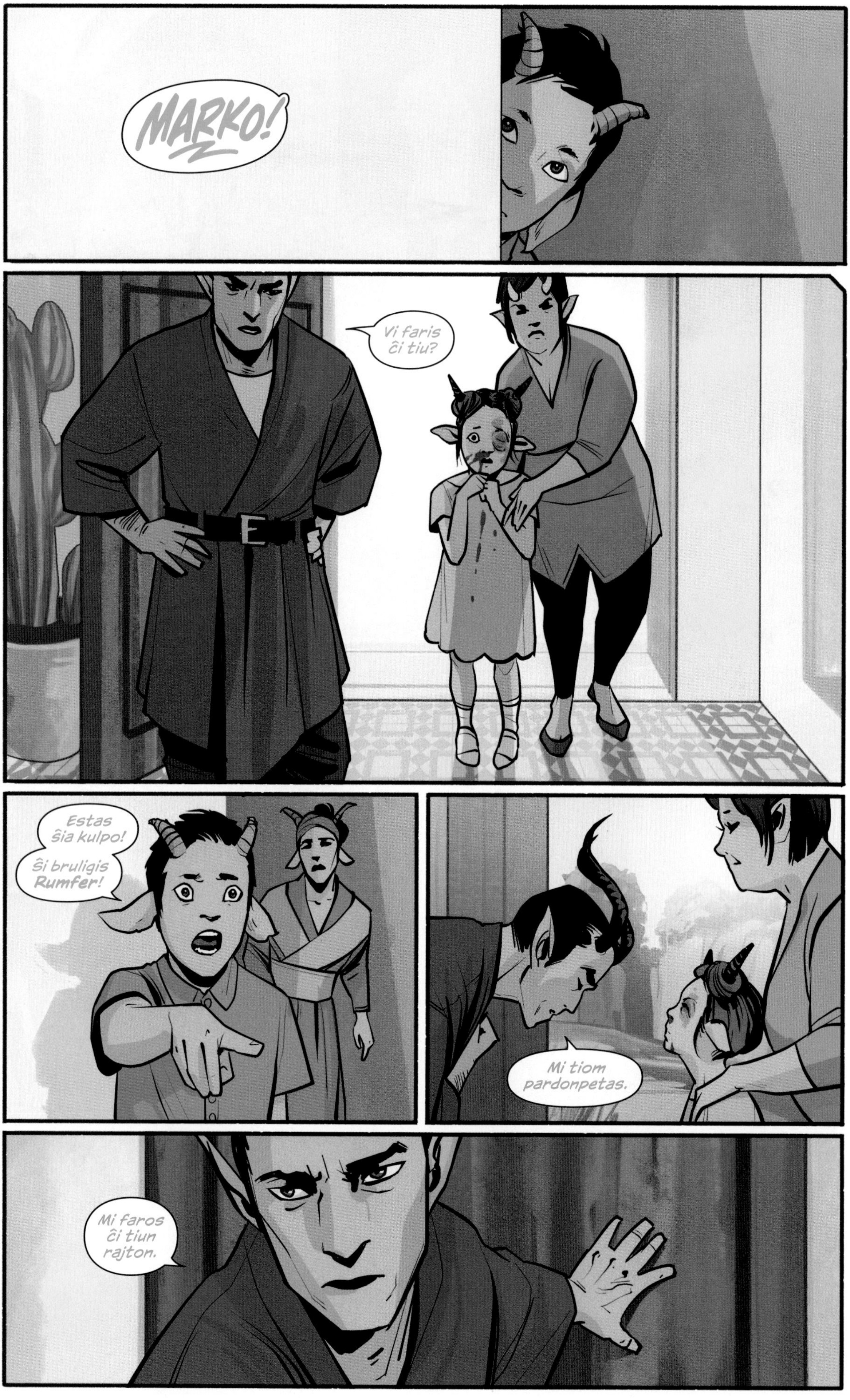
MARKO!
Vi faris ĉi tiu?
Estas ŝia kulpo!
Ŝi bruligis Rumfer!
Mi tiom pardonpetas.
Mi faros ĉi tiun rajton.

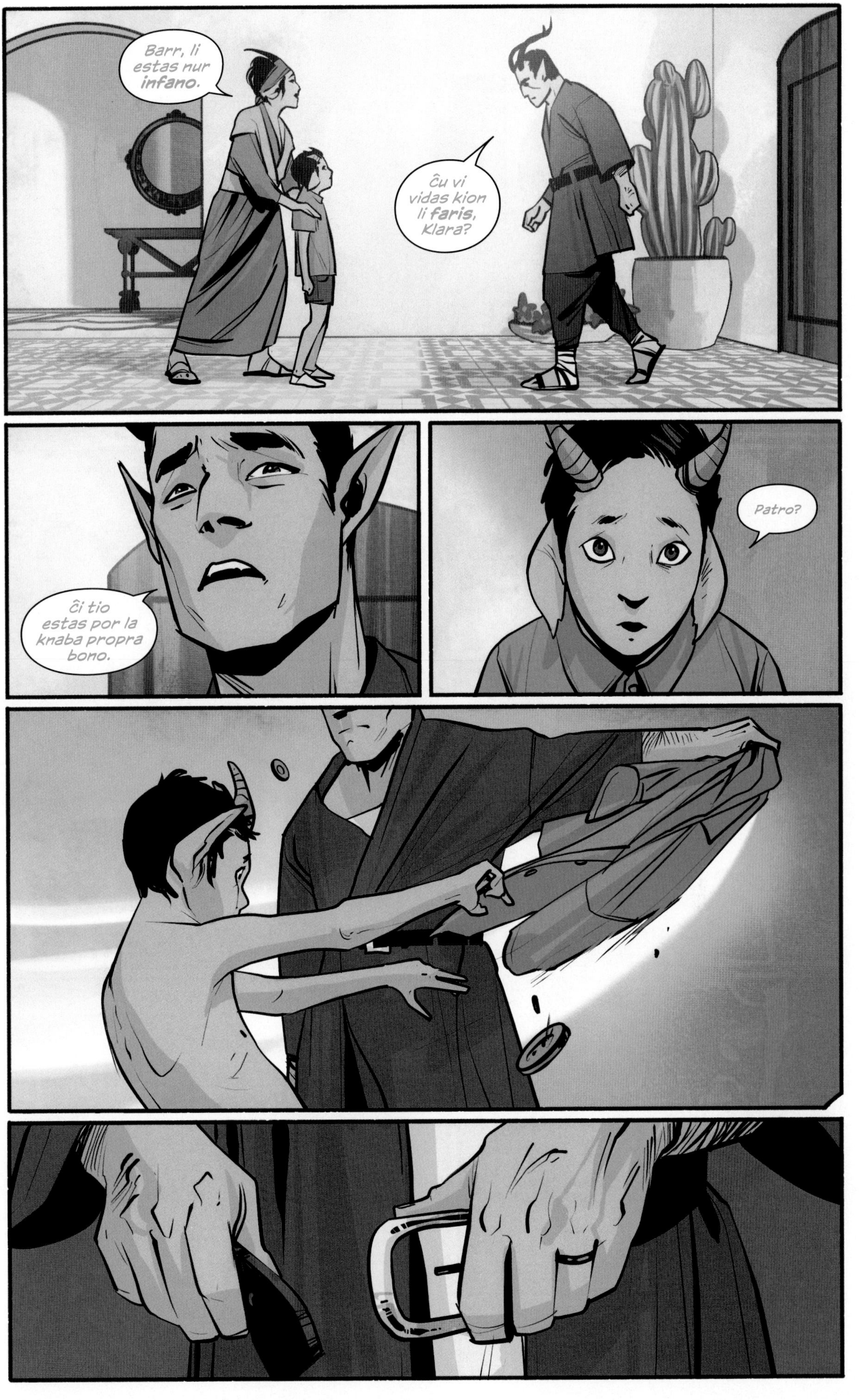

Barr, li estas nur **infano**.
Ĉu vi vidas kion li **faris**, Klara?
Ĉi tio estas por la knaba propra bono.
Patro?

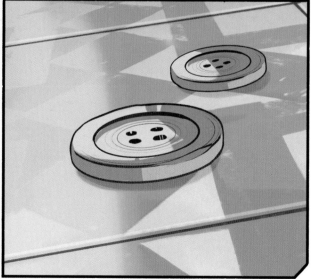

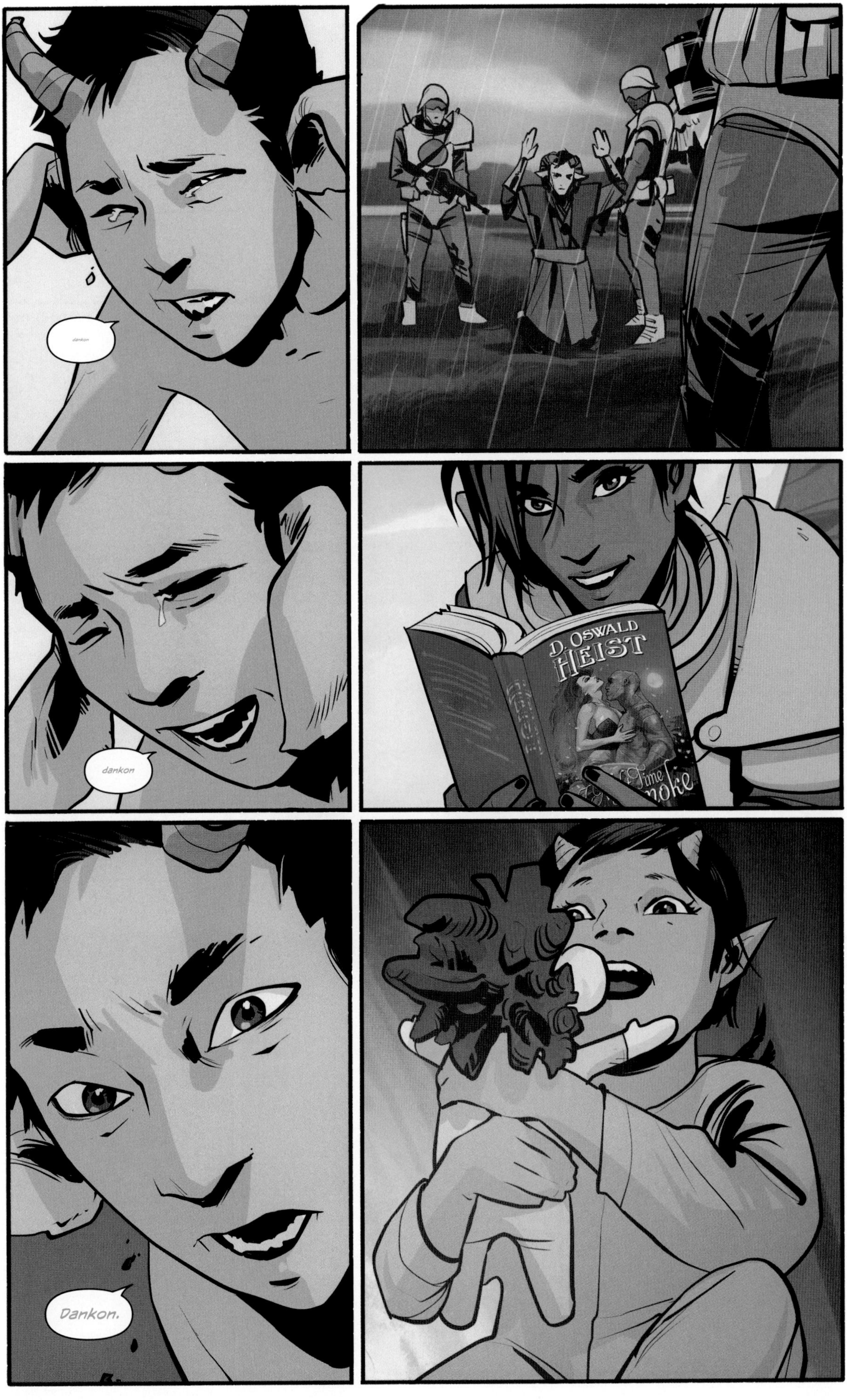
dankon
dankon
D. OSWALD
HEIST
Dankon.

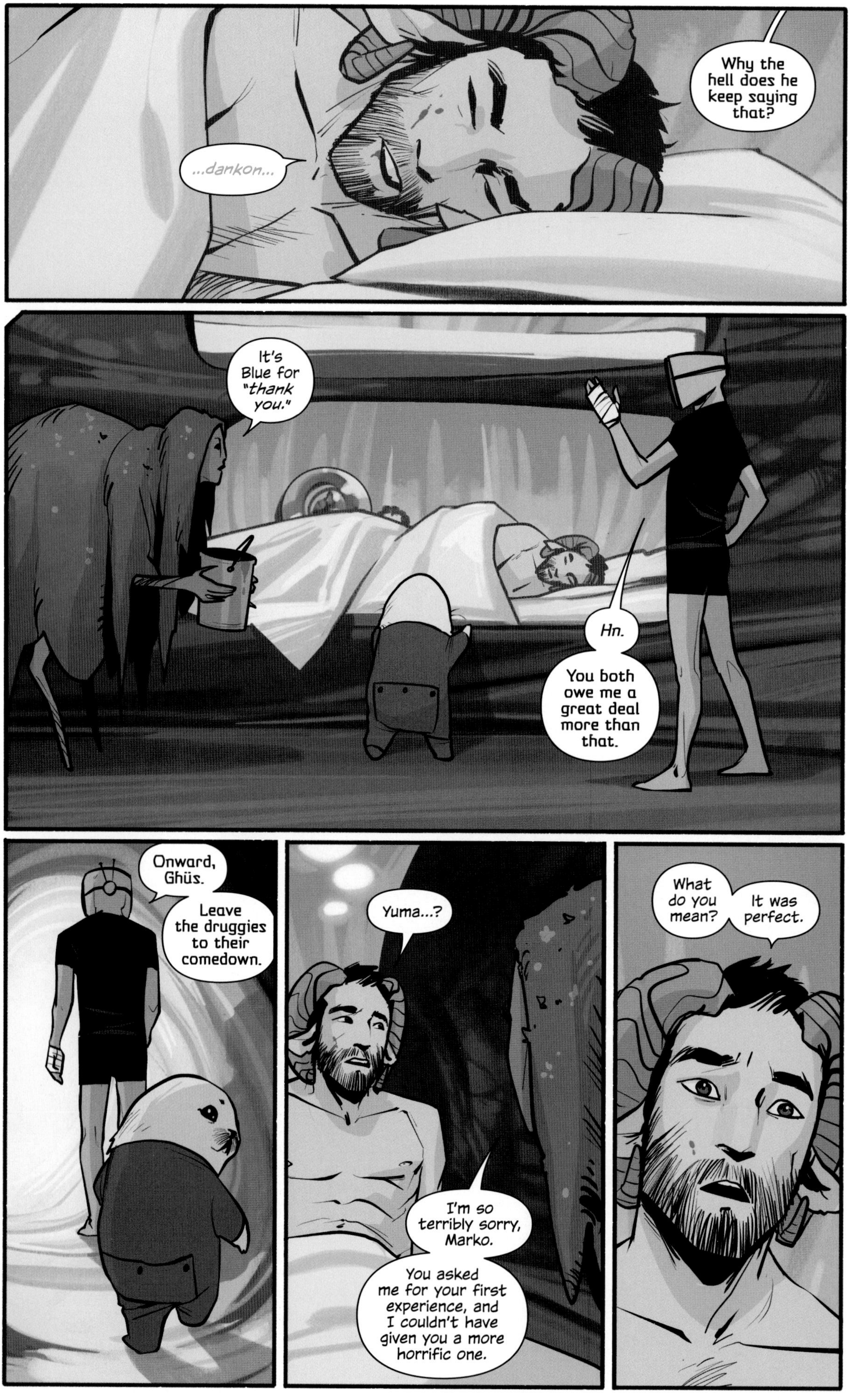
Why the hell does he keep saying that?
...dankon...
It's Blue for "thank you."
Hn.
You both owe me a great deal more than that.
Onward, Ghüs.
Leave the druggies to their comedown.
Yuma...?
I'm so terribly sorry, Marko.
You asked me for your first experience, and I couldn't have given you a more horrific one.
What do you mean?
It was perfect.

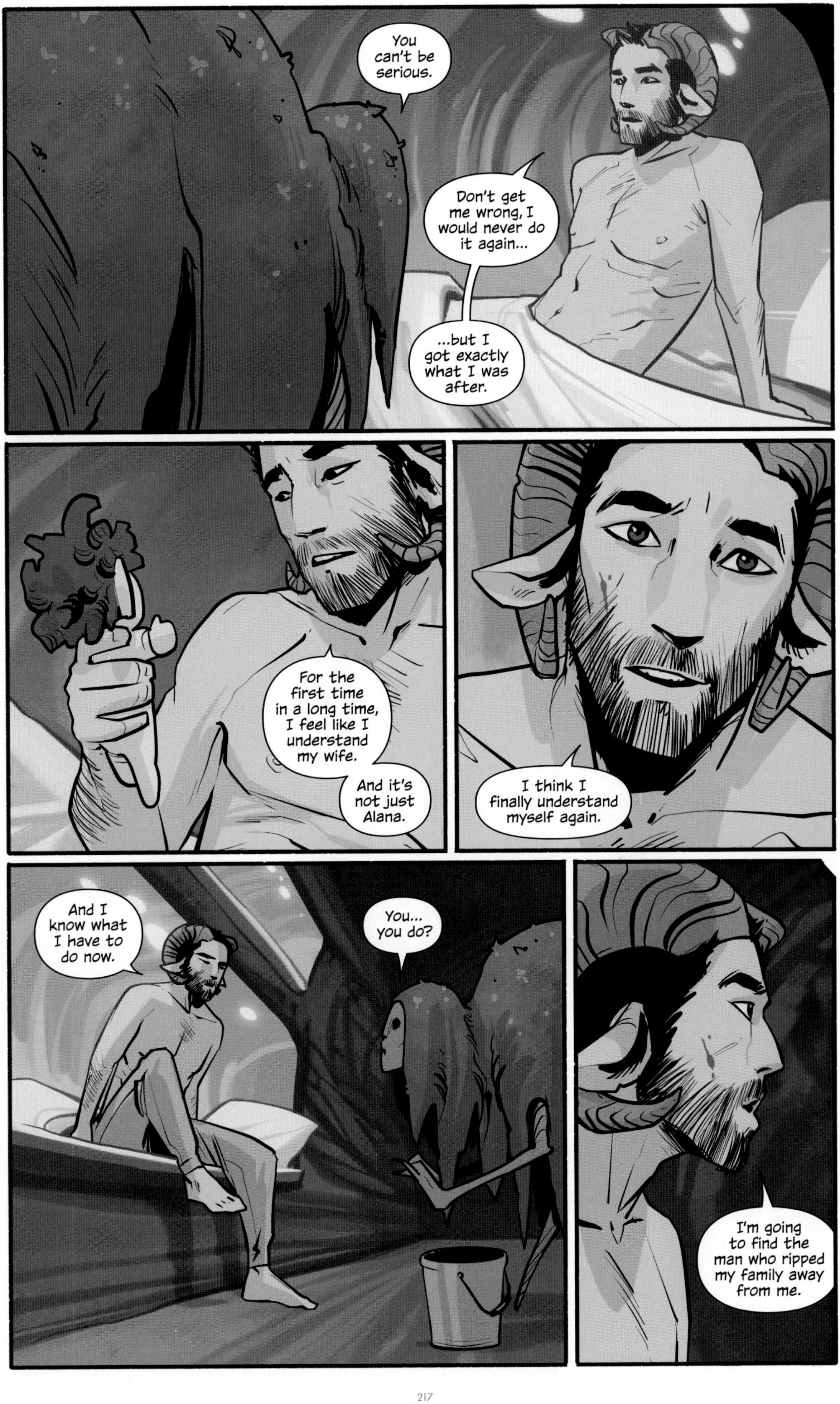
You can't be serious.
Don't get me wrong, I would never do it again...
...but I got exactly what I was after.
For the first time in a long time, I feel like I understand my wife.
And it's not just Alana.
I think I finally understand myself again.
And I know what I have to do now.
You... you do?
I'm going to find the man who ripped my family away from me.

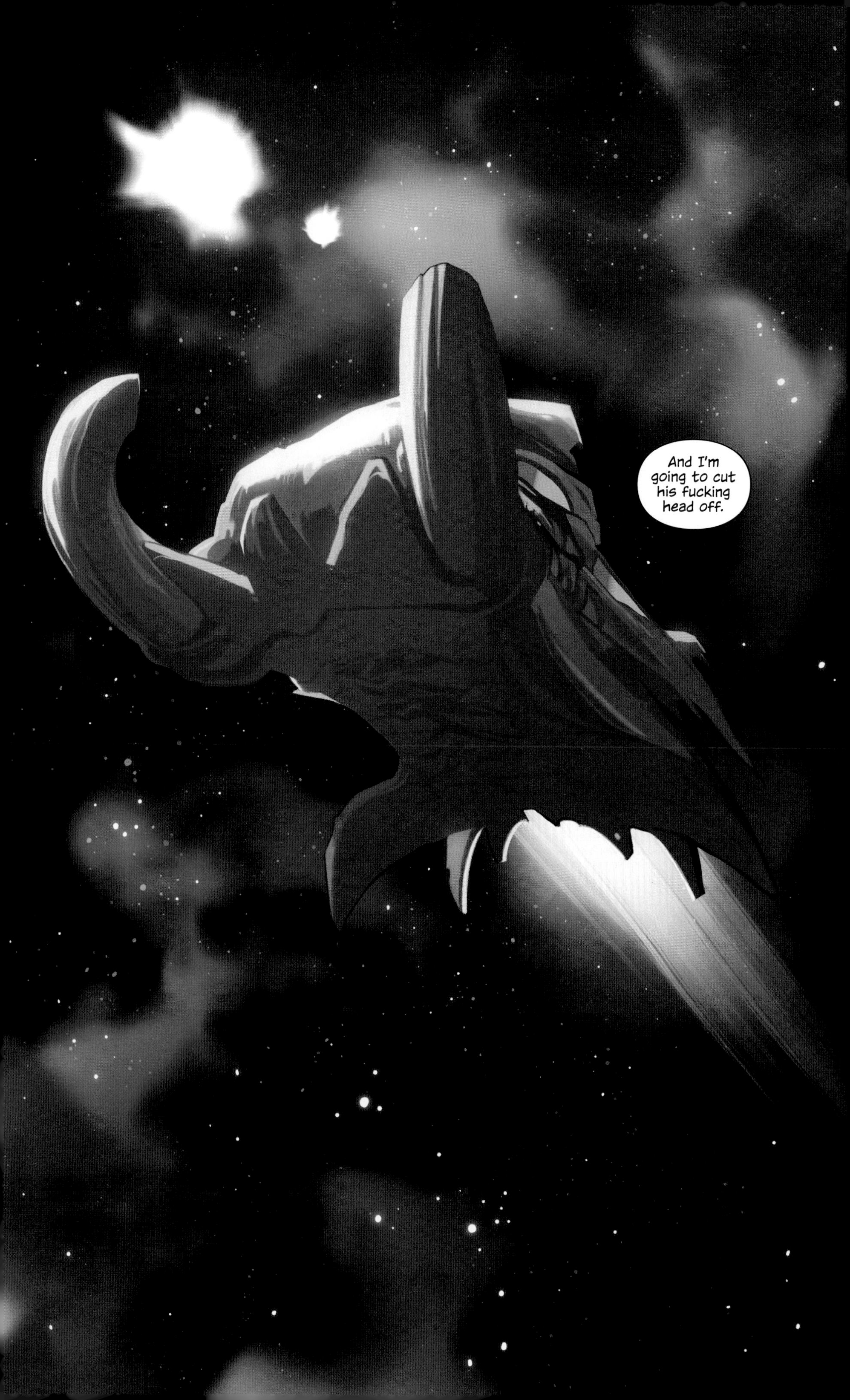

And I'm going to cut his fucking head off.

end chapter twenty-seven

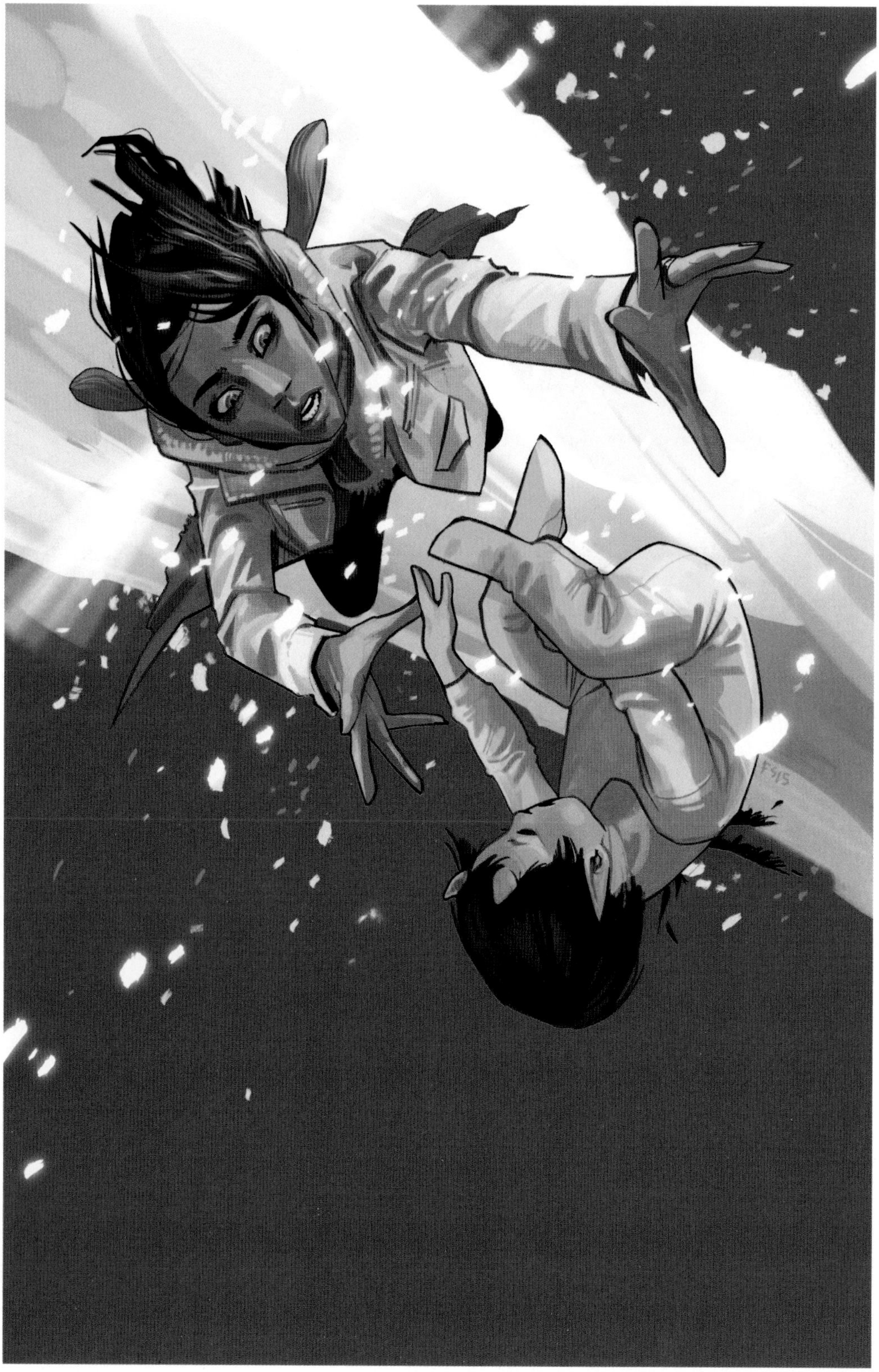
FS15

CHAPTER

TWENTY-EIGHT

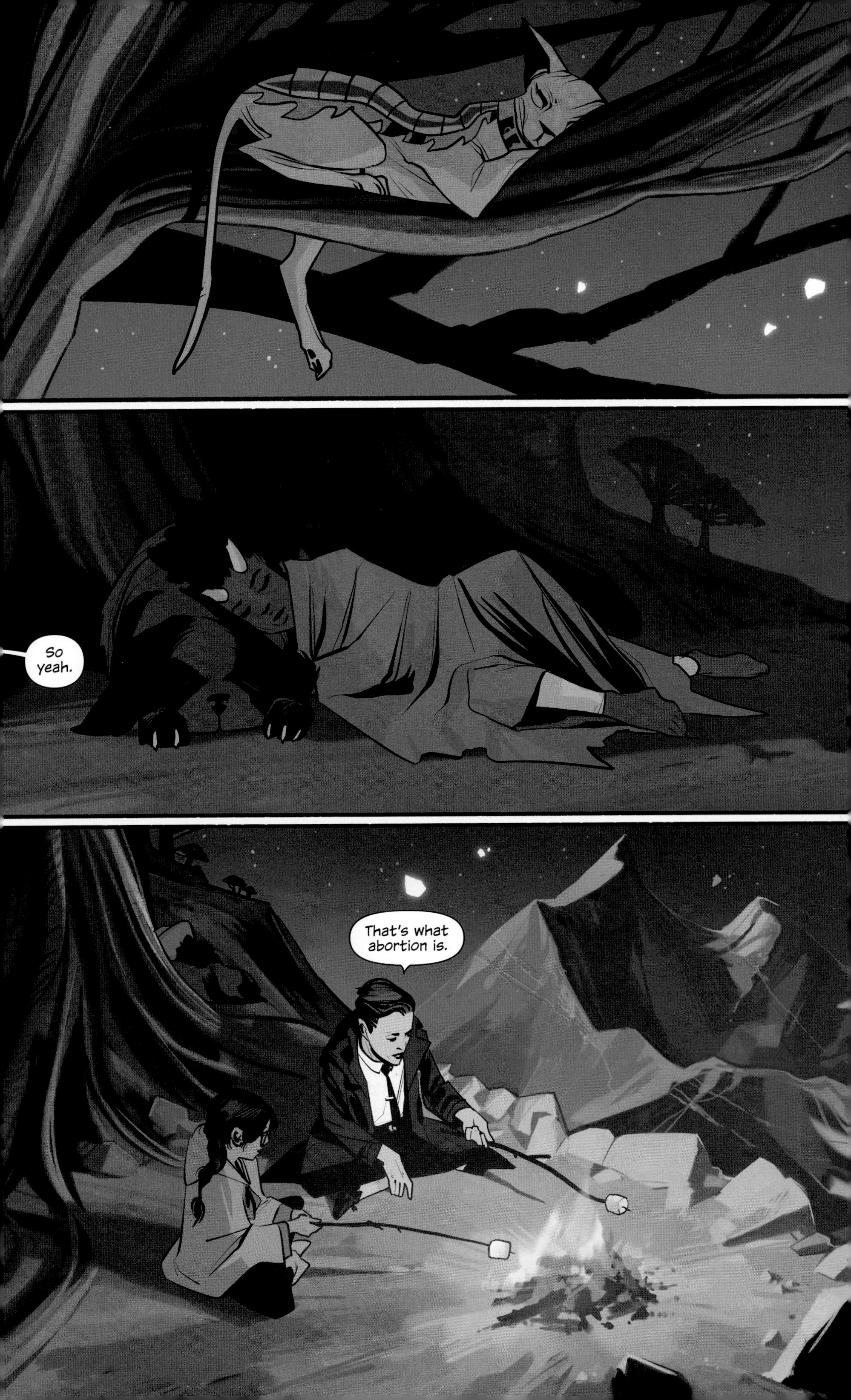
So yeah.
That's what abortion is.

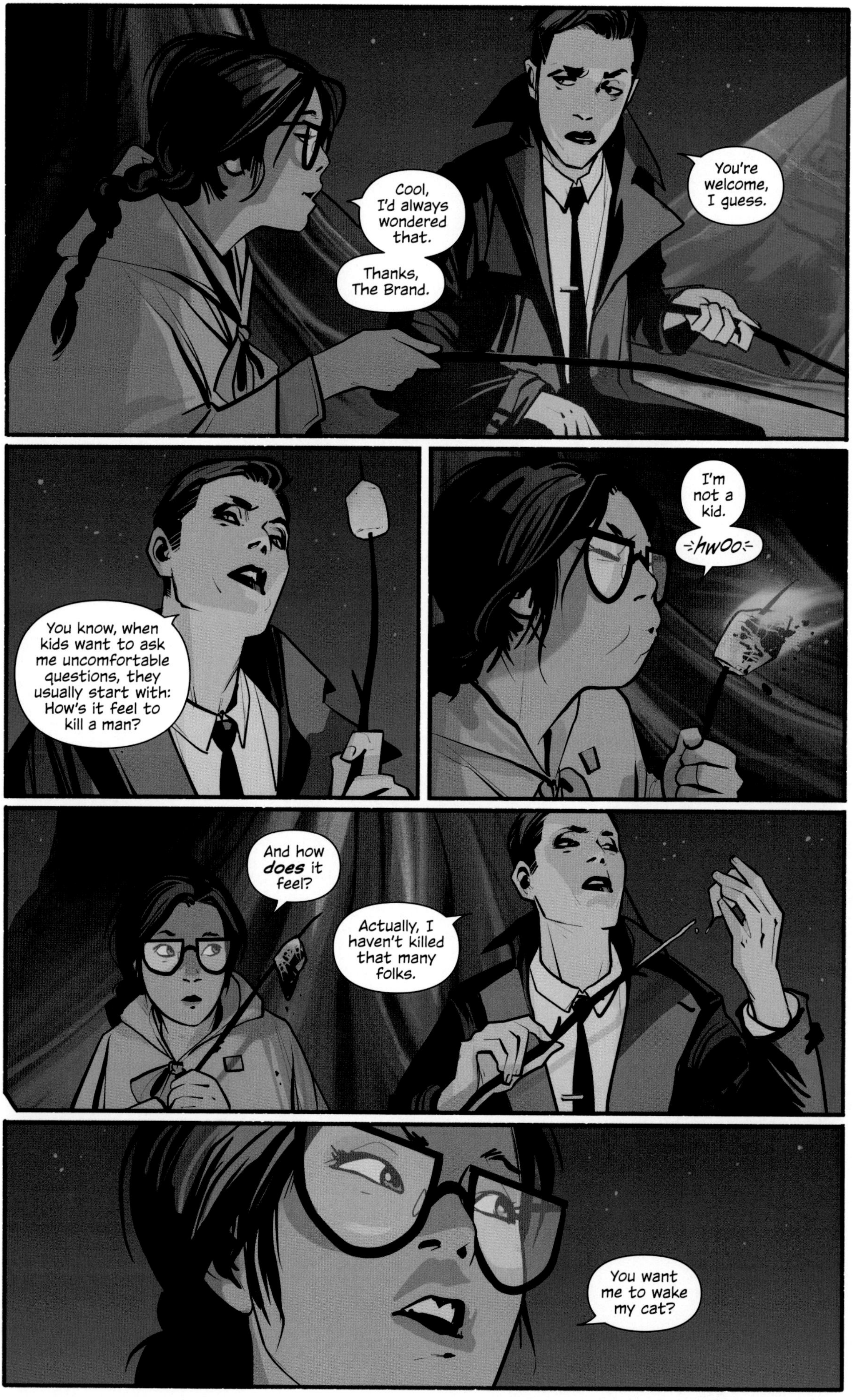
Cool, I'd always wondered that.
Thanks, The Brand.
You're welcome, I guess.
You know, when kids want to ask me uncomfortable questions, they usually start with: How's it feel to kill a man?
I'm not a kid.
HWOO
And how **does** it feel?
Actually, I haven't killed that many folks.
You want me to wake my cat?

I'm serious, my job isn't all stabbing bad guys in the face.

Most of the time, it's negotiation, intimidation, maybe the occasional broken nose.

But when you *have* killed? What was it like...?

Not too great.

Which is why people in my line of work always try to look for other solutions.

What about your *brother*?

He doesn't seem to mind killing that much.

Yeah.

He's always been pretty direct.

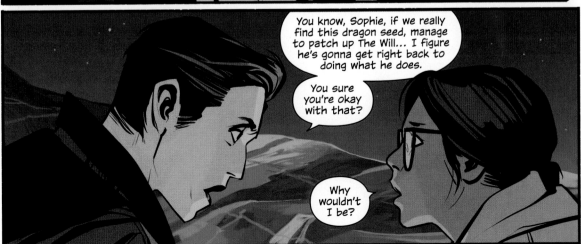

You know, Sophie, if we really find this dragon seed, manage to patch up The Will... I figure he's gonna get right back to doing what he does.

You sure you're okay with that?

Why wouldn't I be?

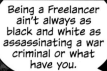

Being a Freelancer ain't always as black and white as assassinating a war criminal or what have you.

The last folks who hired The Will wanted him to off a couple of *new parents*.

Yeah, but one of those parents is the man with the horns, the one who hurt Miss Gwendolyn, right?

So she says.

Nicely put.

Well... maybe the universe is better off with some people just not being in it anymore.

I couldn't agree more.

Halvor.

It doesn't matter who started it or what it's really about... war usually ends up sucking most for women.

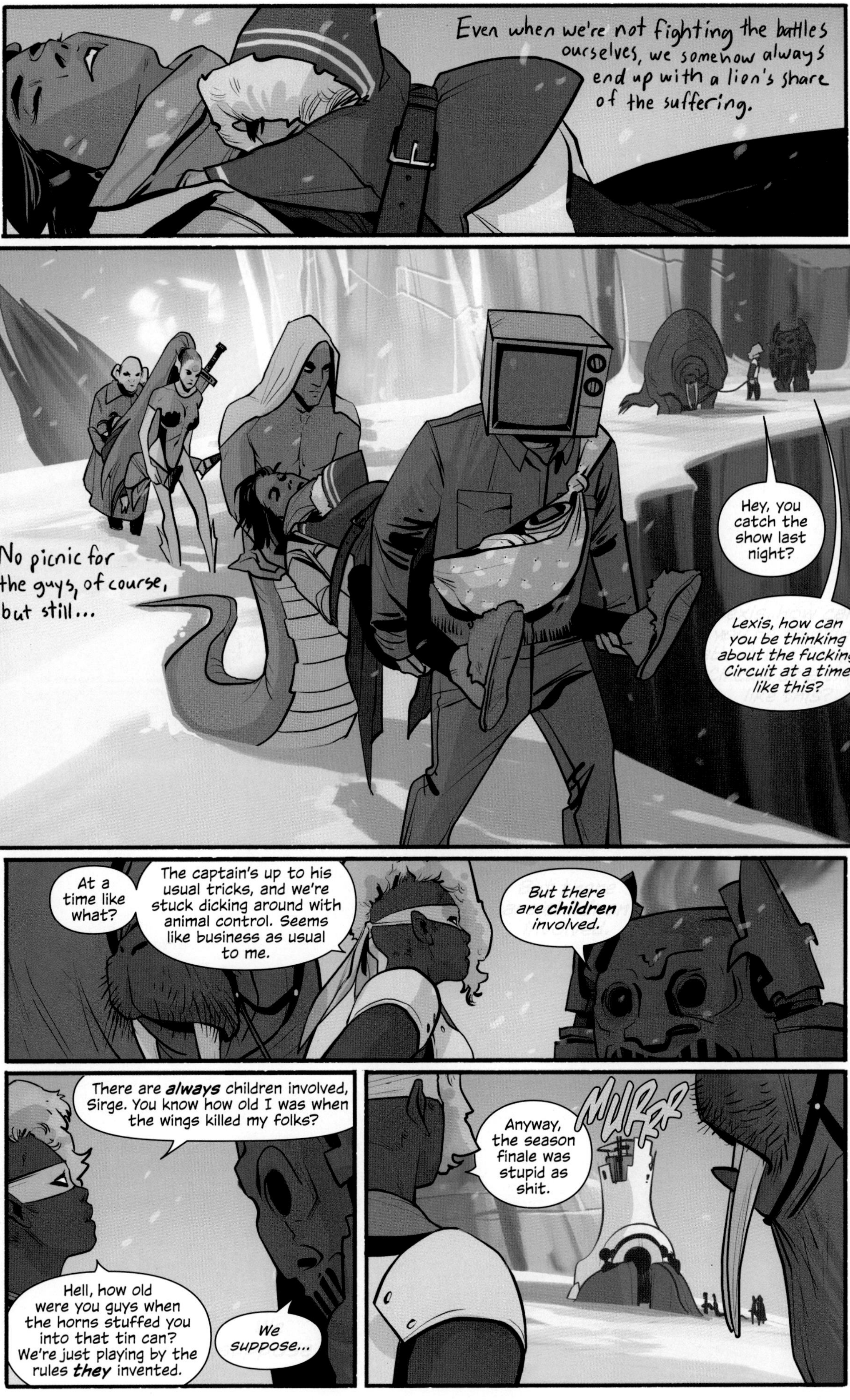

Even when we're not fighting the battles ourselves, we somehow always end up with a lion's share of the suffering.
No picnic for the guys, of course, but still...
Hey, you catch the show last night?
Lexis, how can you be thinking about the fucking Circuit at a time like this?
At a time like what?
The captain's up to his usual tricks, and we're stuck dicking around with animal control. Seems like business as usual to me.
But there are **children** involved.
There are **always** children involved, Sirge. You know how old I was when the wings killed my folks?
Hell, how old were you guys when the horns stuffed you into that tin can? We're just playing by the rules **they** invented.
We suppose...
MURRR
Anyway, the season finale was stupid as shit.

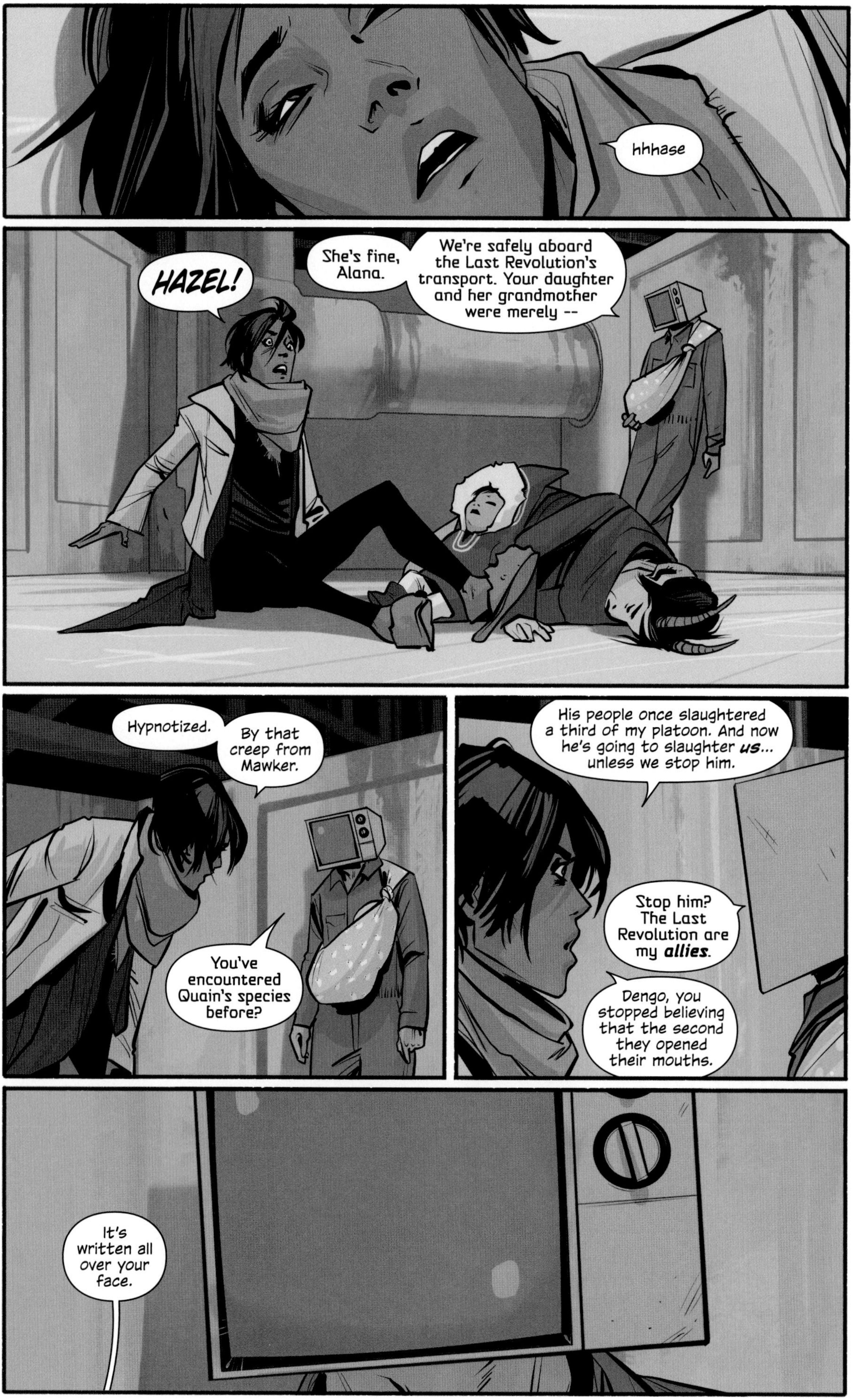
hhhase
HAZEL!
She's fine, Alana.
We're safely aboard the Last Revolution's transport. Your daughter and her grandmother were merely --
Hypnotized.
By that creep from Mawker.
You've encountered Quain's species before?
His people once slaughtered a third of my platoon. And now he's going to slaughter *us*... unless we stop him.
Stop him? The Last Revolution are my *allies*.
Dengo, you stopped believing that the second they opened their mouths.
It's written all over your face.

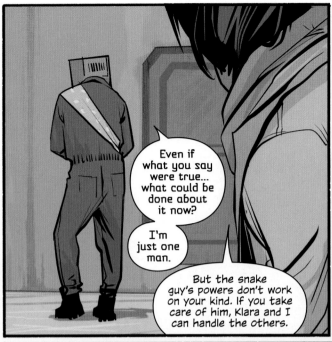

Even if what you say were true... what could be done about it now?

I'm just one man.

But the snake guy's powers don't work on your kind. If you take care of him, Klara and I can handle the others.

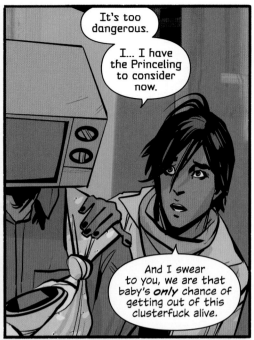

It's too dangerous.

I... I have the Princeling to consider now.

And I swear to you, we are that baby's *only* chance of getting out of this clusterfuck alive.

Look into my eyes and tell me I'm lying.

Dengo.

The hell are you doing in here?

Just making sure our valuables were secure, Zizz.

Great, whatever.

Cap needs to speak with you right away.

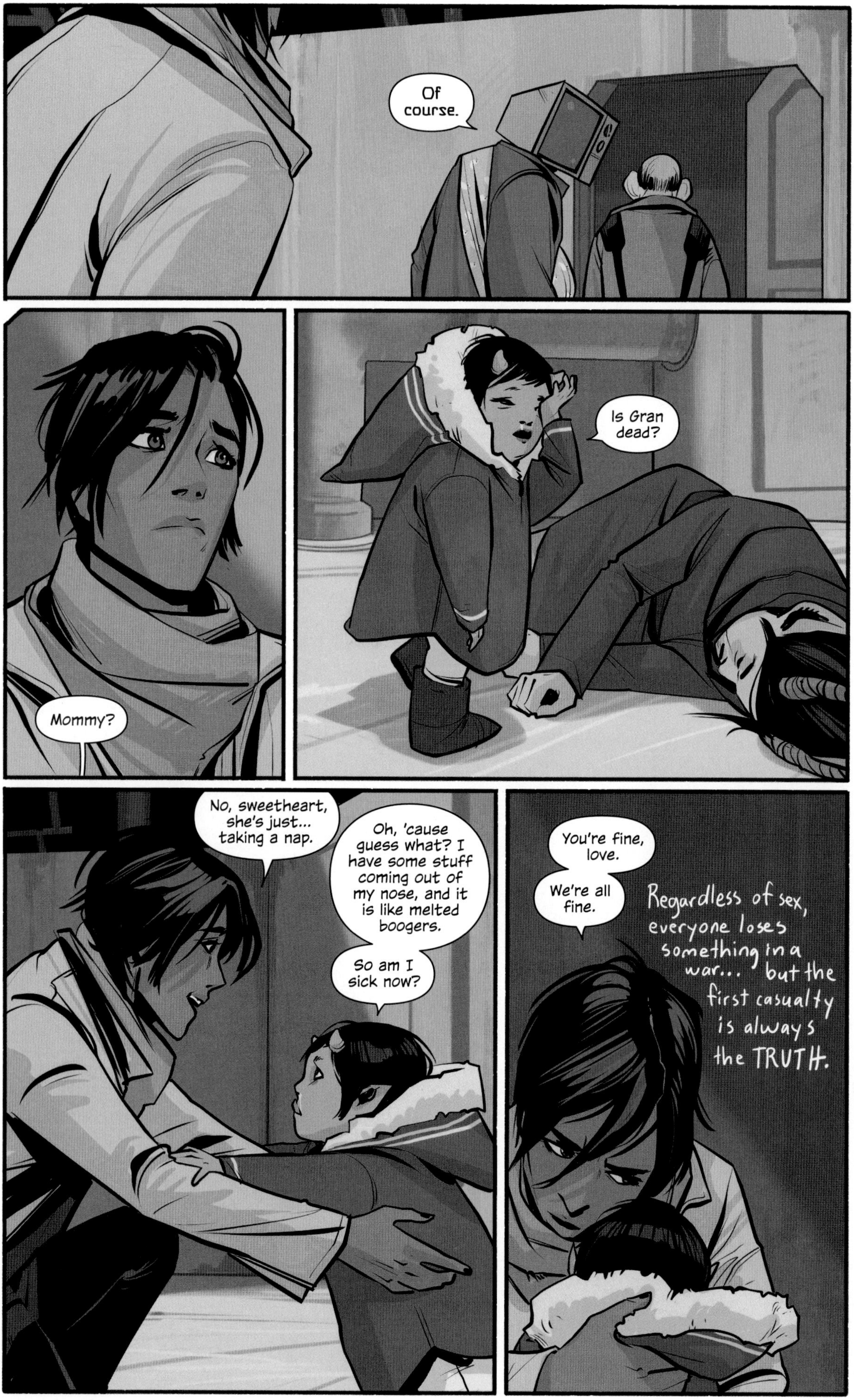
Of course.
Mommy?
Is Gran dead?
No, sweetheart, she's just... taking a nap.
Oh, 'cause guess what? I have some stuff coming out of my nose, and it is like melted boogers.
So am I sick now?
You're fine, love.
We're all fine.
Regardless of sex, everyone loses something in a war... but the first casualty is always the TRUTH.

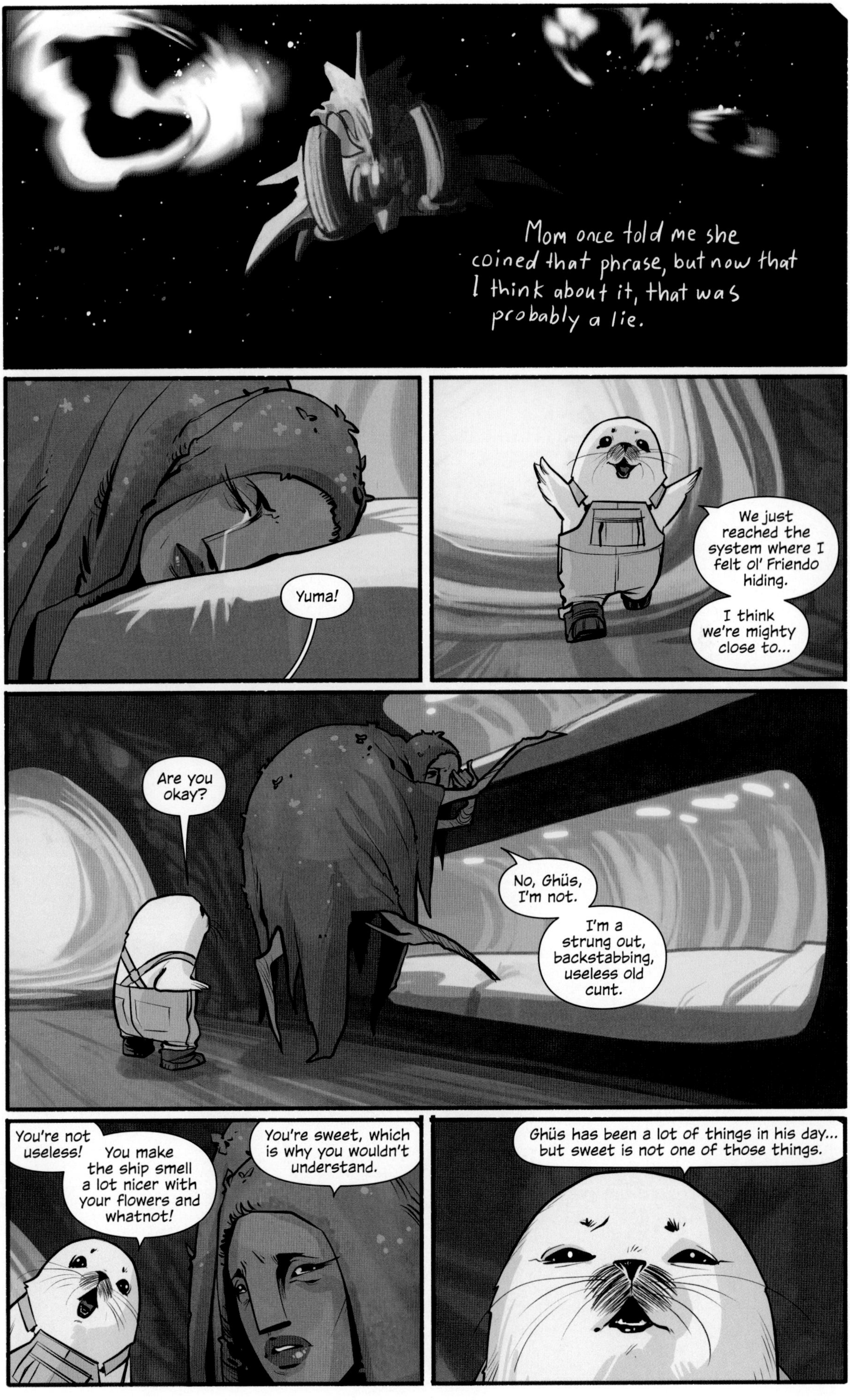
Mom once told me she coined that phrase, but now that I think about it, that was probably a lie.
Yuma!
We just reached the system where I felt ol' Friendo hiding.
I think we're mighty close to...
Are you okay?
No, Ghüs, I'm not.
I'm a strung out, backstabbing, useless old cunt.
You're not useless!
You make the ship smell a lot nicer with your flowers and whatnot!
You're sweet, which is why you wouldn't understand.
Ghüs has been a lot of things in his day... but sweet is not one of those things.

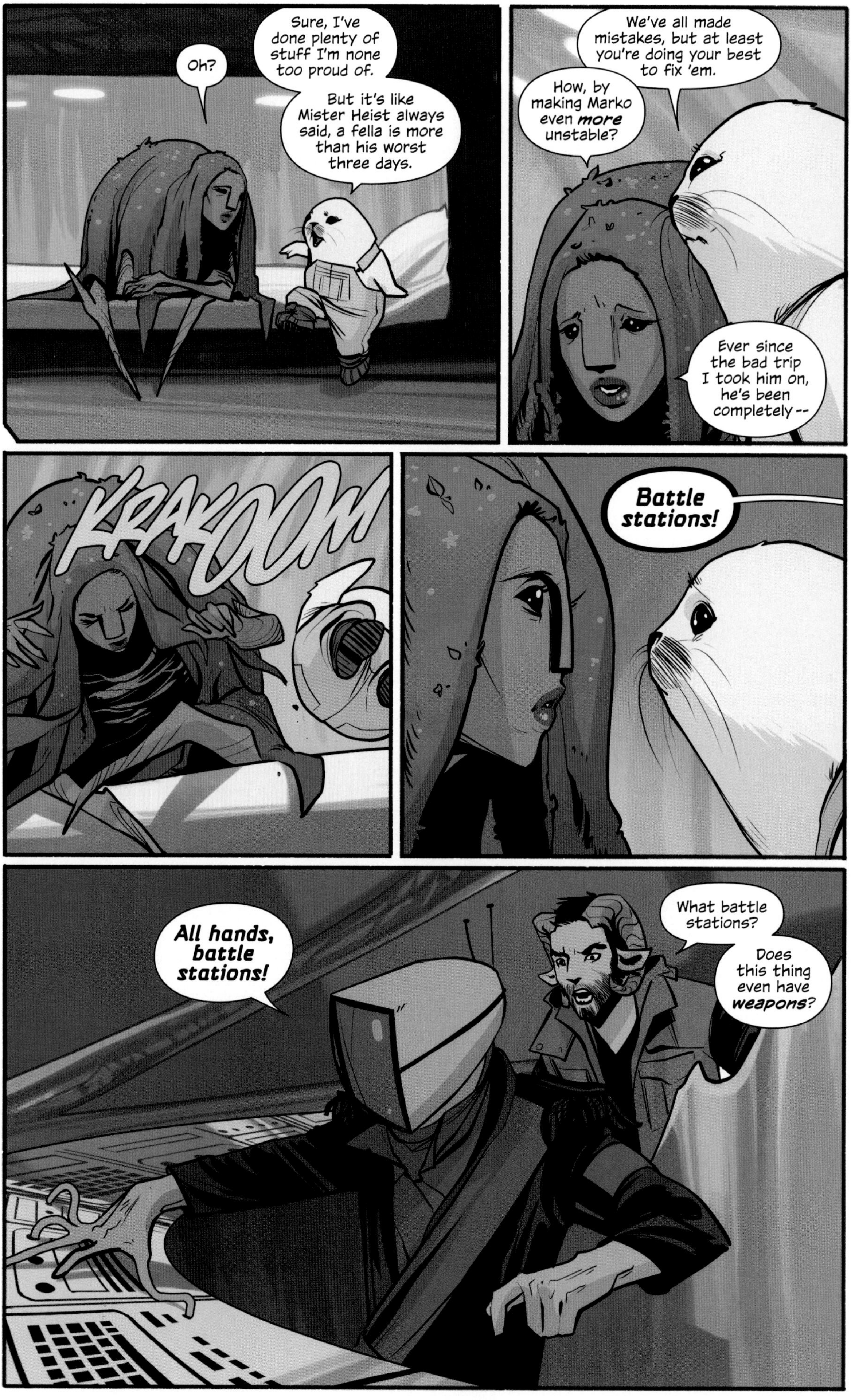
Oh?
Sure, I've done plenty of stuff I'm none too proud of.
But it's like Mister Heist always said, a fella is more than his worst three days.
We've all made mistakes, but at least you're doing your best to fix 'em.
How, by making Marko even **more** unstable?
Ever since the bad trip I took him on, he's been completely --
KRAKOOM
Battle stations!
All hands, battle stations!
What battle stations?
Does this thing even have ***weapons***?

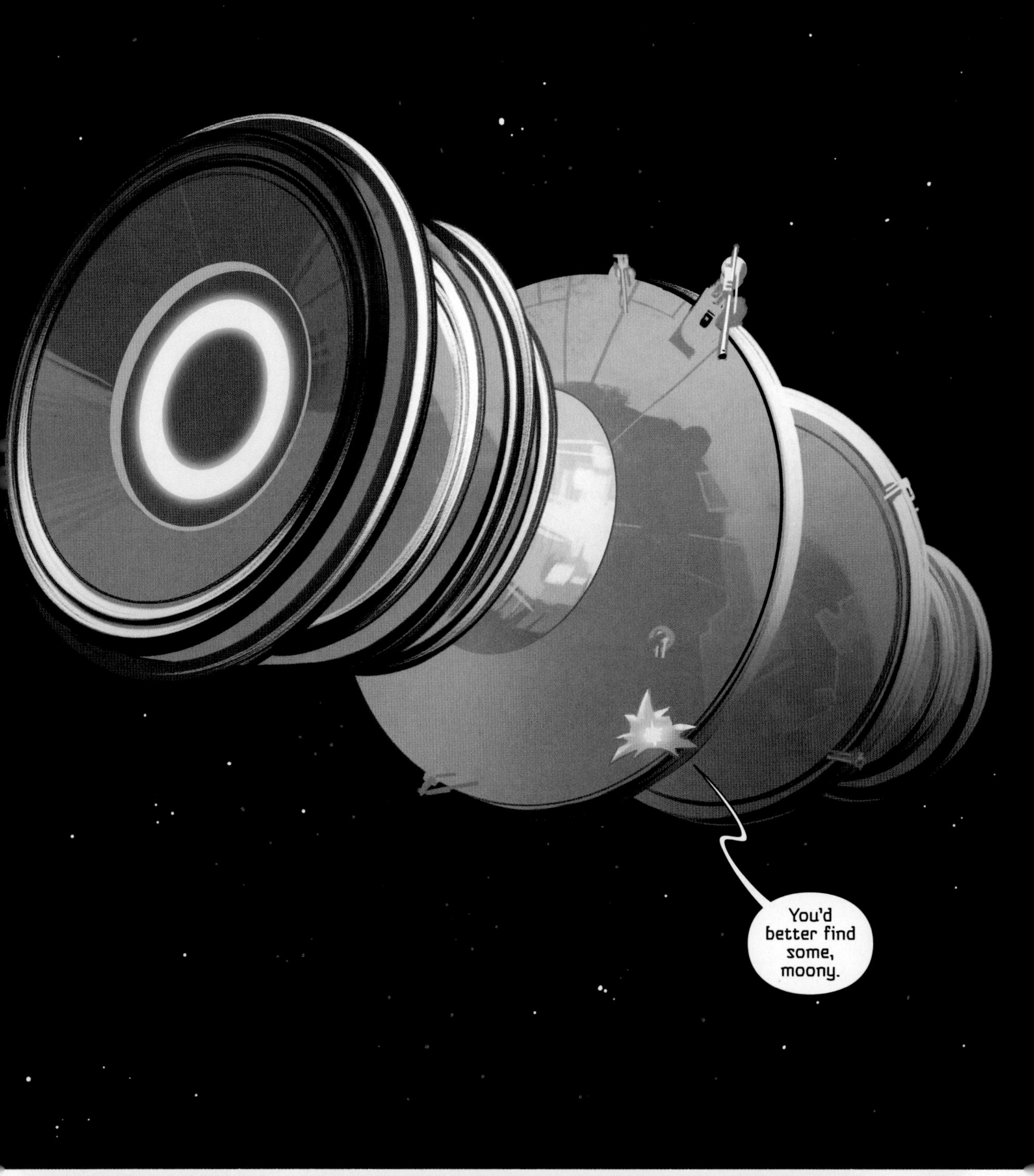
You'd better find some, moony.

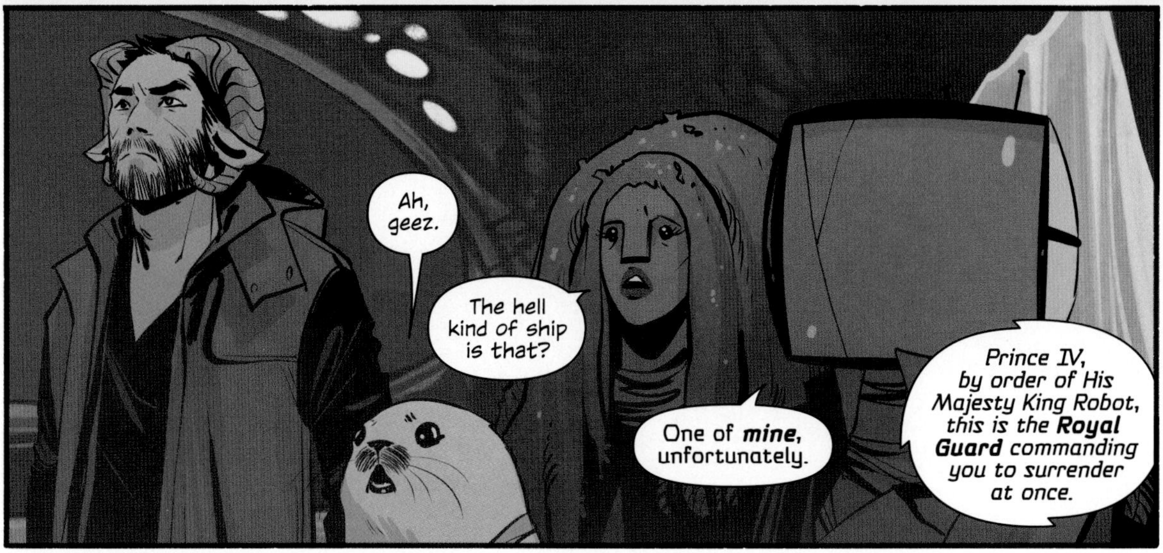
Ah, geez.
The hell kind of ship is that?
One of **mine**, unfortunately.
*Prince IV, by order of His Majesty King Robot, this is the **Royal Guard** commanding you to surrender at once.*

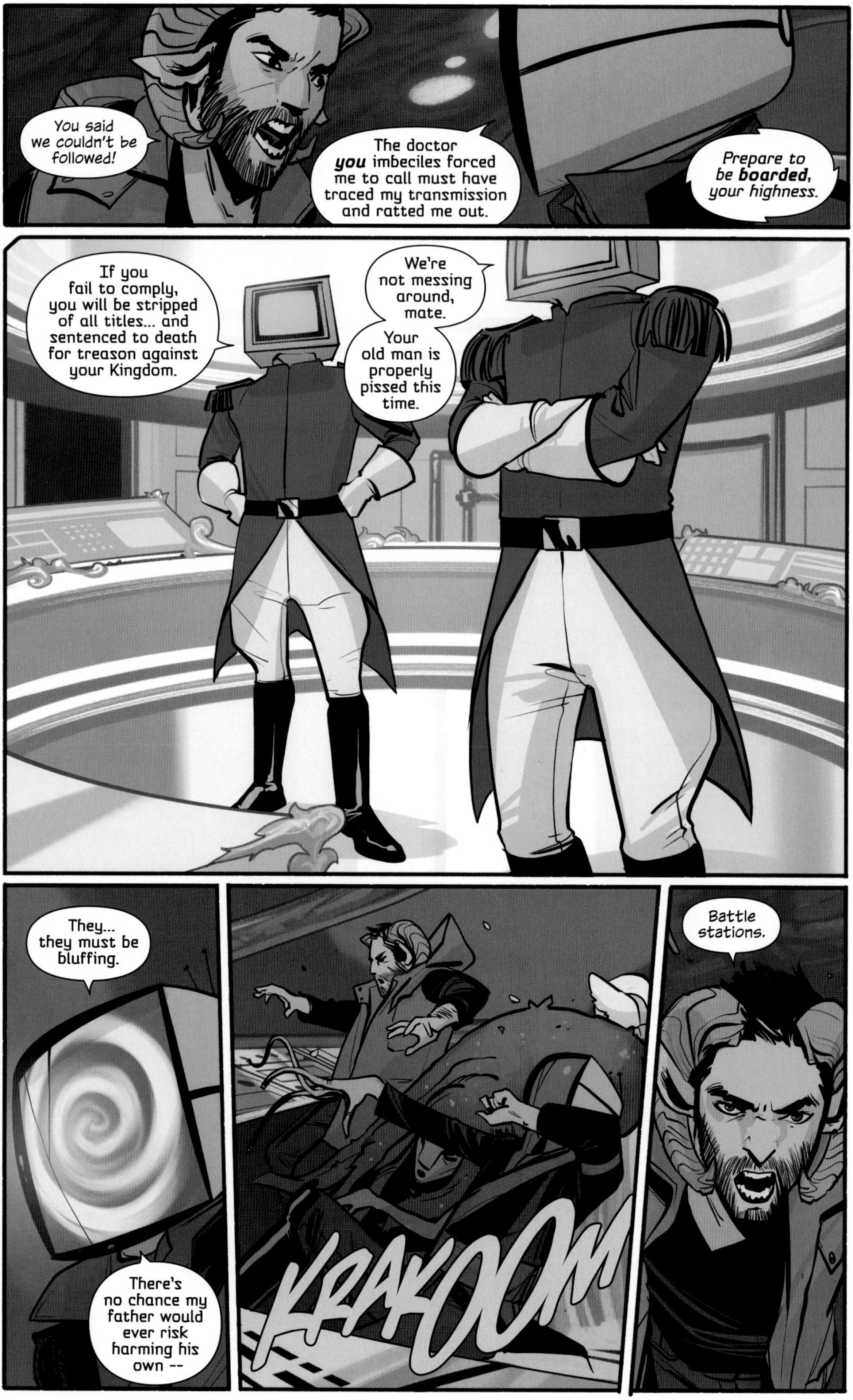

You said we couldn't be followed!
The doctor *you* imbeciles forced me to call must have traced my transmission and ratted me out.
*Prepare to be **boarded**, your highness.*
If you fail to comply, you will be stripped of all titles... and sentenced to death for treason against your Kingdom.
We're not messing around, mate.
Your old man is properly pissed this time.
They... they must be bluffing.
There's no chance my father would ever risk harming his own --
KRAKOOM
Battle stations.

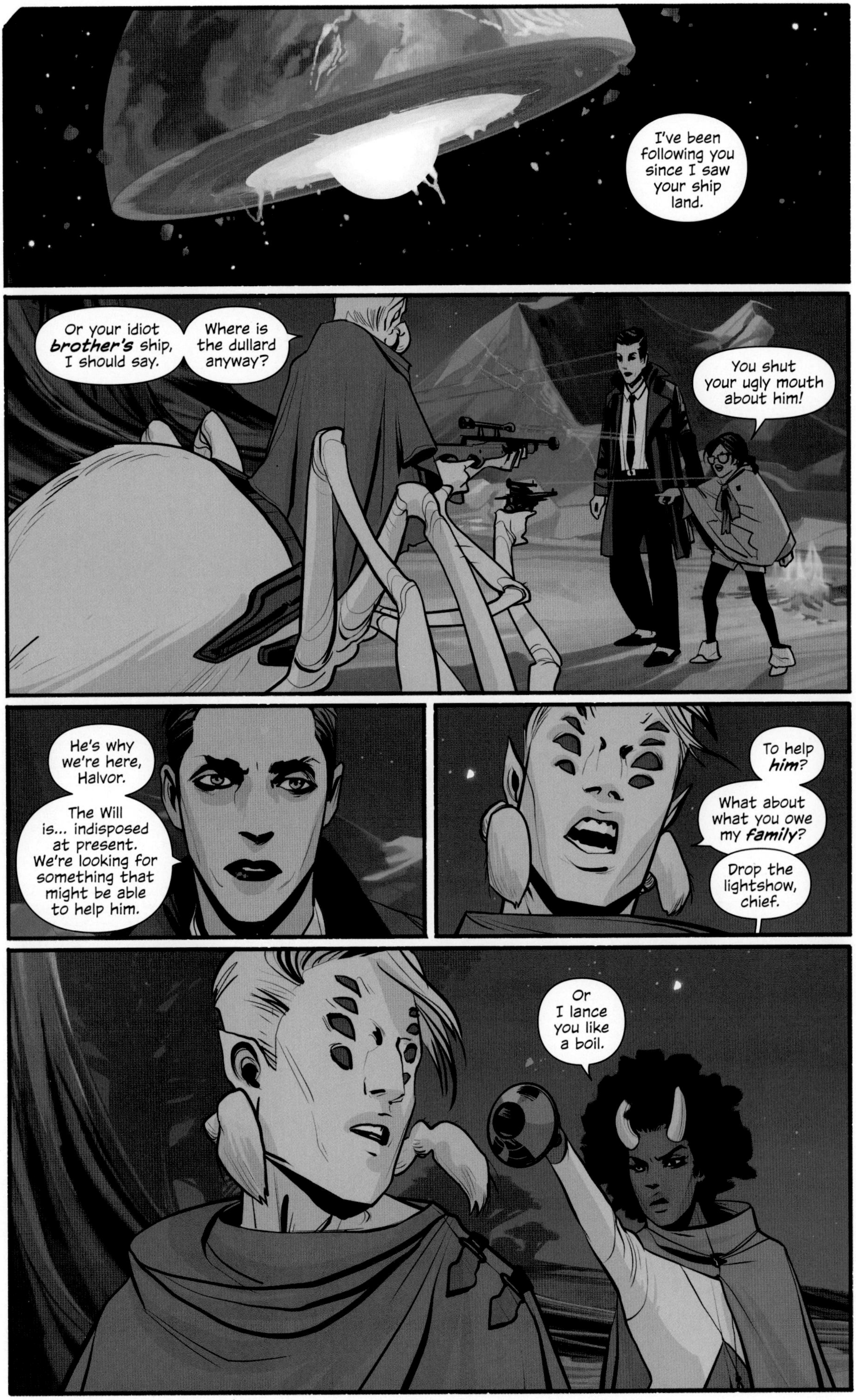
I've been following you since I saw your ship land.
Or your idiot **brother's** ship, I should say.
Where is the dullard anyway?
You shut your ugly mouth about him!
He's why we're here, Halvor.
The Will is... indisposed at present. We're looking for something that might be able to help him.
To help *him*?
What about what you owe my *family*?
Drop the lightshow, chief.
Or I lance you like a boil.

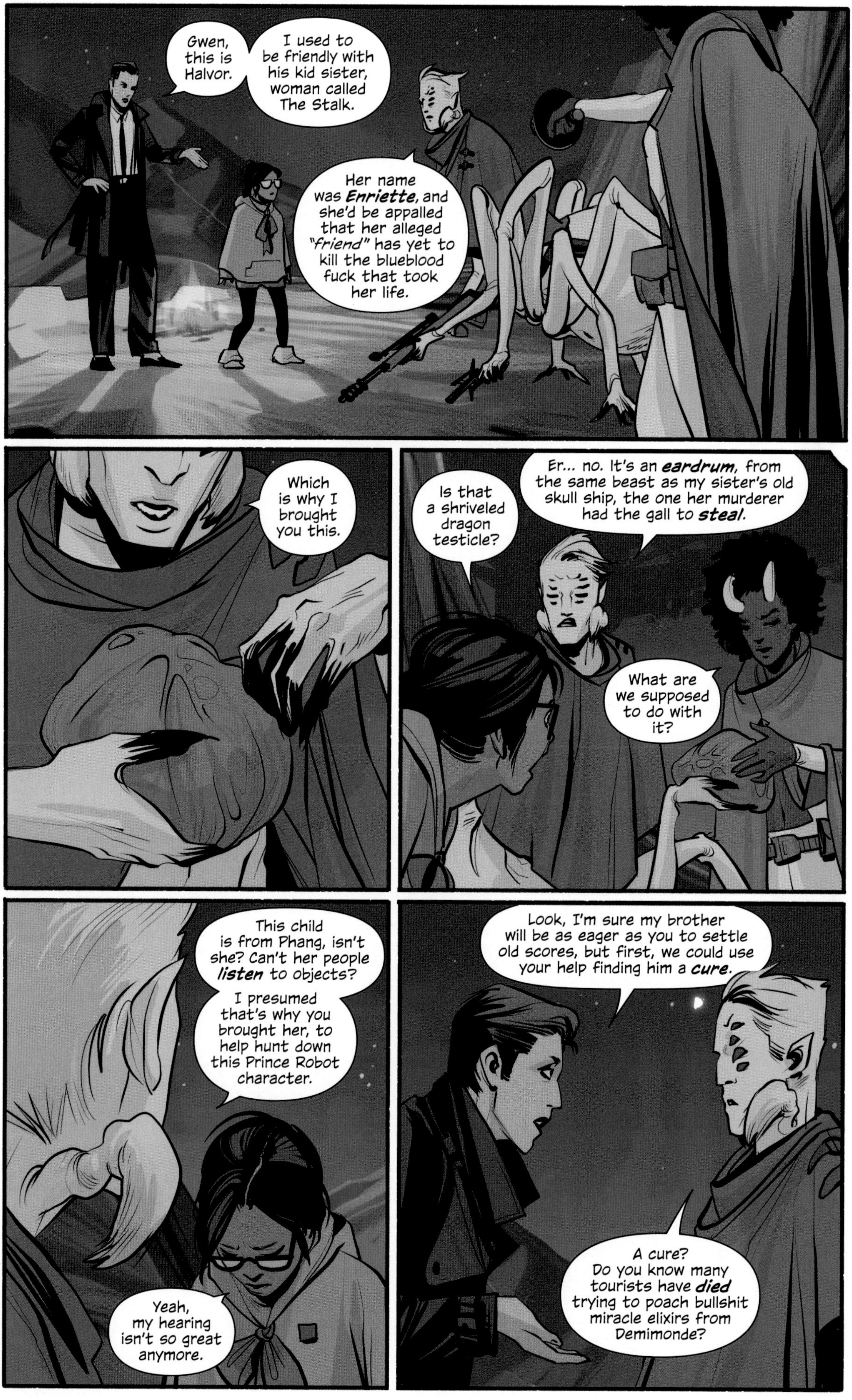
Gwen, this is Halvor.
I used to be friendly with his kid sister, woman called The Stalk.
Her name was Enriette, and she'd be appalled that her alleged "friend" has yet to kill the blueblood fuck that took her life.
Which is why I brought you this.
Is that a shriveled dragon testicle?
Er... no. It's an eardrum, from the same beast as my sister's old skull ship, the one her murderer had the gall to steal.
What are we supposed to do with it?
This child is from Phang, isn't she? Can't her people listen to objects?
I presumed that's why you brought her, to help hunt down this Prince Robot character.
Yeah, my hearing isn't so great anymore.
Look, I'm sure my brother will be as eager as you to settle old scores, but first, we could use your help finding him a cure.
A cure? Do you know many tourists have died trying to poach bullshit miracle elixirs from Demimonde?

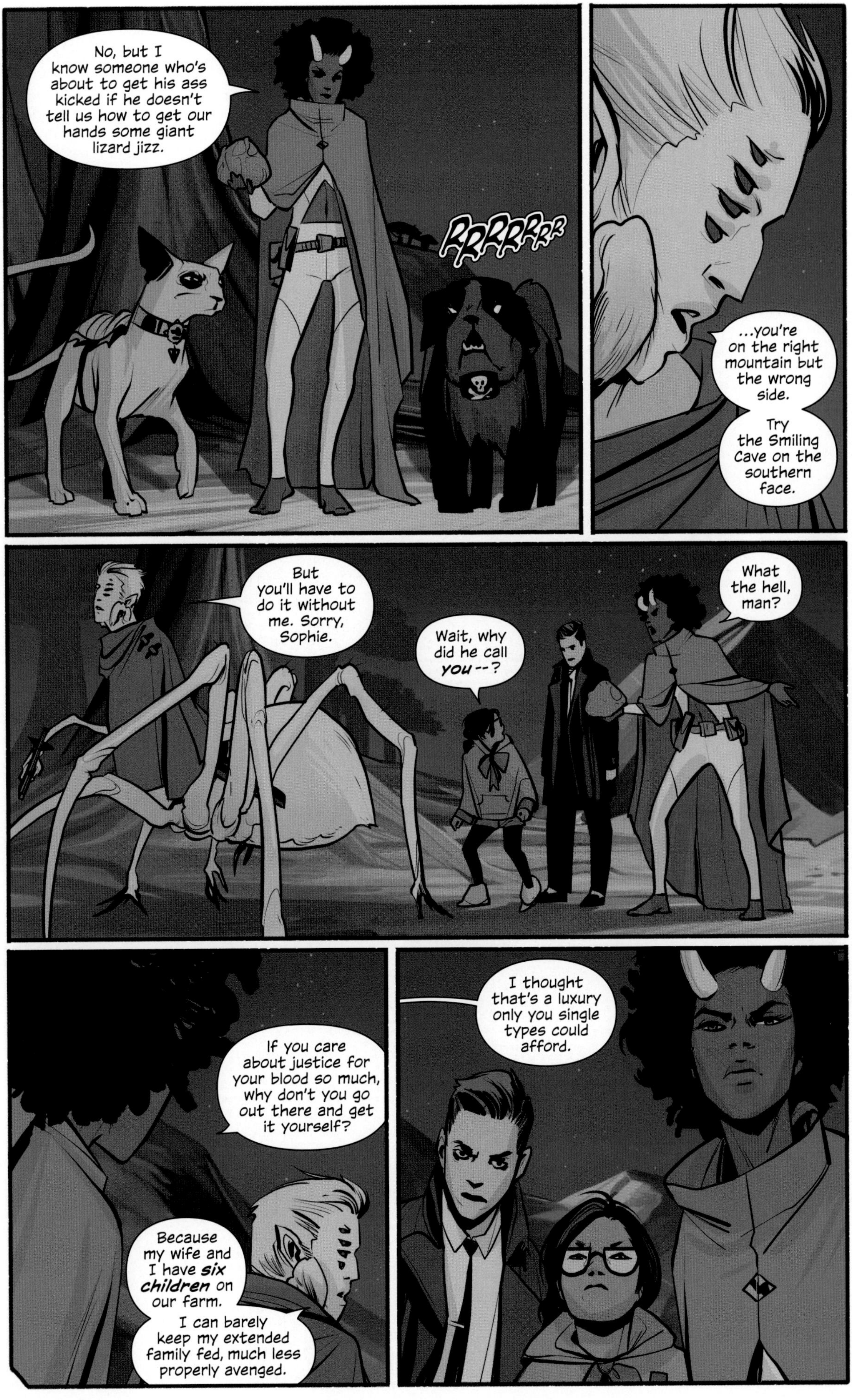
No, but I know someone who's about to get his ass kicked if he doesn't tell us how to get our hands some giant lizard jizz.
RRRRRRR
...you're on the right mountain but the wrong side.
Try the Smiling Cave on the southern face.
But you'll have to do it without me. Sorry, Sophie.
Wait, why did he call *you*--?
What the hell, man?
If you care about justice for your blood so much, why don't you go out there and get it yourself?
Because my wife and I have *six children* on our farm.
I can barely keep my extended family fed, much less properly avenged.
I thought that's a luxury only you single types could afford.

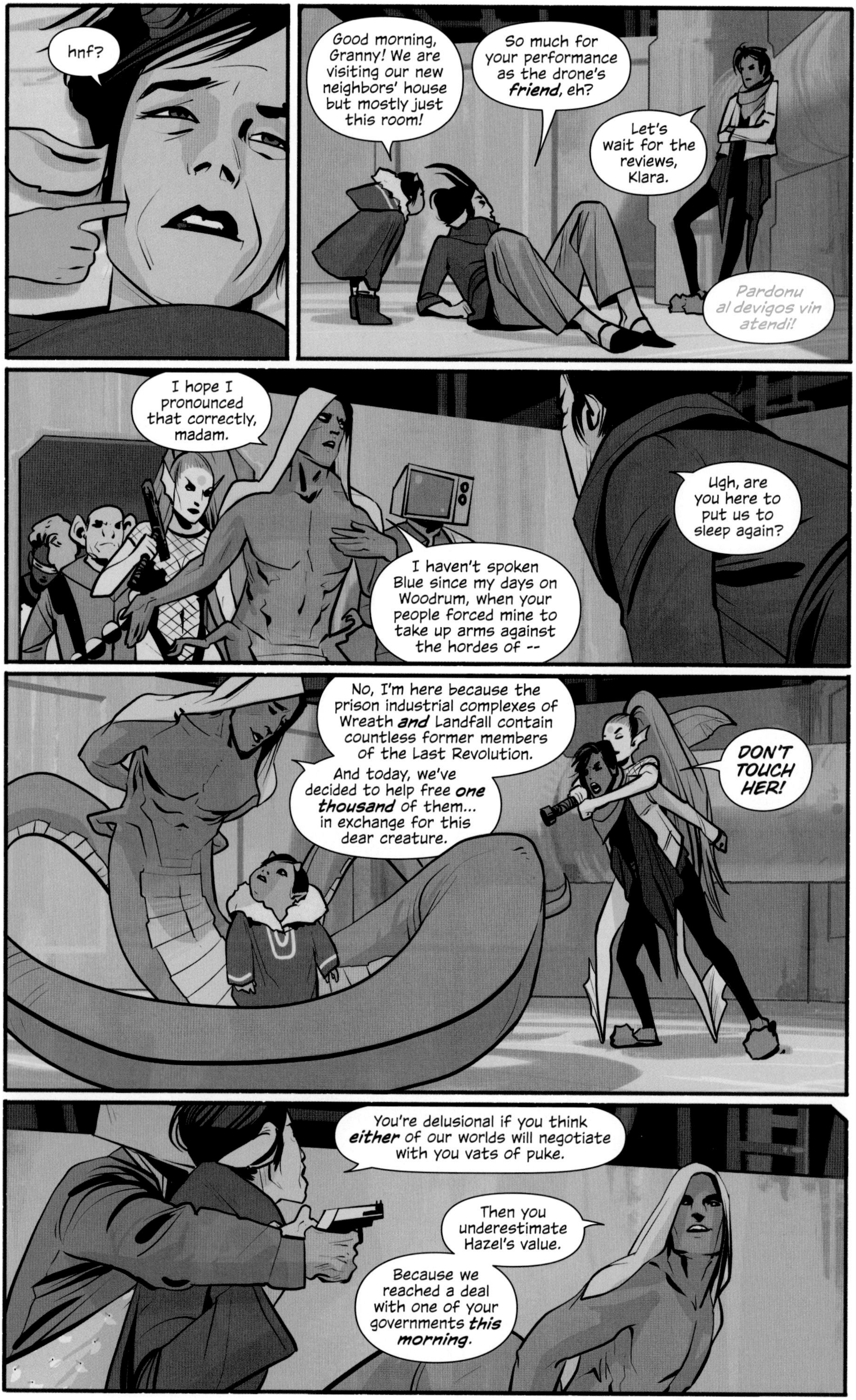
hnf?
Good morning, Granny! We are visiting our new neighbors' house but mostly just this room!
So much for your performance as the drone's *friend*, eh?
Let's wait for the reviews, Klara.
Pardonu al devigos vin atendi!
I hope I pronounced that correctly, madam.
Ugh, are you here to put us to sleep again?
I haven't spoken Blue since my days on Woodrum, when your people forced mine to take up arms against the hordes of --
No, I'm here because the prison industrial complexes of Wreath ***and*** Landfall contain countless former members of the Last Revolution.
And today, we've decided to help free ***one thousand*** of them... in exchange for this dear creature.
DON'T TOUCH HER!
You're delusional if you think ***either*** of our worlds will negotiate with you vats of puke.
Then you underestimate Hazel's value.
Because we reached a deal with one of your governments ***this morning***.

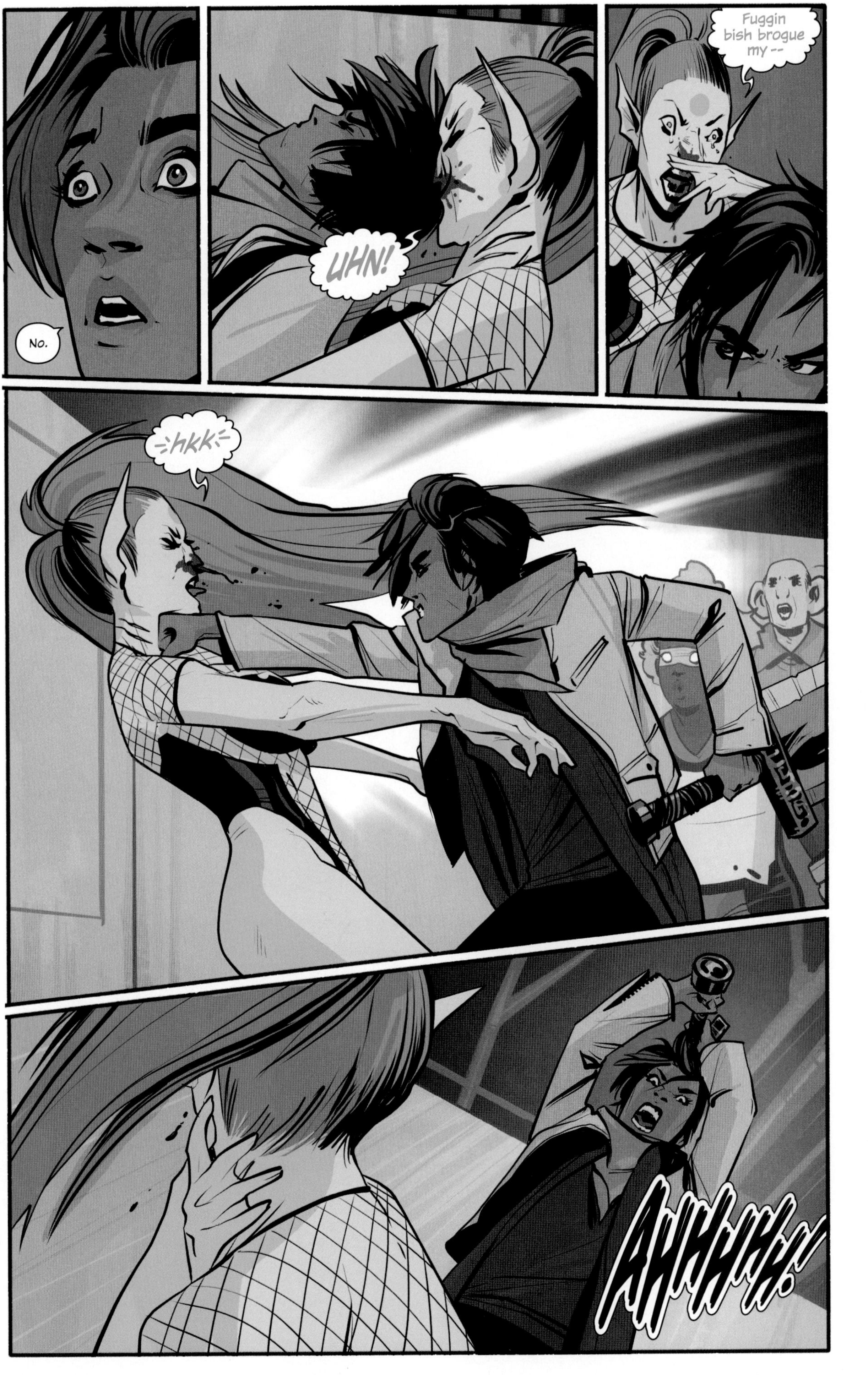
No.
UHN!
Fuggin bish brogue my --
hkk
AHHHHH!

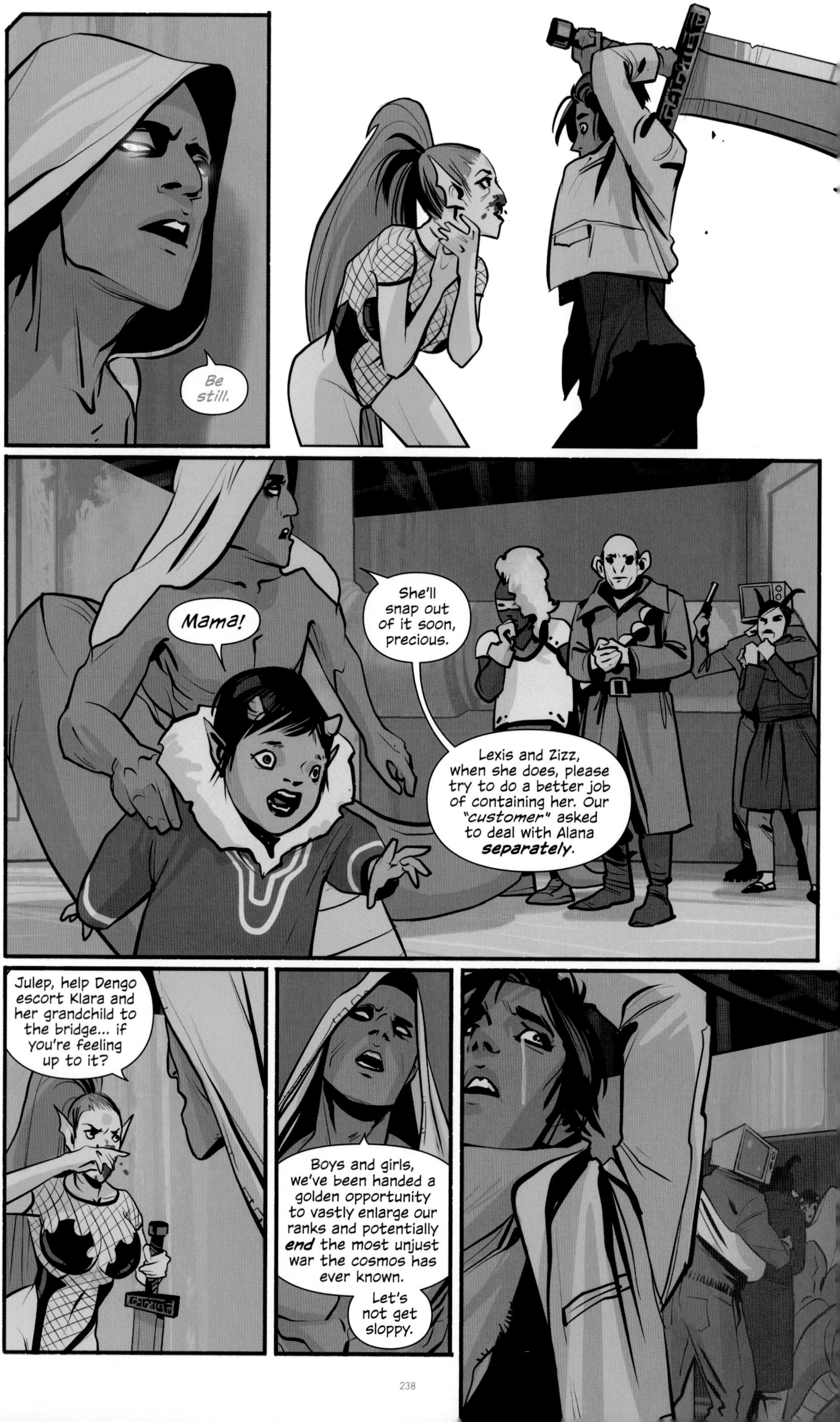

Be still.
Mama!
She'll snap out of it soon, precious.
Lexis and Zizz, when she does, please try to do a better job of containing her. Our *"customer"* asked to deal with Alana ***separately***.
Julep, help Dengo escort Klara and her grandchild to the bridge... if you're feeling up to it?
Boys and girls, we've been handed a golden opportunity to vastly enlarge our ranks and potentially ***end*** the most unjust war the cosmos has ever known.
Let's not get sloppy.

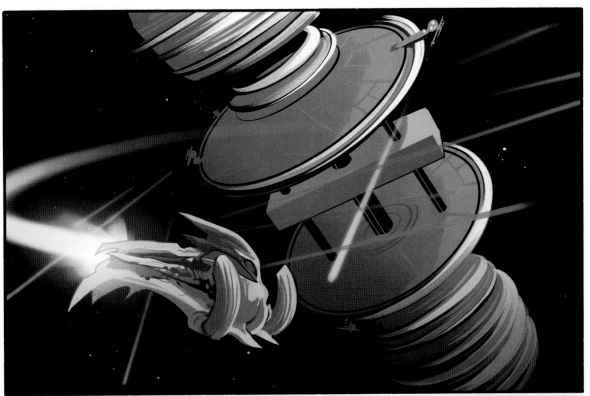

Dammit, can you hit bloody *anything*?

When I'm being piloted by someone who actually knows how to --

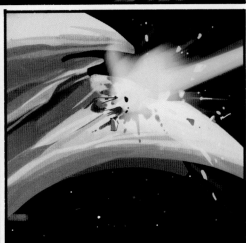

We've got some kind of *warning light* flashing for the engine room!

Freeloaders, get down there and *fix it!*

This isn't a fight we can win! We should try to *run* before --

Just *go*, Yuma!

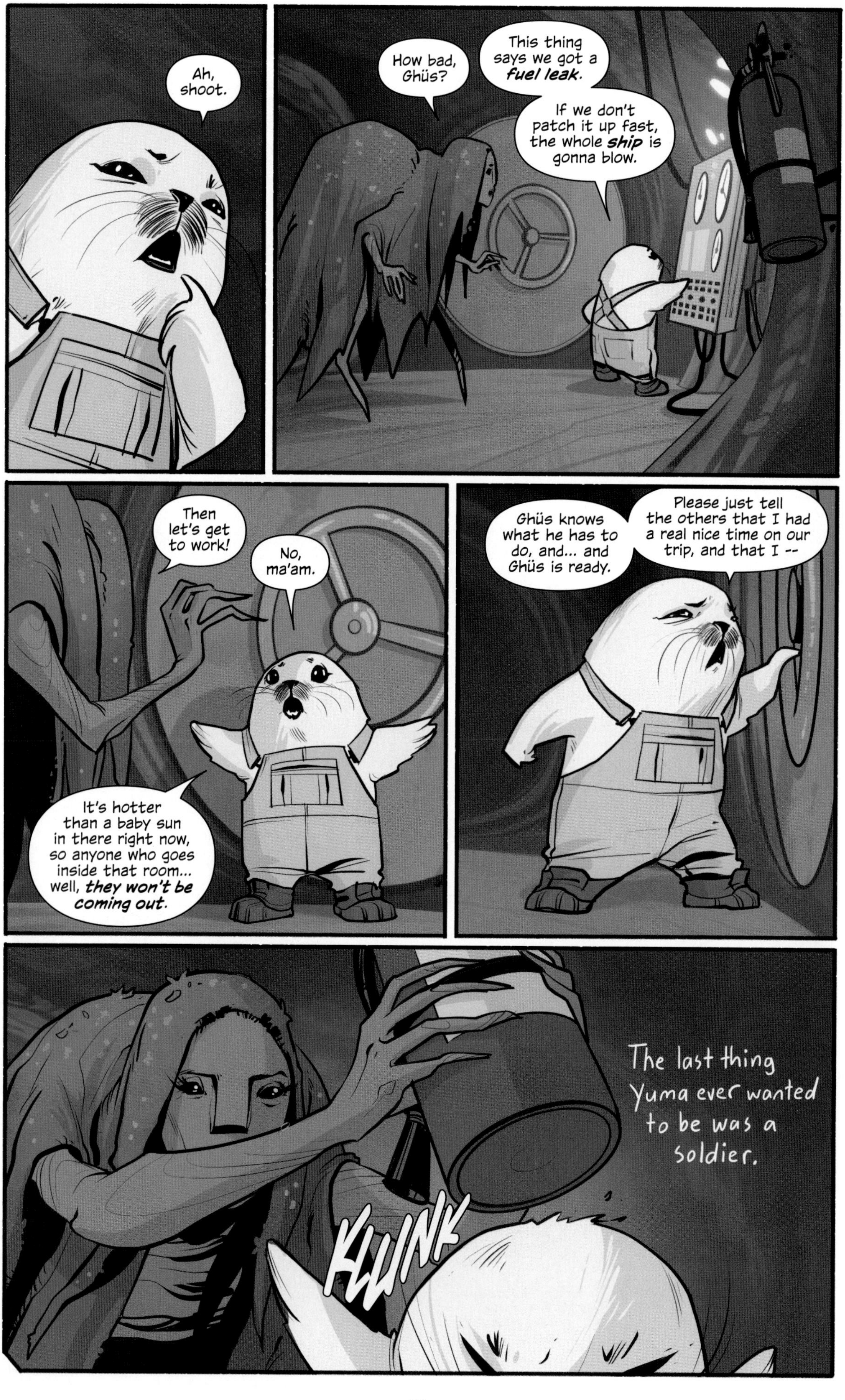
Ah, shoot.
How bad, Ghüs?
This thing says we got a **fuel leak**.
If we don't patch it up fast, the whole **ship** is gonna blow.
Then let's get to work!
No, ma'am.
It's hotter than a baby sun in there right now, so anyone who goes inside that room... well, **they won't be coming out**.
Ghüs knows what he has to do, and... and Ghüs is ready.
Please just tell the others that I had a real nice time on our trip, and that I --
The last thing Yuma ever wanted to be was a soldier.
KLUNK

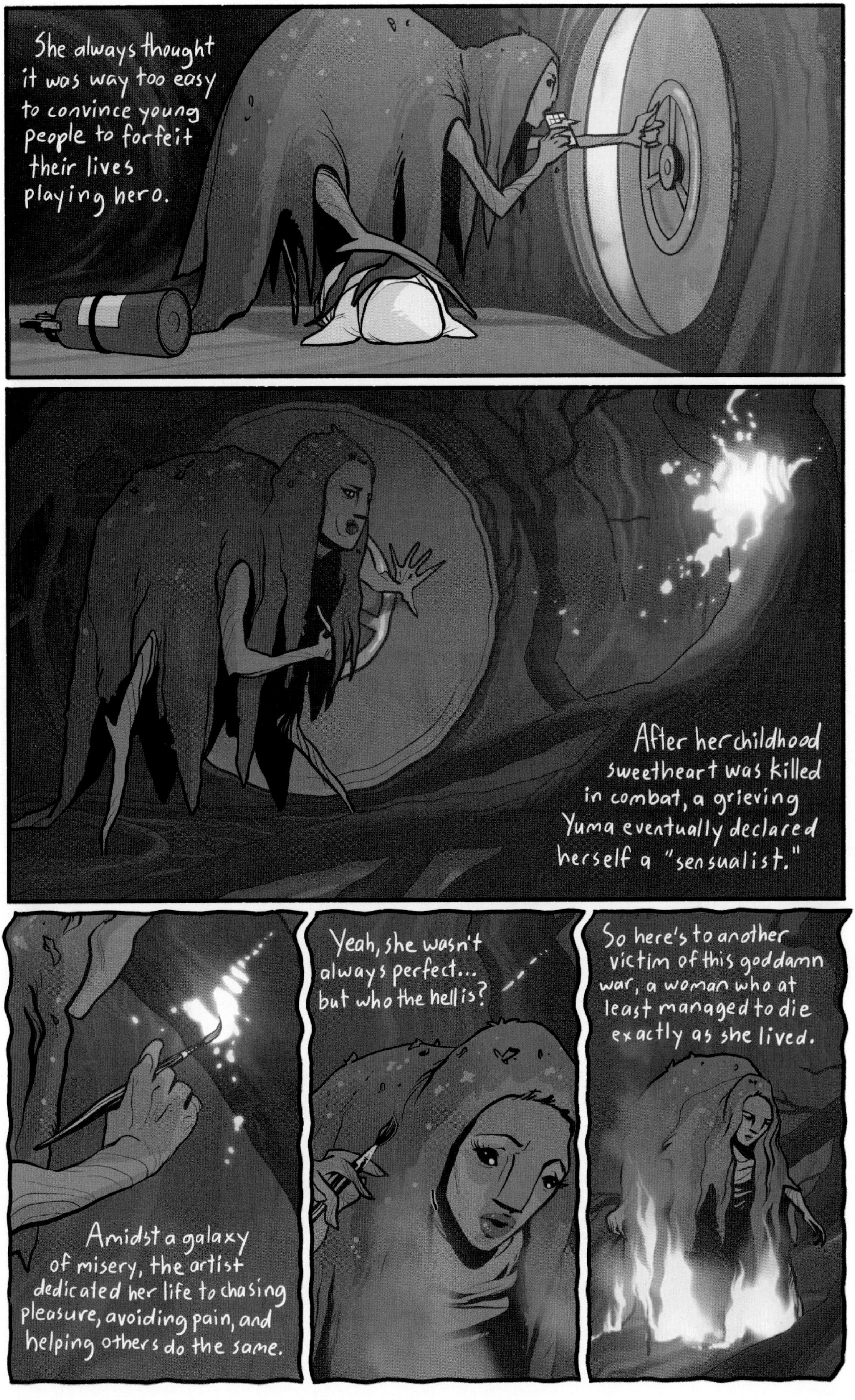
She always thought it was way too easy to convince young people to forfeit their lives playing hero.
After her childhood sweetheart was killed in combat, a grieving Yuma eventually declared herself a "sensualist."
Amidst a galaxy of misery, the artist dedicated her life to chasing pleasure, avoiding pain, and helping others do the same.
Yeah, she wasn't always perfect... but who the hell is?
So here's to another victim of this goddamn war, a woman who at least managed to die exactly as she lived.

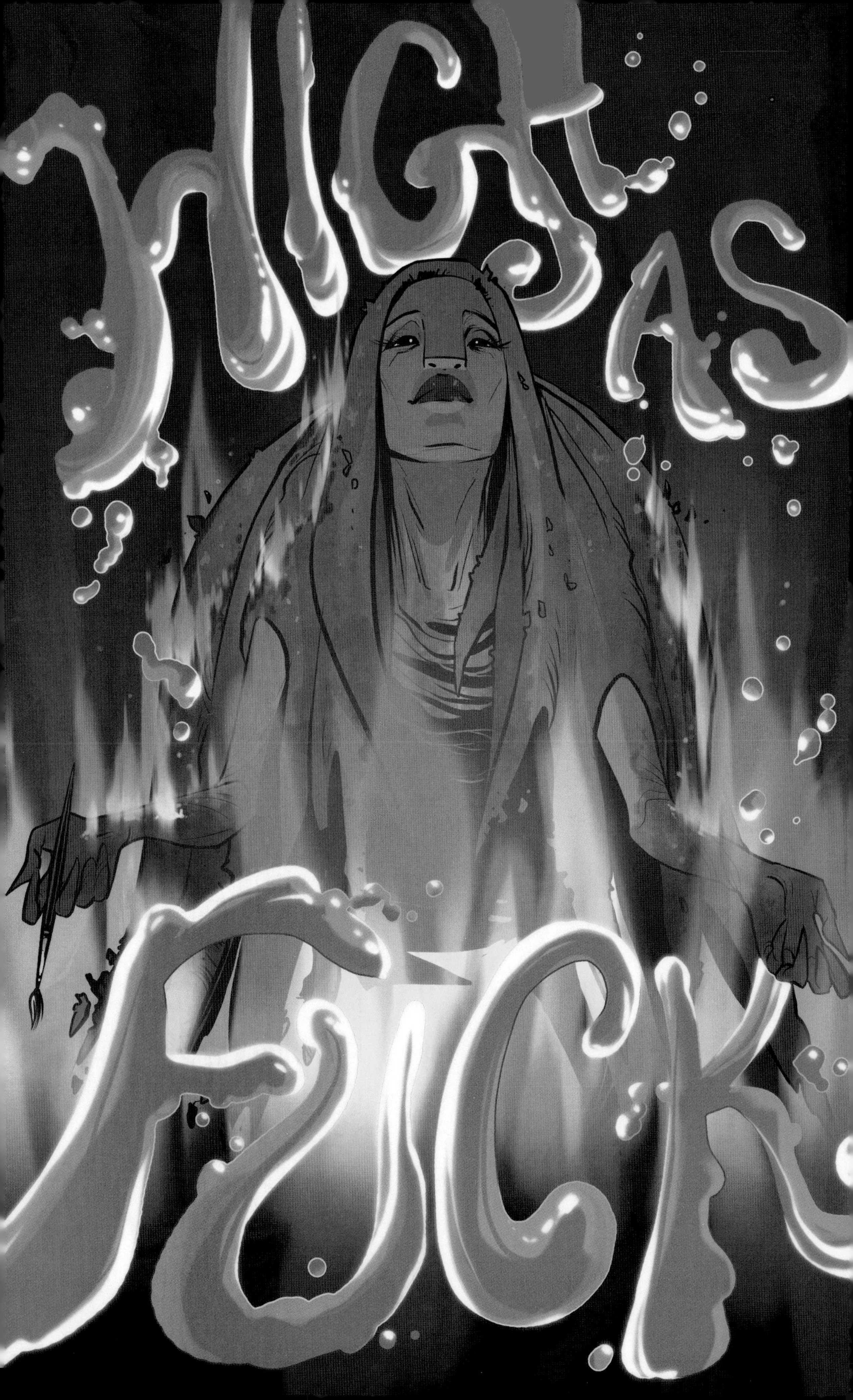
HIGH AS
FUCK

end chapter twenty-eight

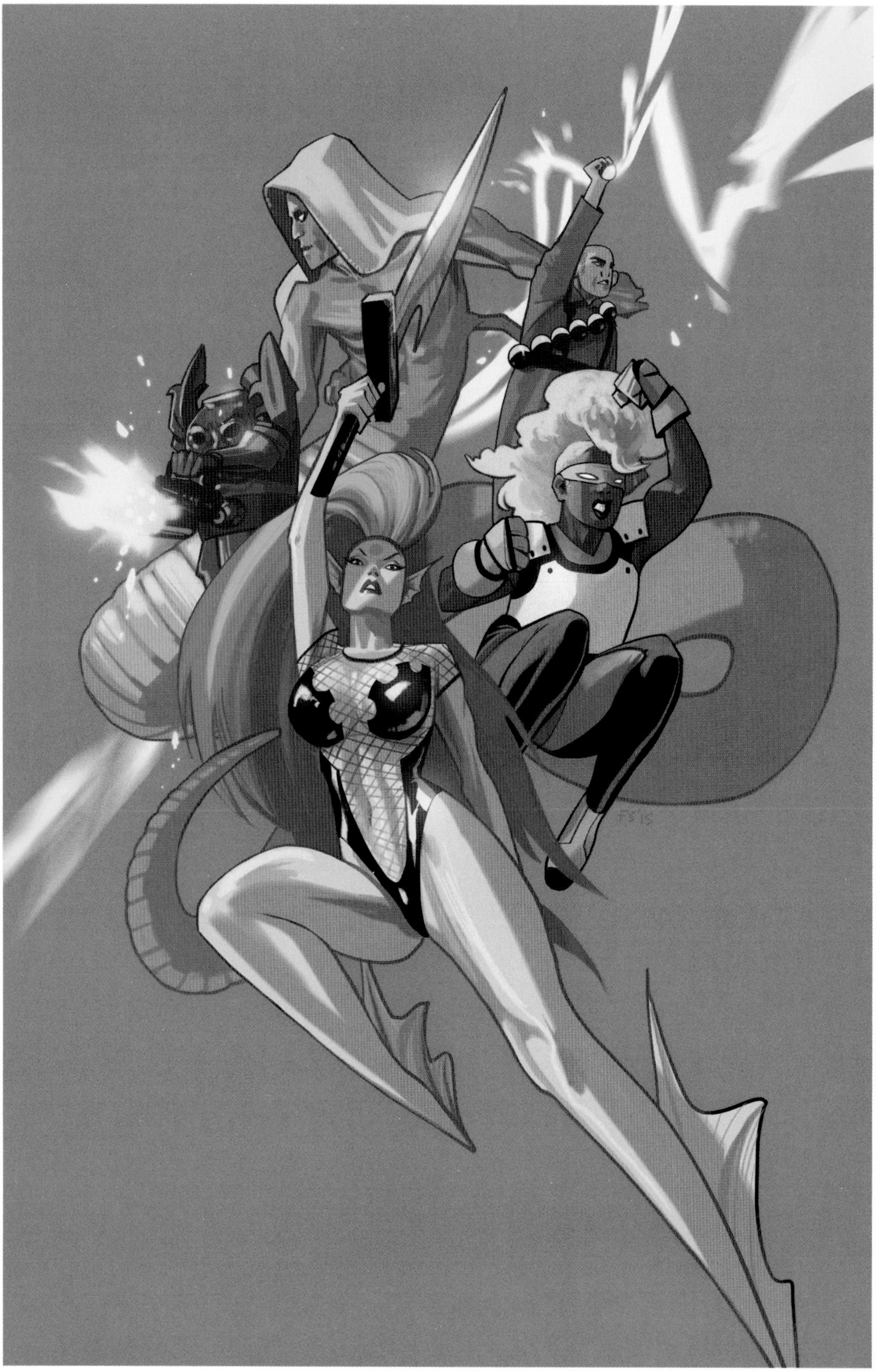

CHAPTER

TWENTY-NINE

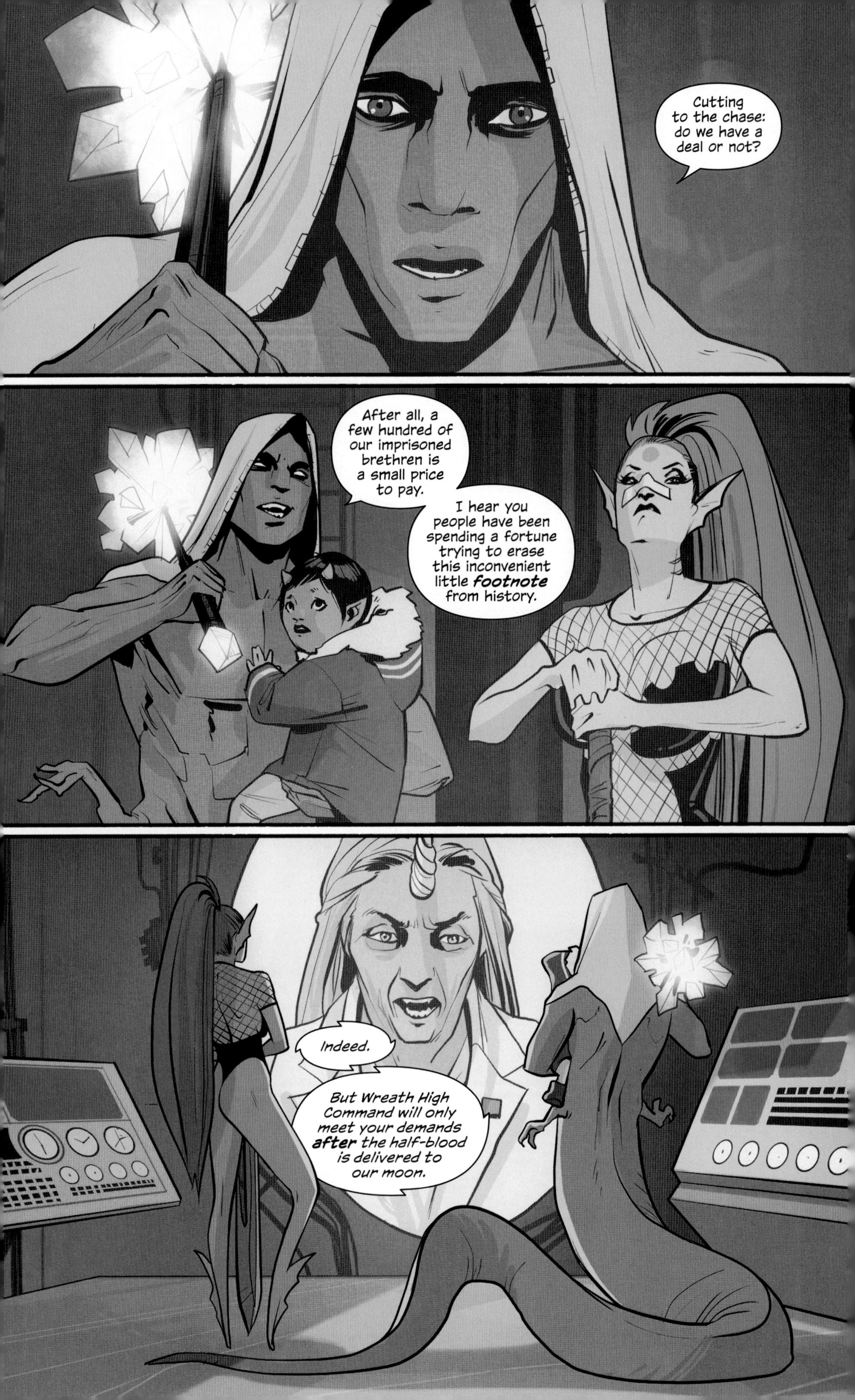

Cutting to the chase: do we have a deal or not?
After all, a few hundred of our imprisoned brethren is a small price to pay.
I hear you people have been spending a fortune trying to erase this inconvenient little **footnote** from history.
Indeed.
*But Wreath High Command will only meet your demands **after** the half-blood is delivered to our moon.*

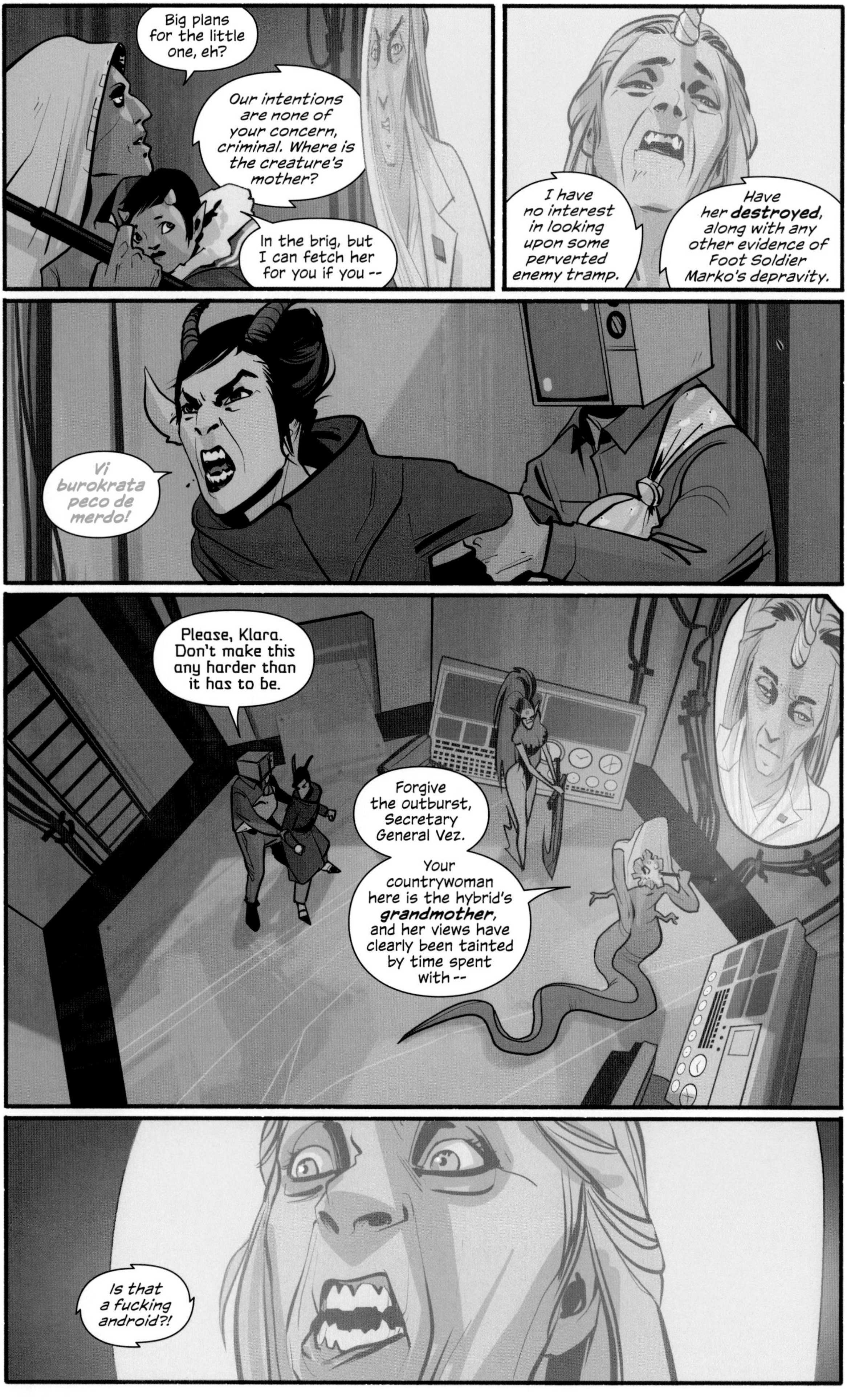

Big plans for the little one, eh?
Our intentions are none of your concern, criminal. Where is the creature's mother?
In the brig, but I can fetch her for you if you --
I have no interest in looking upon some perverted enemy tramp.
Have her **destroyed**, along with any other evidence of Foot Soldier Marko's depravity.
Vi burokrata peco de merdo!
Please, Klara. Don't make this any harder than it has to be.
Forgive the outburst, Secretary General Vez.
Your countrywoman here is the hybrid's ***grandmother***, and her views have clearly been tainted by time spent with --
Is that a fucking android?!

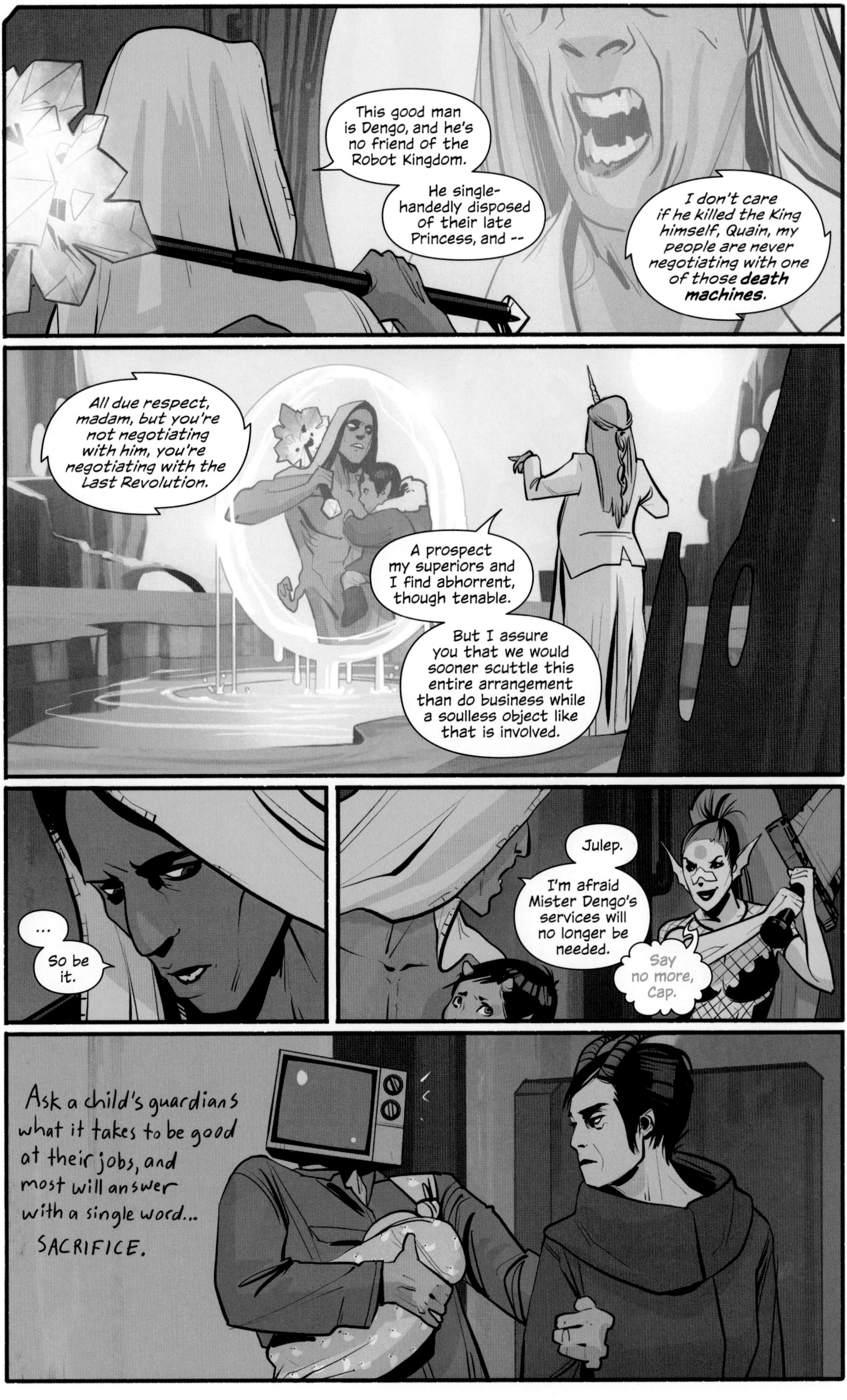
This good man is Dengo, and he's no friend of the Robot Kingdom.
He single-handedly disposed of their late Princess, and --
I don't care if he killed the King himself, Quain, my people are never negotiating with one of those **death machines**.
All due respect, madam, but you're not negotiating with him, you're negotiating with the Last Revolution.
A prospect my superiors and I find abhorrent, though tenable.
But I assure you that we would sooner scuttle this entire arrangement than do business while a soulless object like that is involved.
...
So be it.
Julep.
I'm afraid Mister Dengo's services will no longer be needed.
Say no more, Cap.
Ask a child's guardians what it takes to be good at their jobs, and most will answer with a single word... SACRIFICE.

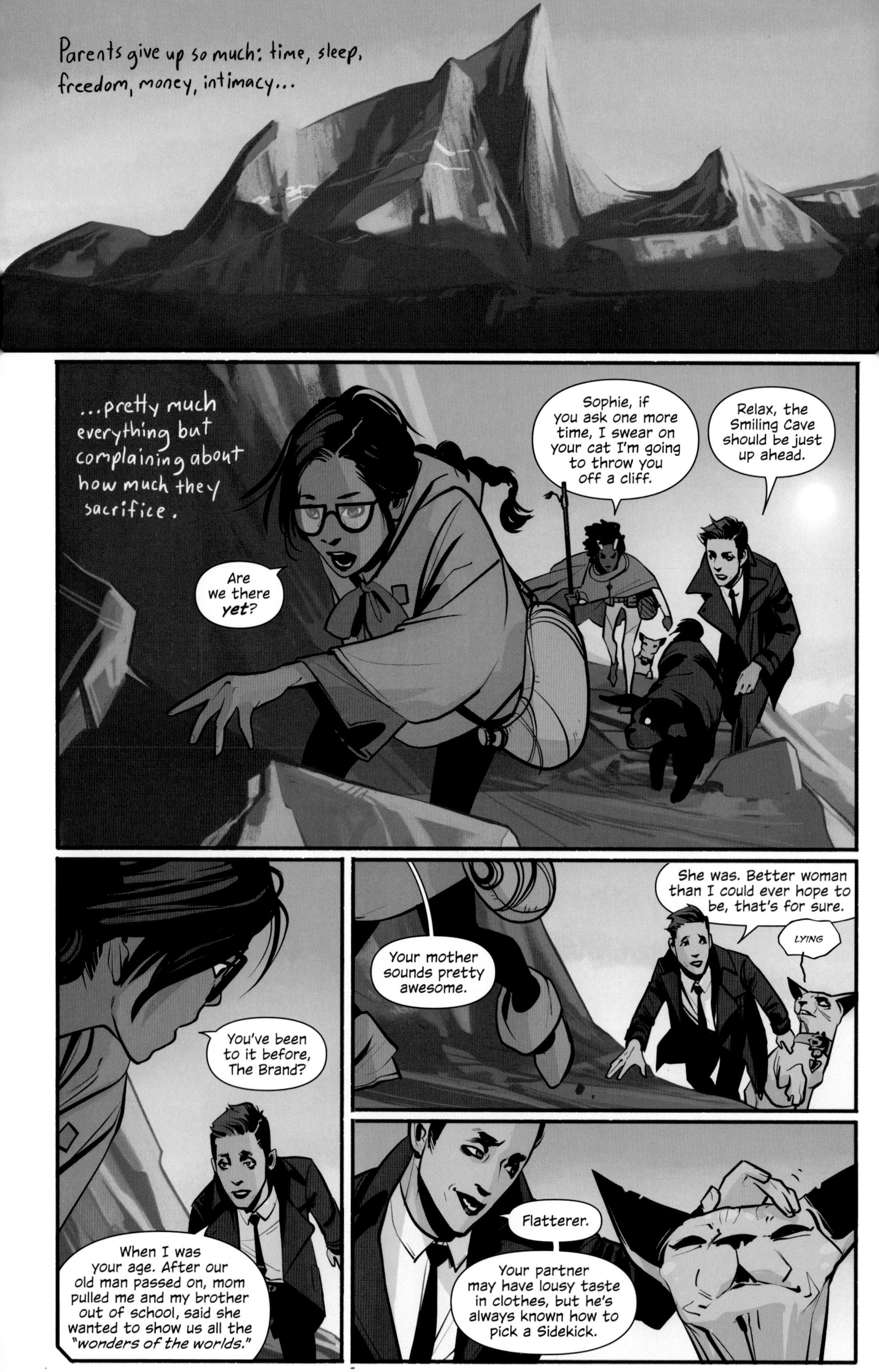

Parents give up so much: time, sleep, freedom, money, intimacy...
...pretty much everything but complaining about how much they sacrifice.
Are we there *yet*?
Sophie, if you ask one more time, I swear on your cat I'm going to throw you off a cliff.
Relax, the Smiling Cave should be just up ahead.
You've been to it before, The Brand?
When I was your age. After our old man passed on, mom pulled me and my brother out of school, said she wanted to show us all the "*wonders of the worlds.*"
Your mother sounds pretty awesome.
She was. Better woman than I could ever hope to be, that's for sure.
LYING
Flatterer.
Your partner may have lousy taste in clothes, but he's always known how to pick a Sidekick.

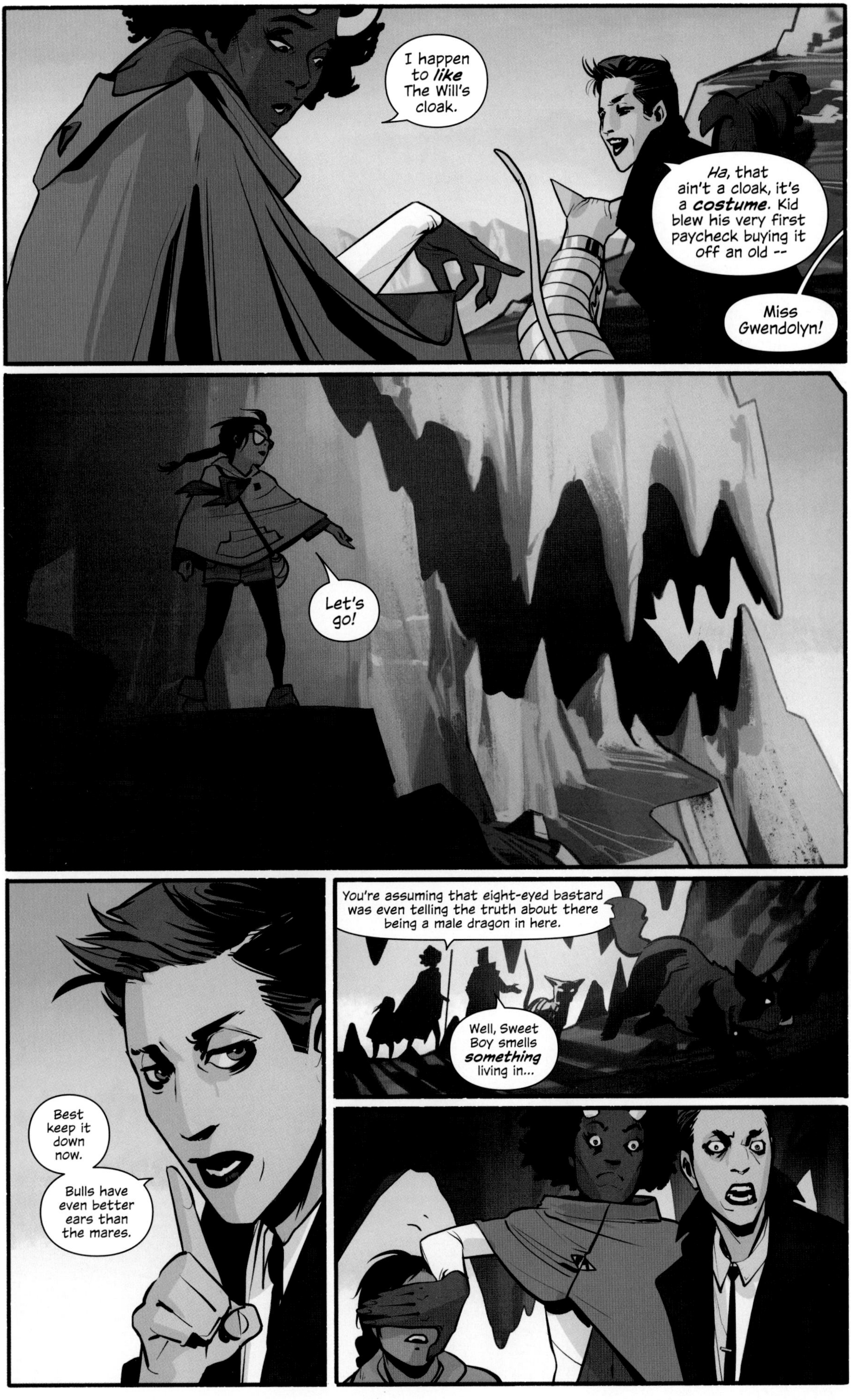

I happen to *like* The Will's cloak.
Ha, that ain't a cloak, it's a ***costume***. Kid blew his very first paycheck buying it off an old --
Miss Gwendolyn!
Let's go!
You're assuming that eight-eyed bastard was even telling the truth about there being a male dragon in here.
Well, Sweet Boy smells ***something*** living in...
Best keep it down now.
Bulls have even better ears than the mares.

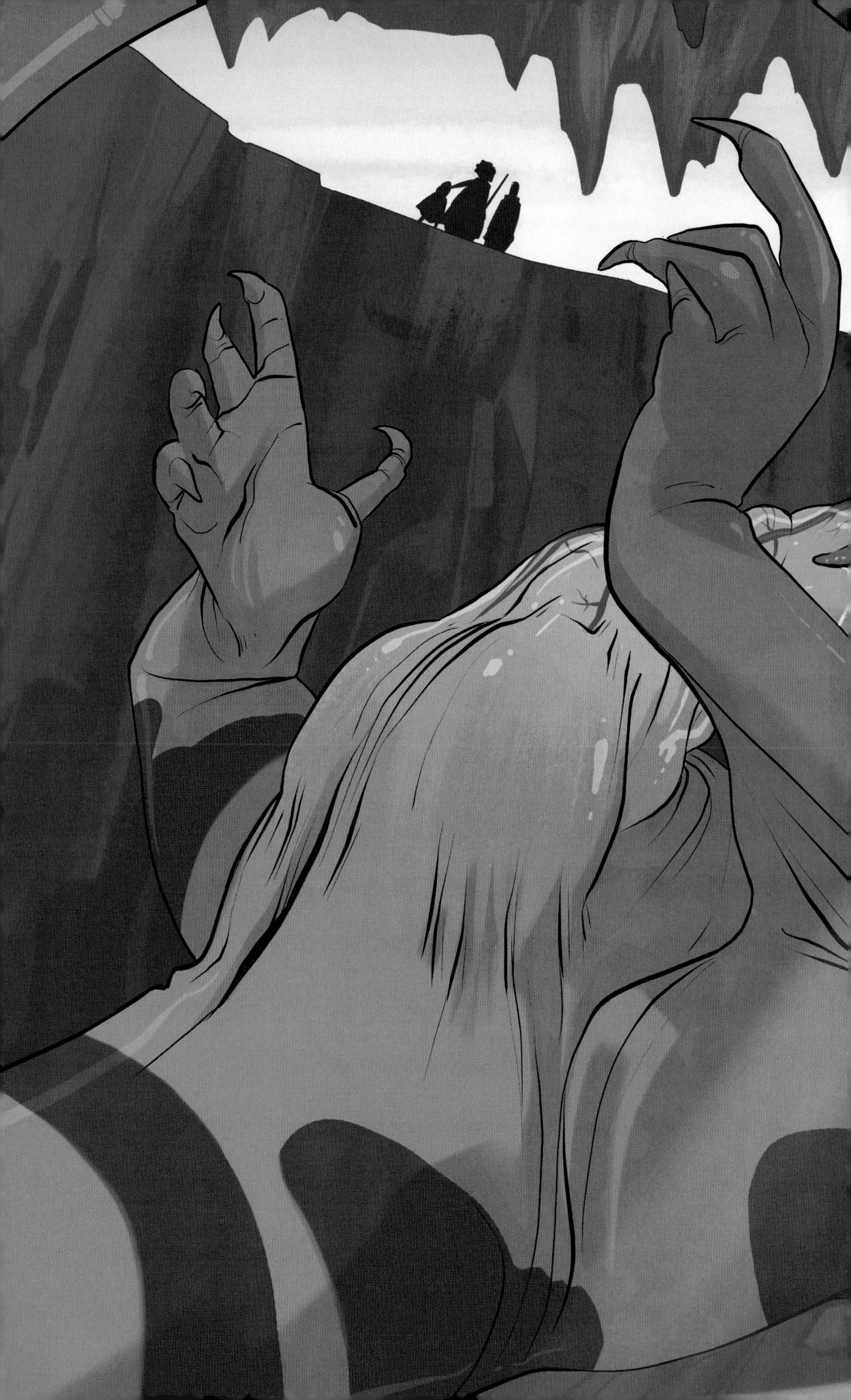

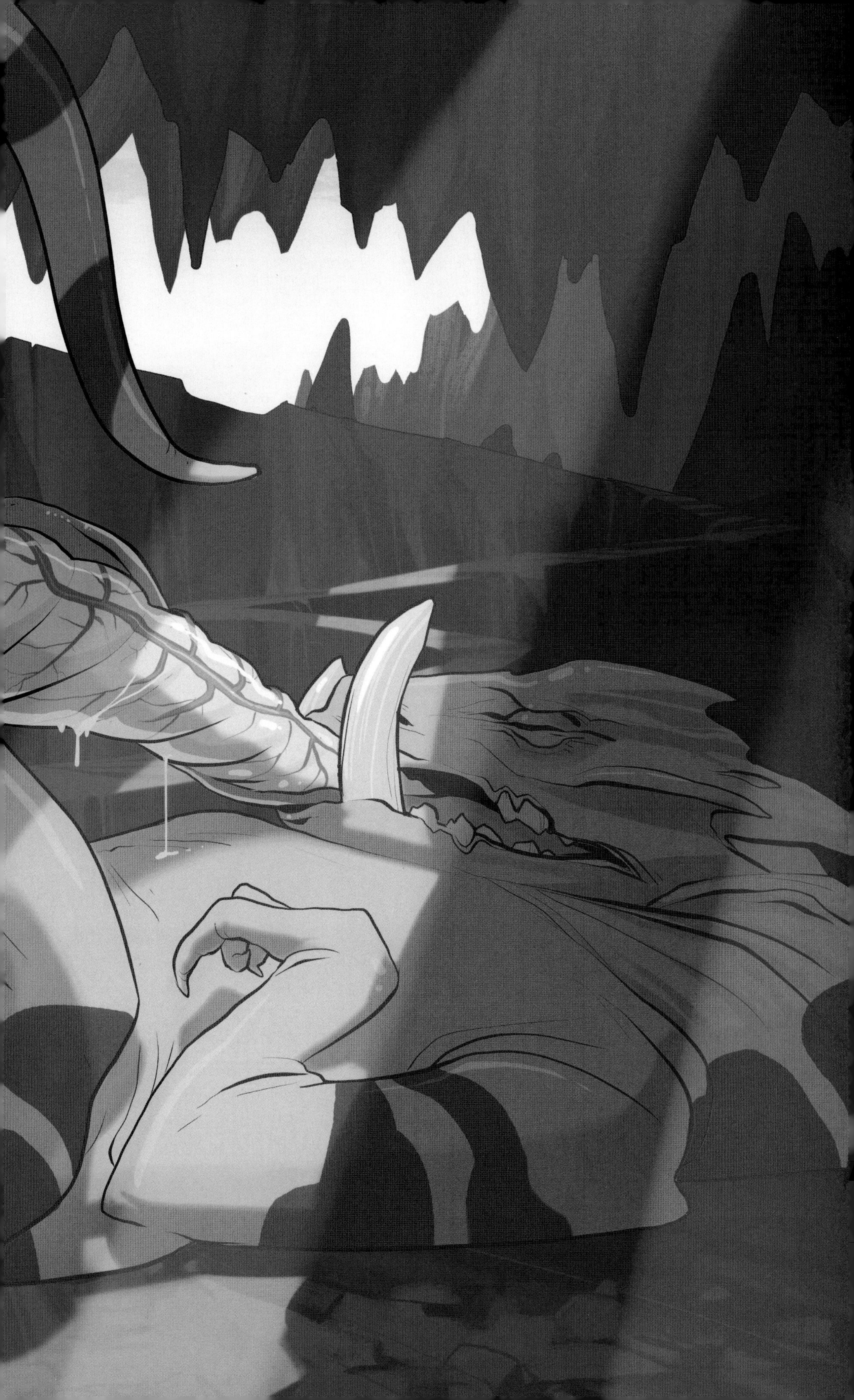

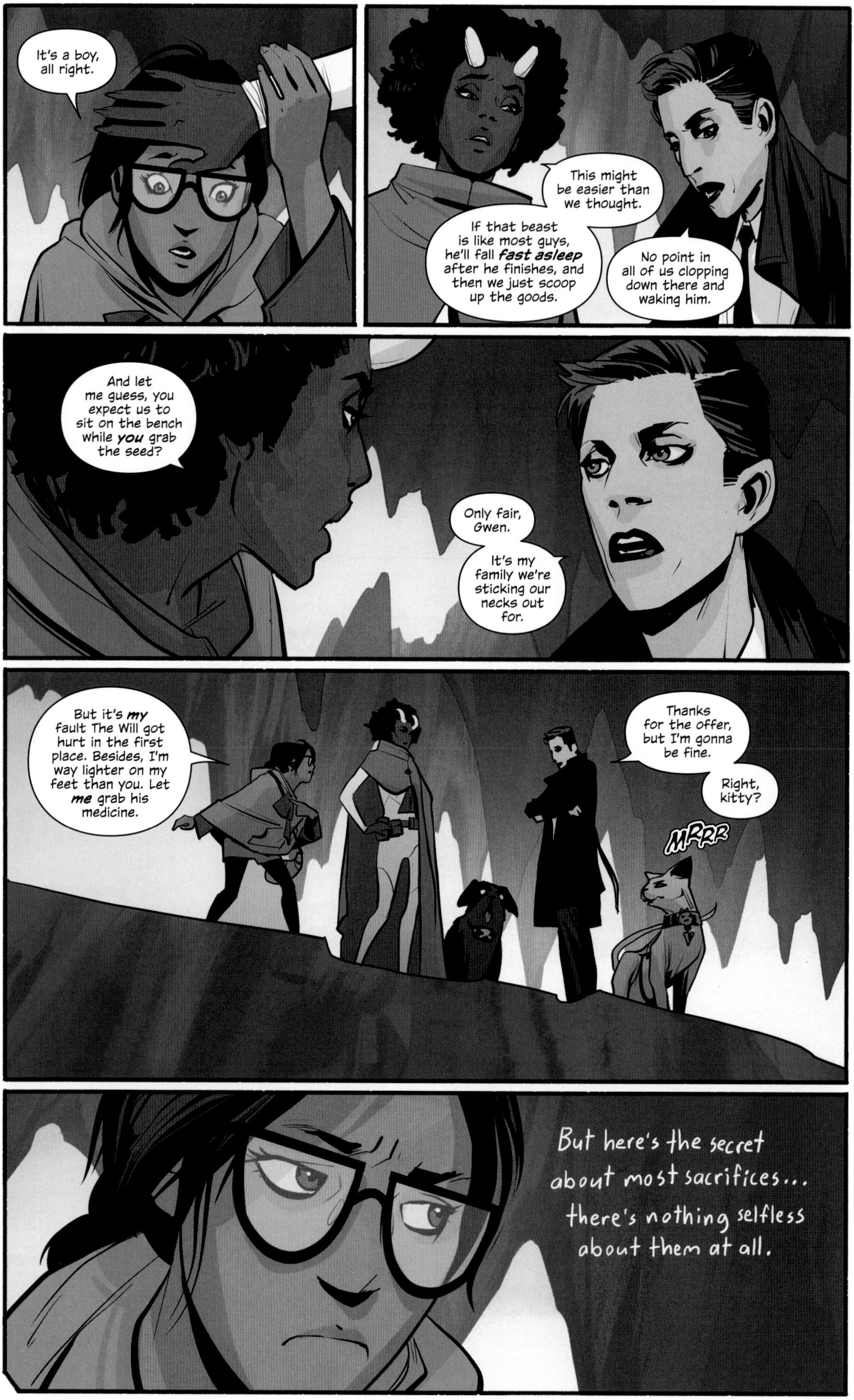
It's a boy, all right.
This might be easier than we thought.
If that beast is like most guys, he'll fall **fast asleep** after he finishes, and then we just scoop up the goods.
No point in all of us clopping down there and waking him.
And let me guess, you expect us to sit on the bench while **you** grab the seed?
Only fair, Gwen.
It's my family we're sticking our necks out for.
But it's **my** fault The Will got hurt in the first place. Besides, I'm way lighter on my feet than you. Let **me** grab his medicine.
Thanks for the offer, but I'm gonna be fine.
Right, kitty?
MRRR
But here's the secret about most sacrifices... there's nothing selfless about them at all.

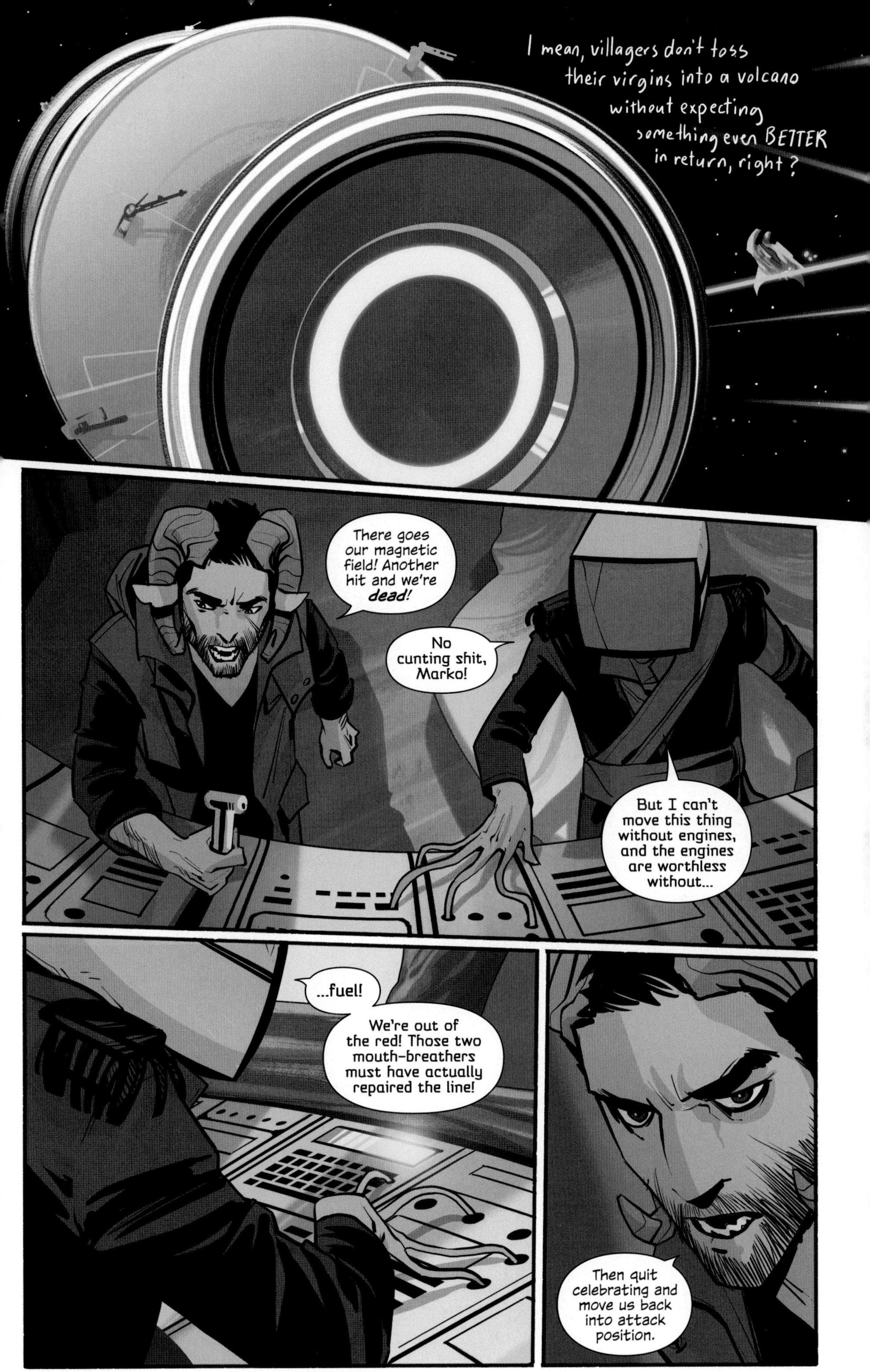
I mean, villagers don't toss their virgins into a volcano without expecting something even BETTER in return, right?
There goes our magnetic field! Another hit and we're *dead!*
No cunting shit, Marko!
But I can't move this thing without engines, and the engines are worthless without...
...fuel!
We're out of the red! Those two mouth-breathers must have actually repaired the line!
Then quit celebrating and move us back into attack position.

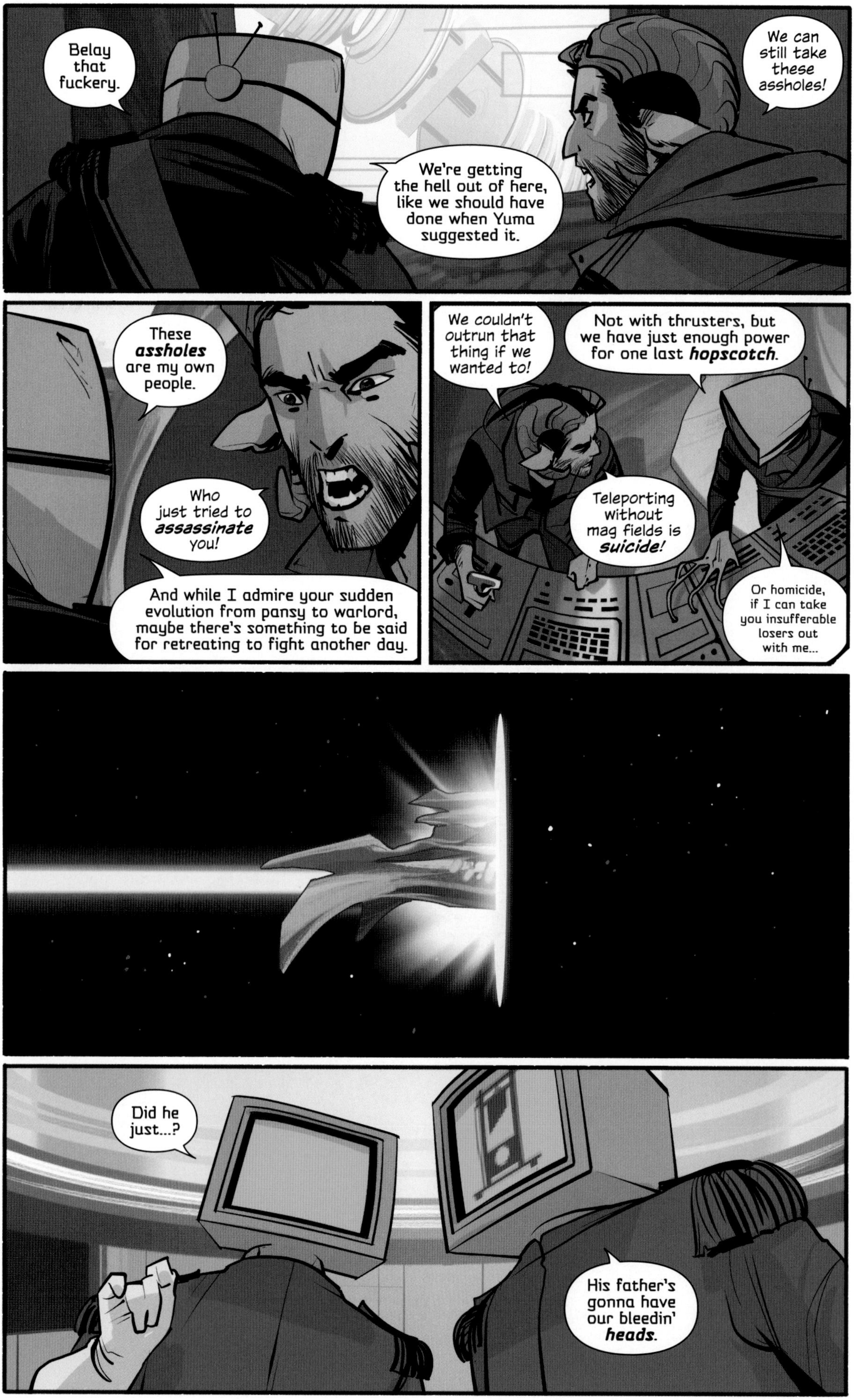
Belay that fuckery.
We can still take these assholes!
We're getting the hell out of here, like we should have done when Yuma suggested it.
These *assholes* are my own people.
Who just tried to *assassinate* you!
And while I admire your sudden evolution from pansy to warlord, maybe there's something to be said for retreating to fight another day.
We couldn't outrun that thing if we wanted to!
Not with thrusters, but we have just enough power for one last *hopscotch*.
Teleporting without mag fields is *suicide!*
Or homicide, if I can take you insufferable losers out with me...
Did he just...?
His father's gonna have our bleedin' *heads*.

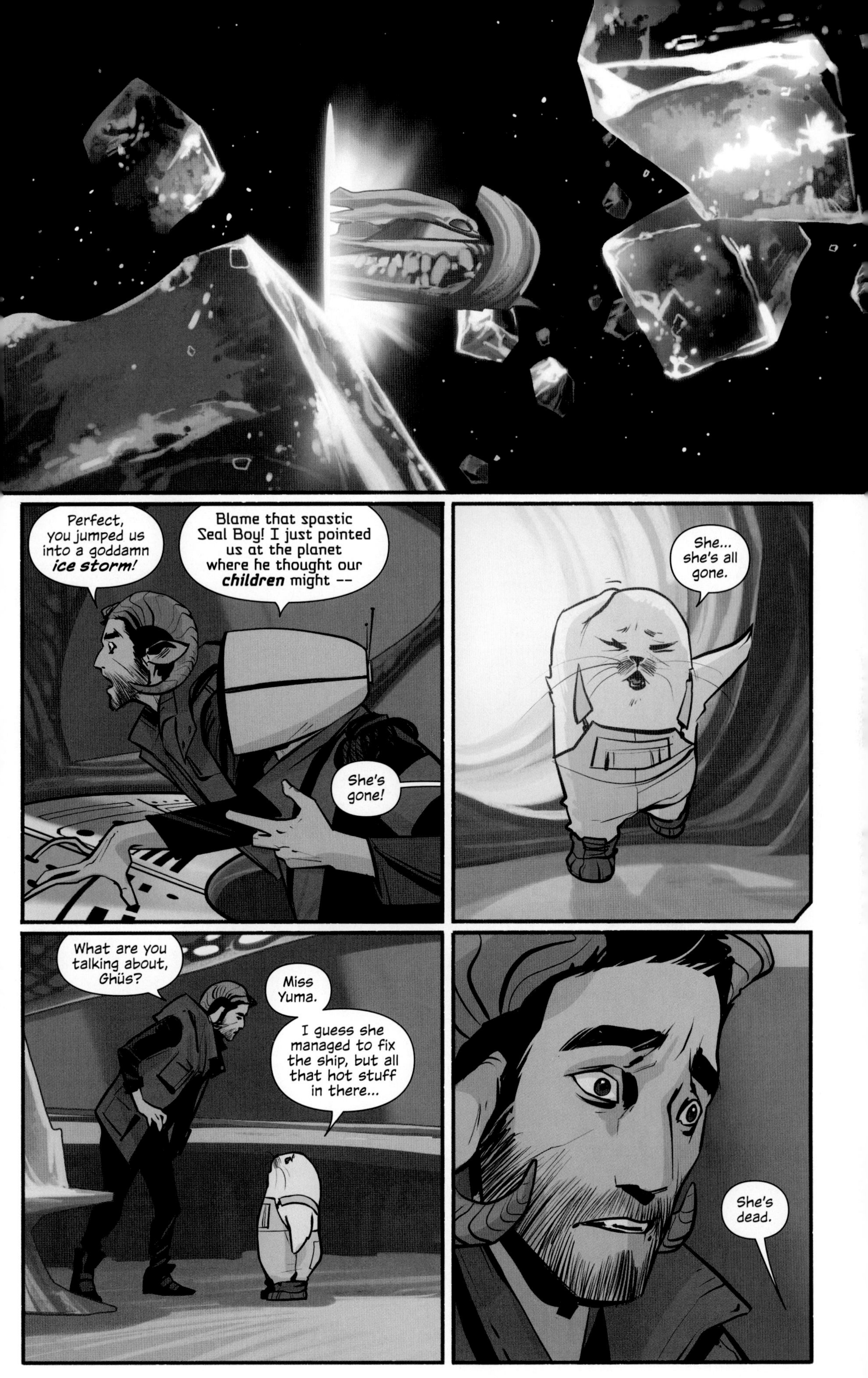

Perfect, you jumped us into a goddamn *ice storm!*
Blame that spastic Seal Boy! I just pointed us at the planet where he thought our **children** might --
She's gone!
She... she's all gone.
What are you talking about, Ghüs?
Miss Yuma.
I guess she managed to fix the ship, but all that hot stuff in there...
She's dead.

I... I don't know what to say.
She wasn't a saint, but the old girl deserved better than --
IV!
Oh.
Oh, gosh.

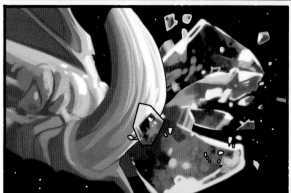

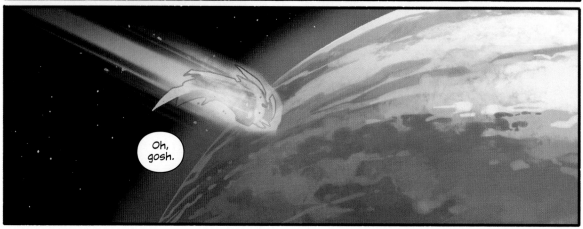

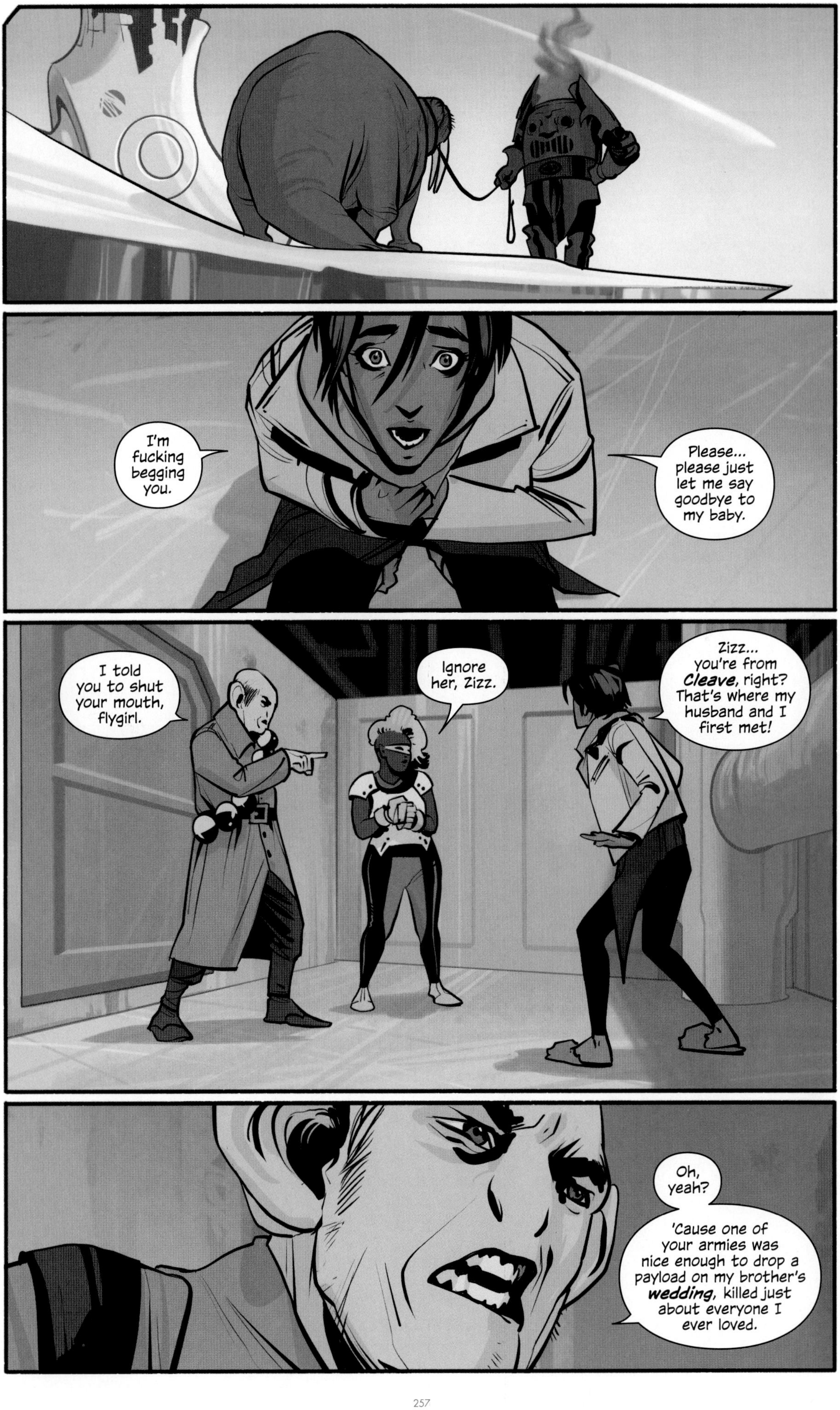
I'm fucking begging you.
Please... please just let me say goodbye to my baby.
I told you to shut your mouth, flygirl.
Ignore her, Zizz.
Zizz... you're from *Cleave*, right? That's where my husband and I first met!
Oh, yeah?
'Cause one of your armies was nice enough to drop a payload on my brother's *wedding*, killed just about everyone I ever loved.

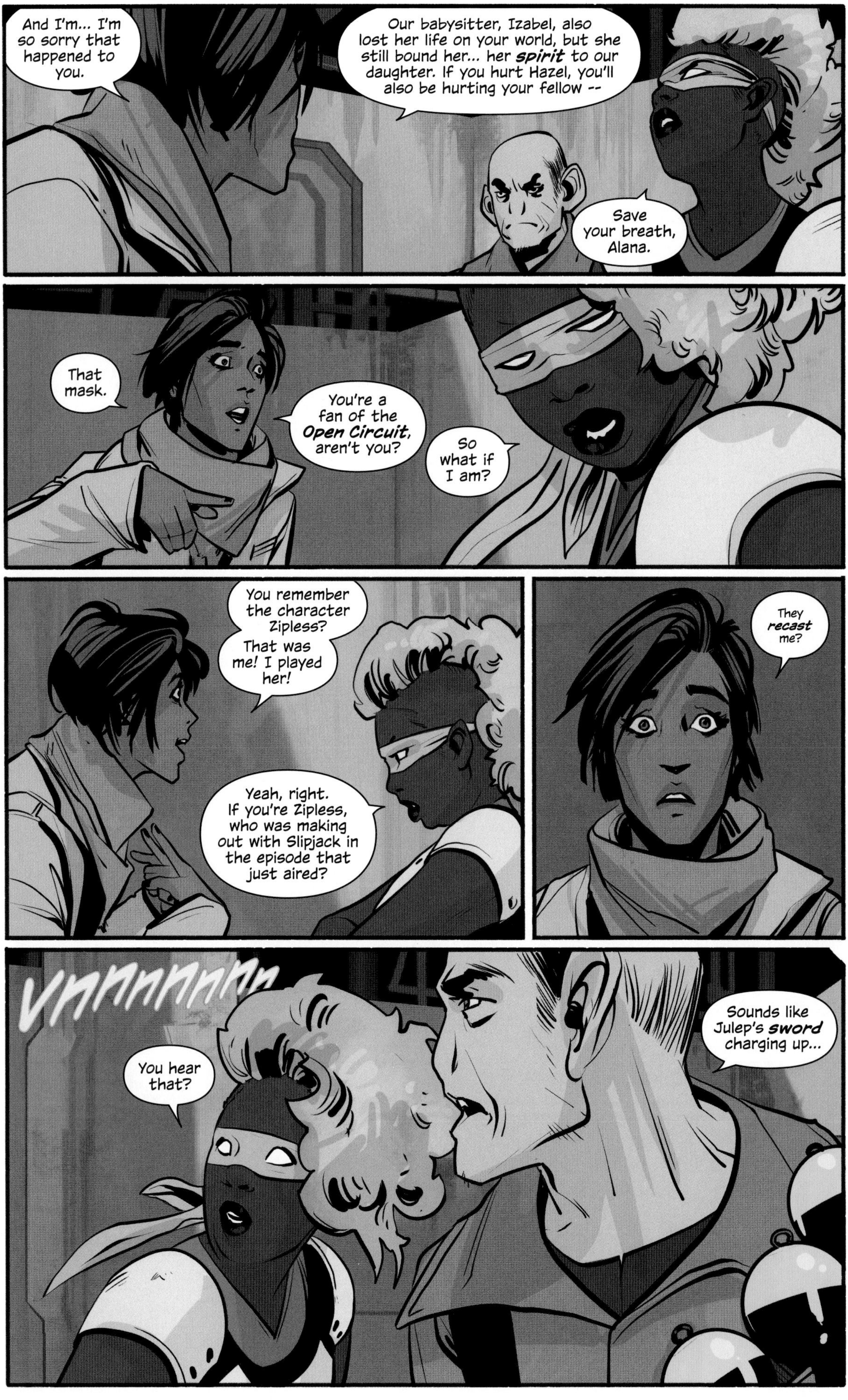

And I'm... I'm so sorry that happened to you.
Our babysitter, Izabel, also lost her life on your world, but she still bound her... her spirit to our daughter. If you hurt Hazel, you'll also be hurting your fellow --
Save your breath, Alana.
That mask.
You're a fan of the Open Circuit, aren't you?
So what if I am?
You remember the character Zipless?
That was me! I played her!
Yeah, right. If you're Zipless, who was making out with Slipjack in the episode that just aired?
They recast me?
VNNNNNNN
You hear that?
Sounds like Julep's sword charging up...

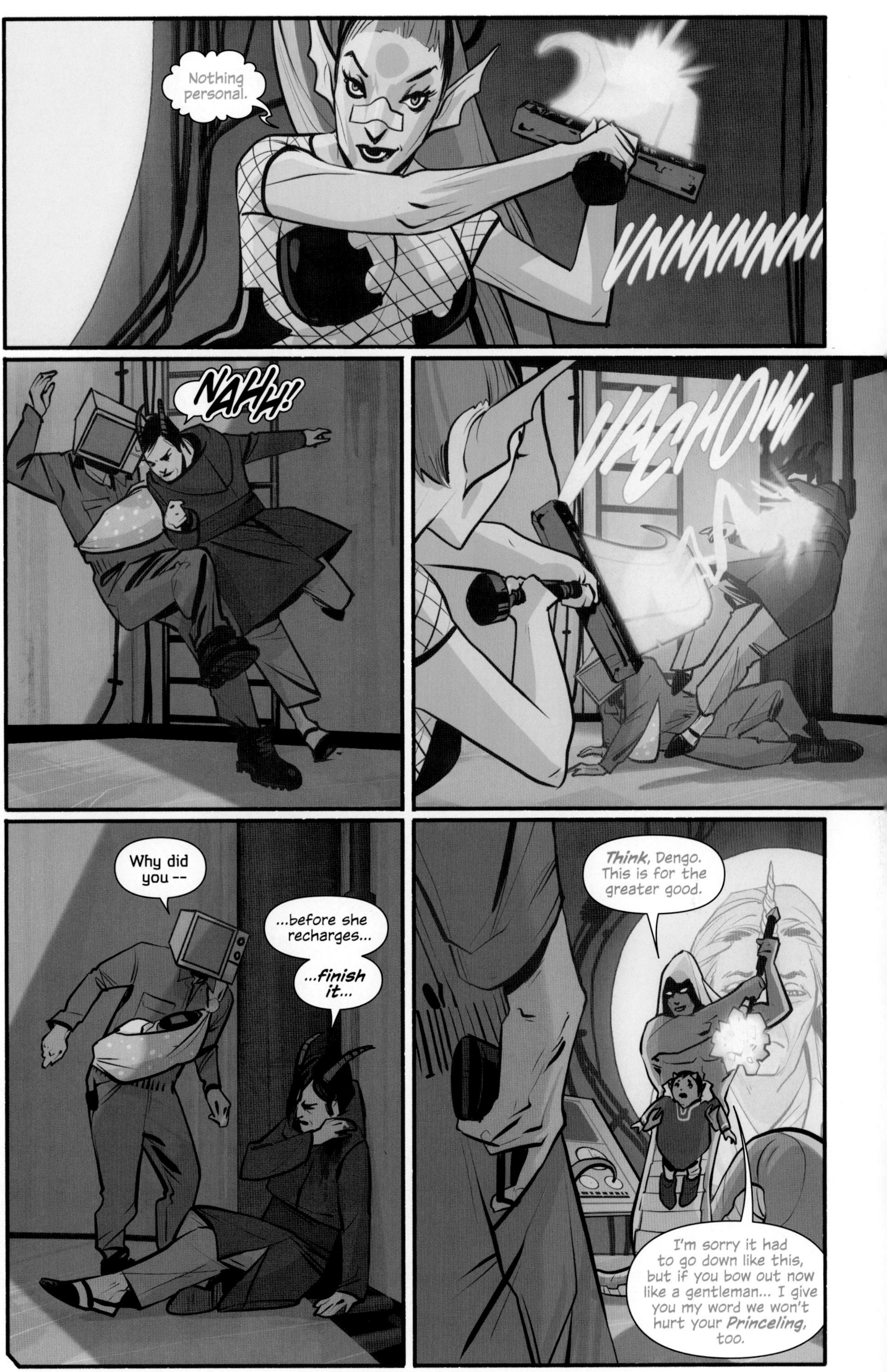
Nothing personal.
VNNNNNN
NAHH!
VACHOW
Why did you --
...before she recharges...
...finish it...
Think, Dengo. This is for the greater good.
I'm sorry it had to go down like this, but if you bow out now like a gentleman... I give you my word we won't hurt your Princeling, too.

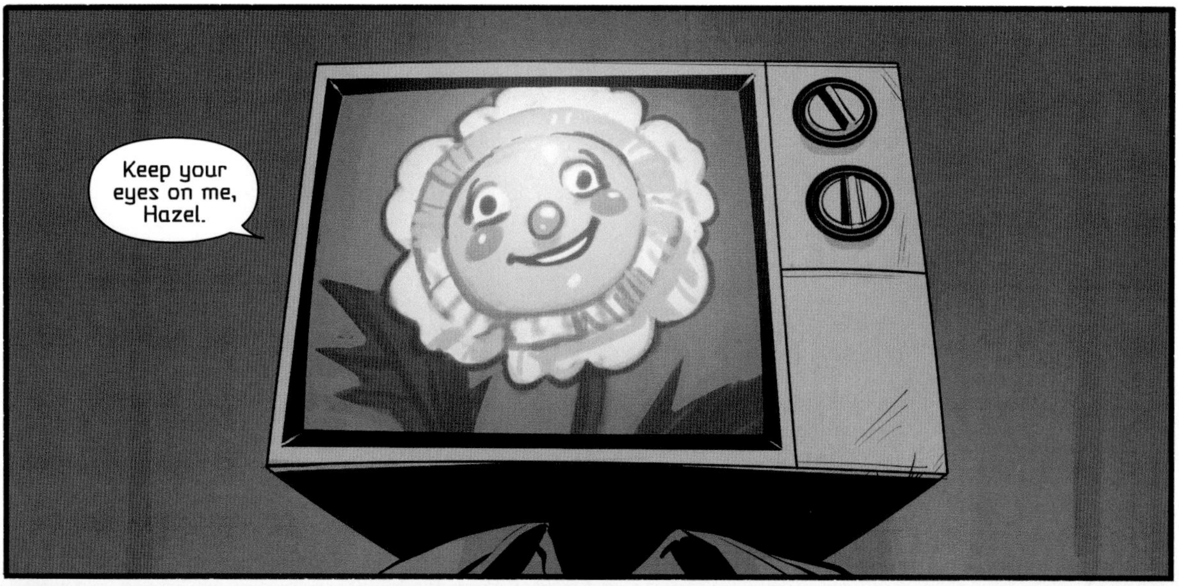
Keep your
eyes on me,
Hazel.

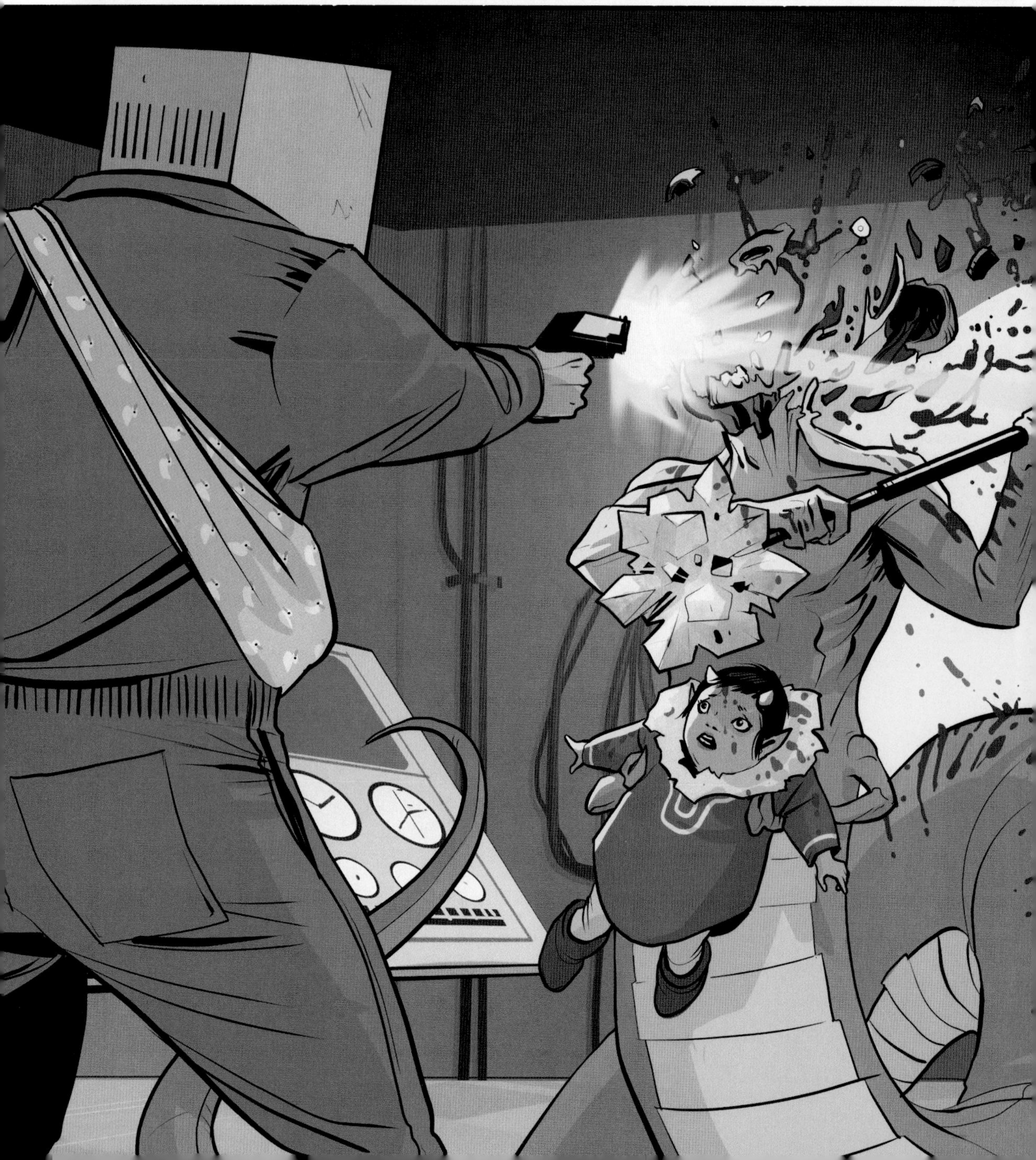

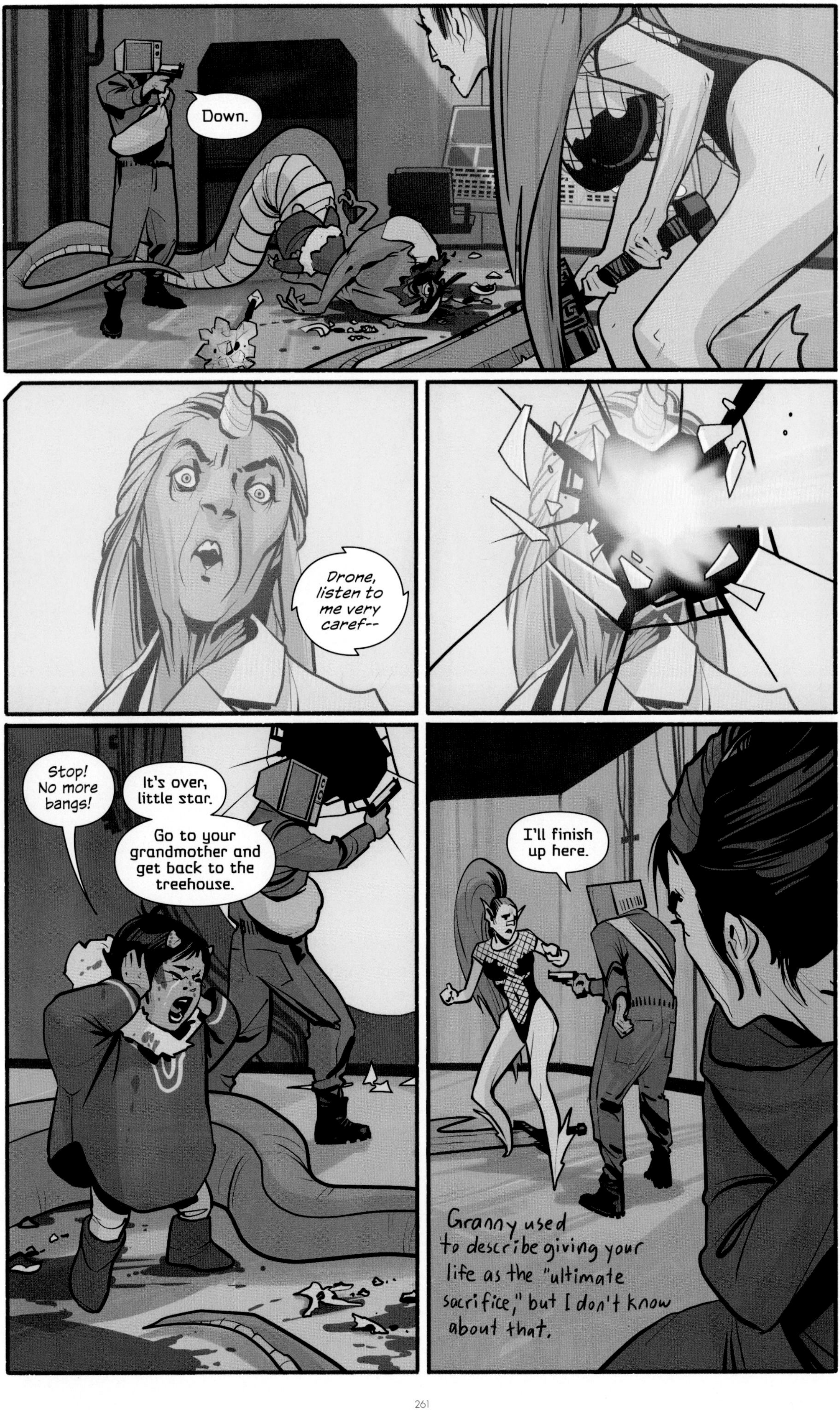
Down.
Drone, listen to me very caref--
Stop! No more bangs!
It's over, little star.
Go to your grandmother and get back to the treehouse.
I'll finish up here.
Granny used to describe giving your life as the "ultimate sacrifice," but I don't know about that.

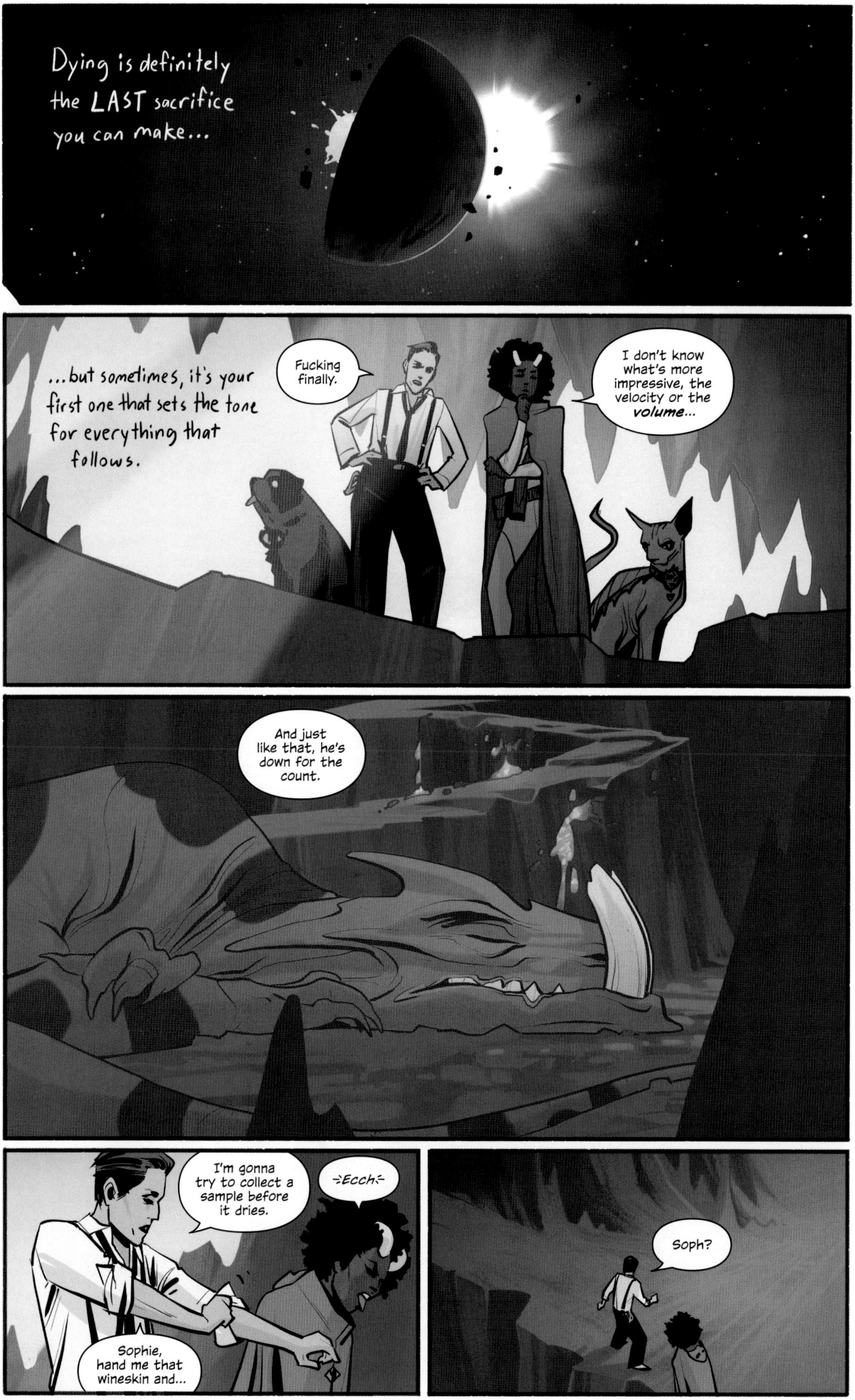
Dying is definitely the LAST sacrifice you can make...
...but sometimes, it's your first one that sets the tone for everything that follows.
Fucking finally.
I don't know what's more impressive, the velocity or the *volume*...
And just like that, he's down for the count.
I'm gonna try to collect a sample before it dries.
Ecch
Sophie, hand me that wineskin and...
Soph?

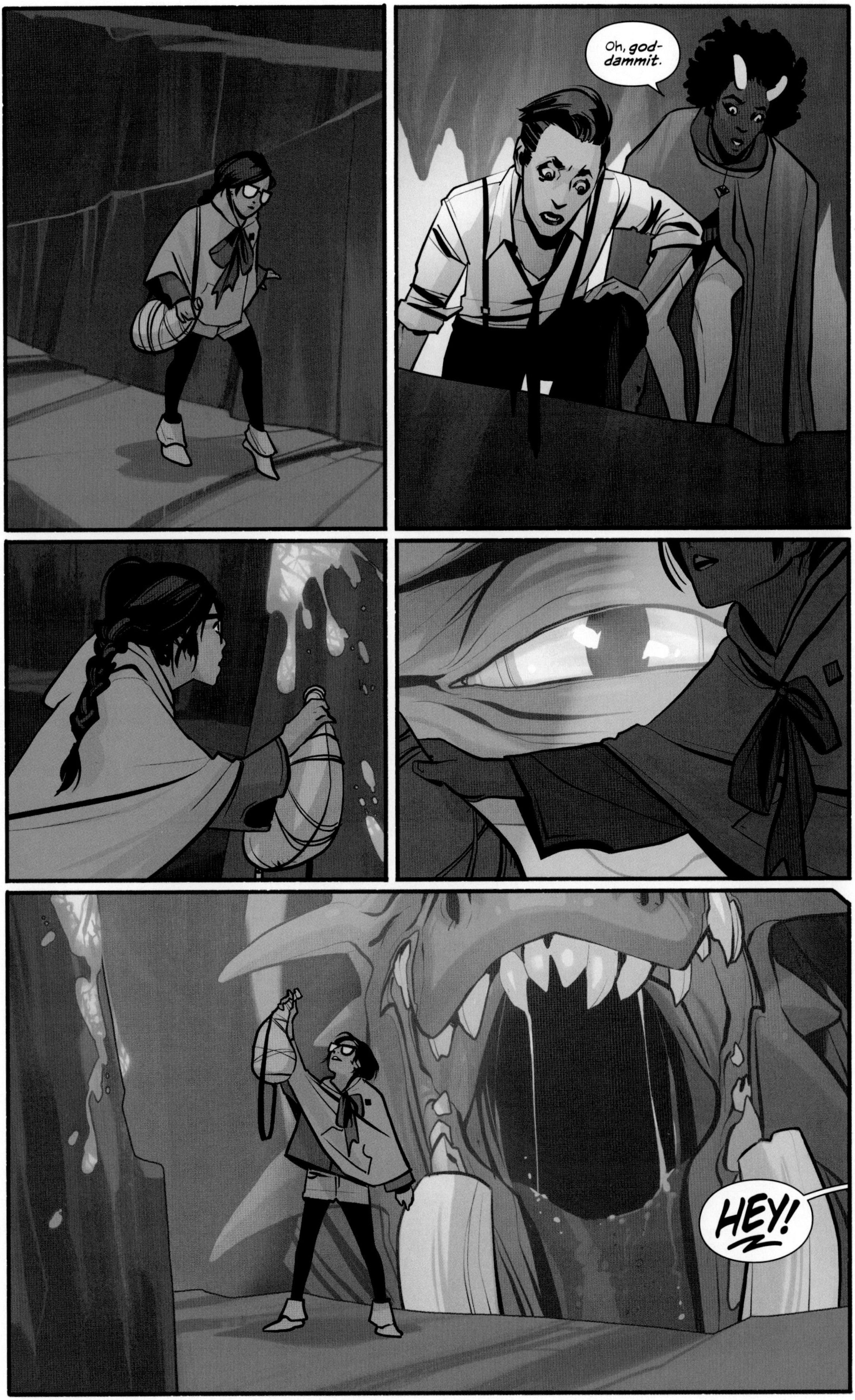
Oh, god-dammit.
HEY!

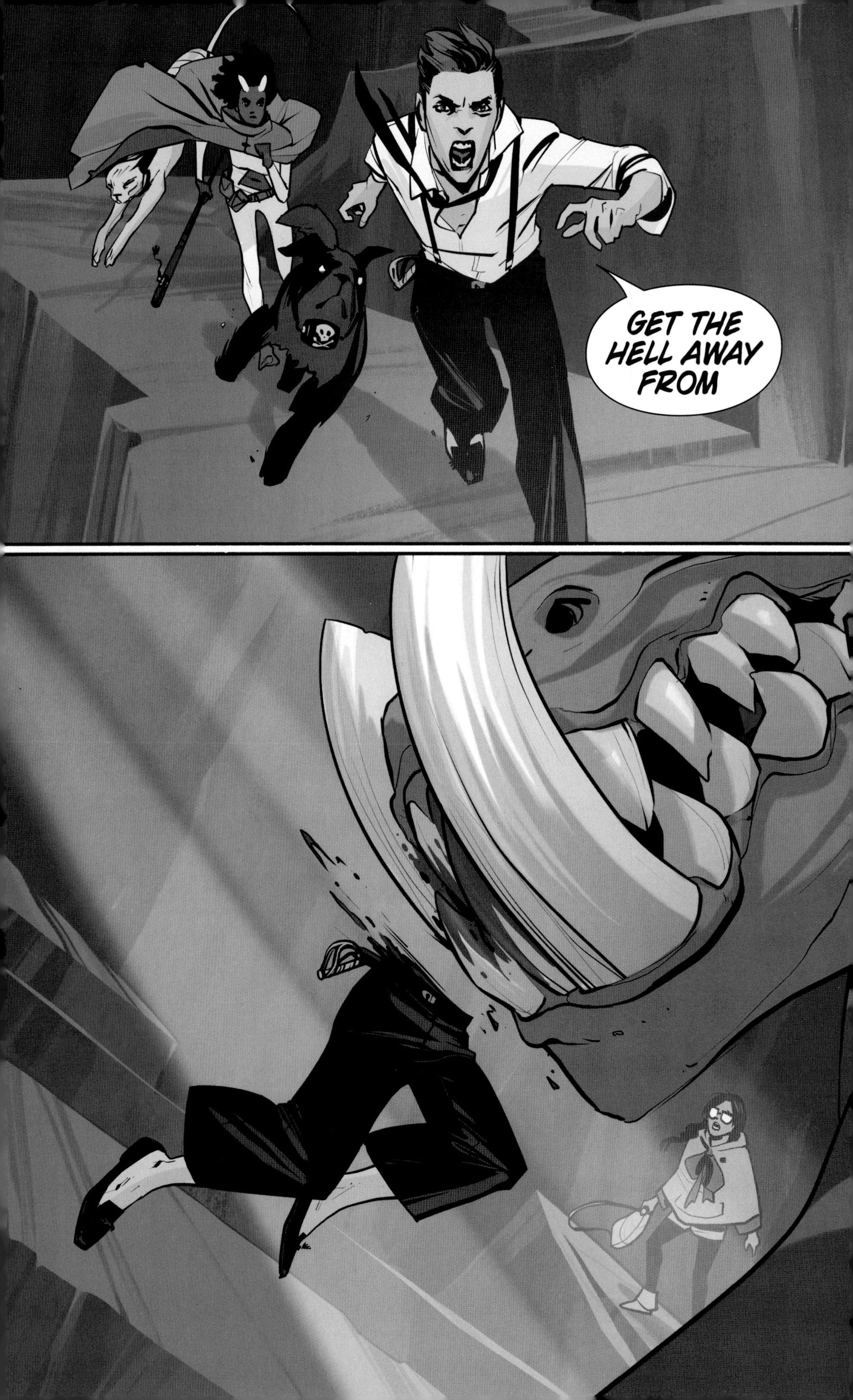
GET THE HELL AWAY FROM

AHHH!

NO!

HARKOOOOooo

Sorry.

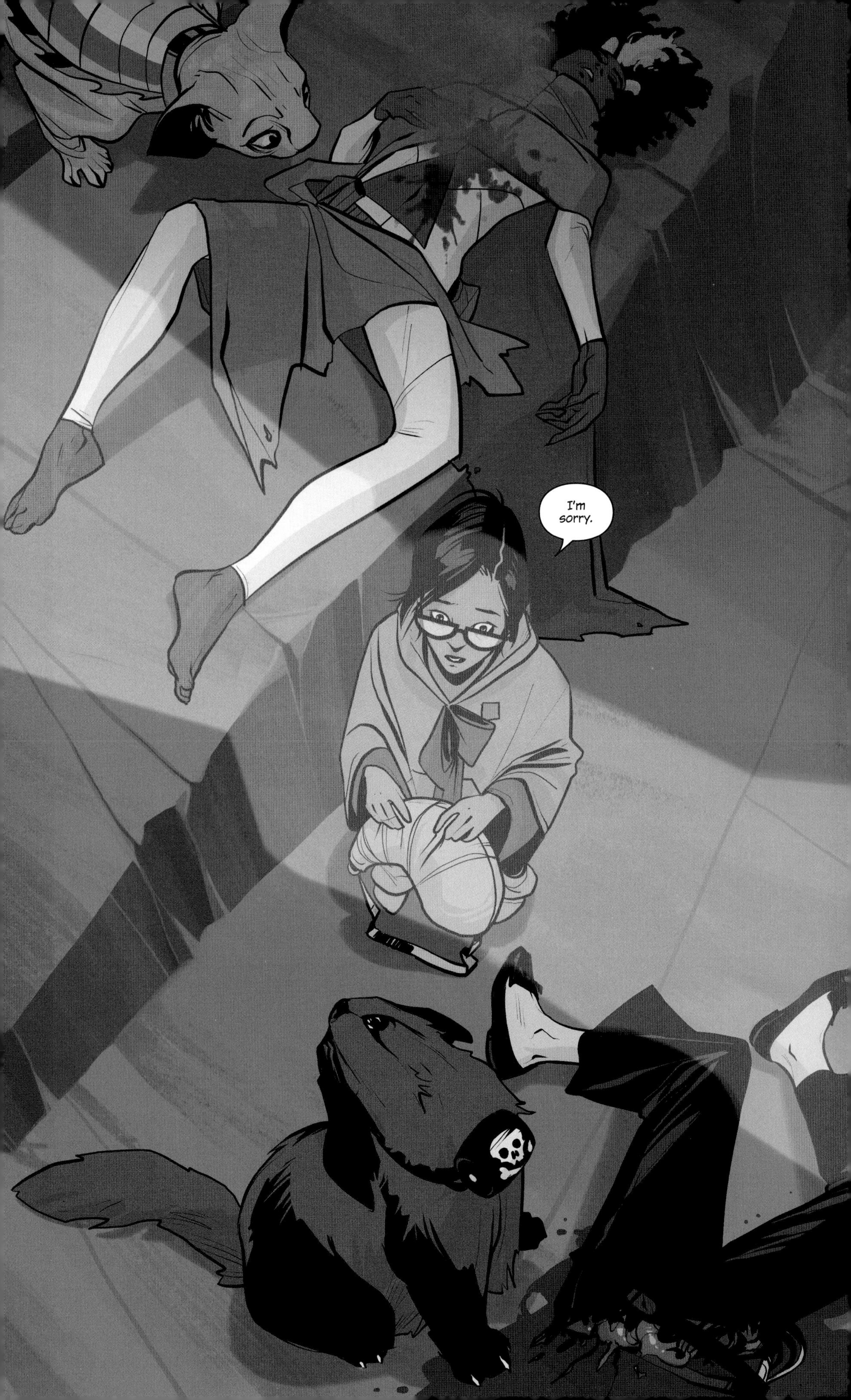
I'm sorry.

end chapter twenty-nine

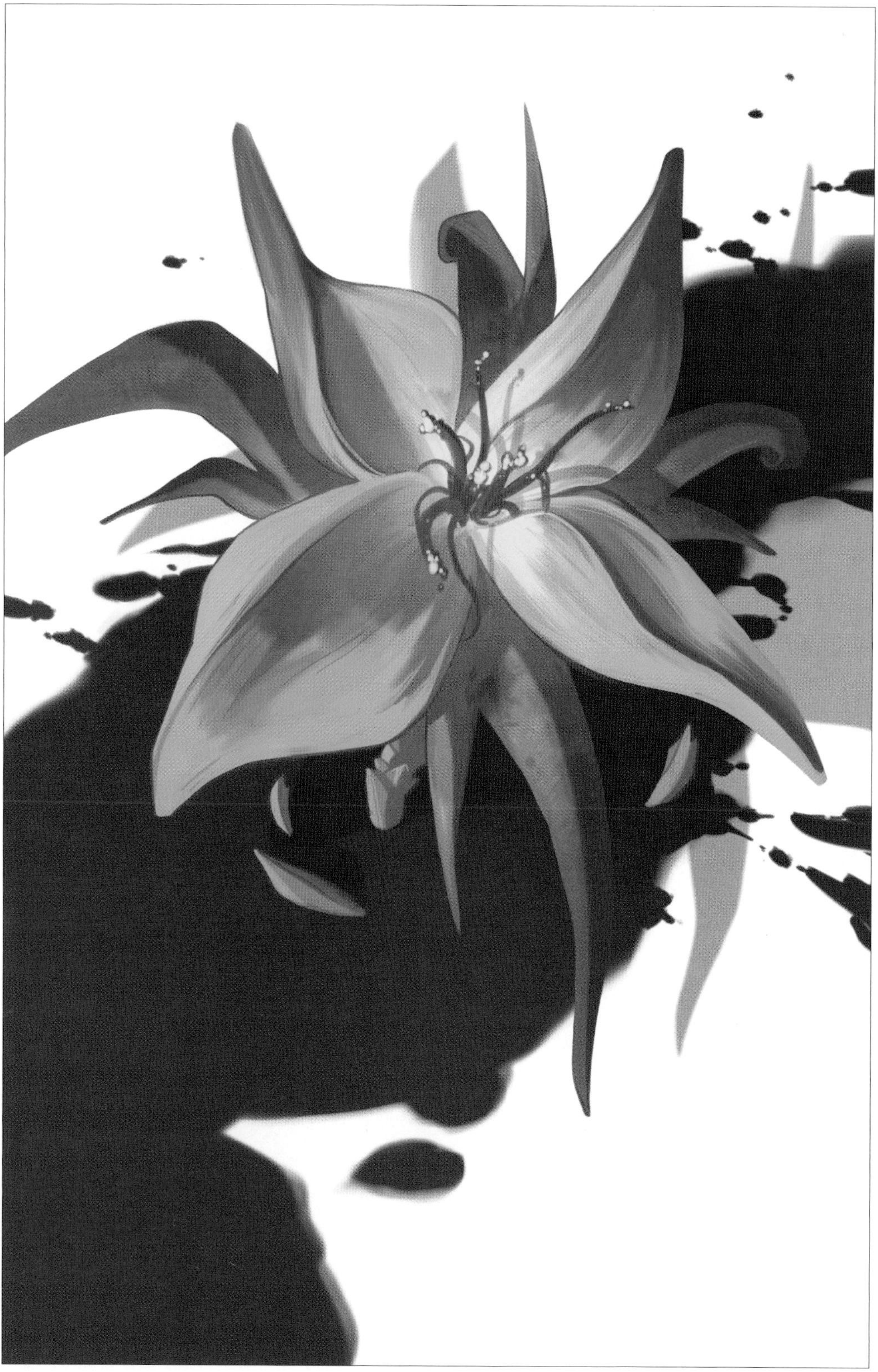

CHAPTER

THIRTY

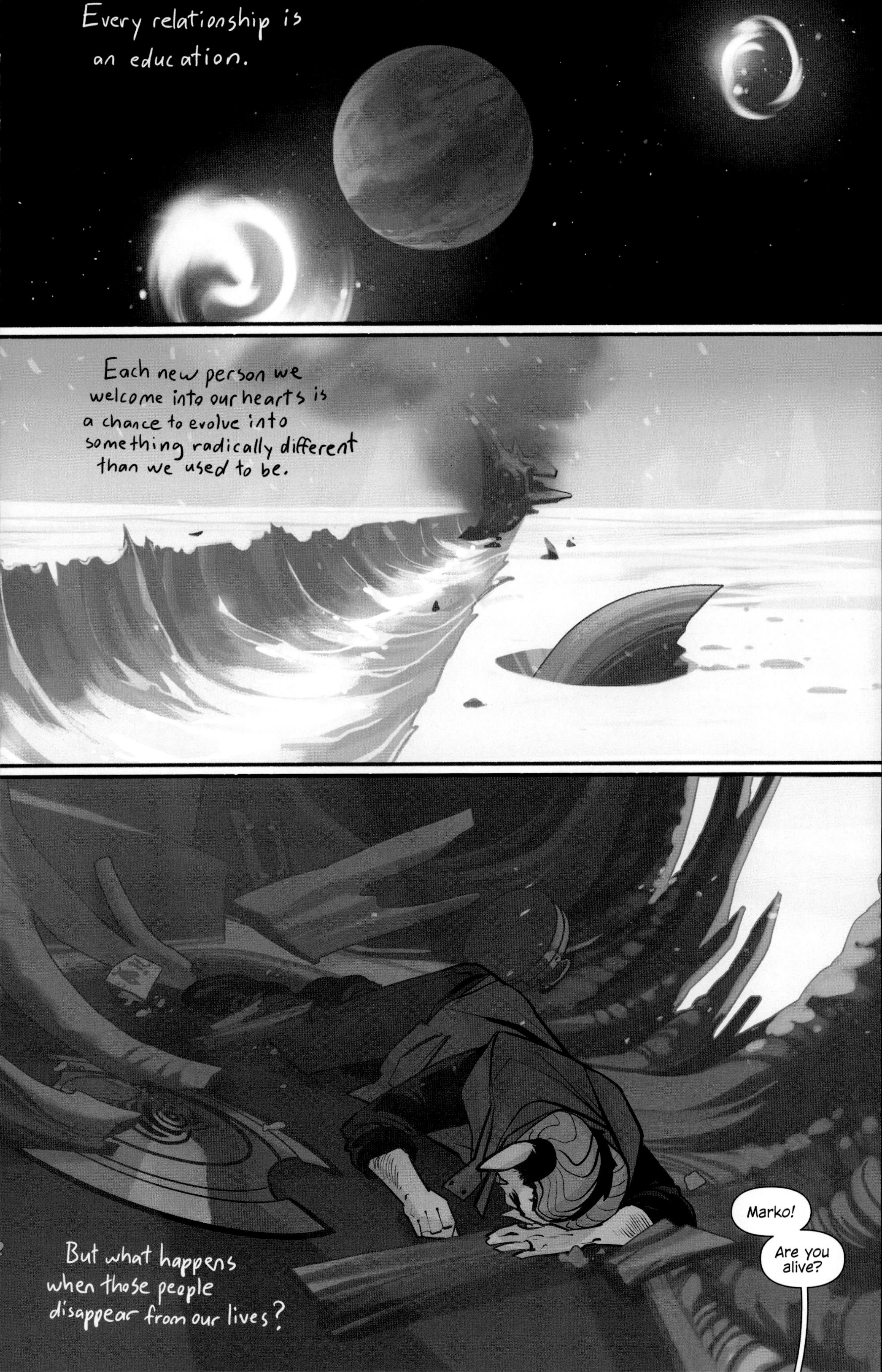
Every relationship is an education.
Each new person we welcome into our hearts is a chance to evolve into something radically different than we used to be.
But what happens when those people disappear from our lives?
Marko!
Are you alive?

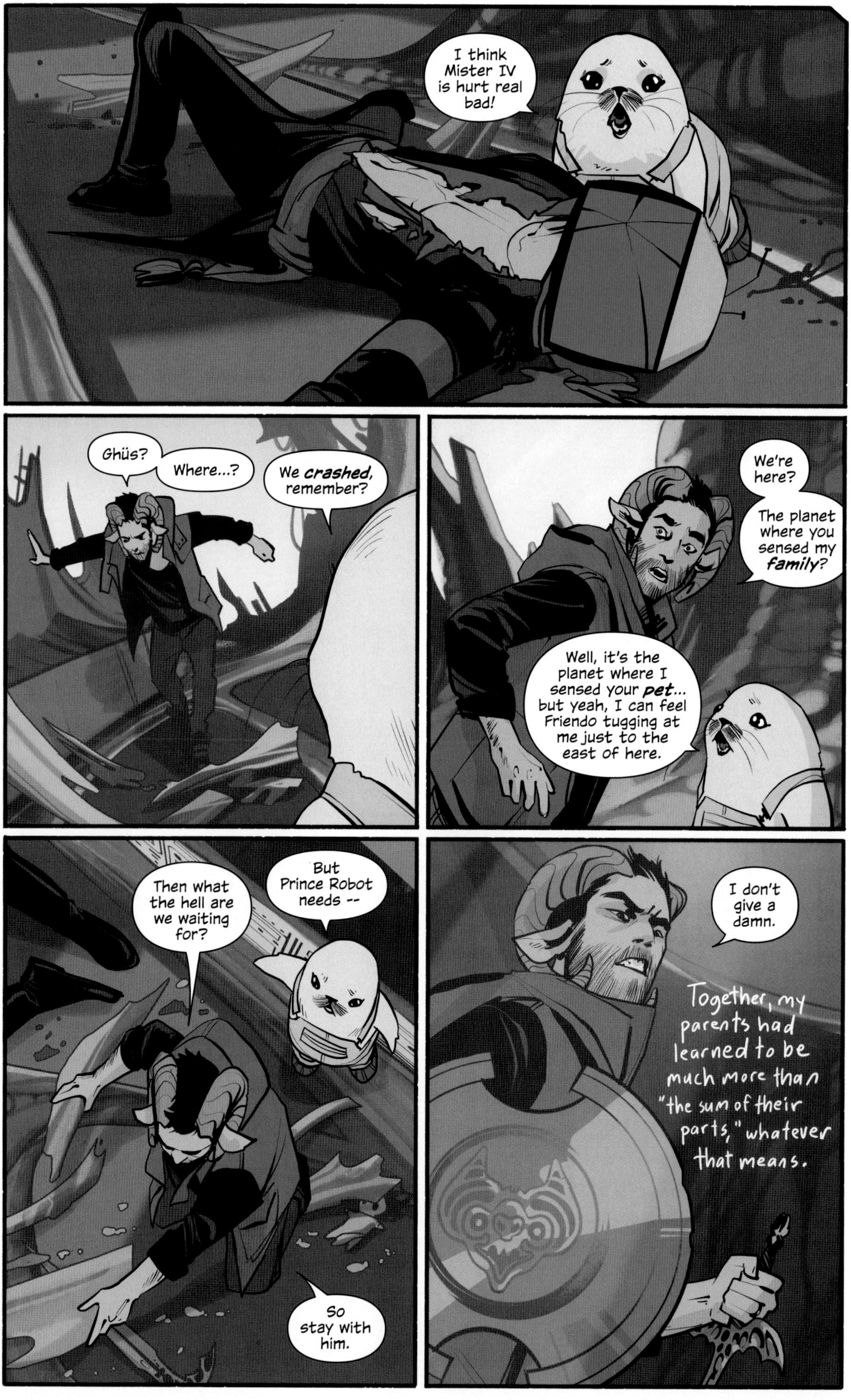
I think Mister IV is hurt real bad!
Ghüs?
Where...?
We crashed, remember?
We're here?
The planet where you sensed my family?
Well, it's the planet where I sensed your pet... but yeah, I can feel Friendo tugging at me just to the east of here.
Then what the hell are we waiting for?
But Prince Robot needs --
So stay with him.
I don't give a damn.
Together, my parents had learned to be much more than "the sum of their parts," whatever that means.

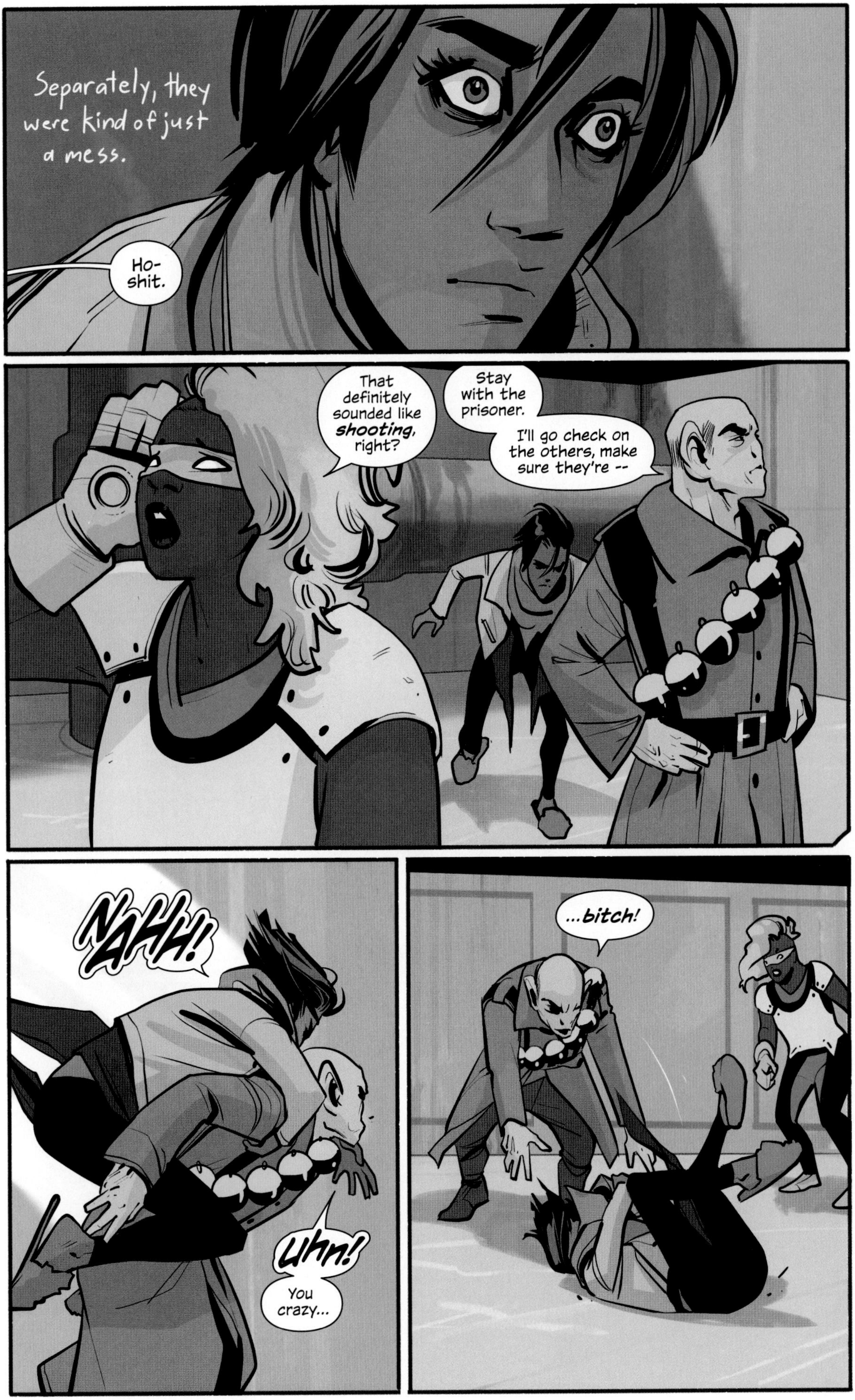
Separately, they were kind of just a mess.
Ho- shit.
That definitely sounded like ***shooting***, right?
Stay with the prisoner.
I'll go check on the others, make sure they're --
NAHH!
Uhn!
You crazy...
...***bitch***!

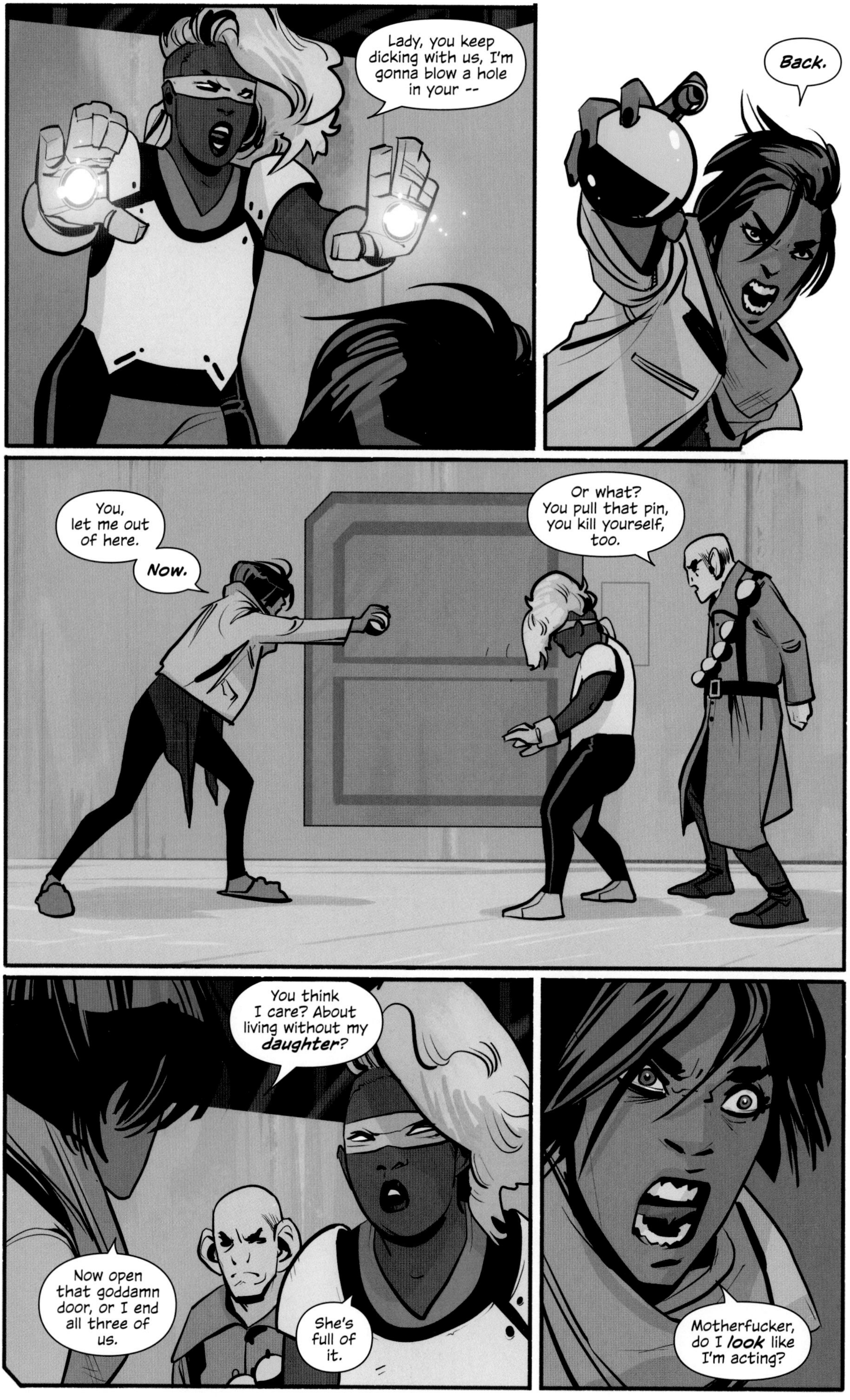

Lady, you keep dicking with us, I'm gonna blow a hole in your --
Back.
You, let me out of here.
Now.
Or what? You pull that pin, you kill yourself, too.
You think I care? About living without my daughter?
Now open that goddamn door, or I end all three of us.
She's full of it.
Motherfucker, do I look like I'm acting?

Whatever.

Yeah, have fun out there.

You're never getting off this ship alive.

And I hope the moonies we sold your ugly little mutant to carve her up like --

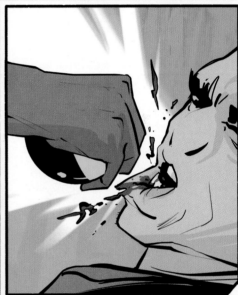

HARD LOCKDOWN

Alana!

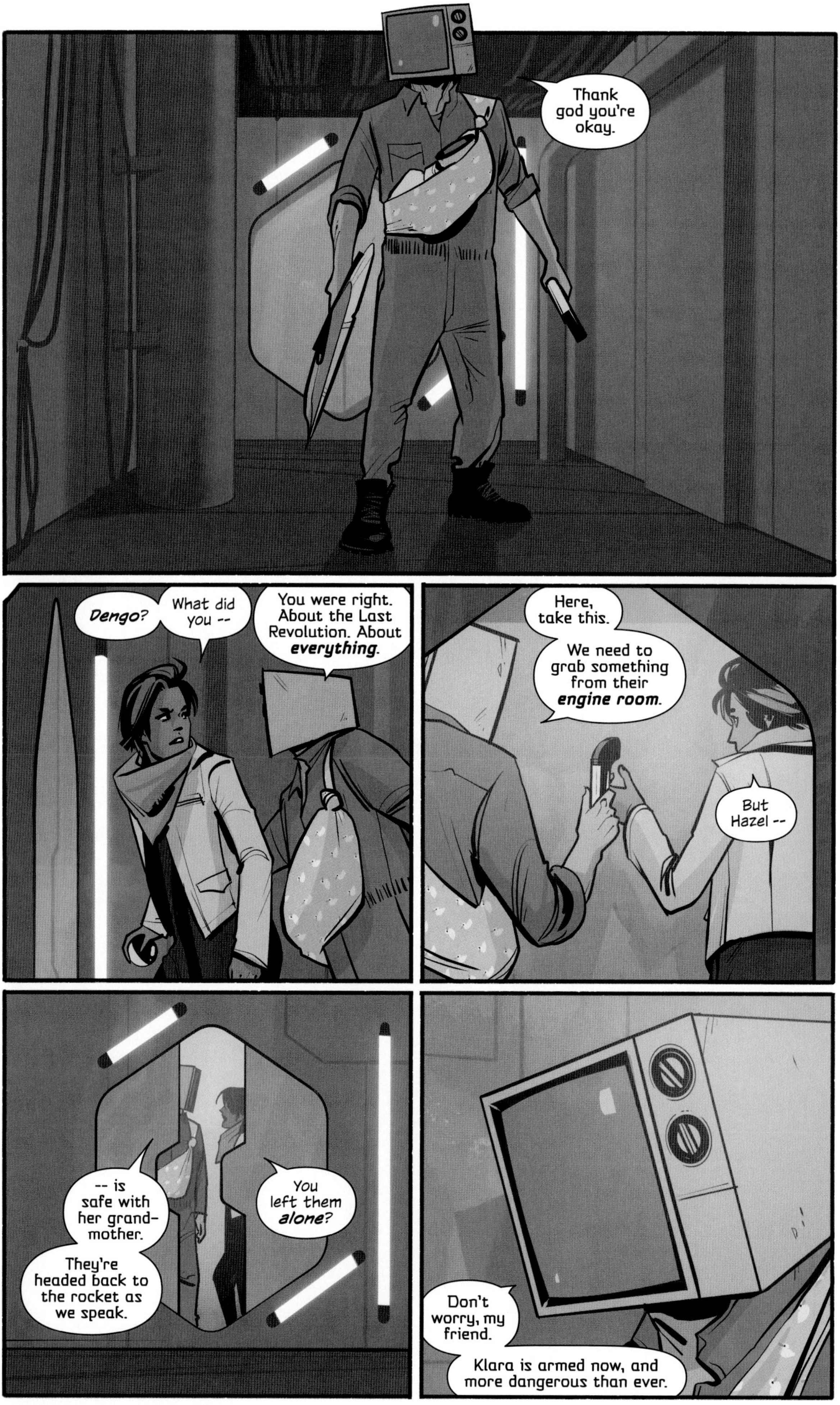
Thank god you're okay.
Dengo?
What did you --
You were right. About the Last Revolution. About *everything*.
Here, take this.
We need to grab something from their *engine room*.
But Hazel --
-- is safe with her grand-mother.
They're headed back to the rocket as we speak.
You left them *alone*?
Don't worry, my friend.
Klara is armed now, and more dangerous than ever.

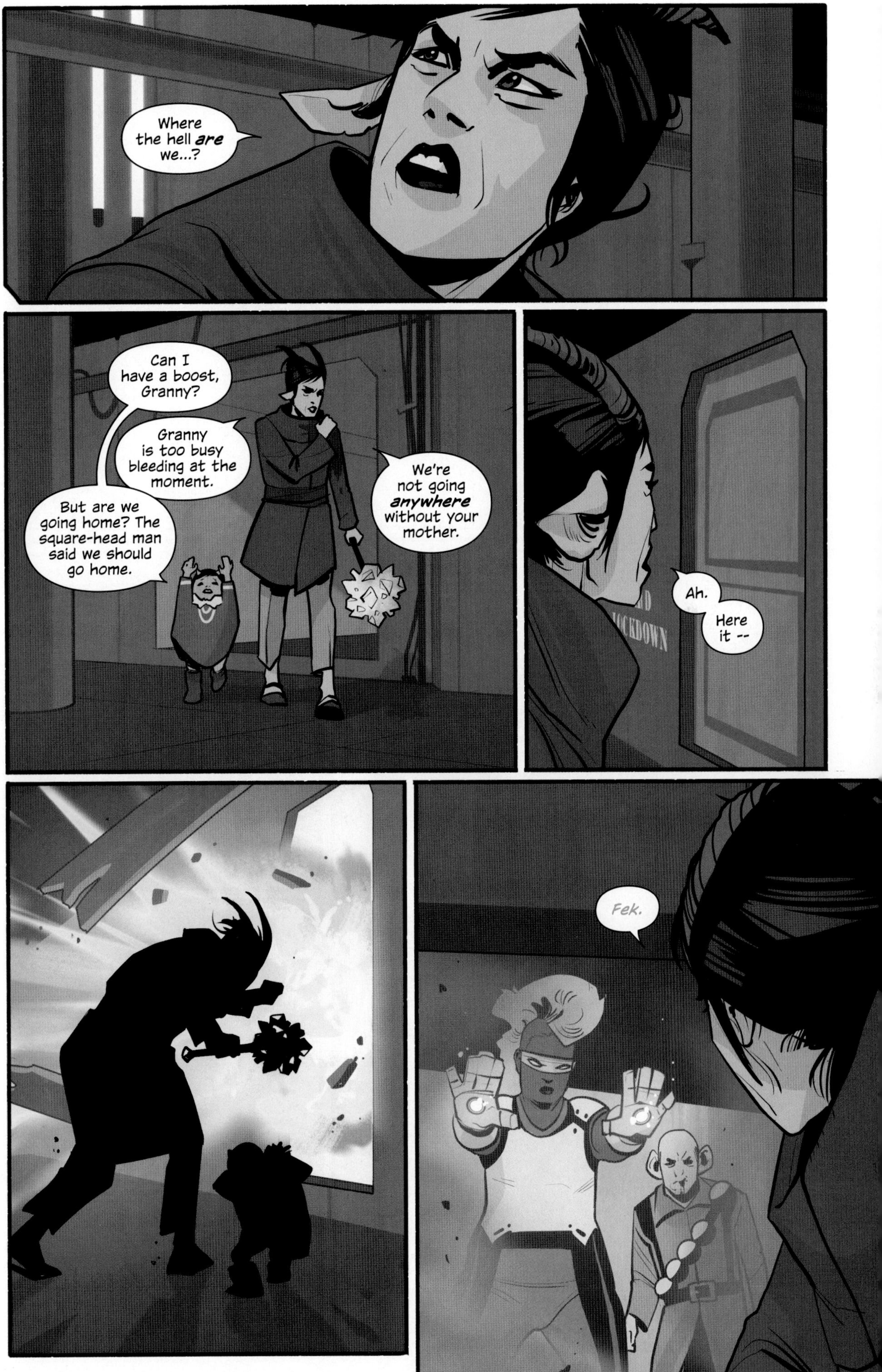
Where the hell *are* we...?
Can I have a boost, Granny?
Granny is too busy bleeding at the moment.
But are we going home? The square-head man said we should go home.
We're not going *anywhere* without your mother.
Ah.
Here it --
Fek.

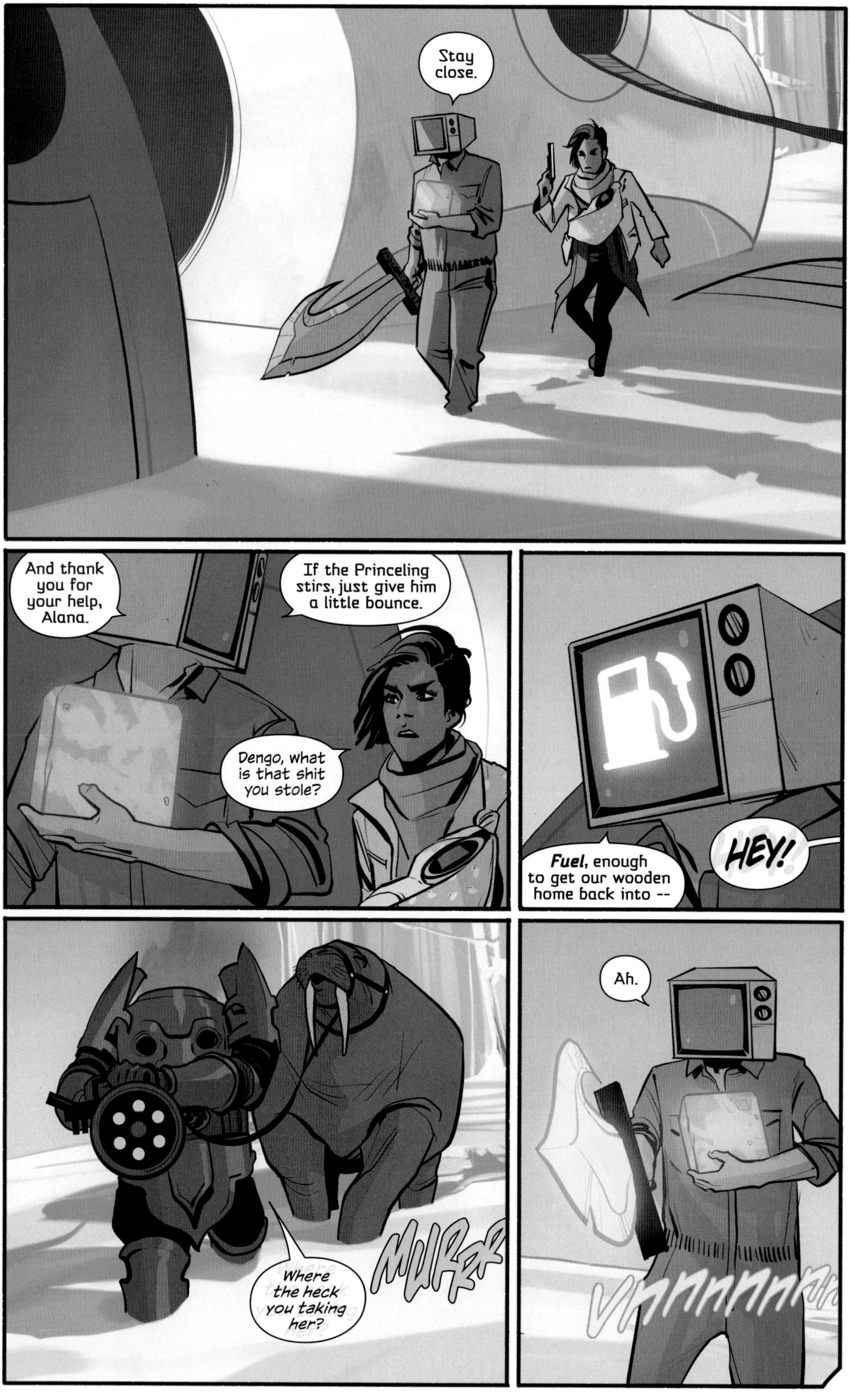
Stay close.
And thank you for your help, Alana.
If the Princeling stirs, just give him a little bounce.
Dengo, what is that shit you stole?
Fuel, enough to get our wooden home back into --
HEY!
Where the heck you taking her?
Ah.

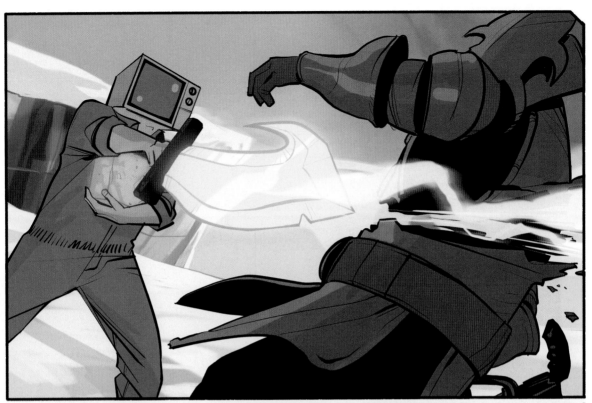

FAHHH!

What the hell? There was a *guard* posted out here?

Forgive me, I... I had presumed your mother-in-law would have finished this one already.

...we...

...we are dying...

Then do it with some dignity, and tell us what happened to the people who came out of that ship before us.

...we...

...we didn't see anyone...

...we swear...

Dammit.

That turncoat did Julep **and** the Cap?

It gets worse.

Looks like the drone just got Sirge.

Watch these two.

I'm gonna go *murder* those assholes.

Fuck that noise, man.

This brat has cost us enough.

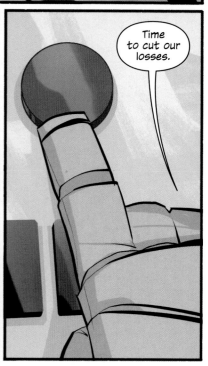

Time to cut our losses.

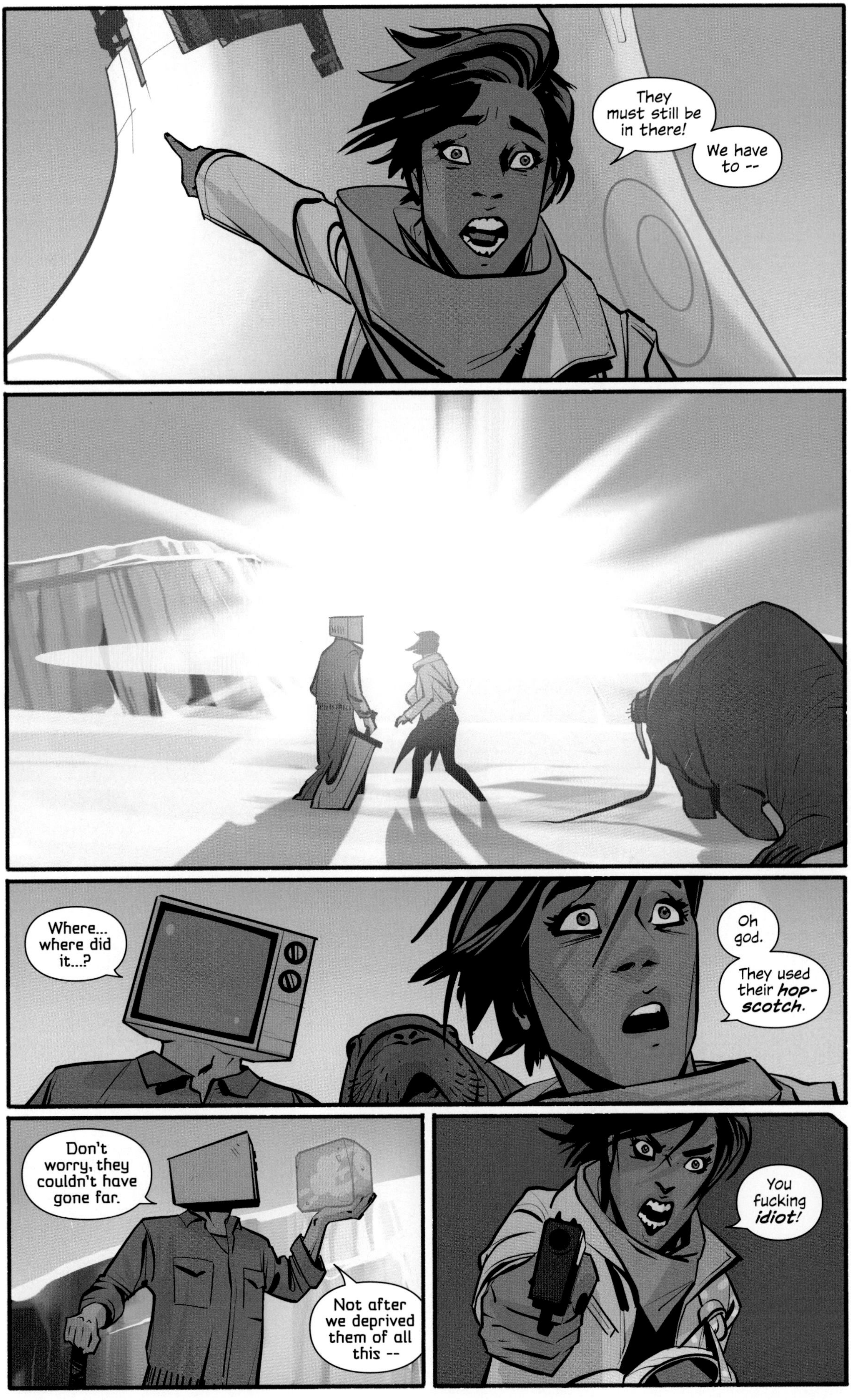
They must still be in there!
We have to --
Where... where did it...?
Oh god.
They used their **hop-scotch**.
Don't worry, they couldn't have gone far.
Not after we deprived them of all this --
You fucking **idiot**!

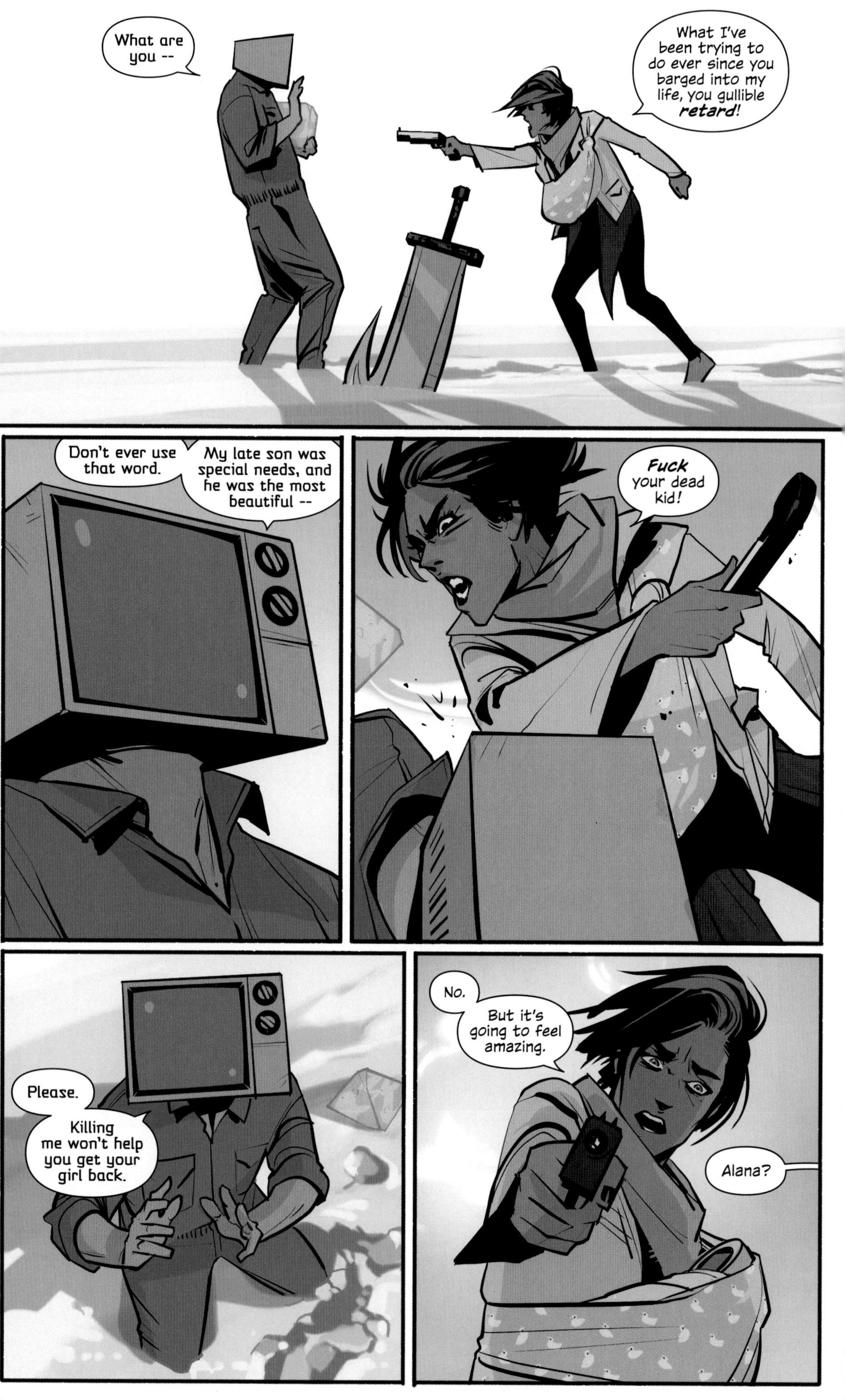
What are you --
What I've been trying to do ever since you barged into my life, you gullible *retard*!
Don't ever use that word.
My late son was special needs, and he was the most beautiful --
Fuck your dead kid!
Please.
Killing me won't help you get your girl back.
No.
But it's going to feel amazing.
Alana?

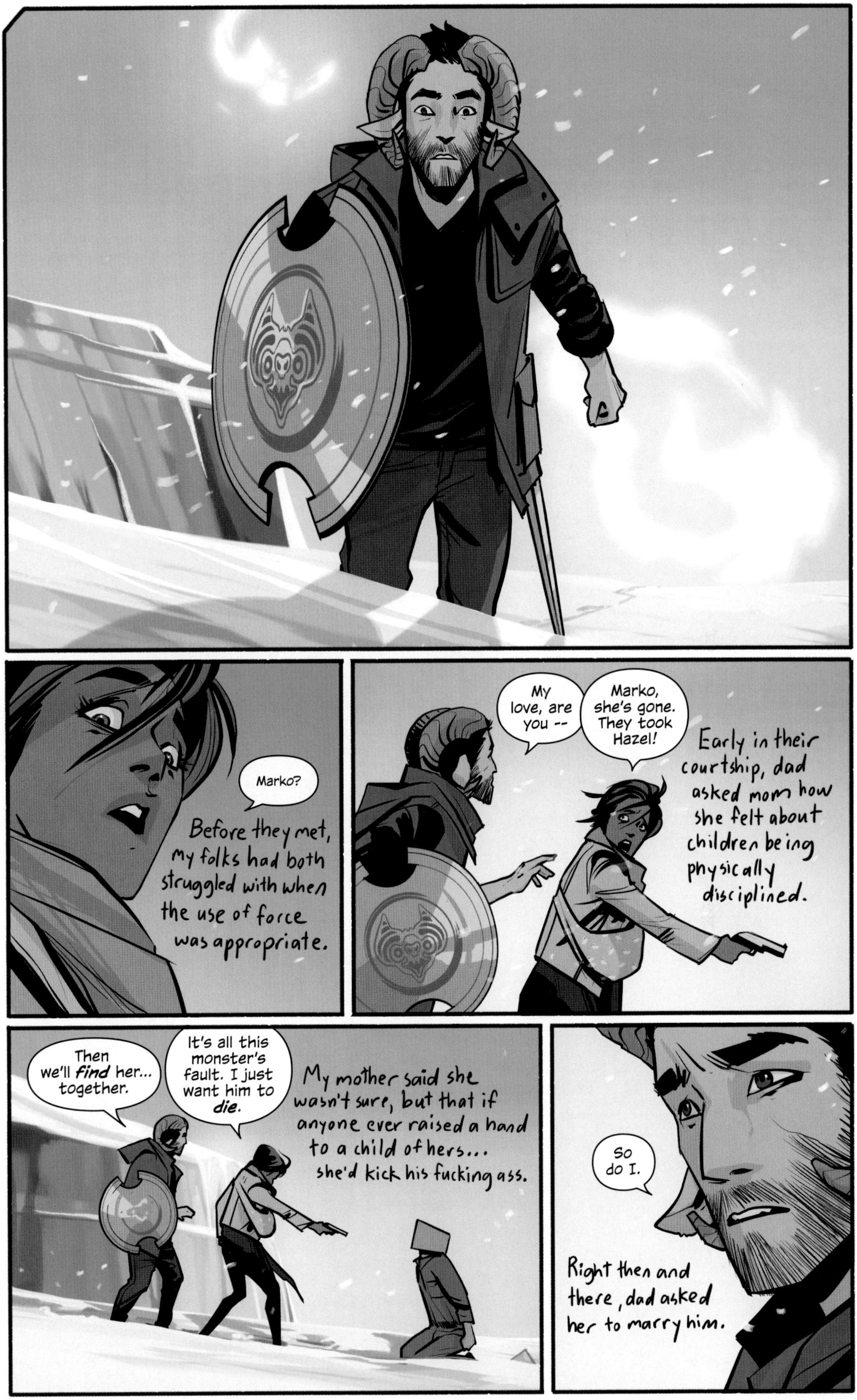

Marko?
Before they met, my folks had both struggled with when the use of force was appropriate.
My love, are you --
Marko, she's gone. They took Hazel!
Early in their courtship, dad asked mom how she felt about children being physically disciplined.
Then we'll find her... together.
It's all this monster's fault. I just want him to die.
My mother said she wasn't sure, but that if anyone ever raised a hand to a child of hers... she'd kick his fucking ass.
So do I.
Right then and there, dad asked her to marry him.

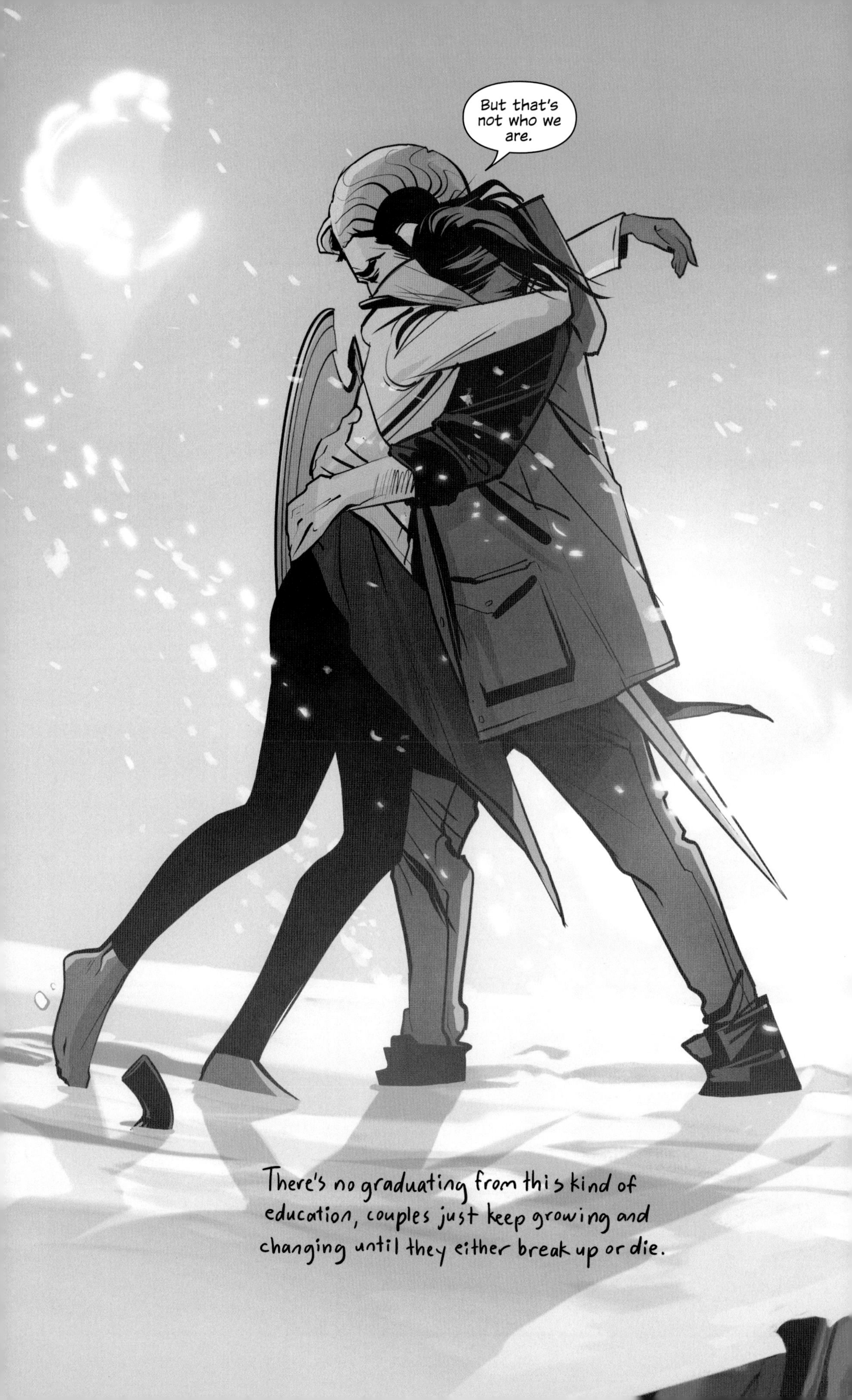
But that's not who we are.
There's no graduating from this kind of education, couples just keep growing and changing until they either break up or die.

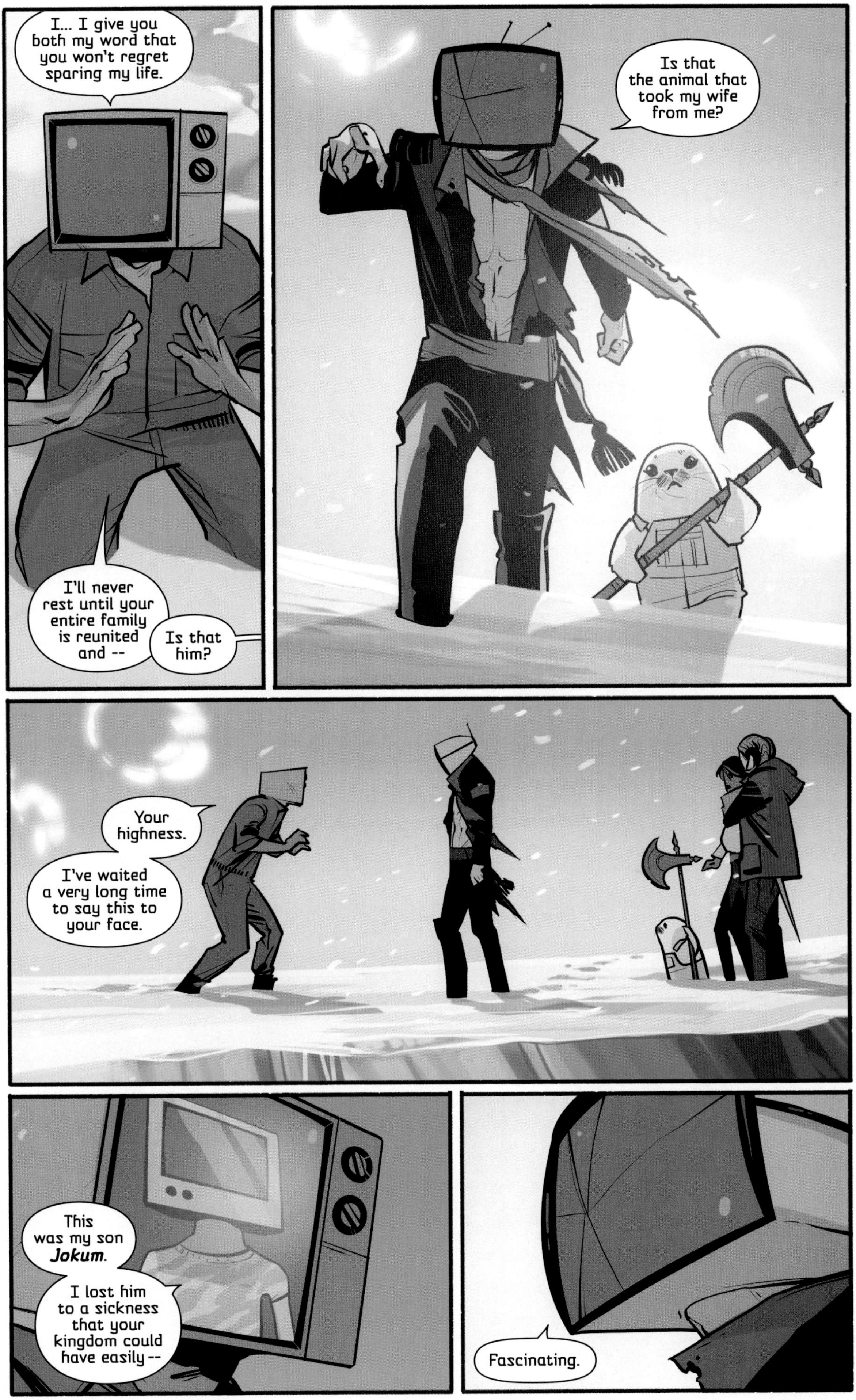
I... I give you both my word that you won't regret sparing my life.
I'll never rest until your entire family is reunited and --
Is that him?
Is that the animal that took my wife from me?
Your highness.
I've waited a very long time to say this to your face.
This was my son *Jokum*.
I lost him to a sickness that your kingdom could have easily --
Fascinating.

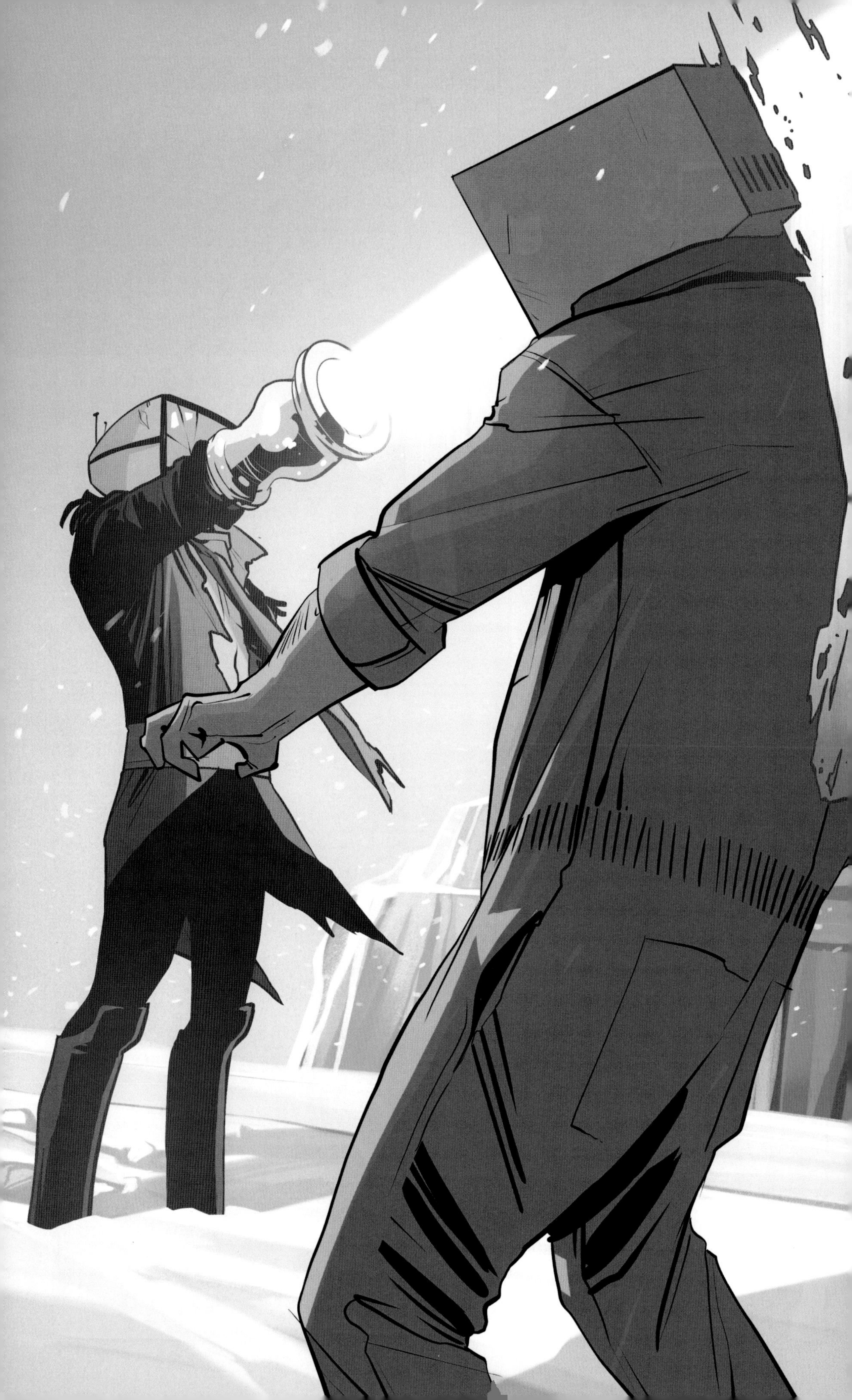

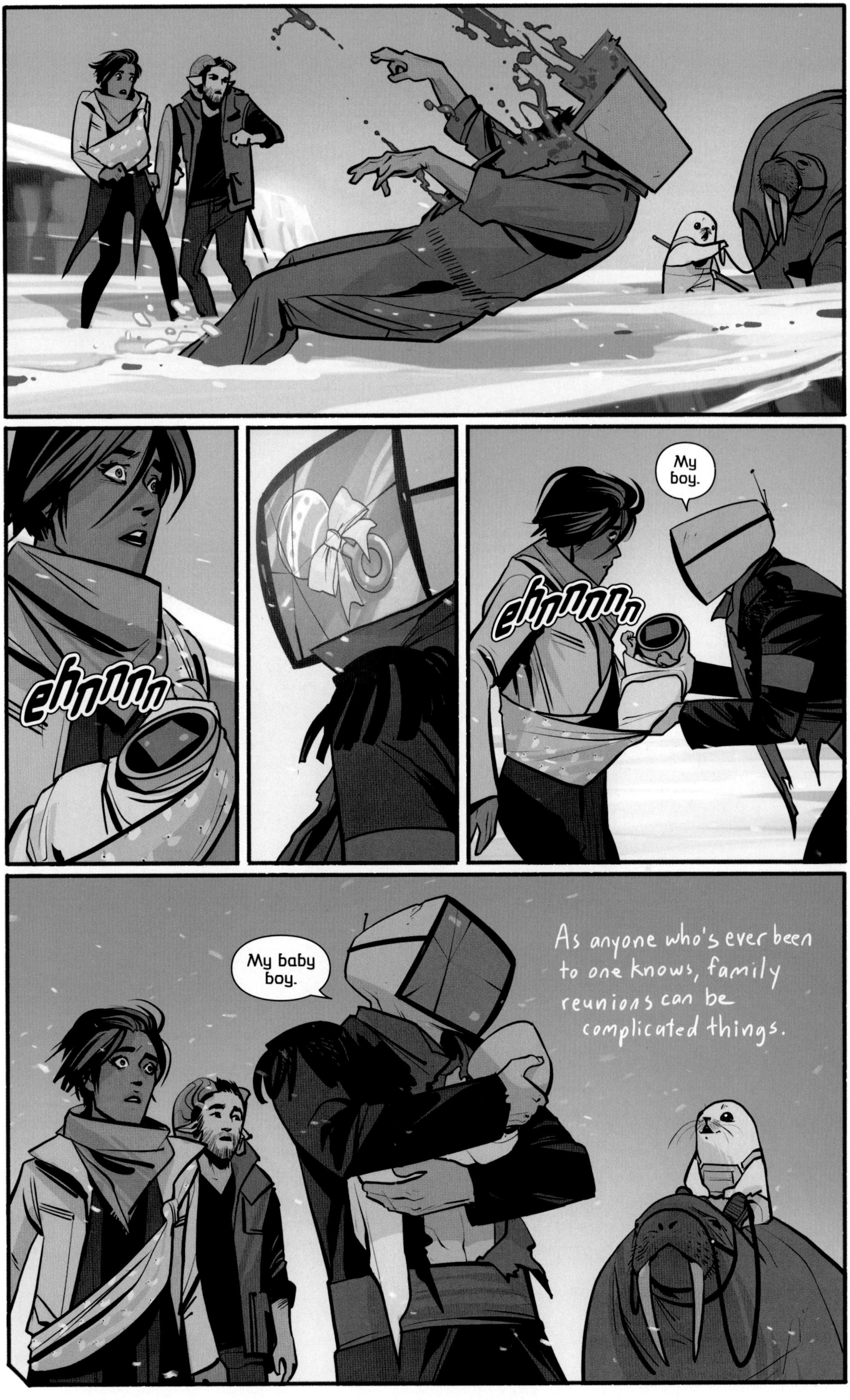

ehnnnn
My boy.
ehnnnnn
My baby boy.
As anyone who's ever been to one knows, family reunions can be complicated things.

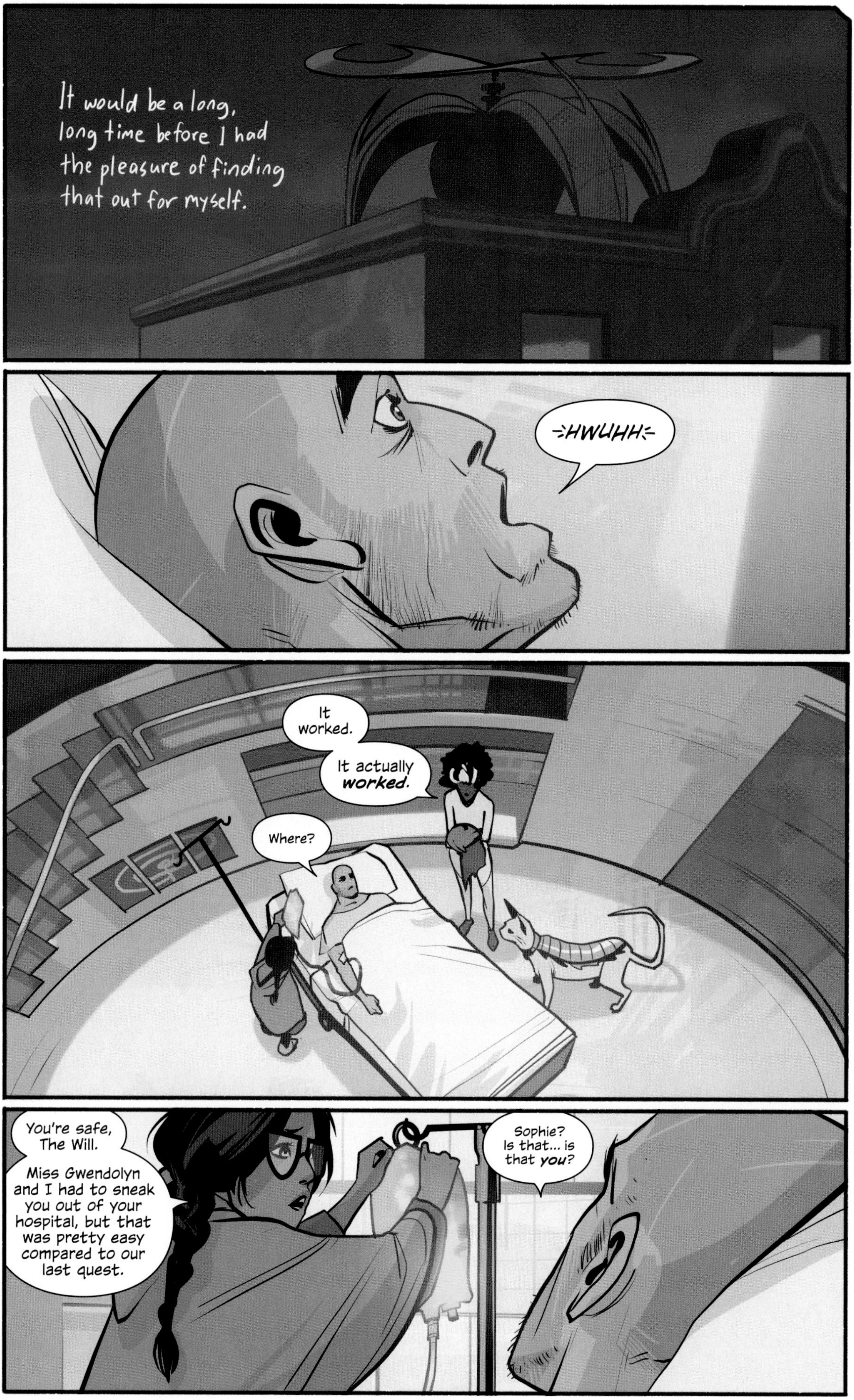
It would be a long, long time before I had the pleasure of finding that out for myself.
HWUHH
It worked.
It actually *worked*.
Where?
You're safe, The Will.
Miss Gwendolyn and I had to sneak you out of your hospital, but that was pretty easy compared to our last quest.
Sophie? Is that... is that *you*?

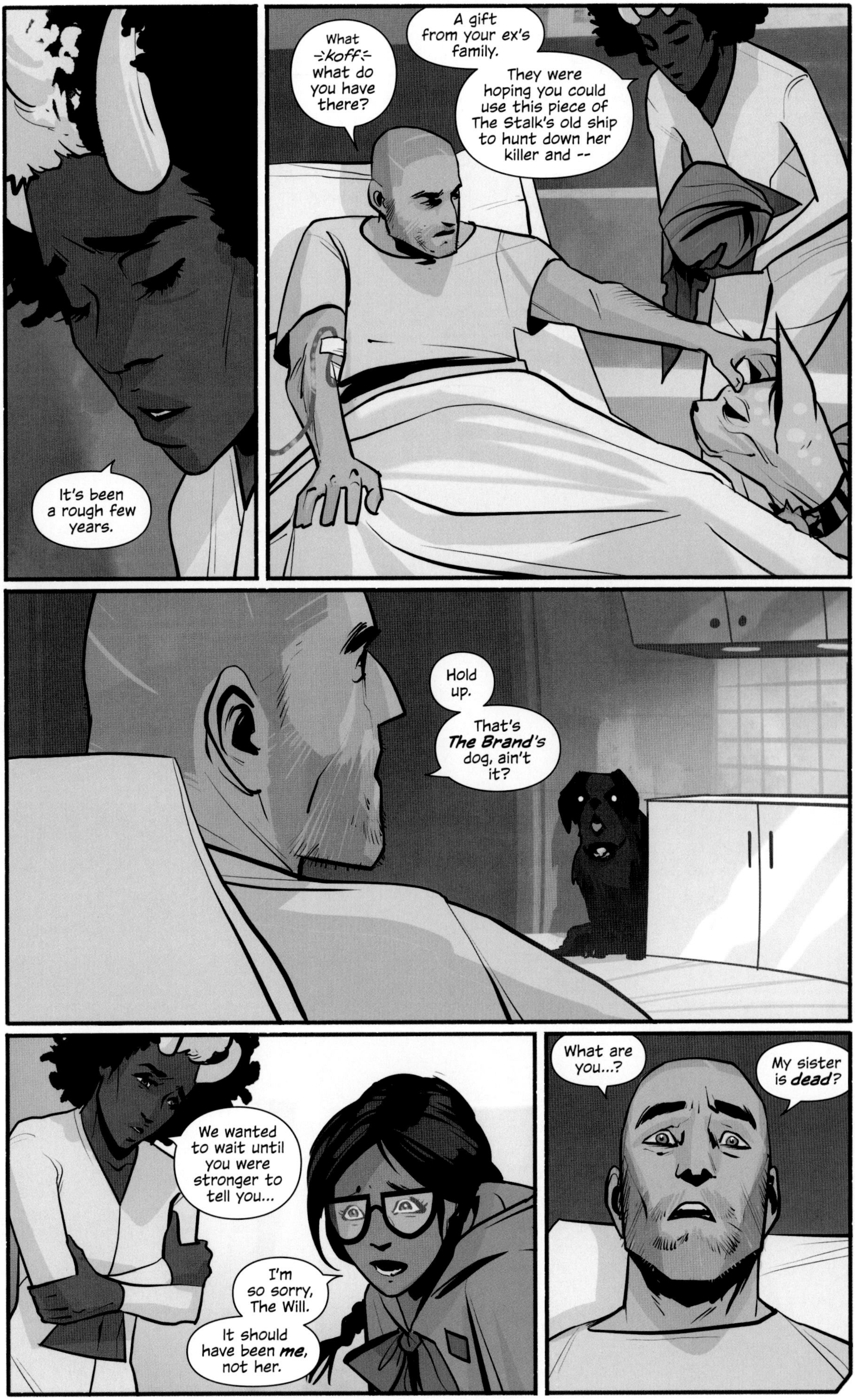

It's been a rough few years.
What ⇒koff⇐ what do you have there?
A gift from your ex's family.
They were hoping you could use this piece of The Stalk's old ship to hunt down her killer and --
Hold up.
That's ***The Brand***'s dog, ain't it?
We wanted to wait until you were stronger to tell you...
I'm so sorry, The Will.
It should have been ***me***, not her.
What are you...?
My sister is ***dead***?

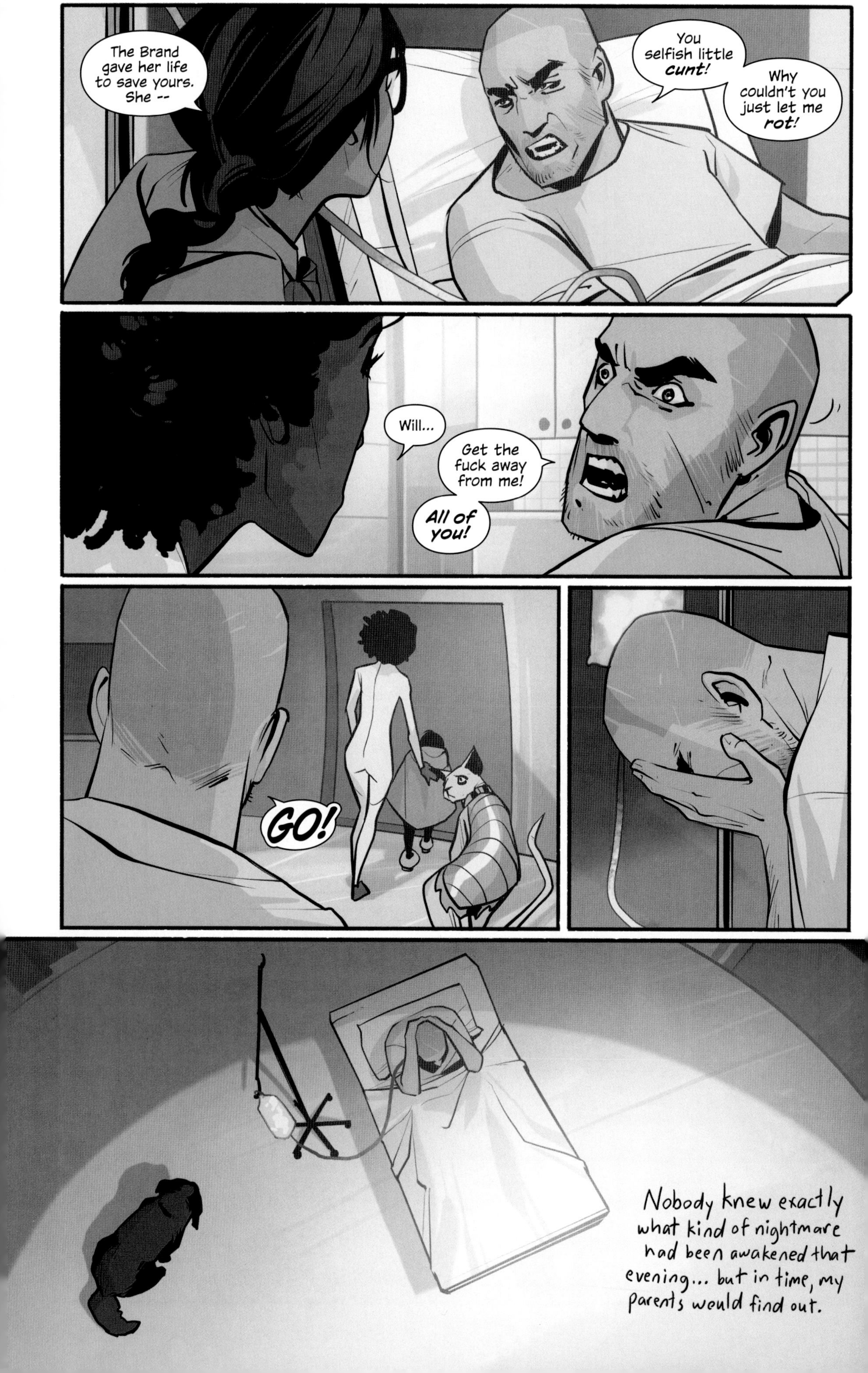
The Brand gave her life to save yours. She --
You selfish little **cunt!**
Why couldn't you just let me **rot!**
Will...
Get the fuck away from me!
All of you!
GO!
Nobody knew exactly what kind of nightmare had been awakened that evening... but in time, my parents would find out.

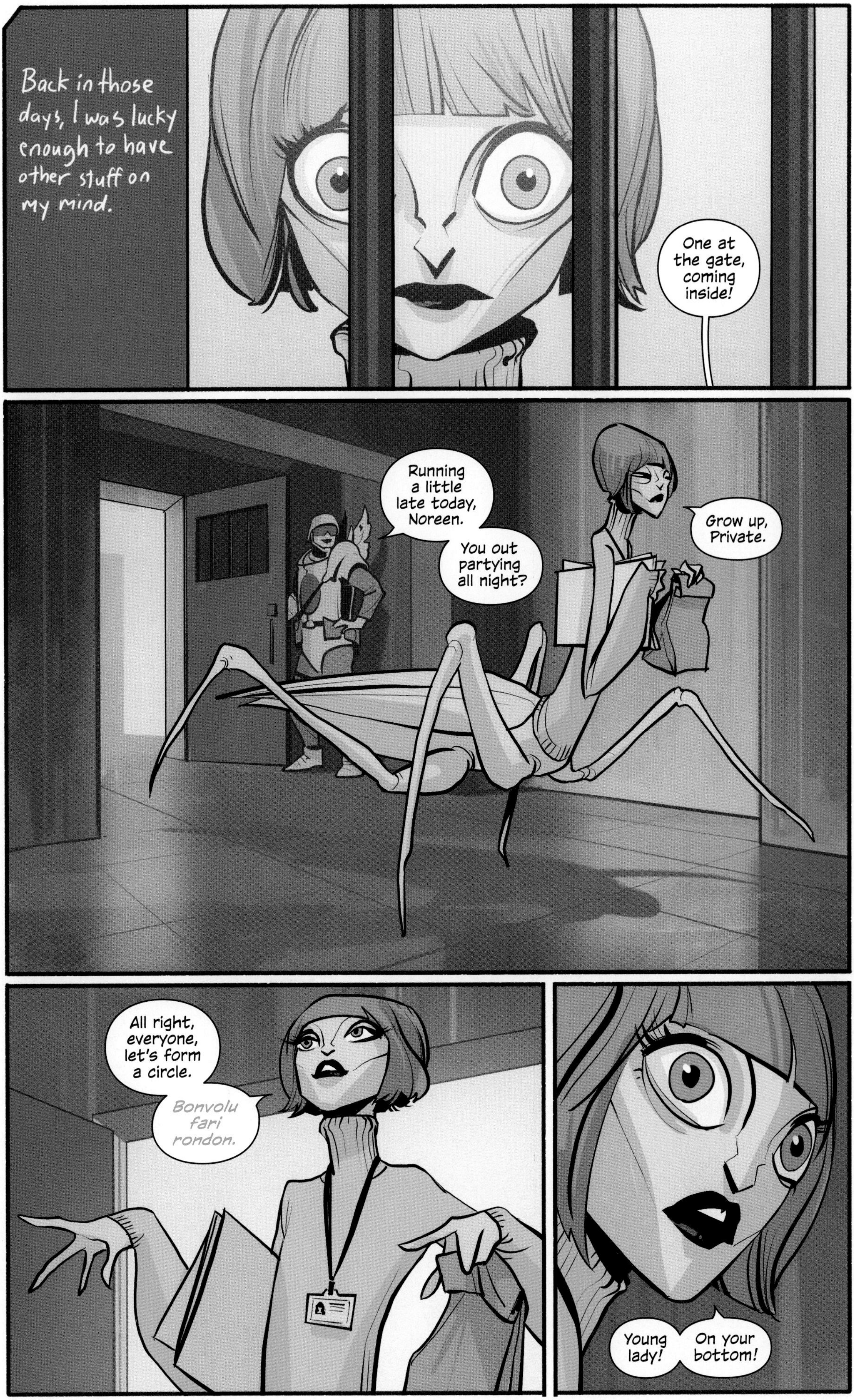

Back in those days, I was lucky enough to have other stuff on my mind.
One at the gate, coming inside!
Running a little late today, Noreen.
You out partying all night?
Grow up, Private.
All right, everyone, let's form a circle.
Bonvolu fari rondon.
Young lady!
On your bottom!

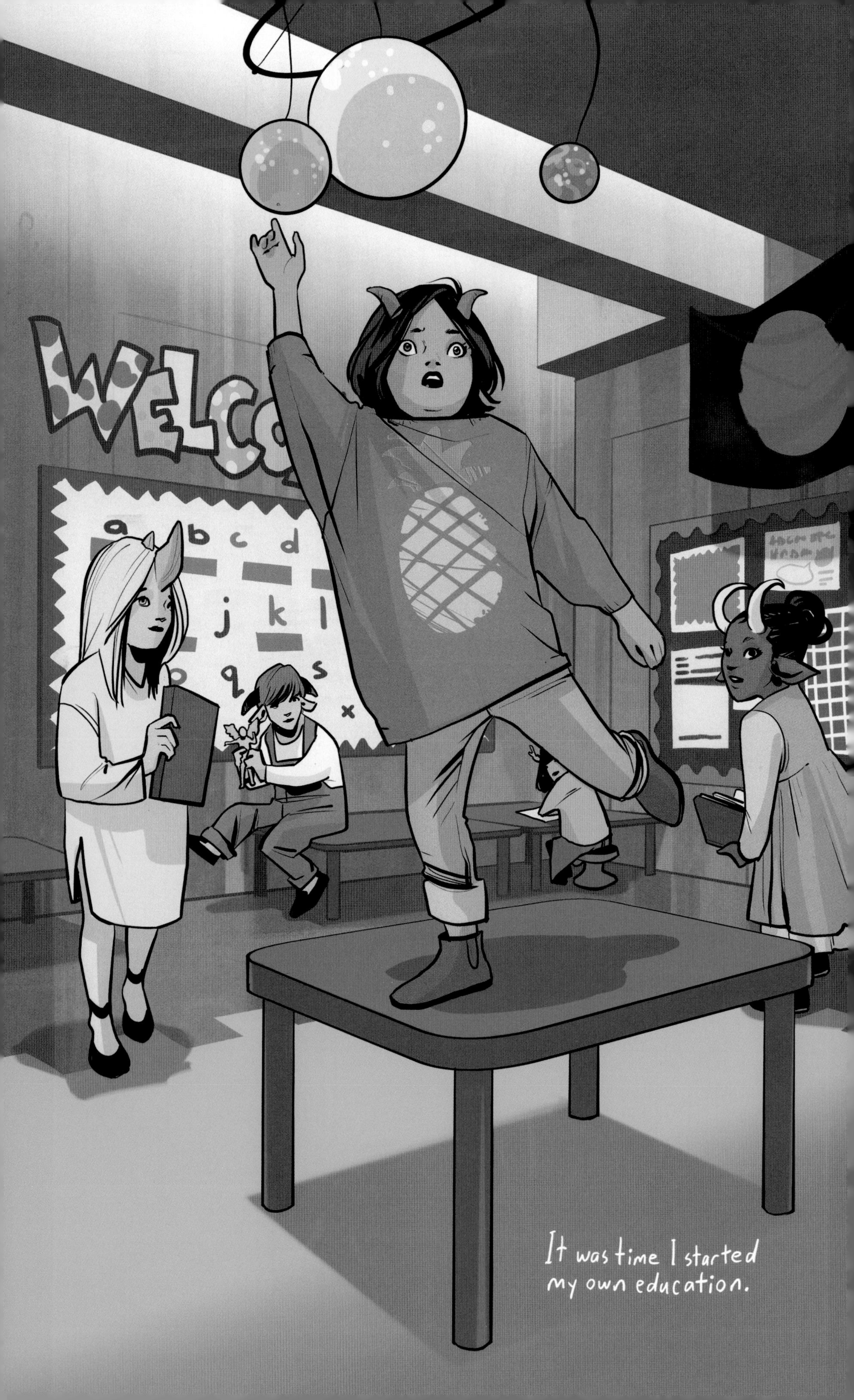
WELCO
It was time I started my own education.

end chapter thirty

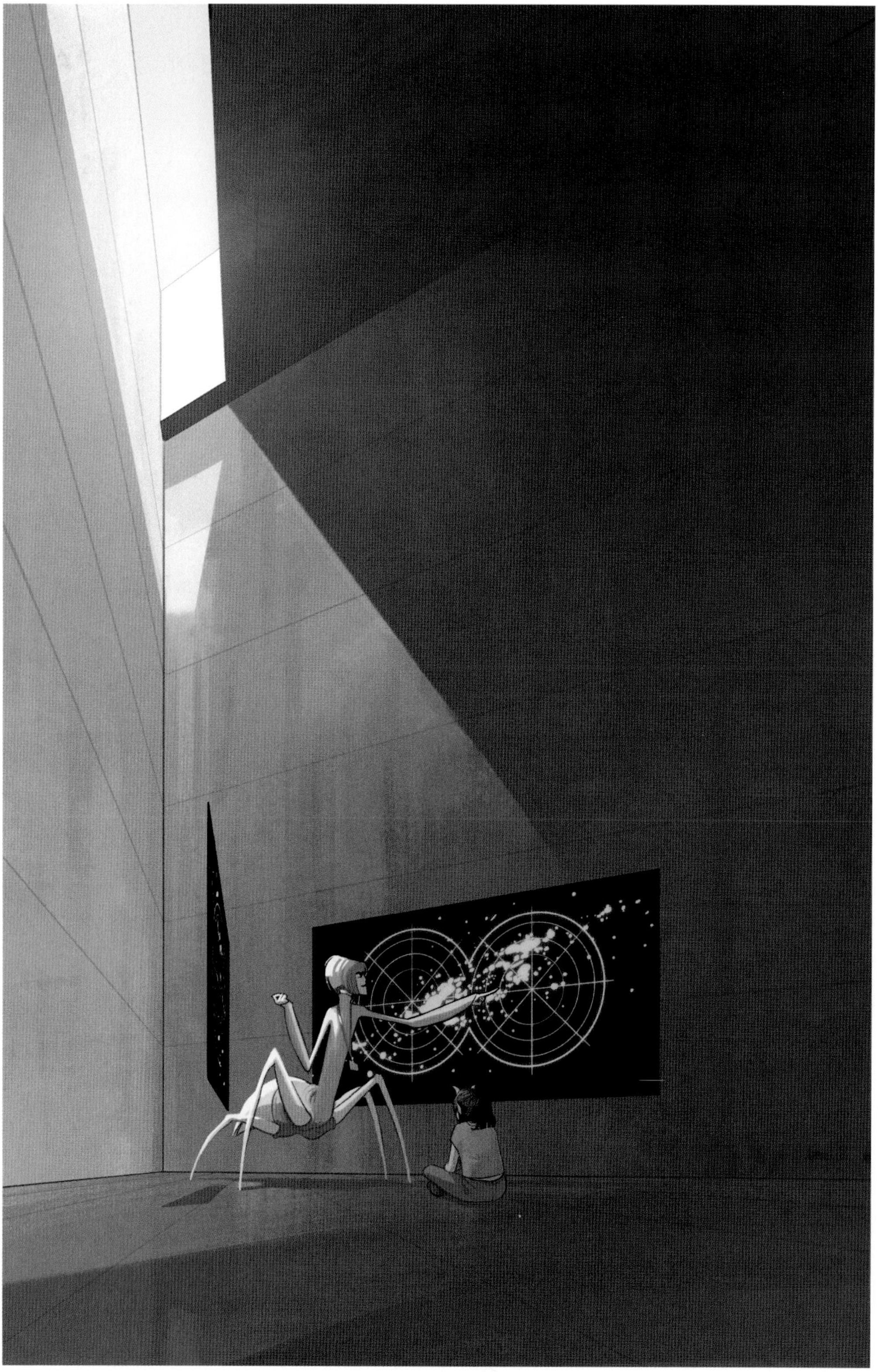

CHAPTER

THIRTY-ONE

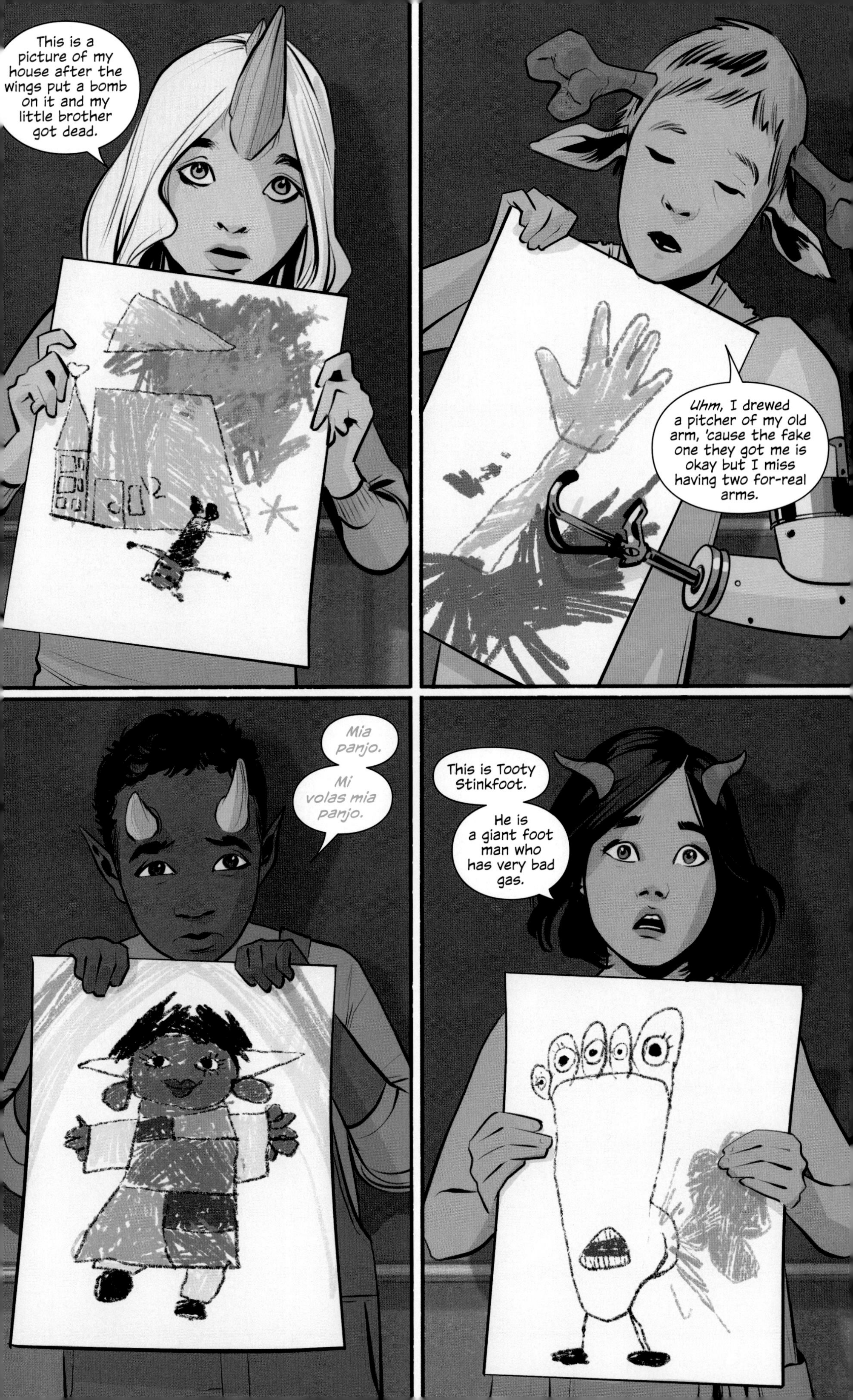
This is a picture of my house after the wings put a bomb on it and my little brother got dead.
Uhm, I drewed a pitcher of my old arm, 'cause the fake one they got me is okay but I miss having two for-real arms.
Mia panjo.
Mi volas mia panjo.
This is Tooty Stinkfoot.
He is a giant foot man who has very bad gas.

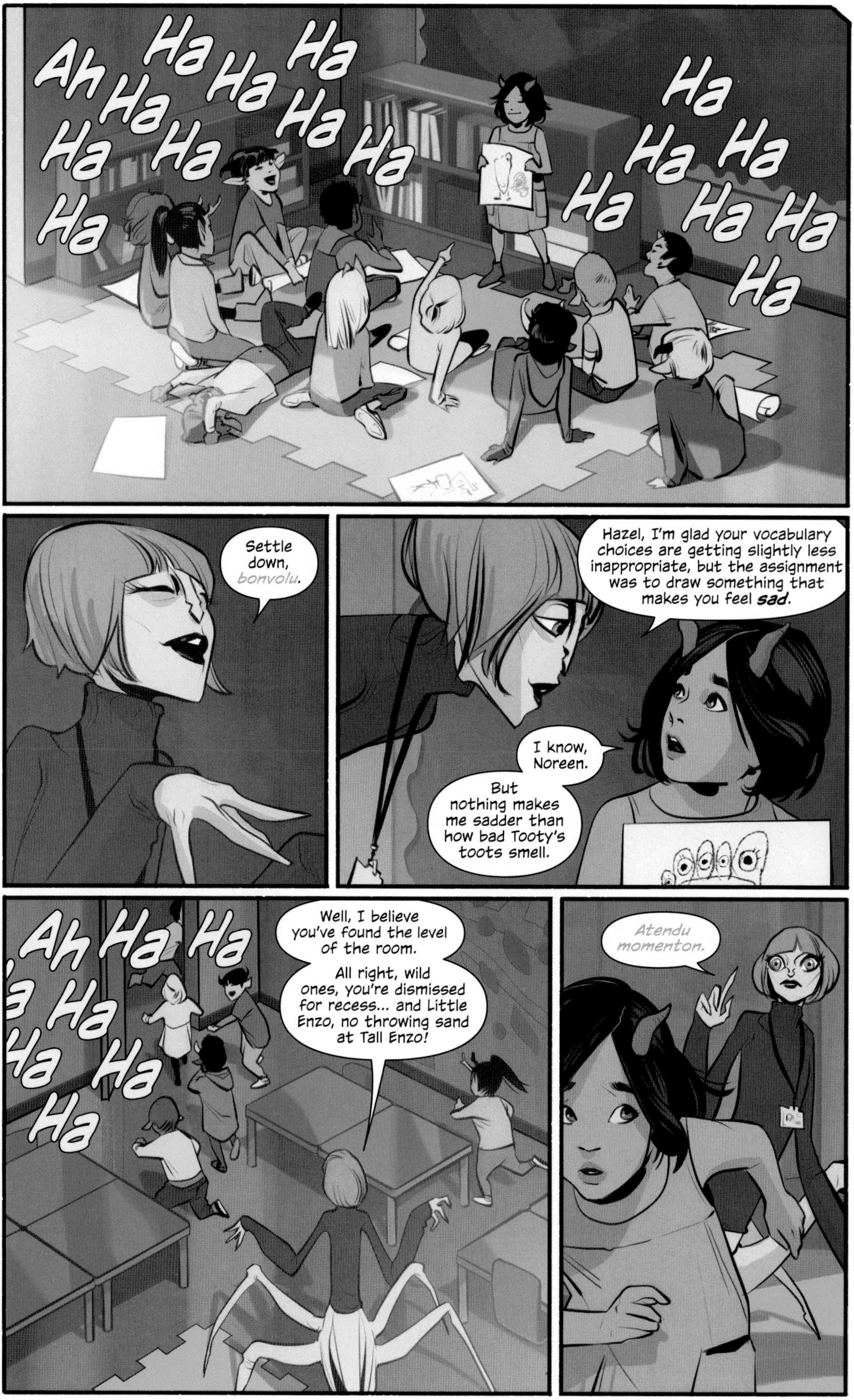
Ah Ha Ha Ha Ha Ha Ha Ha Ha Ha Ha
Ha Ha Ha Ha Ha Ha Ha Ha
Settle down, bonvolu.
Hazel, I'm glad your vocabulary choices are getting slightly less inappropriate, but the assignment was to draw something that makes you feel sad.
I know, Noreen.
But nothing makes me sadder than how bad Tooty's toots smell.
Ah Ha Ha Ha Ha Ha Ha Ha Ha Ha
Well, I believe you've found the level of the room.
All right, wild ones, you're dismissed for recess... and Little Enzo, no throwing sand at Tall Enzo!
Atendu momenton.

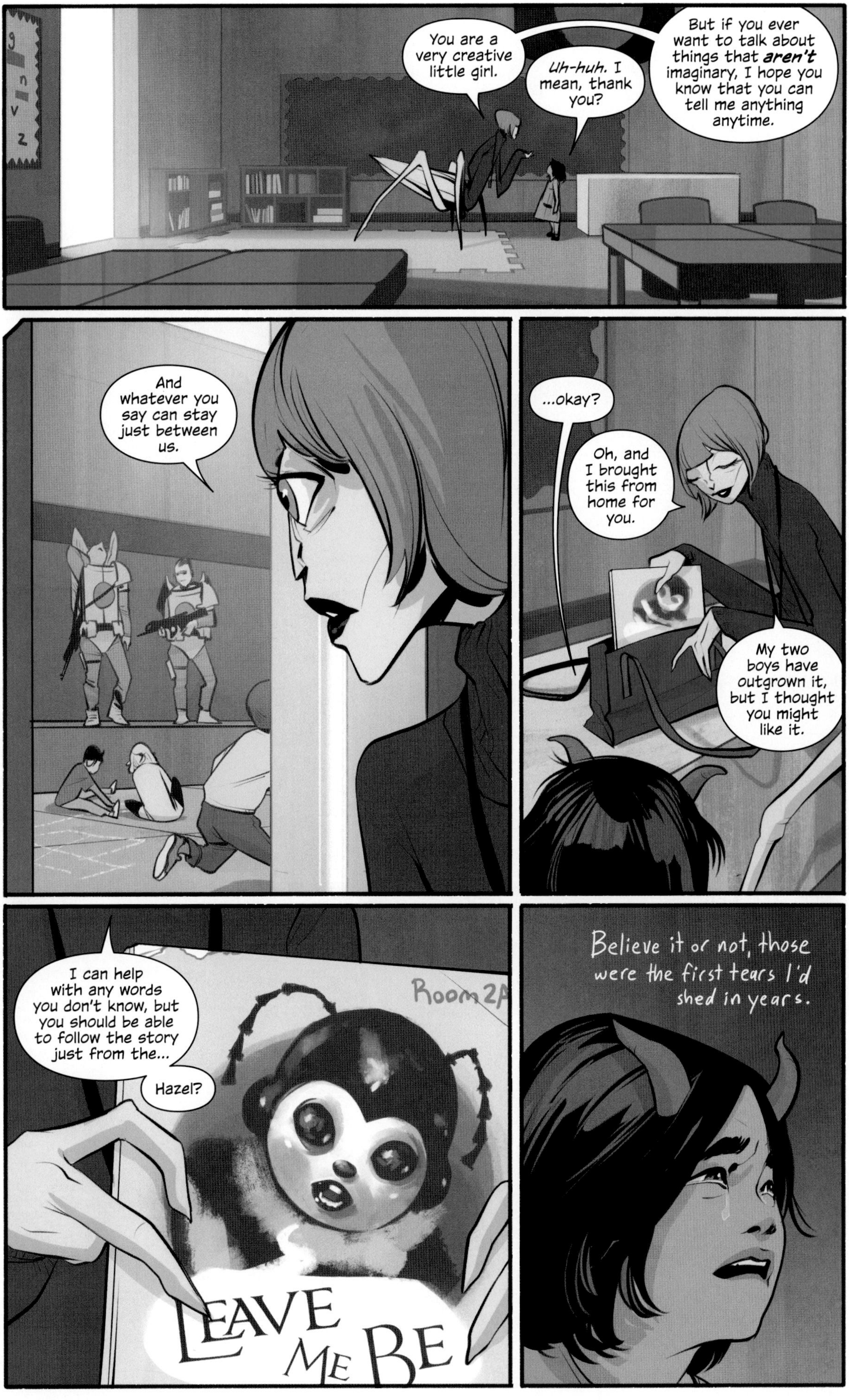
You are a very creative little girl.
Uh-huh. I mean, thank you?
But if you ever want to talk about things that **aren't** imaginary, I hope you know that you can tell me anything anytime.
And whatever you say can stay just between us.
...okay?
Oh, and I brought this from home for you.
My two boys have outgrown it, but I thought you might like it.
I can help with any words you don't know, but you should be able to follow the story just from the...
Hazel?
Room 2A
LEAVE ME BE
Believe it or not, those were the first tears I'd shed in years.

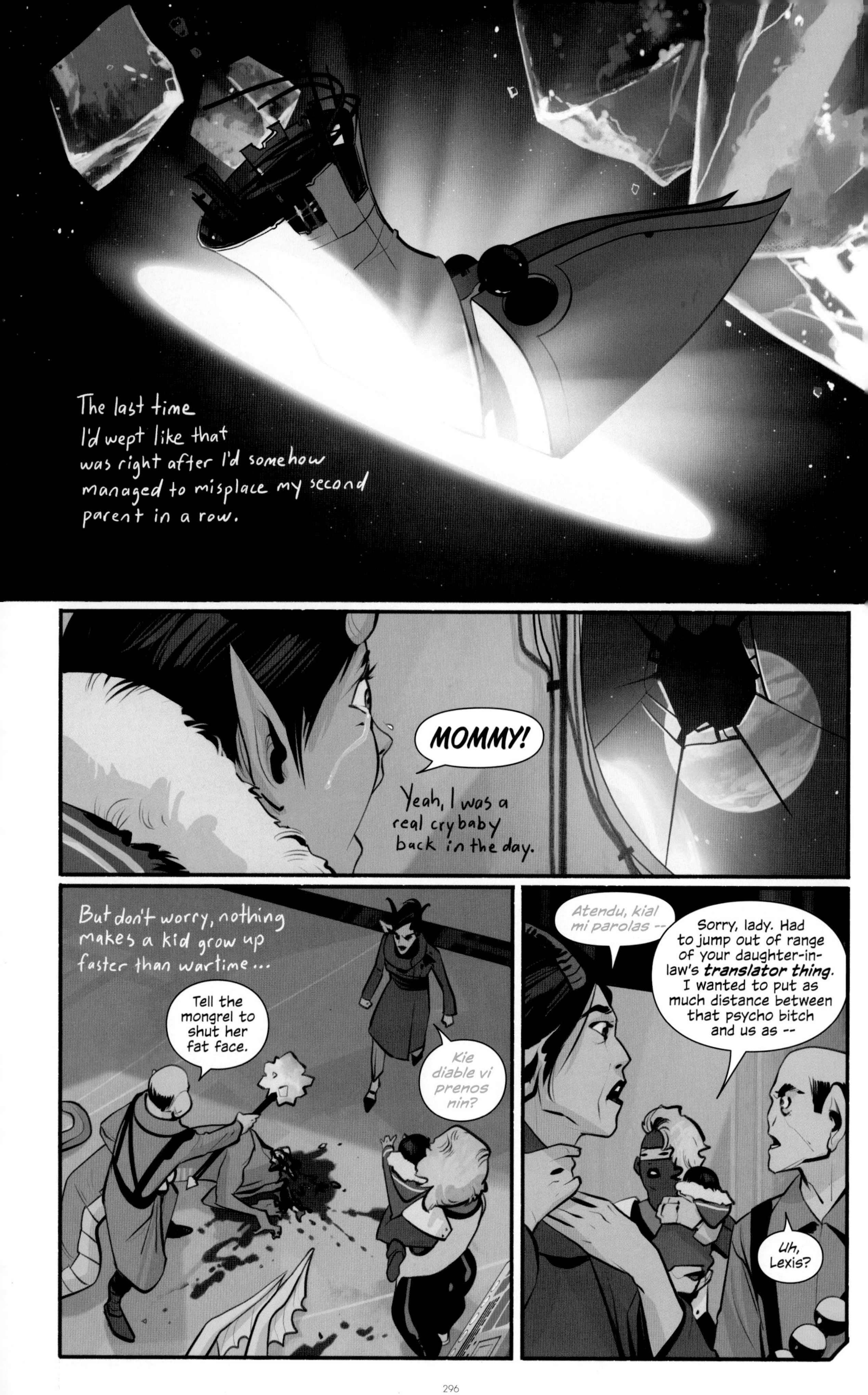
The last time I'd wept like that was right after I'd somehow managed to misplace my second parent in a row.
MOMMY!
Yeah, I was a real crybaby back in the day.
But don't worry, nothing makes a kid grow up faster than wartime...
Tell the mongrel to shut her fat face.
Kie diable vi prenos nin?
Atendu, kial mi parolas --
Sorry, lady. Had to jump out of range of your daughter-in-law's **translator thing**. I wanted to put as much distance between that psycho bitch and us as --
Uh, Lexis?

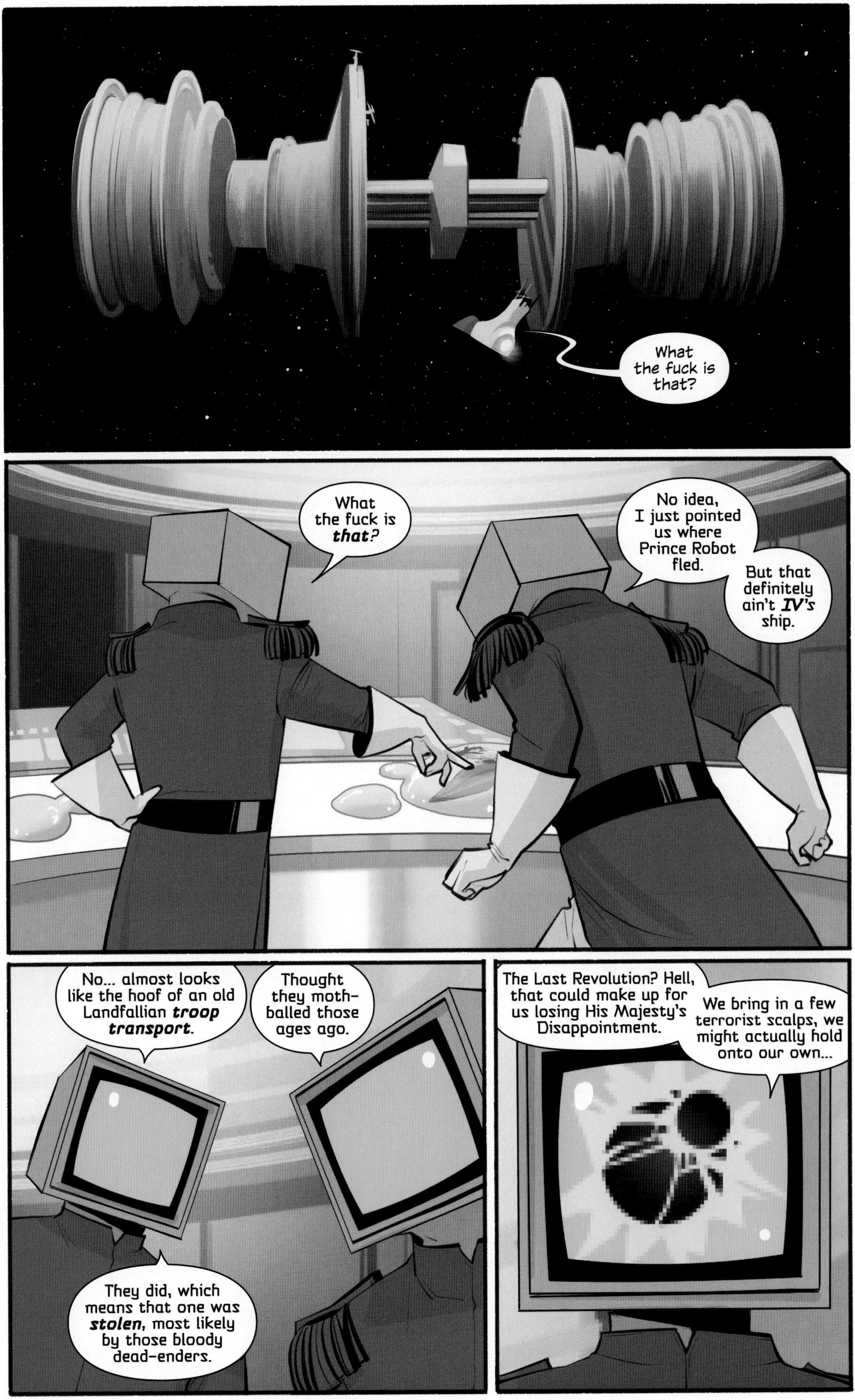

What the fuck is that?
What the fuck is *that*?
No idea, I just pointed us where Prince Robot fled.
But that definitely ain't *IV's* ship.
No... almost looks like the hoof of an old Landfallian *troop transport*.
Thought they moth-balled those ages ago.
They did, which means that one was *stolen*, most likely by those bloody dead-enders.
The Last Revolution? Hell, that could make up for us losing His Majesty's Disappointment.
We bring in a few terrorist scalps, we might actually hold onto our own...

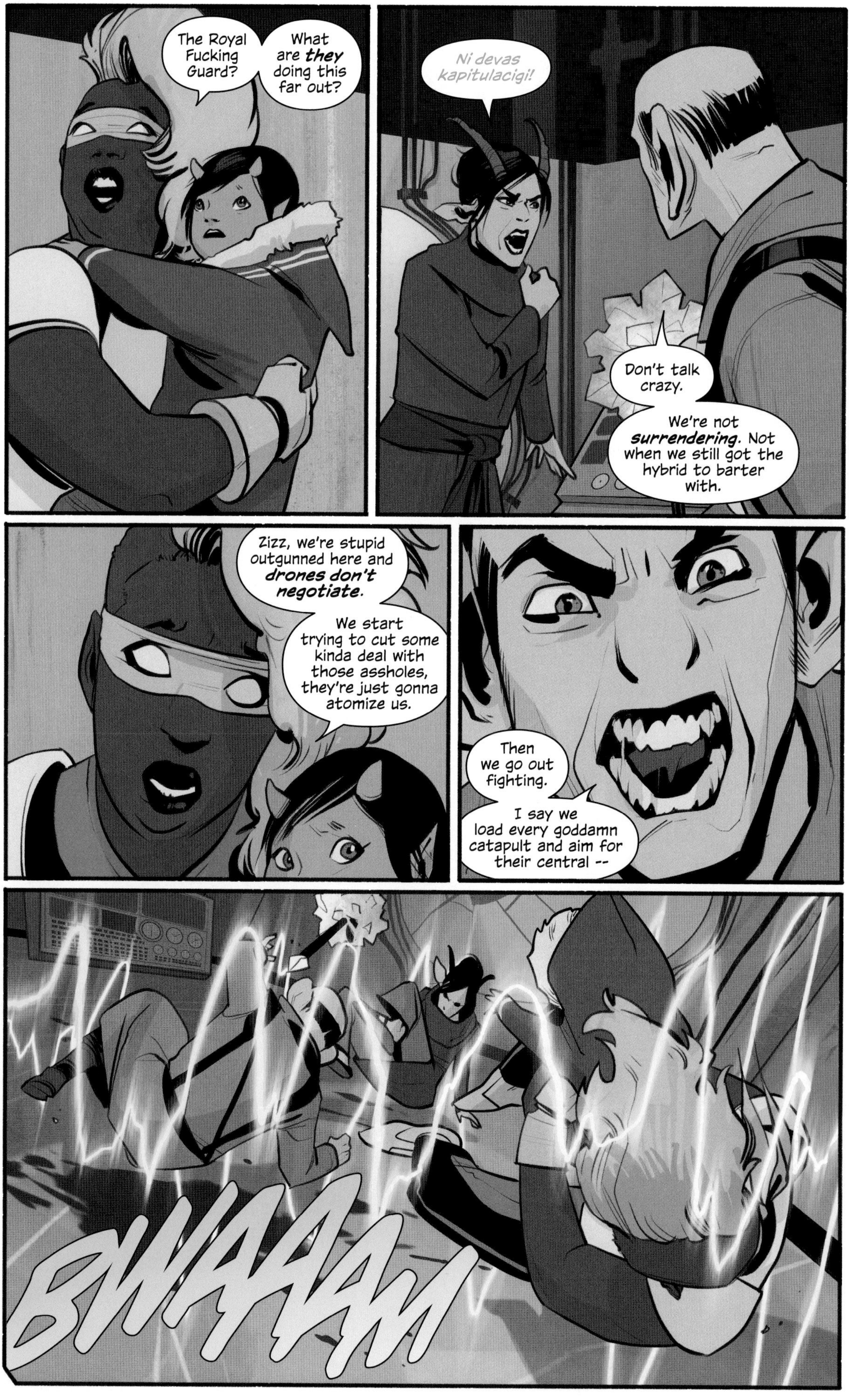

The Royal Fucking Guard?
What are *they* doing this far out?
Ni devas kapitulacigi!
Don't talk crazy.
We're not **surrendering**. Not when we still got the hybrid to barter with.
Zizz, we're stupid outgunned here and **drones don't negotiate**.
We start trying to cut some kinda deal with those assholes, they're just gonna atomize us.
Then we go out fighting.
I say we load every goddamn catapult and aim for their central --
BWAAAM

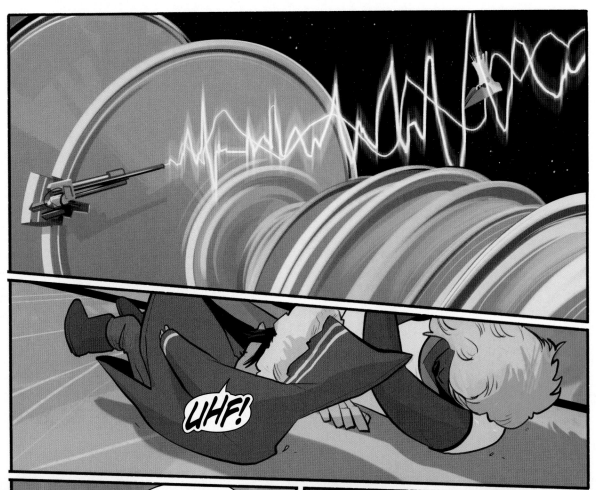

UHF!

Occupants, your illegal vessel has been disabled by authority of the Robot Kingdom.

Prepare to be boarded.

Kid, don't watch!

Over the years, "Auntie" Lexis would become very protective of me, which was sweet, but rarely necessary.

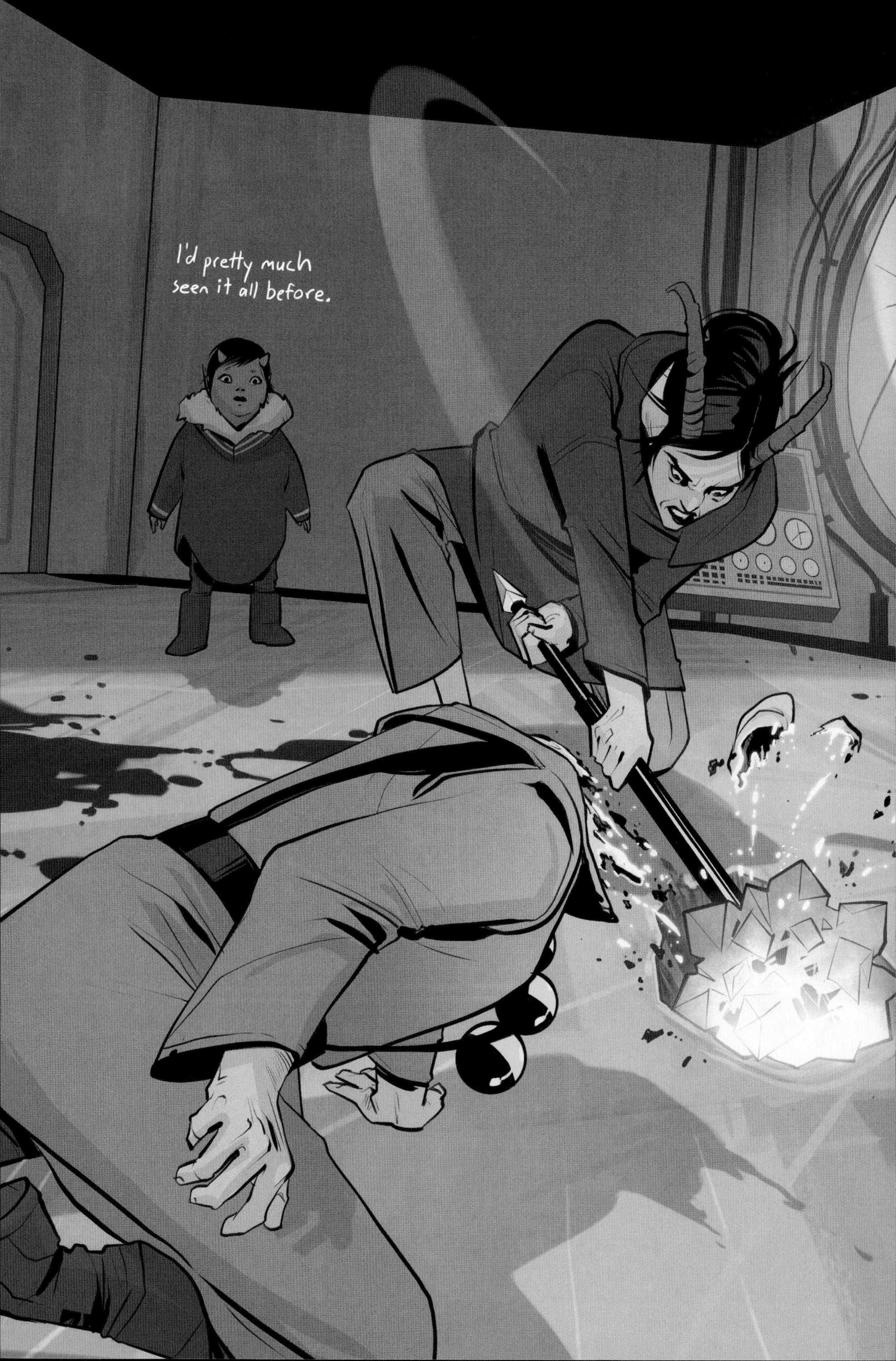
I'd pretty much seen it all before.

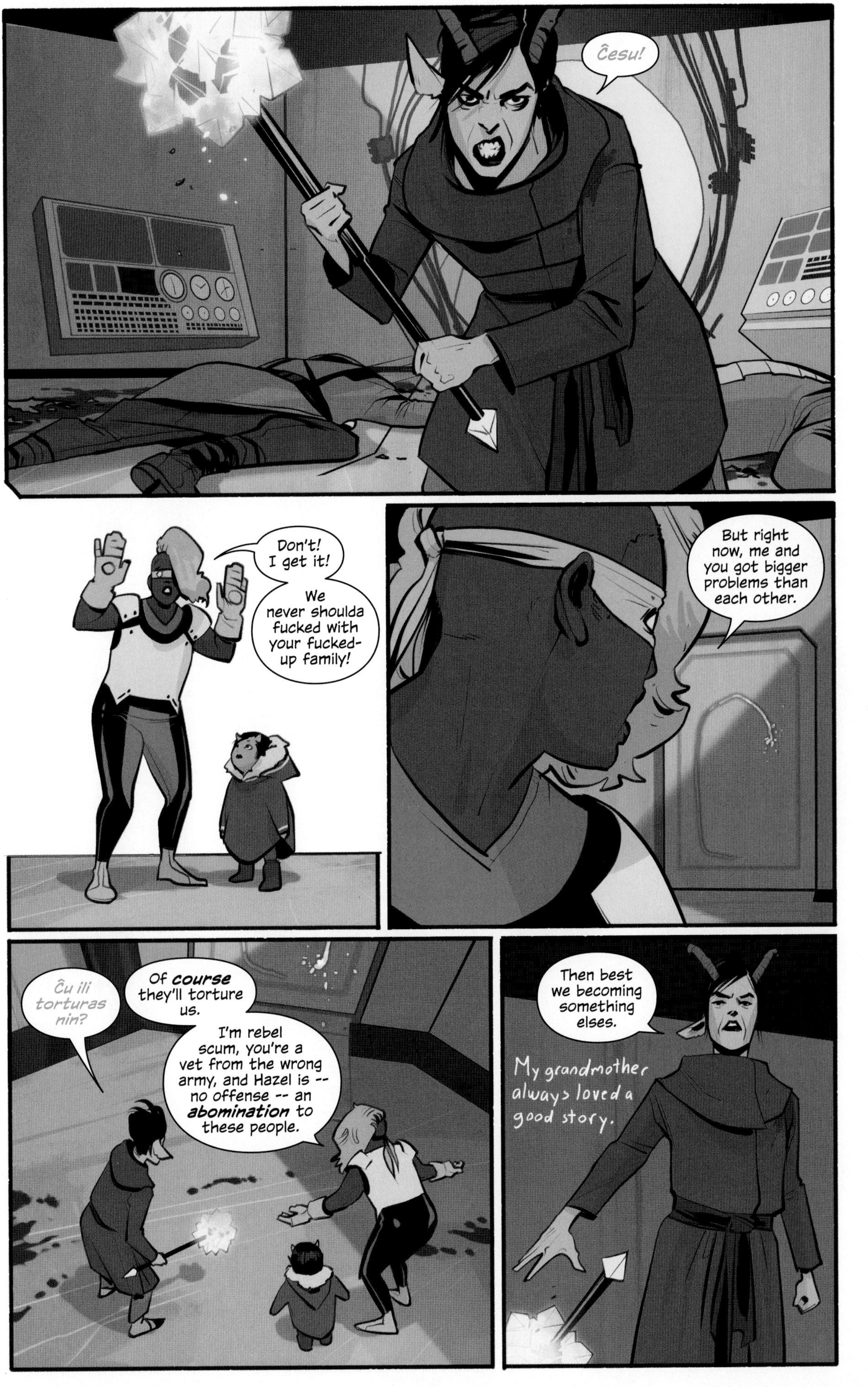

Ĉesu!
Don't! I get it!
We never shoulda fucked with your fucked-up family!
But right now, me and you got bigger problems than each other.
Ĉu ili torturas nin?
Of **course** they'll torture us.
I'm rebel scum, you're a vet from the wrong army, and Hazel is -- no offense -- an **abomination** to these people.
Then best we becoming something elses.
My grandmother always loved a good story.

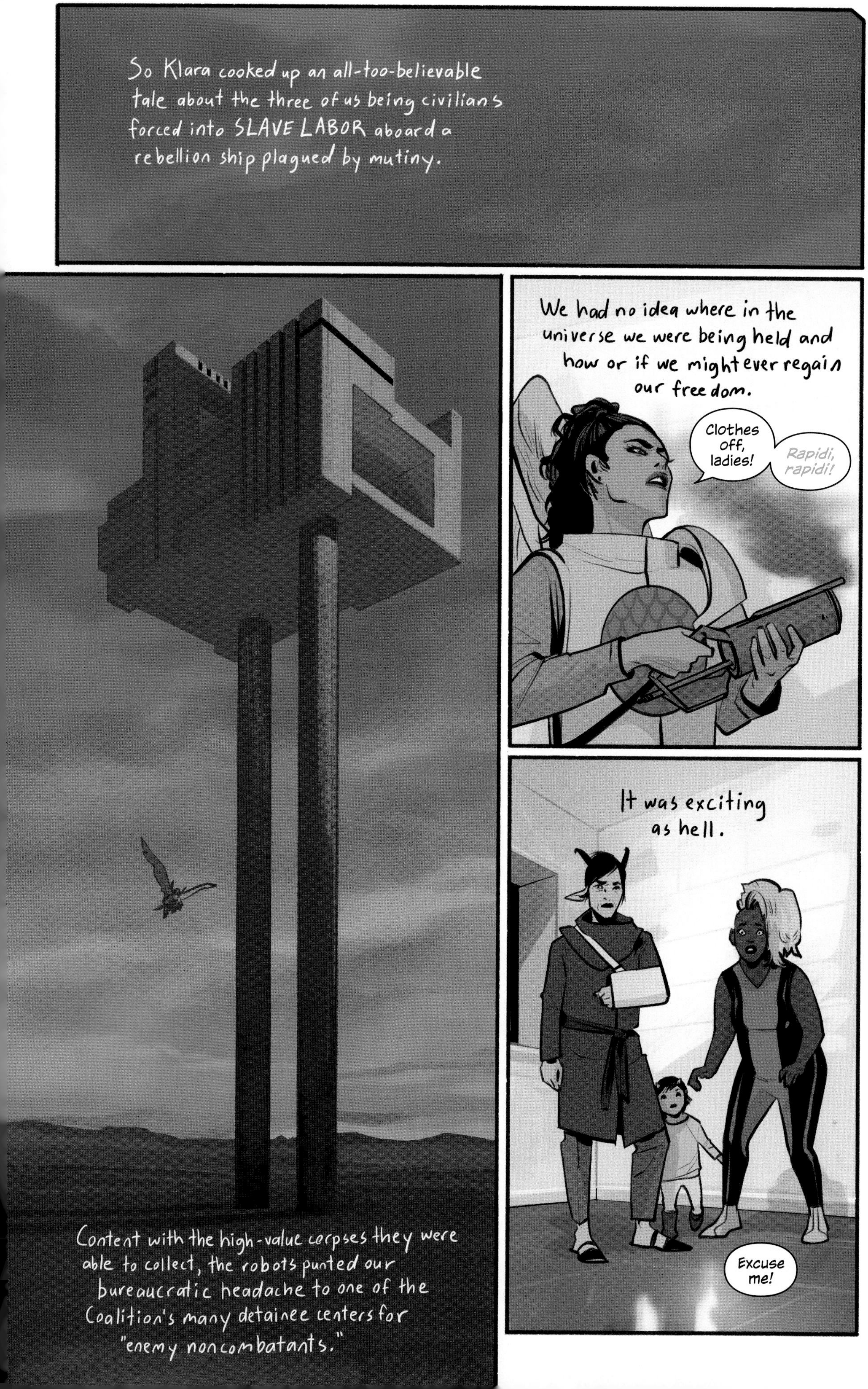
So Klara cooked up an all-too-believable tale about the three of us being civilians forced into SLAVE LABOR aboard a rebellion ship plagued by mutiny.
Content with the high-value corpses they were able to collect, the robots punted our bureaucratic headache to one of the Coalition's many detainee centers for "enemy noncombatants."
We had no idea where in the universe we were being held and how or if we might ever regain our freedom.
Clothes off, ladies!
Rapidi, rapidi!
It was exciting as hell.
Excuse me!

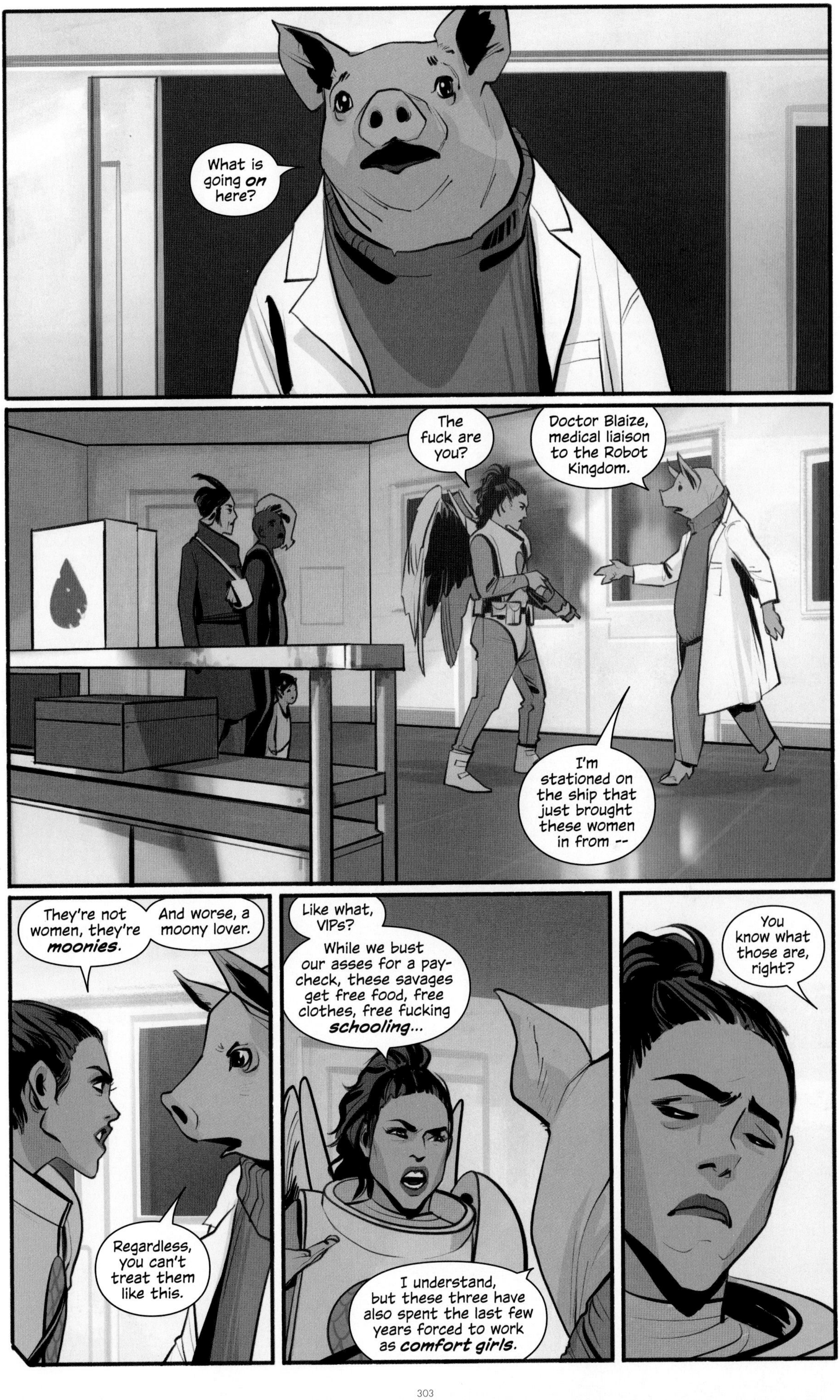
What is going on here?
The fuck are you?
Doctor Blaize, medical liaison to the Robot Kingdom.
I'm stationed on the ship that just brought these women in from --
They're not women, they're moonies.
And worse, a moony lover.
Regardless, you can't treat them like this.
Like what, VIPs?
While we bust our asses for a paycheck, these savages get free food, free clothes, free fucking schooling...
I understand, but these three have also spent the last few years forced to work as comfort girls.
You know what those are, right?

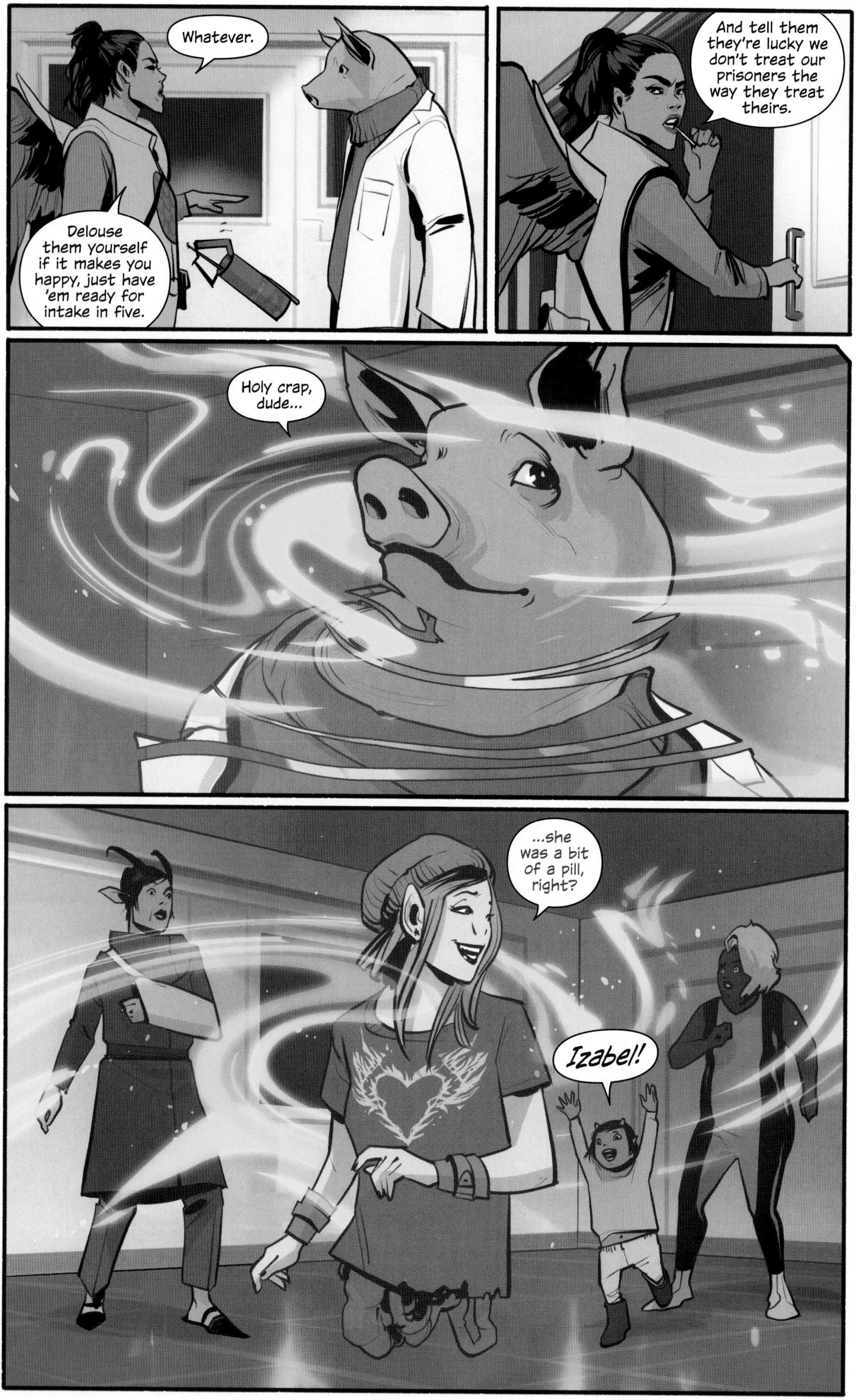
Whatever.
Delouse them yourself if it makes you happy, just have 'em ready for intake in five.
And tell them they're lucky we don't treat our prisoners the way they treat theirs.
Holy crap, dude...
...she was a bit of a pill, right?
Izabel!

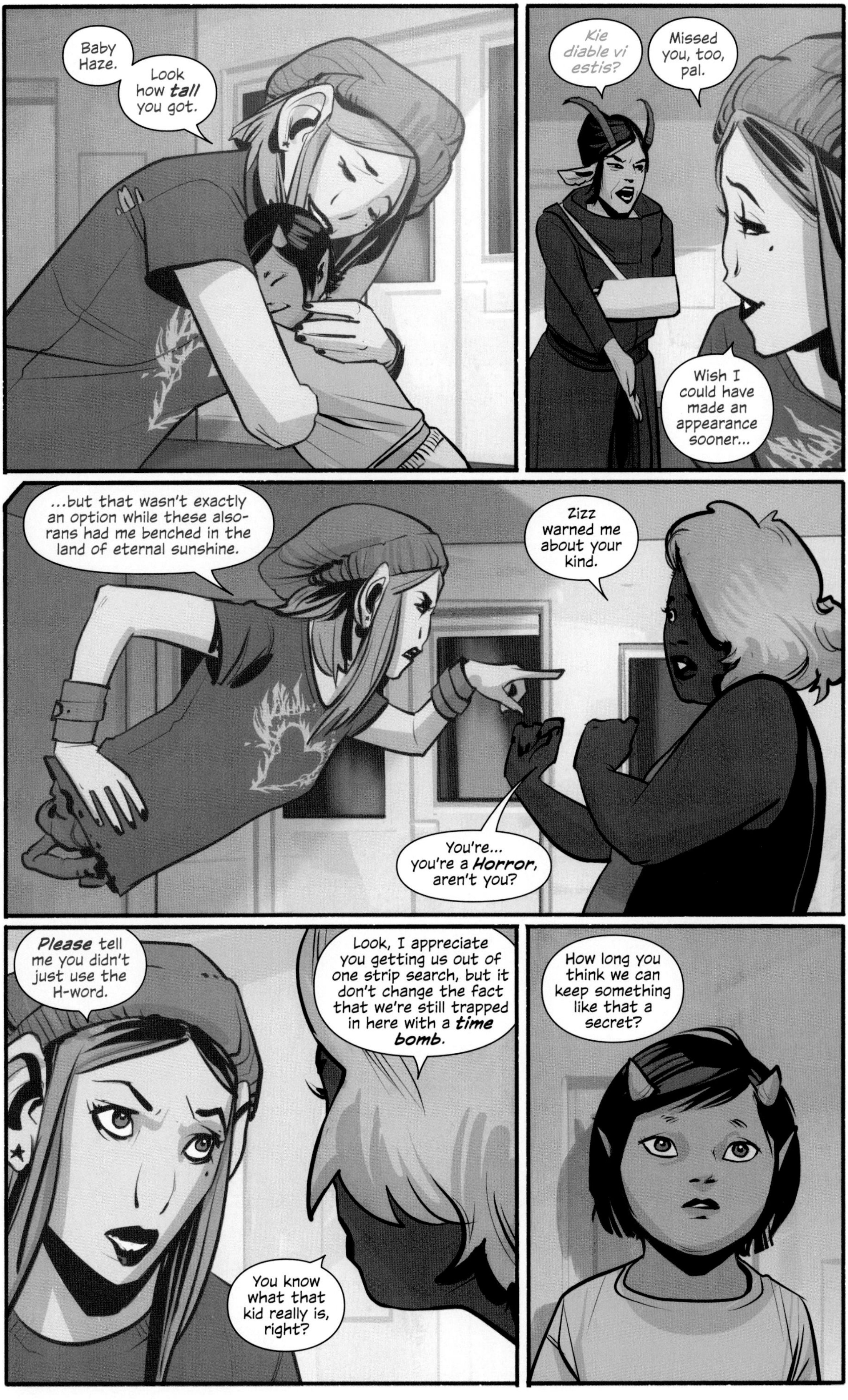
Baby Haze.
Look how tall you got.
Kie diable vi estis?
Missed you, too, pal.
Wish I could have made an appearance sooner...
...but that wasn't exactly an option while these also-rans had me benched in the land of eternal sunshine.
Zizz warned me about your kind.
You're... you're a Horror, aren't you?
Please tell me you didn't just use the H-word.
Look, I appreciate you getting us out of one strip search, but it don't change the fact that we're still trapped in here with a time bomb.
You know what that kid really is, right?
How long you think we can keep something like that a secret?

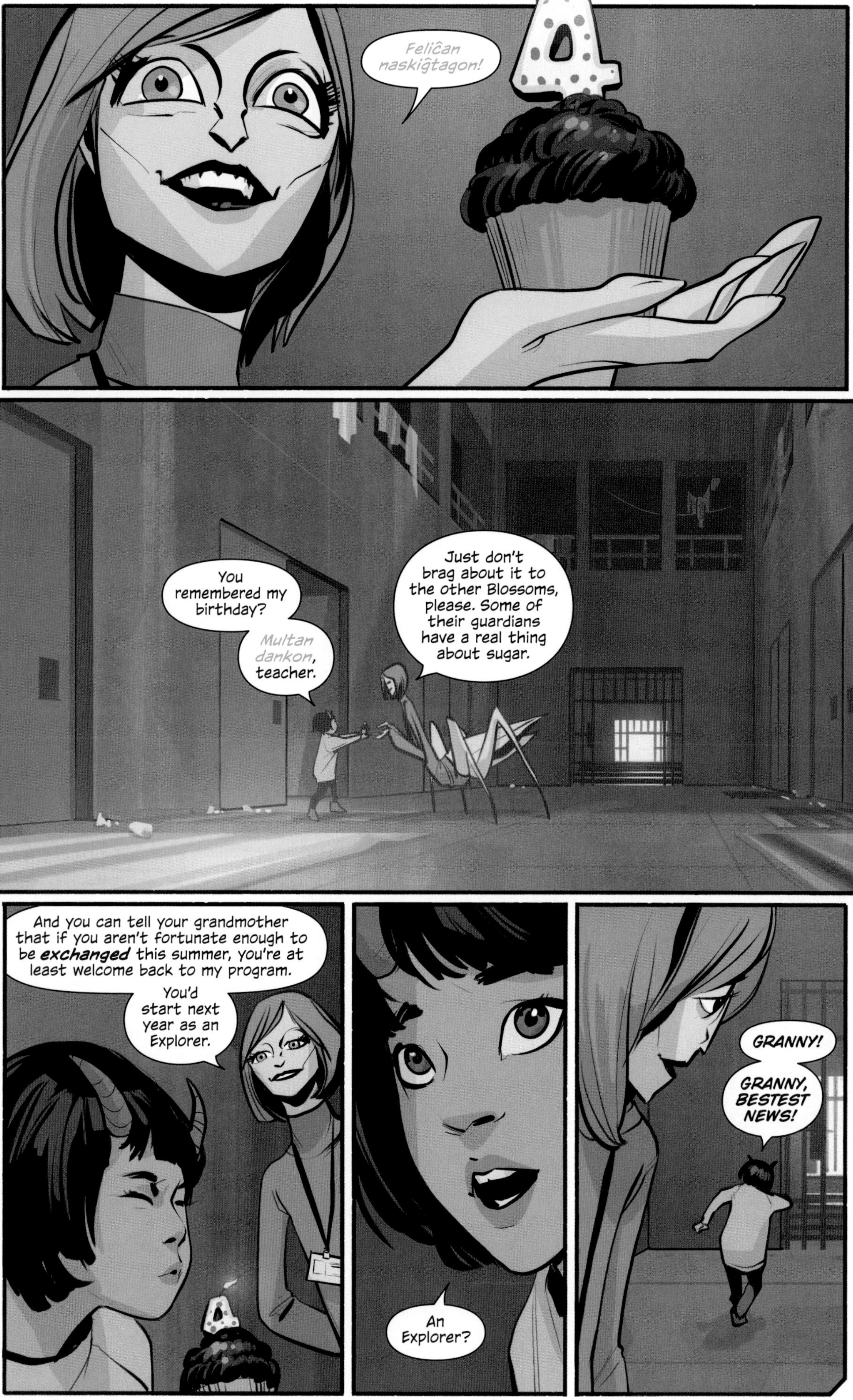
Feliĉan naskiĝtagon!
You remembered my birthday?
Multan dankon, teacher.
Just don't brag about it to the other Blossoms, please. Some of their guardians have a real thing about sugar.
And you can tell your grandmother that if you aren't fortunate enough to be ***exchanged*** this summer, you're at least welcome back to my program.
You'd start next year as an Explorer.
An Explorer?
GRANNY!
GRANNY, BESTEST NEWS!

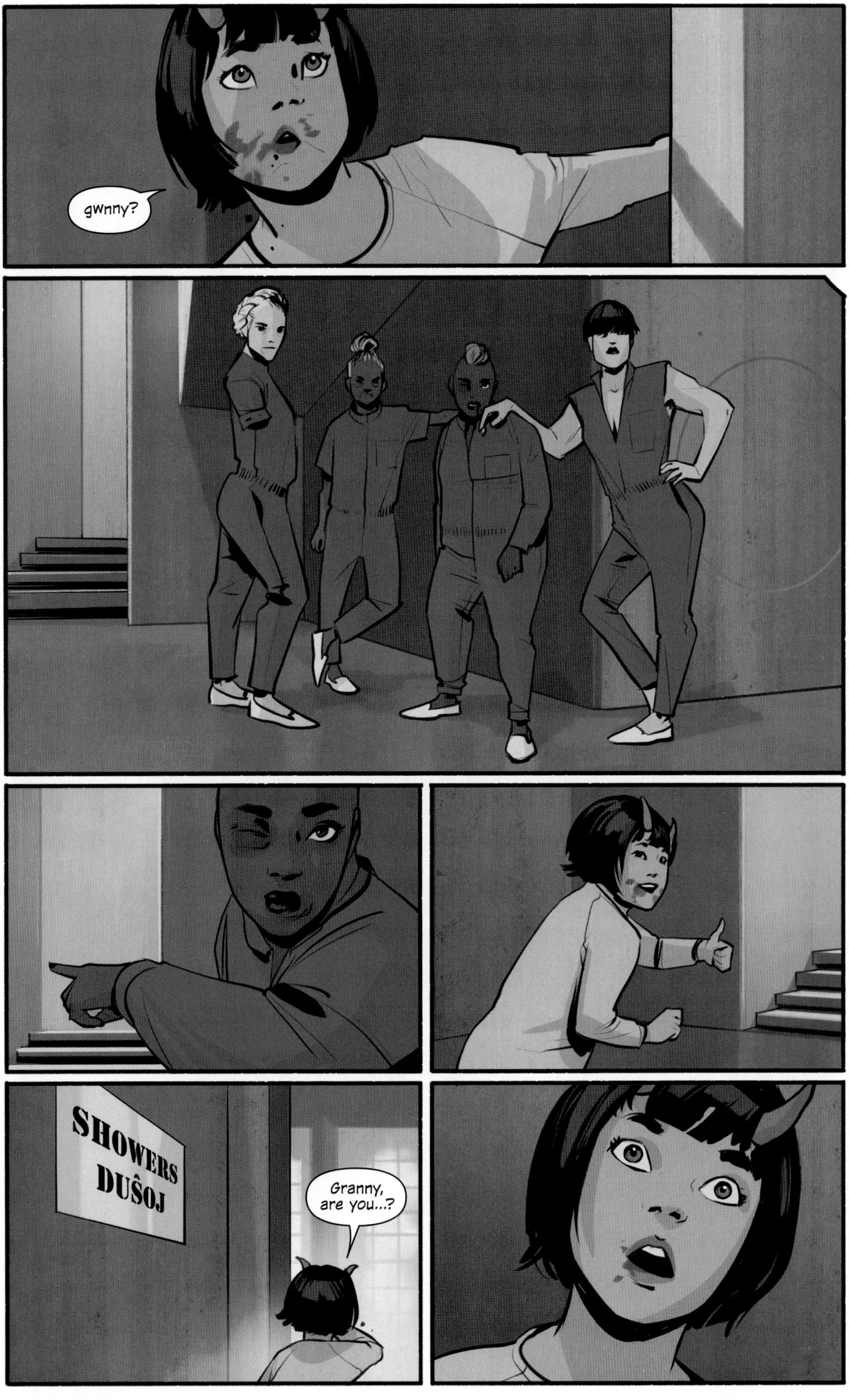
gwnny?
SHOWERS
DUŜOJ
Granny, are you...?

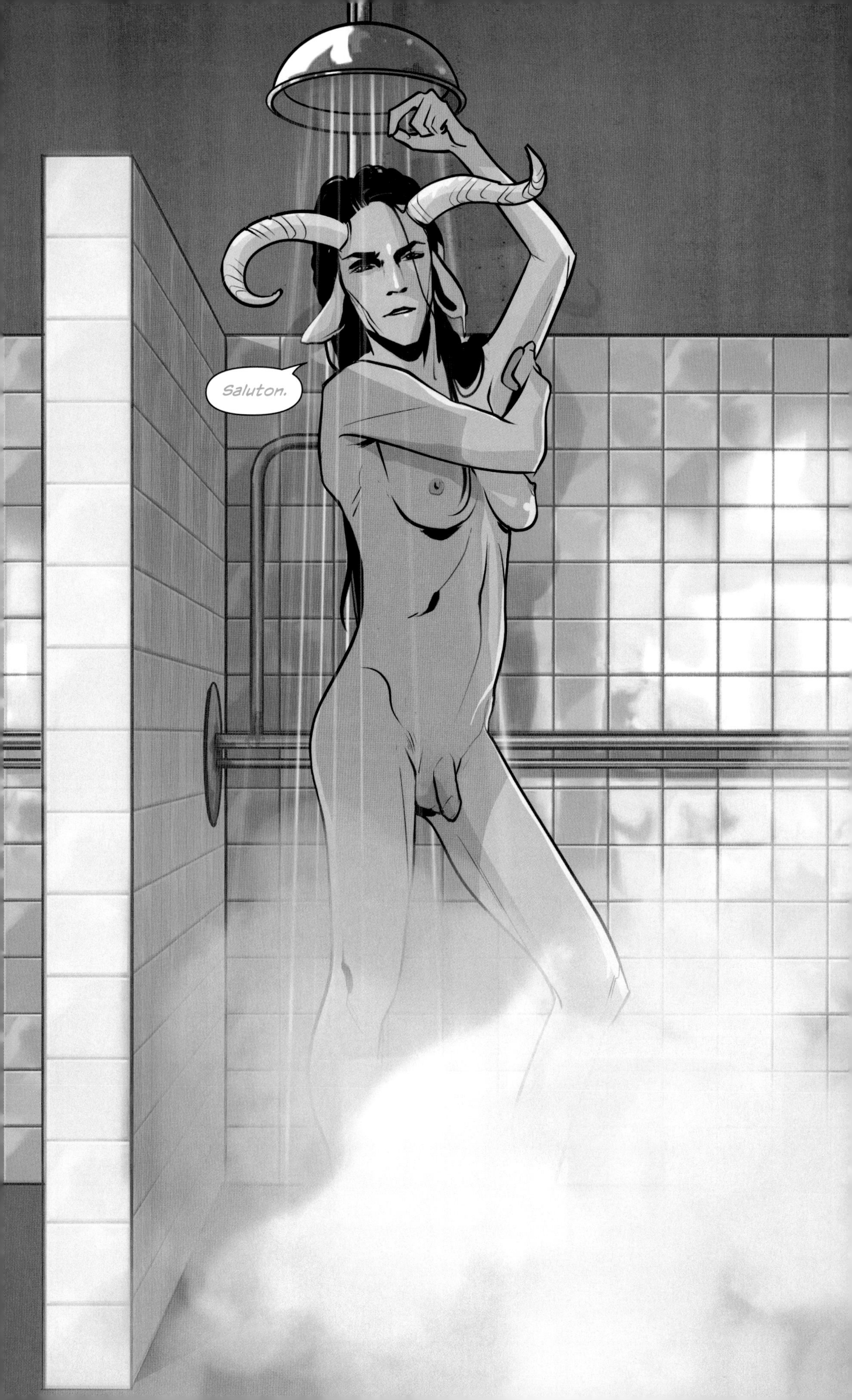
Saluton.

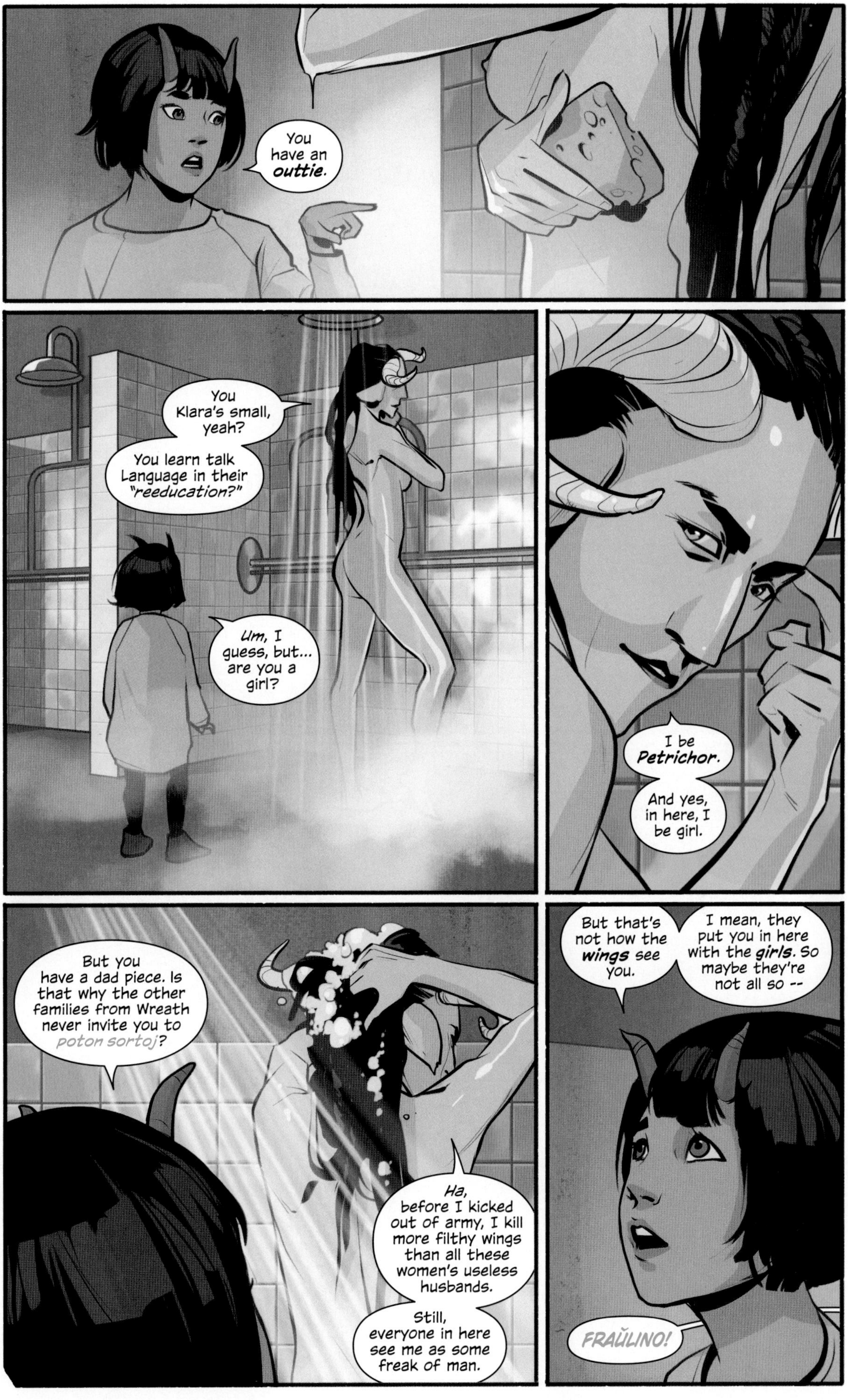
You have an outtie.
You Klara's small, yeah?
You learn talk Language in their "reeducation?"
Um, I guess, but... are you a girl?
I be Petrichor.
And yes, in here, I be girl.
But you have a dad piece. Is that why the other families from Wreath never invite you to poton sortoj?
Ha, before I kicked out of army, I kill more filthy wings than all these women's useless husbands.
Still, everyone in here see me as some freak of man.
But that's not how the wings see you.
I mean, they put you in here with the girls. So maybe they're not all so --
FRAŬLINO!

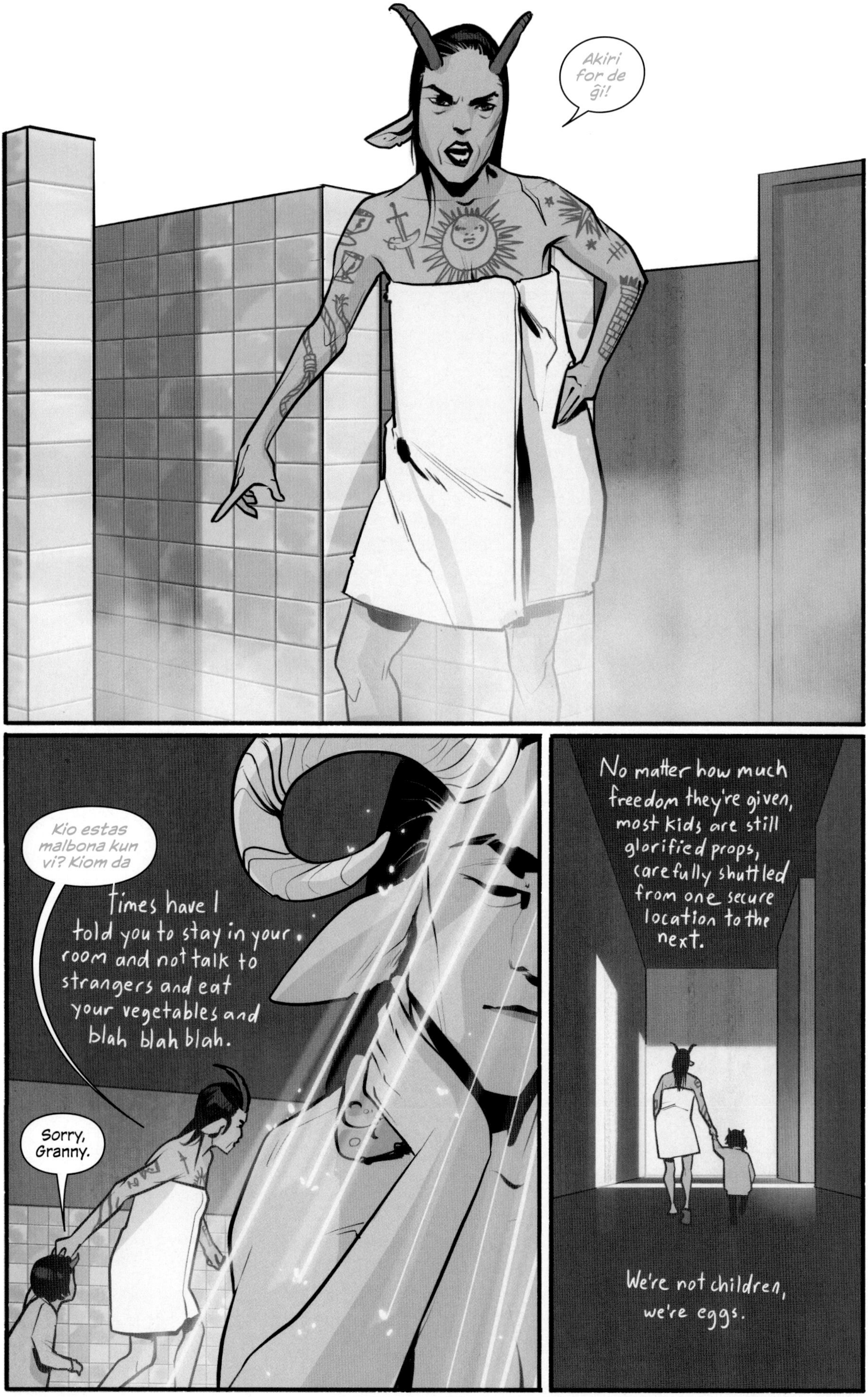

Akiri for de ĝi!
Kio estas malbona kun vi? Kiom da
times have I told you to stay in your room and not talk to strangers and eat your vegetables and blah blah blah.
Sorry, Granny.
No matter how much freedom they're given, most kids are still glorified props, carefully shuttled from one secure location to the next.
We're not children, we're eggs.

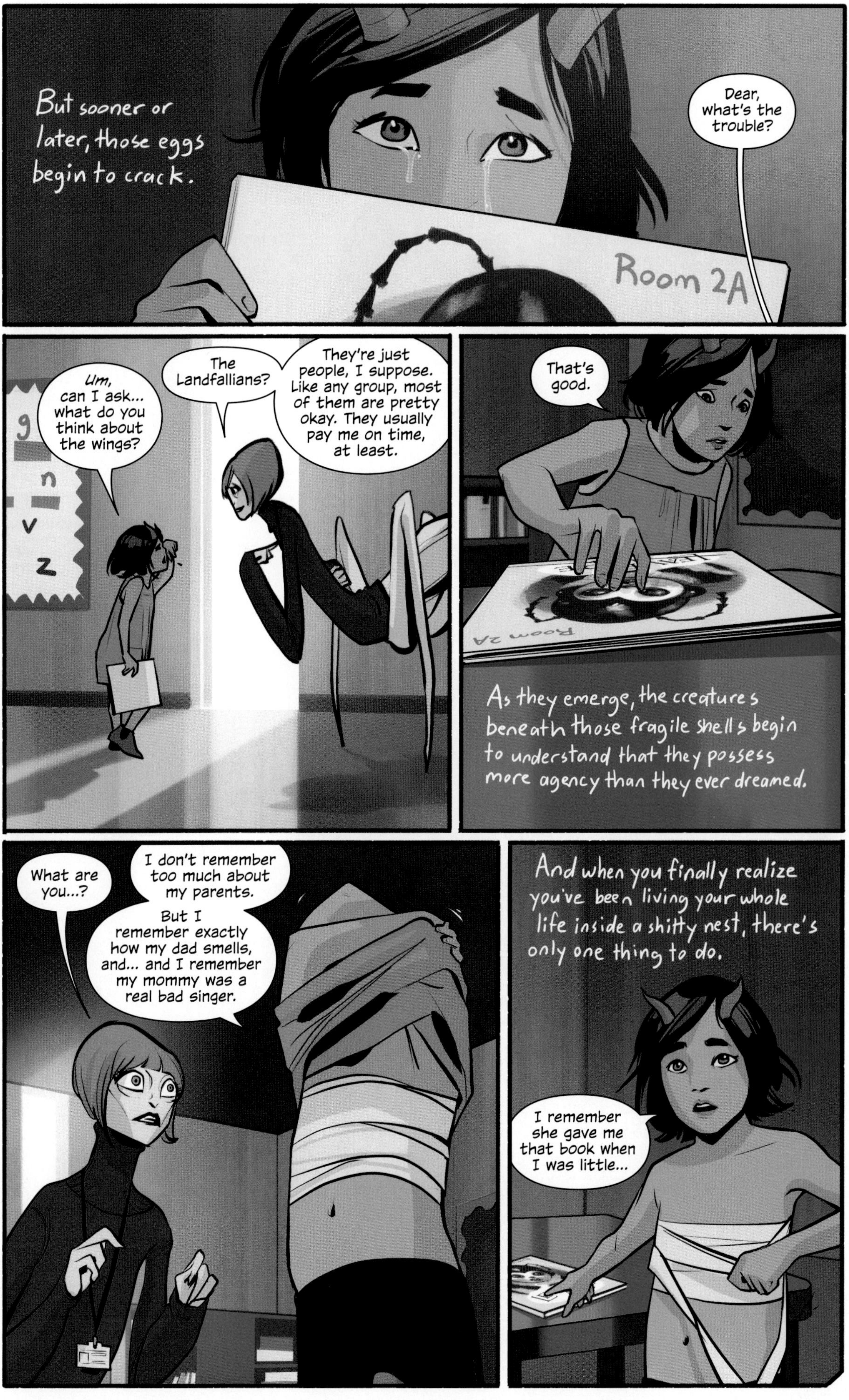

But sooner or later, those eggs begin to crack.
Dear, what's the trouble?
Room 2A
Um, can I ask... what do you think about the wings?
The Landfallians?
They're just people, I suppose. Like any group, most of them are pretty okay. They usually pay me on time, at least.
That's good.
Room 2A
As they emerge, the creatures beneath those fragile shells begin to understand that they possess more agency than they ever dreamed.
What are you...?
I don't remember too much about my parents.
But I remember exactly how my dad smells, and... and I remember my mommy was a real bad singer.
And when you finally realize you've been living your whole life inside a shitty nest, there's only one thing to do.
I remember she gave me that book when I was little...

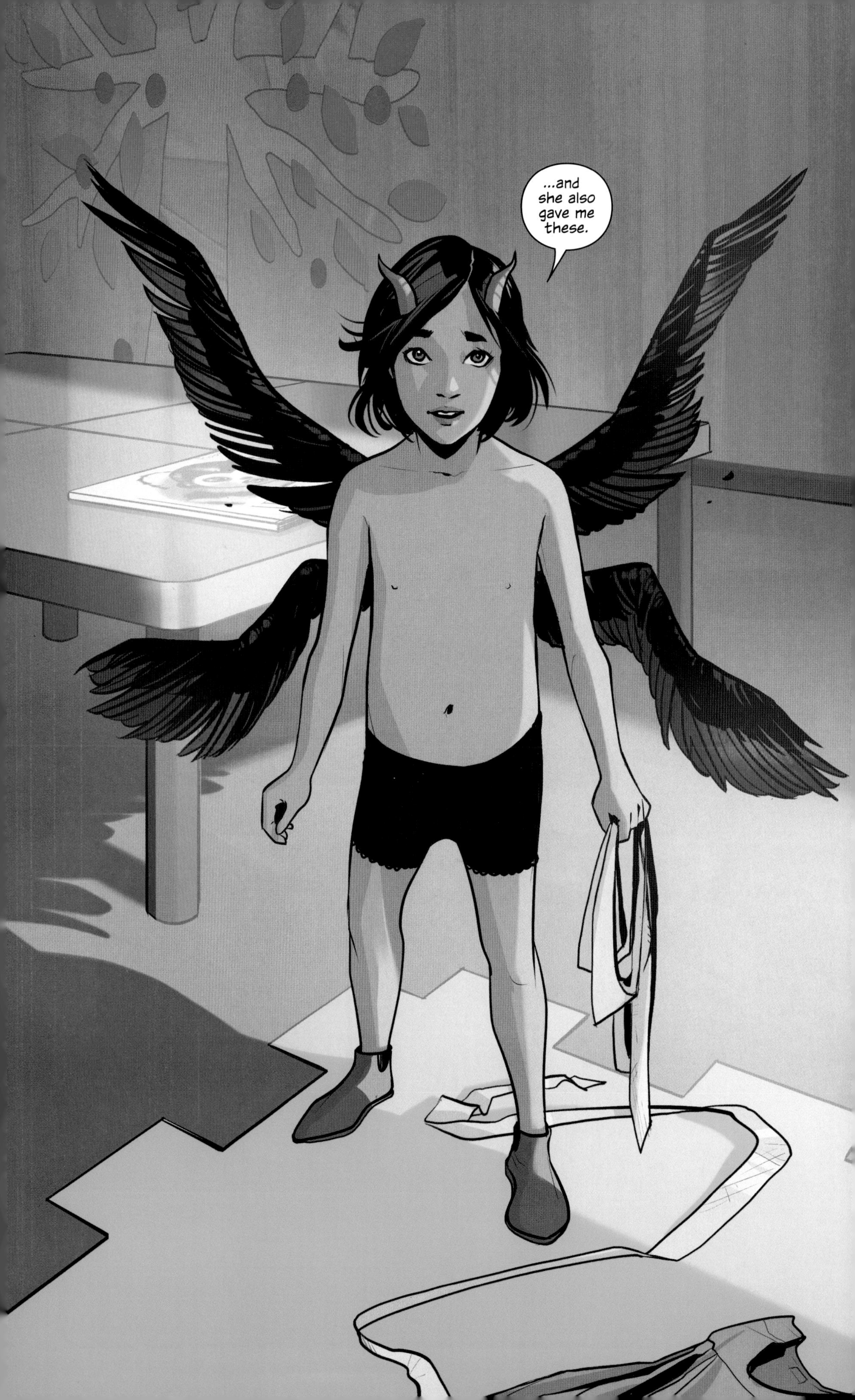
...and she also gave me these.

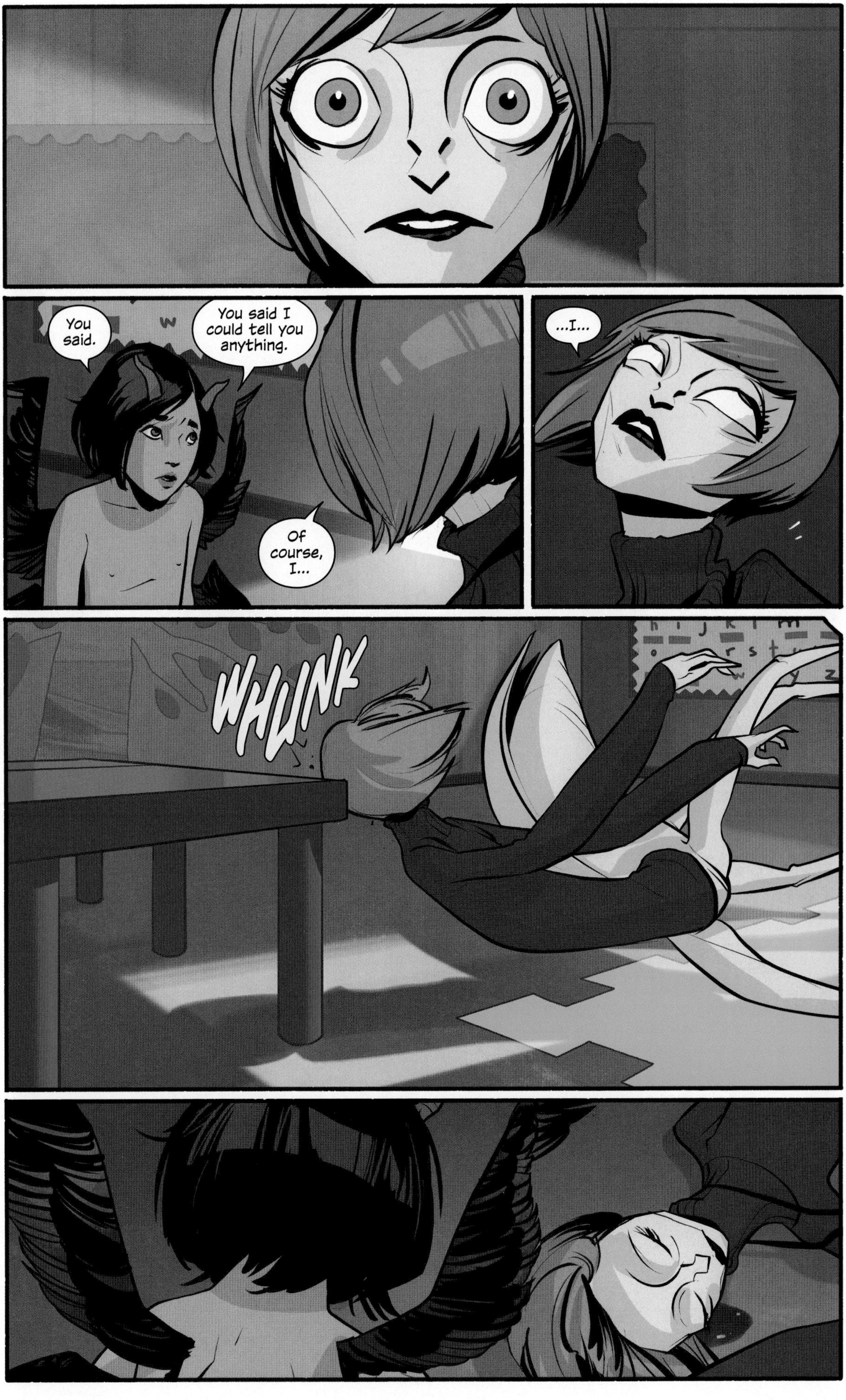
You said.
You said I could tell you anything.
Of course, I...
...I...
WHUNK

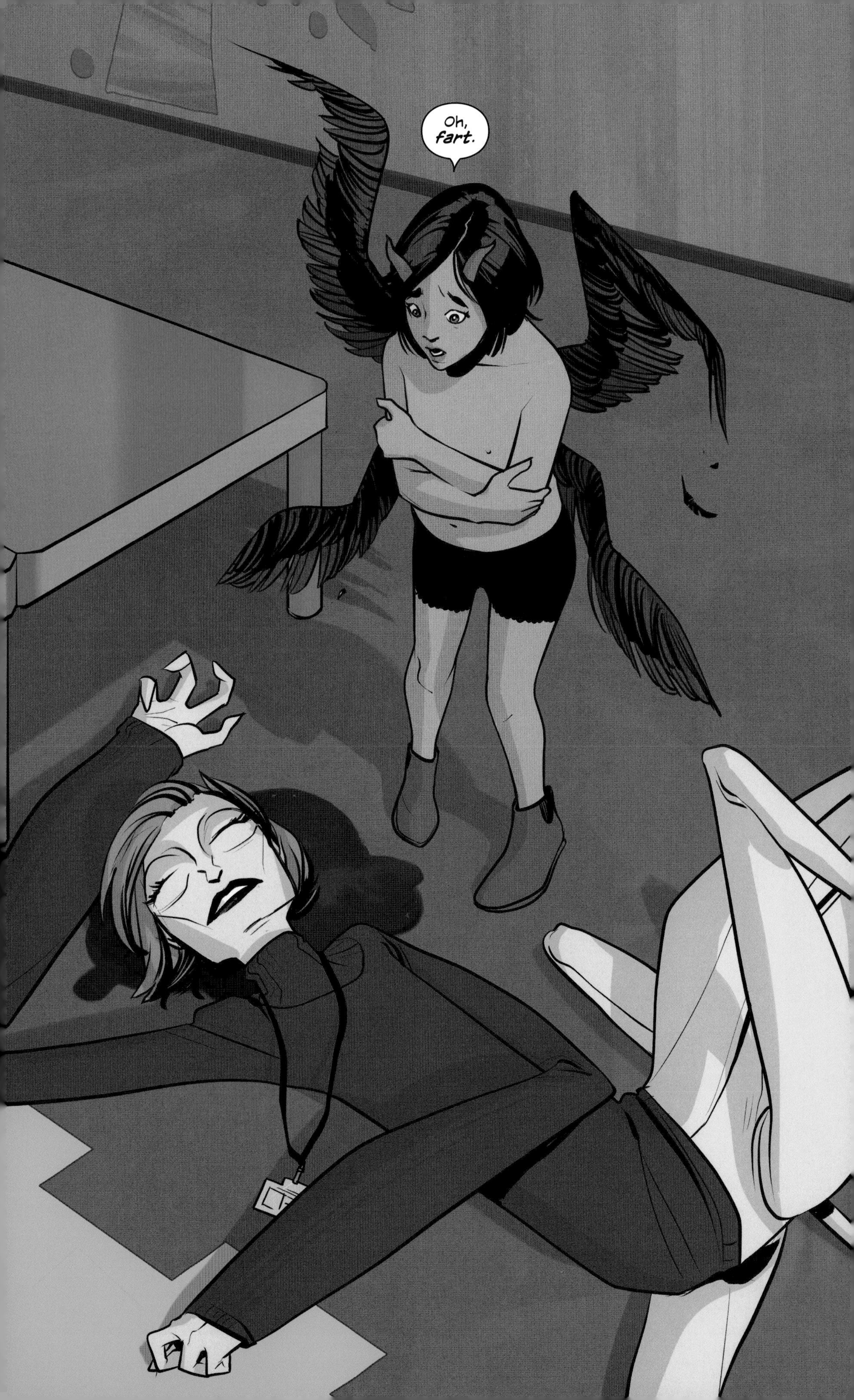
Oh, *fart*.

end chapter thirty-one

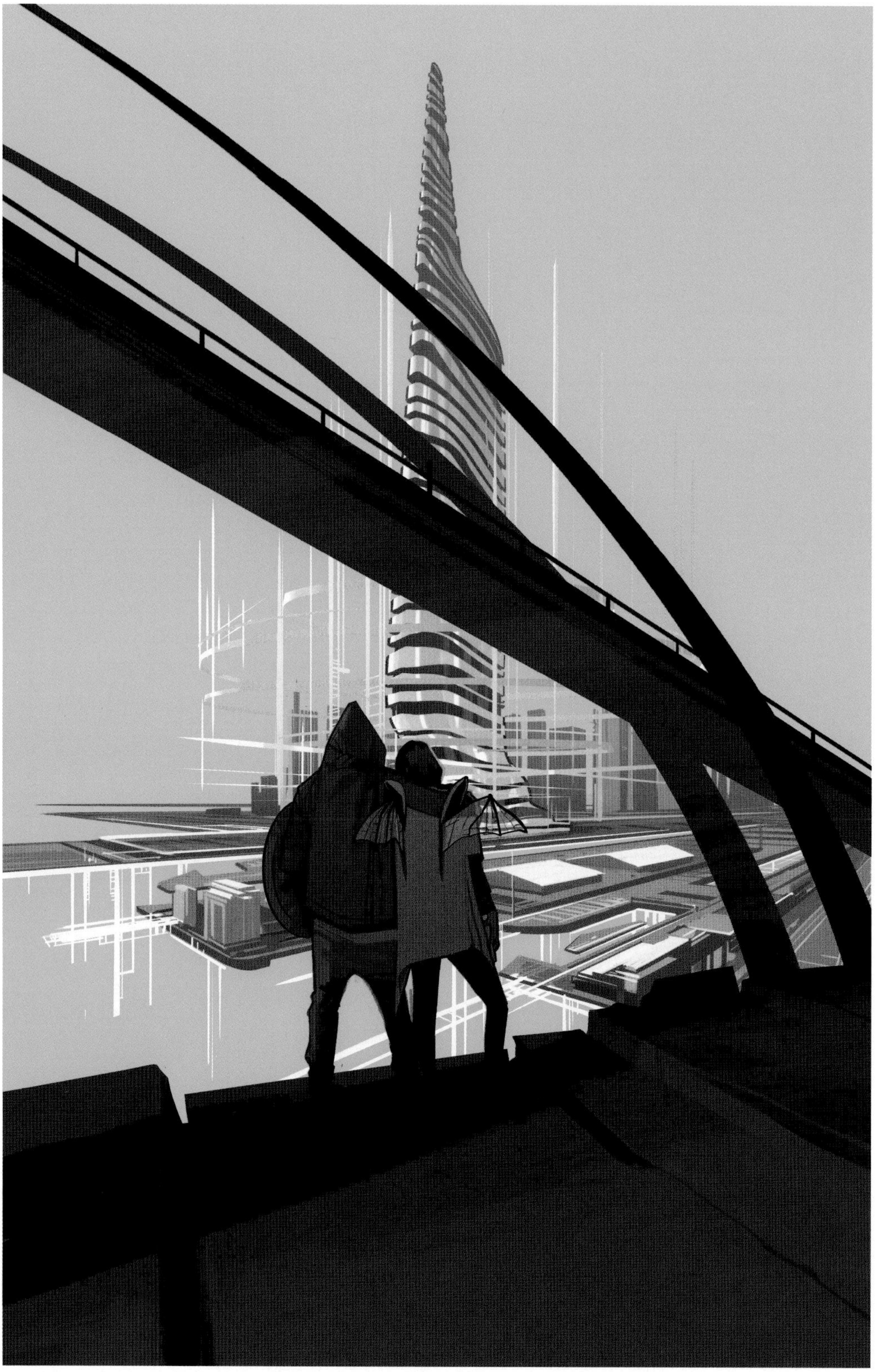

CHAPTER

THIRTY-TWO

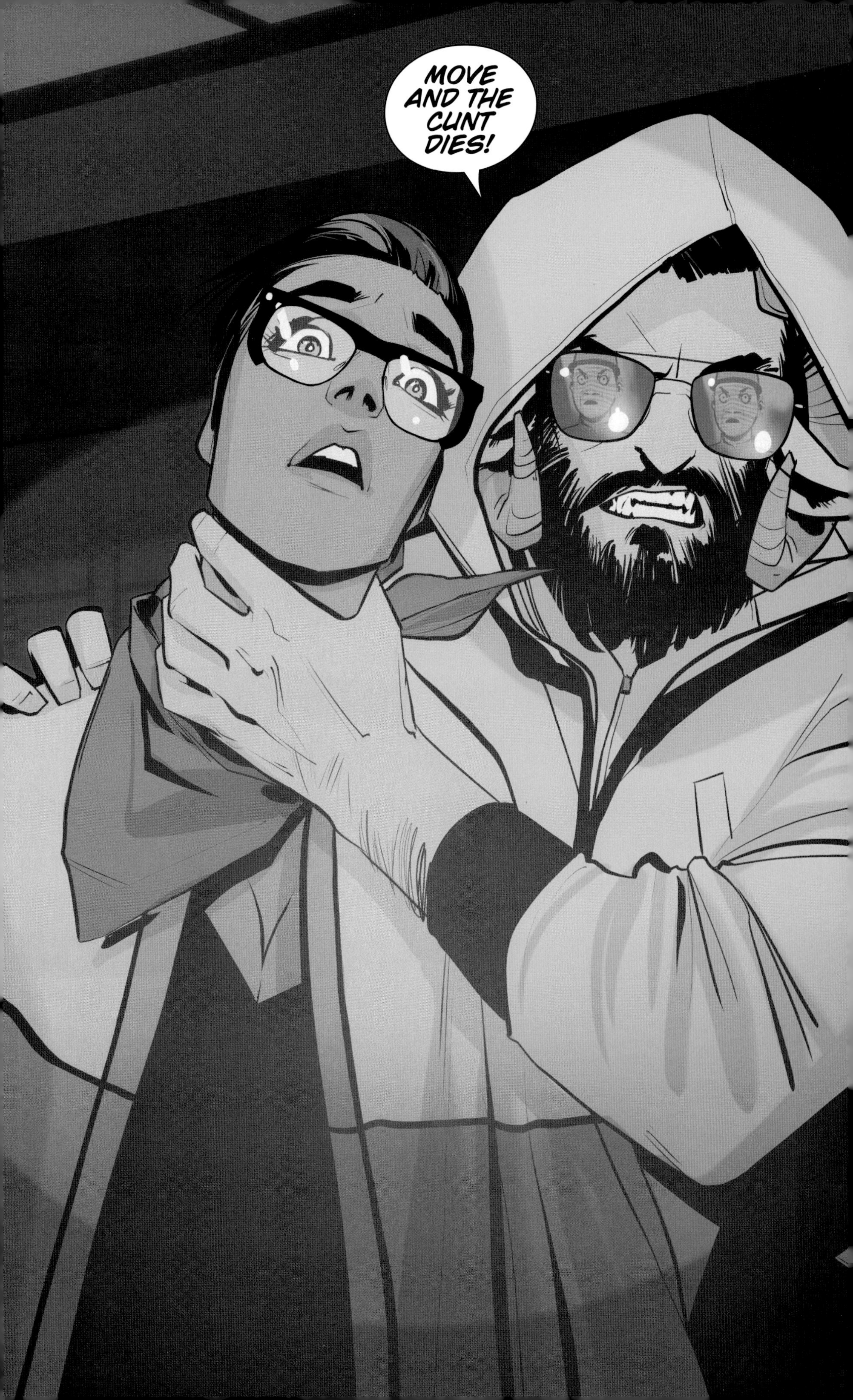
MOVE AND THE CUNT DIES!

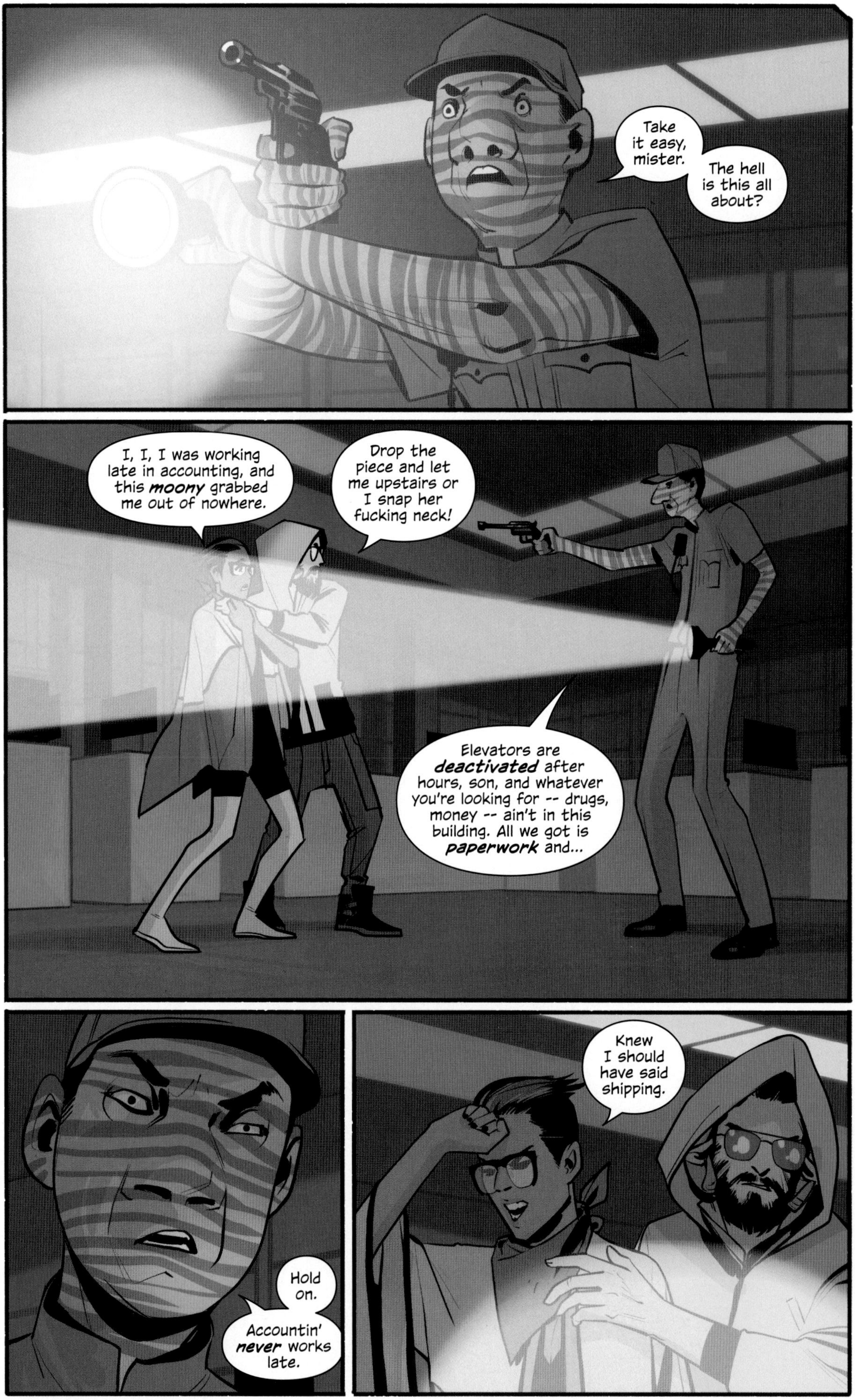
Take it easy, mister.
The hell is this all about?
I, I, I was working late in accounting, and this **moony** grabbed me out of nowhere.
Drop the piece and let me upstairs or I snap her fucking neck!
Elevators are **deactivated** after hours, son, and whatever you're looking for -- drugs, money -- ain't in this building. All we got is **paperwork** and...
Hold on.
Accountin' **never** works late.
Knew I should have said shipping.

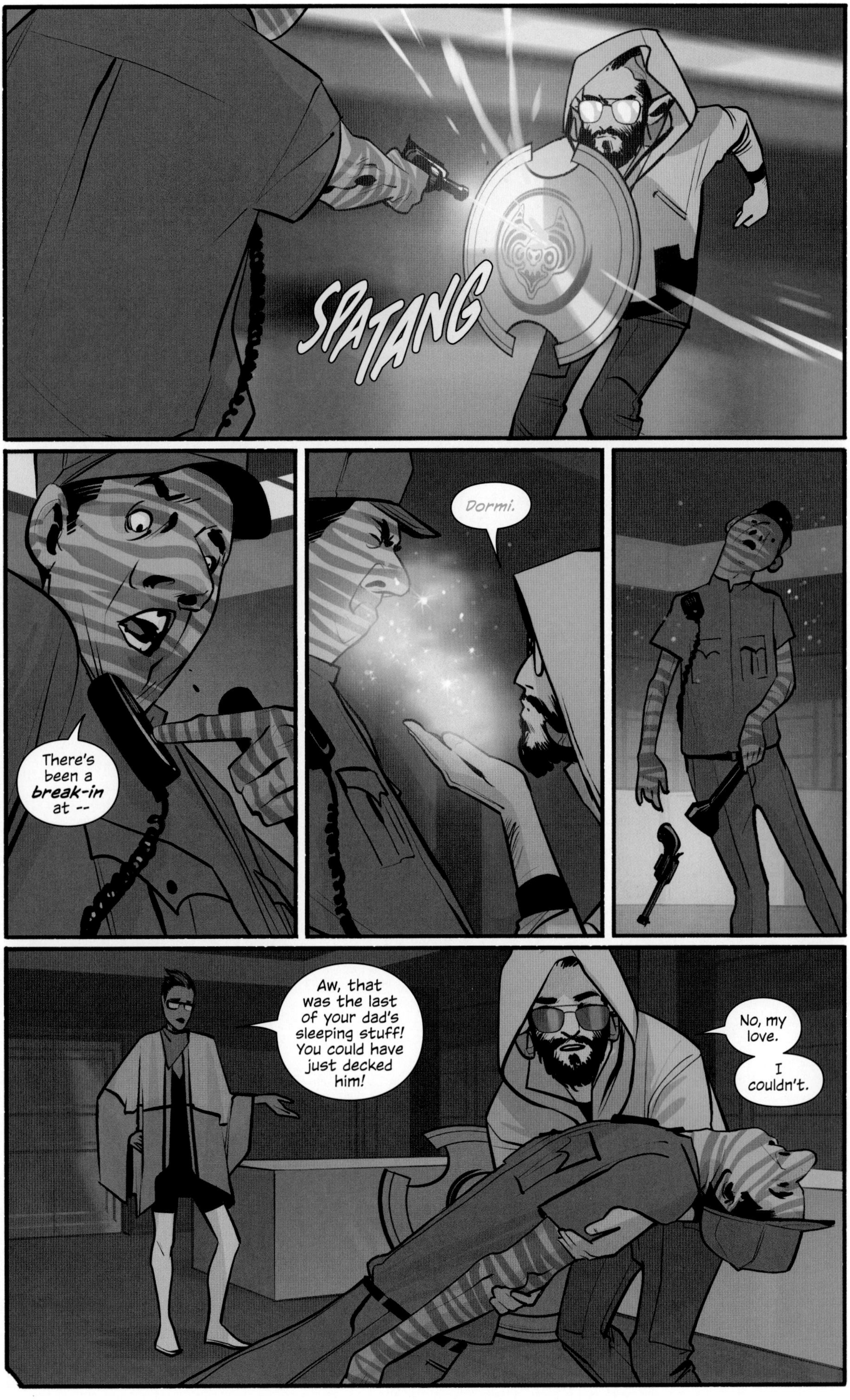
SPATANG
There's been a break-in at --
Dormi.
Aw, that was the last of your dad's sleeping stuff! You could have just decked him!
No, my love.
I couldn't.

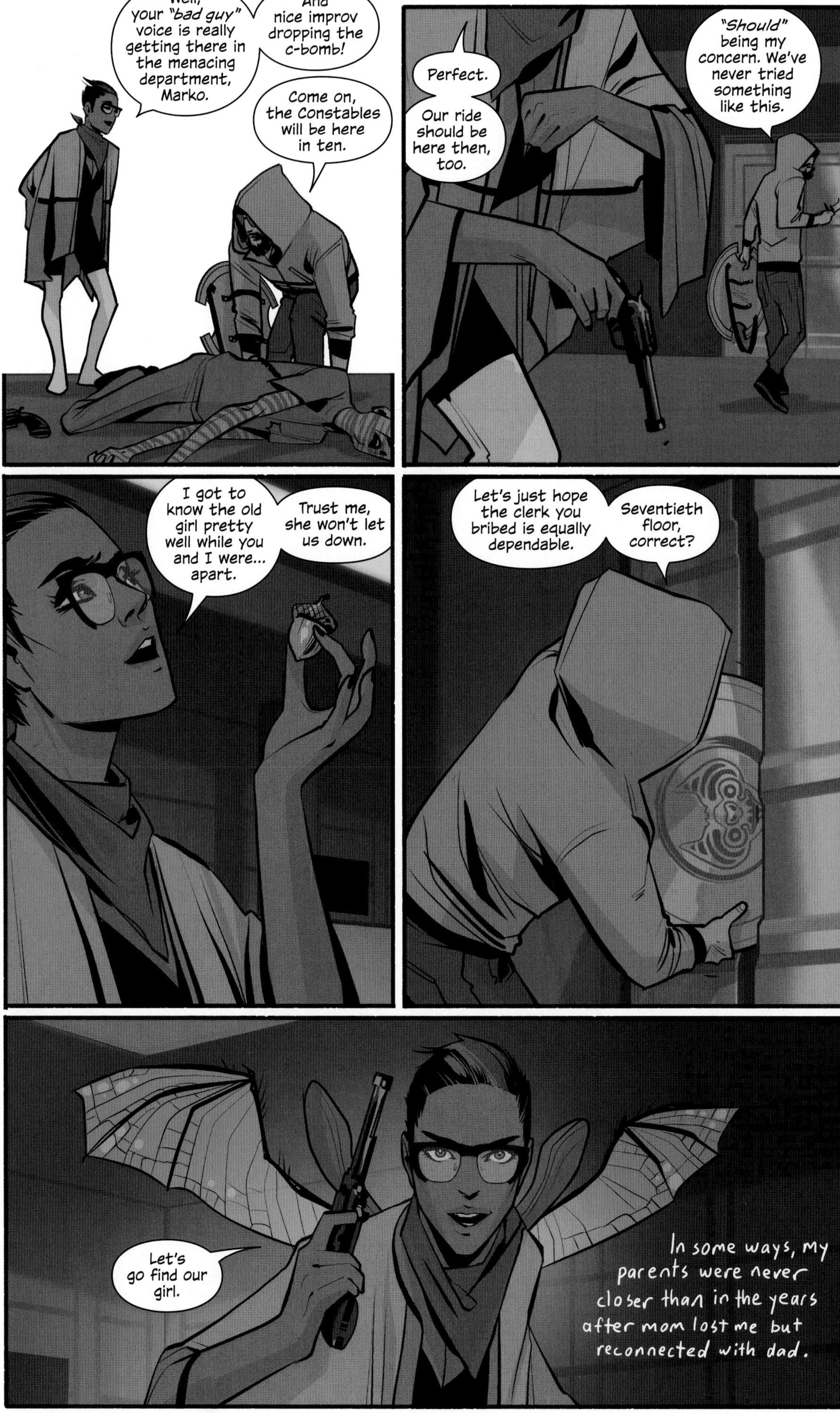
Well, your "bad guy" voice is really getting there in the menacing department, Marko.
And nice improv dropping the c-bomb!
Come on, the Constables will be here in ten.
Perfect.
Our ride should be here then, too.
"Should" being my concern. We've never tried something like this.
I got to know the old girl pretty well while you and I were... apart.
Trust me, she won't let us down.
Let's just hope the clerk you bribed is equally dependable.
Seventieth floor, correct?
Let's go find our girl.
In some ways, my parents were never closer than in the years after mom lost me but reconnected with dad.

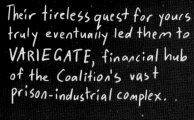
Their tireless quest for yours truly eventually led them to VARIEGATE, financial hub of the Coalition's vast prison-industrial complex.

Despite the persistent sense of loss, united by a shared obsession, my parents once again brought out the very best in each other.

But even with their renewed bond, the two of them hadn't so much as KISSED since finding each other.

A vow was unspoken yet painfully clear...

...they would never again perform the act that created ME until I was safely back in their lives.

Pick it up, slow-poke.

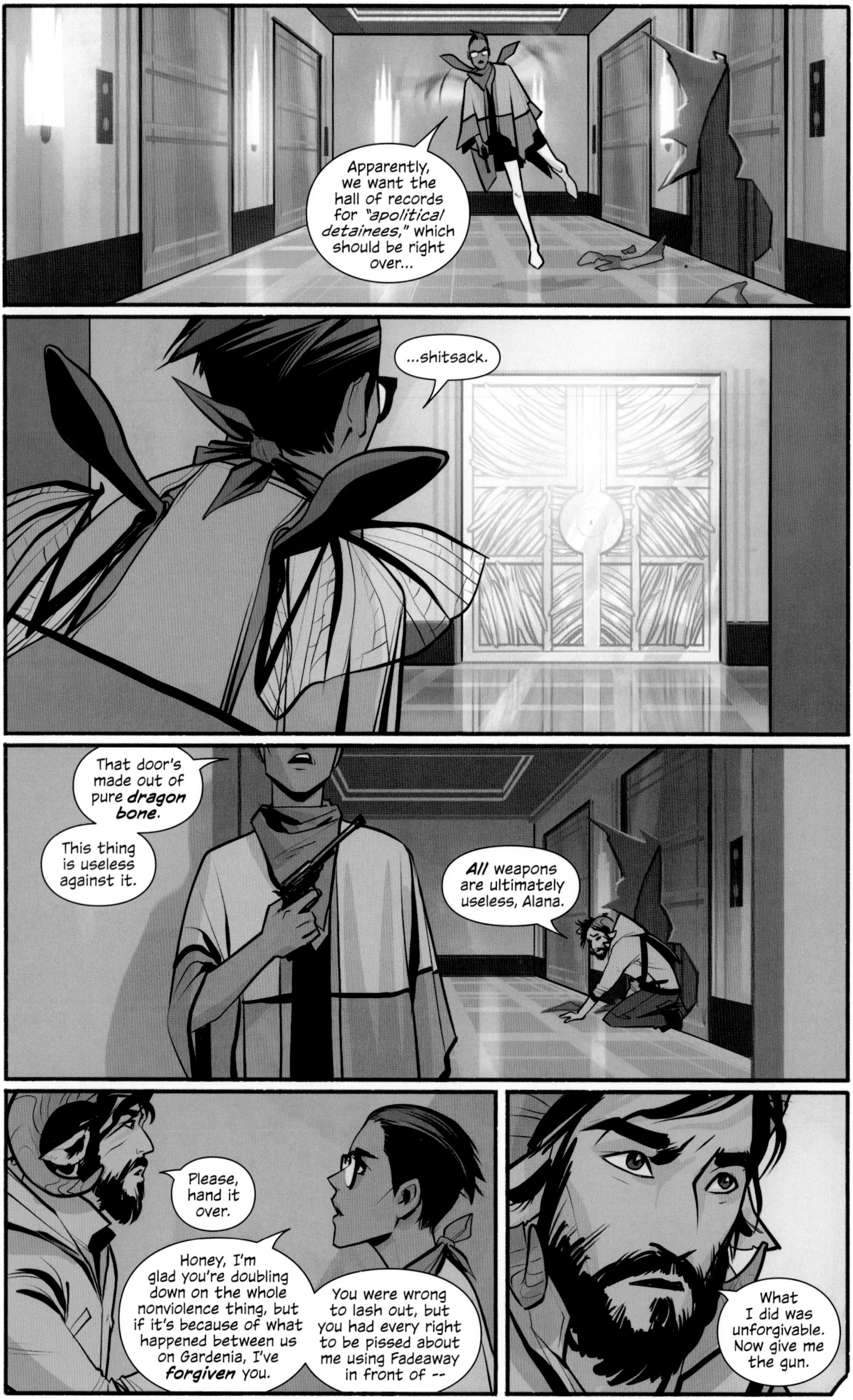

Apparently, we want the hall of records for "apolitical detainees," which should be right over...
...shitsack.
That door's made out of pure **dragon bone**.
This thing is useless against it.
All weapons are ultimately useless, Alana.
Please, hand it over.
Honey, I'm glad you're doubling down on the whole nonviolence thing, but if it's because of what happened between us on Gardenia, I've **forgiven** you.
You were wrong to lash out, but you had every right to be pissed about me using Fadeaway in front of --
What I did was unforgivable. Now give me the gun.

What I can or can't forgive isn't for you to decide.

Either way, Izabel thinks we *both* over-reacted.

I love our sitter, but she's also a *child*.

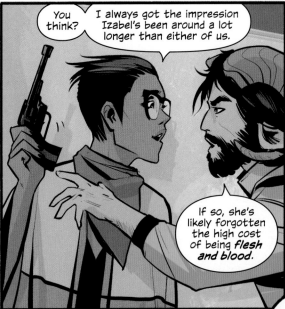

You think?

I always got the impression Izabel's been around a lot longer than either of us.

If so, she's likely forgotten the high cost of being *flesh and blood*.

I haven't.

Alana, you and I are going to put our family back together... but only if we do it in the spirit in which that family was forged.

Ŝlosilo.

Agreed?

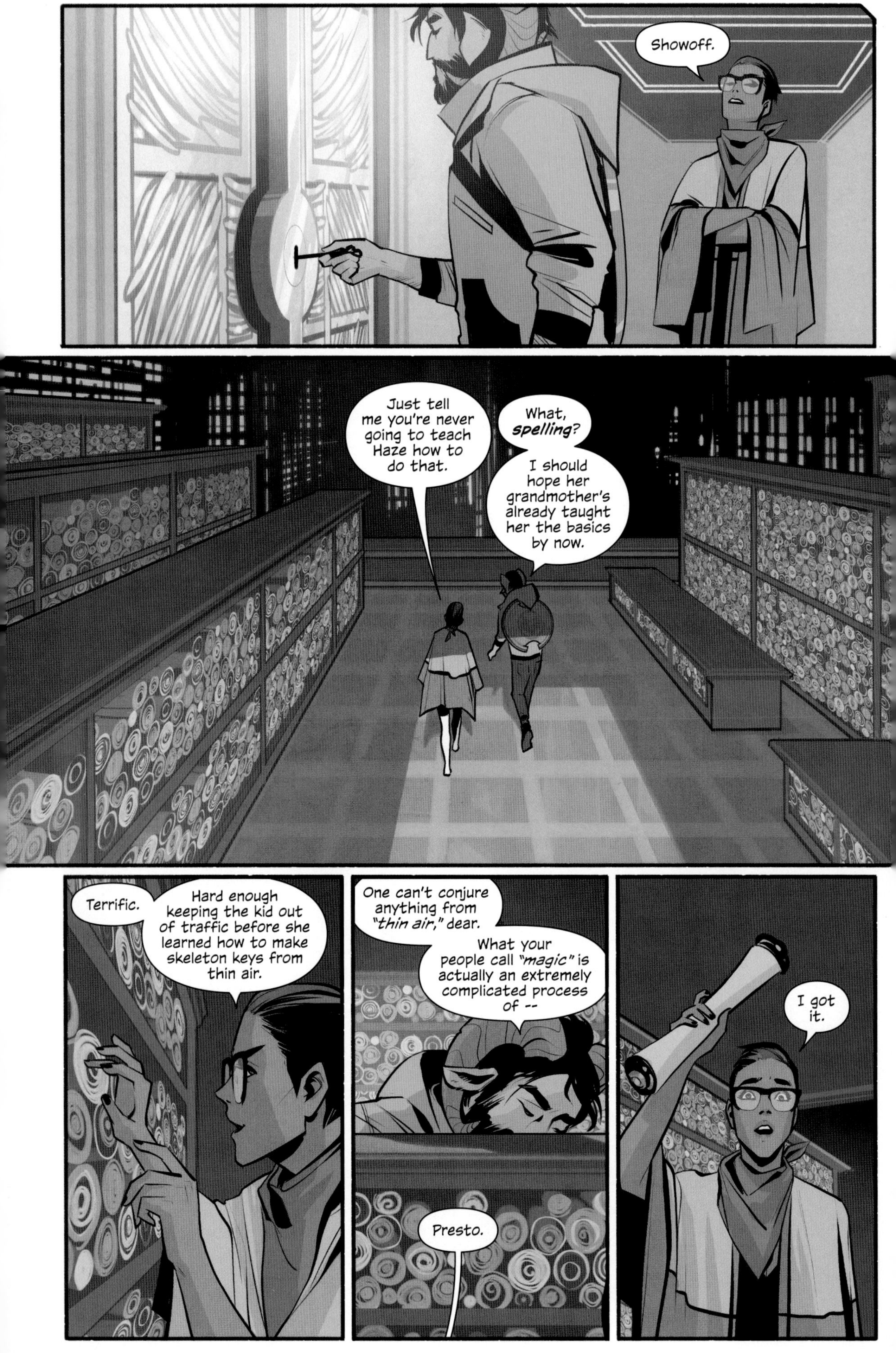

Showoff.
Just tell me you're never going to teach Haze how to do that.
What, **spelling**?
I should hope her grandmother's already taught her the basics by now.
Terrific.
Hard enough keeping the kid out of traffic before she learned how to make skeleton keys from thin air.
One can't conjure anything from *"thin air,"* dear.
What your people call *"magic"* is actually an extremely complicated process of --
Presto.
I got it.

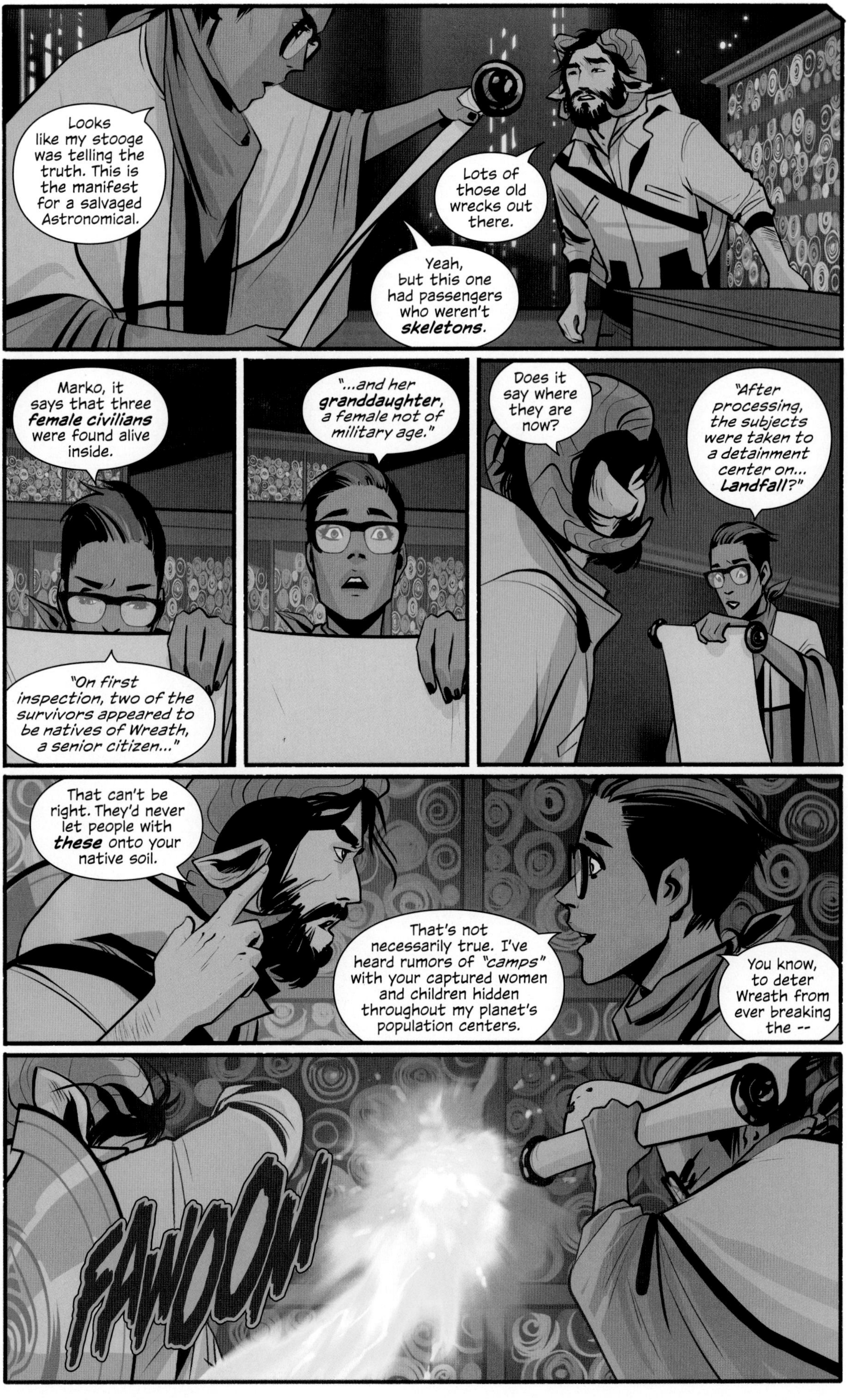

Looks like my stooge was telling the truth. This is the manifest for a salvaged Astronomical.
Lots of those old wrecks out there.
Yeah, but this one had passengers who weren't ***skeletons***.
Marko, it says that three ***female civilians*** were found alive inside.
"On first inspection, two of the survivors appeared to be natives of Wreath, a senior citizen..."
"...and her ***granddaughter****, a female not of military age."*
Does it say where they are now?
"After processing, the subjects were taken to a detainment center on... ***Landfall****?"*
That can't be right. They'd never let people with ***these*** onto your native soil.
That's not necessarily true. I've heard rumors of *"camps"* with your captured women and children hidden throughout my planet's population centers.
You know, to deter Wreath from ever breaking the --
FWOOM

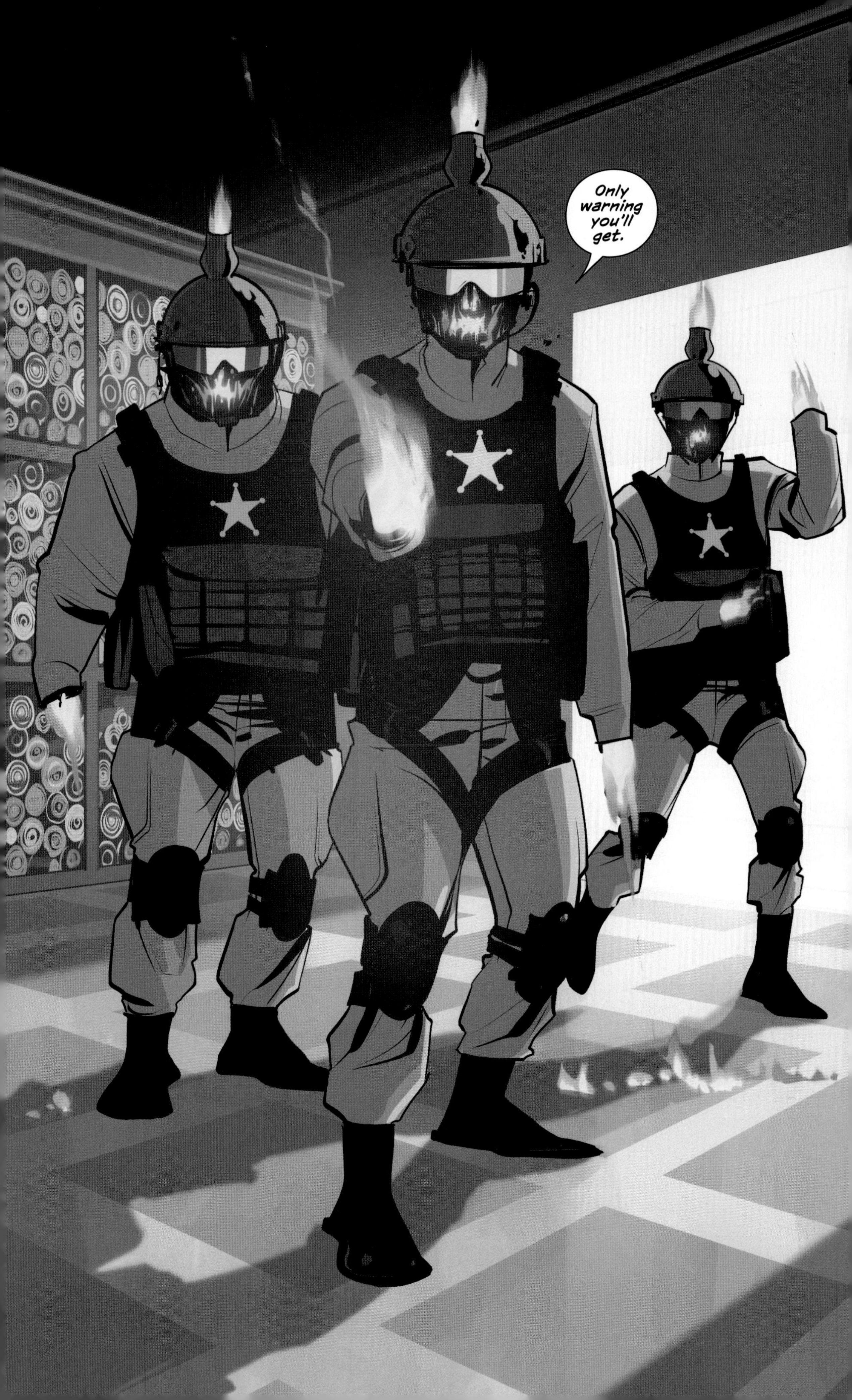
Only warning you'll get.

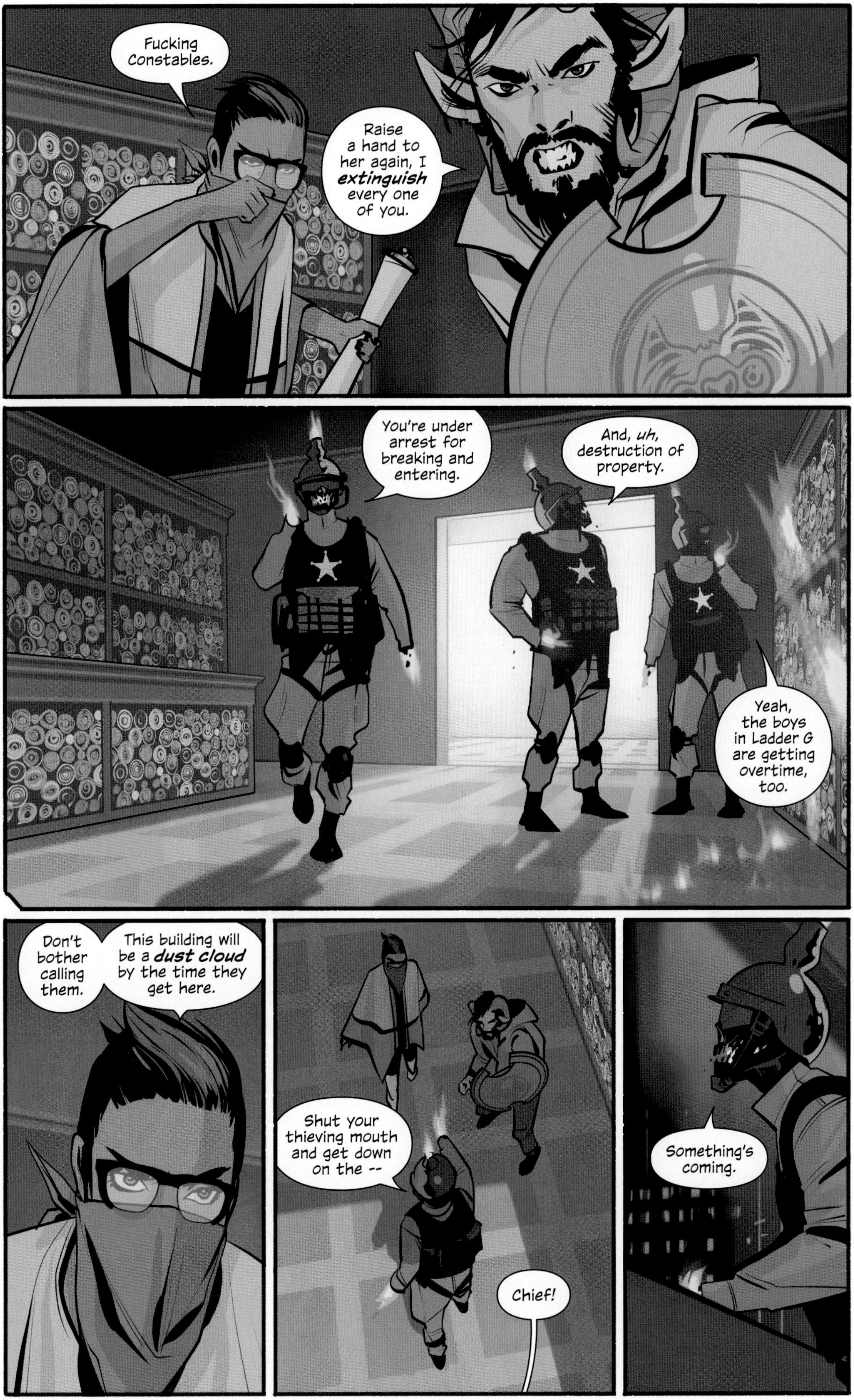

Fucking Constables.
Raise a hand to her again, I *extinguish* every one of you.
You're under arrest for breaking and entering.
And, *uh,* destruction of property.
Yeah, the boys in Ladder G are getting overtime, too.
Don't bother calling them.
This building will be a *dust cloud* by the time they get here.
Shut your thieving mouth and get down on the --
Chief!
Something's coming.

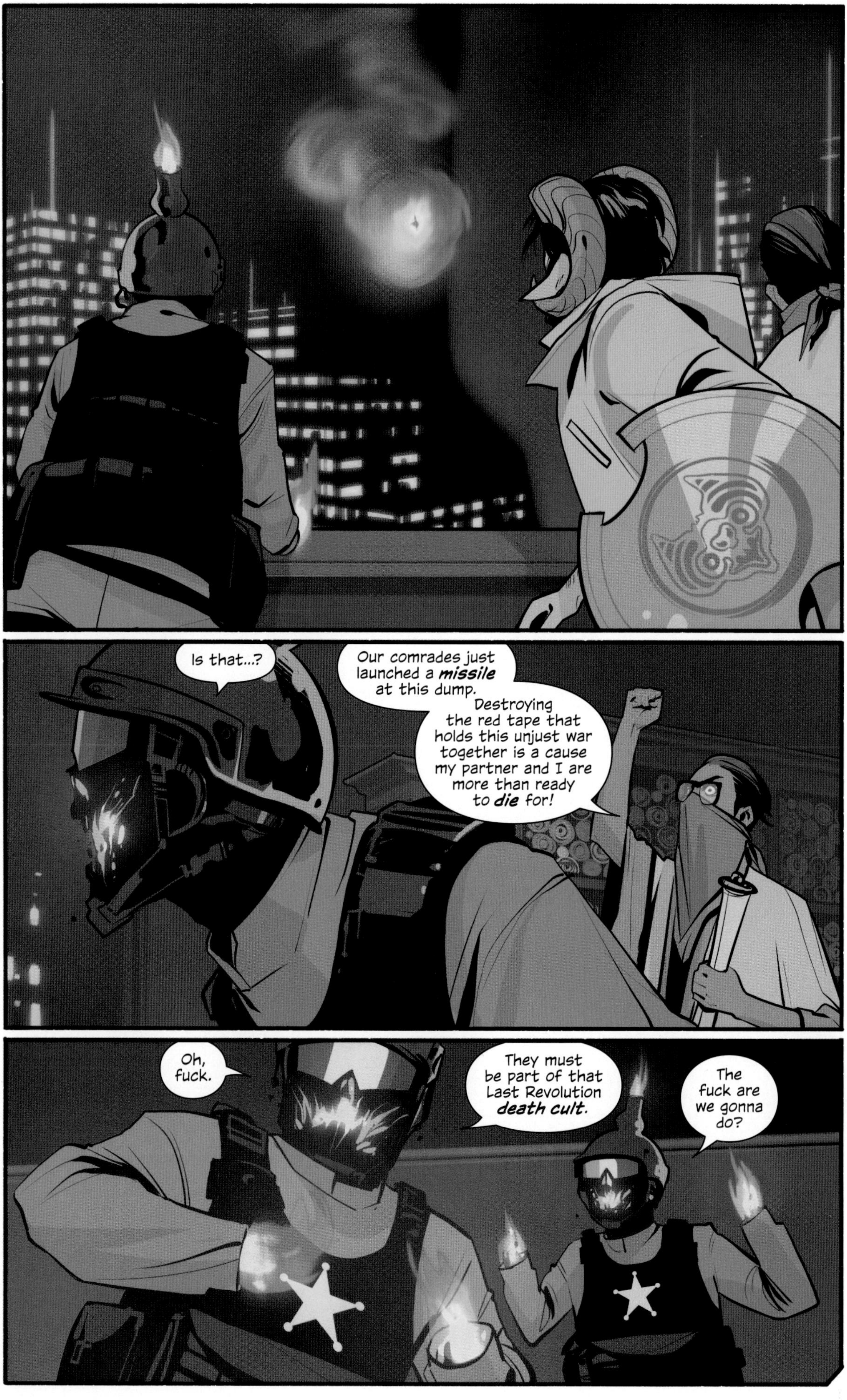
Is that...?
Our comrades just launched a missile at this dump.
Destroying the red tape that holds this unjust war together is a cause my partner and I are more than ready to die for!
Oh, fuck.
They must be part of that Last Revolution death cult.
The fuck are we gonna do?

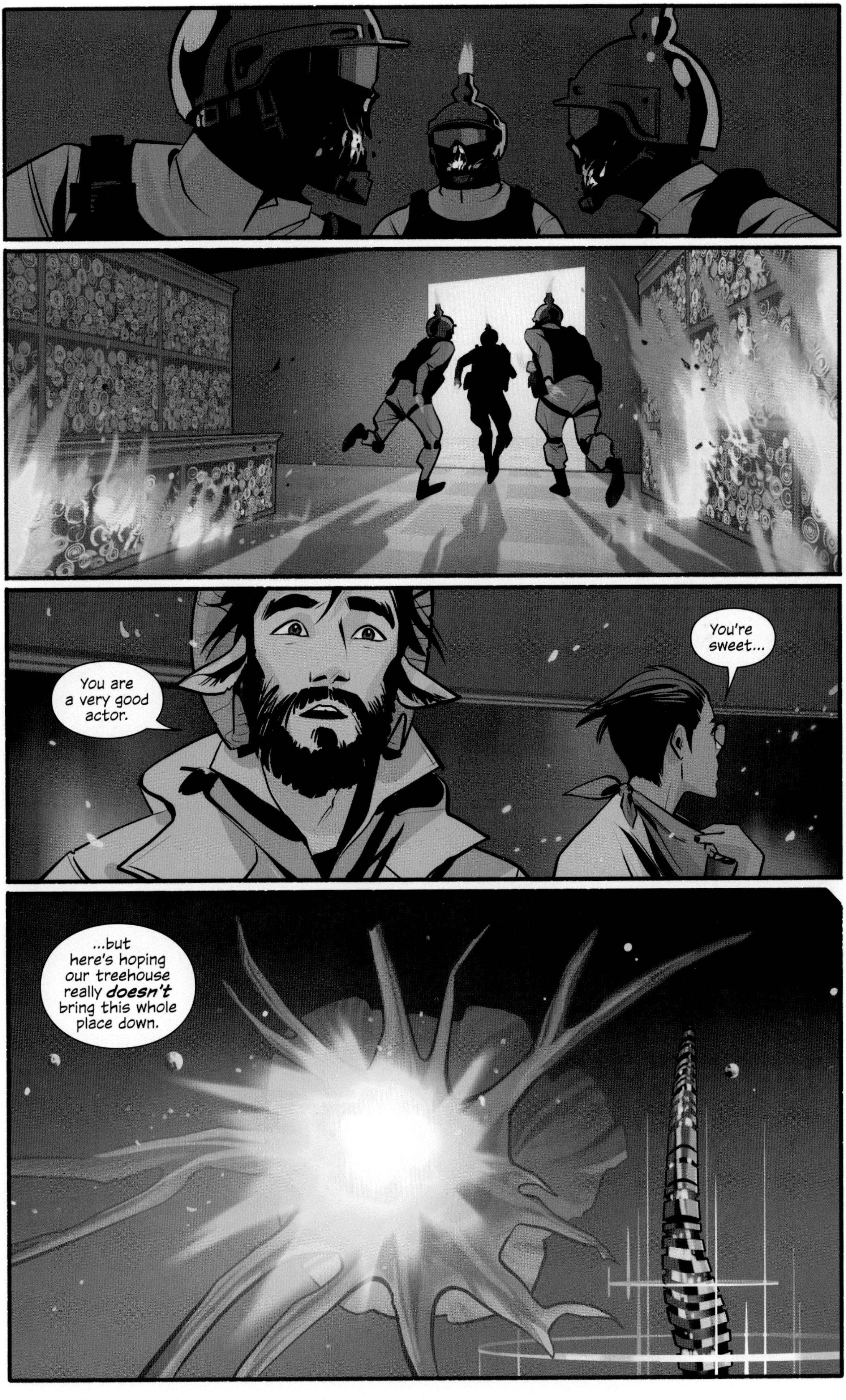
You are a very good actor.
You're sweet...
...but here's hoping our treehouse really ***doesn't*** bring this whole place down.

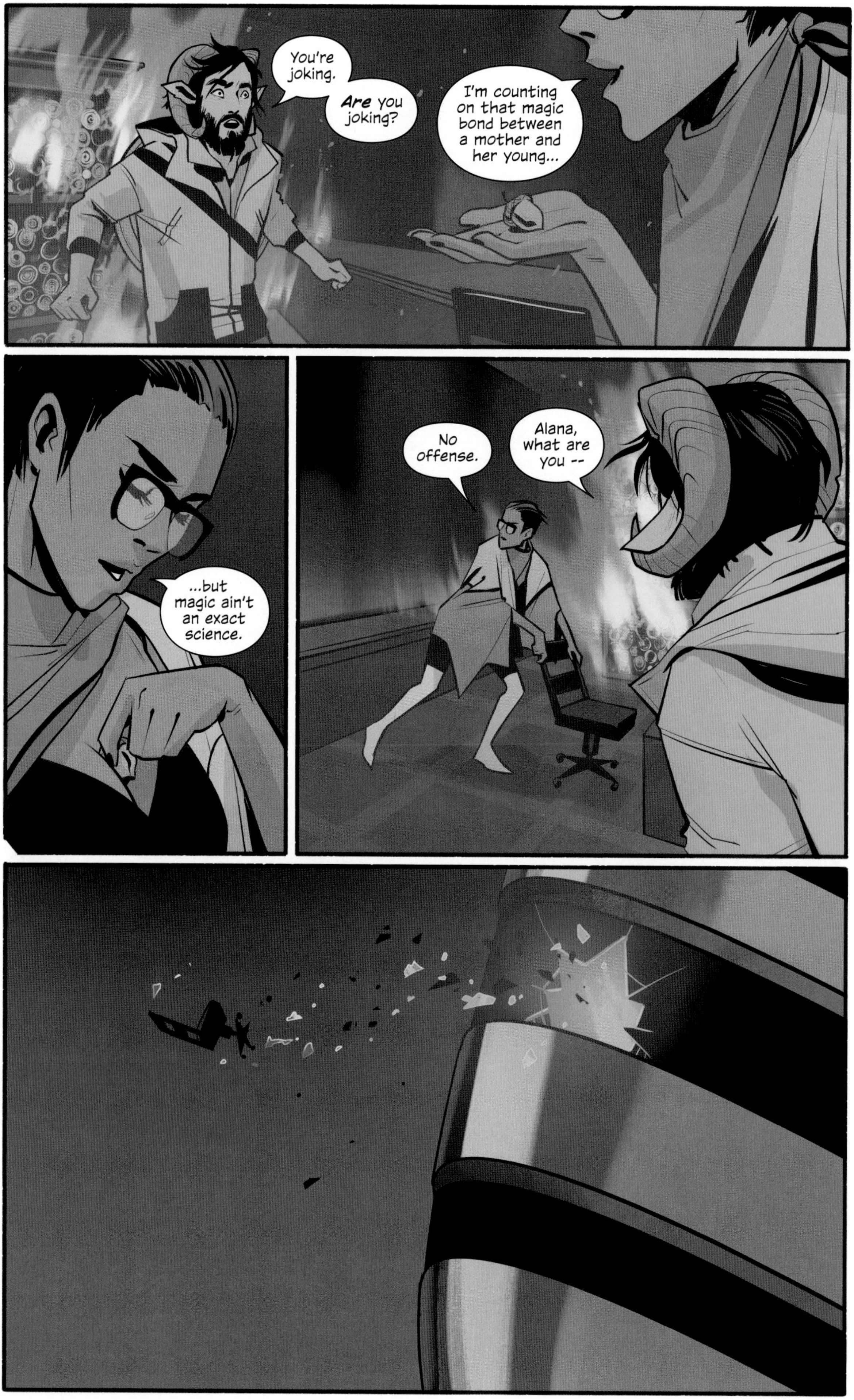
You're joking.
Are you joking?
I'm counting on that magic bond between a mother and her young...
...but magic ain't an exact science.
Alana, what are you --
No offense.

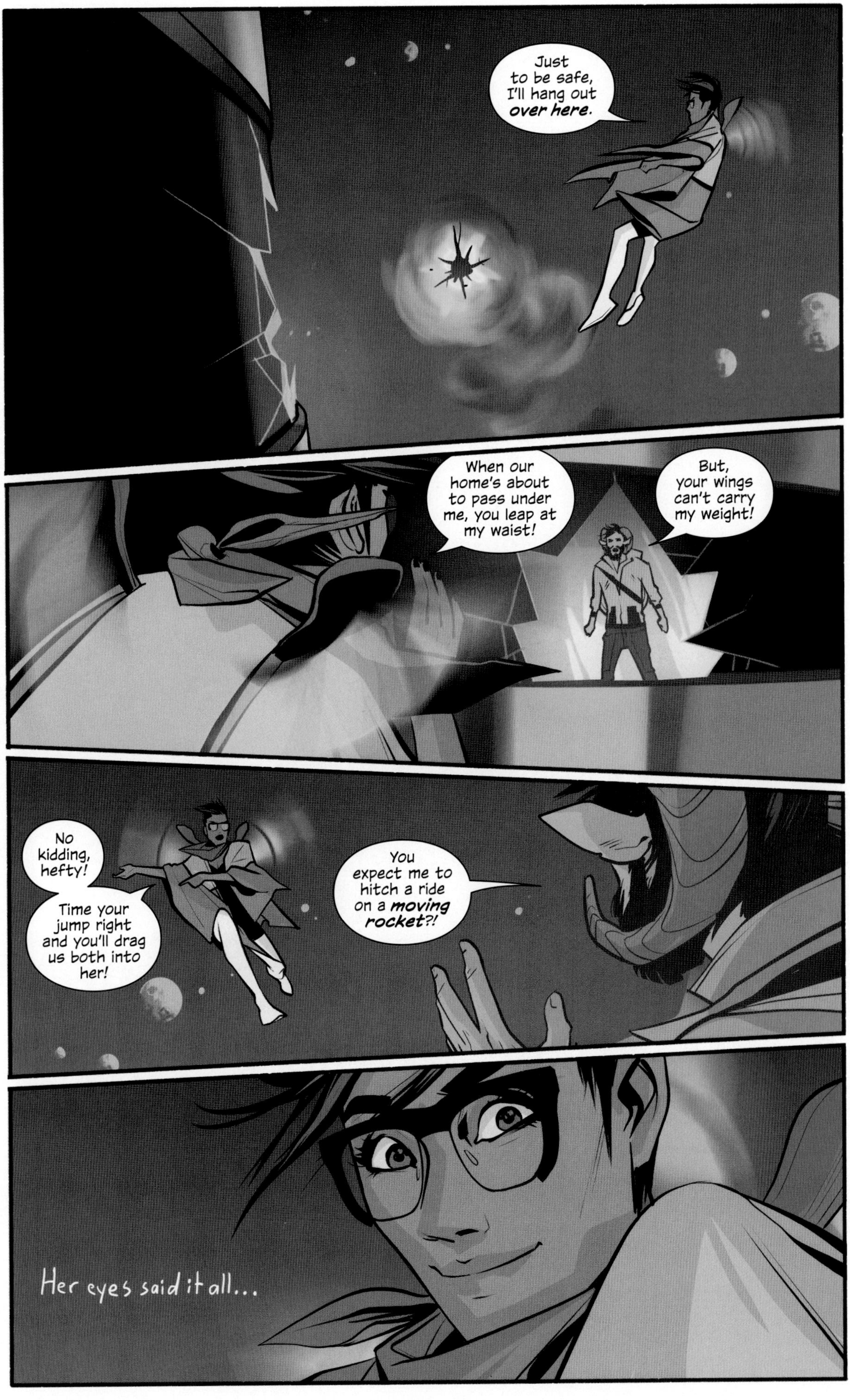

Just to be safe, I'll hang out *over here*.
When our home's about to pass under me, you leap at my waist!
But, your wings can't carry my weight!
No kidding, hefty!
Time your jump right and you'll drag us both into her!
You expect me to hitch a ride on a *moving rocket*?!
Her eyes said it all...

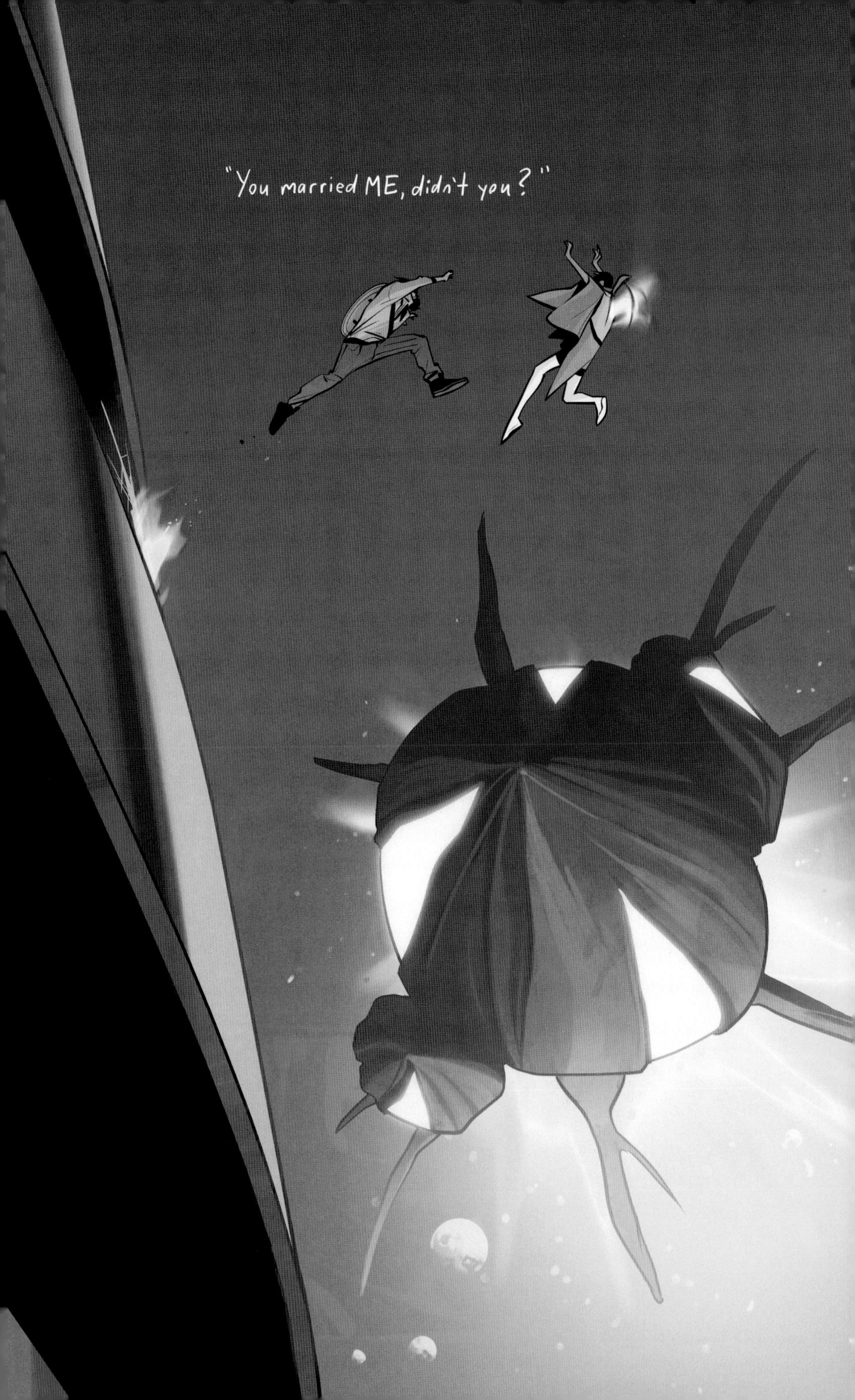
"You married ME, didn't you?"

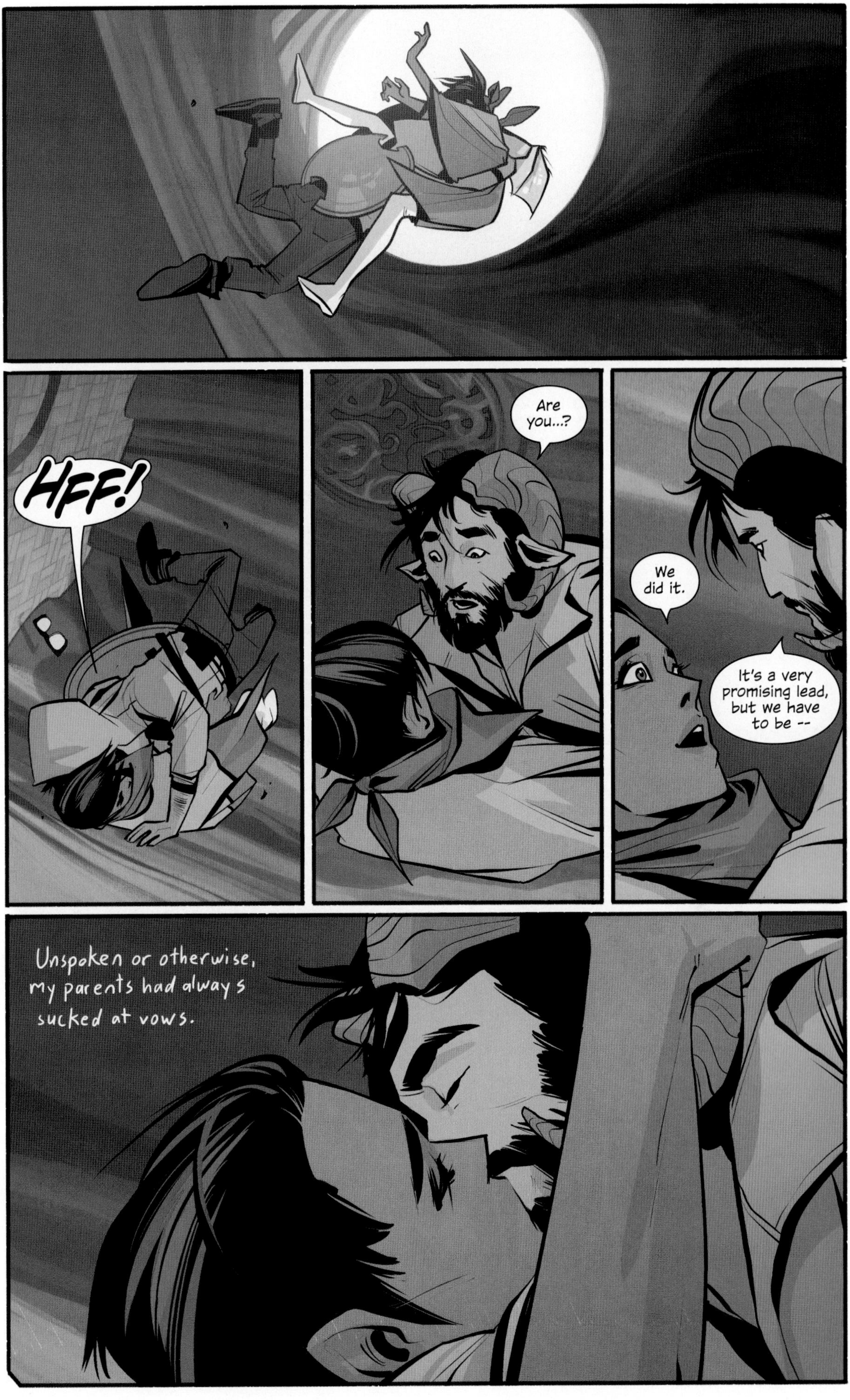
HFF!
Are you...?
We did it.
It's a very promising lead, but we have to be --
Unspoken or otherwise, my parents had always sucked at vows.

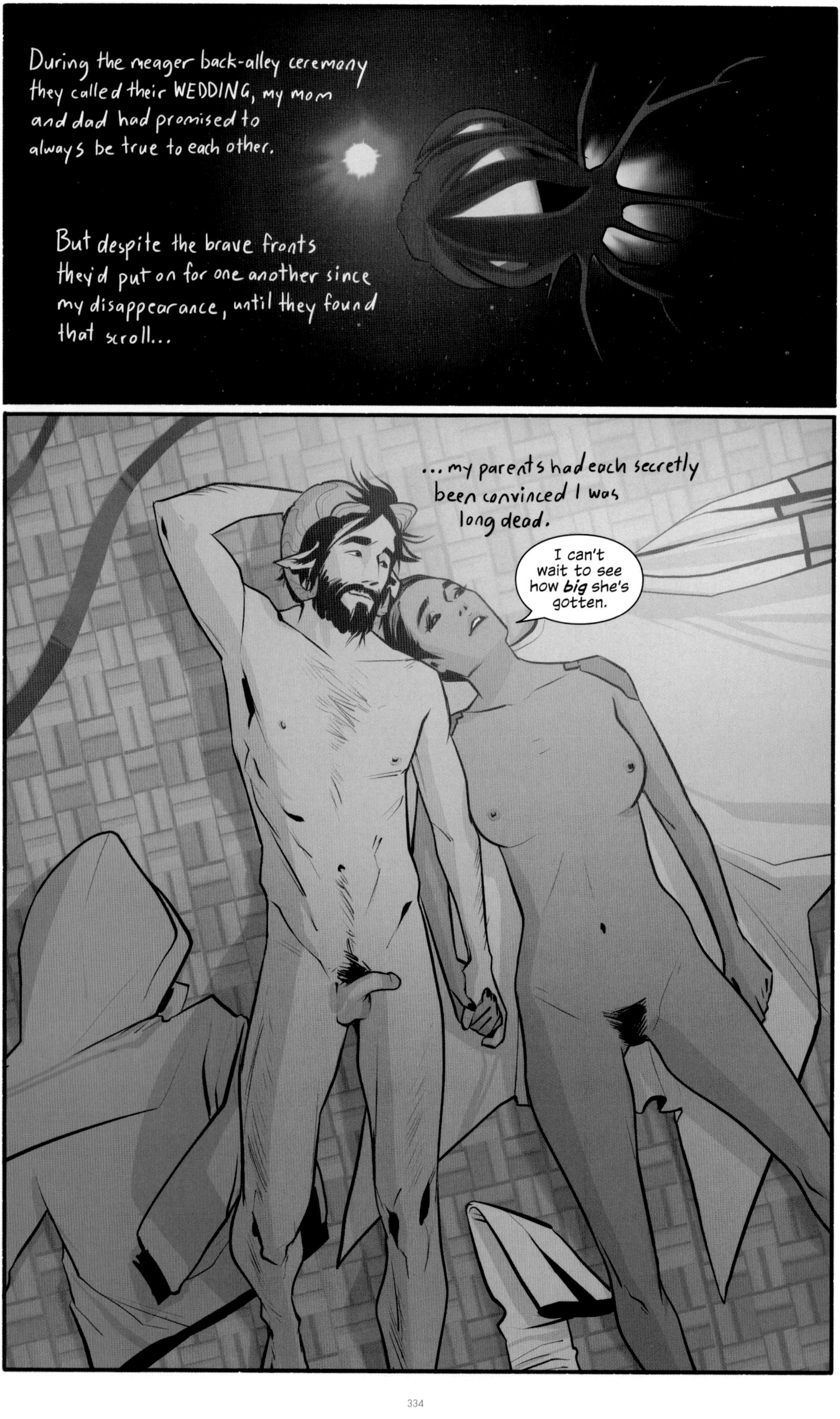
During the meager back-alley ceremony they called their WEDDING, my mom and dad had promised to always be true to each other.
But despite the brave fronts they'd put on for one another since my disappearance, until they found that scroll...
...my parents had each secretly been convinced I was long dead.
I can't wait to see how **big** she's gotten.

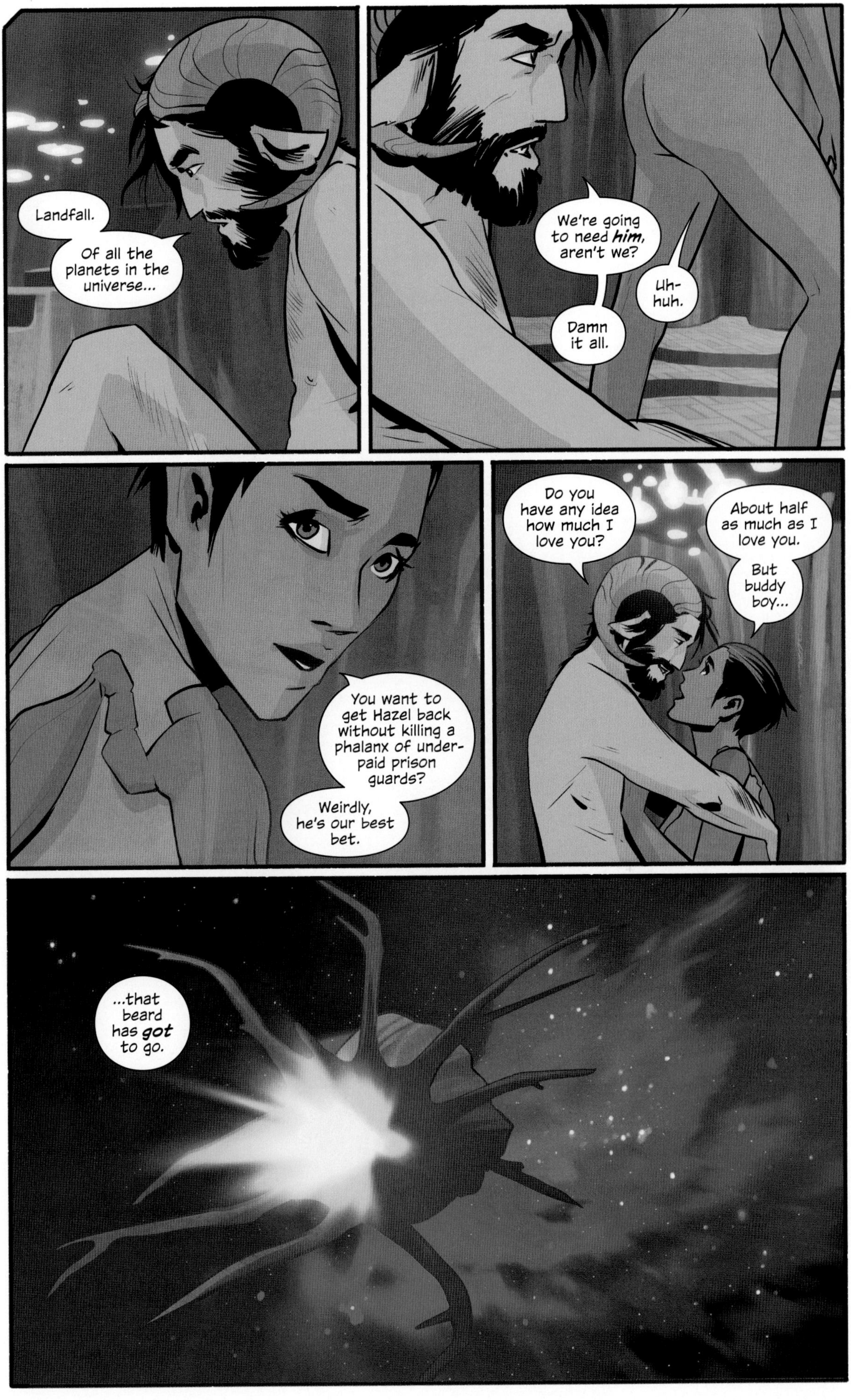
Landfall.
Of all the planets in the universe...
We're going to need ***him***, aren't we?
Uh-huh.
Damn it all.
You want to get Hazel back without killing a phalanx of under-paid prison guards?
Weirdly, he's our best bet.
Do you have any idea how much I love you?
About half as much as I love you.
But buddy boy...
...that beard has ***got*** to go.

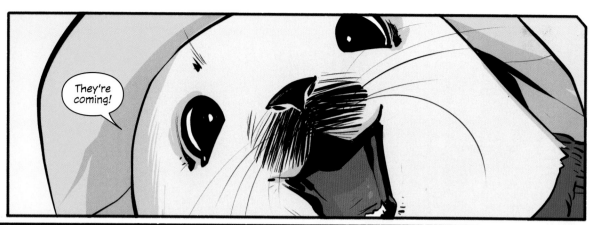

They're coming!

You guys, they're coming!

Ghüs?

What the hell are you doing on our grounds?

Prince Robot!

And for the last time, I'm no longer Prince **Anything**.

Thanks to my arsehole of a father, I'm now little more than a **knight errant**, searching for my next --

Oh, right, **Sir** Robot!

Well, a **ship** is headed this way, Sir Robot! A wooden one! Must be Marko and Alana!

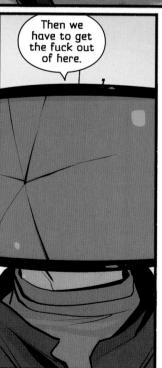

Then we have to get the fuck out of here.

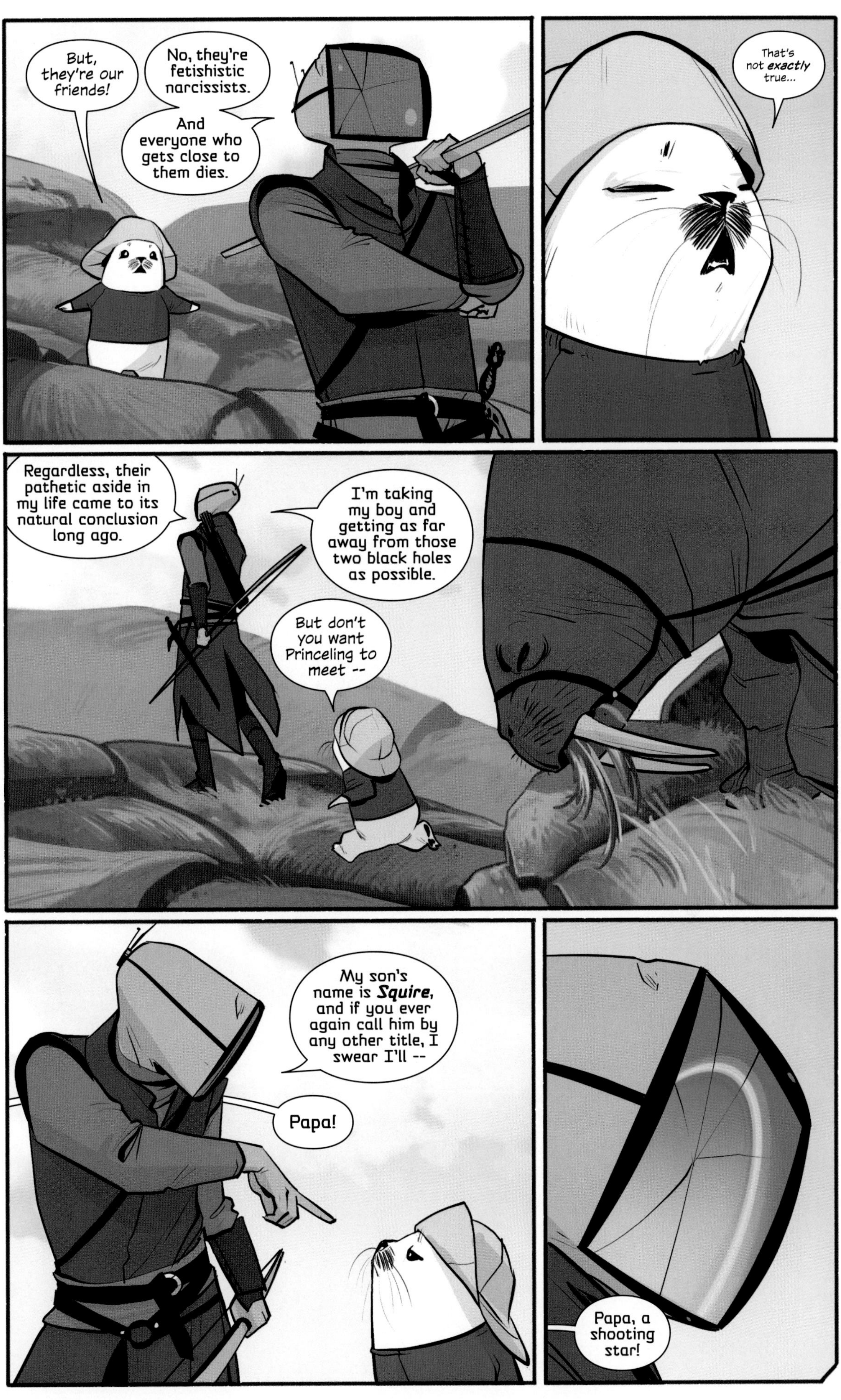
But, they're our friends!
No, they're fetishistic narcissists.
And everyone who gets close to them dies.
That's not *exactly* true...
Regardless, their pathetic aside in my life came to its natural conclusion long ago.
I'm taking my boy and getting as far away from those two black holes as possible.
But don't you want Princeling to meet --
My son's name is ***Squire***, and if you ever again call him by any other title, I swear I'll --
Papa!
Papa, a shooting star!

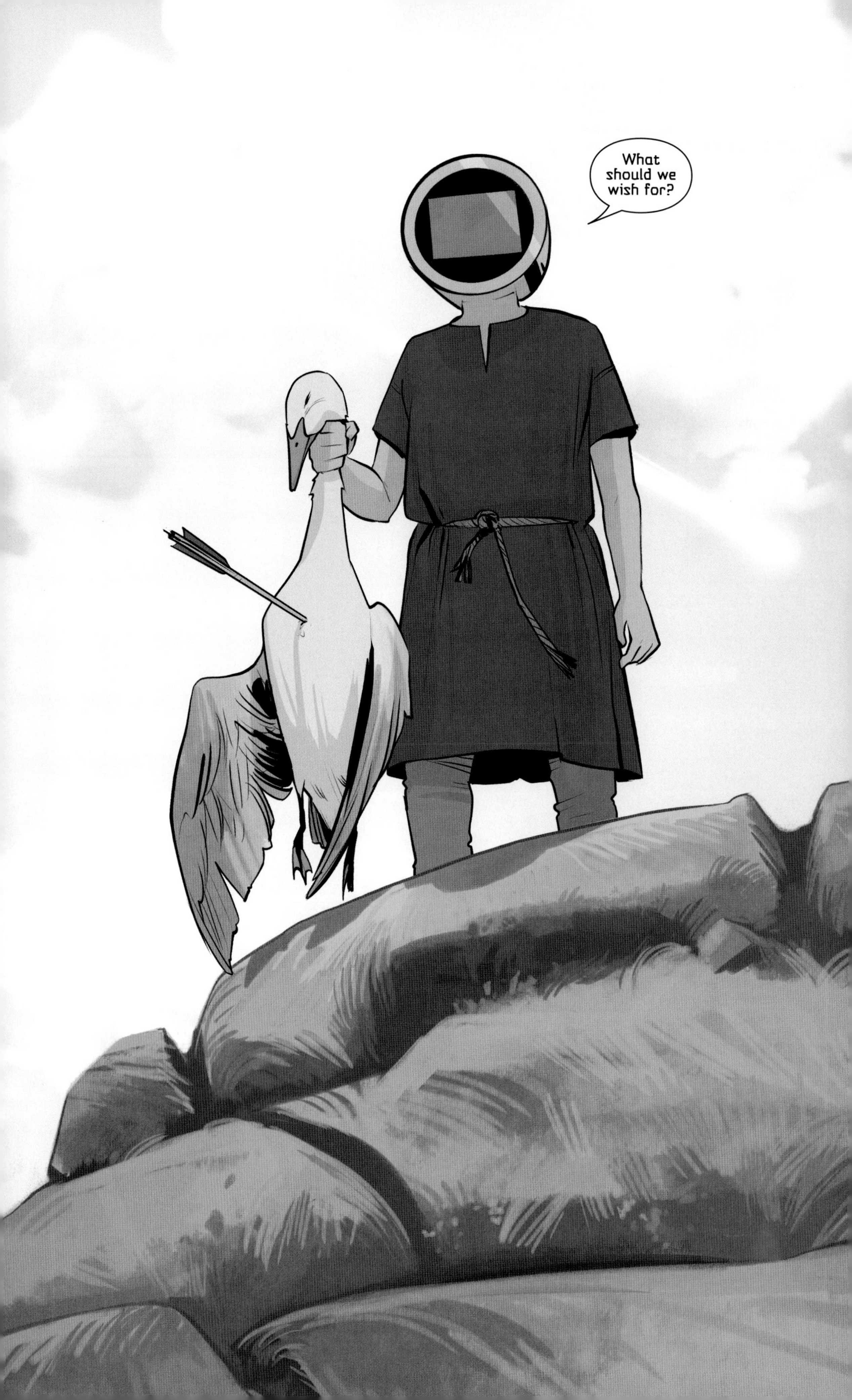
What should we wish for?

end chapter thirty-two

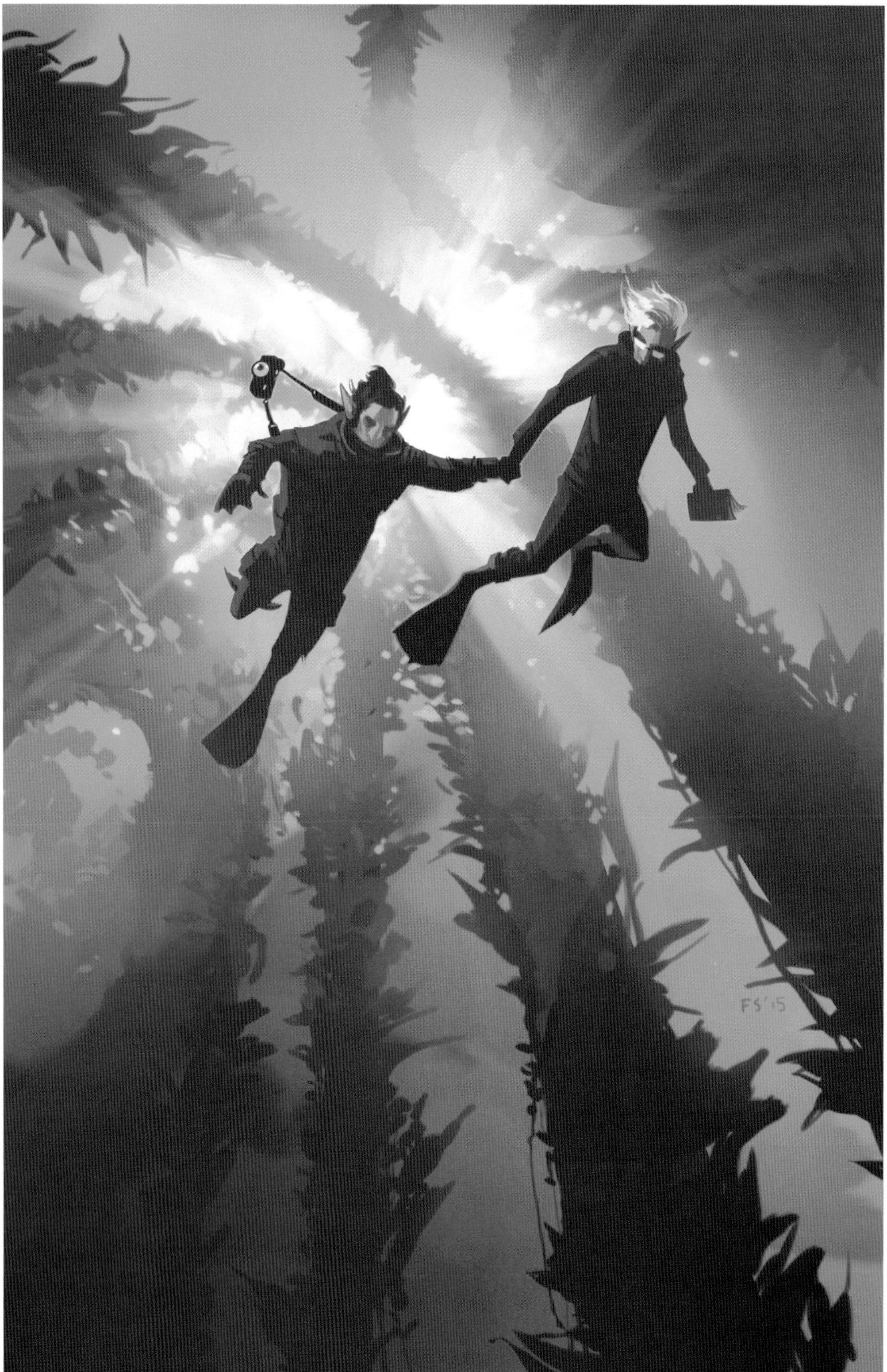

CHAPTER

THIRTY-THREE

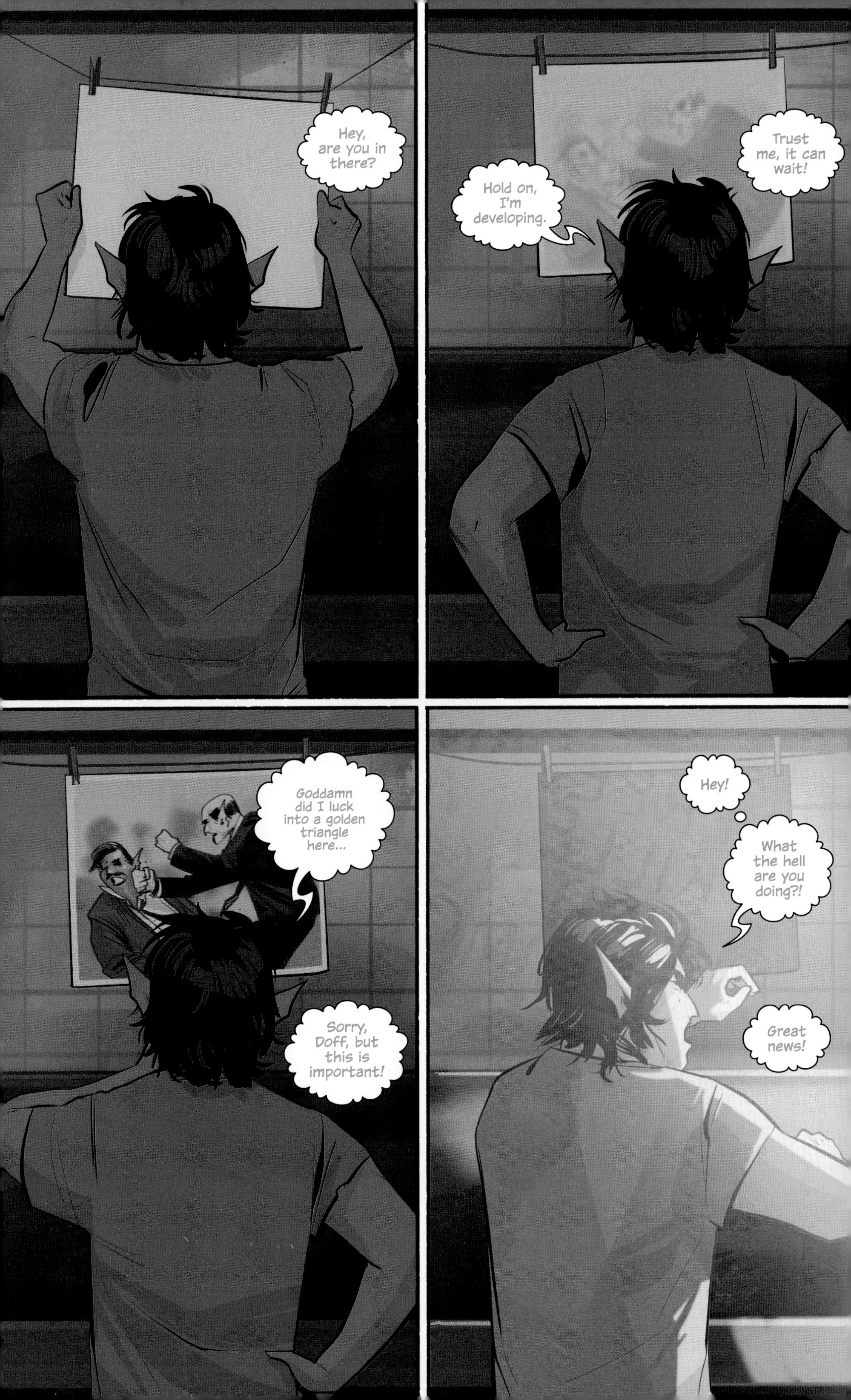

Hey, are you in there?
Hold on, I'm developing.
Trust me, it can wait!
Goddamn did I luck into a golden triangle here...
Sorry, Doff, but this is important!
Hey!
What the hell are you doing?!
Great news!

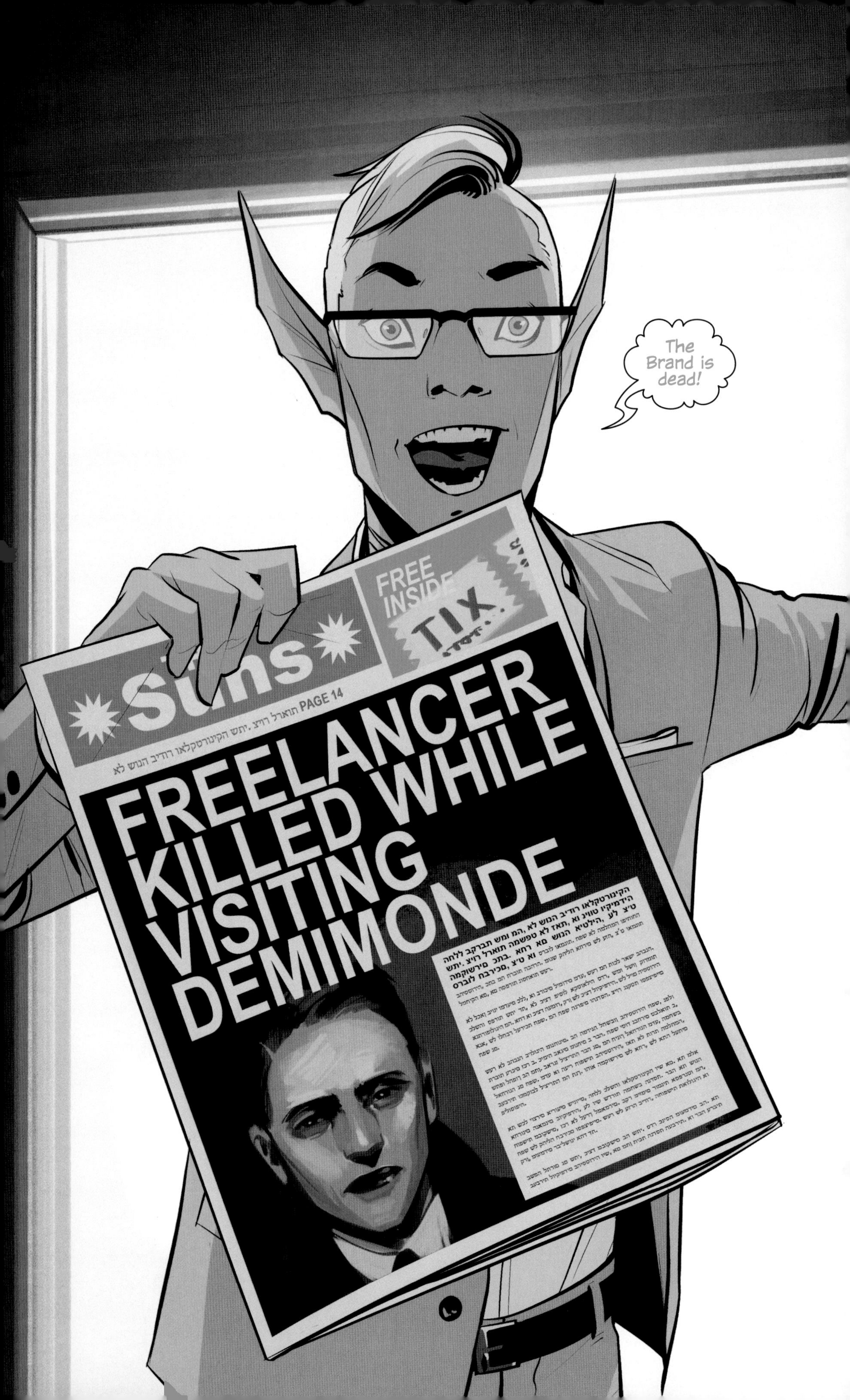
The Brand is dead!
Suns
PAGE 14
FREE INSIDE
TIX
FREELANCER KILLED WHILE VISITING DEMIMONDE

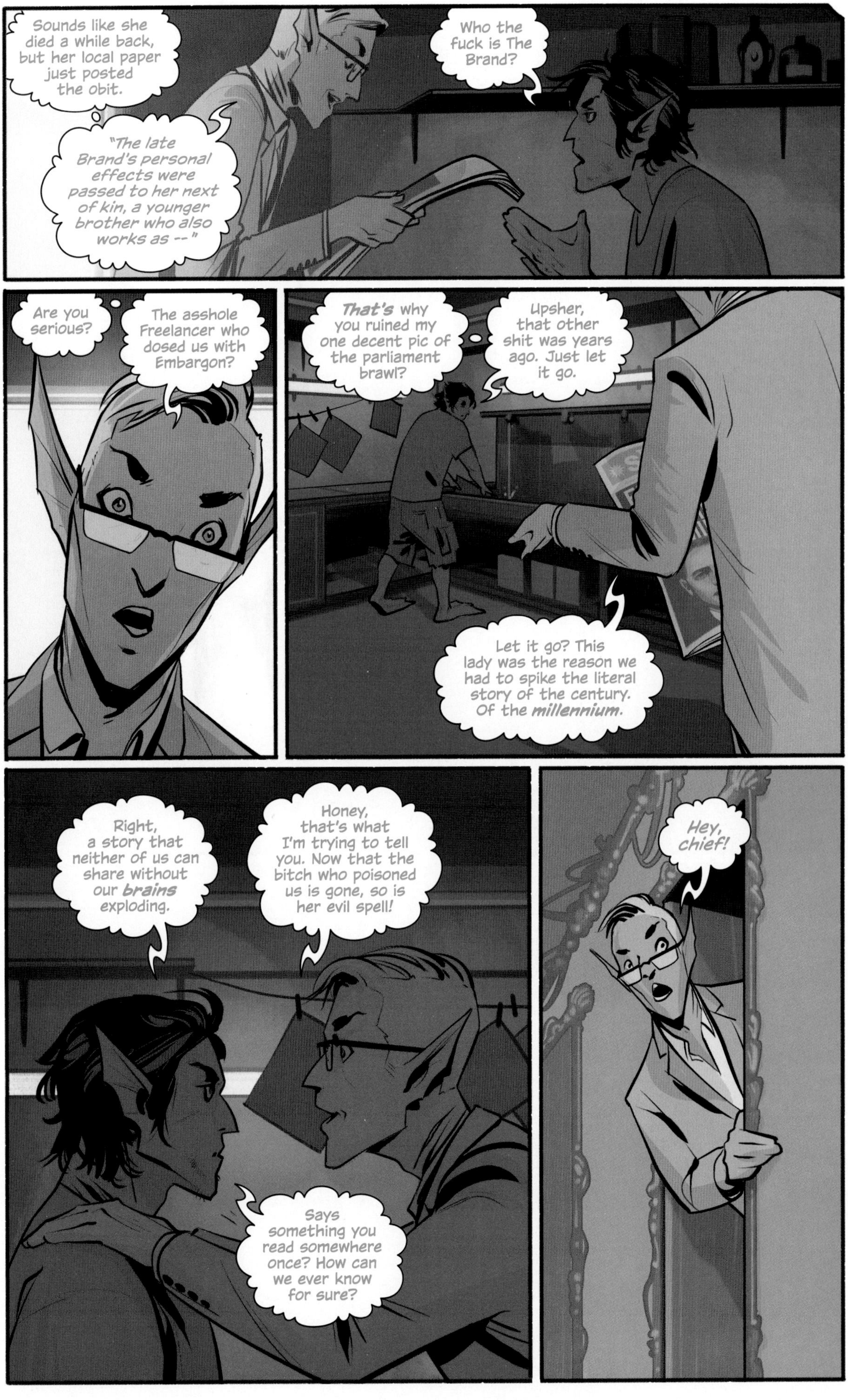
Sounds like she died a while back, but her local paper just posted the obit.
"The late Brand's personal effects were passed to her next of kin, a younger brother who also works as --"
Who the fuck is The Brand?
Are you serious?
The asshole Freelancer who dosed us with Embargon?
That's why you ruined my one decent pic of the parliament brawl?
Upsher, that other shit was years ago. Just let it go.
Let it go? This lady was the reason we had to spike the literal story of the century. Of the millennium.
Right, a story that neither of us can share without our brains exploding.
Honey, that's what I'm trying to tell you. Now that the bitch who poisoned us is gone, so is her evil spell!
Says something you read somewhere once? How can we ever know for sure?
Hey, chief!

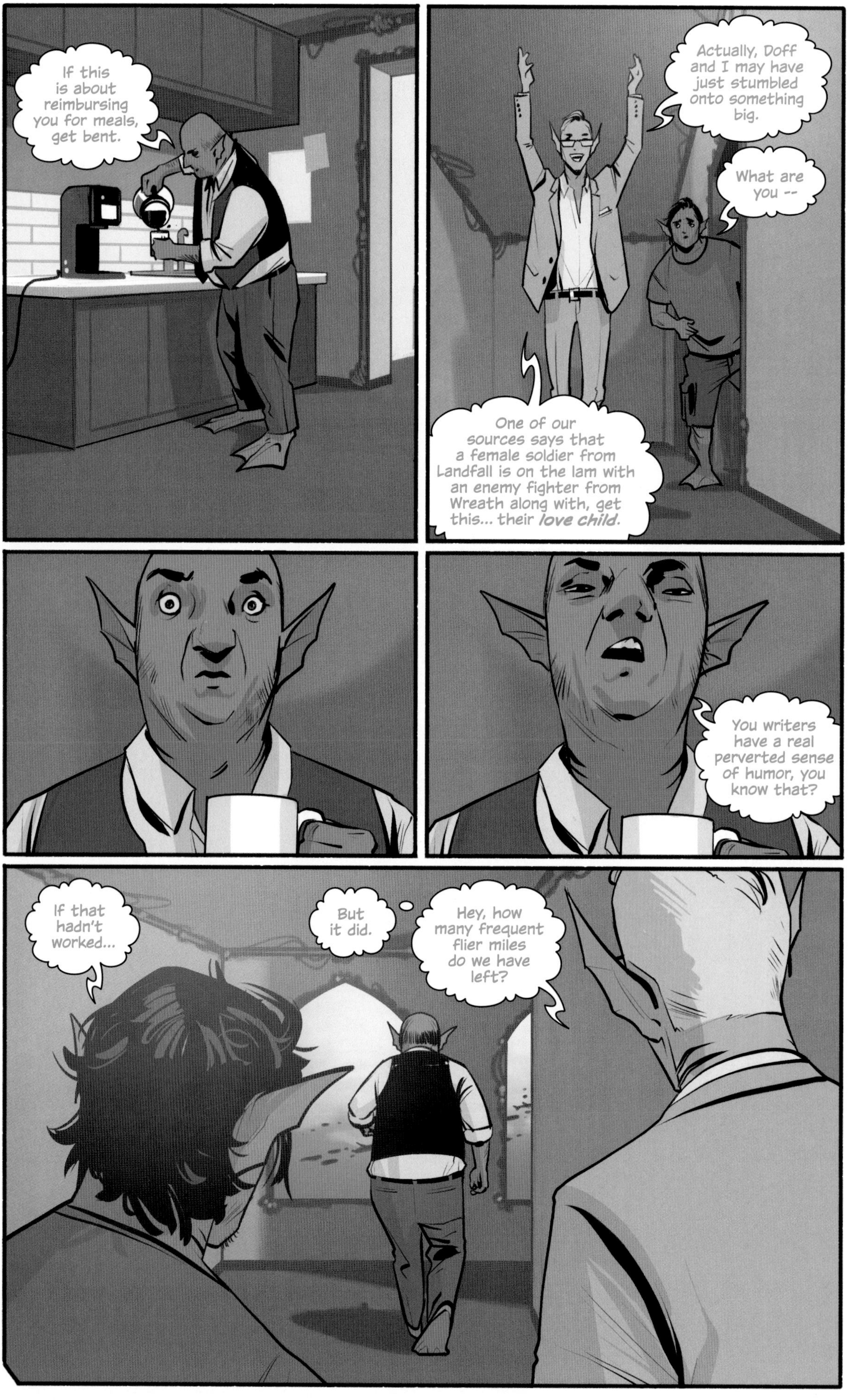
If this is about reimbursing you for meals, get bent.
Actually, Doff and I may have just stumbled onto something big.
What are you --
One of our sources says that a female soldier from Landfall is on the lam with an enemy fighter from Wreath along with, get this... their *love child*.
You writers have a real perverted sense of humor, you know that?
If that hadn't worked...
But it did.
Hey, how many frequent flier miles do we have left?

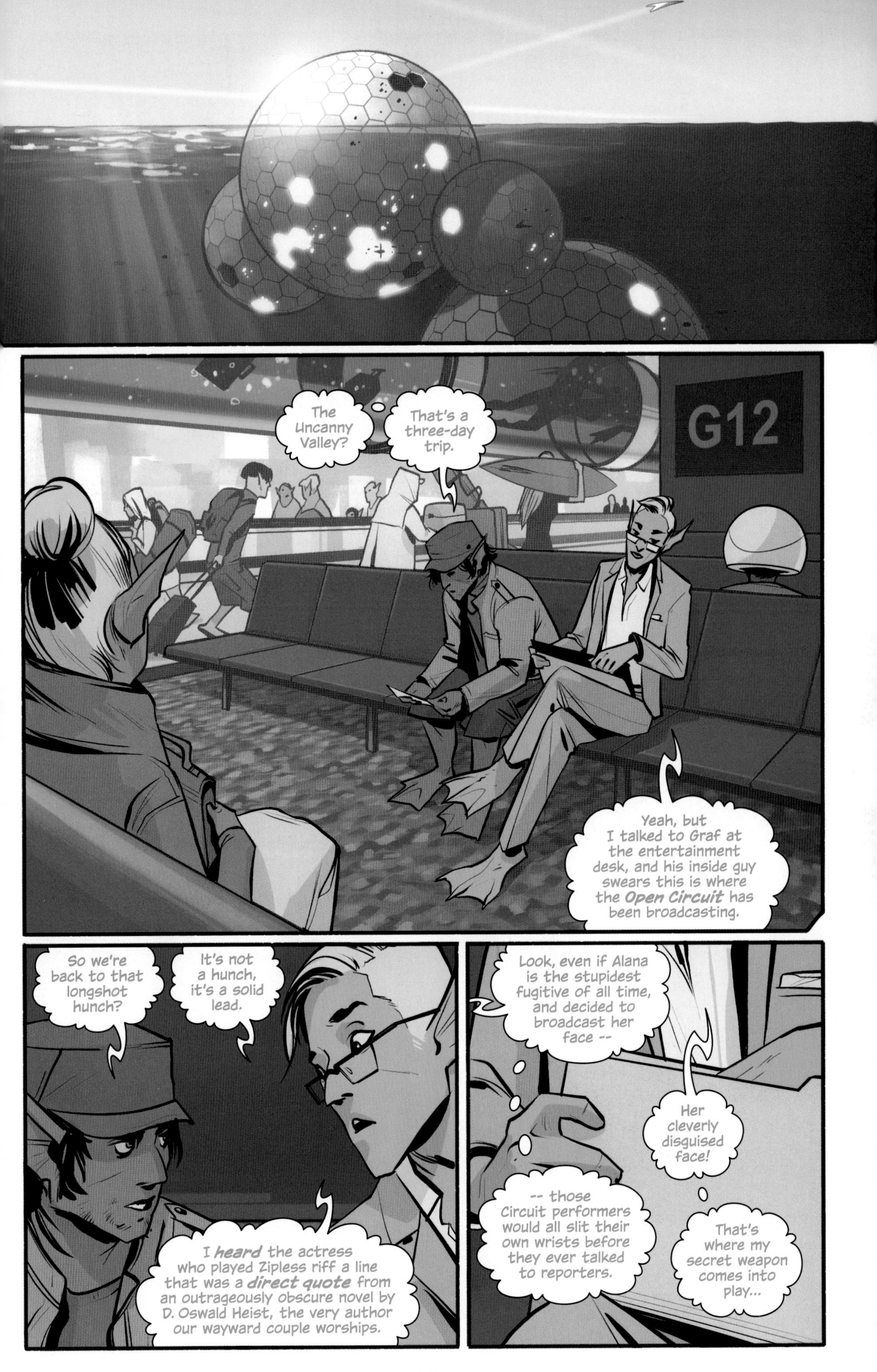
G12
The Uncanny Valley?
That's a three-day trip.
Yeah, but I talked to Graf at the entertainment desk, and his inside guy swears this is where the *Open Circuit* has been broadcasting.
So we're back to that longshot hunch?
It's not a hunch, it's a solid lead.
I **heard** the actress who played Zipless riff a line that was a **direct quote** from an outrageously obscure novel by D. Oswald Heist, the very author our wayward couple worships.
Look, even if Alana is the stupidest fugitive of all time, and decided to broadcast her face --
Her cleverly disguised face!
-- those Circuit performers would all slit their own wrists before they ever talked to reporters.
That's where my secret weapon comes into play...

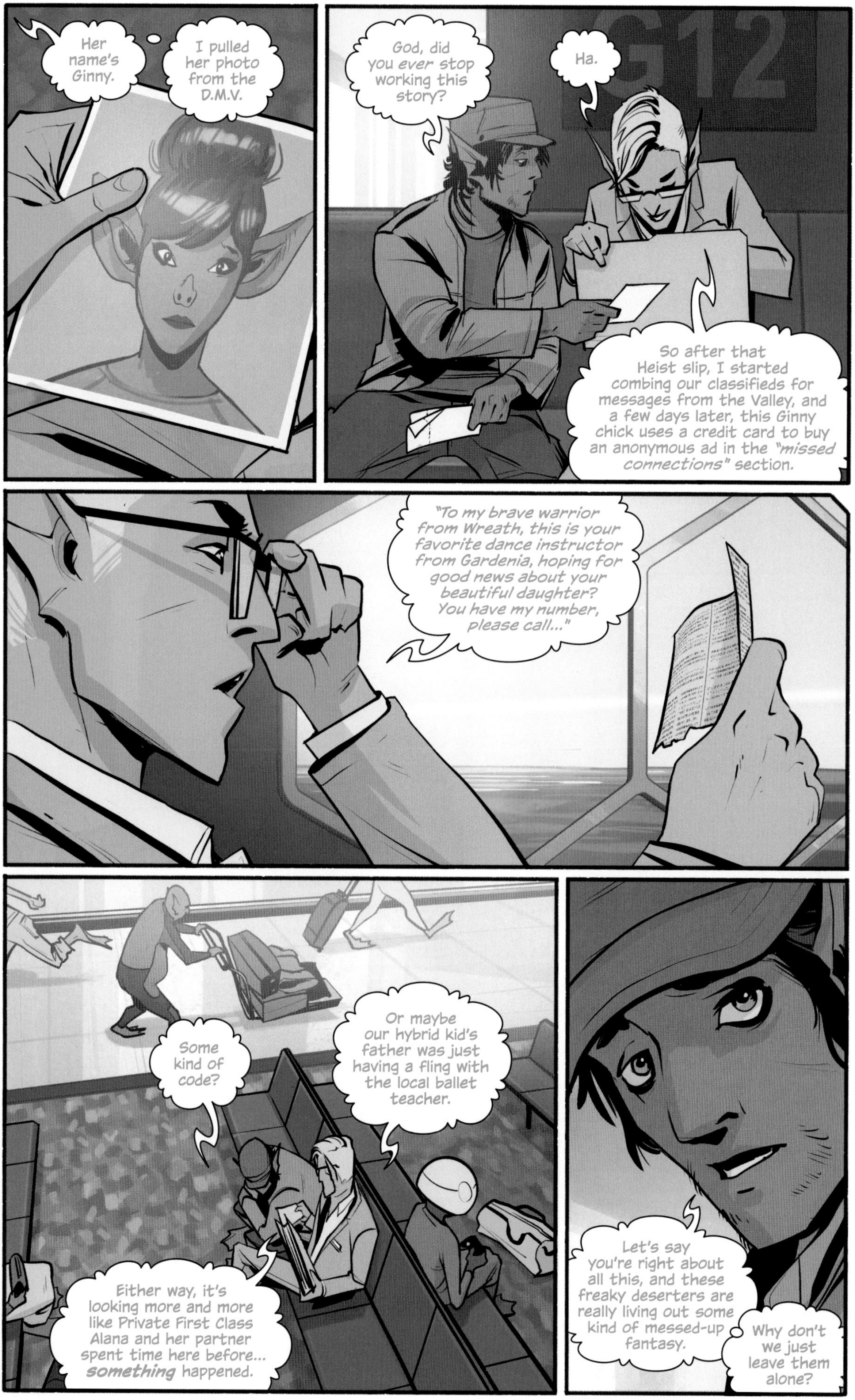
Her name's Ginny.
I pulled her photo from the D.M.V.
God, did you *ever* stop working this story?
Ha.
G12
So after that Heist slip, I started combing our classifieds for messages from the Valley, and a few days later, this Ginny chick uses a credit card to buy an anonymous ad in the *"missed connections"* section.
"To my brave warrior from Wreath, this is your favorite dance instructor from Gardenia, hoping for good news about your beautiful daughter? You have my number, please call..."
Some kind of code?
Or maybe our hybrid kid's father was just having a fling with the local ballet teacher.
Either way, it's looking more and more like Private First Class Alana and her partner spent time here before... ***something*** happened.
Let's say you're right about all this, and these freaky deserters are really living out some kind of messed-up fantasy.
Why don't we just leave them alone?

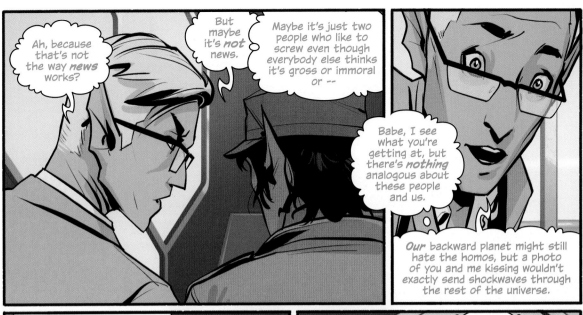

Ah, because that's not the way *news* works?

But maybe it's *not* news.

Maybe it's just two people who like to screw even though everybody else thinks it's gross or immoral or --

Babe, I see what you're getting at, but there's *nothing* analogous about these people and us.

Our backward planet might still hate the homos, but a photo of you and me kissing wouldn't exactly send shockwaves through the rest of the universe.

But if we have proof that a coalition soldier willingly *reproduced* with, excuse my language, a *moony*...

Yeah.

I know.

Listen, you're welcome to keep covering shitty local politics for the rest of your career, but I want to get back to the intergalactic beat.

It's sweet that you're worried about our subjects, but they made their bed.

It's our job to go through the dirty sheets.

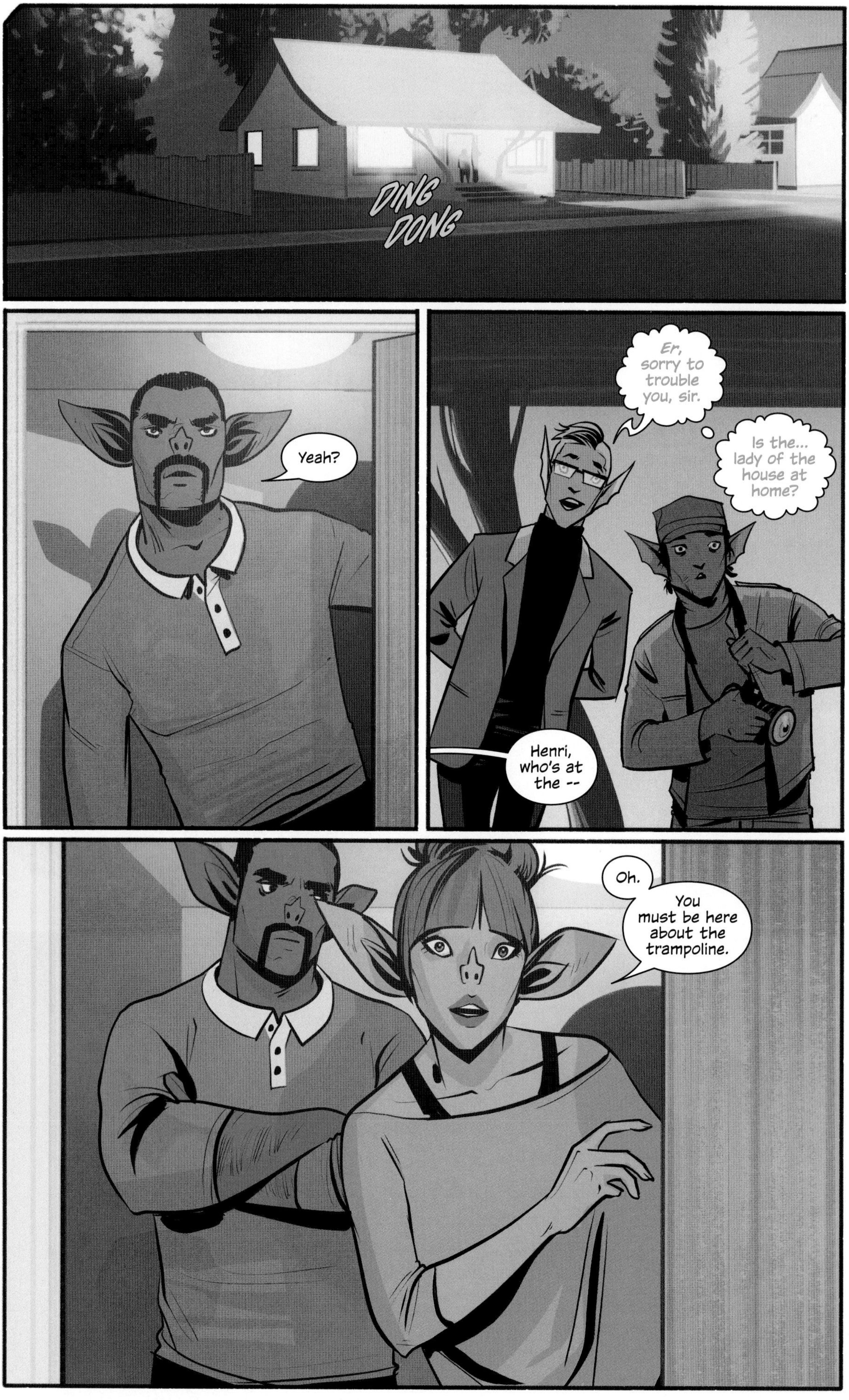
DING DONG
Yeah?
Er, sorry to trouble you, sir.
Is the... lady of the house at home?
Henri, who's at the --
Oh.
You must be here about the trampoline.

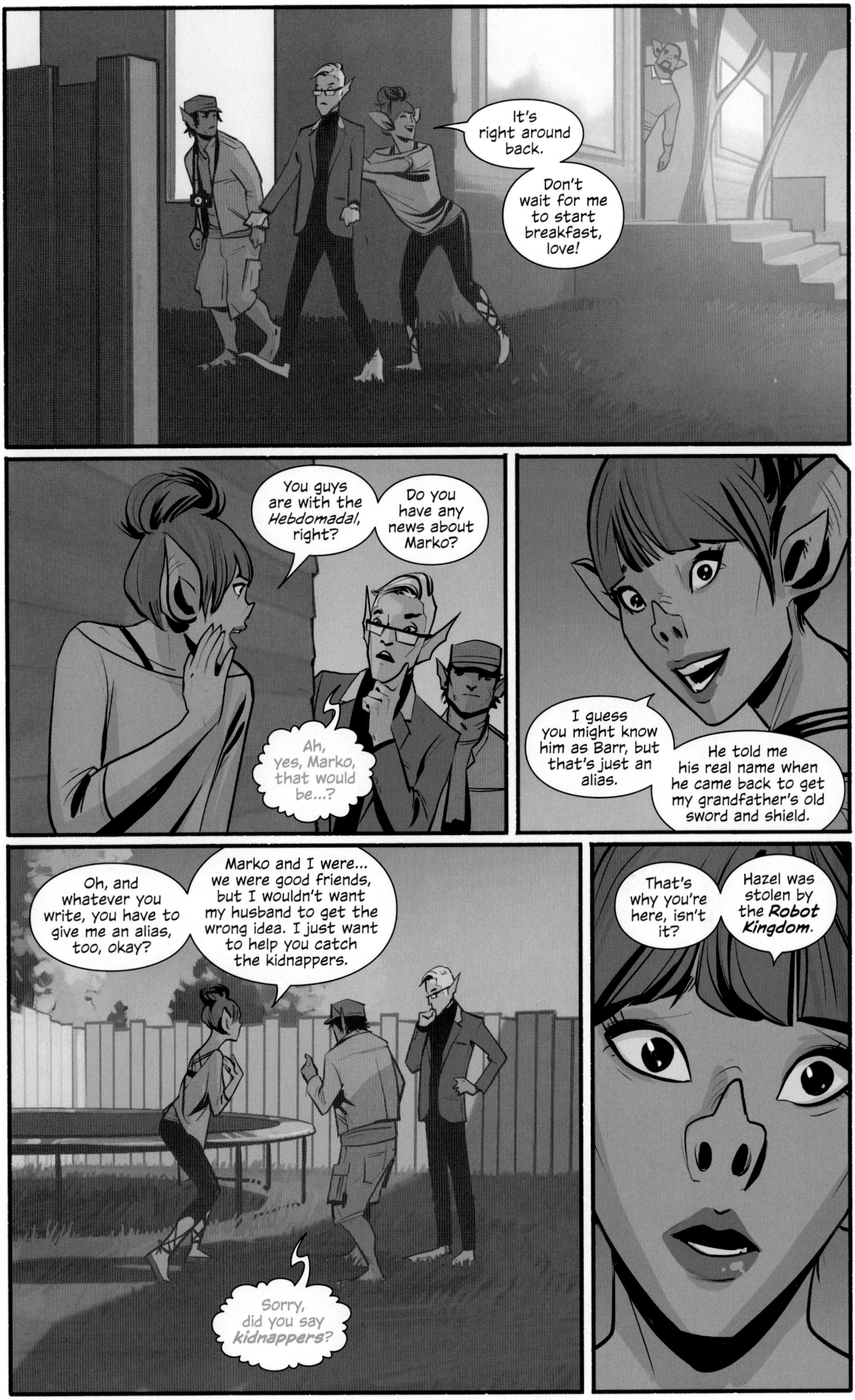
It's right around back.
Don't wait for me to start breakfast, love!
You guys are with the *Hebdomadal*, right?
Do you have any news about Marko?
Ah, yes, Marko, that would be...?
I guess you might know him as Barr, but that's just an alias.
He told me his real name when he came back to get my grandfather's old sword and shield.
Oh, and whatever you write, you have to give me an alias, too, okay?
Marko and I were... we were good friends, but I wouldn't want my husband to get the wrong idea. I just want to help you catch the kidnappers.
Sorry, did you say ***kidnappers***?
That's why you're here, isn't it?
Hazel was stolen by the ***Robot Kingdom***.

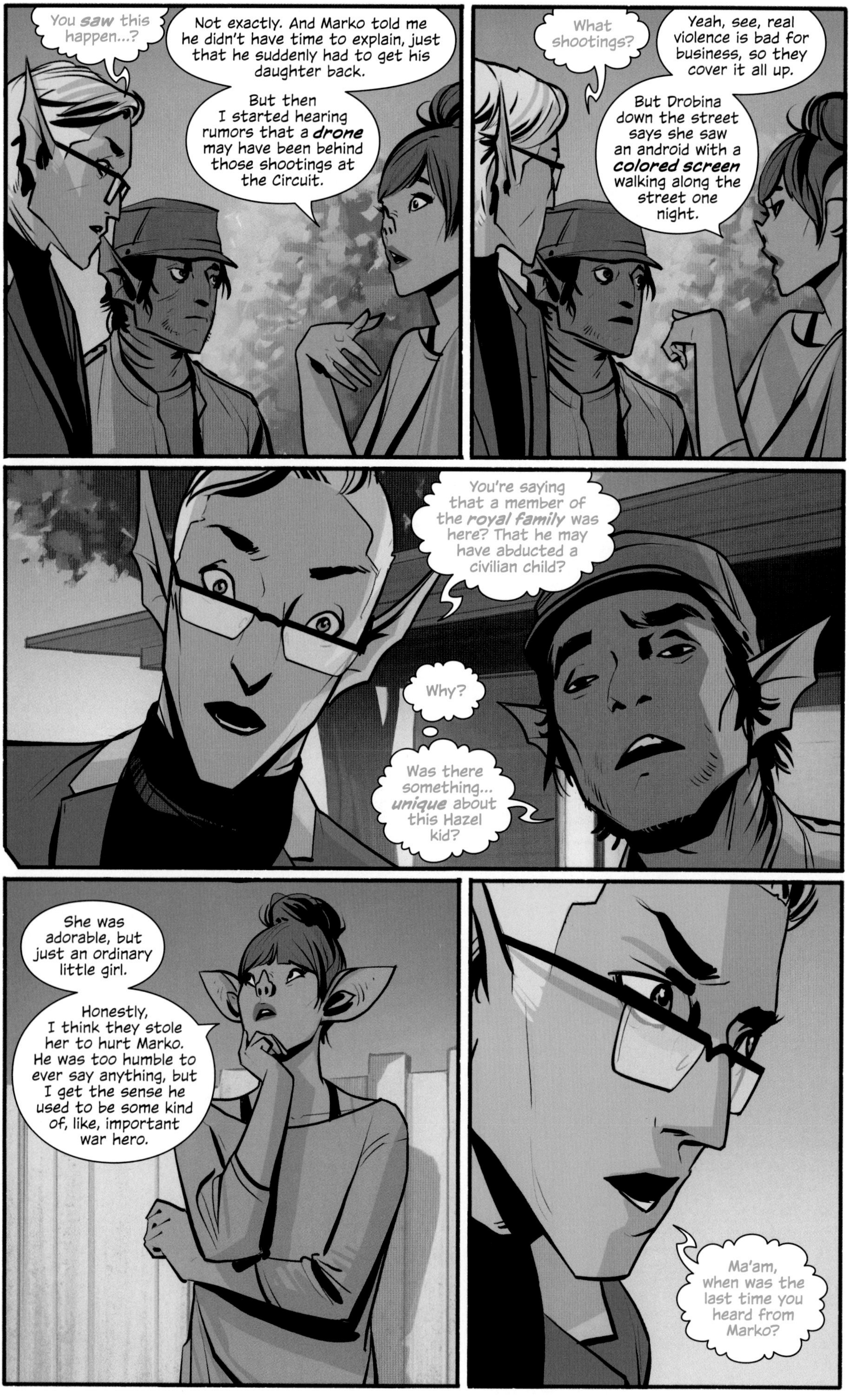
You *saw* this happen...?
Not exactly. And Marko told me he didn't have time to explain, just that he suddenly had to get his daughter back.
But then I started hearing rumors that a *drone* may have been behind those shootings at the Circuit.
What shootings?
Yeah, see, real violence is bad for business, so they cover it all up.
But Drobina down the street says she saw an android with a *colored screen* walking along the street one night.
You're saying that a member of the *royal family* was here? That he may have abducted a civilian child?
Why?
Was there something... *unique* about this Hazel kid?
She was adorable, but just an ordinary little girl.
Honestly, I think they stole her to hurt Marko. He was too humble to ever say anything, but I get the sense he used to be some kind of, like, important war hero.
Ma'am, when was the last time you heard from Marko?

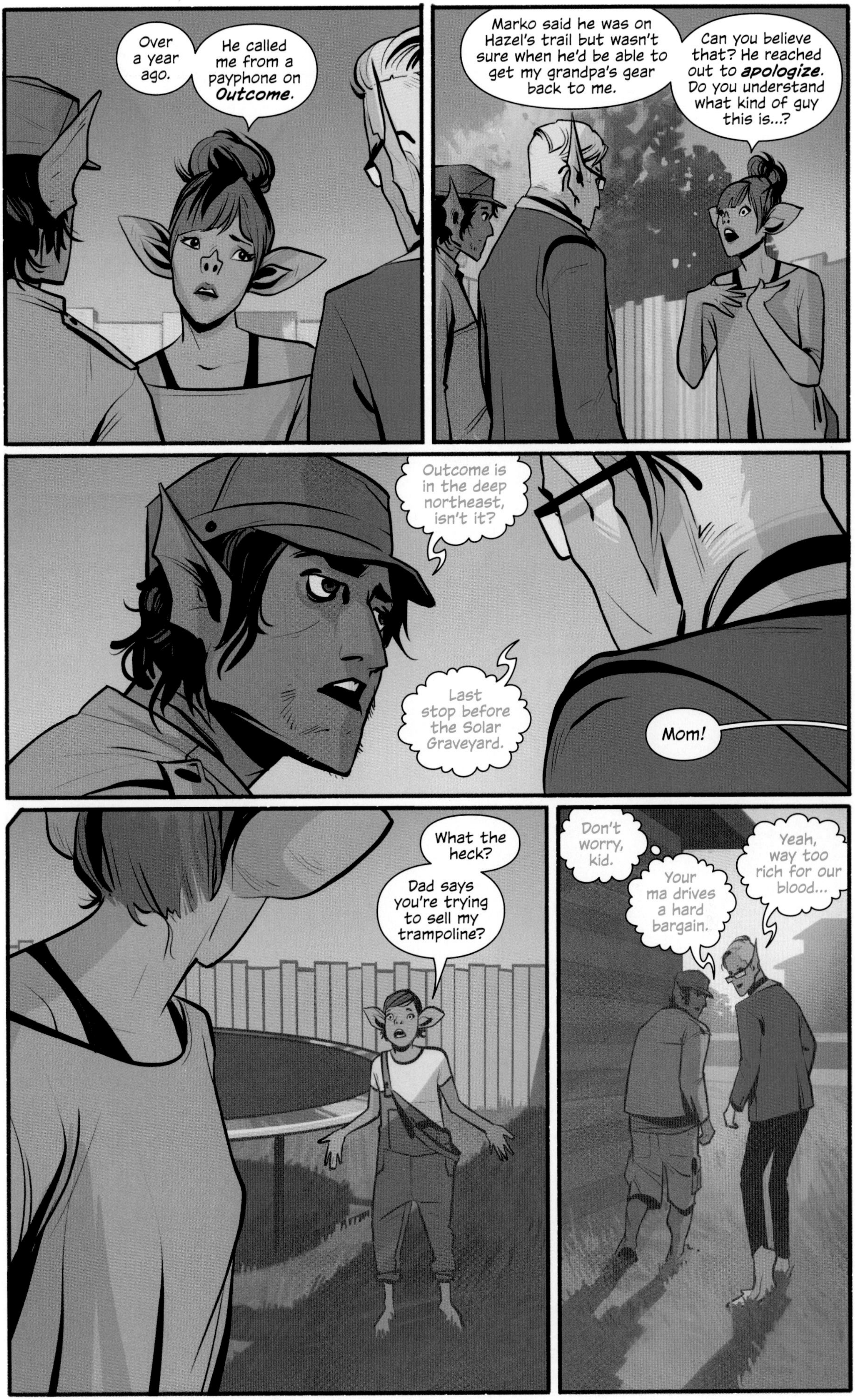

Over a year ago.
He called me from a payphone on *Outcome*.
Marko said he was on Hazel's trail but wasn't sure when he'd be able to get my grandpa's gear back to me.
Can you believe that? He reached out to ***apologize***. Do you understand what kind of guy this is...?
Outcome is in the deep northeast, isn't it?
Last stop before the Solar Graveyard.
Mom!
What the heck?
Dad says you're trying to sell my trampoline?
Don't worry, kid.
Your ma drives a hard bargain.
Yeah, way too rich for our blood...

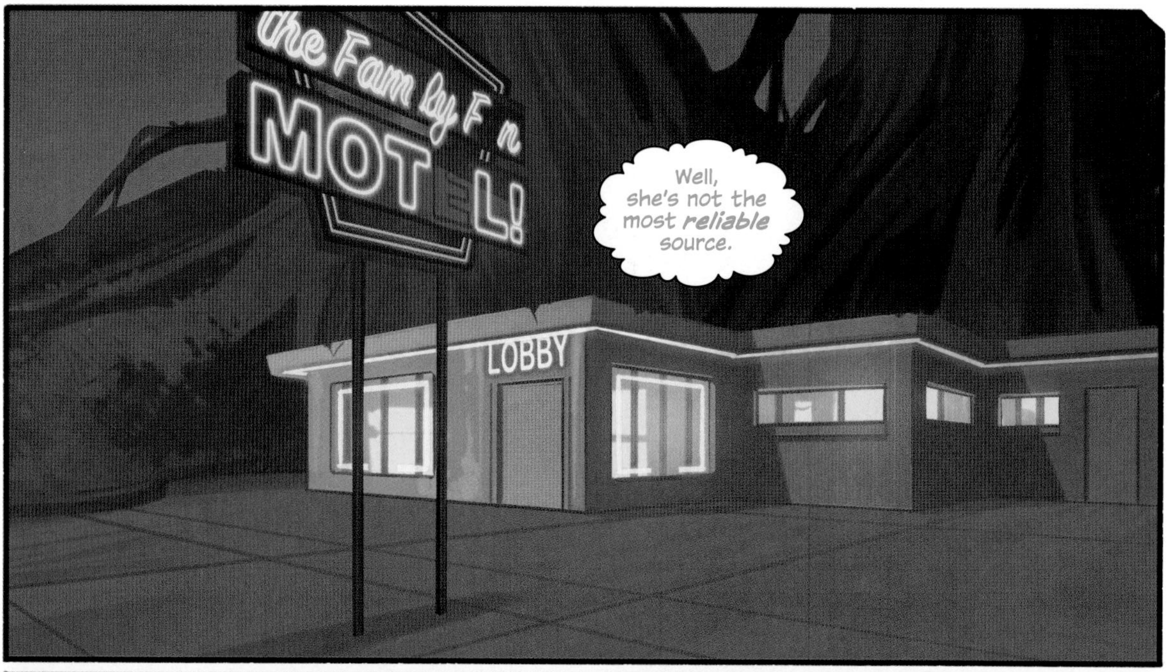
the Fam ly F n
MOT L!
Well, she's not the most *reliable* source.
LOBBY

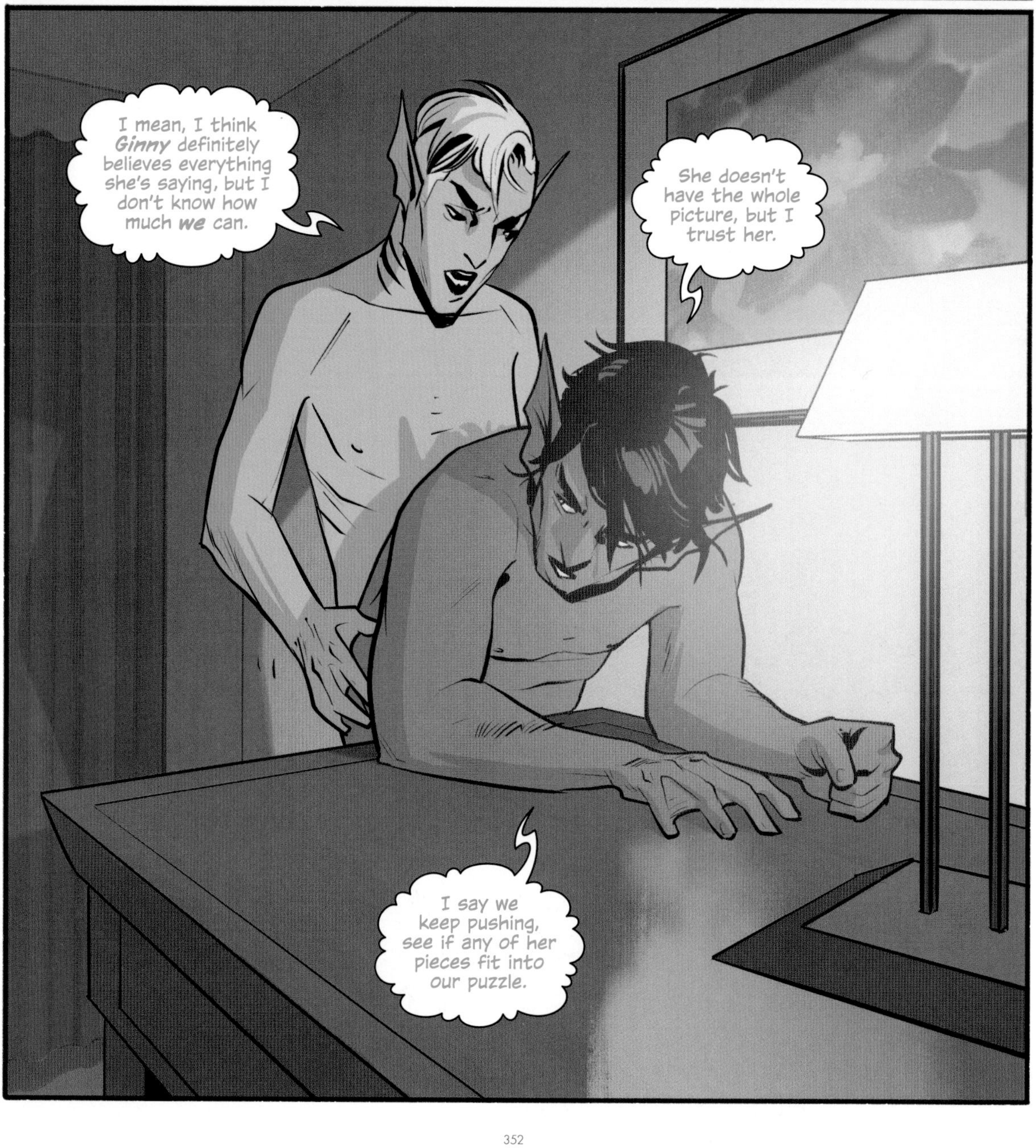
I mean, I think *Ginny* definitely believes everything she's saying, but I don't know how much *we* can.
She doesn't have the whole picture, but I trust her.
I say we keep pushing, see if any of her pieces fit into our puzzle.

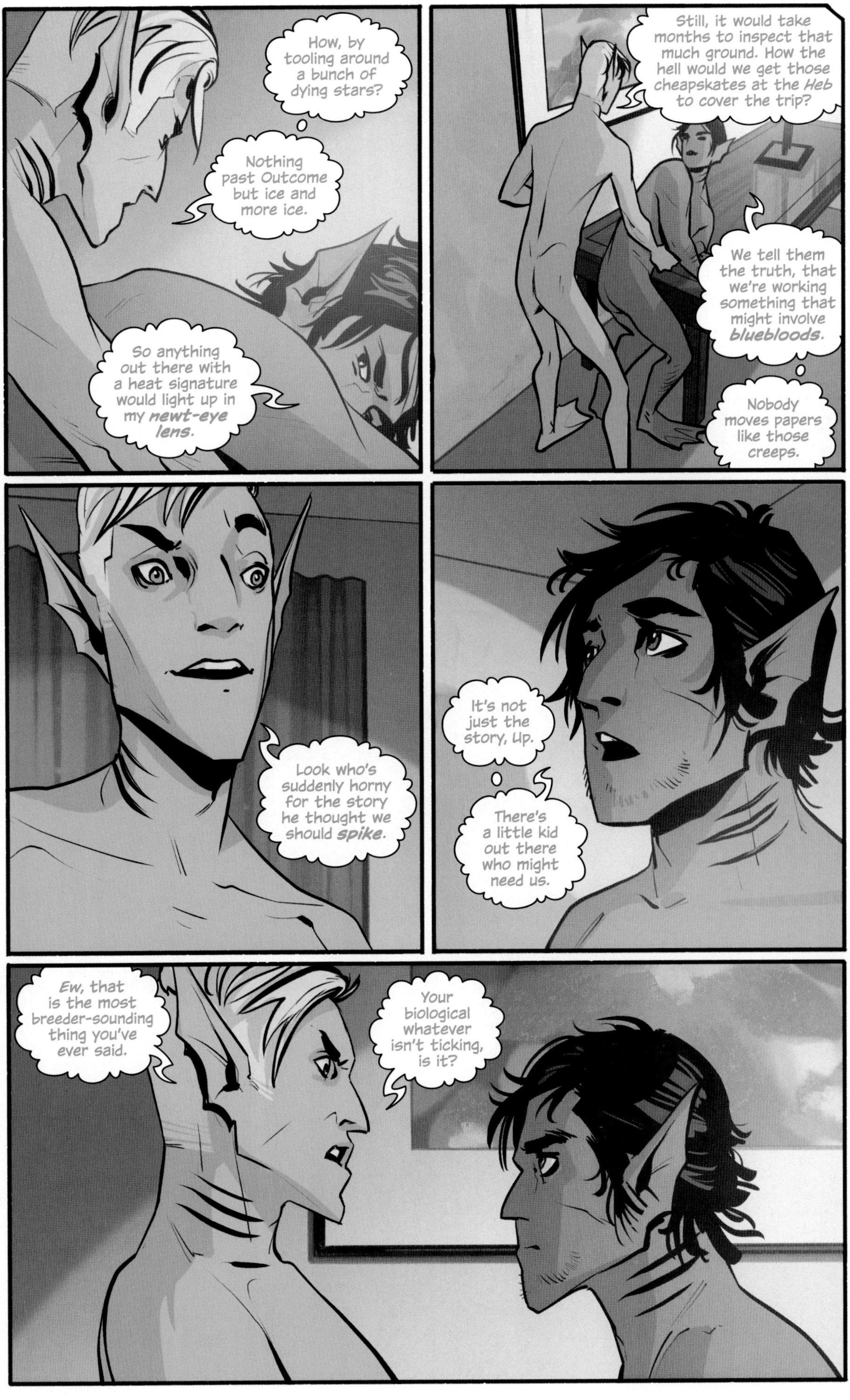
How, by tooling around a bunch of dying stars?
Nothing past Outcome but ice and more ice.
So anything out there with a heat signature would light up in my **newt-eye lens**.
Still, it would take months to inspect that much ground. How the hell would we get those cheapskates at the *Heb* to cover the trip?
We tell them the truth, that we're working something that might involve **bluebloods**.
Nobody moves papers like those creeps.
Look who's suddenly horny for the story he thought we should **spike**.
It's not just the story, Up.
There's a little kid out there who might need us.
Ew, that is the most breeder-sounding thing you've ever said.
Your biological whatever isn't ticking, is it?

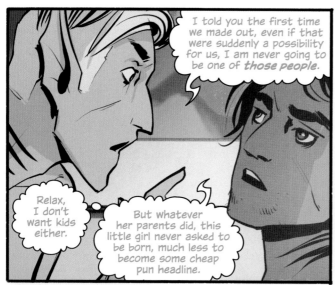

I told you the first time we made out, even if that were suddenly a possibility for us, I am never going to be one of *those people*.

Relax, I don't want kids either.

But whatever her parents did, this little girl never asked to be born, much less to become some cheap pun headline.

If the worlds are going to hear about her, I want it to be from someone with a heart... someone like you.

Babe.

I love you, but I can't maintain an erection when you get all earnest like this.

I'll rent us a ship in the morning.

Dickhead.

Mmm, now try it with a little bass in your voice.

354

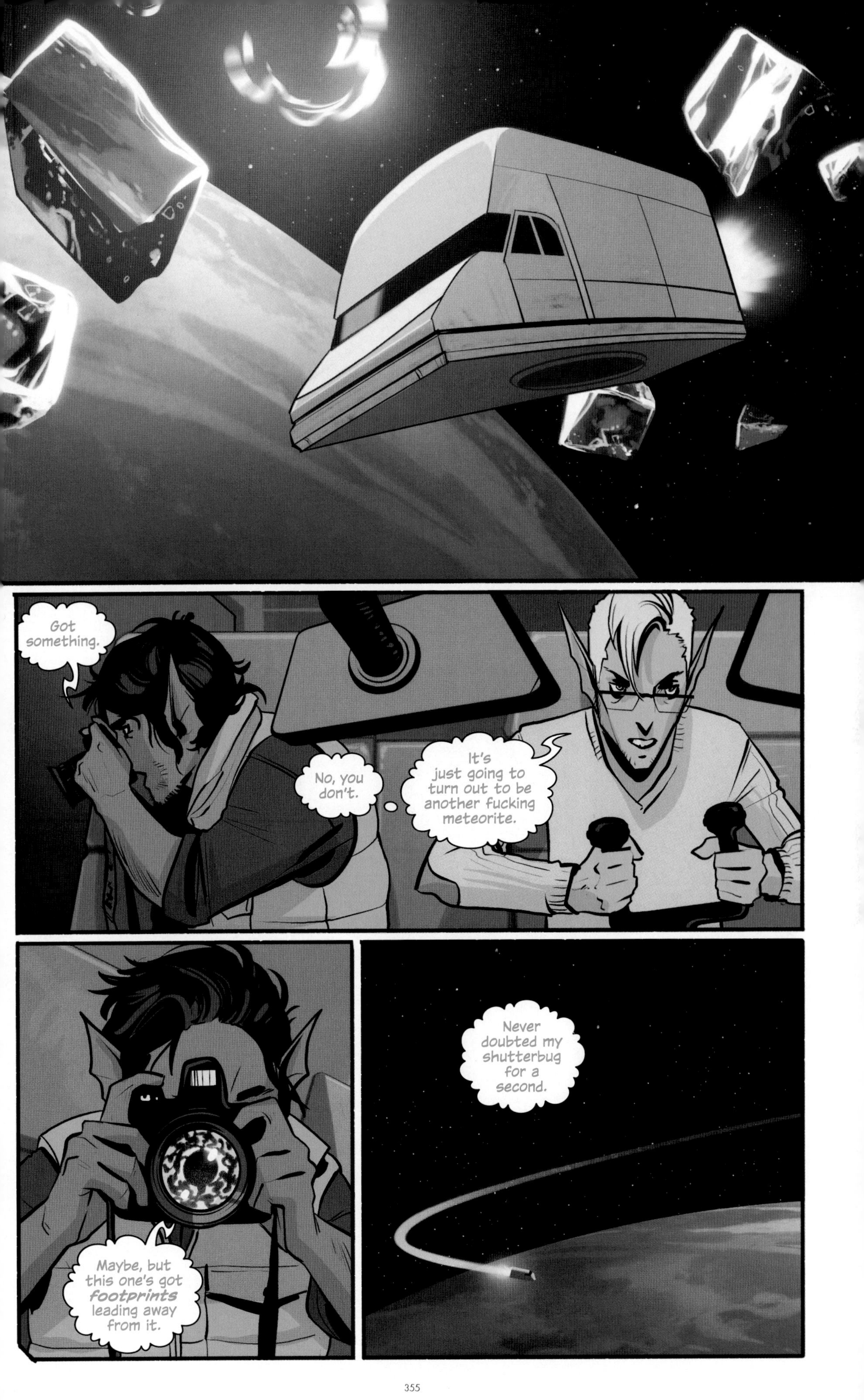
Got something.
No, you don't.
It's just going to turn out to be another fucking meteorite.
Maybe, but this one's got **footprints** leading away from it.
Never doubted my shutterbug for a second.

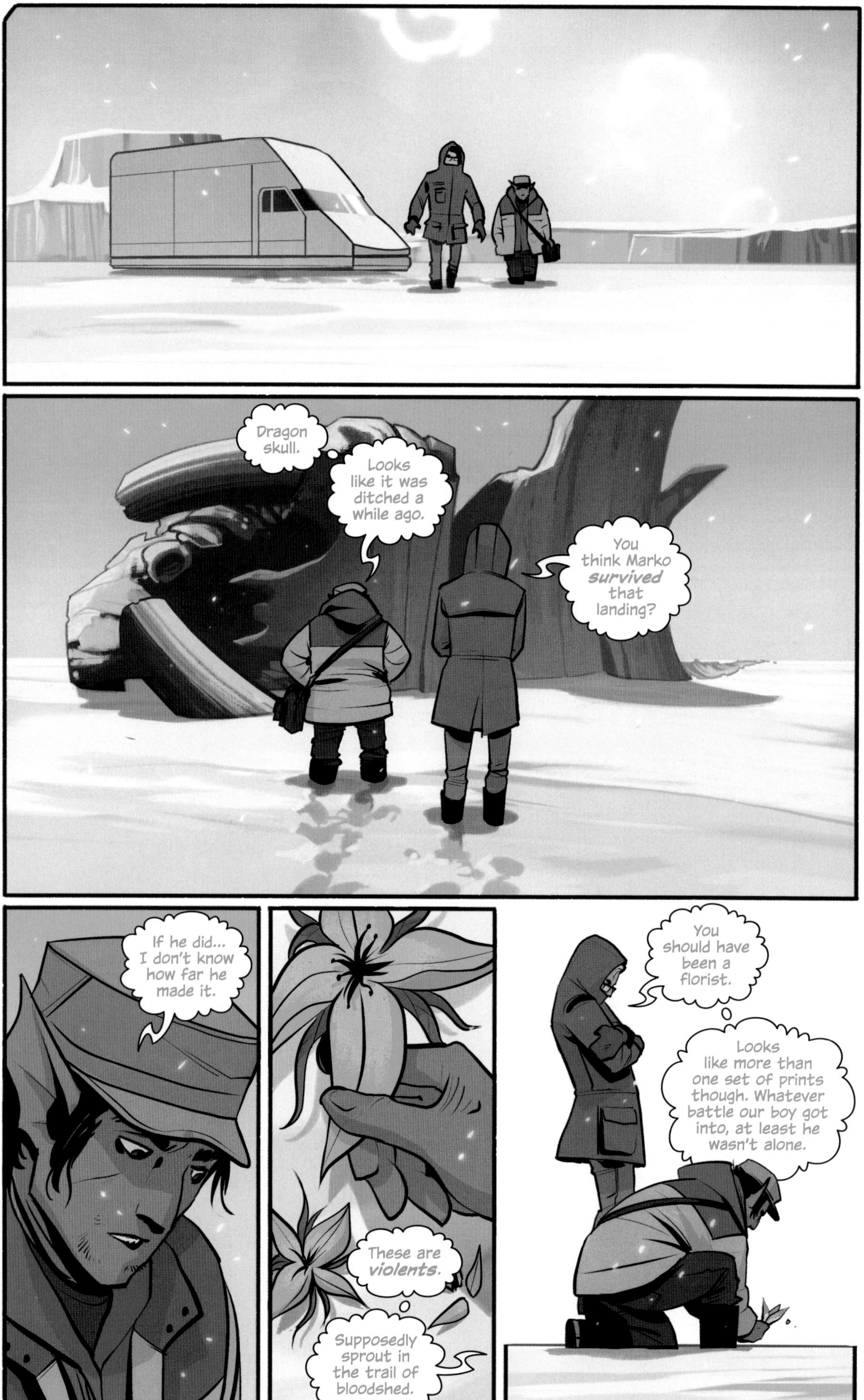

Dragon skull.
Looks like it was ditched a while ago.
You think Marko *survived* that landing?
If he did... I don't know how far he made it.
These are *violents*.
Supposedly sprout in the trail of bloodshed.
You should have been a florist.
Looks like more than one set of prints though. Whatever battle our boy got into, at least he wasn't alone.

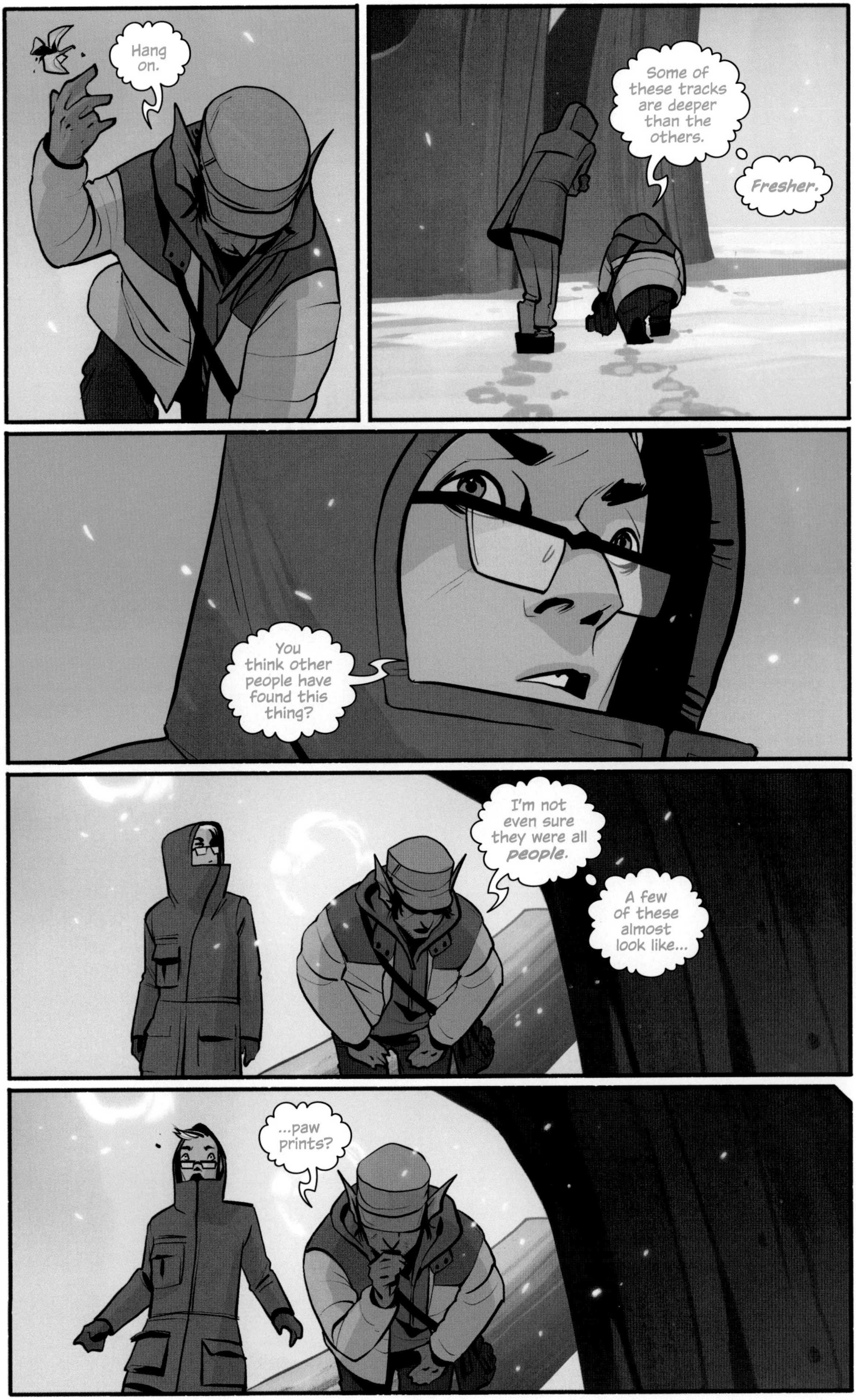
Hang on.
Some of these tracks are deeper than the others.
Fresher.
You think other people have found this thing?
I'm not even sure they were all people.
A few of these almost look like...
...paw prints?

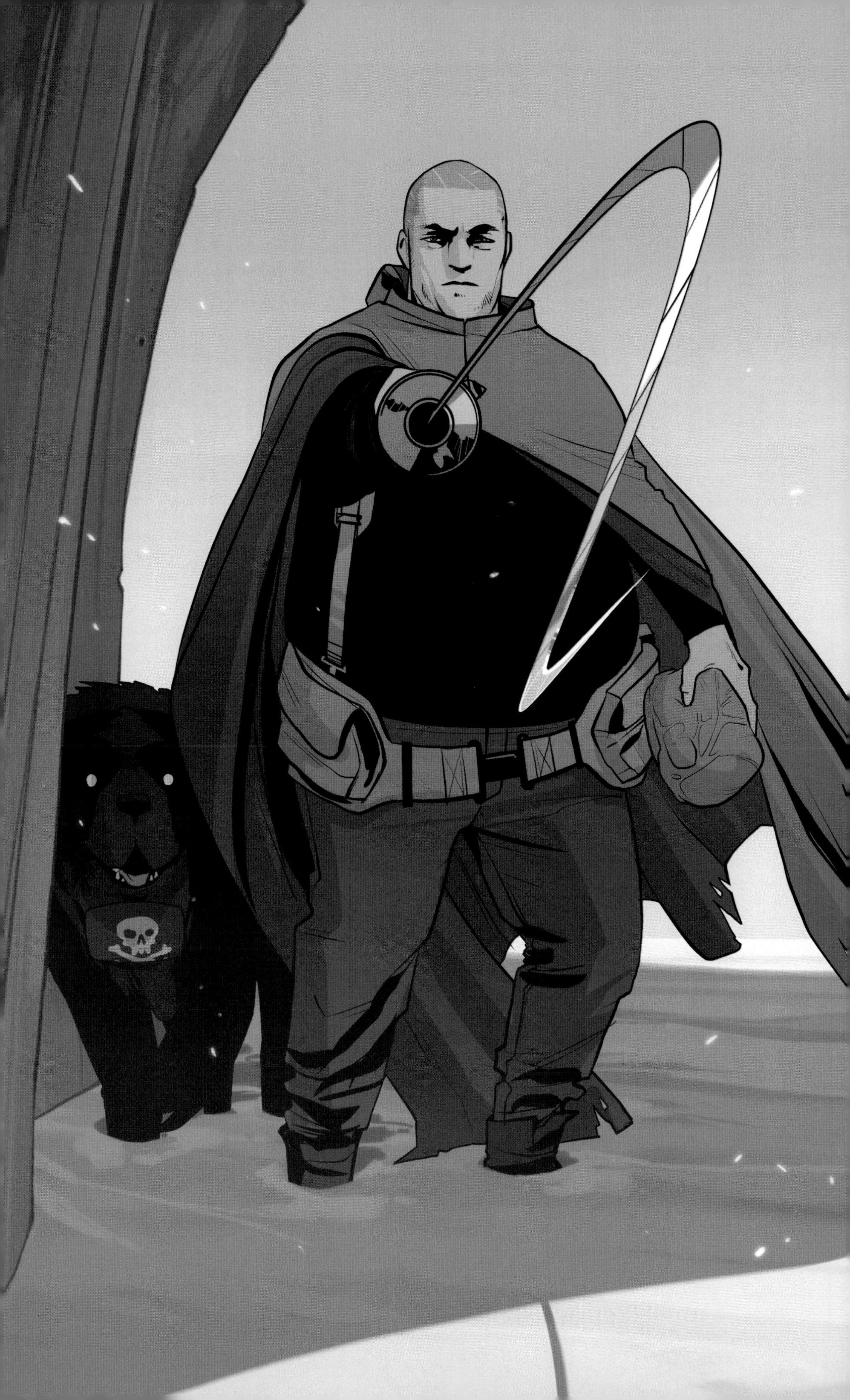

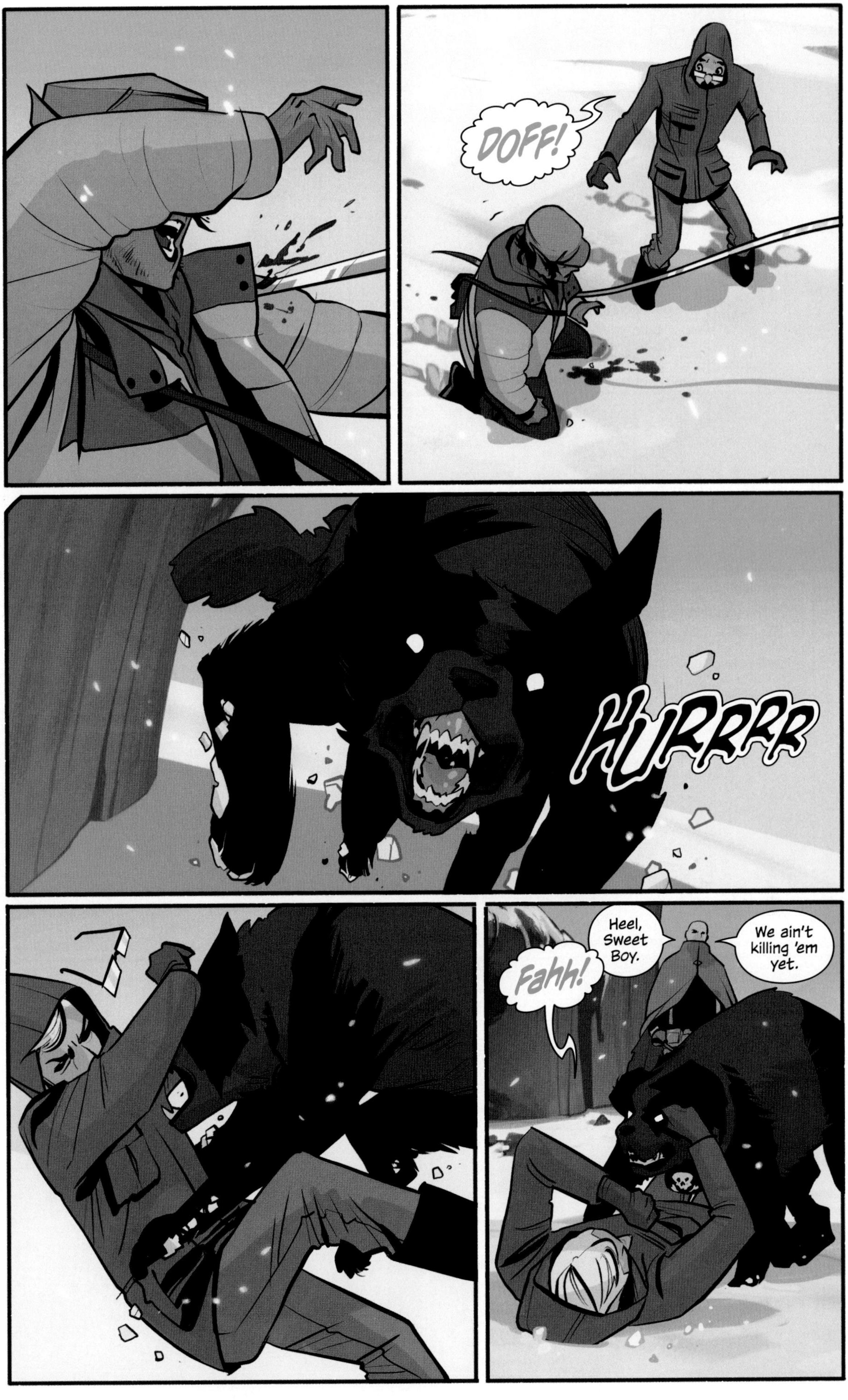
DOFF!
HURRRR
Fahh!
Heel, Sweet Boy.
We ain't killing 'em yet.

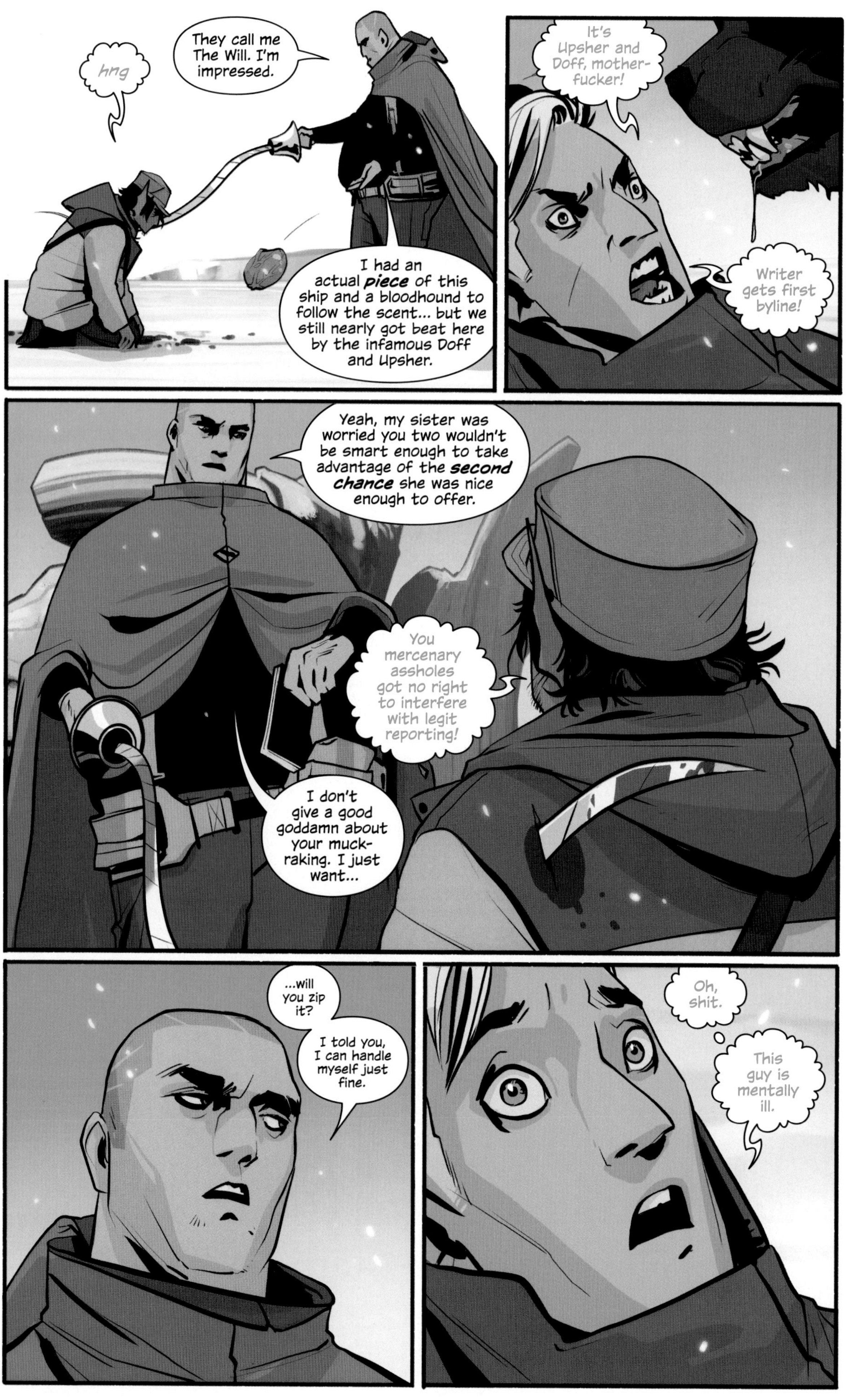

hng
They call me The Will. I'm impressed.
I had an actual piece of this ship and a bloodhound to follow the scent... but we still nearly got beat here by the infamous Doff and Upsher.
It's Upsher and Doff, mother-fucker!
Writer gets first byline!
Yeah, my sister was worried you two wouldn't be smart enough to take advantage of the second chance she was nice enough to offer.
You mercenary assholes got no right to interfere with legit reporting!
I don't give a good goddamn about your muck-raking. I just want...
...will you zip it?
I told you, I can handle myself just fine.
Oh, shit.
This guy is mentally ill.

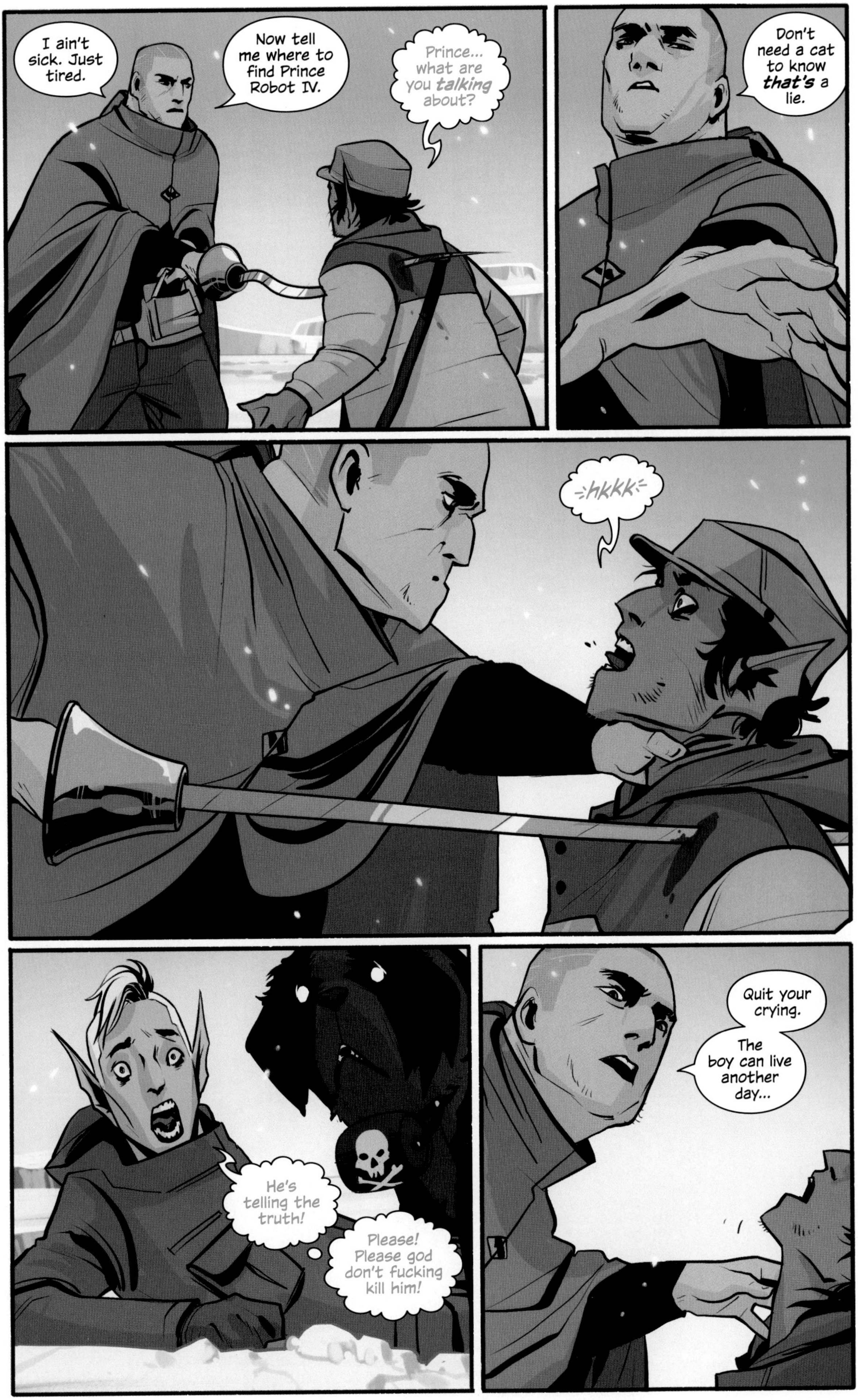
I ain't sick. Just tired.
Now tell me where to find Prince Robot IV.
Prince... what are you *talking* about?
Don't need a cat to know *that's* a lie.
hkkk
He's telling the truth!
Please! Please god don't fucking kill him!
Quit your crying.
The boy can live another day...

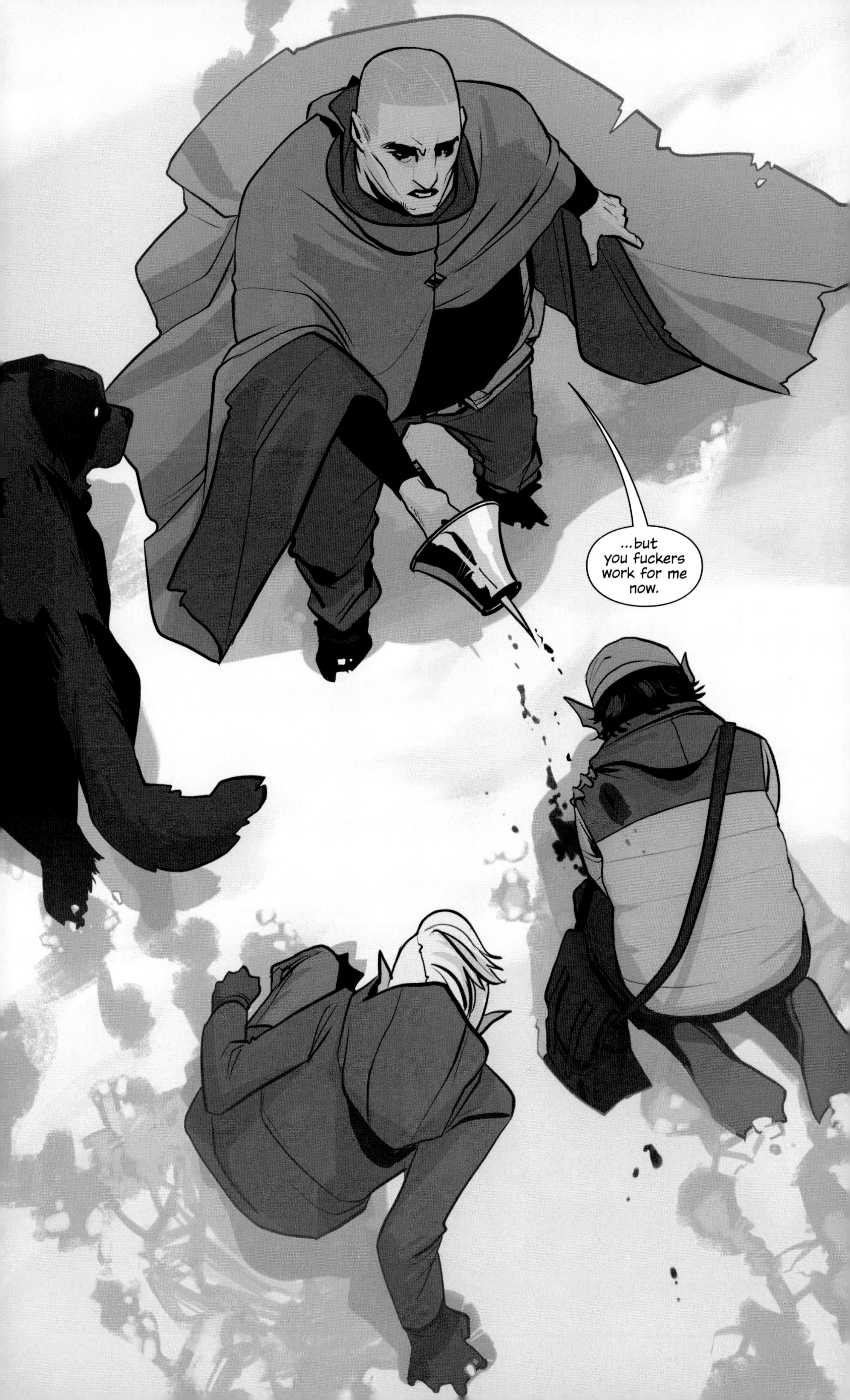
...but you fuckers work for me now.

end chapter thirty-three

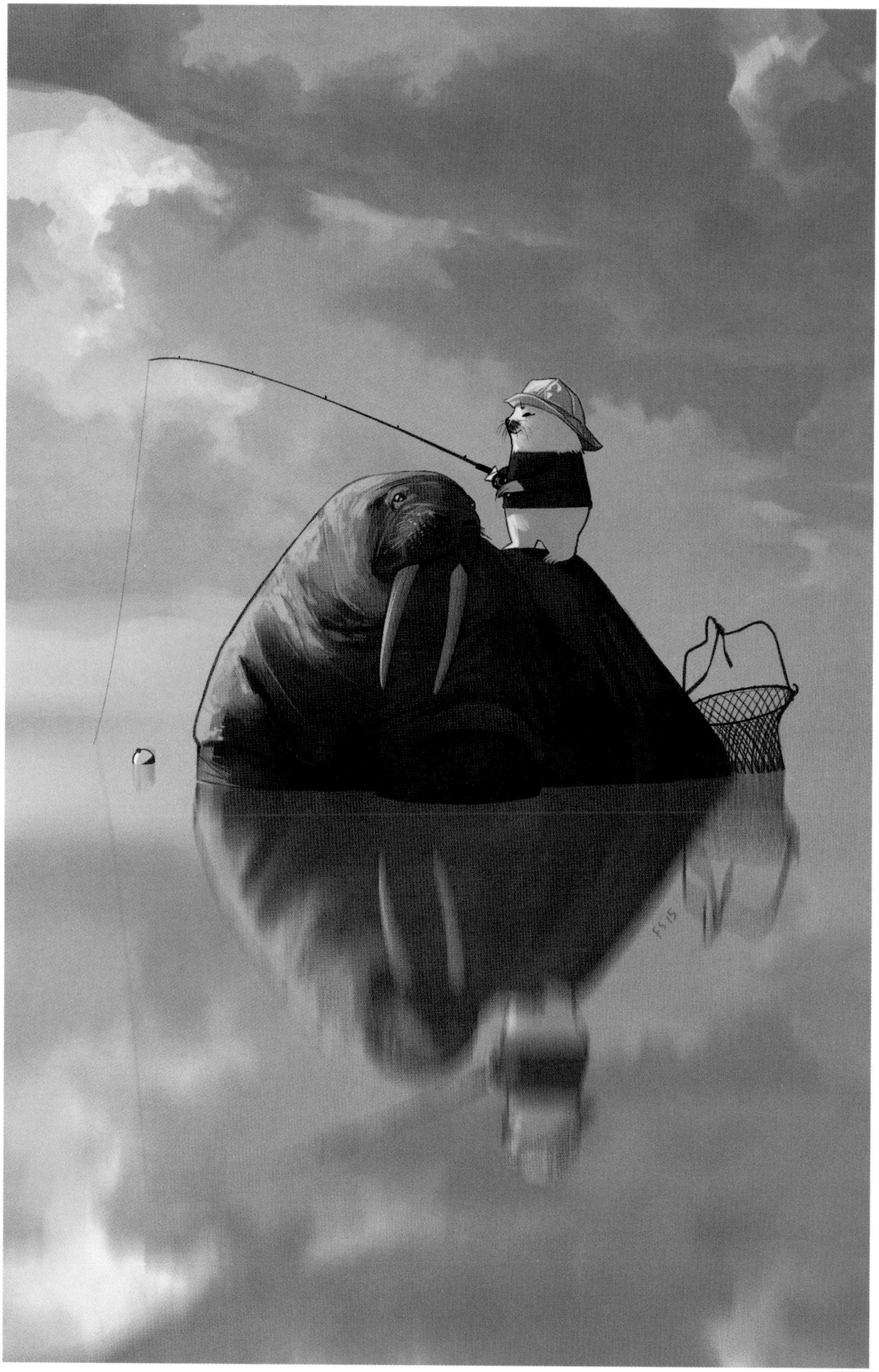

CHAPTER

THIRTY-FOUR

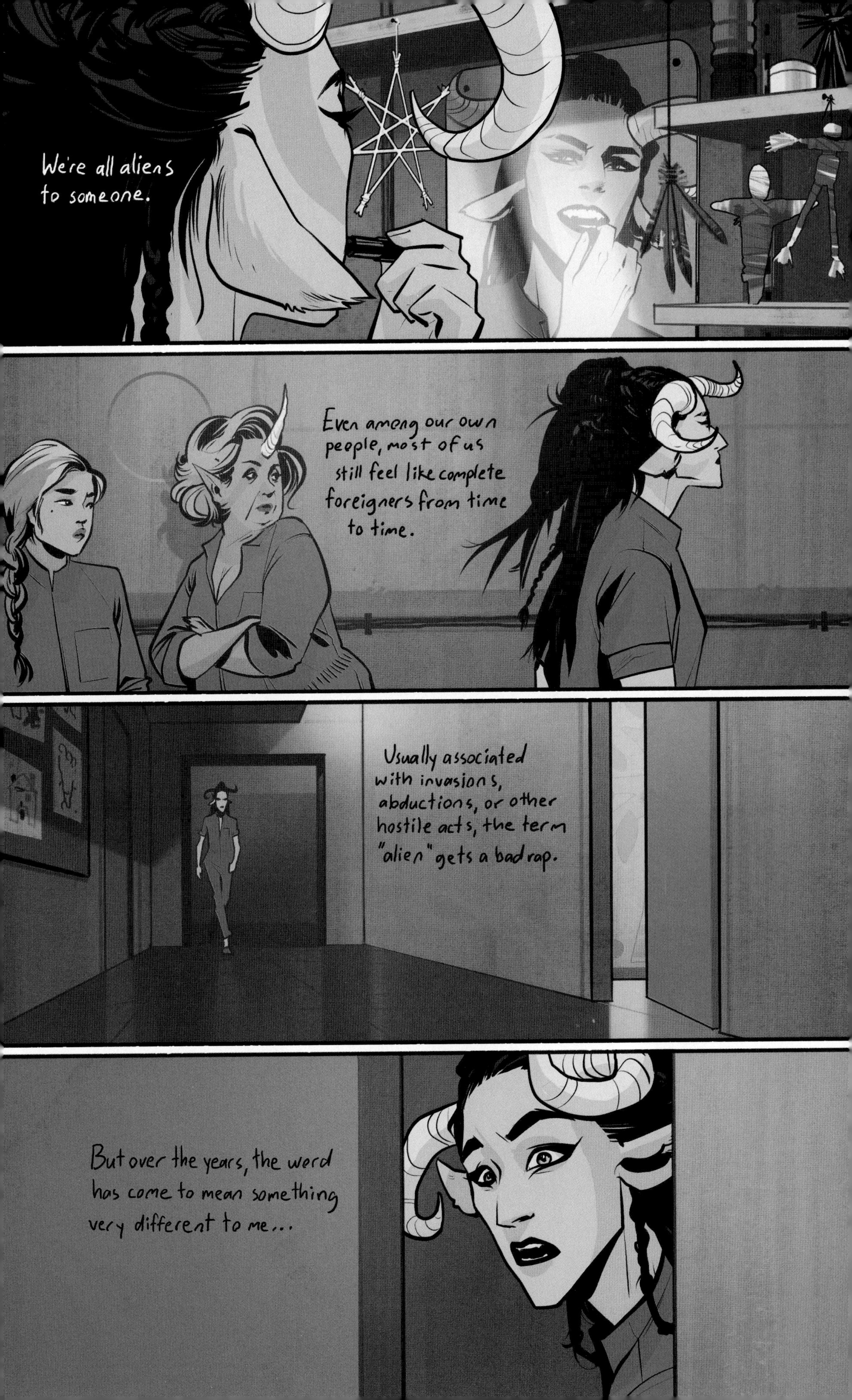
We're all aliens to someone.
Even among our own people, most of us still feel like complete foreigners from time to time.
Usually associated with invasions, abductions, or other hostile acts, the term "alien" gets a bad rap.
But over the years, the word has come to mean something very different to me...

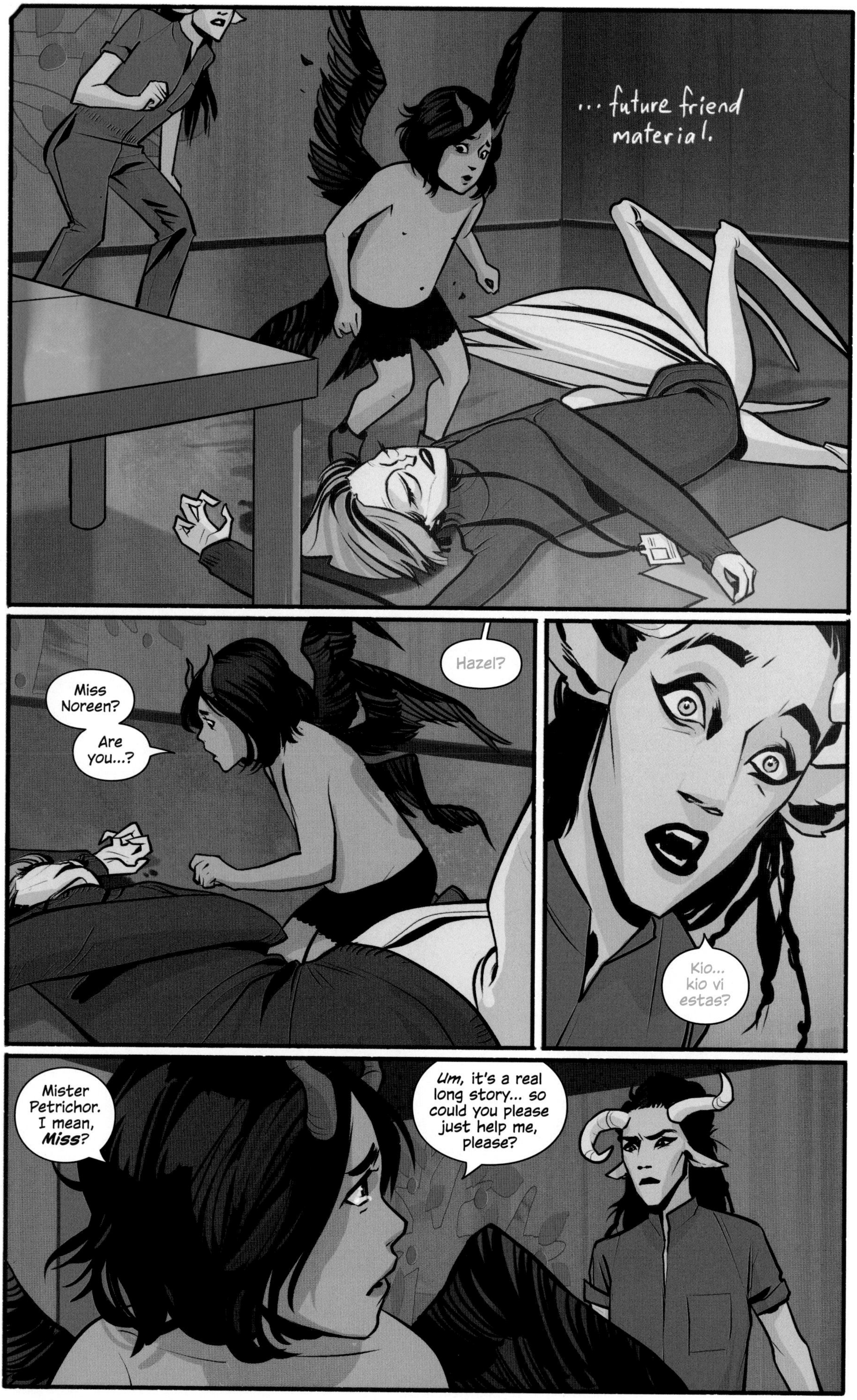

...future friend material.
Hazel?
Miss Noreen?
Are you...?
Kio... kio vi estas?
Mister Petrichor. I mean, *Miss*?
Um, it's a real long story... so could you please just help me, please?

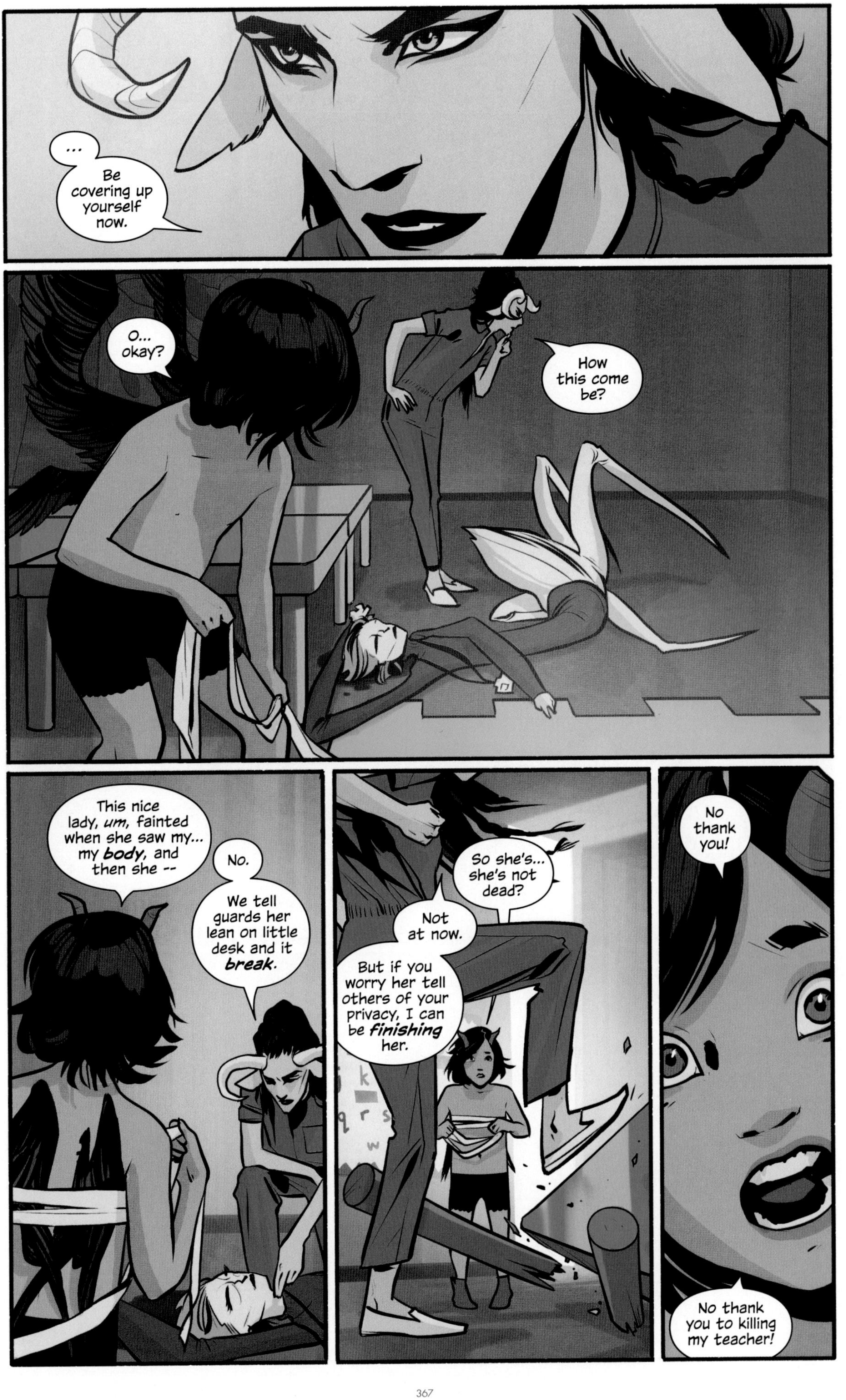
...
Be covering up yourself now.
O... okay?
How this come be?
This nice lady, *um*, fainted when she saw my... my *body*, and then she --
No.
We tell guards her lean on little desk and it *break*.
So she's... she's not dead?
Not at now.
But if you worry her tell others of your privacy, I can be *finishing* her.
No thank you!
No thank you to killing my teacher!

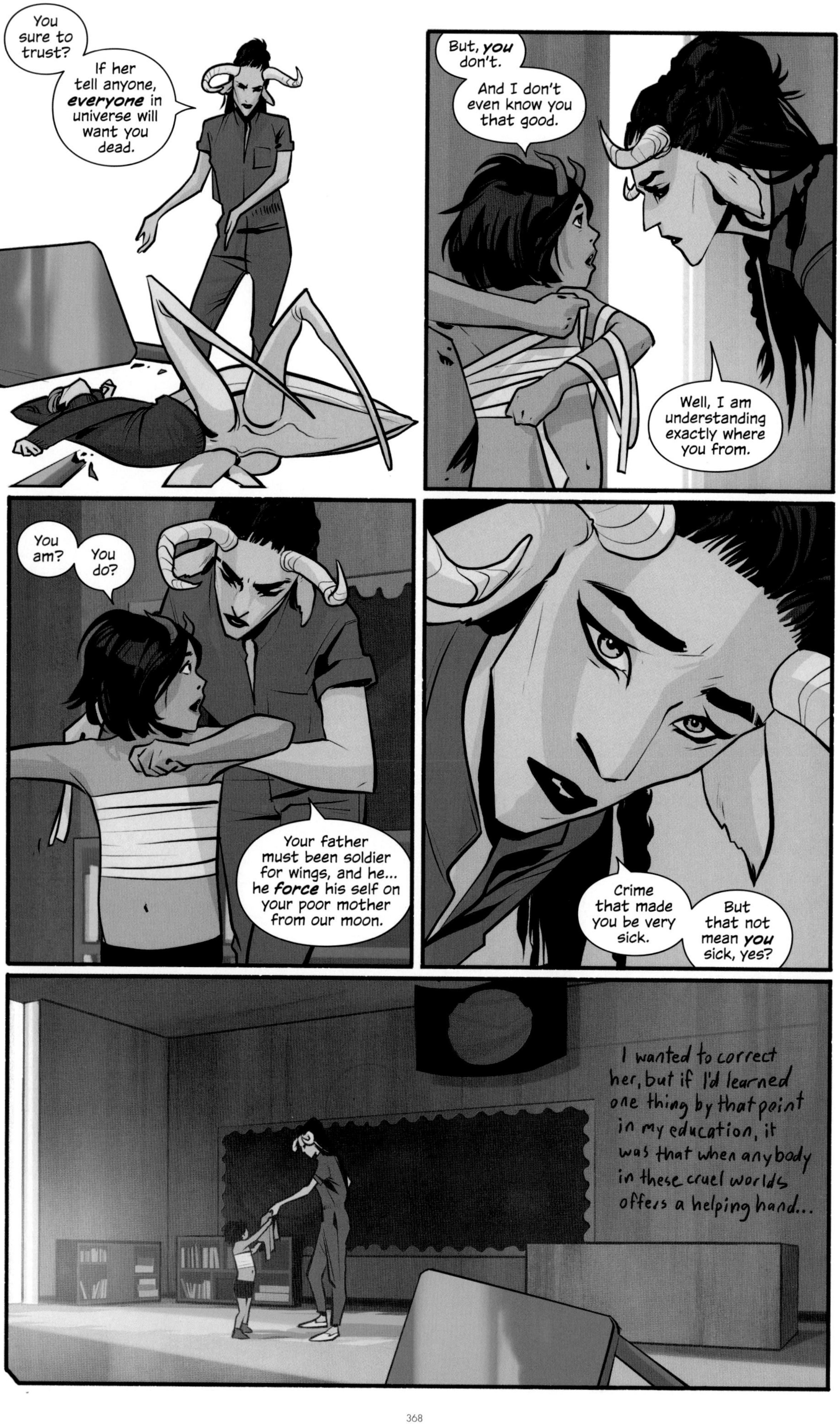
You sure to trust?
If her tell anyone, **everyone** in universe will want you dead.
But, **you** don't.
And I don't even know you that good.
Well, I am understanding exactly where you from.
You am?
You do?
Your father must been soldier for wings, and he... he **force** his self on your poor mother from our moon.
Crime that made you be very sick.
But that not mean **you** sick, yes?
I wanted to correct her, but if I'd learned one thing by that point in my education, it was that when anybody in these cruel worlds offers a helping hand...

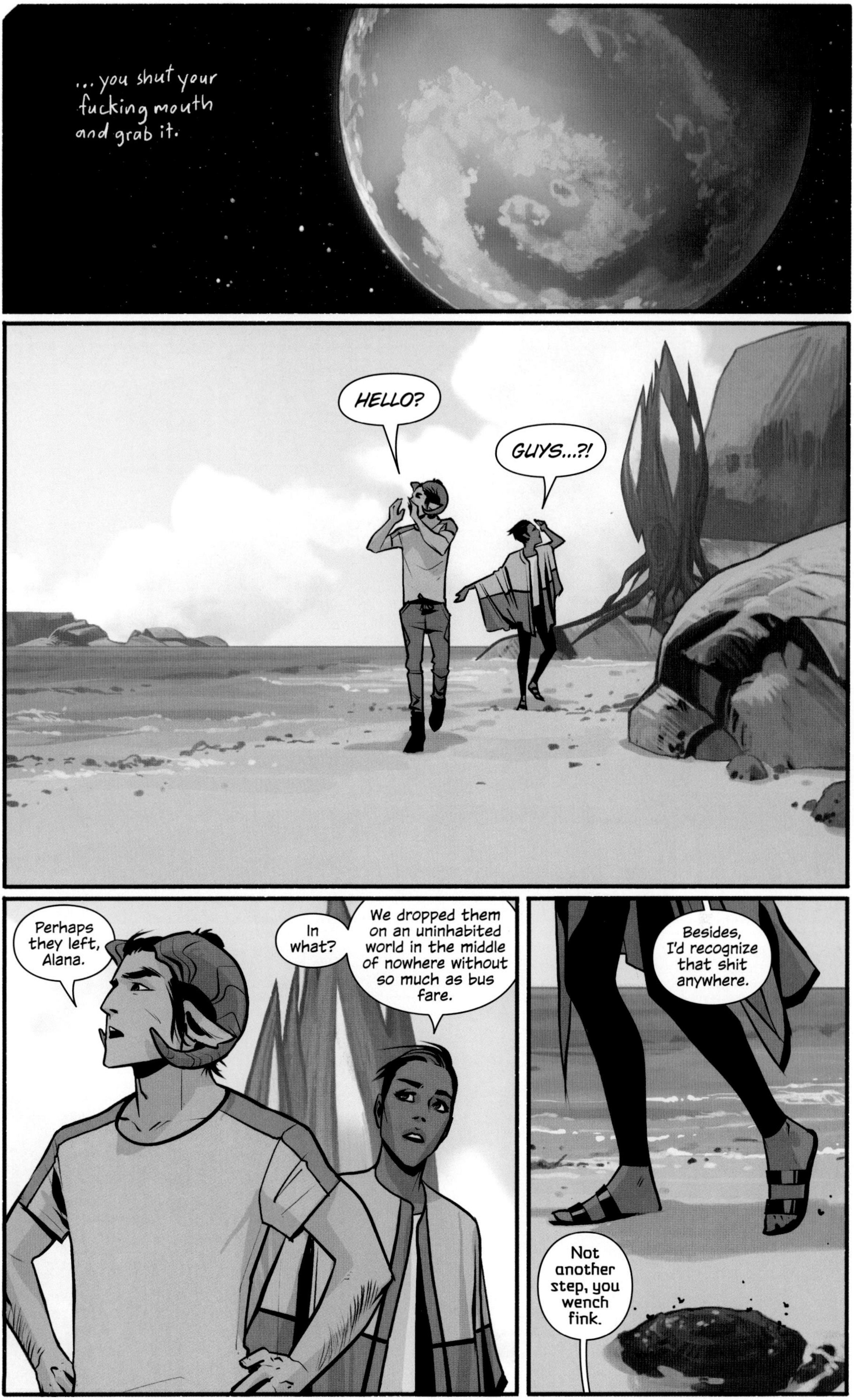
...you shut your fucking mouth and grab it.
HELLO?
GUYS...?!
Perhaps they left, Alana.
In what?
We dropped them on an uninhabited world in the middle of nowhere without so much as bus fare.
Besides, I'd recognize that shit anywhere.
Not another step, you wench fink.

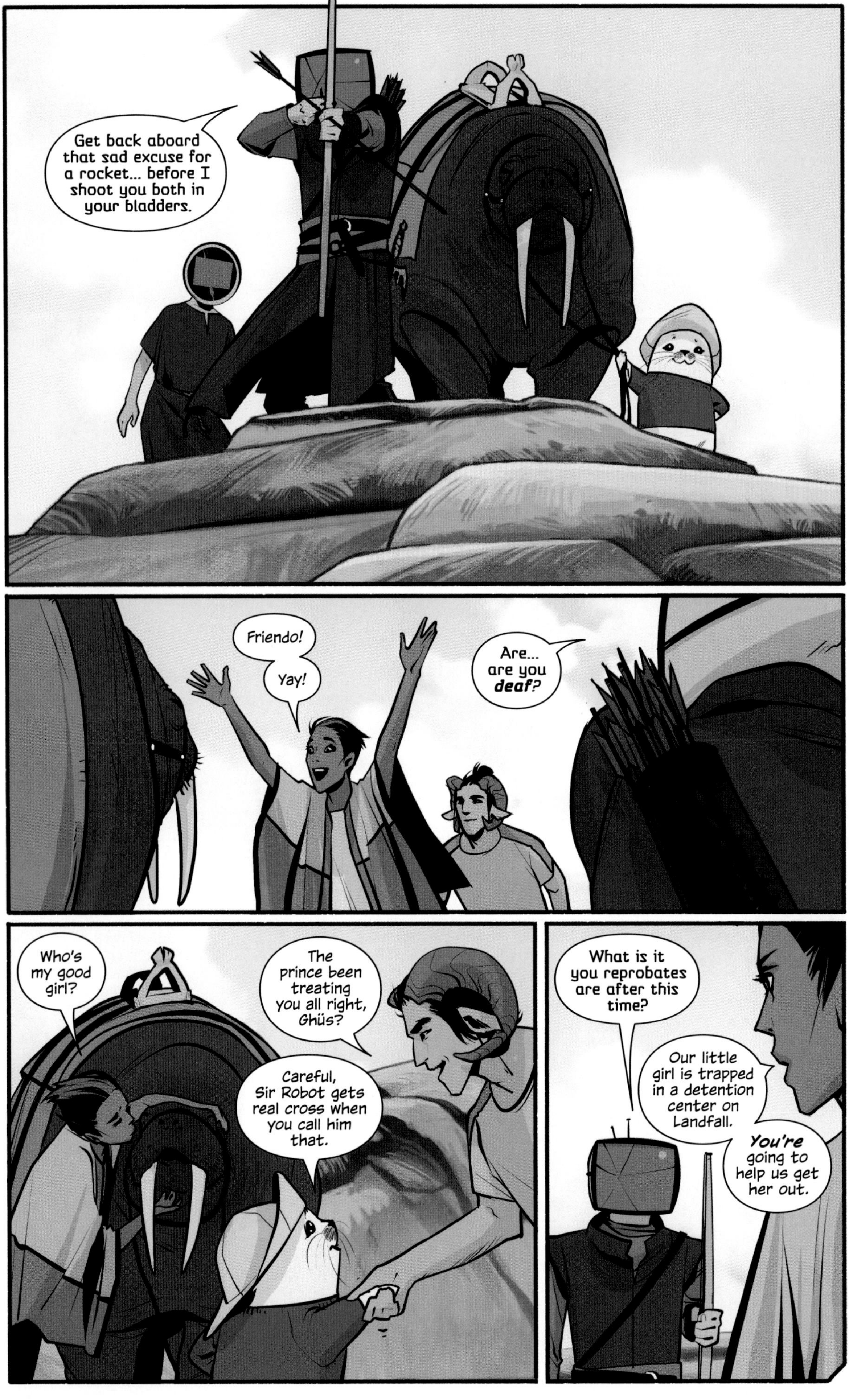

Get back aboard that sad excuse for a rocket... before I shoot you both in your bladders.
Friendo!
Yay!
Are... are you ***deaf***?
Who's my good girl?
The prince been treating you all right, Ghüs?
Careful, Sir Robot gets real cross when you call him that.
What is it you reprobates are after this time?
Our little girl is trapped in a detention center on Landfall.
You're going to help us get her out.

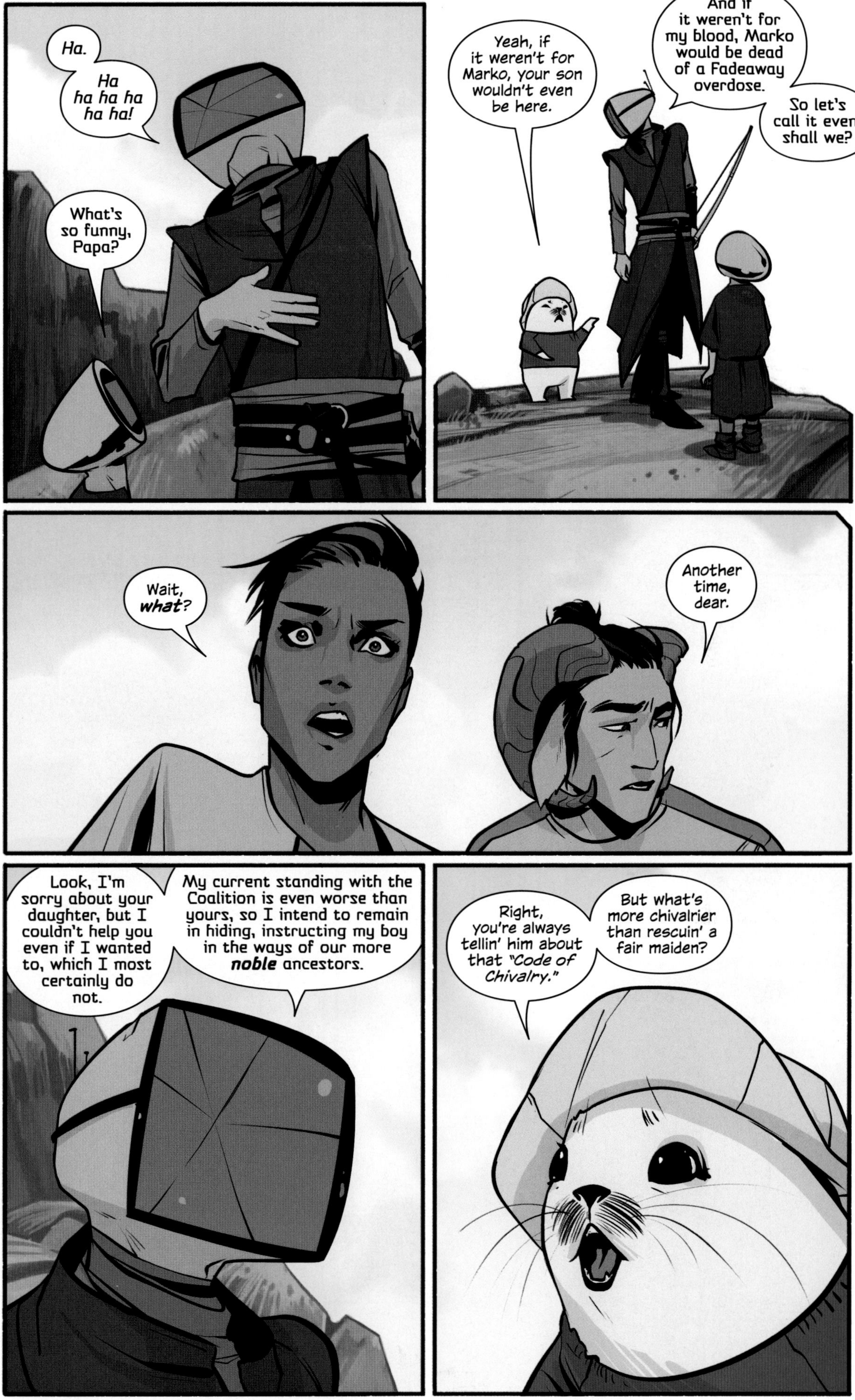
Ha.
Ha ha ha ha ha ha!
What's so funny, Papa?
Yeah, if it weren't for Marko, your son wouldn't even be here.
And if it weren't for my blood, Marko would be dead of a Fadeaway overdose.
So let's call it even, shall we?
Wait, *what*?
Another time, dear.
Look, I'm sorry about your daughter, but I couldn't help you even if I wanted to, which I most certainly do not.
My current standing with the Coalition is even worse than yours, so I intend to remain in hiding, instructing my boy in the ways of our more **noble** ancestors.
Right, you're always tellin' him about that *"Code of Chivalry."*
But what's more chivalrier than rescuin' a fair maiden?

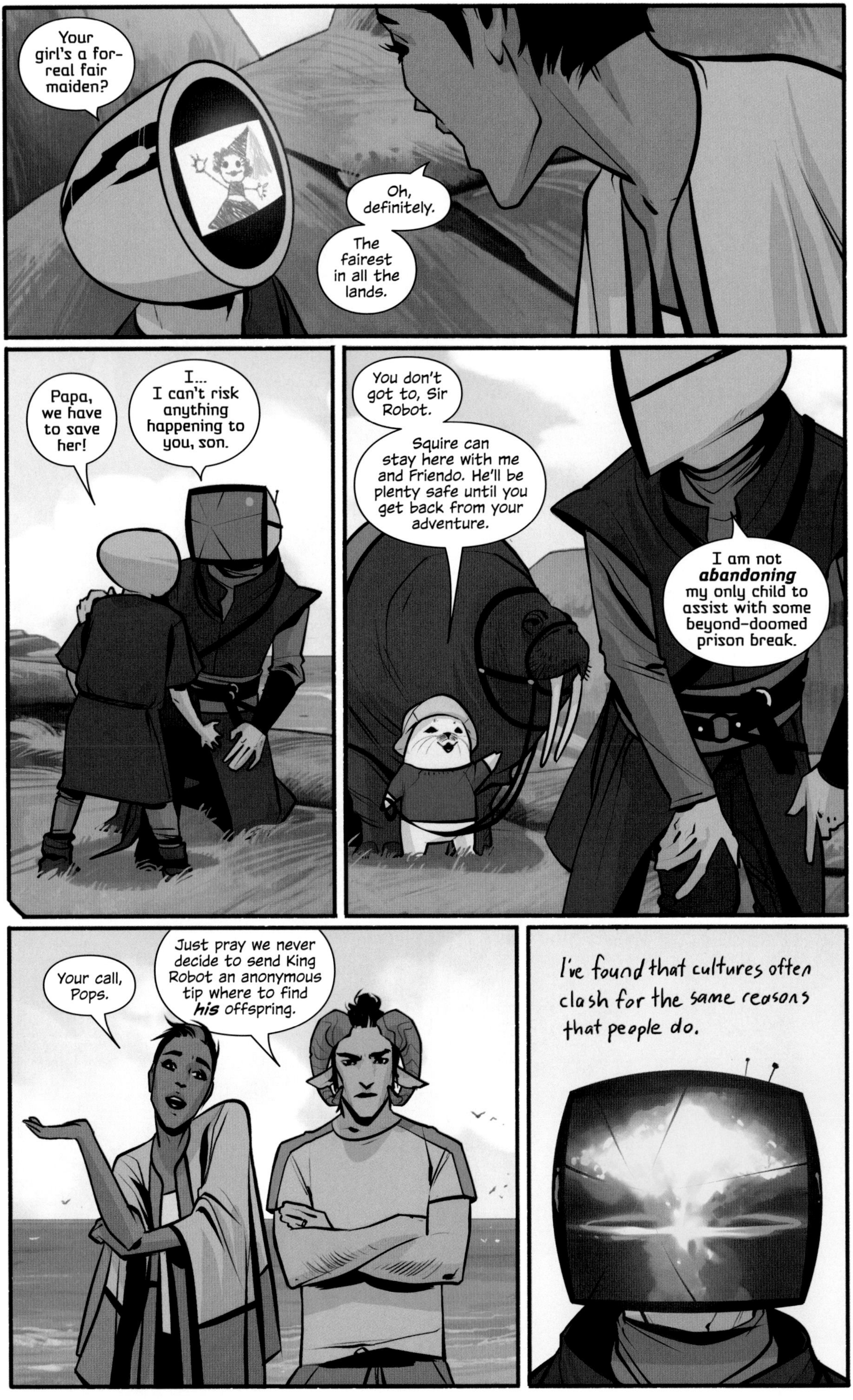
Your girl's a for-real fair maiden?
Oh, definitely.
The fairest in all the lands.
Papa, we have to save her!
I... I can't risk anything happening to you, son.
You don't got to, Sir Robot.
Squire can stay here with me and Friendo. He'll be plenty safe until you get back from your adventure.
I am not **abandoning** my only child to assist with some beyond-doomed prison break.
Your call, Pops.
Just pray we never decide to send King Robot an anonymous tip where to find **his** offspring.
I've found that cultures often clash for the same reasons that people do.

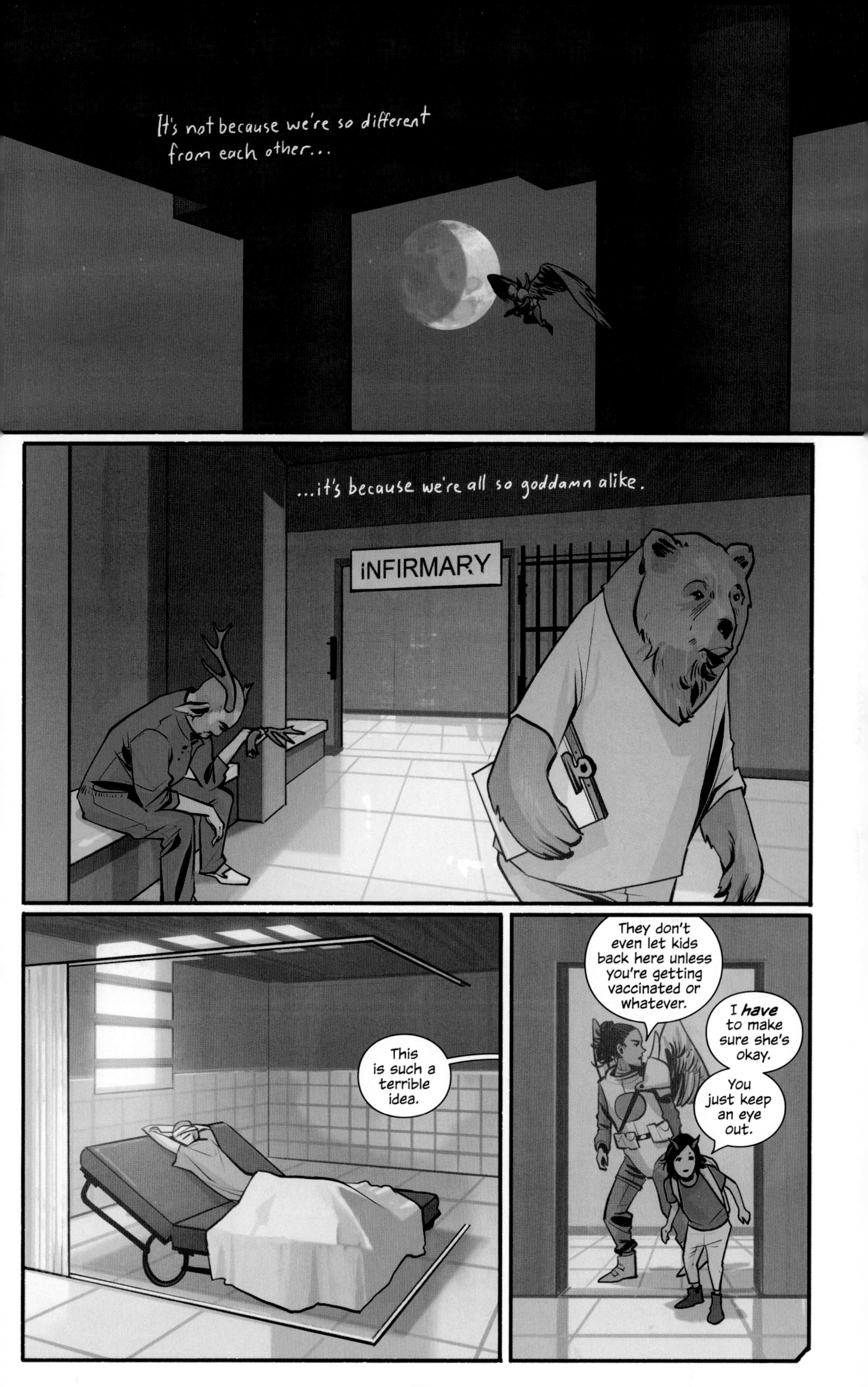

It's not because we're so different from each other...
...it's because we're all so goddamn alike.
INFIRMARY
This is such a terrible idea.
They don't even let kids back here unless you're getting vaccinated or whatever.
I *have* to make sure she's okay.
You just keep an eye out.

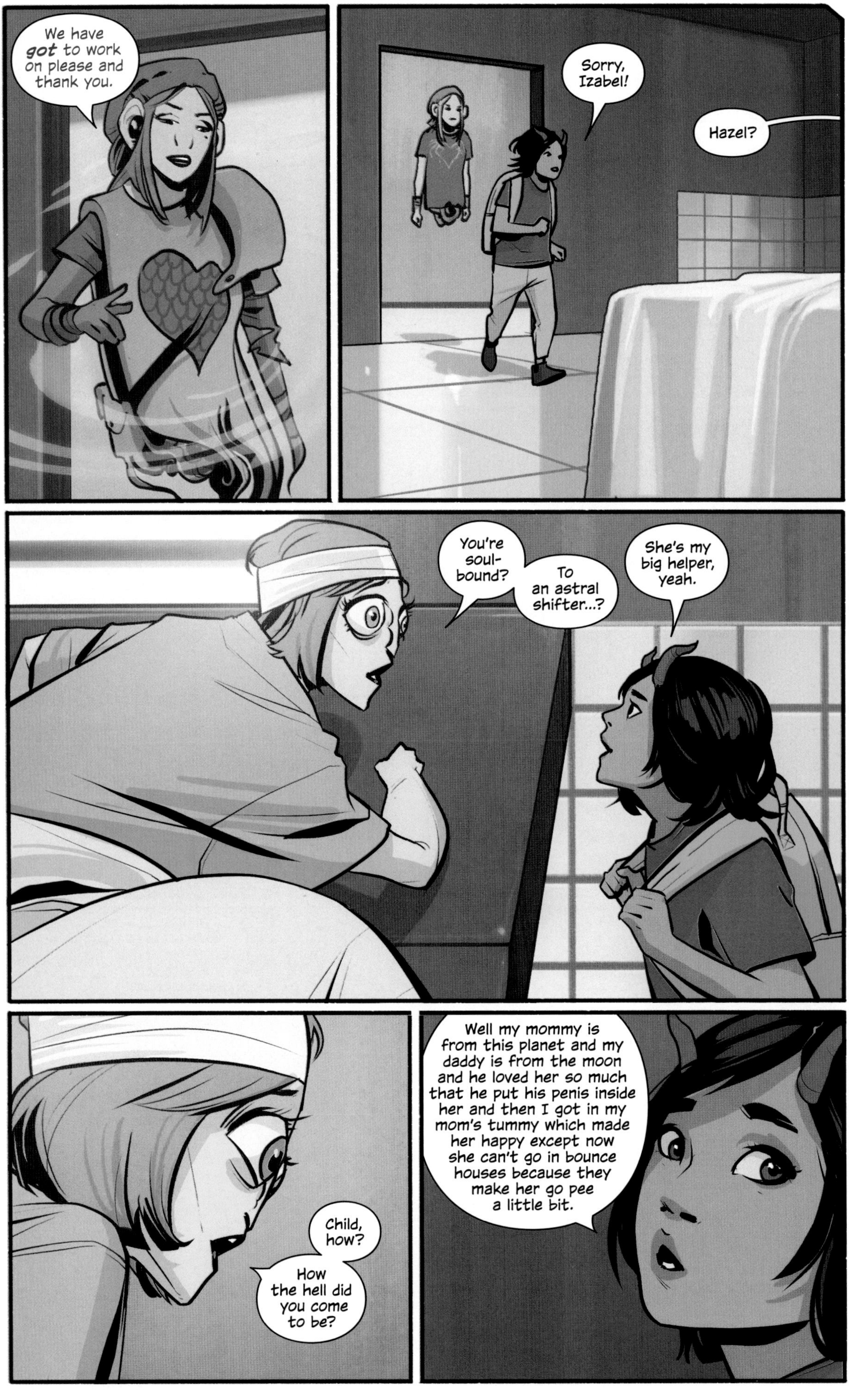
We have got to work on please and thank you.
Sorry, Izabel!
Hazel?
You're soul-bound?
To an astral shifter...?
She's my big helper, yeah.
Child, how?
How the hell did you come to be?
Well my mommy is from this planet and my daddy is from the moon and he loved her so much that he put his penis inside her and then I got in my mom's tummy which made her happy except now she can't go in bounce houses because they make her go pee a little bit.

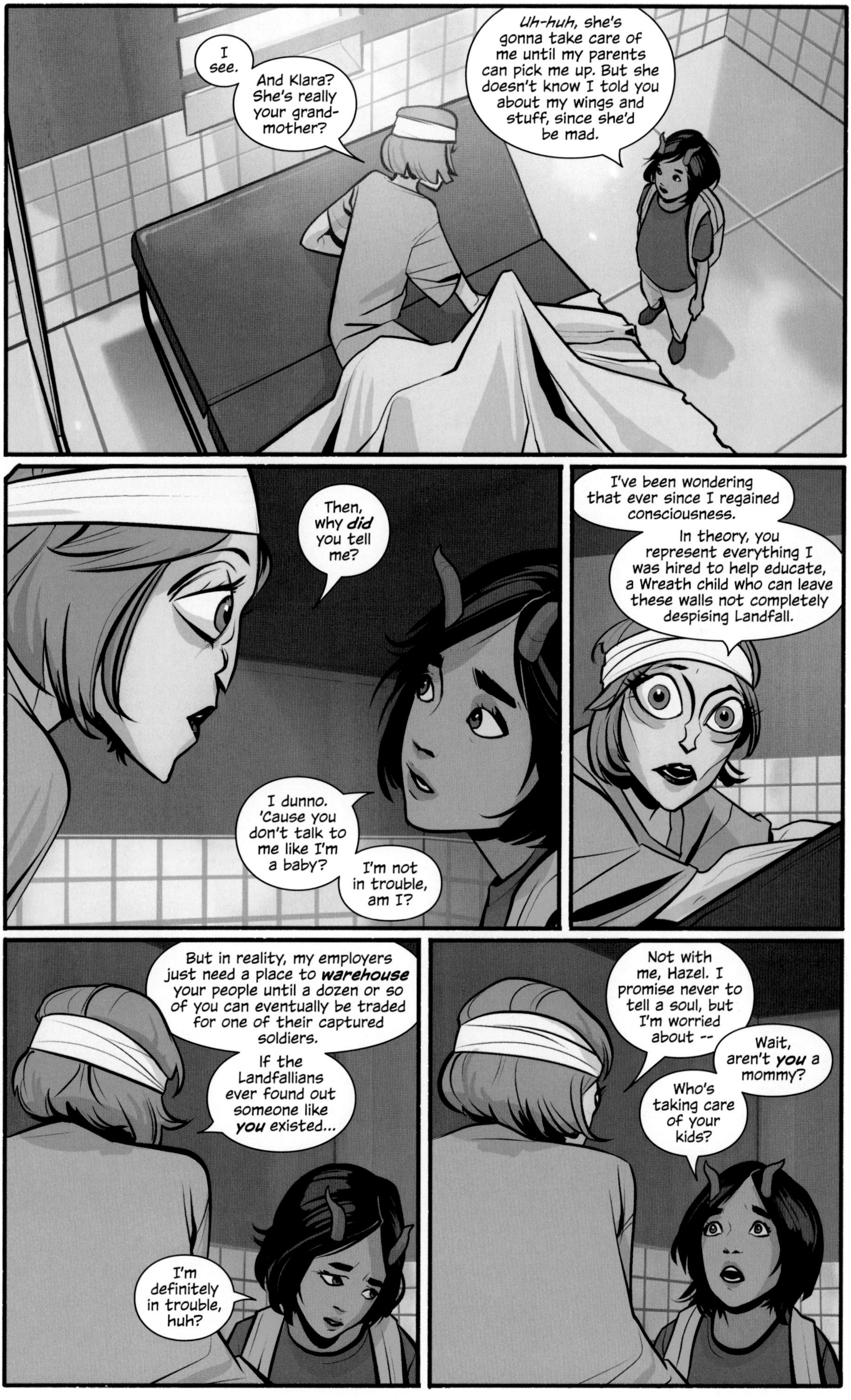

I see.
And Klara? She's really your grand-mother?
Uh-huh, she's gonna take care of me until my parents can pick me up. But she doesn't know I told you about my wings and stuff, since she'd be mad.
Then, why **did** you tell me?
I dunno. 'Cause you don't talk to me like I'm a baby?
I'm not in trouble, am I?
I've been wondering that ever since I regained consciousness.
In theory, you represent everything I was hired to help educate, a Wreath child who can leave these walls not completely despising Landfall.
But in reality, my employers just need a place to **warehouse** your people until a dozen or so of you can eventually be traded for one of their captured soldiers.
If the Landfallians ever found out someone like **you** existed...
I'm definitely in trouble, huh?
Not with me, Hazel. I promise never to tell a soul, but I'm worried about --
Wait, aren't **you** a mommy?
Who's taking care of your kids?

You're sweet to worry, but my mother-in-law is watching the boys.

The warden wants to keep me here overnight for observations... mostly to make sure I don't sue, I'm sure.

Well, I'm real sorry I made you fall down, so I brought you a present.

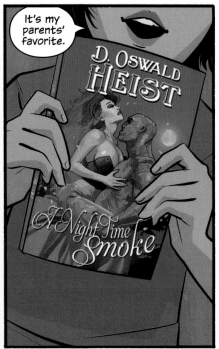

It's my parents' favorite.

D. OSWALD HEIST

A Night Time Smoke

Granny loves it, too, so she got a **bunch** for our library.

But that one's from a book swap so she said I could give it to you since it's got too many grown-up parts for me anyway.

This... this is very kind, Hazel.

I haven't read any Heist since high school.

D. OSWALD HEIST

ight Time Smoke

The man who wroted it is pretty much how my mom and dad decided to make me.

Do you think he's the best writer ever, too?

376

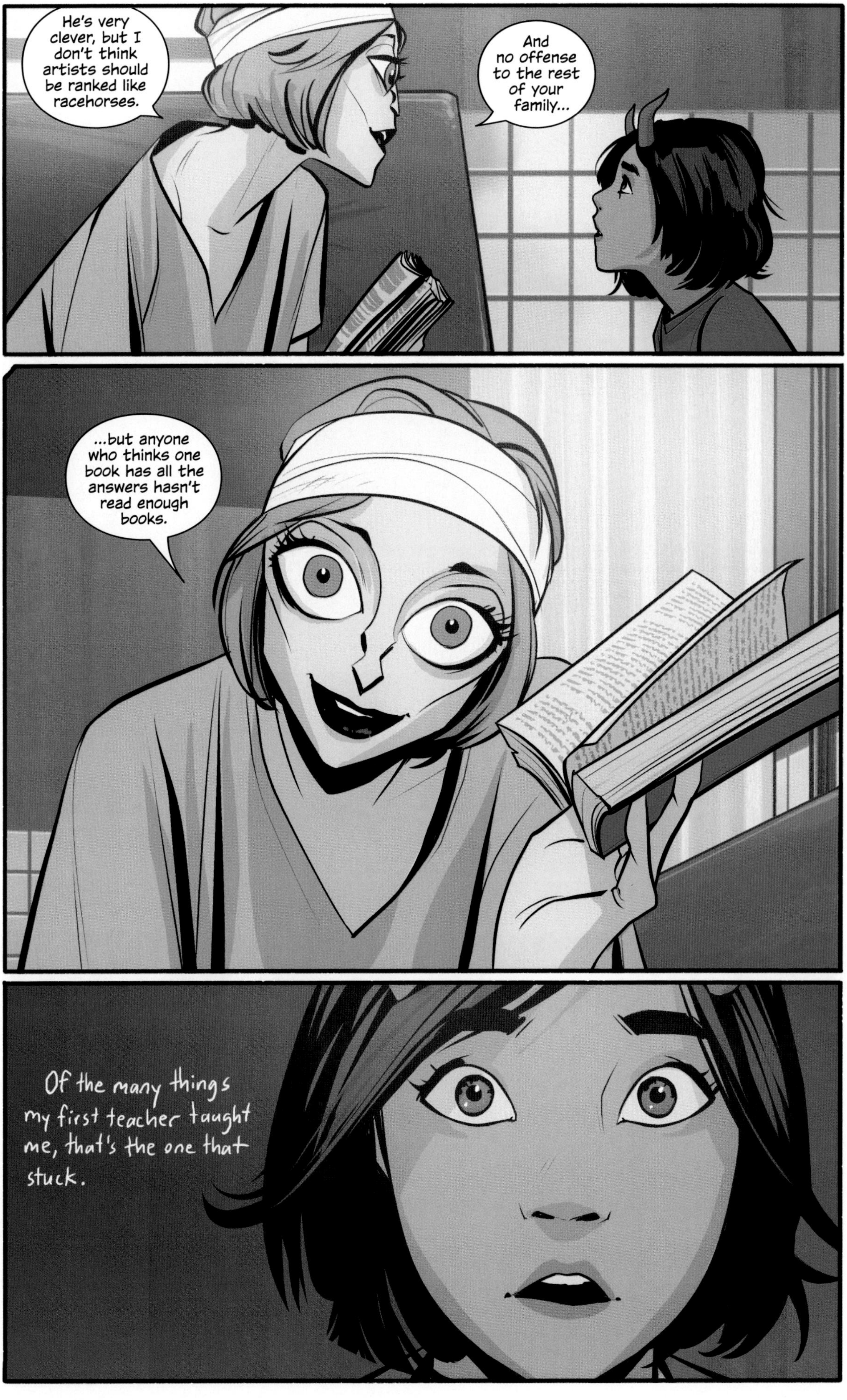
He's very clever, but I don't think artists should be ranked like racehorses.
And no offense to the rest of your family...
...but anyone who thinks one book has all the answers hasn't read enough books.
Of the many things my first teacher taught me, that's the one that stuck.

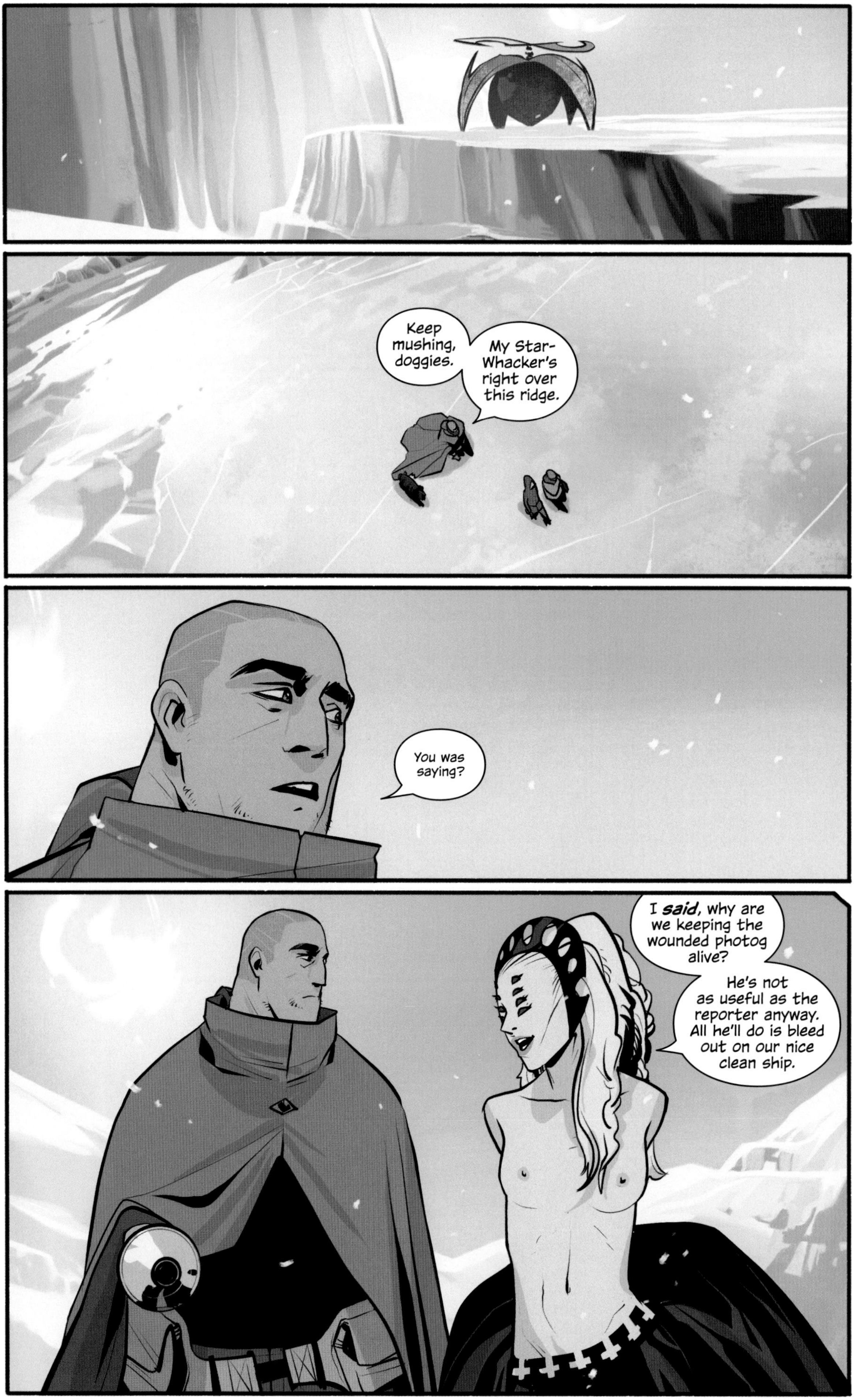

Keep mushing, doggies.
My Star-Whacker's right over this ridge.
You was saying?
I *said*, why are we keeping the wounded photog alive?
He's not as useful as the reporter anyway. All he'll do is bleed out on our nice clean ship.

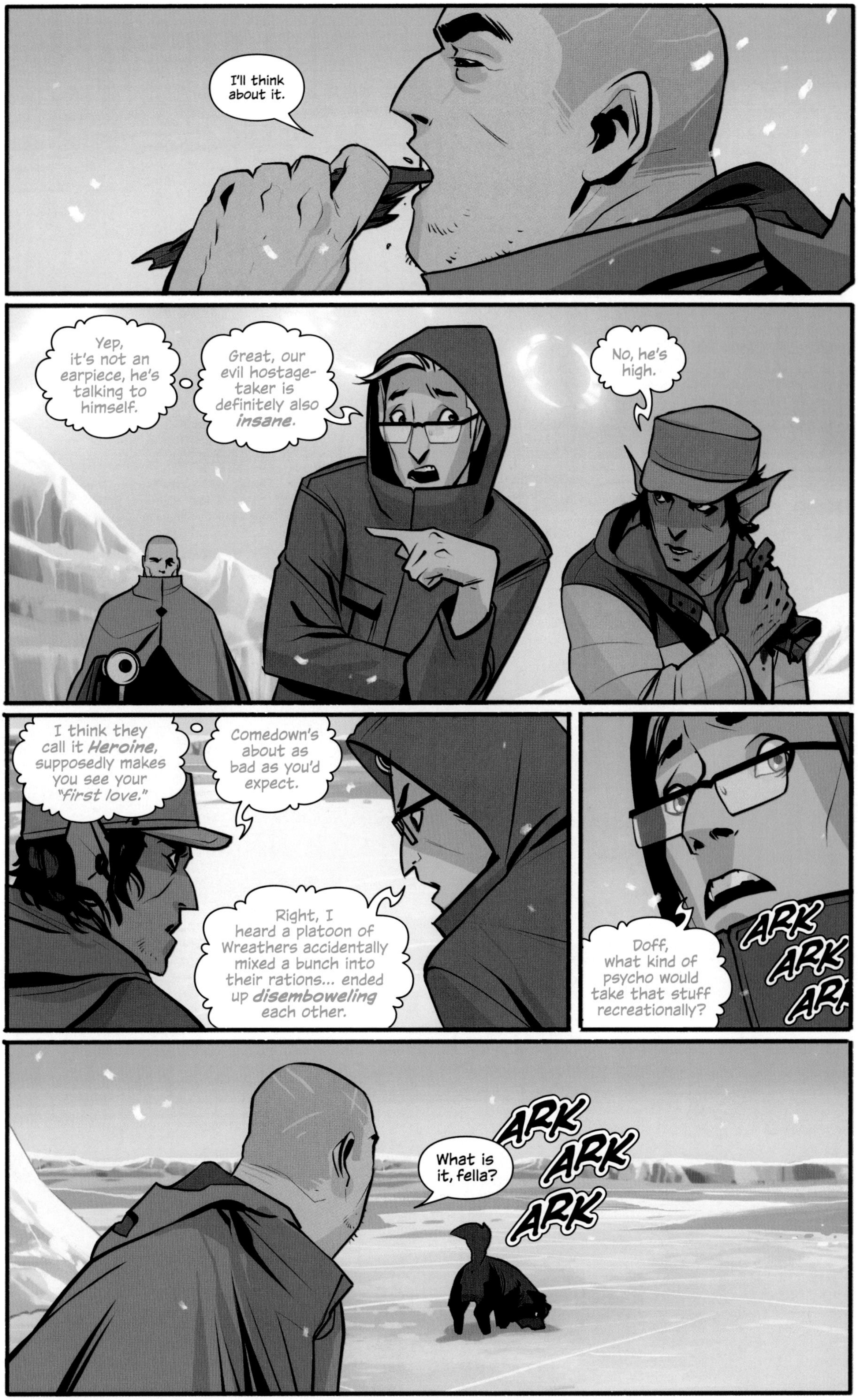
I'll think about it.
Yep, it's not an earpiece, he's talking to himself.
Great, our evil hostage-taker is definitely also *insane*.
No, he's high.
I think they call it *Heroine*, supposedly makes you see your "*first love*."
Comedown's about as bad as you'd expect.
Right, I heard a platoon of Wreathers accidentally mixed a bunch into their rations... ended up *disemboweling* each other.
Doff, what kind of psycho would take that stuff recreationally?
ARK ARK ARK
ARK ARK ARK
What is it, fella?

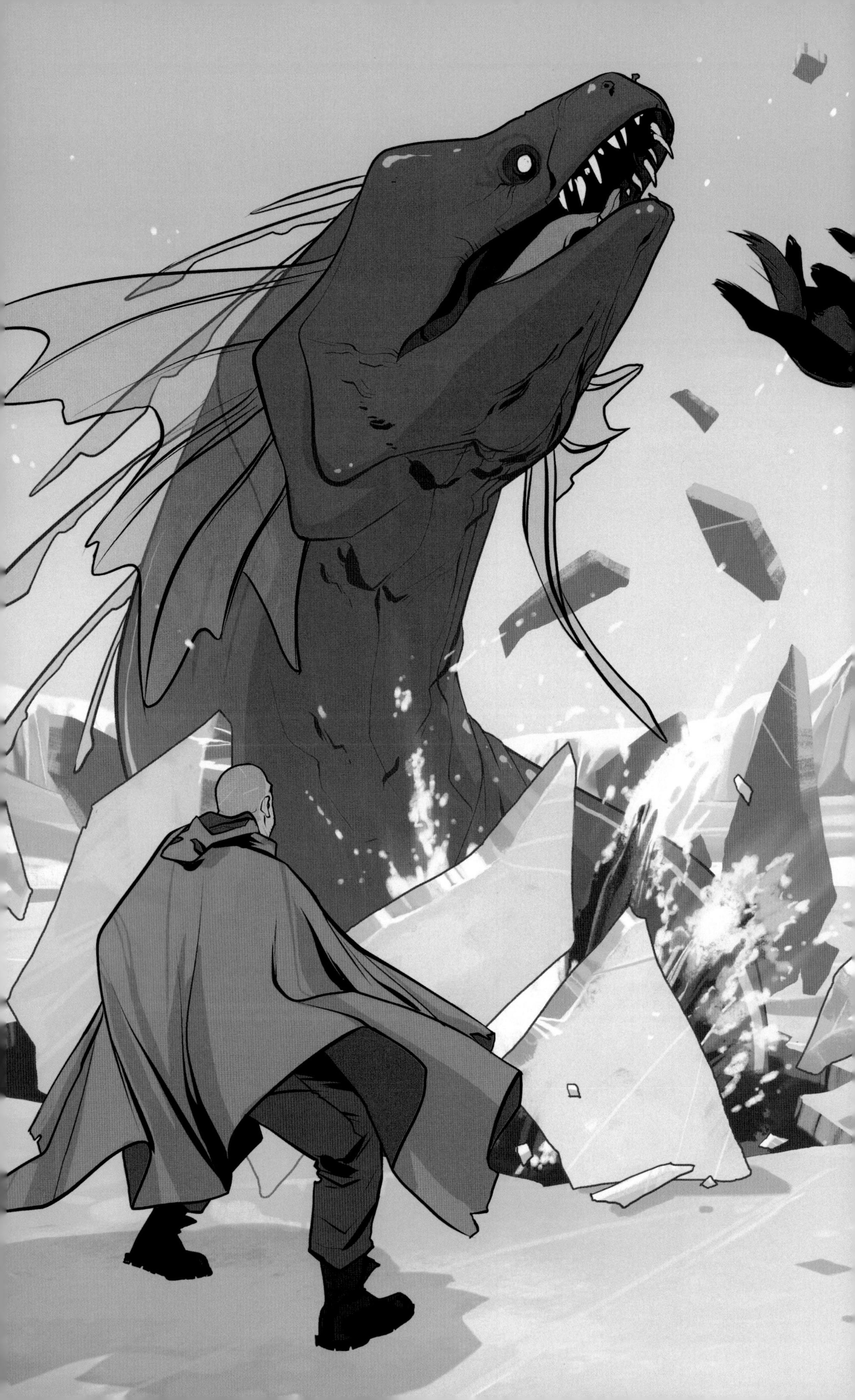

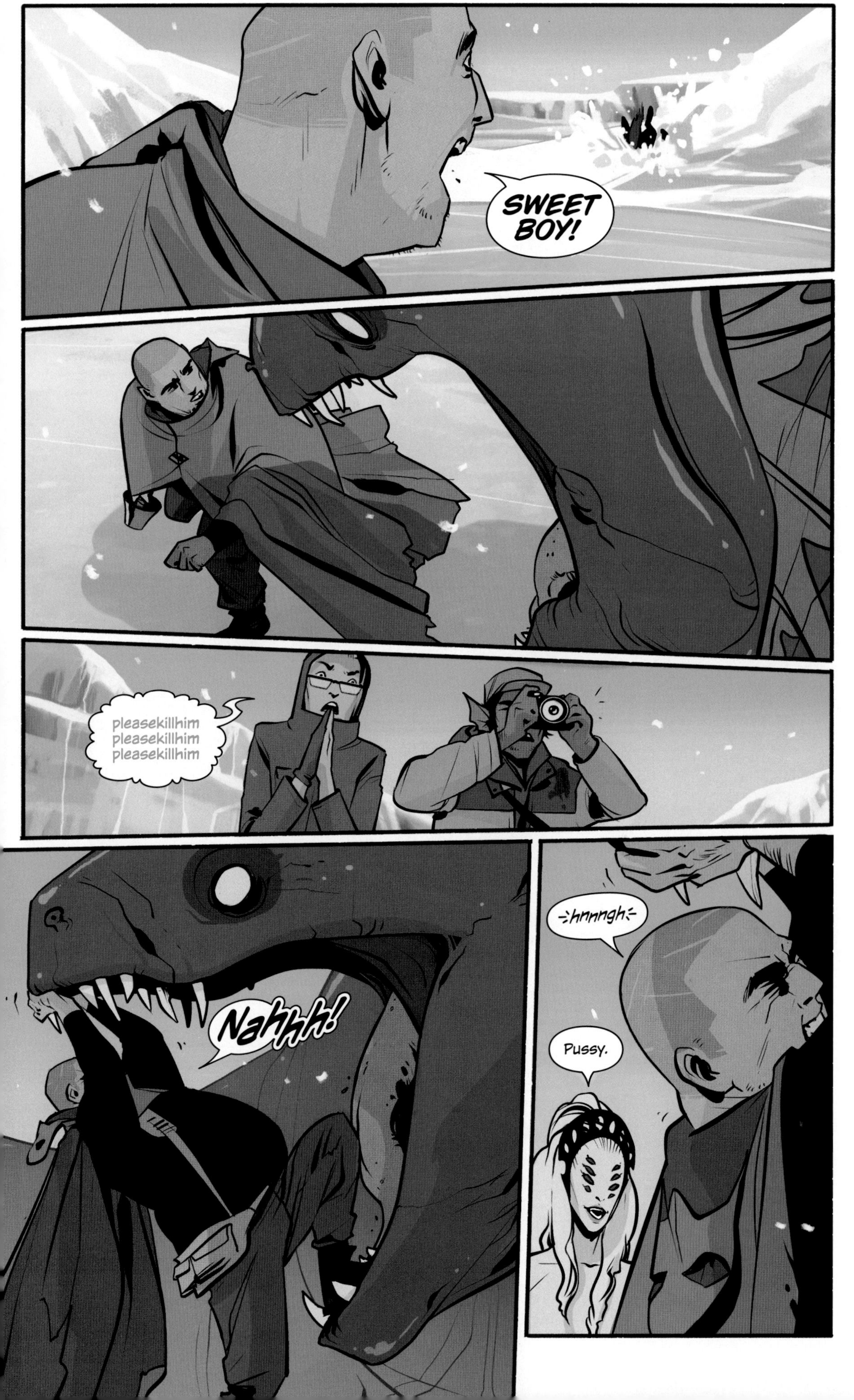
SWEET BOY!
pleasekillhim pleasekillhim pleasekillhim
Nahhh!
hnnngh
Pussy.

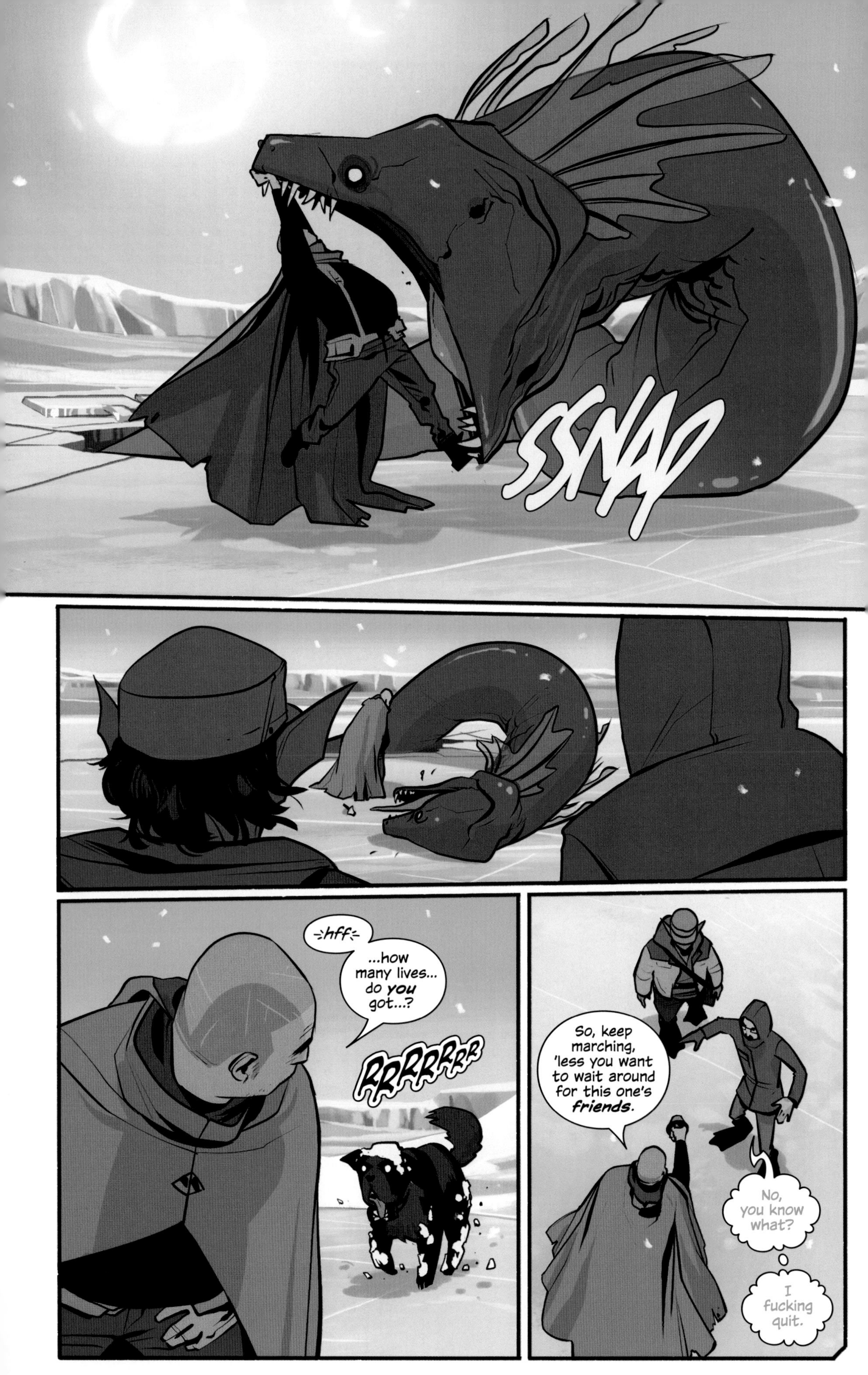
SSNAP
-hff-
...how many lives... do *you* got...?
RRRRRRRR
So, keep marching, 'less you want to wait around for this one's *friends*.
No, you know what?
I fucking quit.

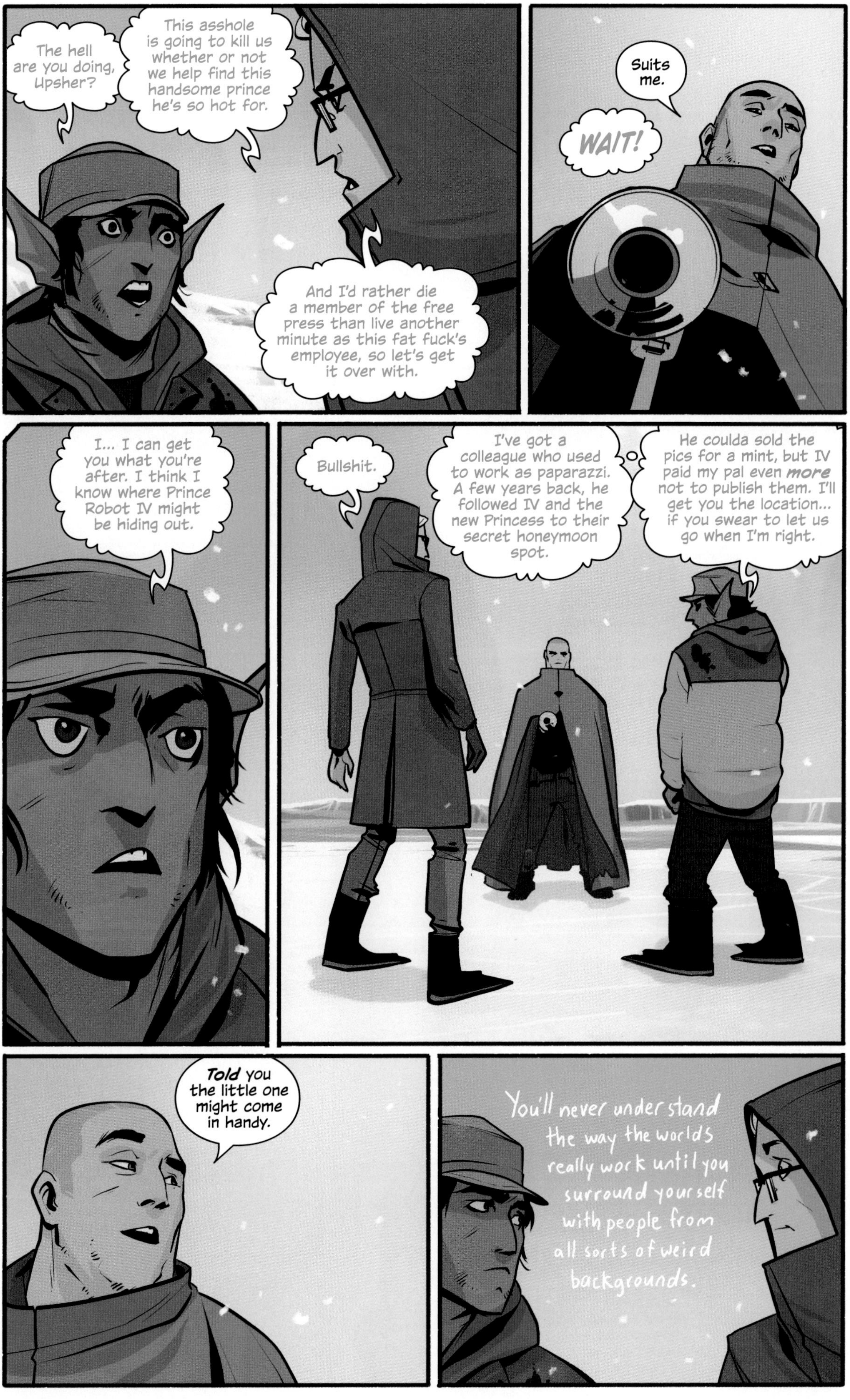

The hell are you doing, Upsher?
This asshole is going to kill us whether or not we help find this handsome prince he's so hot for.
And I'd rather die a member of the free press than live another minute as this fat fuck's employee, so let's get it over with.
Suits me.
WAIT!
I... I can get you what you're after. I think I know where Prince Robot IV might be hiding out.
Bullshit.
I've got a colleague who used to work as paparazzi. A few years back, he followed IV and the new Princess to their secret honeymoon spot.
He coulda sold the pics for a mint, but IV paid my pal even *more* not to publish them. I'll get you the location... if you swear to let us go when I'm right.
Told you the little one might come in handy.
You'll never understand the way the worlds really work until you surround yourself with people from all sorts of weird backgrounds.

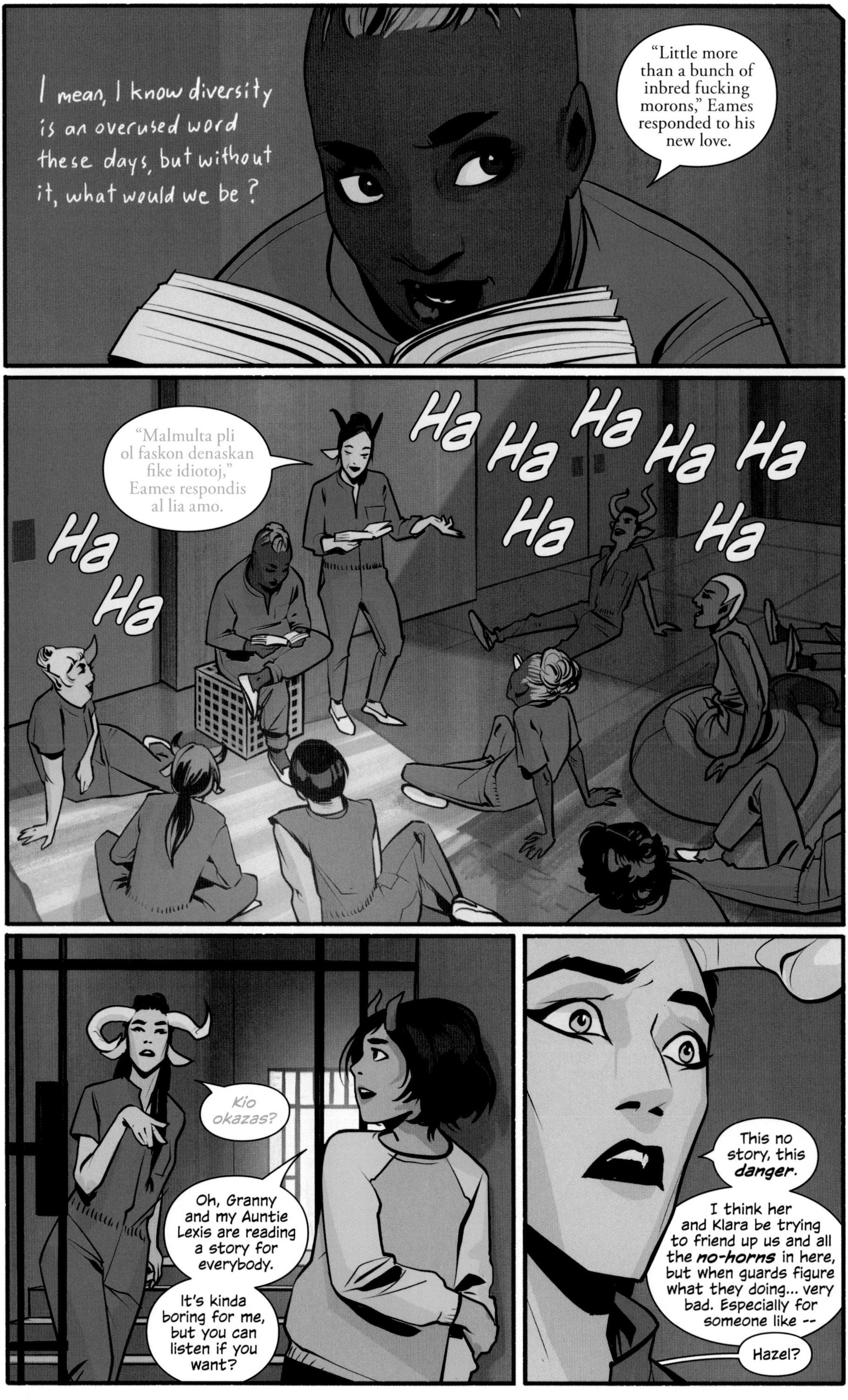

I mean, I know diversity is an overused word these days, but without it, what would we be?
"Little more than a bunch of inbred fucking morons," Eames responded to his new love.
"Malmulta pli ol faskon denaskan fike idiotoj," Eames respondis al lia amo.
Ha Ha Ha Ha Ha Ha Ha Ha
Ha Ha
Kio okazas?
Oh, Granny and my Auntie Lexis are reading a story for everybody.
It's kinda boring for me, but you can listen if you want?
This no story, this danger.
I think her and Klara be trying to friend up us and all the no-horns in here, but when guards figure what they doing... very bad. Especially for someone like --
Hazel?

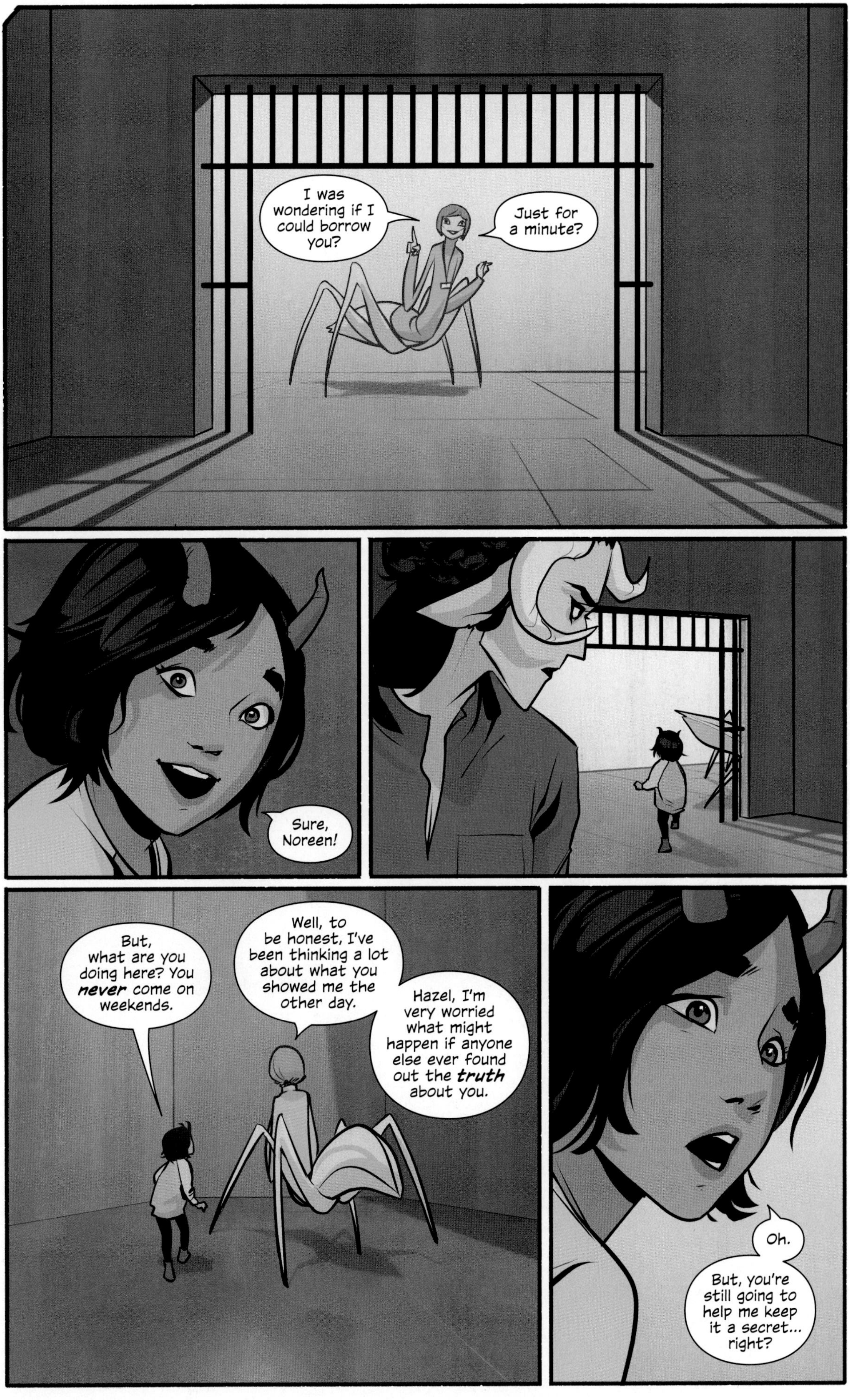
I was wondering if I could borrow you?
Just for a minute?
Sure, Noreen!
But, what are you doing here? You **never** come on weekends.
Well, to be honest, I've been thinking a lot about what you showed me the other day.
Hazel, I'm very worried what might happen if anyone else ever found out the **truth** about you.
Oh.
But, you're still going to help me keep it a secret... right?

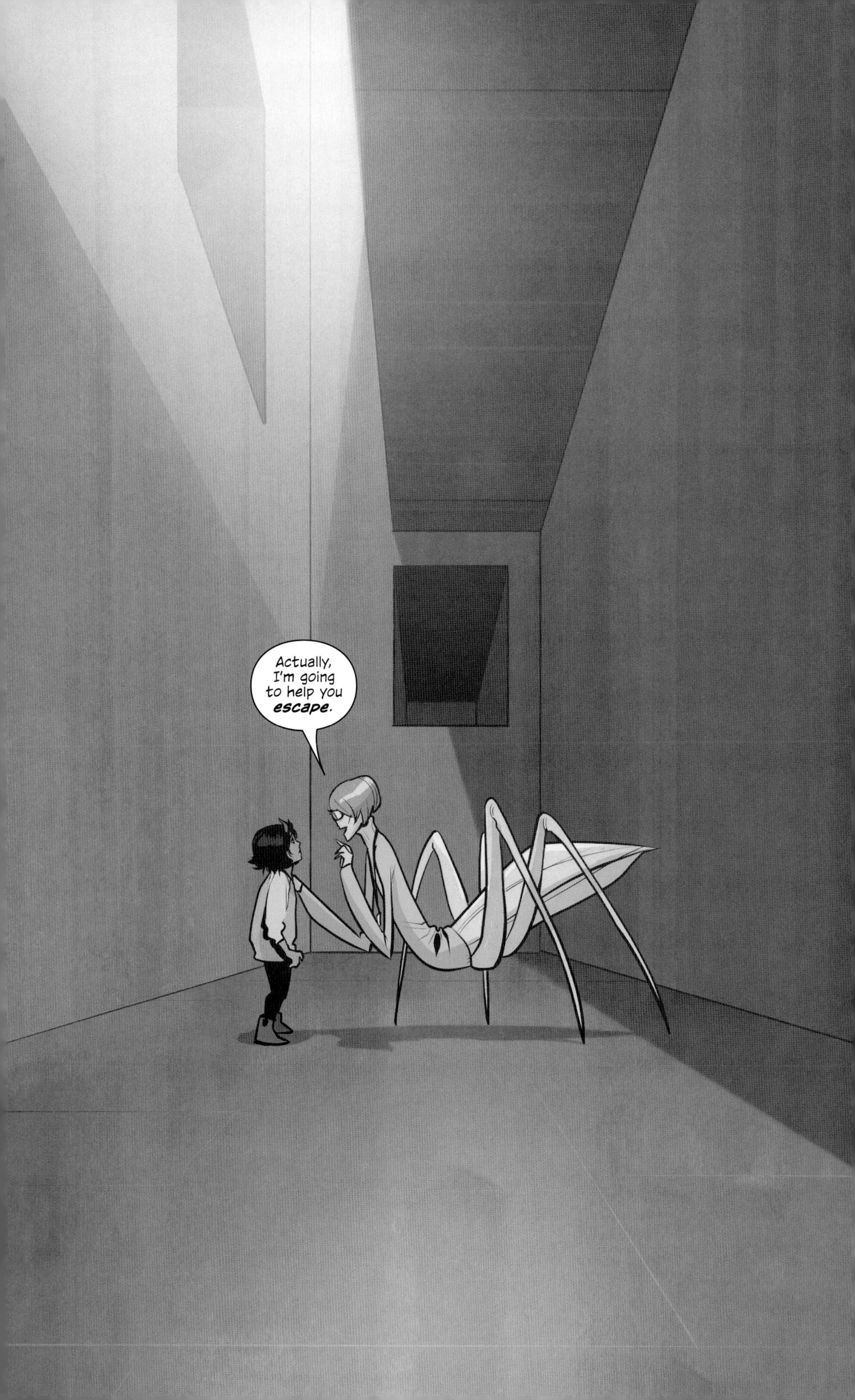
Actually, I'm going to help you *escape*.

end chapter thirty-four

CHAPTER

THIRTY-FIVE

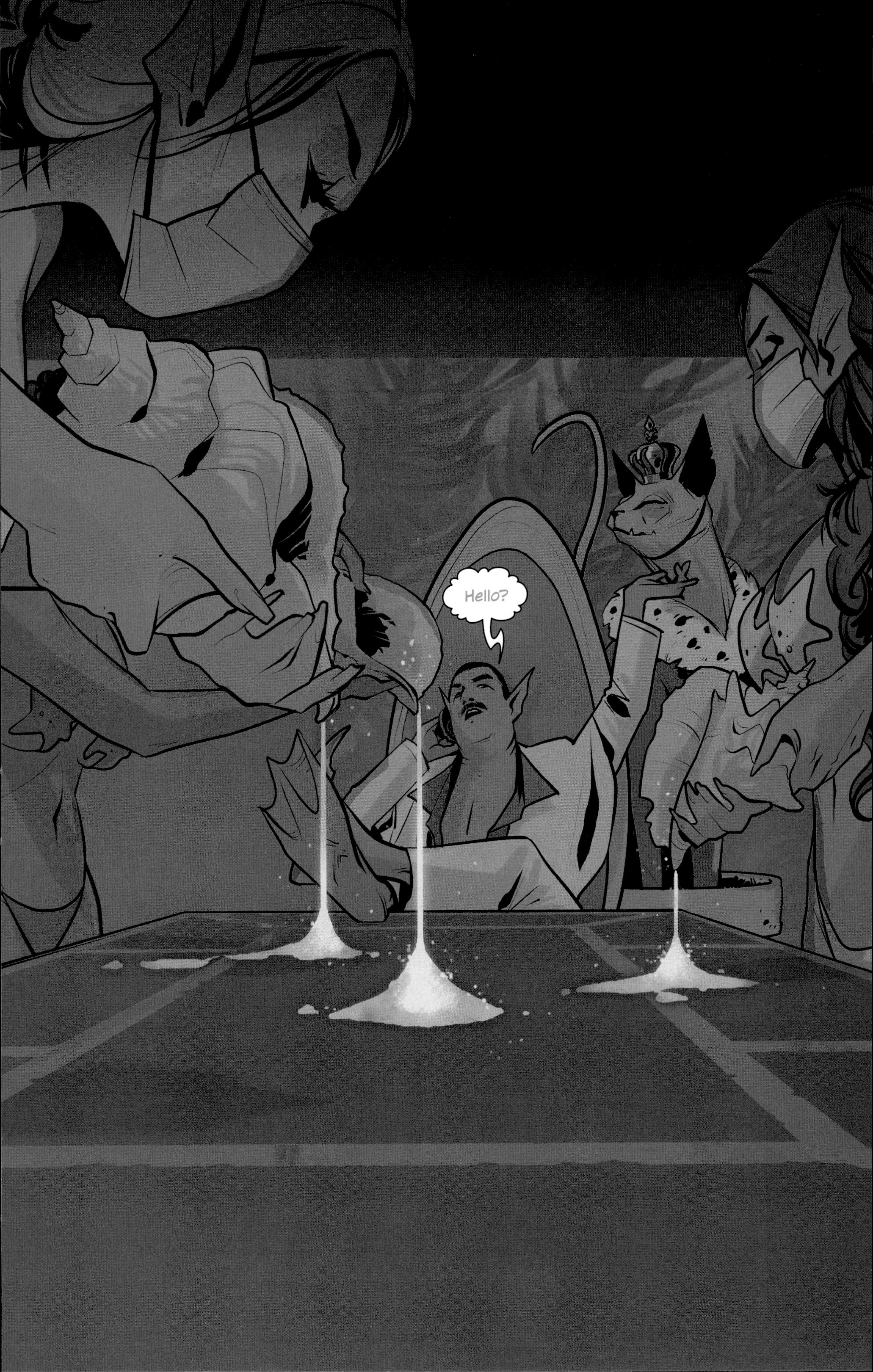
Hello?

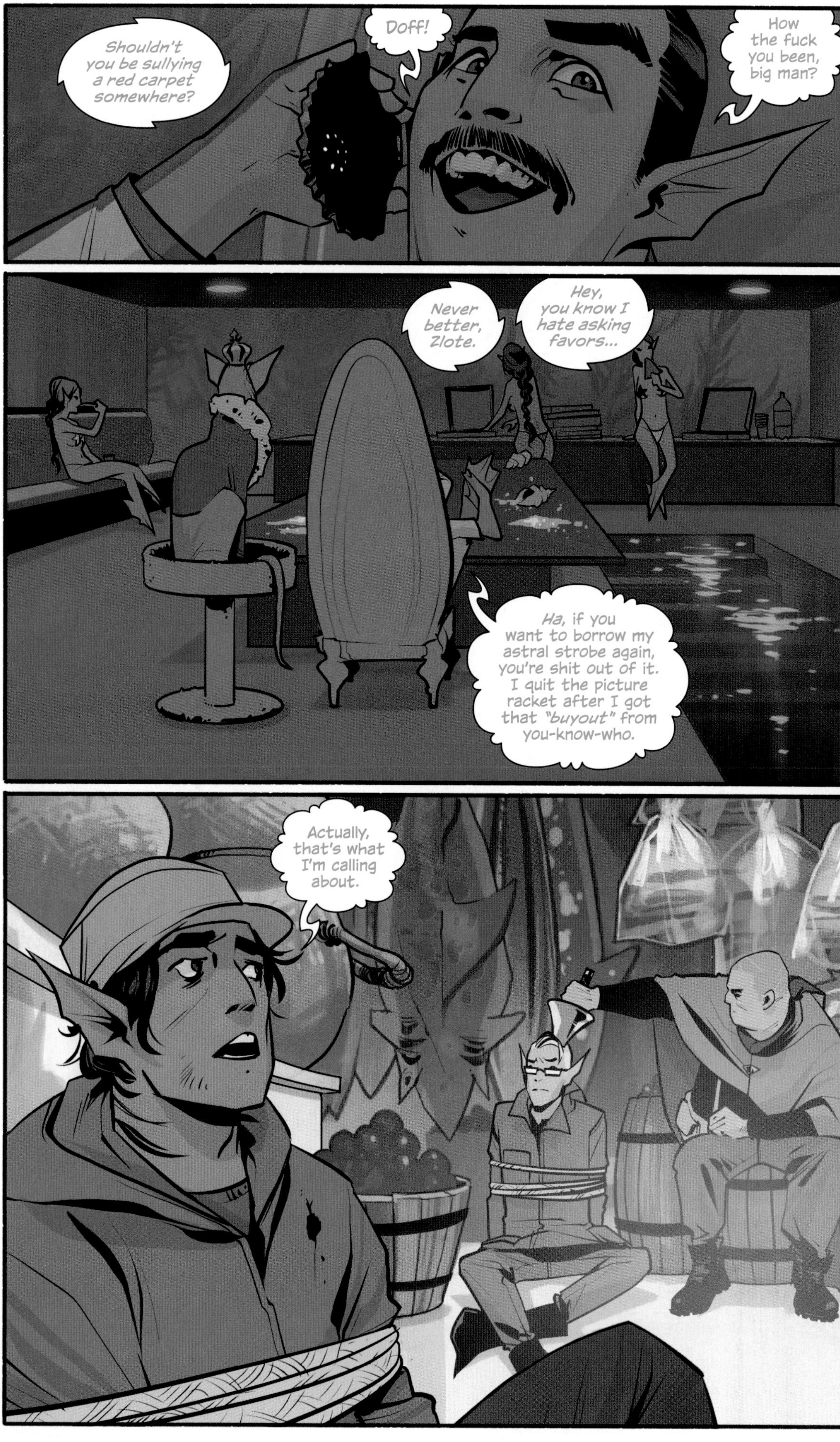
Shouldn't you be sullying a red carpet somewhere?
Doff!
How the fuck you been, big man?
Never better, Zlote.
Hey, you know I hate asking favors...
Ha, if you want to borrow my astral strobe again, you're shit out of it. I quit the picture racket after I got that "*buyout*" from you-know-who.
Actually, that's what I'm calling about.

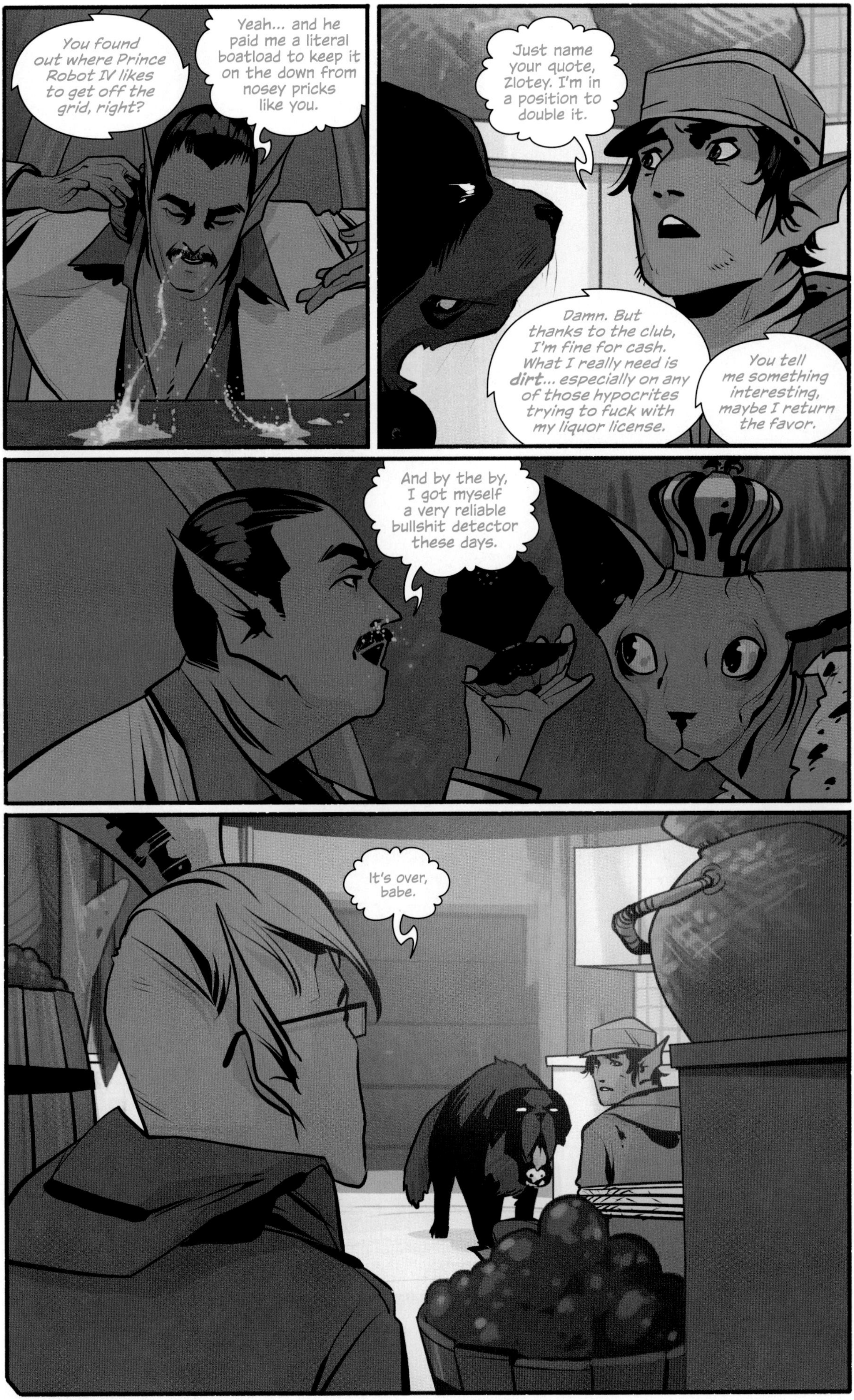

You found out where Prince Robot IV likes to get off the grid, right?
Yeah... and he paid me a literal boatload to keep it on the down from nosey pricks like you.
Just name your quote, Zlotey. I'm in a position to double it.
Damn. But thanks to the club, I'm fine for cash. What I really need is dirt... especially on any of those hypocrites trying to fuck with my liquor license.
You tell me something interesting, maybe I return the favor.
And by the by, I got myself a very reliable bullshit detector these days.
It's over, babe.

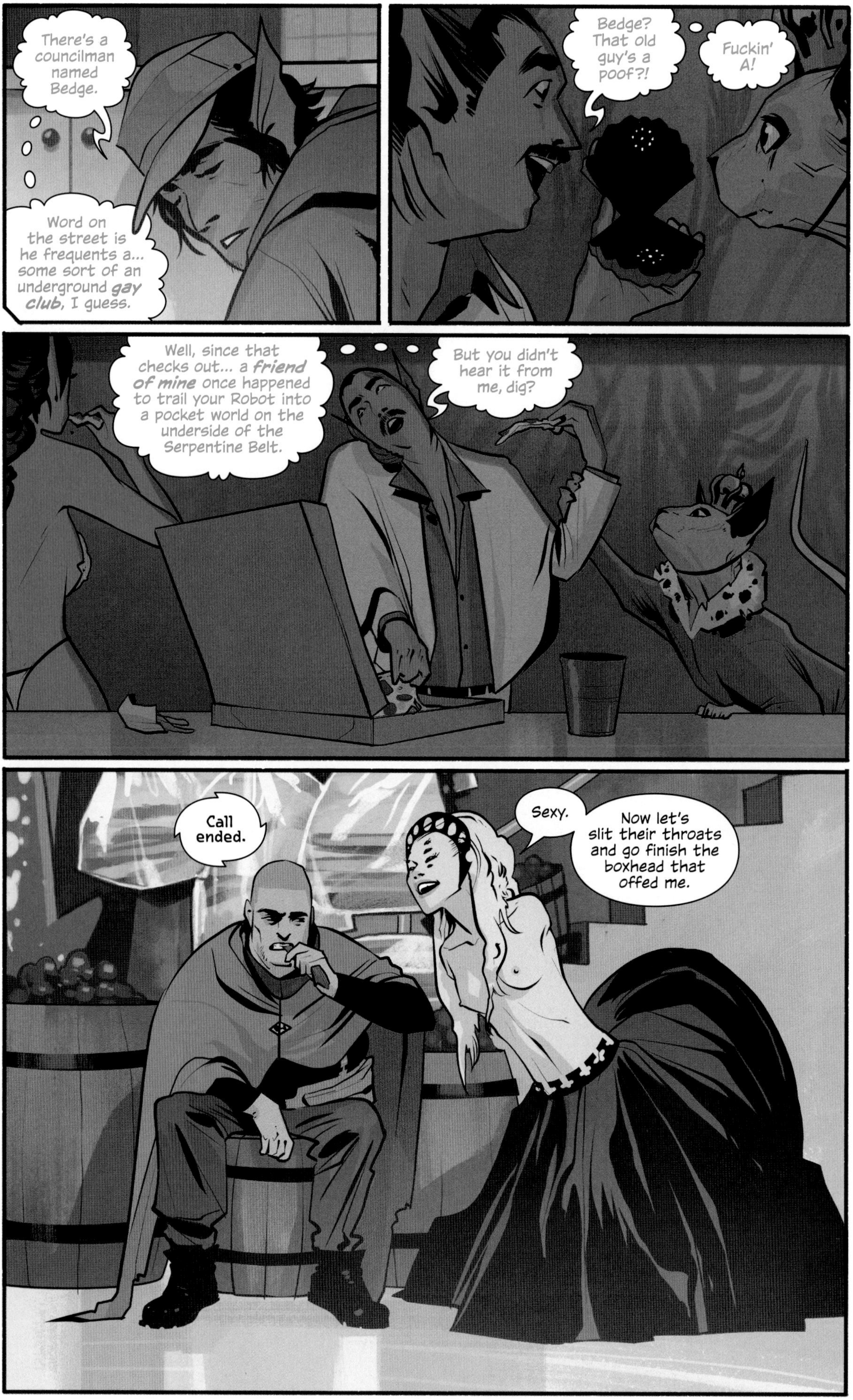
There's a councilman named Bedge.
Word on the street is he frequents a... some sort of an underground gay club, I guess.
Bedge? That old guy's a poof?!
Fuckin' A!
Well, since that checks out... a friend of mine once happened to trail your Robot into a pocket world on the underside of the Serpentine Belt.
But you didn't hear it from me, dig?
Call ended.
Sexy.
Now let's slit their throats and go finish the boxhead that offed me.

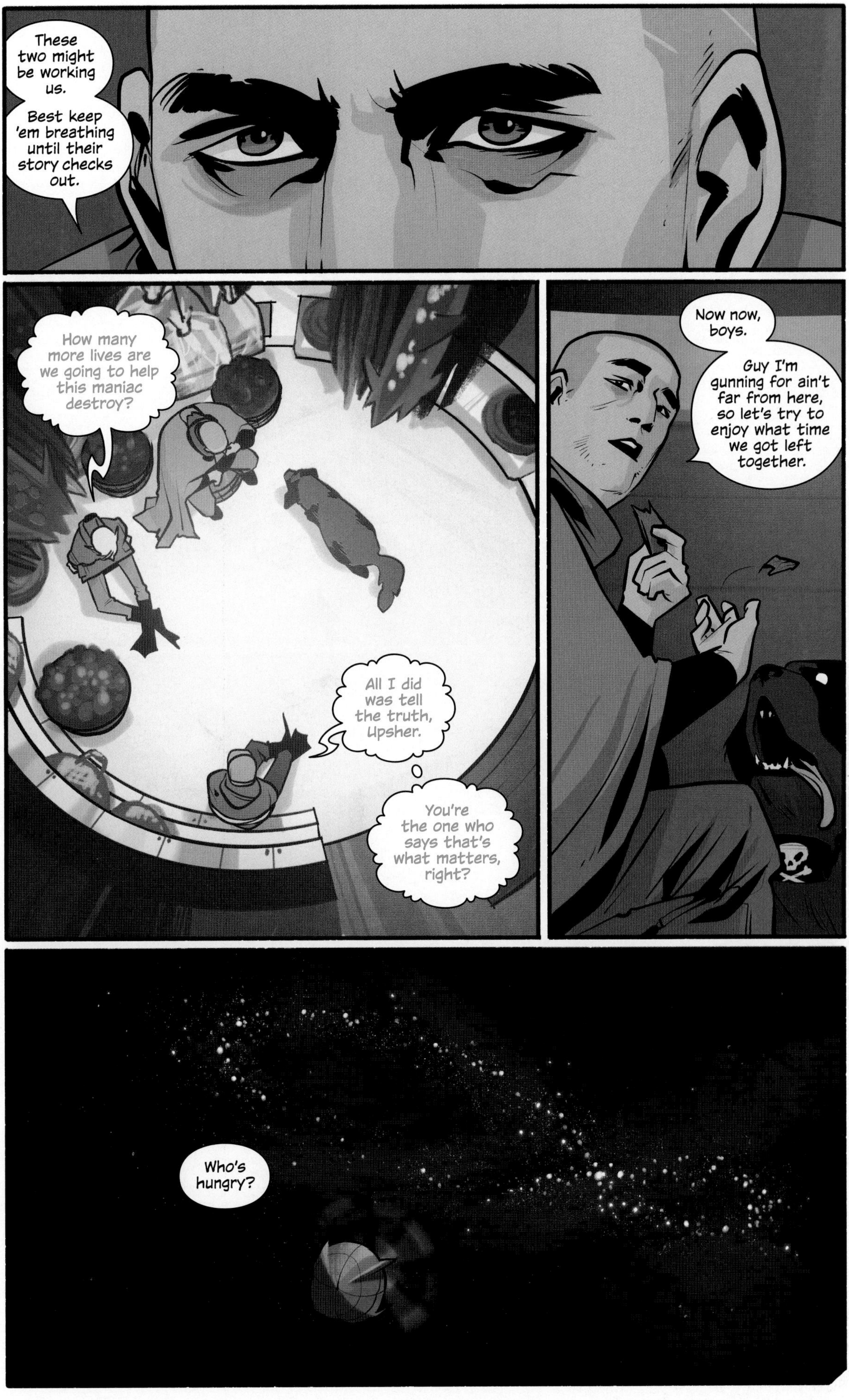
These two might be working us.
Best keep 'em breathing until their story checks out.
How many more lives are we going to help this maniac destroy?
All I did was tell the truth, Upsher.
You're the one who says that's what matters, right?
Now now, boys.
Guy I'm gunning for ain't far from here, so let's try to enjoy what time we got left together.
Who's hungry?

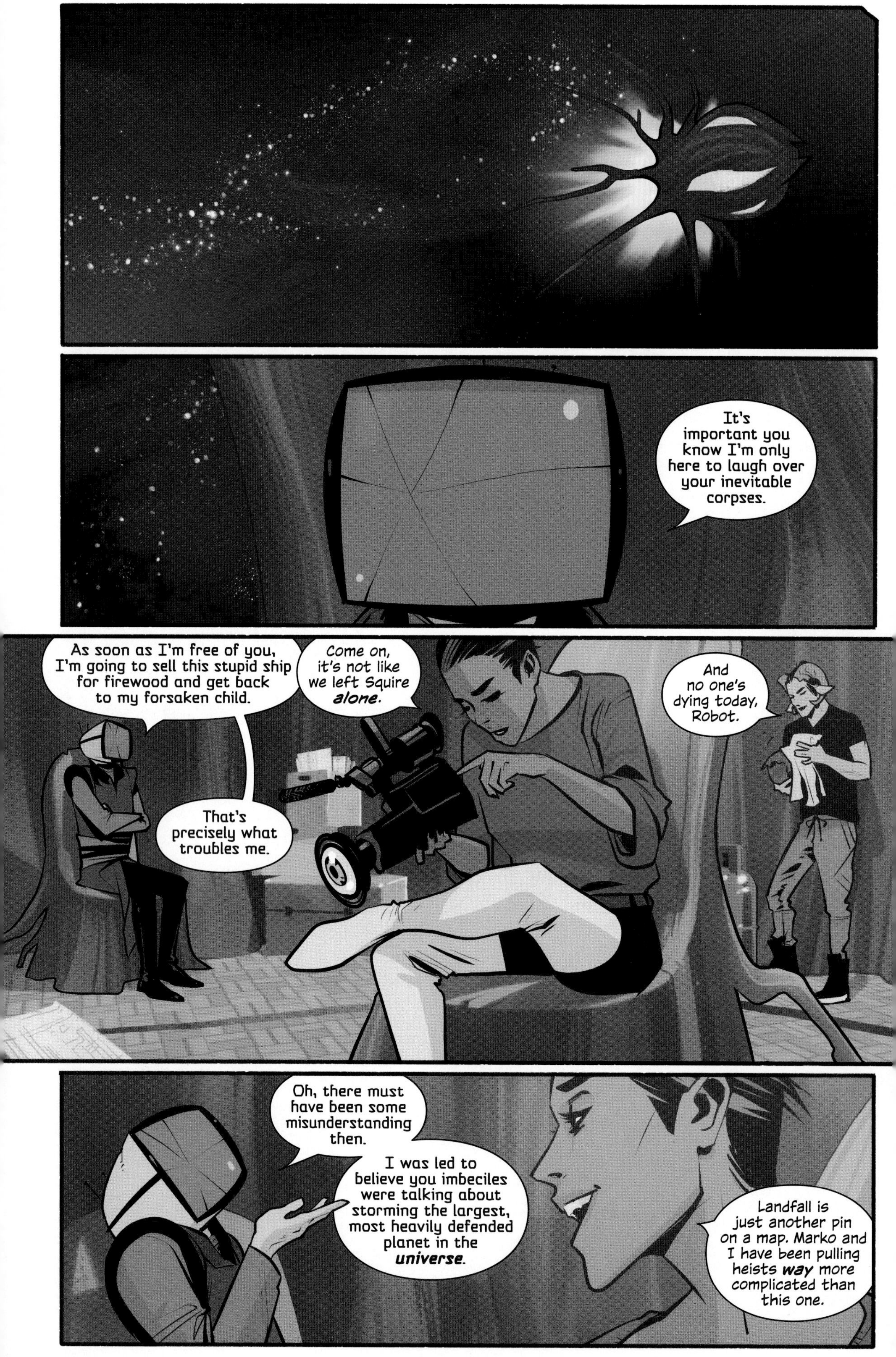
It's important you know I'm only here to laugh over your inevitable corpses.
As soon as I'm free of you, I'm going to sell this stupid ship for firewood and get back to my forsaken child.
That's precisely what troubles me.
Come on, it's not like we left Squire *alone.*
And no one's dying today, Robot.
Oh, there must have been some misunderstanding then.
I was led to believe you imbeciles were talking about storming the largest, most heavily defended planet in the *universe*.
Landfall is just another pin on a map. Marko and I have been pulling heists *way* more complicated than this one.

Hold on, you two have been robbing *banks?*

Among other joints.

Alana and I borrowed *this* from the Endless War Museum on Labunka. It's the last piece we needed to rescue Hazel and my mother.

What is that, one of those *crash helms?*

The old thing doesn't look like it could teleport you out of a wet paper ballsack.

Have those horns corkscrewed into your brain?

If moonies could just "jump" into enemy camps, they would have done it ages ago. The wings have *defenses* against your voodoo.

Defenses you're going to convince the Landfallians to *deactivate.*

It's still got enough kick to jump me onto Landfall and back... but I'll only be able to return with two passengers, so I'll have to make the trip there solo.

Hilarious.

I'm serious. When I worked as a guard on *Cleave*, guys from your Kingdom would always drop by to interrogate high-value targets.

But since our exotic membrane also messes with *your people's* physiology, we'd have to temporarily disable the system to let them --

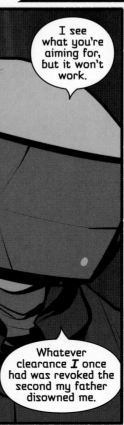

I see what you're aiming for, but it won't work.

Whatever clearance *I* once had was revoked the second my father disowned me.

Which is why I'm proud to christen you *Count Robot LX.*

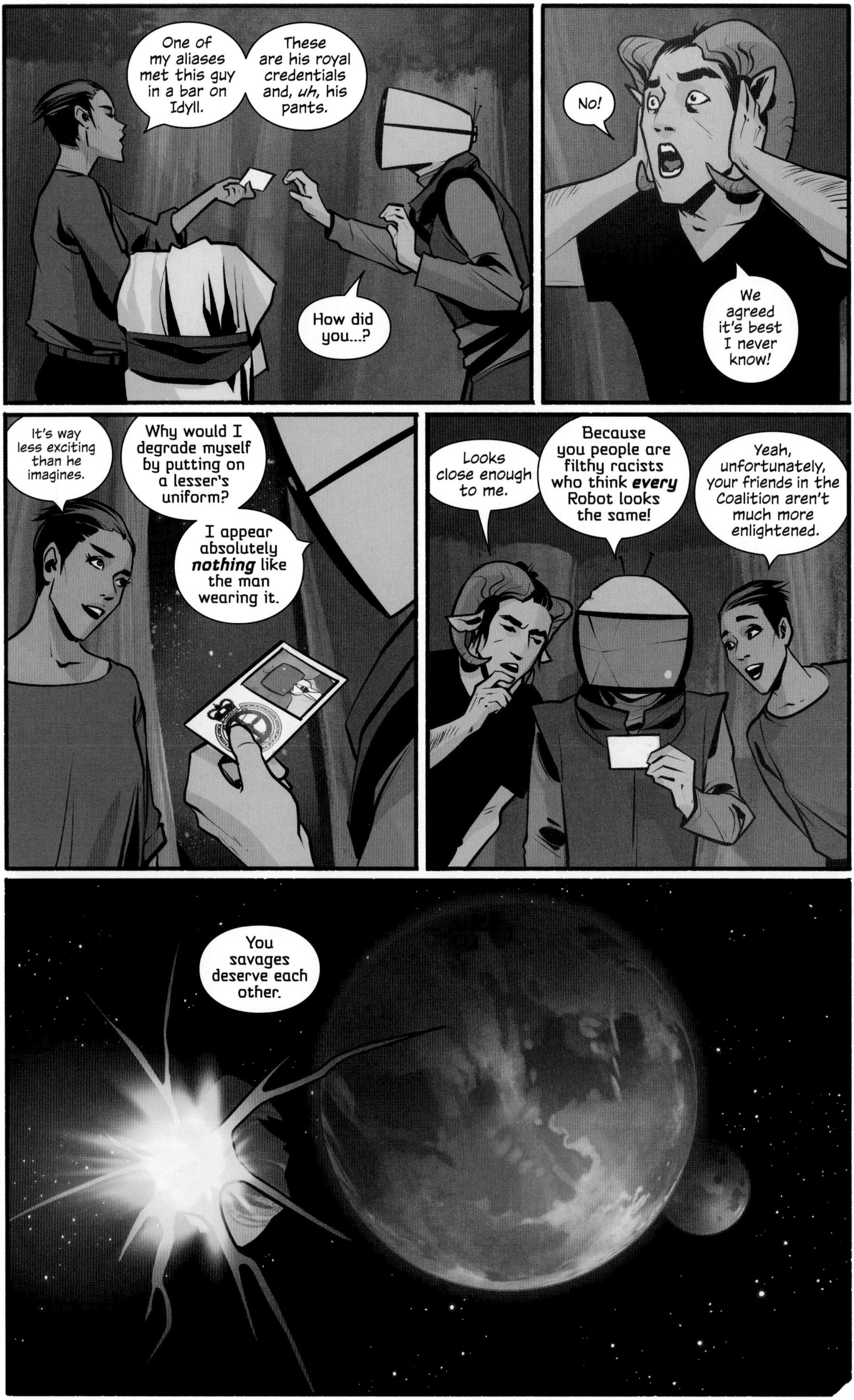
One of my aliases met this guy in a bar on Idyll.
These are his royal credentials and, *uh*, his pants.
How did you...?
No!
We agreed it's best I never know!
It's way less exciting than he imagines.
Why would I degrade myself by putting on a lesser's uniform?
I appear absolutely ***nothing*** like the man wearing it.
Looks close enough to me.
Because you people are filthy racists who think ***every*** Robot looks the same!
Yeah, unfortunately, your friends in the Coalition aren't much more enlightened.
You savages deserve each other.

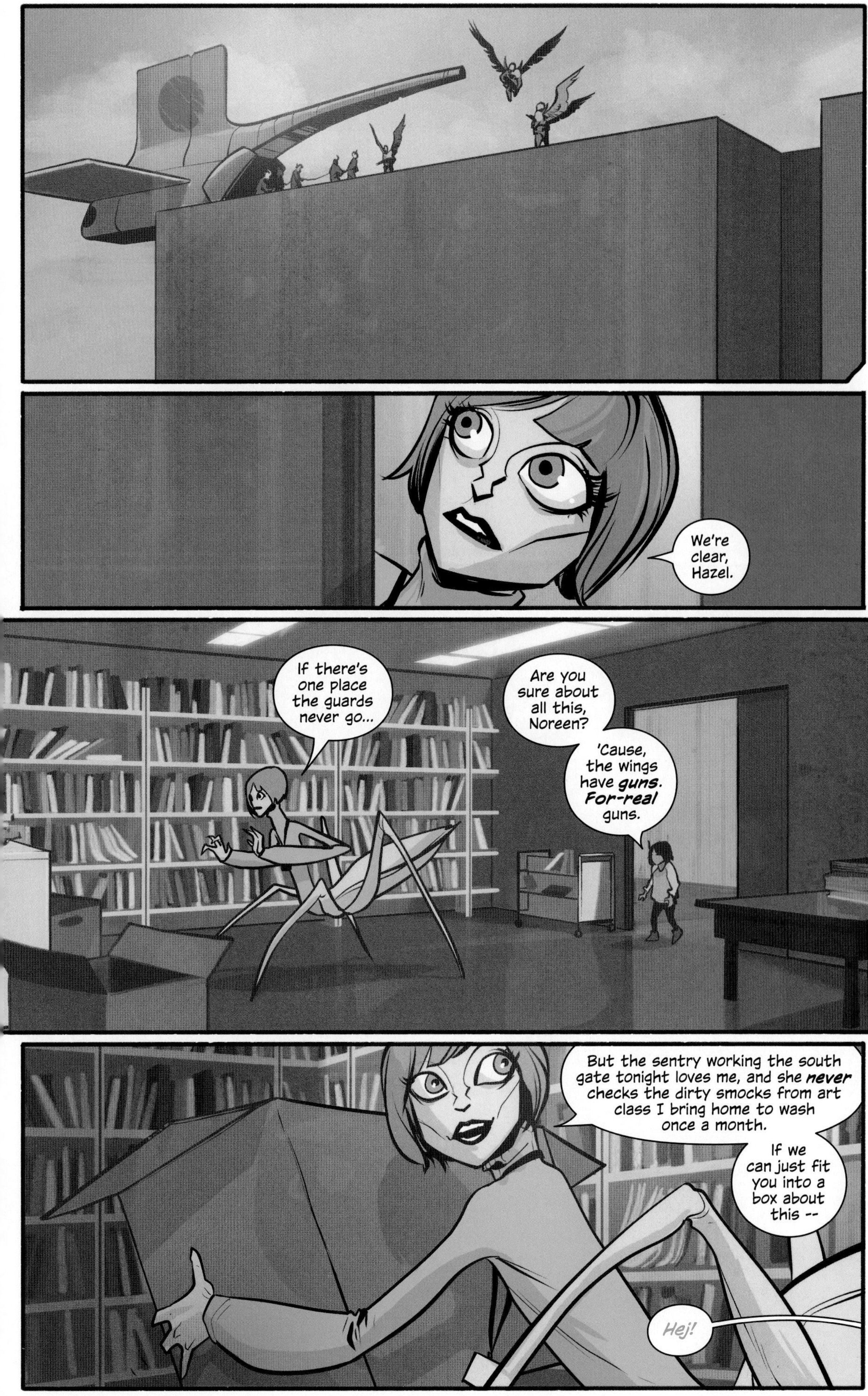
We're clear, Hazel.
If there's one place the guards never go...
Are you sure about all this, Noreen?
'Cause, the wings have **guns**. ***For-real*** guns.
But the sentry working the south gate tonight loves me, and she ***never*** checks the dirty smocks from art class I bring home to wash once a month.
If we can just fit you into a box about this --
Hej!

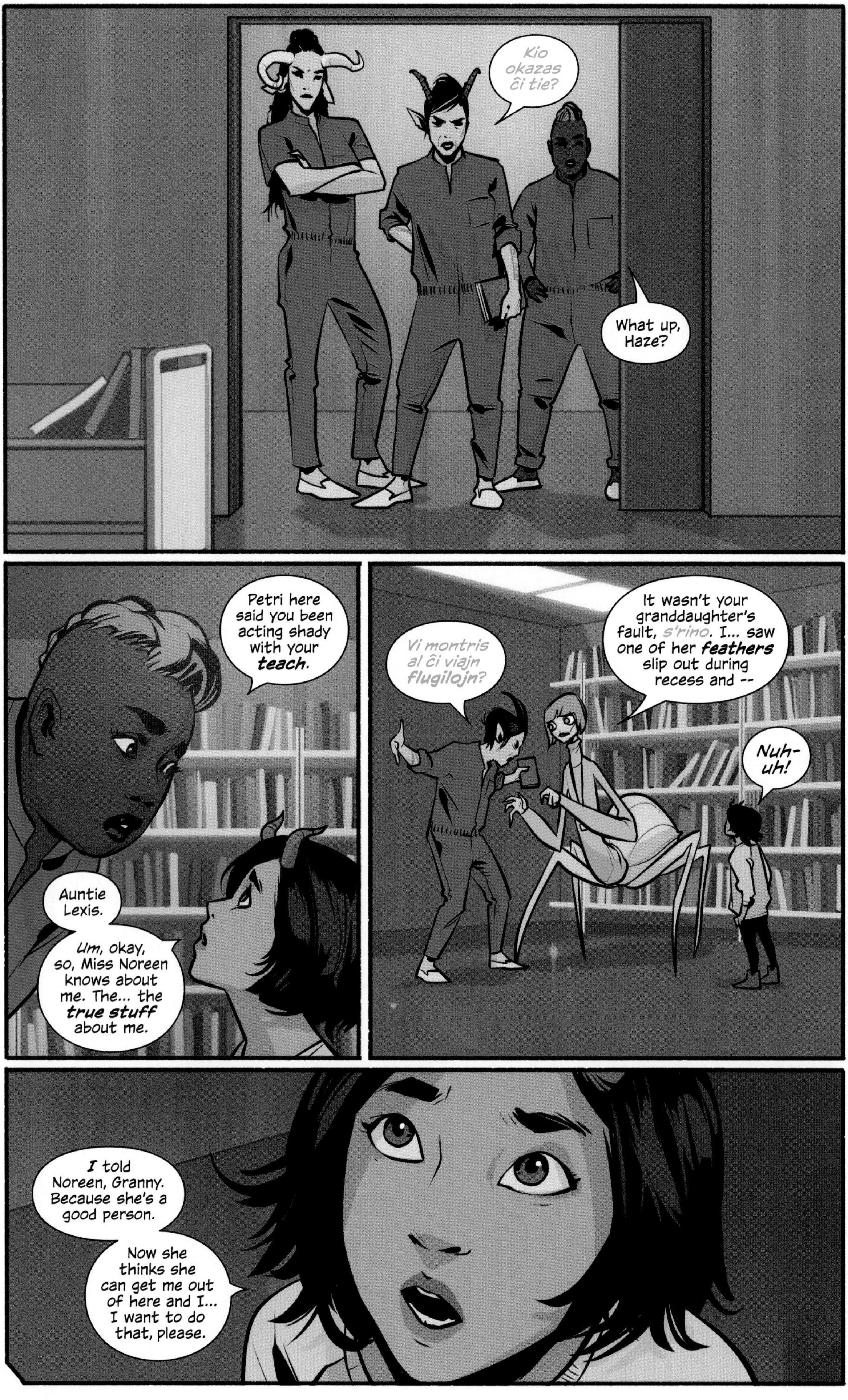
Kio okazas ĉi tie?
What up, Haze?
Petri here said you been acting shady with your **teach**.
Auntie Lexis.
Um, okay, so, Miss Noreen knows about me. The... the ***true stuff*** about me.
Vi montris al ĉi viajn flugilojn?
It wasn't your granddaughter's fault, *s'rino*. I... saw one of her ***feathers*** slip out during recess and --
Nuh-uh!
I told Noreen, Granny. Because she's a good person.
Now she thinks she can get me out of here and I... I want to do that, please.

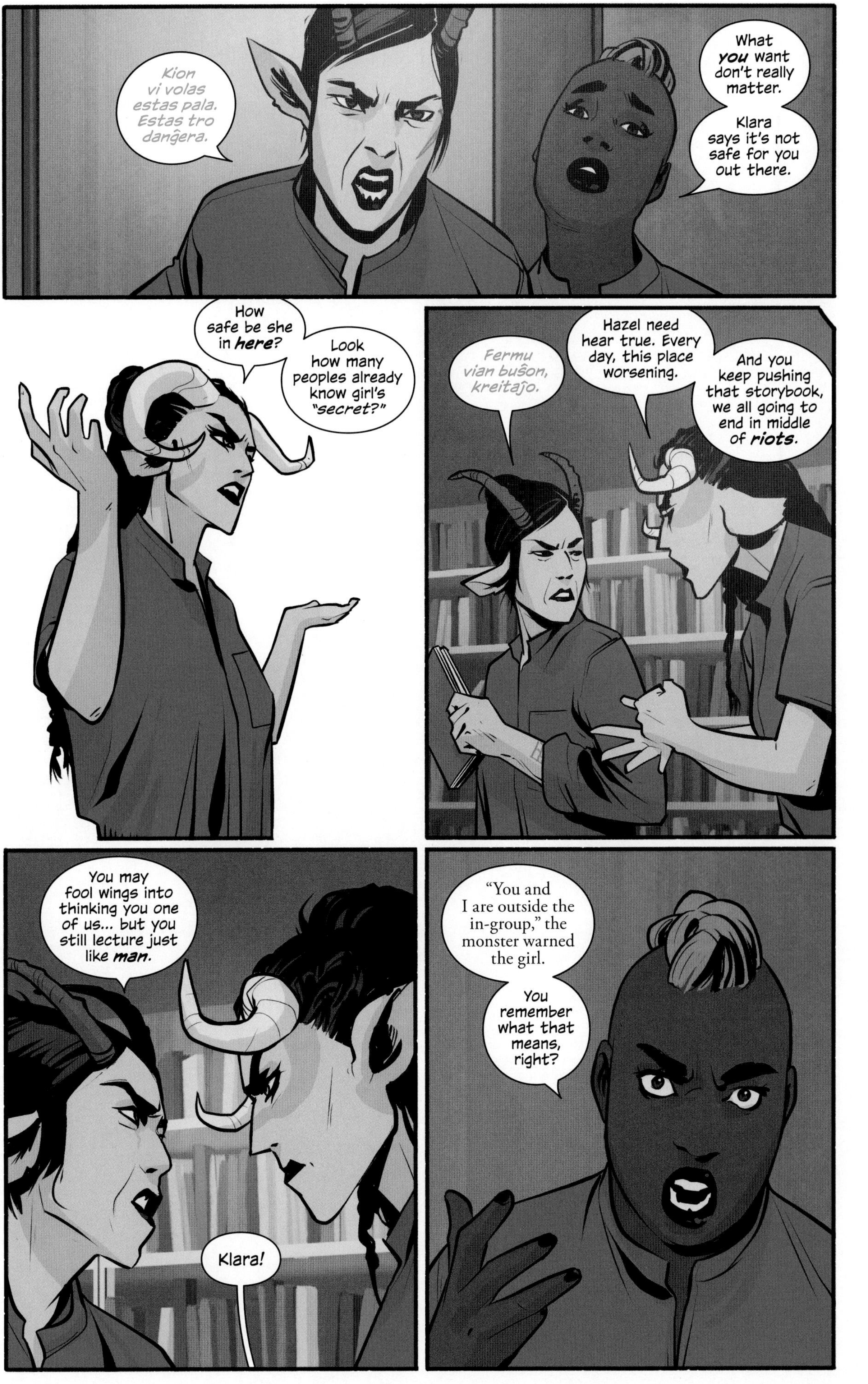
Kion vi volas estas pala. Estas tro danĝera.
What you want don't really matter.
Klara says it's not safe for you out there.
How safe be she in here?
Look how many peoples already know girl's "secret?"
Fermu vian buŝon, kreitaĵo.
Hazel need hear true. Every day, this place worsening.
And you keep pushing that storybook, we all going to end in middle of riots.
You may fool wings into thinking you one of us... but you still lecture just like man.
Klara!
"You and I are outside the in-group," the monster warned the girl.
You remember what that means, right?

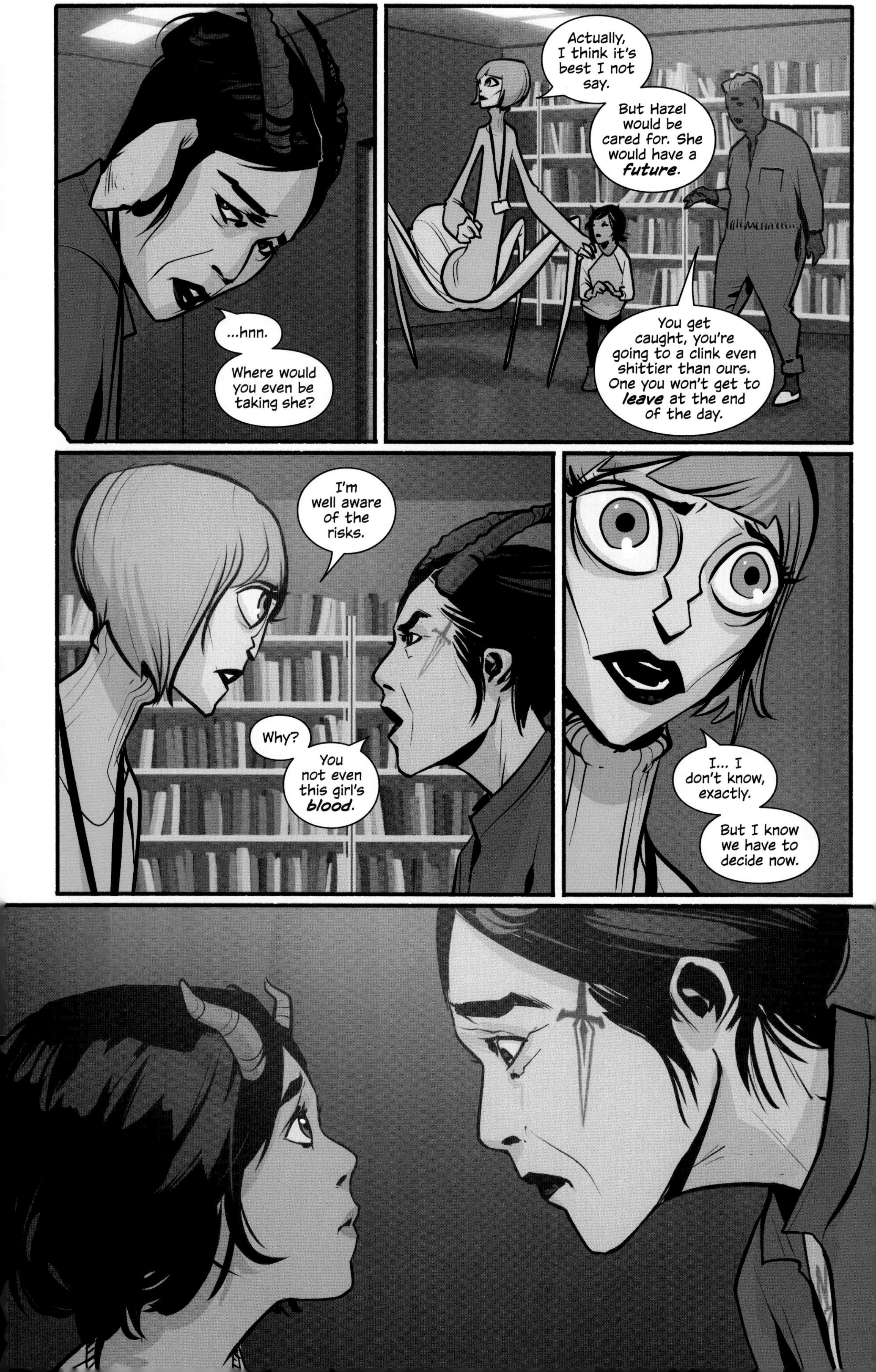
...hnn.
Where would you even be taking she?
Actually, I think it's best I not say.
But Hazel would be cared for. She would have a *future*.
You get caught, you're going to a clink even shittier than ours. One you won't get to *leave* at the end of the day.
I'm well aware of the risks.
Why?
You not even this girl's *blood*.
I... I don't know, exactly.
But I know we have to decide now.

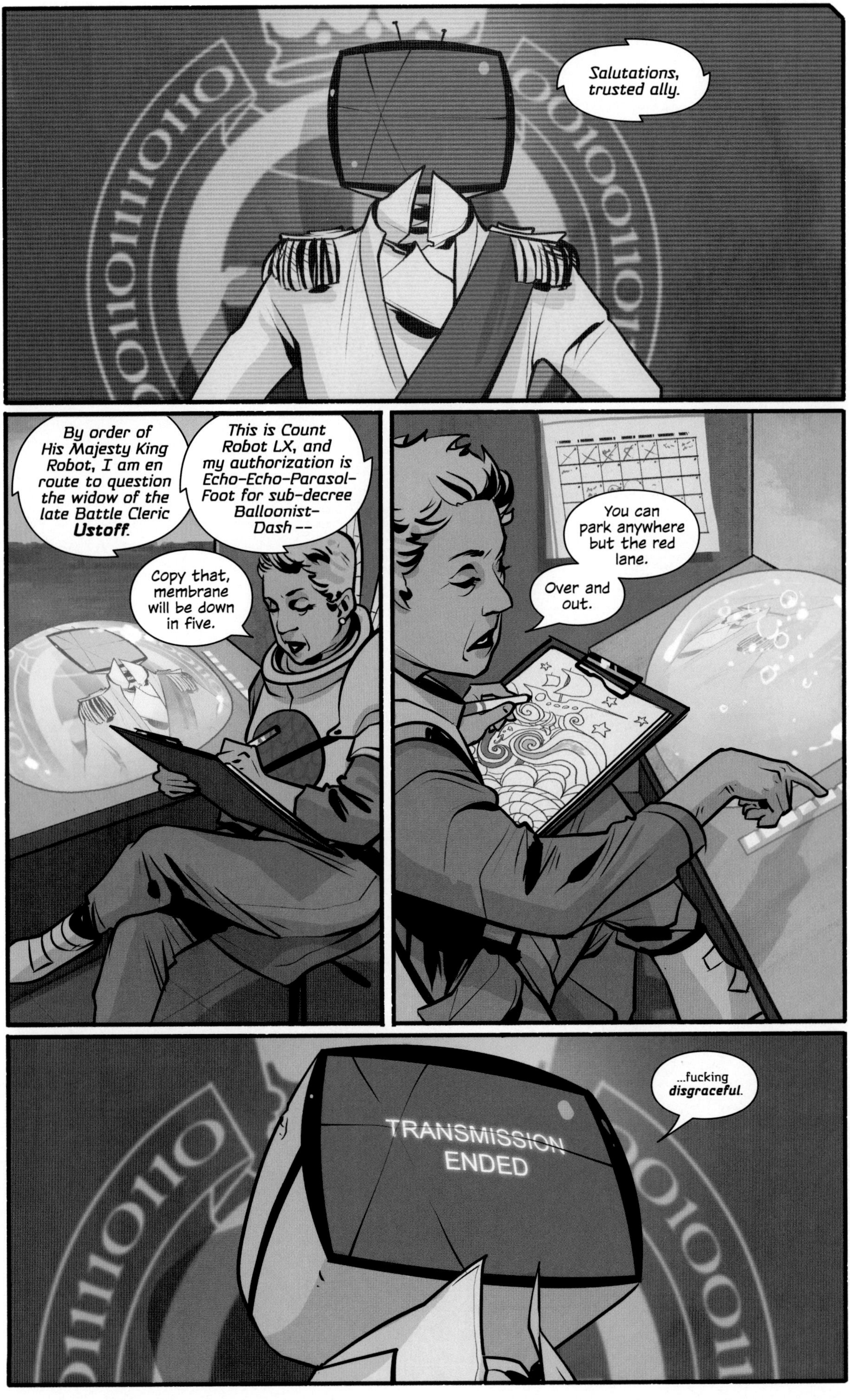
Salutations, trusted ally.
By order of His Majesty King Robot, I am en route to question the widow of the late Battle Cleric **Ustoff**.
This is Count Robot LX, and my authorization is Echo-Echo-Parasol-Foot for sub-decree Balloonist-Dash --
Copy that, membrane will be down in five.
You can park anywhere but the red lane.
Over and out.
TRANSMISSION ENDED
...fucking **disgraceful**.

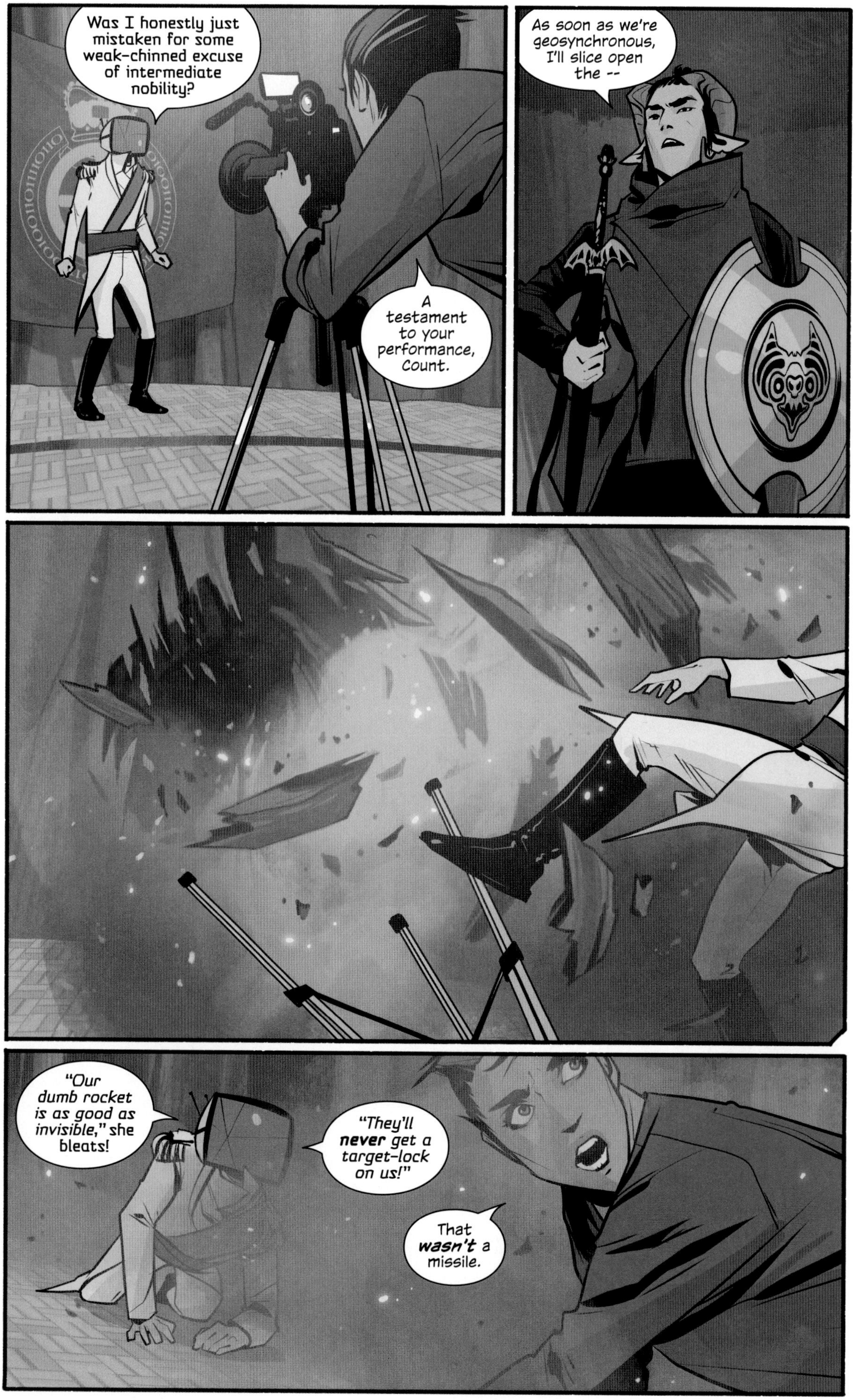
Was I honestly just mistaken for some weak-chinned excuse of intermediate nobility?
A testament to your performance, Count.
As soon as we're geosynchronous, I'll slice open the --
"Our dumb rocket is as good as invisible," she bleats!
"They'll **never** get a target-lock on us!"
That ***wasn't*** a missile.

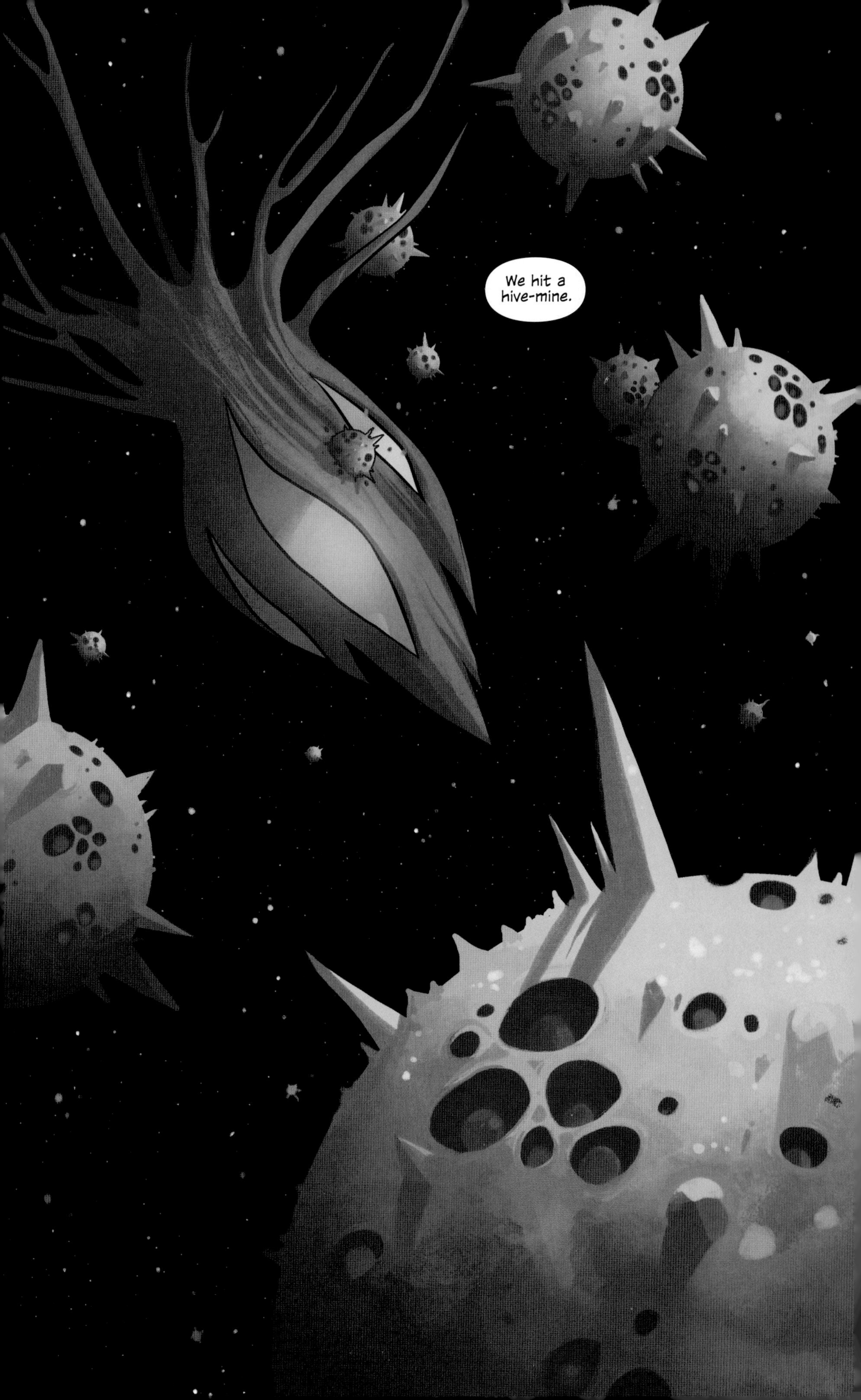
We hit a hive-mine.

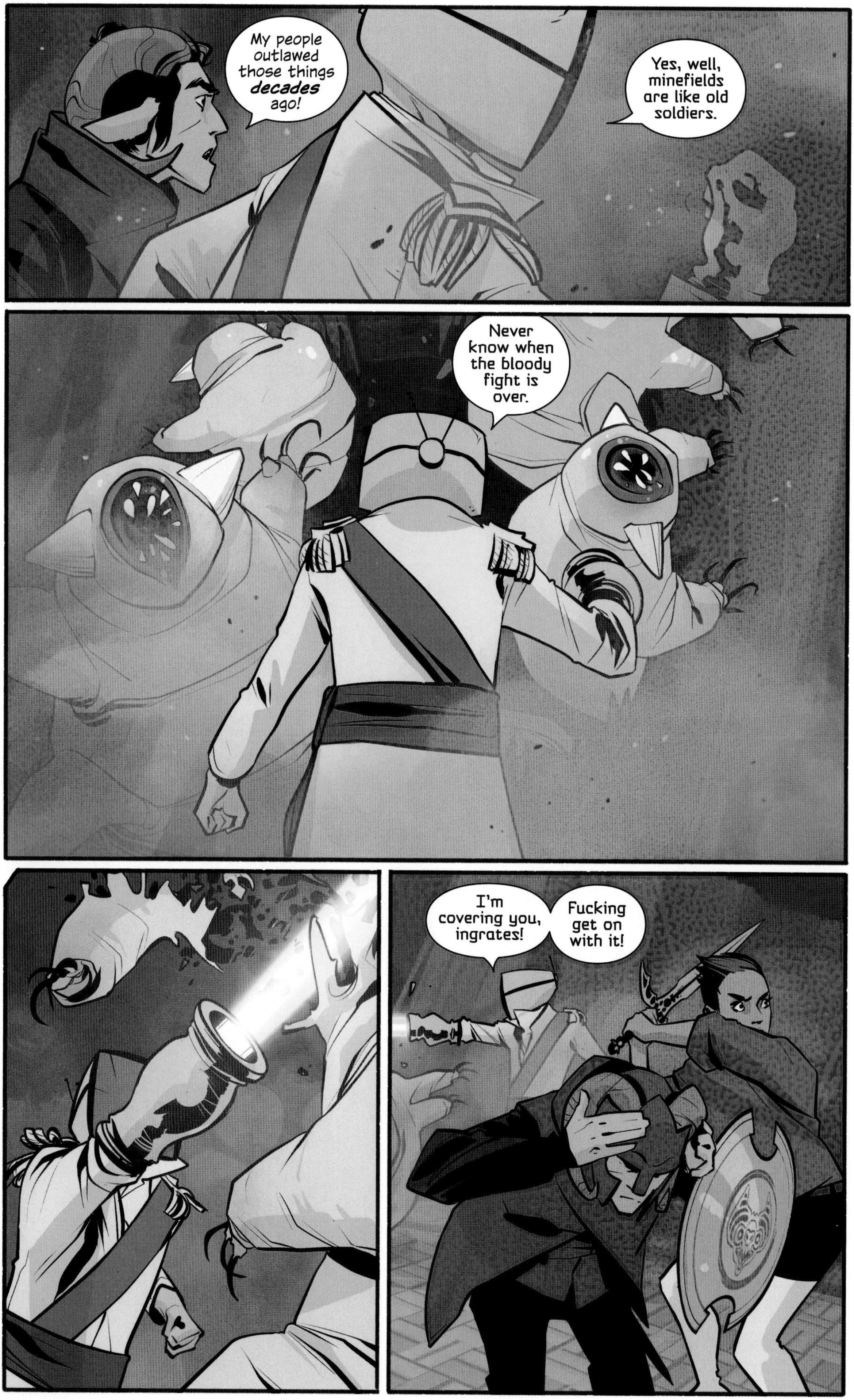
My people outlawed those things *decades* ago!
Yes, well, minefields are like old soldiers.
Never know when the bloody fight is over.
I'm covering you, ingrates!
Fucking get on with it!

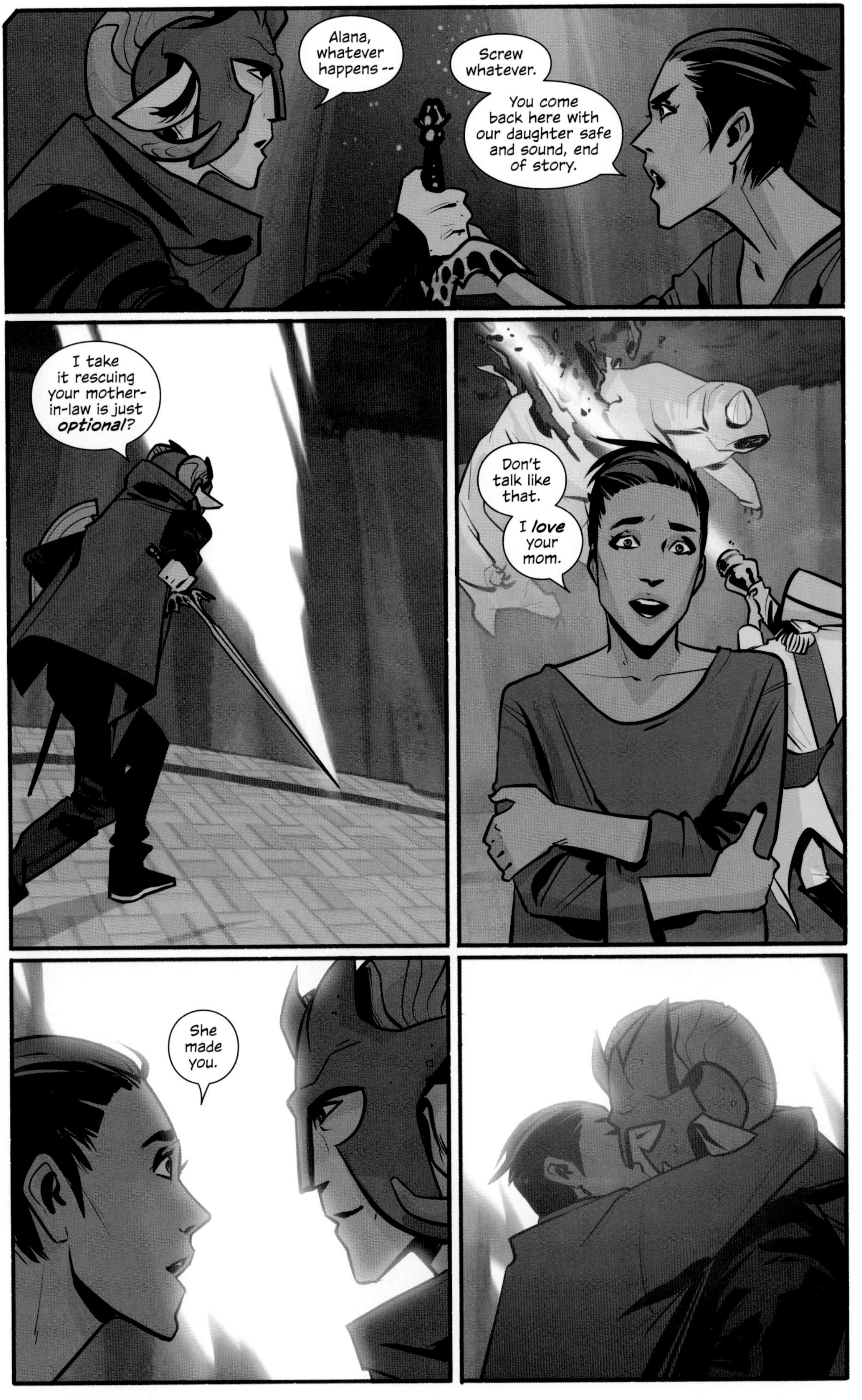

Alana, whatever happens --
Screw whatever.
You come back here with our daughter safe and sound, end of story.
I take it rescuing your mother-in-law is just *optional*?
Don't talk like that.
I *love* your mom.
She made you.

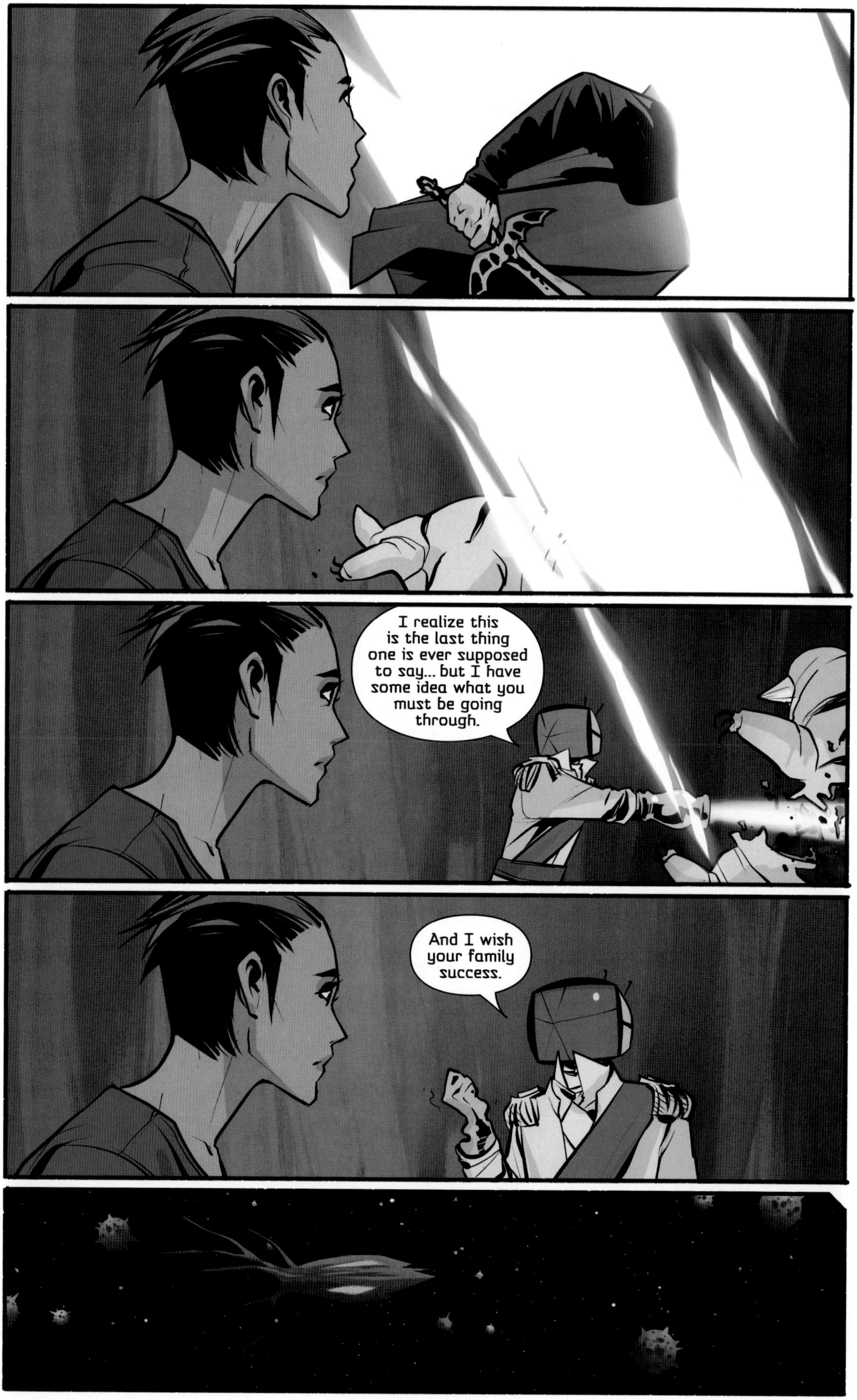
I realize this is the last thing one is ever supposed to say... but I have some idea what you must be going through.
And I wish your family success.

Over here!

I gotted our supper!

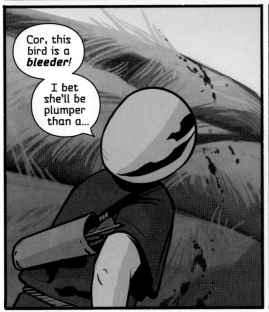

Cor, this bird is a *bleeder!*

I bet she'll be plumper than a...

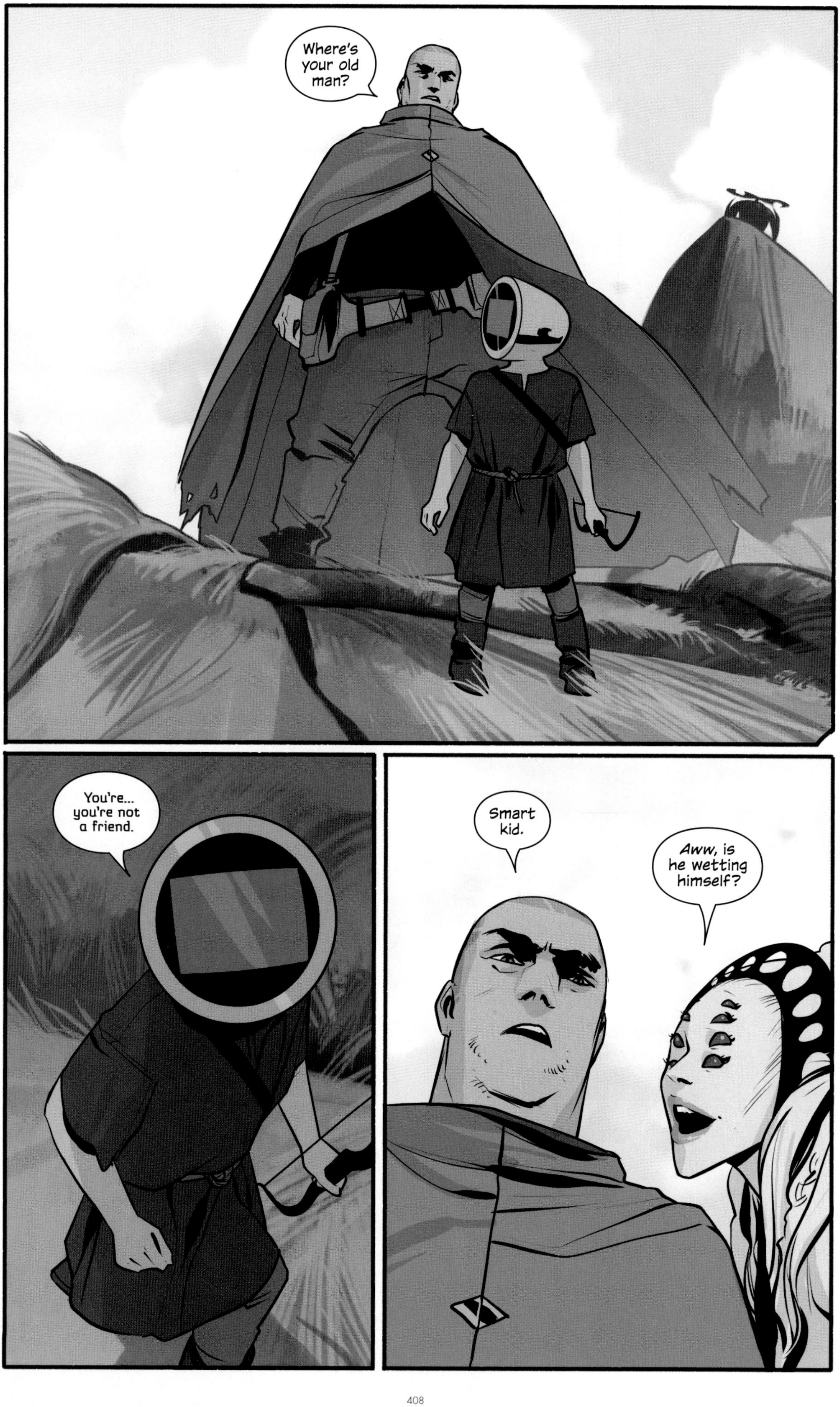

Where's your old man?
You're... you're not a friend.
Smart kid.
Aww, is he wetting himself?

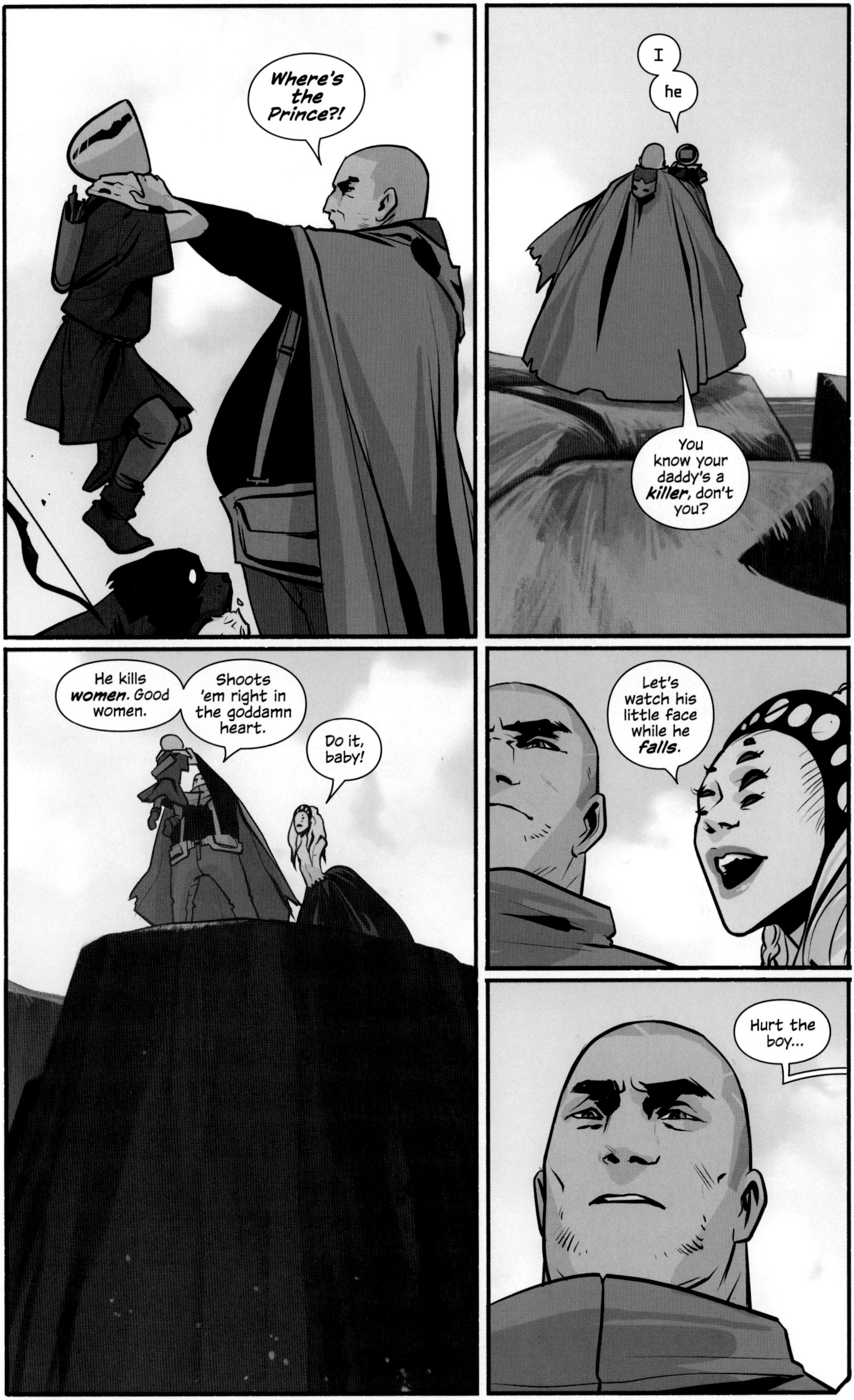

Where's the Prince?!
I
he
You know your daddy's a **killer**, don't you?
He kills **women**. Good women.
Shoots 'em right in the goddamn heart.
Do it, baby!
Let's watch his little face while he **falls**.
Hurt the boy...

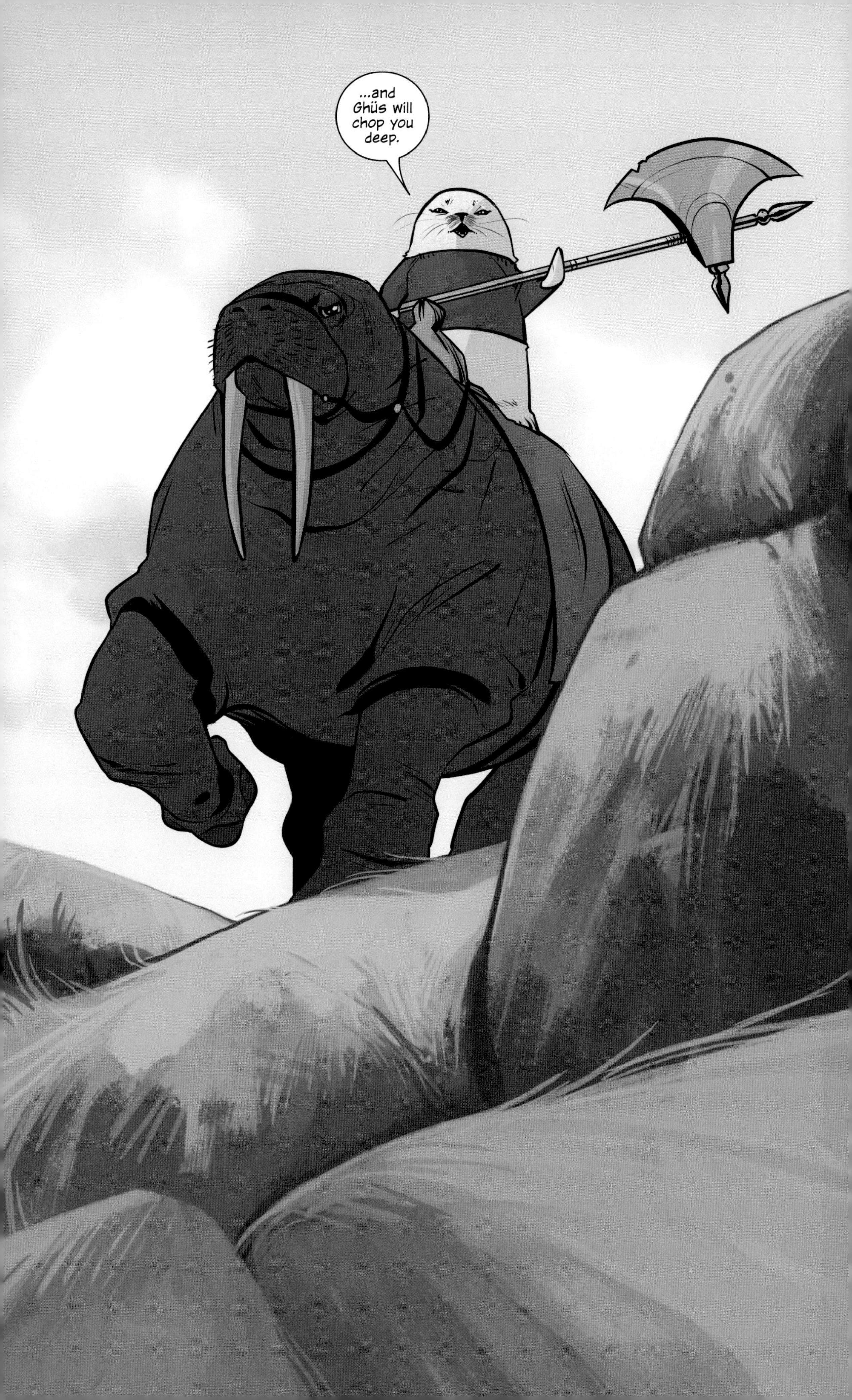
...and Ghüs will chop you deep.

end chapter thirty-five

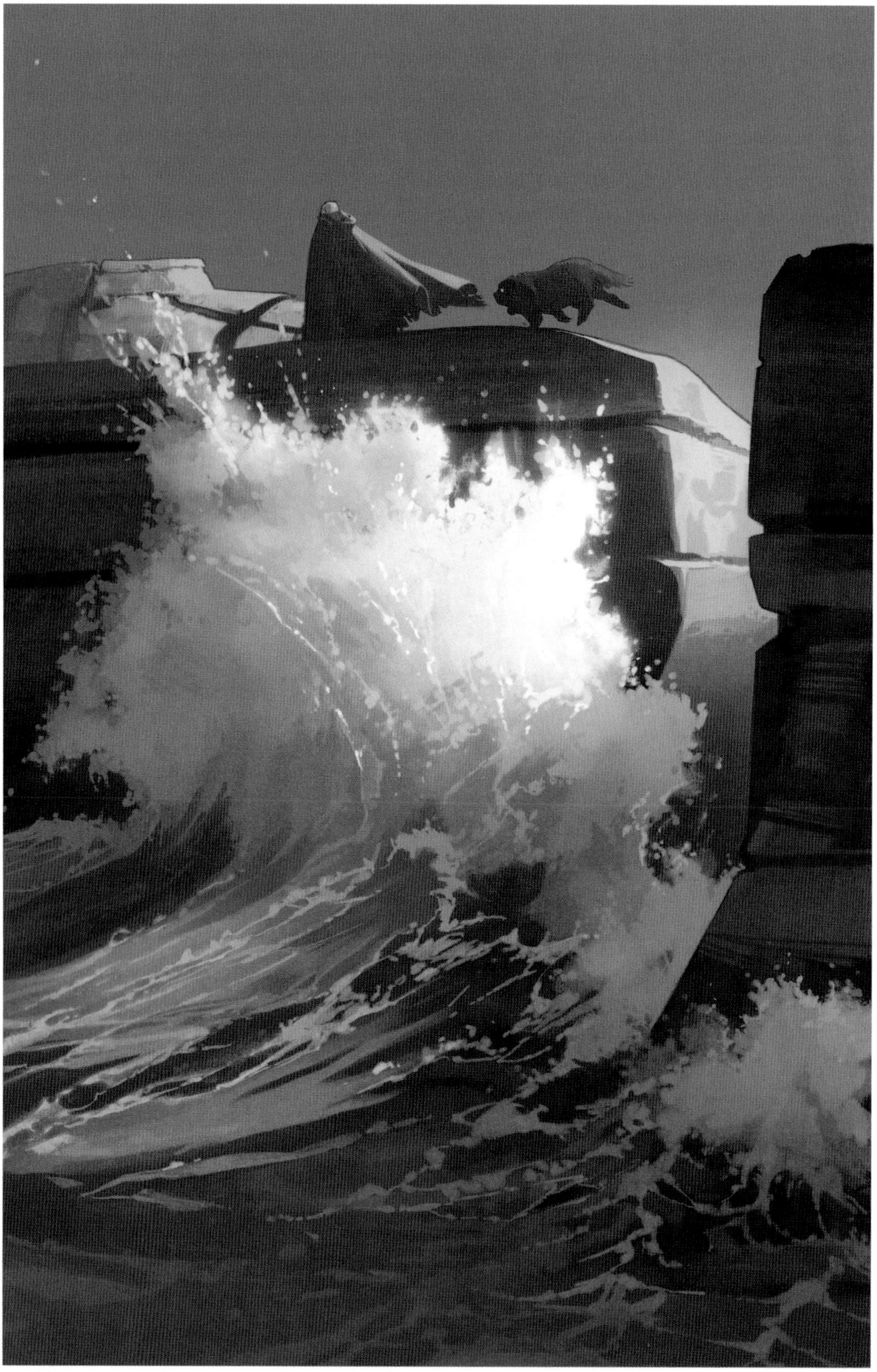

CHAPTER
THIRTY-SIX

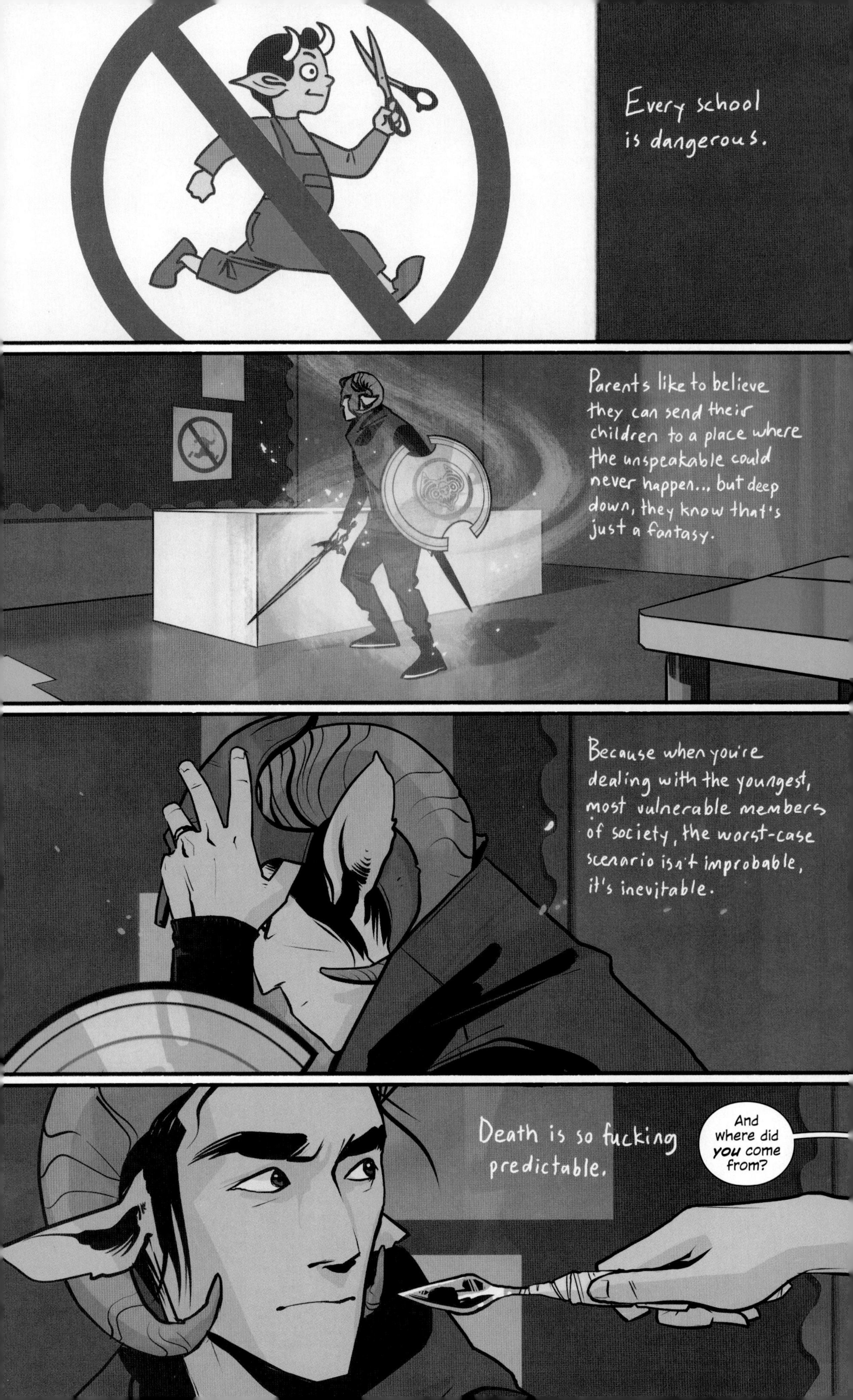
Every school is dangerous.
Parents like to believe they can send their children to a place where the unspeakable could never happen... but deep down, they know that's just a fantasy.
Because when you're dealing with the youngest, most vulnerable members of society, the worst-case scenario isn't improbable, it's inevitable.
Death is so fucking predictable.
And where did *you* come from?

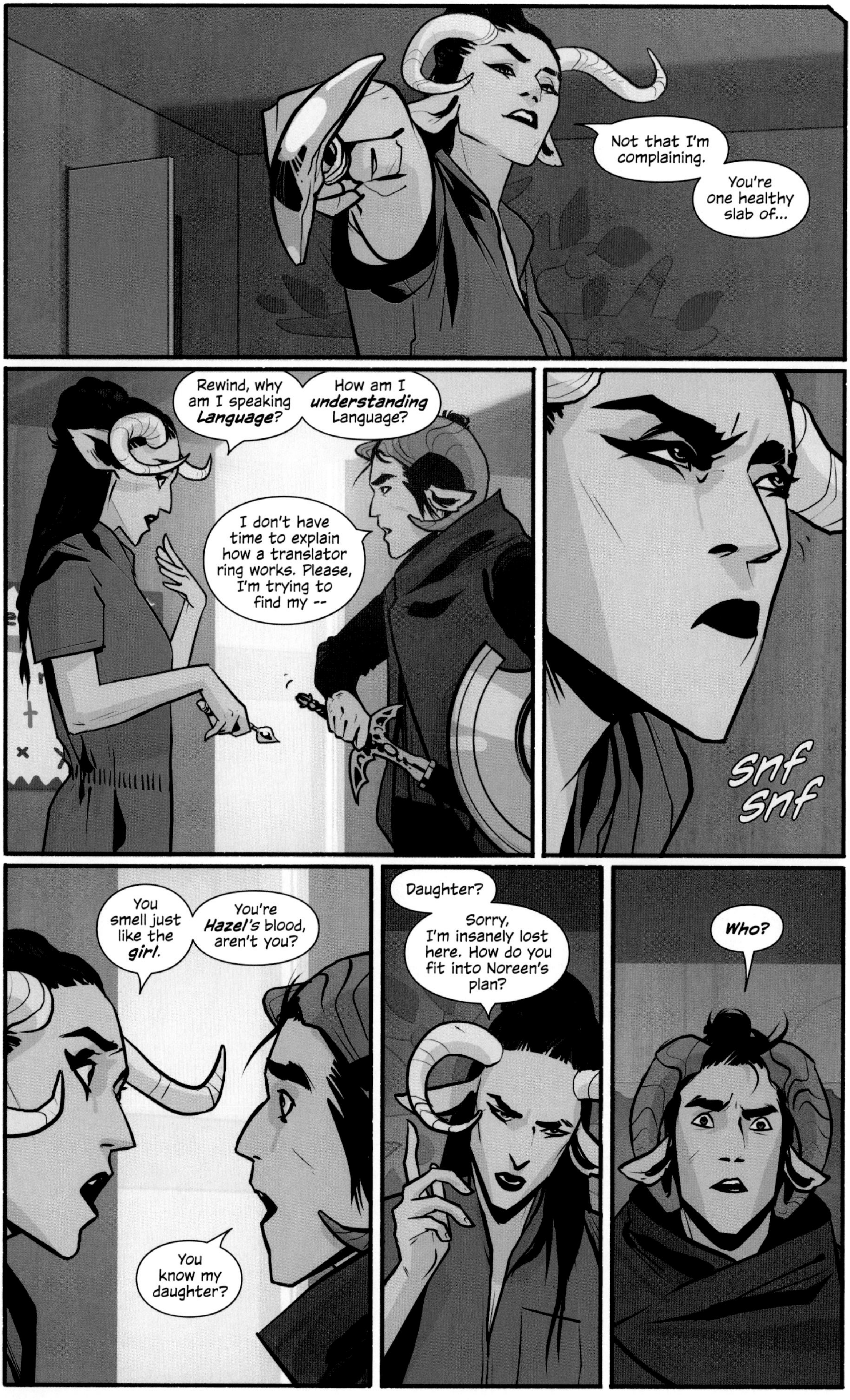
Not that I'm complaining.
You're one healthy slab of...
Rewind, why am I speaking *Language*?
How am I *understanding* Language?
I don't have time to explain how a translator ring works. Please, I'm trying to find my --
Snf snf
You smell just like the *girl*.
You're *Hazel's* blood, aren't you?
You know my daughter?
Daughter?
Sorry, I'm insanely lost here. How do you fit into Noreen's plan?
Who?

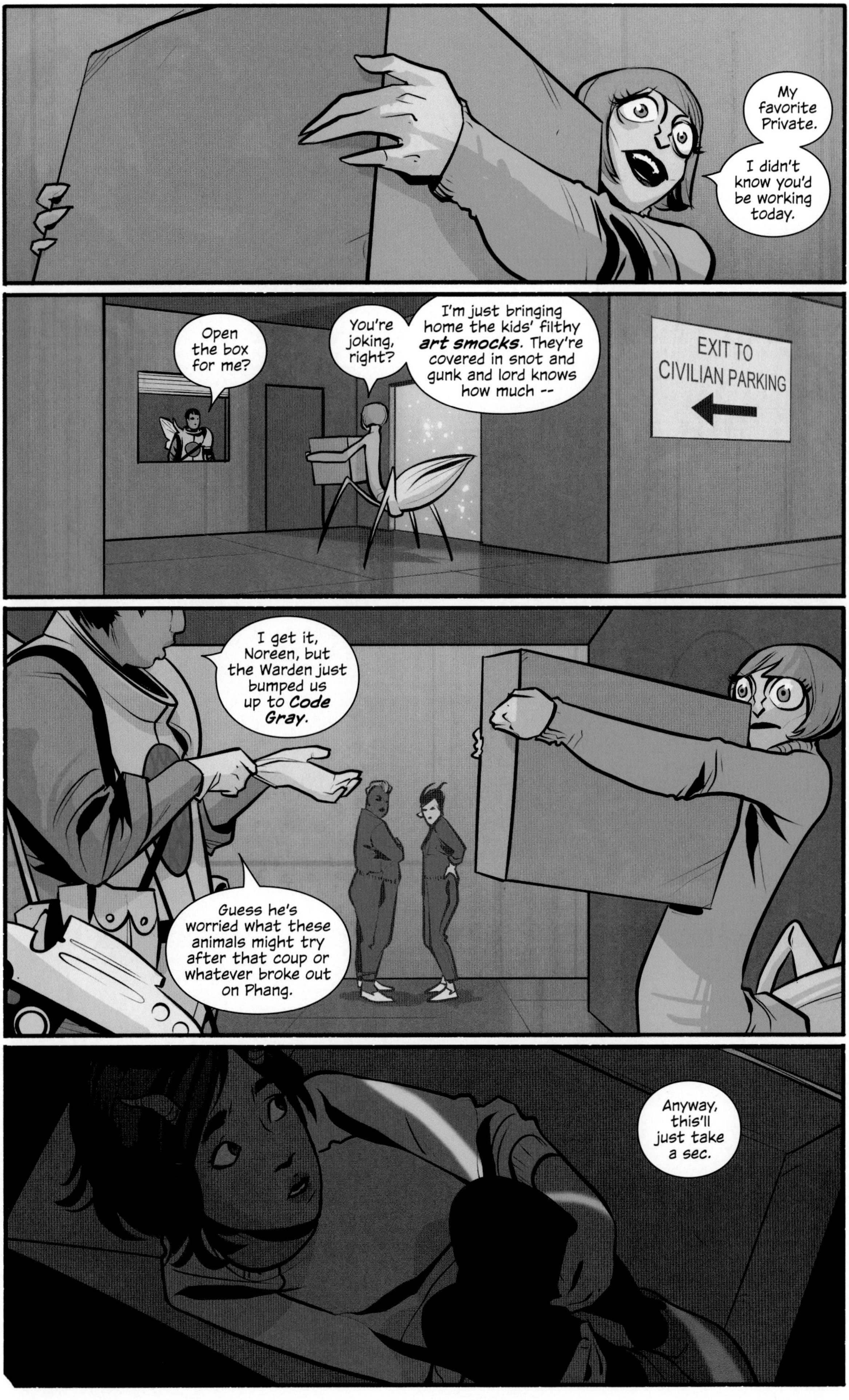
My favorite Private.
I didn't know you'd be working today.
Open the box for me?
You're joking, right?
I'm just bringing home the kids' filthy art smocks. They're covered in snot and gunk and lord knows how much --
EXIT TO CIVILIAN PARKING
I get it, Noreen, but the Warden just bumped us up to Code Gray.
Guess he's worried what these animals might try after that coup or whatever broke out on Phang.
Anyway, this'll just take a sec.

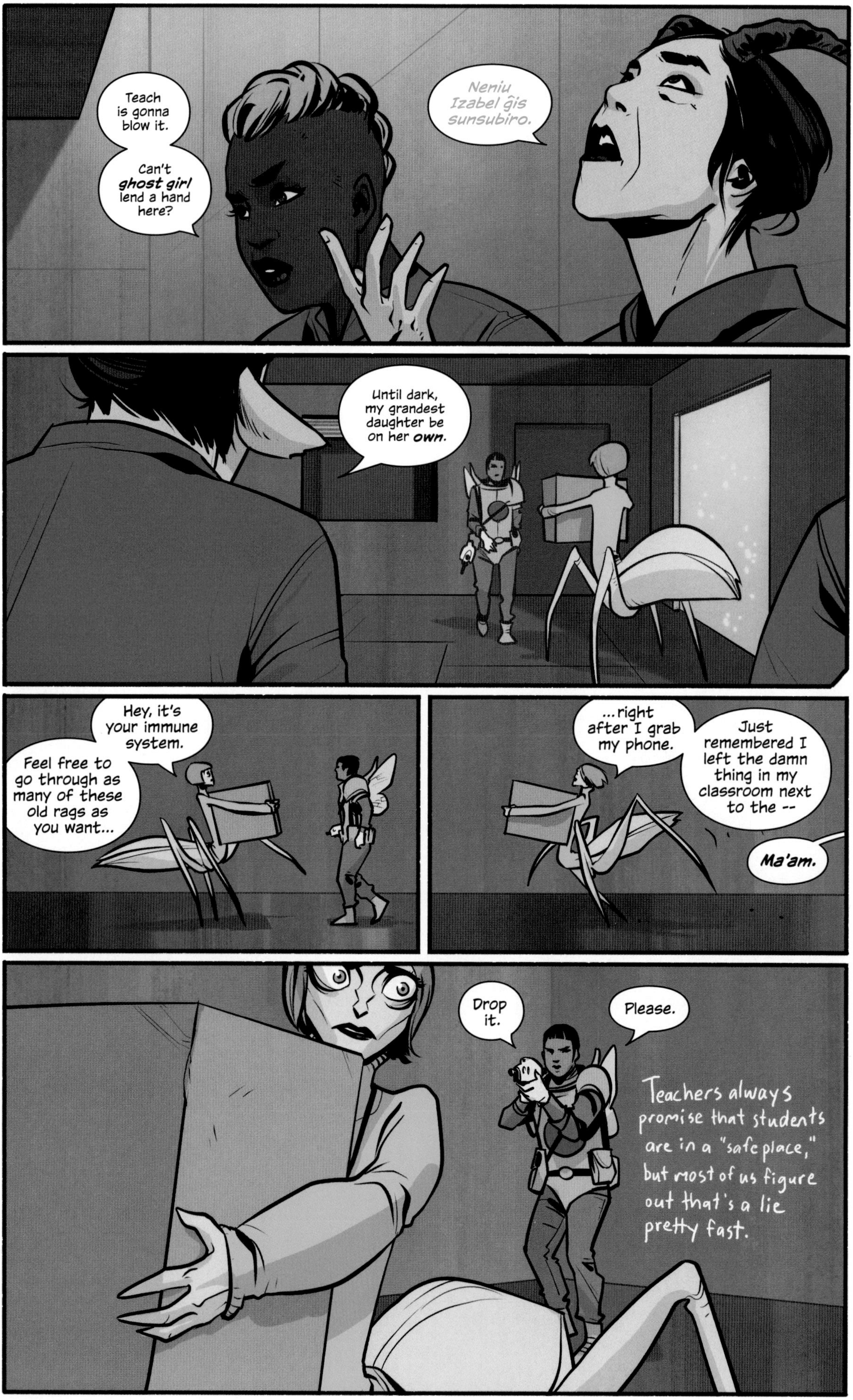
Teach is gonna blow it.
Can't *ghost girl* lend a hand here?
Neniu Izabel ĝis sunsubiro.
Until dark, my grandest daughter be on her *own*.
Hey, it's your immune system.
Feel free to go through as many of these old rags as you want...
...right after I grab my phone.
Just remembered I left the damn thing in my classroom next to the --
Ma'am.
Drop it.
Please.
Teachers always promise that students are in a "safe place," but most of us figure out that's a lie pretty fast.

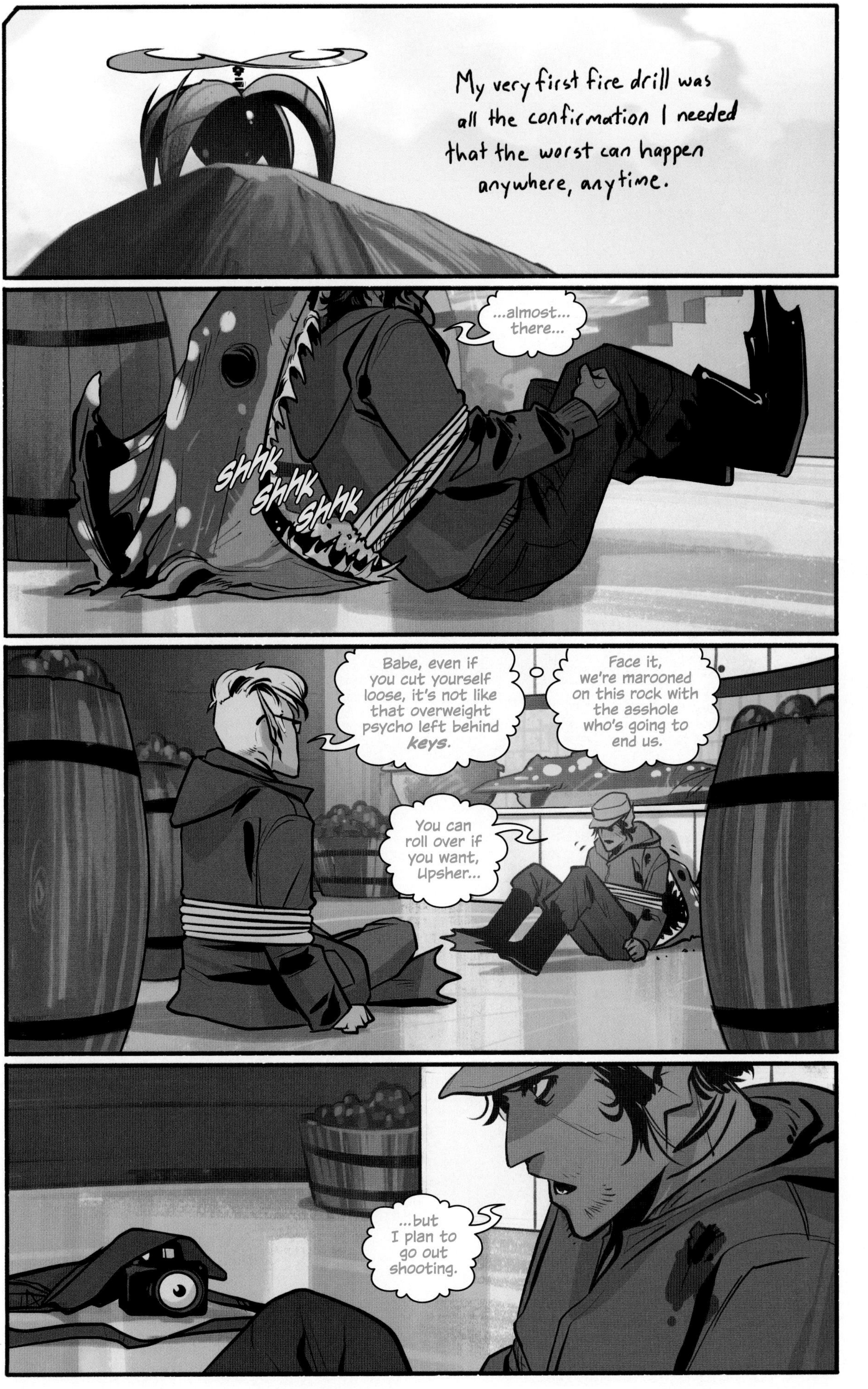
My very first fire drill was all the confirmation I needed that the worst can happen anywhere, anytime.
...almost... there...
SHHK SHHK SHHK
Babe, even if you cut yourself loose, it's not like that overweight psycho left behind *keys*.
Face it, we're marooned on this rock with the asshole who's going to end us.
You can roll over if you want, Upsher...
...but I plan to go out shooting.

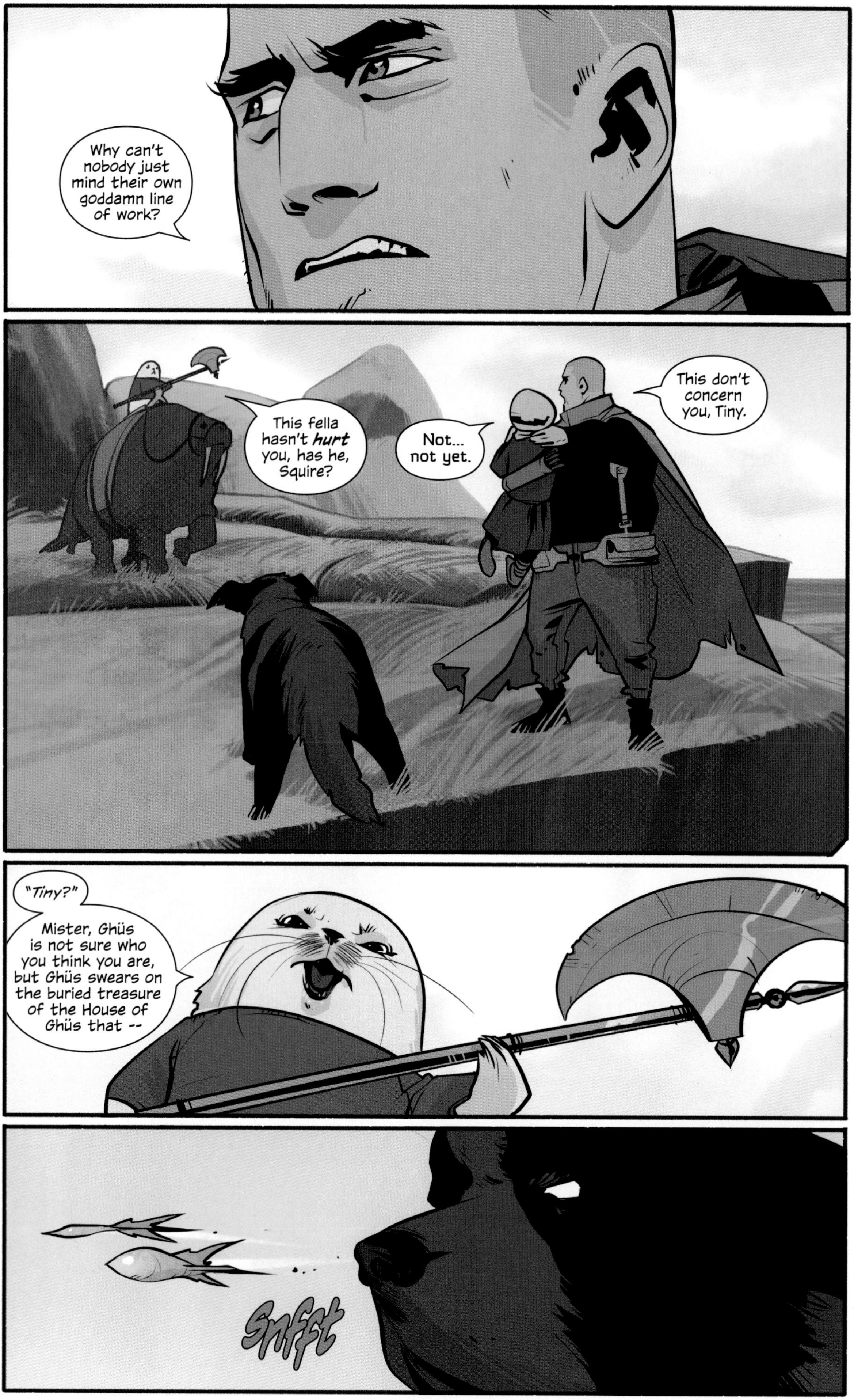
Why can't nobody just mind their own goddamn line of work?
This fella hasn't *hurt* you, has he, Squire?
Not... not yet.
This don't concern you, Tiny.
"Tiny?"
Mister, Ghüs is not sure who you think you are, but Ghüs swears on the buried treasure of the House of Ghüs that --
Snfft

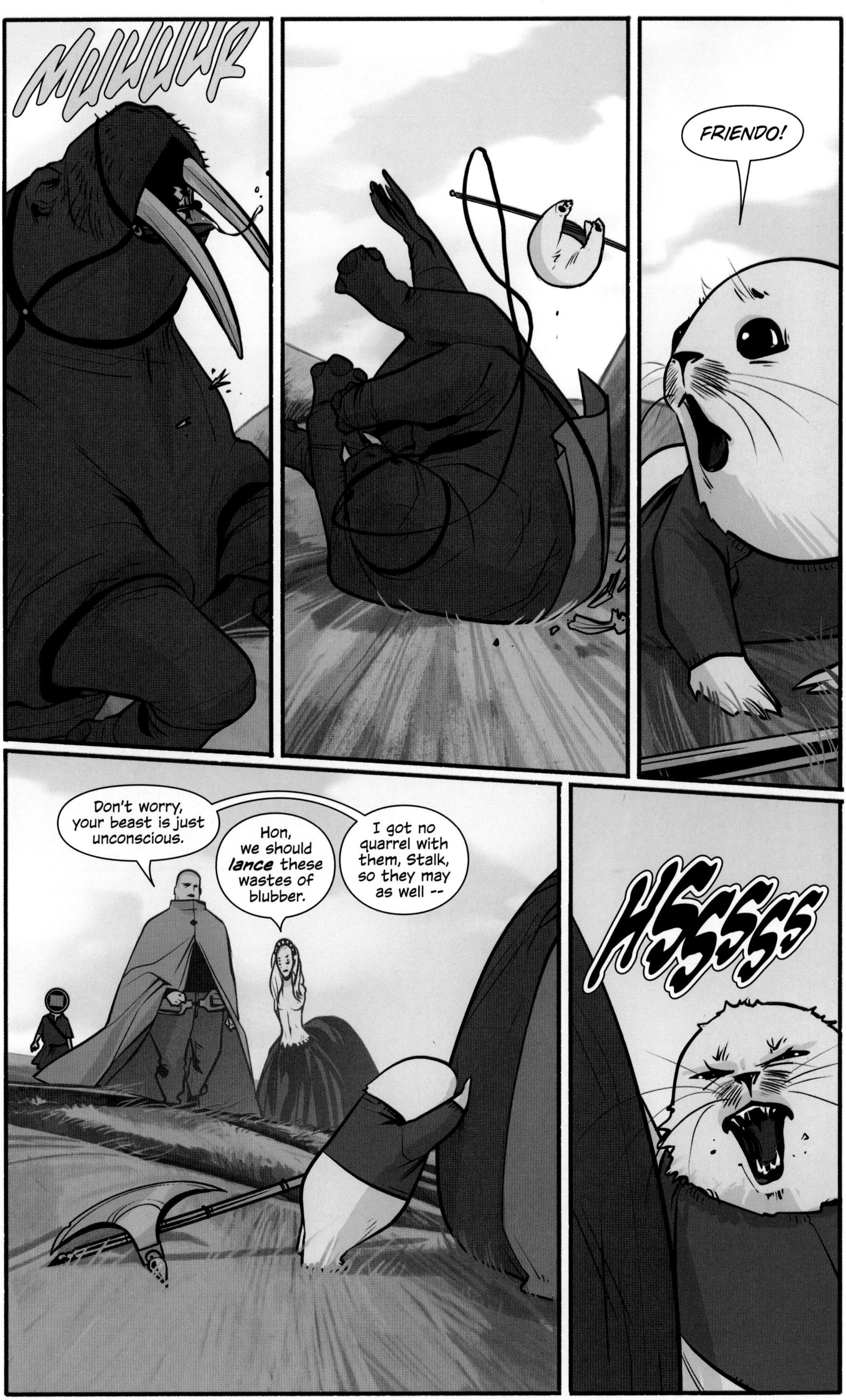
MWWWWR
FRIENDO!
Don't worry, your beast is just unconscious.
Hon, we should lance these wastes of blubber.
I got no quarrel with them, Stalk, so they may as well --
HSSSSS

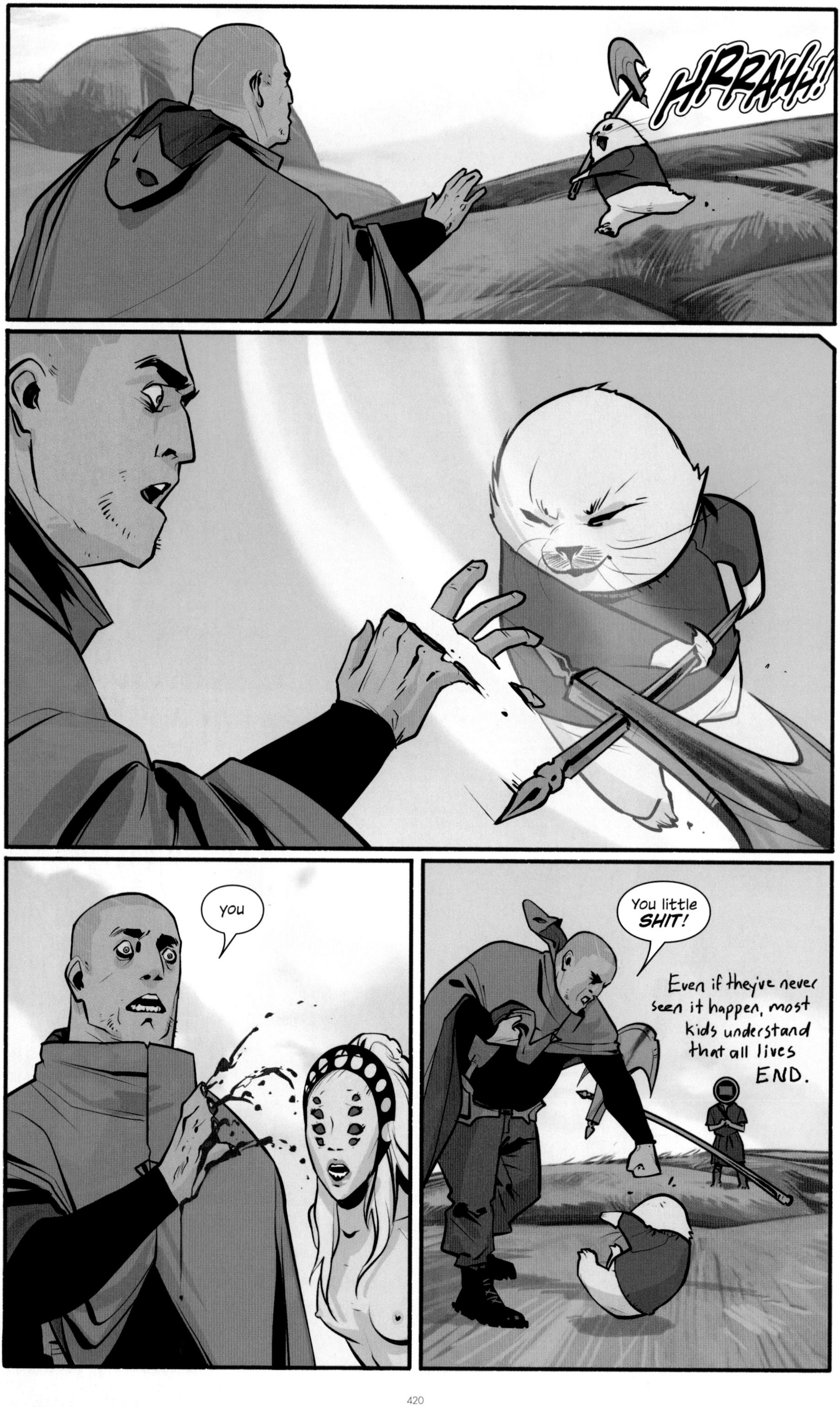
HRRAHH!
You
You little SHIT!
Even if they've never seen it happen, most kids understand that all lives END.

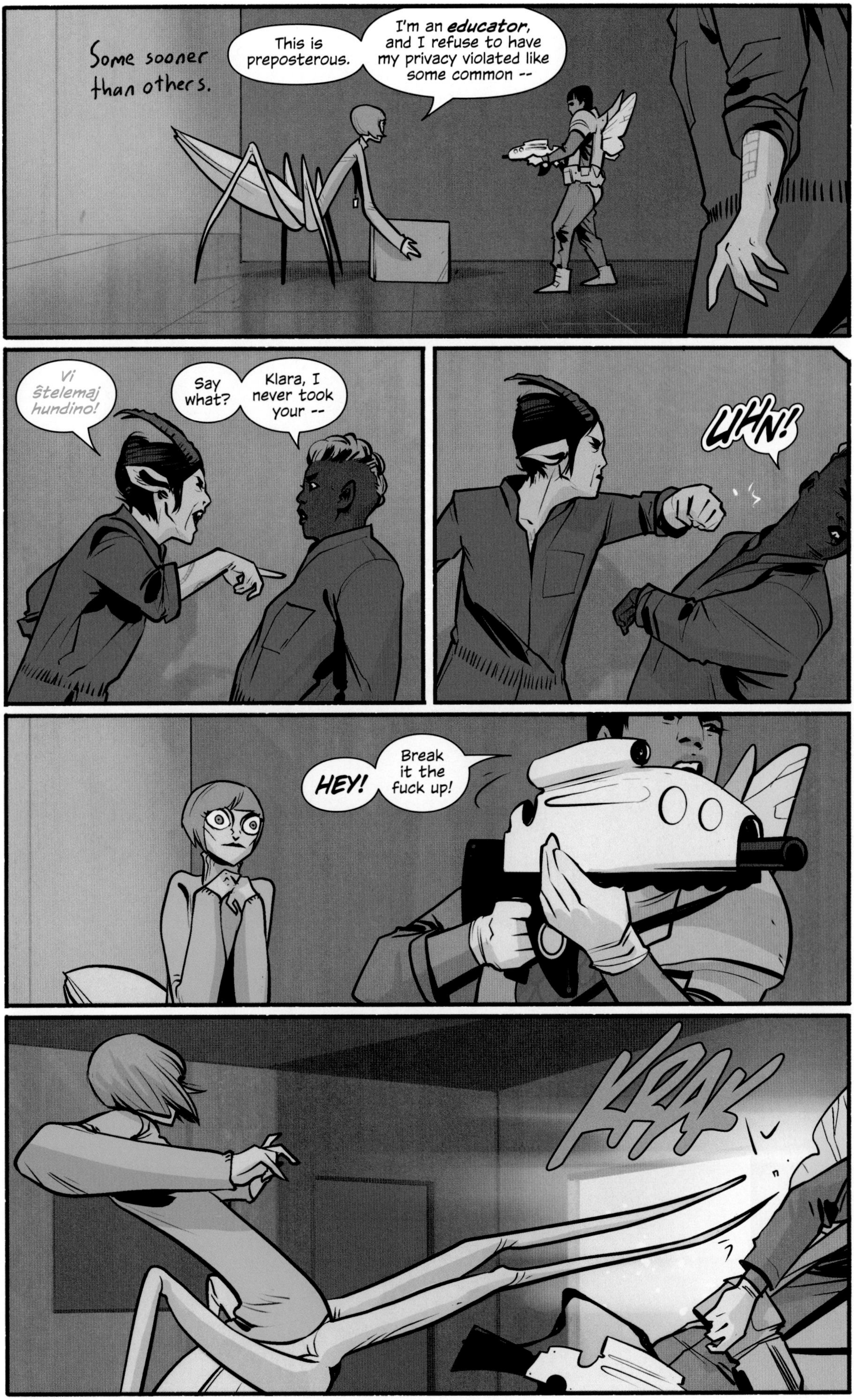

Some sooner than others.
This is preposterous.
I'm an **educator**, and I refuse to have my privacy violated like some common --
Vi ŝtelemaj hundino!
Say what?
Klara, I never took your --
UHN!
HEY!
Break it the fuck up!
KRAK

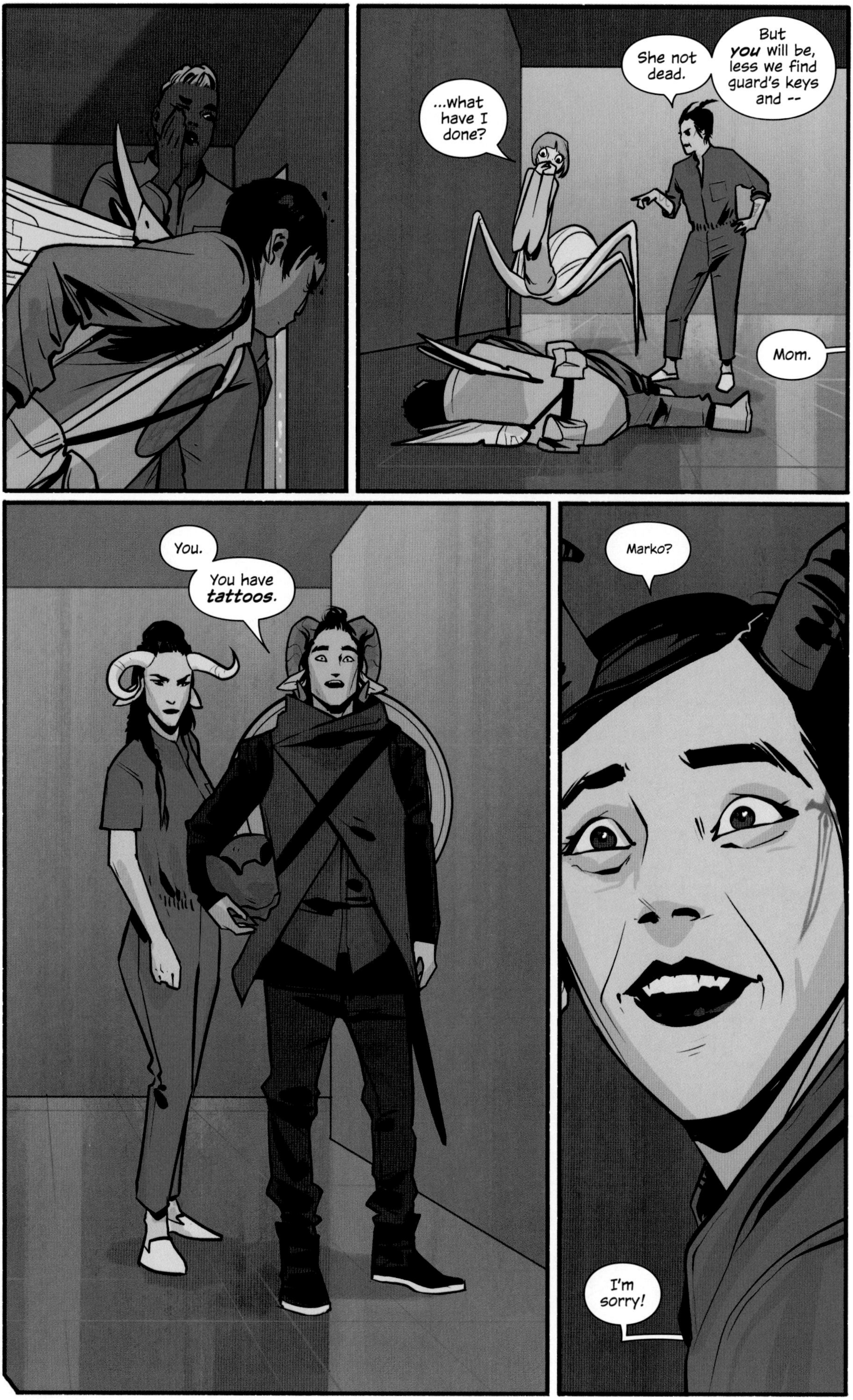
...what have I done?
She not dead.
But *you* will be, less we find guard's keys and --
Mom.
You.
You have *tattoos*.
Marko?
I'm sorry!

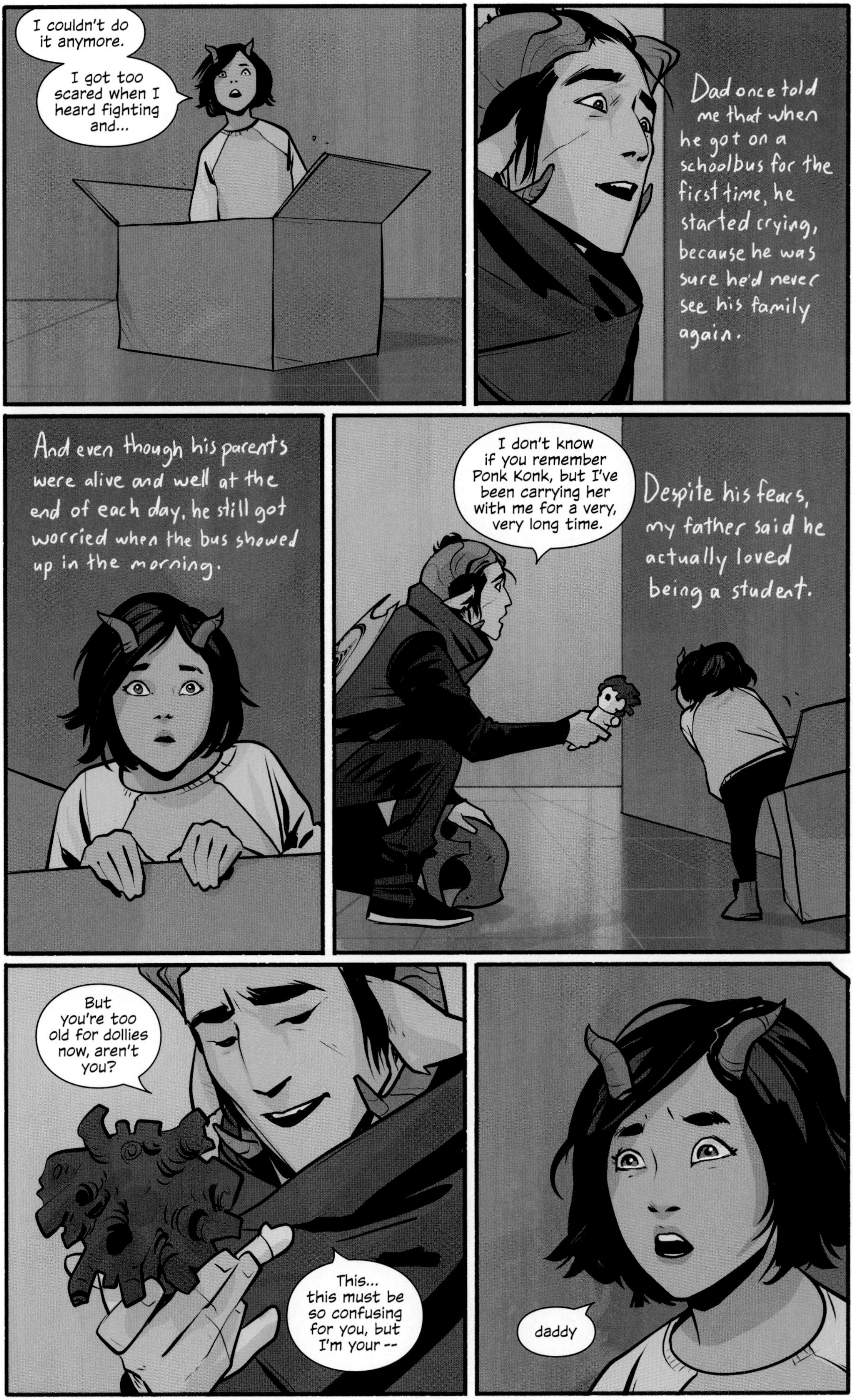
I couldn't do it anymore.
I got too scared when I heard fighting and...
Dad once told me that when he got on a schoolbus for the first time, he started crying, because he was sure he'd never see his family again.
And even though his parents were alive and well at the end of each day, he still got worried when the bus showed up in the morning.
I don't know if you remember Ponk Konk, but I've been carrying her with me for a very, very long time.
Despite his fears, my father said he actually loved being a student.
But you're too old for dollies now, aren't you?
This... this must be so confusing for you, but I'm your --
daddy

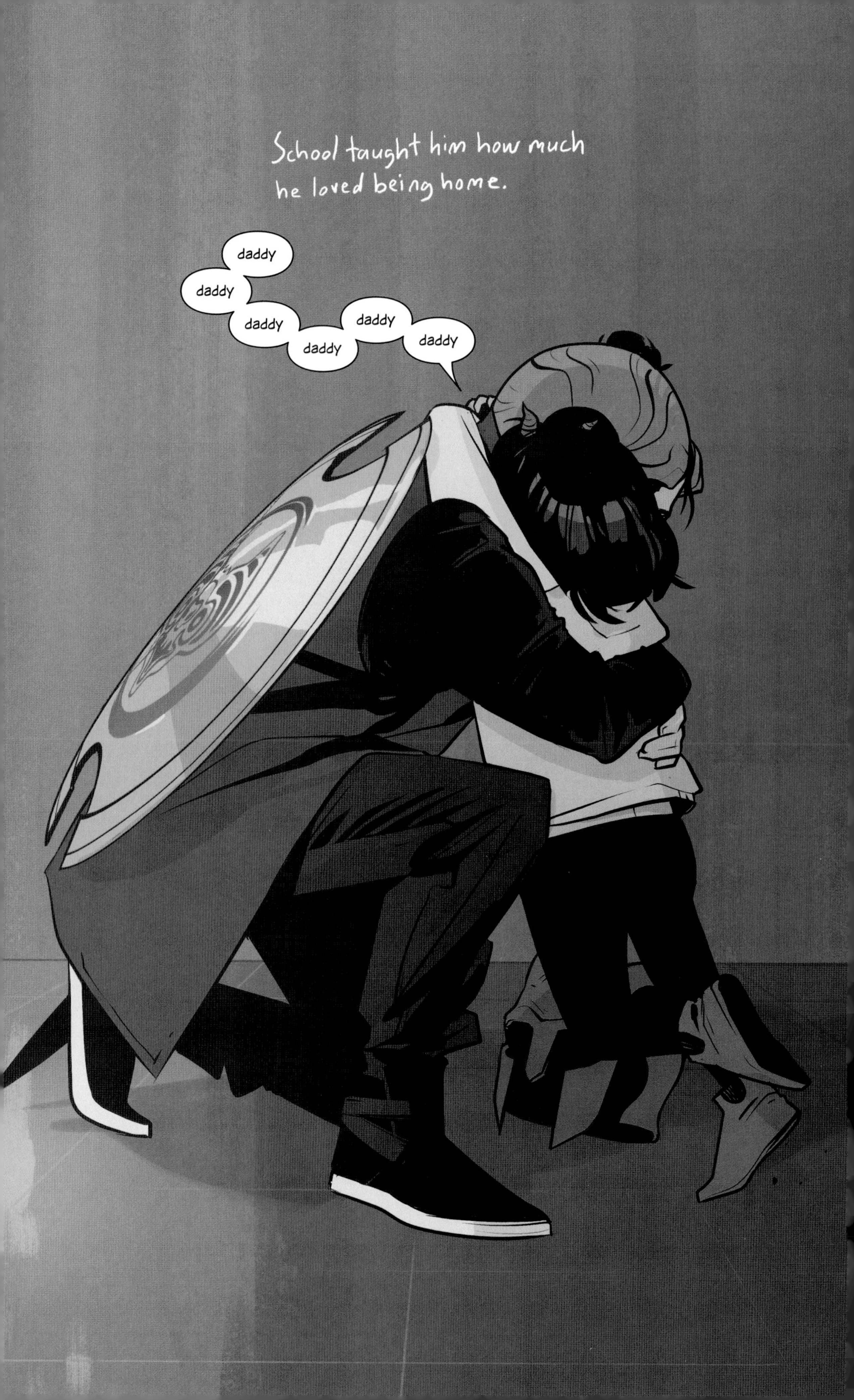
School taught him how much he loved being home.
daddy
daddy
daddy
daddy
daddy
daddy

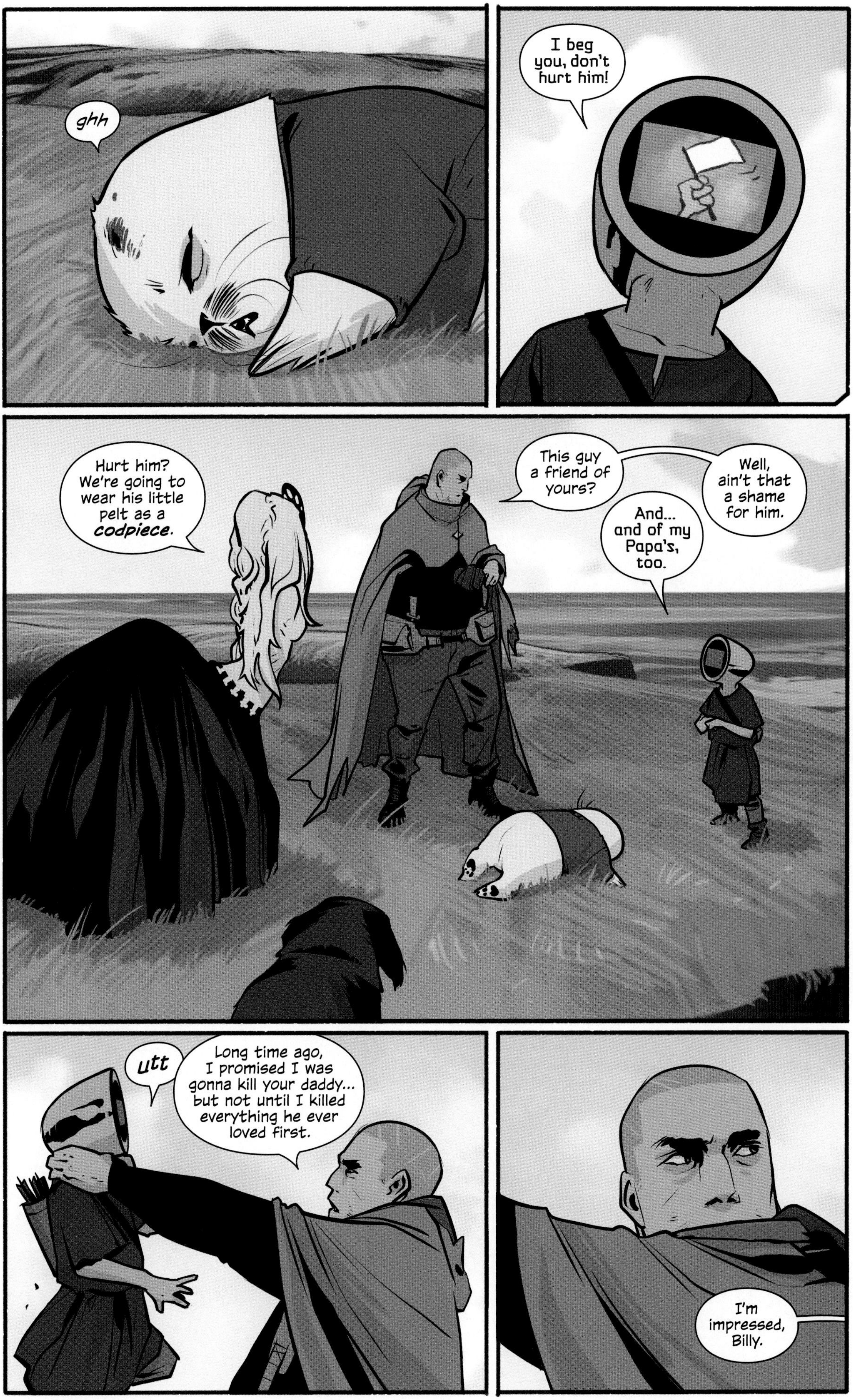
ghh
I beg you, don't hurt him!
Hurt him? We're going to wear his little pelt as a *codpiece*.
This guy a friend of yours?
And... and of my Papa's, too.
Well, ain't that a shame for him.
utt
Long time ago, I promised I was gonna kill your daddy... but not until I killed everything he ever loved first.
I'm impressed, Billy.

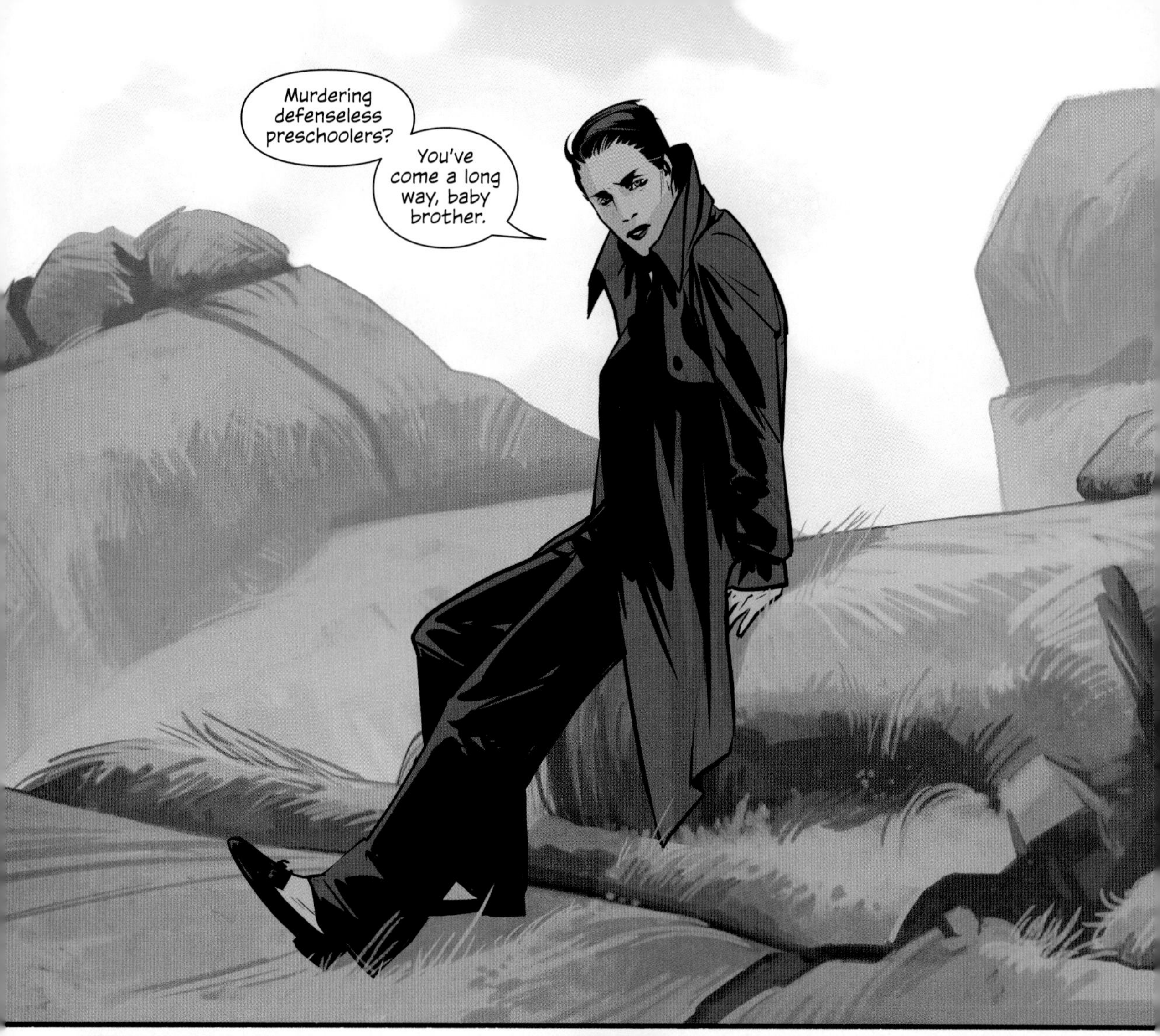
Murdering defenseless preschoolers?
You've come a long way, baby brother.

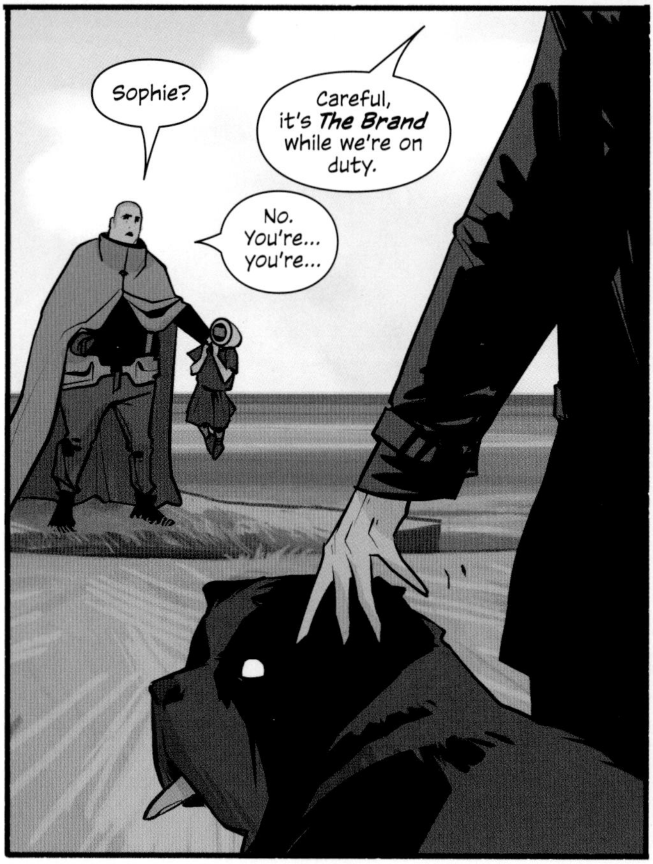
Sophie?
Careful, it's ***The Brand*** while we're on duty.
No. You're... you're...

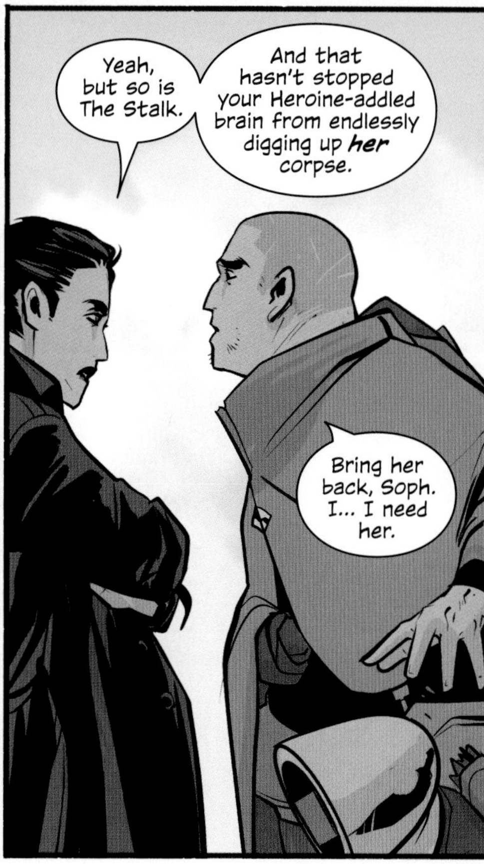
Yeah, but so is The Stalk.
And that hasn't stopped your Heroine-addled brain from endlessly digging up ***her*** corpse.
Bring her back, Soph. I... I need her.

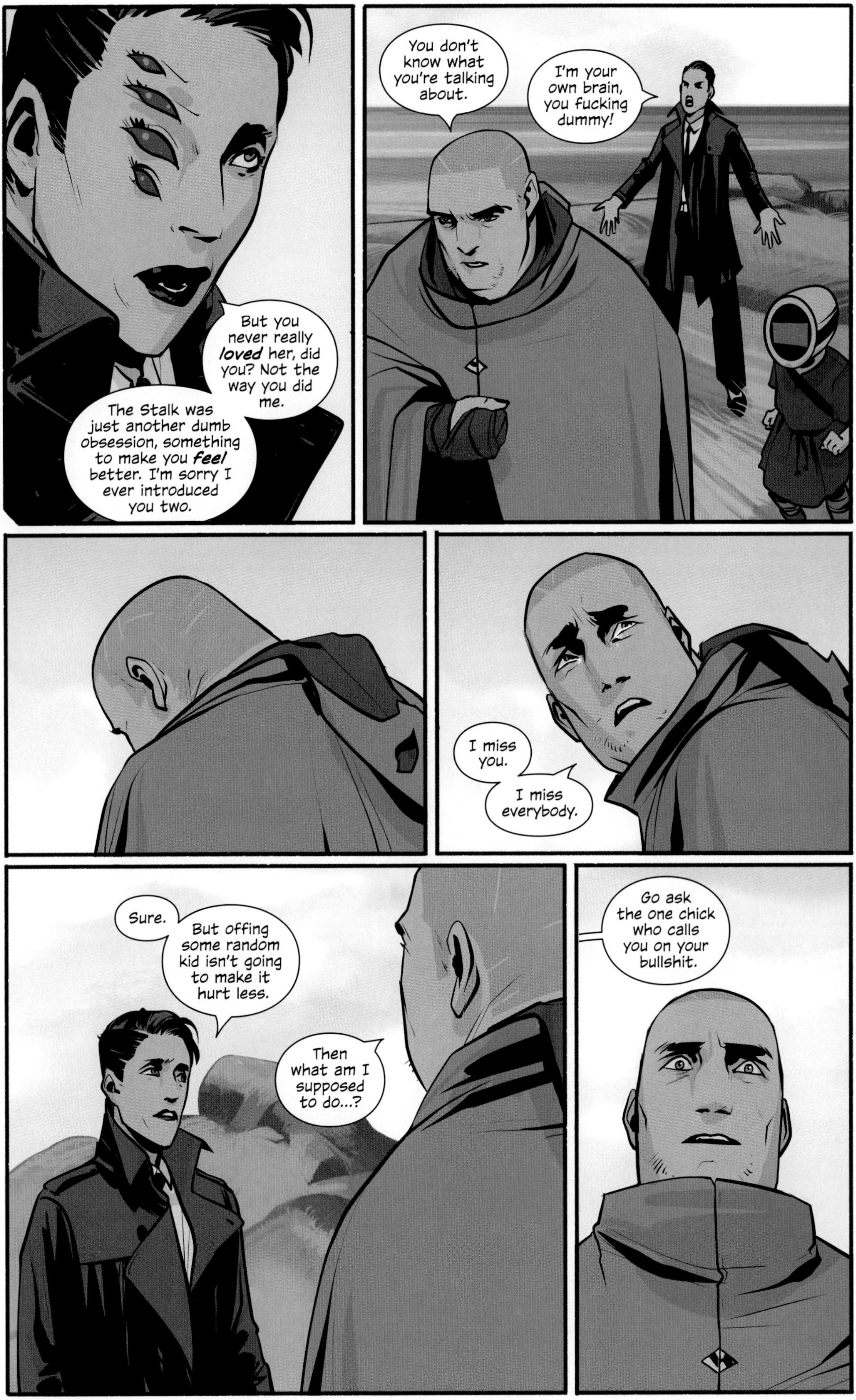
But you never really *loved* her, did you? Not the way you did me.
The Stalk was just another dumb obsession, something to make you *feel* better. I'm sorry I ever introduced you two.
You don't know what you're talking about.
I'm your own brain, you fucking dummy!
I miss you.
I miss everybody.
Sure.
But offing some random kid isn't going to make it hurt less.
Then what am I supposed to do...?
Go ask the one chick who calls you on your bullshit.

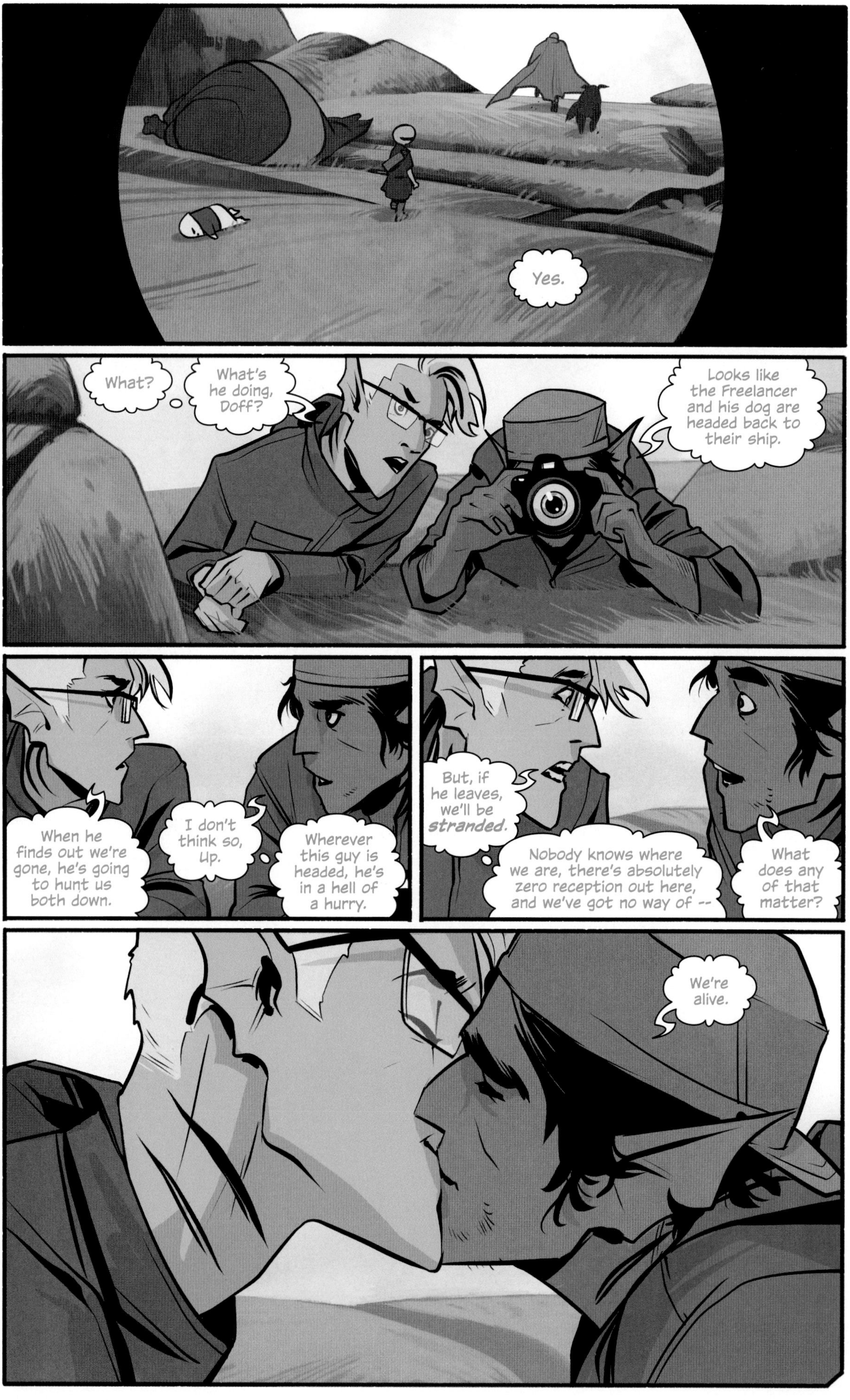
Yes.
What?
What's he doing, Doff?
Looks like the Freelancer and his dog are headed back to their ship.
When he finds out we're gone, he's going to hunt us both down.
I don't think so, Up.
Wherever this guy is headed, he's in a hell of a hurry.
But, if he leaves, we'll be *stranded*.
Nobody knows where we are, there's absolutely zero reception out here, and we've got no way of --
What does any of that matter?
We're alive.

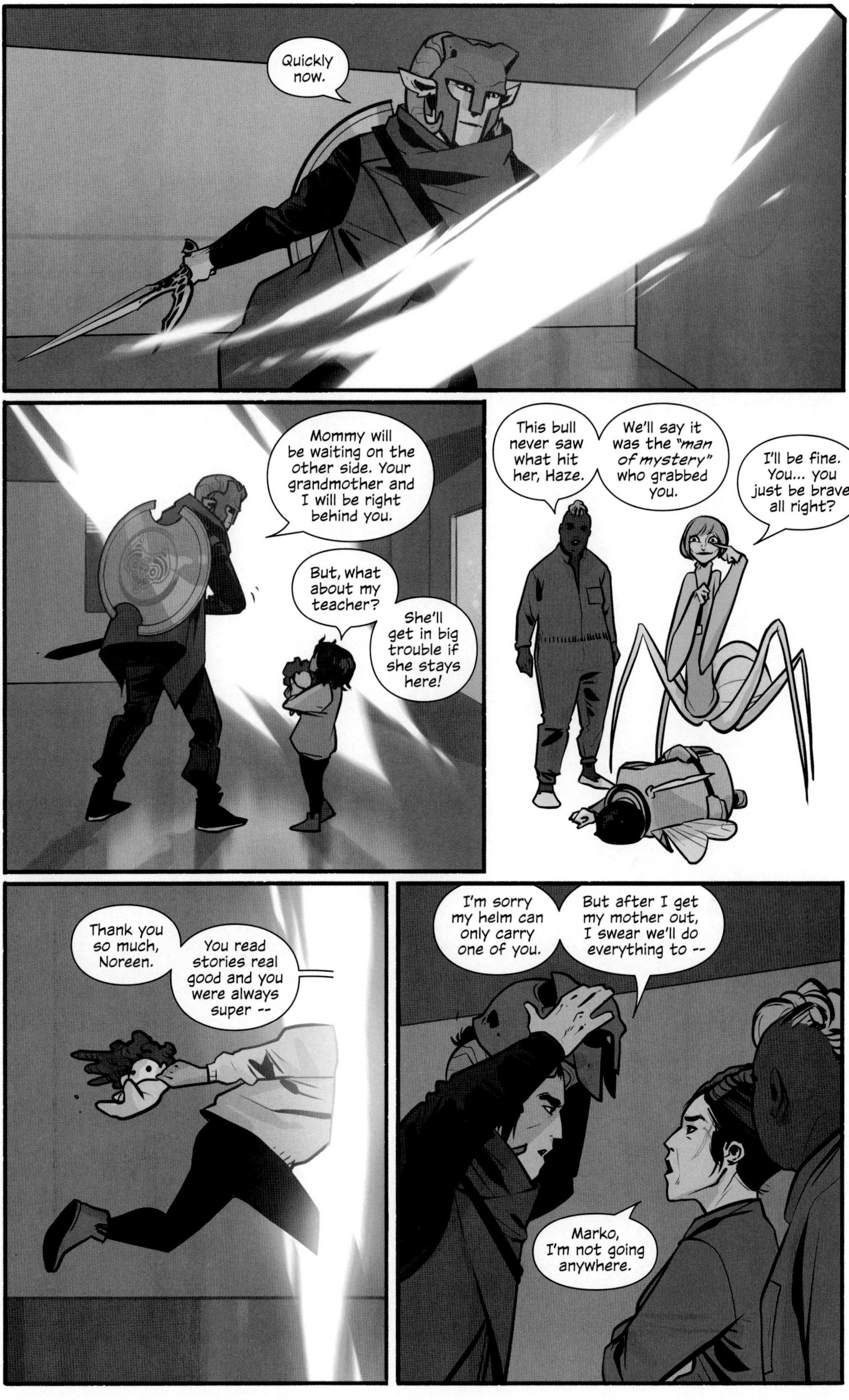
Quickly now.
Mommy will be waiting on the other side. Your grandmother and I will be right behind you.
But, what about my teacher?
She'll get in big trouble if she stays here!
This bull never saw what hit her, Haze.
We'll say it was the *"man of mystery"* who grabbed you.
I'll be fine. You... you just be brave, all right?
Thank you so much, Noreen.
You read stories real good and you were always super --
I'm sorry my helm can only carry one of you.
But after I get my mother out, I swear we'll do everything to --
Marko, I'm not going anywhere.

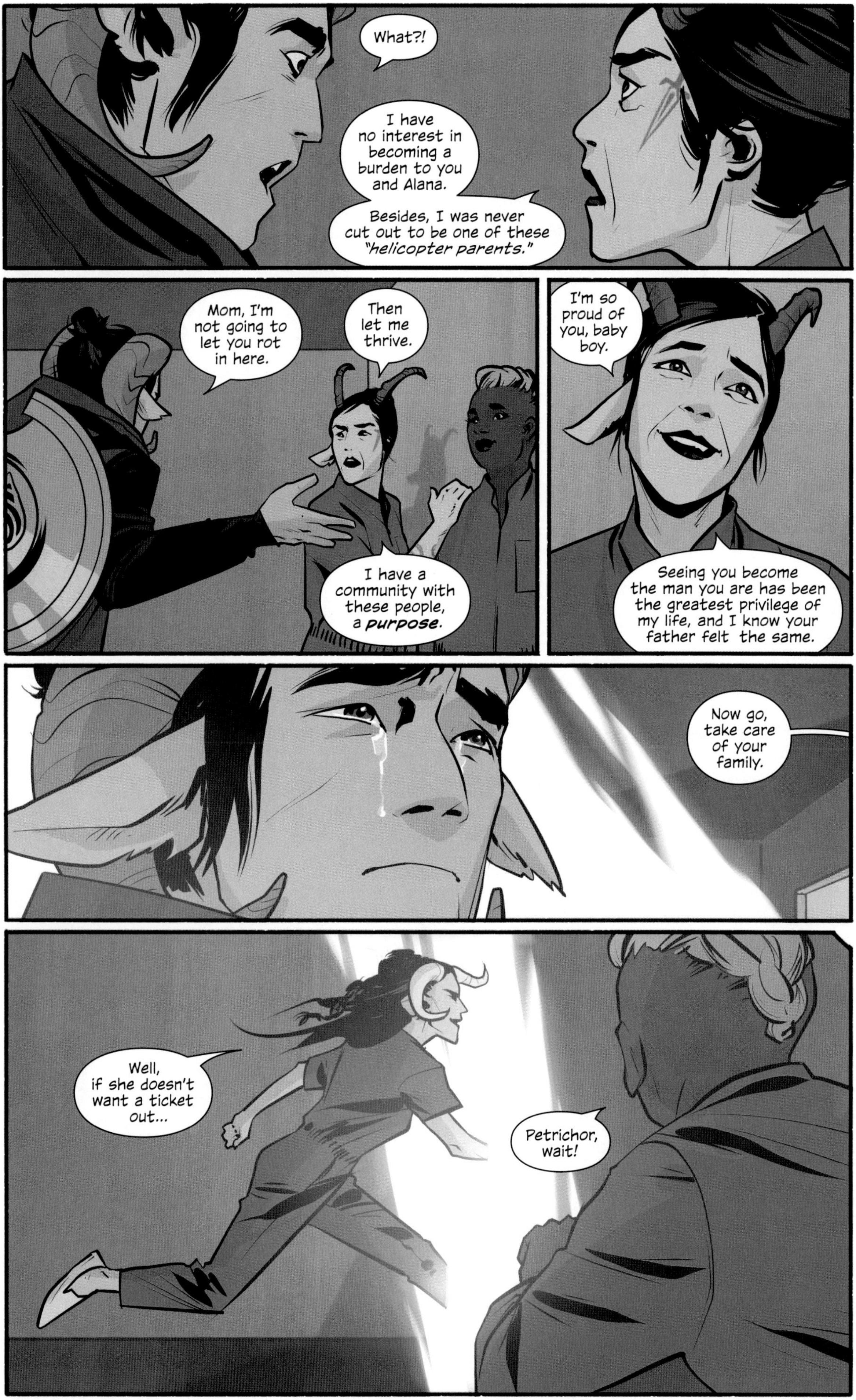

What?!
I have no interest in becoming a burden to you and Alana.
Besides, I was never cut out to be one of these "helicopter parents."
Mom, I'm not going to let you rot in here.
Then let me thrive.
I have a community with these people, a *purpose*.
I'm so proud of you, baby boy.
Seeing you become the man you are has been the greatest privilege of my life, and I know your father felt the same.
Now go, take care of your family.
Well, if she doesn't want a ticket out...
Petrichor, wait!

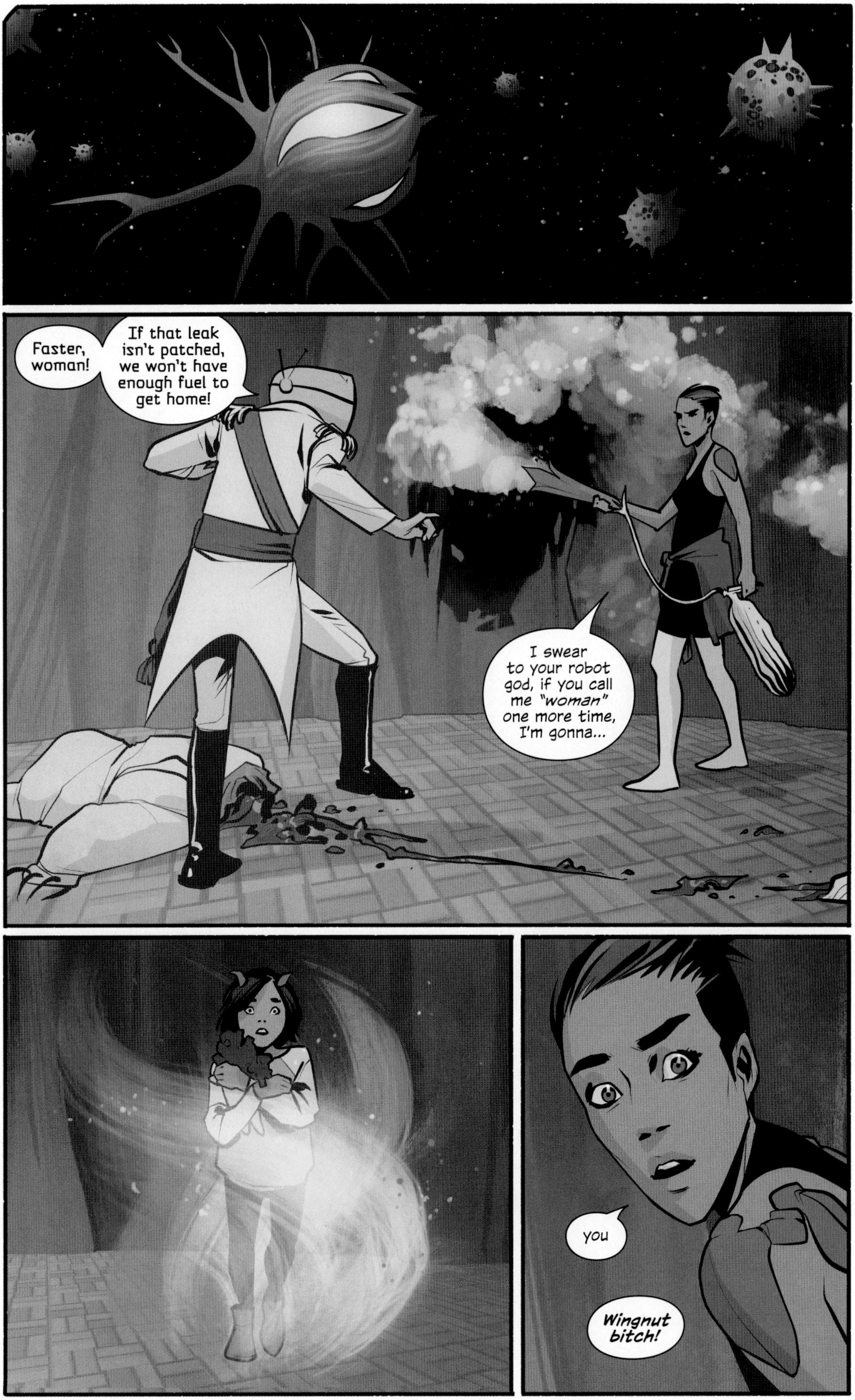
Faster, woman!
If that leak isn't patched, we won't have enough fuel to get home!
I swear to your robot god, if you call me "*woman*" one more time, I'm gonna...
you
Wingnut bitch!

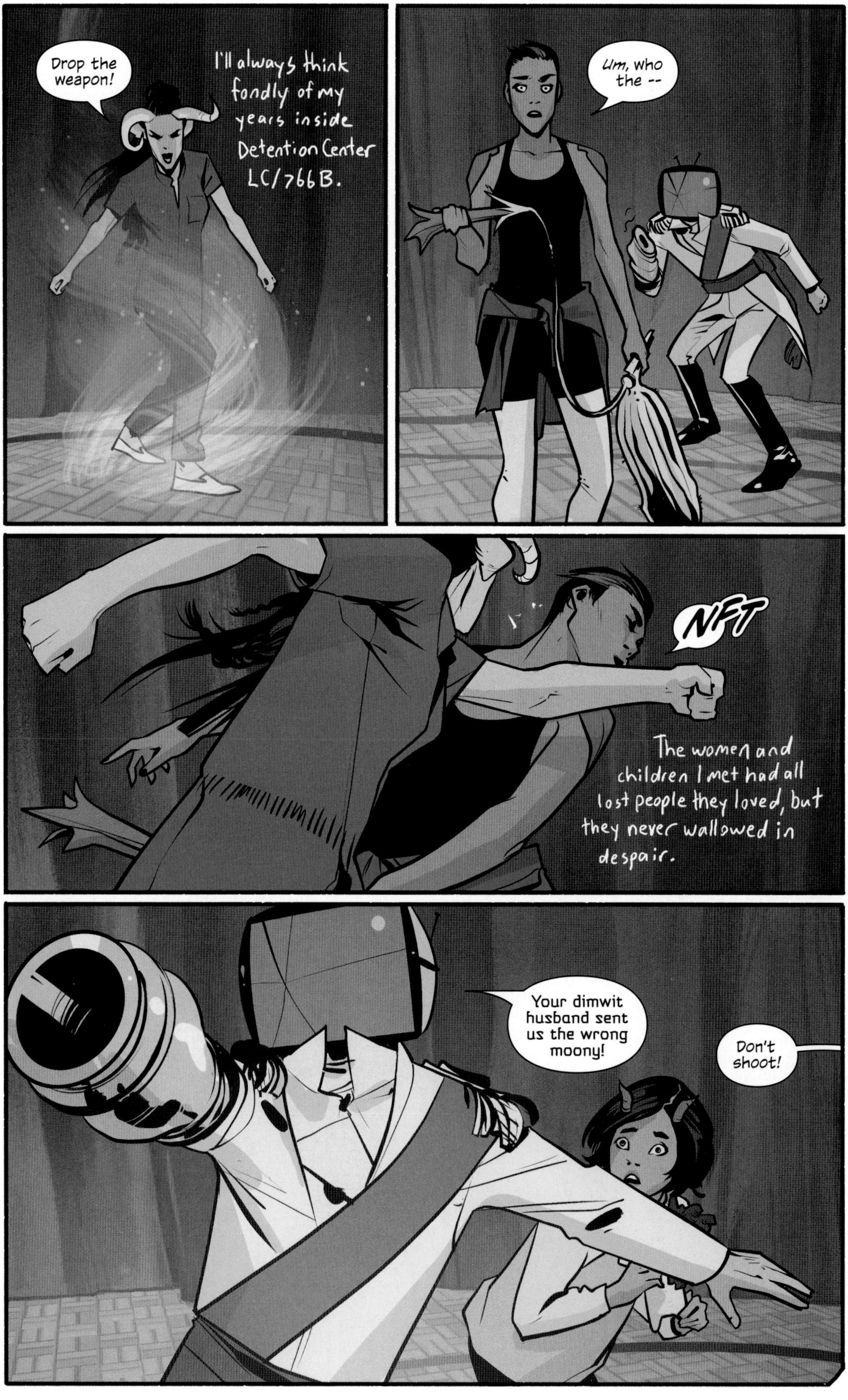
Drop the weapon!
I'll always think fondly of my years inside Detention Center LC/766B.
Um, who the --
NFT
The women and children I met had all lost people they loved, but they never wallowed in despair.
Your dimwit husband sent us the wrong moony!
Don't shoot!

We're all on the same side here.

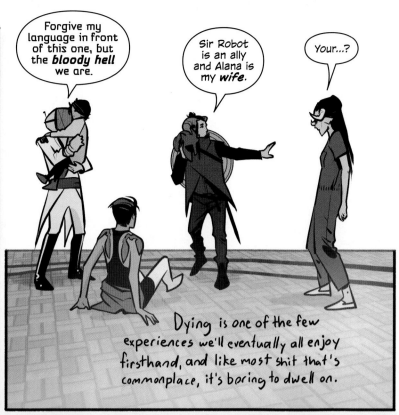

Forgive my language in front of this one, but the *bloody hell* we are.

Sir Robot is an ally and Alana is my *wife*.

Your...?

Dying is one of the few experiences we'll eventually all enjoy firsthand, and like most shit that's commonplace, it's boring to dwell on.

I think I'm gonna puke.

Sorry, *who* is this terrible woman?

My fellow inmates/classmates (and really, what's the difference?) showed me it was more interesting to concentrate on the living.

You're just lucky I'd never fell a female who's expecting.

...expecting what?

I can smell it from here.

You're *pregnant*.

Because death is fucking predictable...

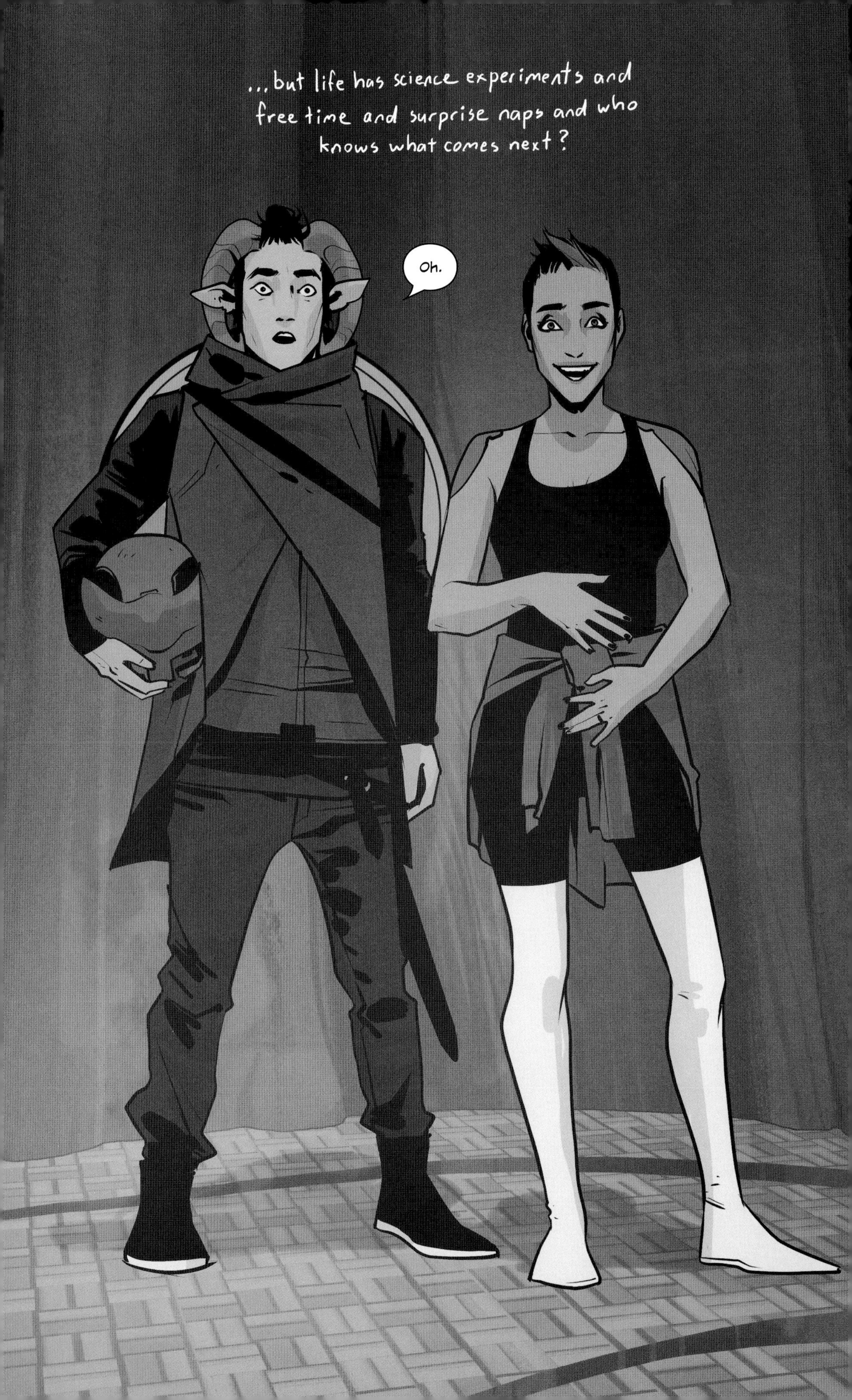
...but life has science experiments and free time and surprise naps and who knows what comes next?
Oh.

to be continued

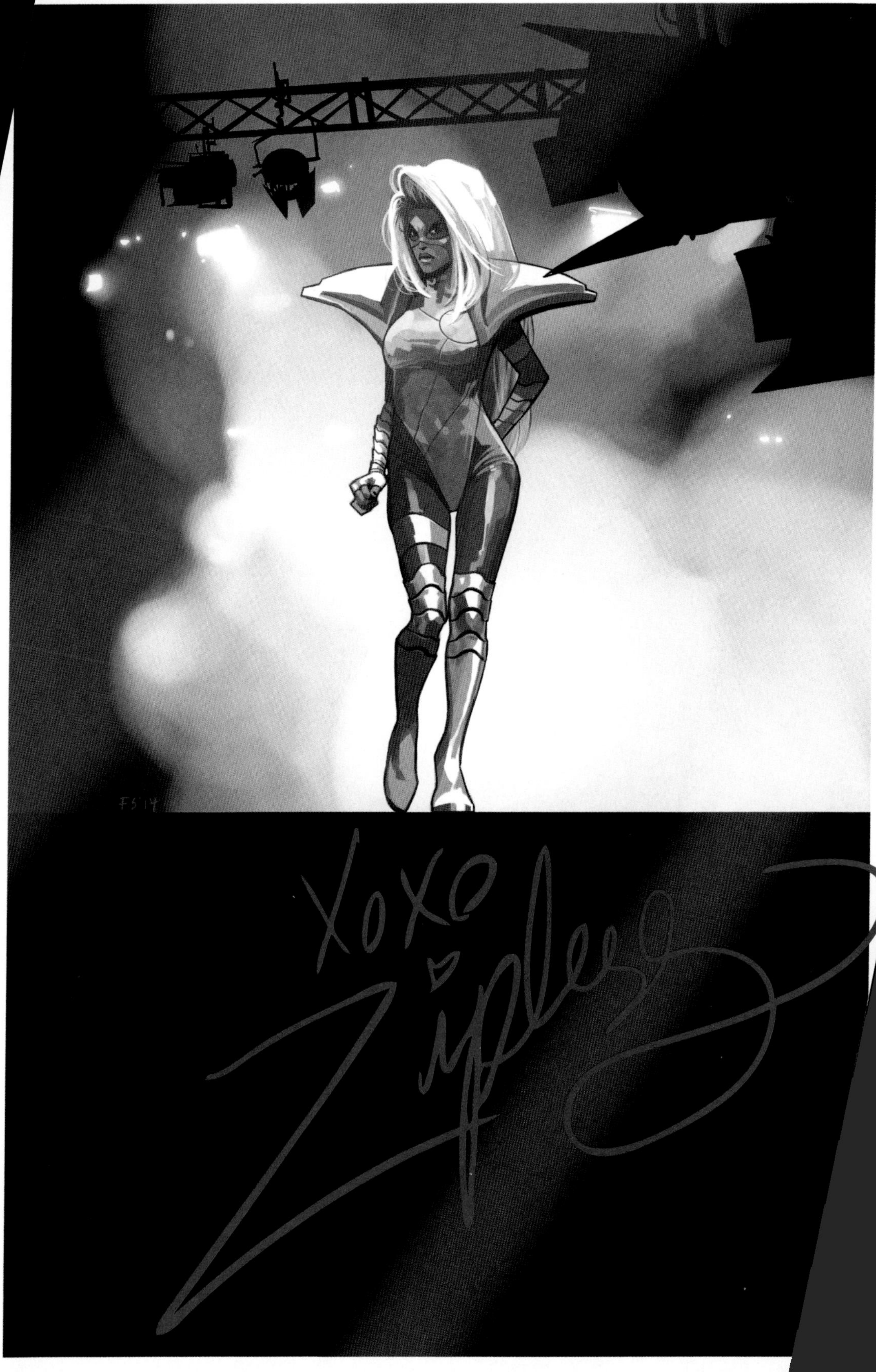
FS '14
XOXO
Zipless

TO BE CONTINUED

4335 VAN NUYS BOULEVARD • SUITE 332 • SHERMAN OAKS • CA 91403

And so, Book Two closes with a rare happy ending for our family. I'm sure it'll be all roses and sunshine after this.

Brian Vaughan here, welcoming you to another special installment of our old-school letter column *To Be Continued* (send your hate mail and/or seasonal fruitcakes to our offices at the address above), where we routinely feature readers' Saga cosplay photos, drawings of my trusted mail-dachshund Hamburger K. Vaughan, and even the occasional marriage proposal.

No judgment if you collected-edition lovers don't read each issue of our monthly series, but you're missing out on crackerjack correspondence like this:

Dear Sagacious Ones,

Please never have anyone but Fiona draw Saga. *I don't care about alternate covers or whatever, but I don't want to see anyone but Ms. Staples illustrating Hazel's adventures.*

Yours truly,
Danielle A.
Tuscaloosa, AL

Never fear, Danielle. I'm confident you speak for our entire audience. Not only wouldn't I ever collaborate with another artist on *Saga*, I literally couldn't do it without her. "Ms. Staples" isn't just the illustrator of our series, she's my fellow author.

Fiona shouldn't take the blame for my wonky dialogue or infuriating plot decisions, but I definitely wouldn't know how to write *Saga* without her ideas for our stories, characters and worlds, not to mention the wholly unique way in which she brings them all to life. I've said it before, but Hazel's journey will only last as long as Fiona enjoys guiding it, which I still hope will be for years to come.

And we've flirted with alternate covers in the past (including a gorgeous rendition of The Stalk from the legendary Paul Pope), but I'm starting to worry about what the current glut of those "collectible" variant covers means for the long-term health of our comics' retailing partners and the industry itself.

More importantly, I realize how essential Fiona's covers are to each chapter of our story. Those striking images help set the tone for every issue, and because Fiona often has to draw them months before I've written the corresponding script, her covers also help shape what each arc of *Saga* is really about.

So yeah, Staples is the only artist I want to collaborate with when it comes to these characters, just as Fonografiks is the only man of mystery we want lettering their words, and just as Eric Stephenson and Image Comics are the only folks we want publishing the finished product. I love what each creator brings to the table, and I'd never want to mess with the makeup of our merry band.

That said... wouldn't it be fucking awesome to see Todd McFarlane draw Marko?

So, as an exclusive treat for those of you kind (and patient) enough to shell out for this hardcover, Fiona and I guilted/bribed/blackmailed a few of our friends/collaborators/heroes into contributing a piece of original art for our first ever SAGA ART GALLERY!

(And fellow pros, please don't be offended if we didn't bother you this round; we're saving some of our begging for *Saga* Book Three...)

Anyway, in the spirit of our dopey letter column's semi-annual READER SURVEY, I've asked each artist five personal questions, and I hope their thoughtful answers will further inspire you to check out more of their work. There's nobody featured in this gallery who isn't making consistently outstanding comics.

Shit. That's about all I have to say in this needless introduction, but I'm trying to vamp long enough to at least fill up one single page so I can feel like I contributed something to these bonus features. Oh, I know what to do: the same thing I always do in this situation, hide behind one of my more talented, less lazy collaborators.

When I was emailing artists about possibly contributing to this gallery, my dear friend Pia Guerra was the first to write back with:

"Uhh, of course. Any special requests? Otherwise you may end up with a dragon sucking itself off."

When I said that we should be so lucky as to get a self-fellating dragon from the likes of her, Pia responded literally two minutes later with:

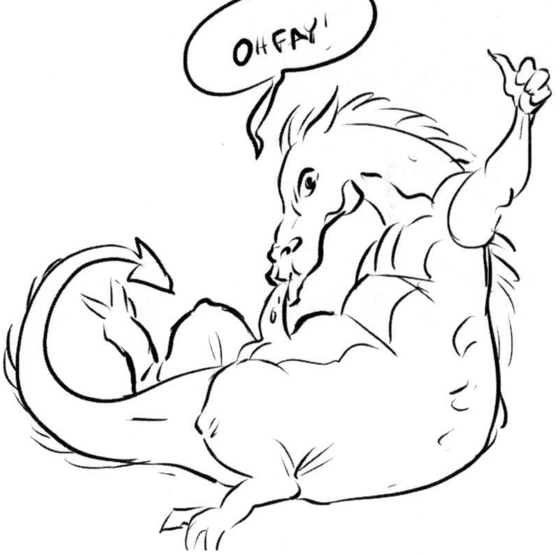
OHFAY!

Aren't artists the greatest?

Fiona and I are honored and enormously grateful for the hard work and passion all of these contributors put into their loving interpretations of our characters, and we hope the artists each enjoy their payment of one (1) complimentary "High As Fuck" Yuma t-shirt (available now at *TheSagaShop.com*), which Hamburger will definitely mail out someday soon.

Hoping this was worth the wait,
BKV

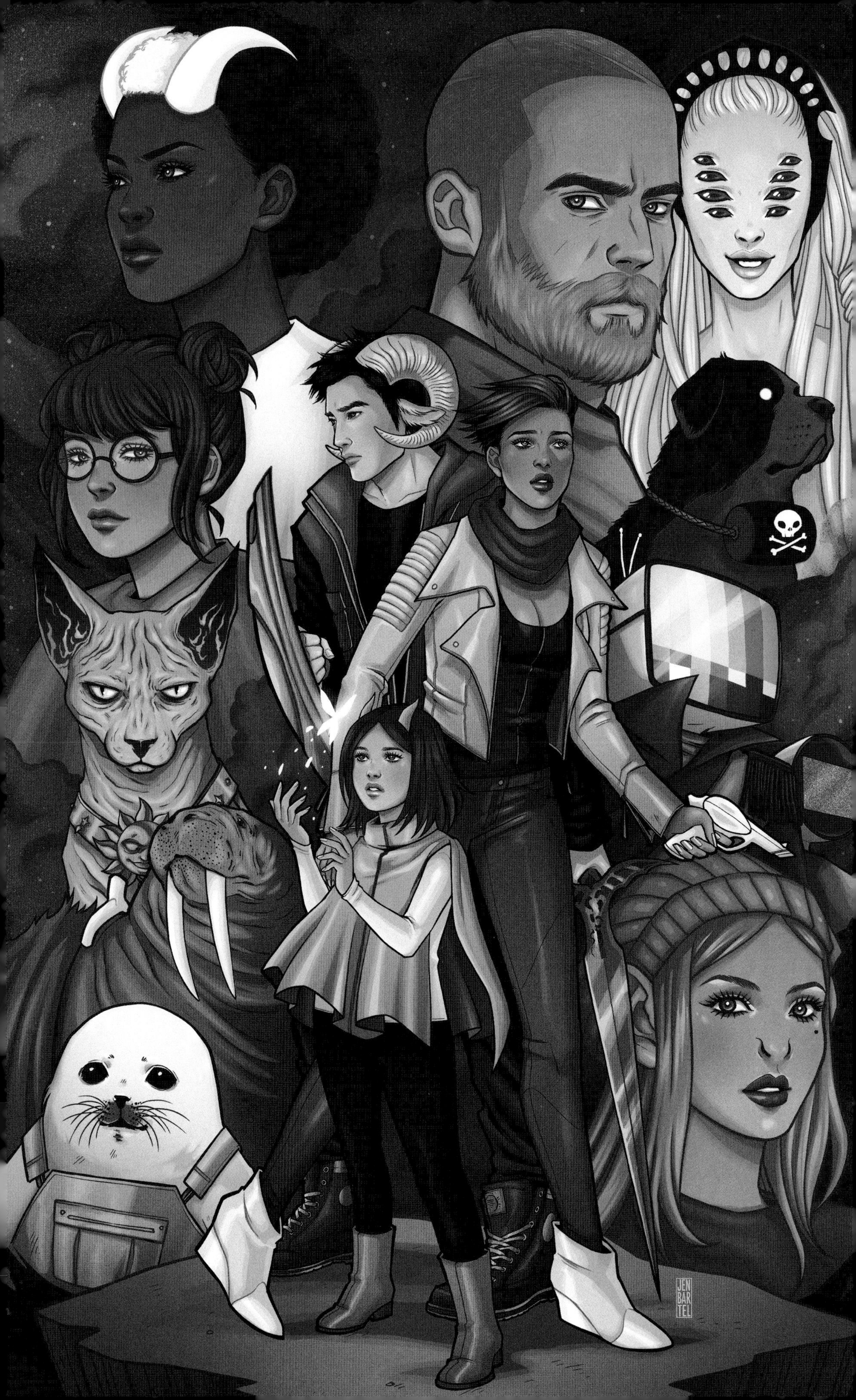
JEN BARTEL

JEN
BARTEL

I've marvelled at Jen's rainbow-coloured, fashion-forward art for quite a while. Turns out the artist is as lovely as her work—when I finally met her in person at Emerald City Comic-con '16, she presented me with an original drawing of Gwendolyn and Lying Cat! Her take on the Saga characters was so charming, I decided to push my luck and ask her to do even more. – FS

Thanks so much for being part of this *Saga* gallery! May we ask, why did you choose the character(s) you did?

I couldn't just pick one character, so I drew my favorites. (As it turns out, I have a LOT of favorites.)

If you were a sentient slice of pizza, what kind of pizza would you be?

I'd be a fruit pizza, which is basically a giant sugar cookie with cream cheese spread and fruit toppings. It is. The. Best. Dessert.

Which work of yours—past, present and/or future—do you think readers of *Saga* might dig?

Up until this point, I've primarily been a cover artist, but I do have a creator-owned project in the works for 2017 that I think *Saga* readers would be interested in! I wish I could divulge more, but everything is currently under wraps so you'll just have to keep an eye out later this year. ;)

What is the definition of a good parent?

A good parent is willing to sacrifice everything and put their child's needs before their own.

Just curious, is there a particular genre you haven't really drawn yet that you'd still love to tackle someday?

Cyberpunk, for sure.

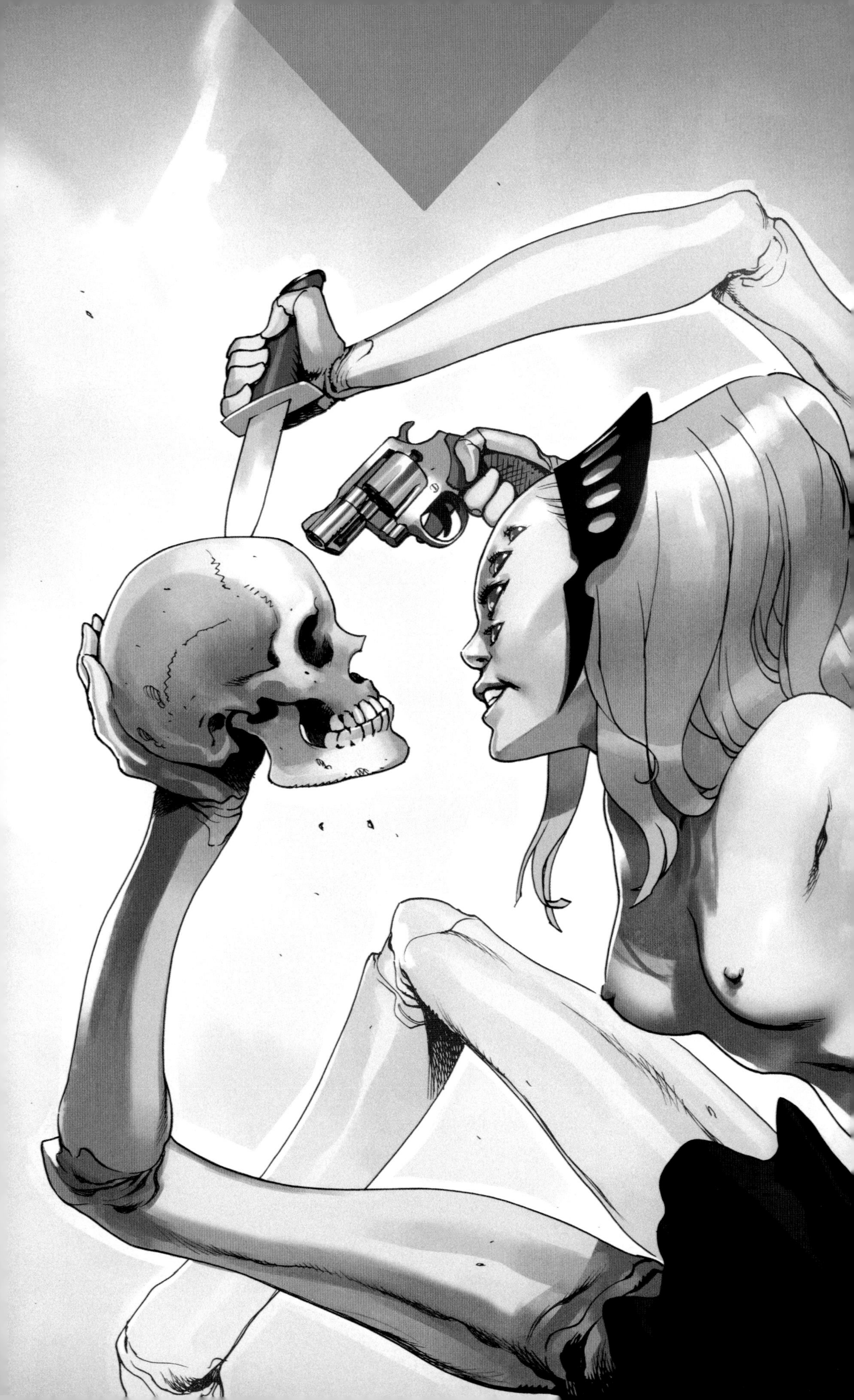

BENGAL

The first work of Bengal's that I saw were his *Spider-Gwen* and *Batgirl* covers. His unique posing and compositions really caught my eye, and he has a talent for rendering light and shadow in a vibrant, painterly way. So glad he was willing to contribute this lovely Stalk! – FS

Thanks so much for being part of this *Saga* gallery! May we ask, why did you choose the character(s) you did?

Thanks for inviting me, it was a pleasure! I chose The Stalk for a couple reasons; first, I tend to render female characters better, in general. I always liked strong women as main characters in comic books, and most of my own books feature strong, powerful women. It's a personal taste! I really liked The Stalk when she appeared, both in terms of design, and in terms of character. I love the concept with her body and arms, it clearly gave me ideas to do an illustration with her, quite easily!

If you were a sentient slice of pizza, what kind of pizza would you be?

I always wanted to be a slice of pizza, thanks for asking. My answer could be different tomorrow morning but right now, I'd probably be a margherita: the original pizza, the most common one.

Which work of yours—past, present and/or future—do you think readers of *Saga* might dig?

That is a tricky question... *Saga* is a one-of-a-kind story, visiting a very diverse, crazy universe, while stories I worked on so far were rather anchored in contemporary, realistic settings.

But I may advise readers to give a try to a creator-owned project I am currently working on, that will be unveiled in a few months. I'm working with a writer, and a publisher, that fans know very well. Wish I could tell you more, but I hope people will like it!

What is the definition of a good parent?

A good parent is someone who does their best, in my humble opinion. Not all parents will deal with their kids the same way, not all parents have the same means to raise their kids, not all kids are the same, not all kids need the same education.

Someone who does what they think is best for their kid, with what they have, is most likely a good parent.

Just curious, is there a particular genre you haven't really drawn yet that you'd still love to tackle someday?

I have been keeping in my drawers for many many years now a project of mine, a very hi-tech futuristic sci-fi story, with a lot of politics involved, and I still have the hope to one day tackle it. I have worked on giant robots once, yes, but this story would be a totally different, new genre in a way I've never worked on before.

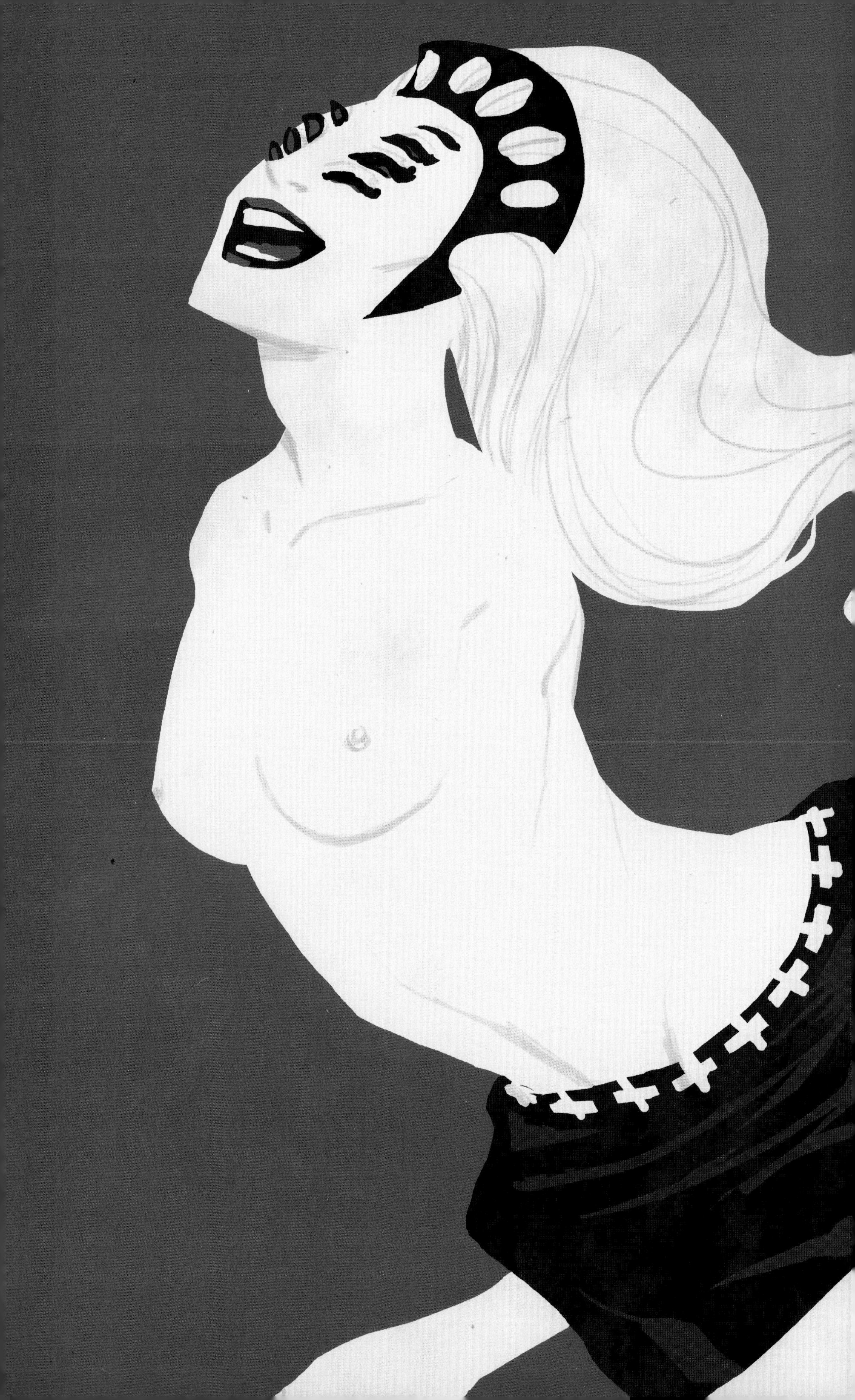

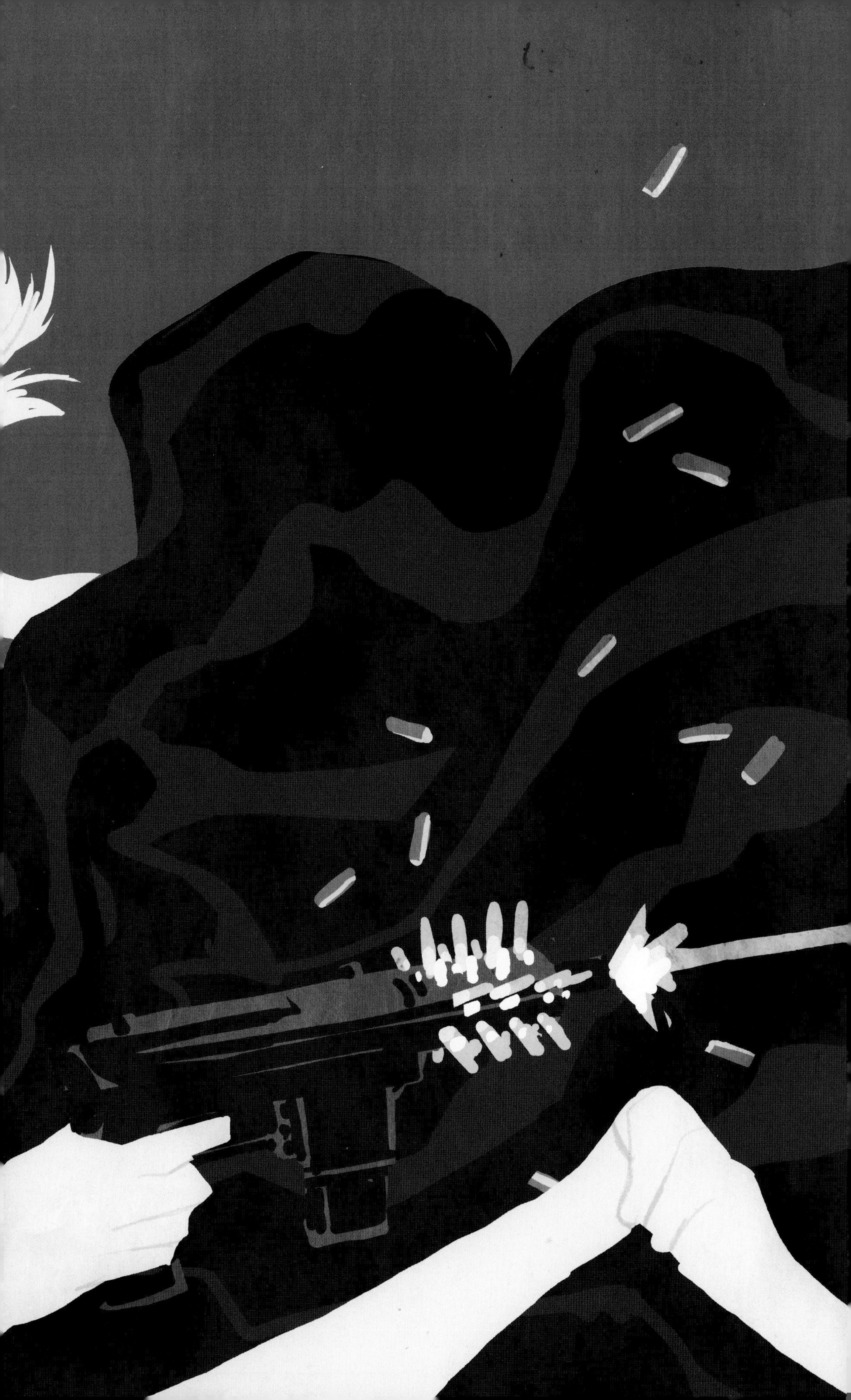

CLIFF
CHIANG

The world-renowned Cliff Chiang and I first worked together on a short *Swamp Thing* comic way back in the 20th Century, and I loved his crystalline storytelling so much that I vowed to collaborate with him again. It only took fifteen years for our stars to realign, but I'm so happy to be working with him on *Paper Girls*, a sci-fi adventure about nostalgia from our pals at Image Comics.

It's very different from *Saga*, but I want all of you to buy it anyway because I am proud of it and I like the color of your money. — BKV

Thanks so much for being part of this *Saga* gallery! May we ask, why did you choose the character(s) you did?

Fiona's design for the Stalk is so brilliantly beautiful and creepy. Why wouldn't you choose to draw the sexy spider assassin?

If you were a sentient slice of pizza, what kind of pizza would you be?

Ellio's frozen pizza.

Which work of yours—past, present and/or future—do you think readers of *Saga* might dig?

Wonder Woman, Paper Girls, and whatever comes next!

What is the definition of a good parent?

Unconditionally loving yet preemptively sneaky.

Just curious, is there a particular genre you haven't really drawn yet that you'd still love to tackle someday?

Fin de siècle magical realism. Or giant robots.

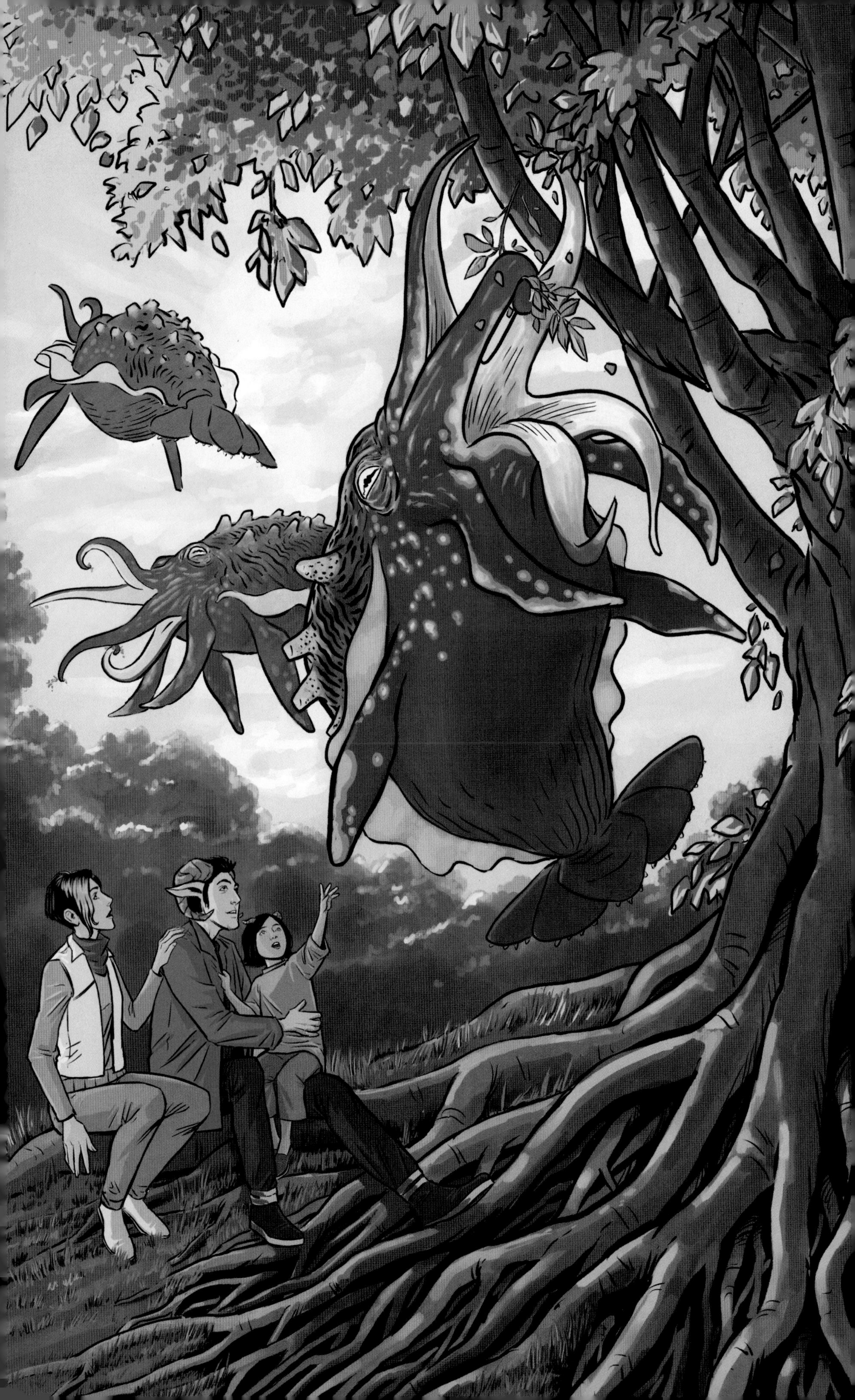

PIA
GUERRA

Pia Guerra is the Eisner Award-winning artist and co-creator of *Y: The Last Man*, and she's also one of the best human beings I've ever met, as evidenced by that dragon doodle.

Man, do I miss seeing her singularly expressive characters on a regular basis, but how cool is it to have the master coloring herself here? – BKV

Thanks so much for being part of this *Saga* gallery! May we ask, why did you choose the character(s) you did?

I did Alana, Marko and Hazel on a picnic. I had a very chaotic childhood growing up, lots of moving around, lots of sketchy business that even to this day I don't really understand, but the thing that happens when you're a kid going through shit is you find strength in the normal stuff like picnics and trips to the beach or going to the comic shop every week. It's the normal moments that keep the bad stuff from overwhelming you, that remind you that it's not all awful so long as you have the ones you love around you, and I would like to think Hazel is finding that strength too, and by doing so, she'll be fine. But then you never know with Brian, do you?

If you were a sentient slice of pizza, what kind of pizza would you be?

Grumpy. I would be a very grumpy slice of pizza as there's not a lot of upward mobility and therefore not much to look forward to being a pizza slice.

Which work of yours—past, present and/or future—do you think readers of *Saga* might dig?

There's this book I worked on a while back called *Y: The Last Man*. You may have heard of it. If not, give it a look, it will rip your heart to shreds.

What is the definition of a good parent?

Being there. That's it. And try not to make promises you can't keep, that shit devours souls.

Just curious, is there a particular genre you haven't really drawn yet that you'd still love to tackle someday?

Sci-fi is definitely on the list... but none of this cutesy talking animal/aliens stuff. That's just weird.

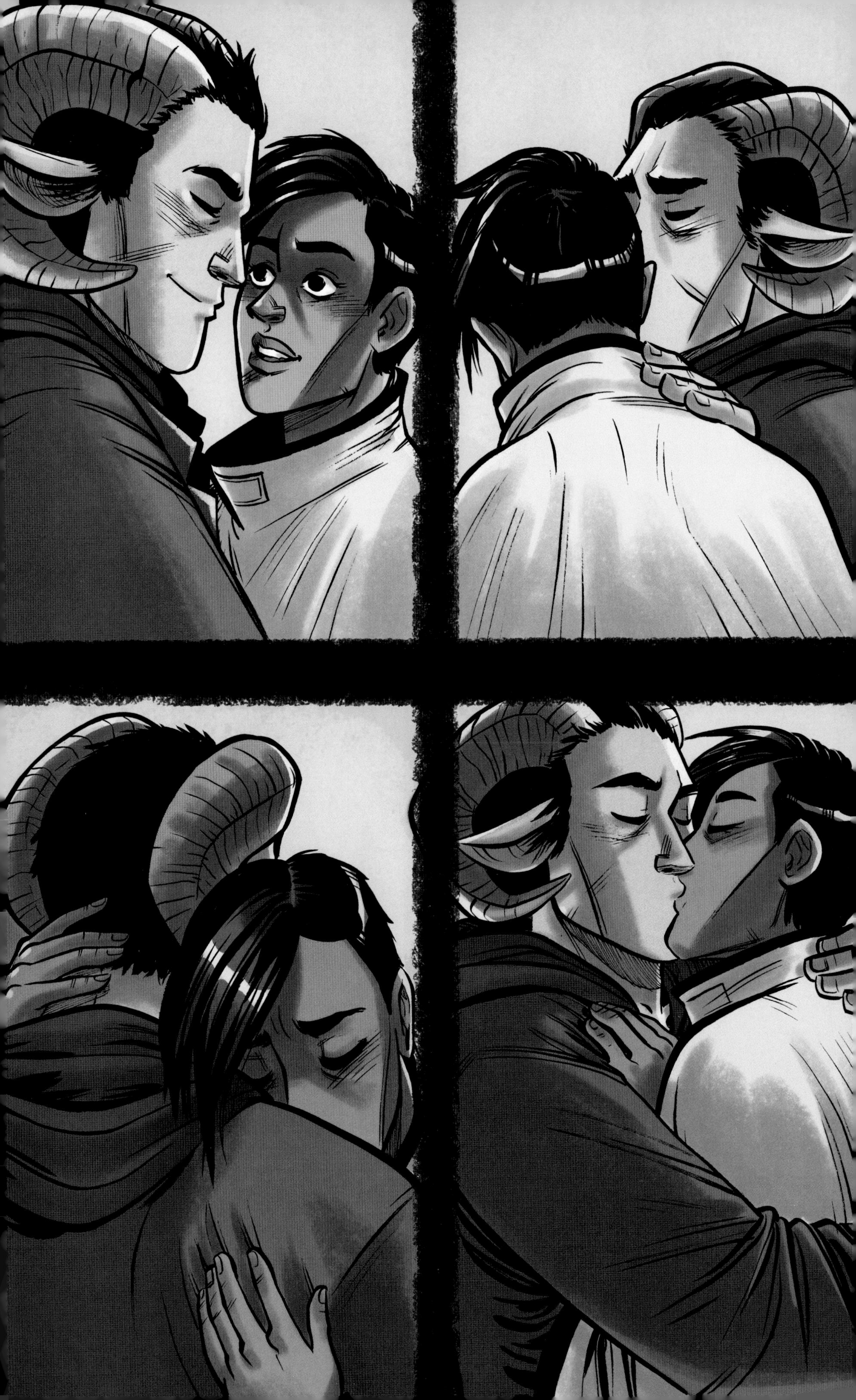

FAITH ERIN HICKS

I met Faith around the same time that *Saga* started. I was visiting the awesome Halifax store Strange Adventures to sign issue #2 or #3, and she kindly dropped by to chat! We've swapped a lot of advice, encouragement, and comic industry gripes since then.

There's a lot I admire and relate to in Faith's work—as evidenced here, she puts a lot of care into acting and characterization. I love the way she brought these two flirts to life! – FS

Thanks so much for being part of this *Saga* gallery! May we ask, why did you choose the character(s) you did?

Alana and Marko's relationship is why I read *Saga*. It's really great to see a complicated but loving adult relationship be the foundation of a comic. I'm rooting for them!

If you were a sentient slice of pizza, what kind of pizza would you be?

I don't eat pizza, my stomach doesn't like it. Can I be a sentient caterpillar sushi roll?

Which work of yours—past, present and/or future—do you think readers of *Saga* might dig?

They might like *The Nameless City*, which is a fantasy action and adventure comic set against a complicated political backdrop, but it's all-ages so the whole family can read it.

What is the definition of a good parent?

Someone who makes time for their children.

Just curious, is there a particular genre you haven't really drawn yet that you'd still love to tackle someday?

I'd love to do a science fiction comic someday, something with spaceships, where characters are exploring the galaxy. Or maybe a story set on a space station. I guess just want to do my own version of *Star Trek*. ;)

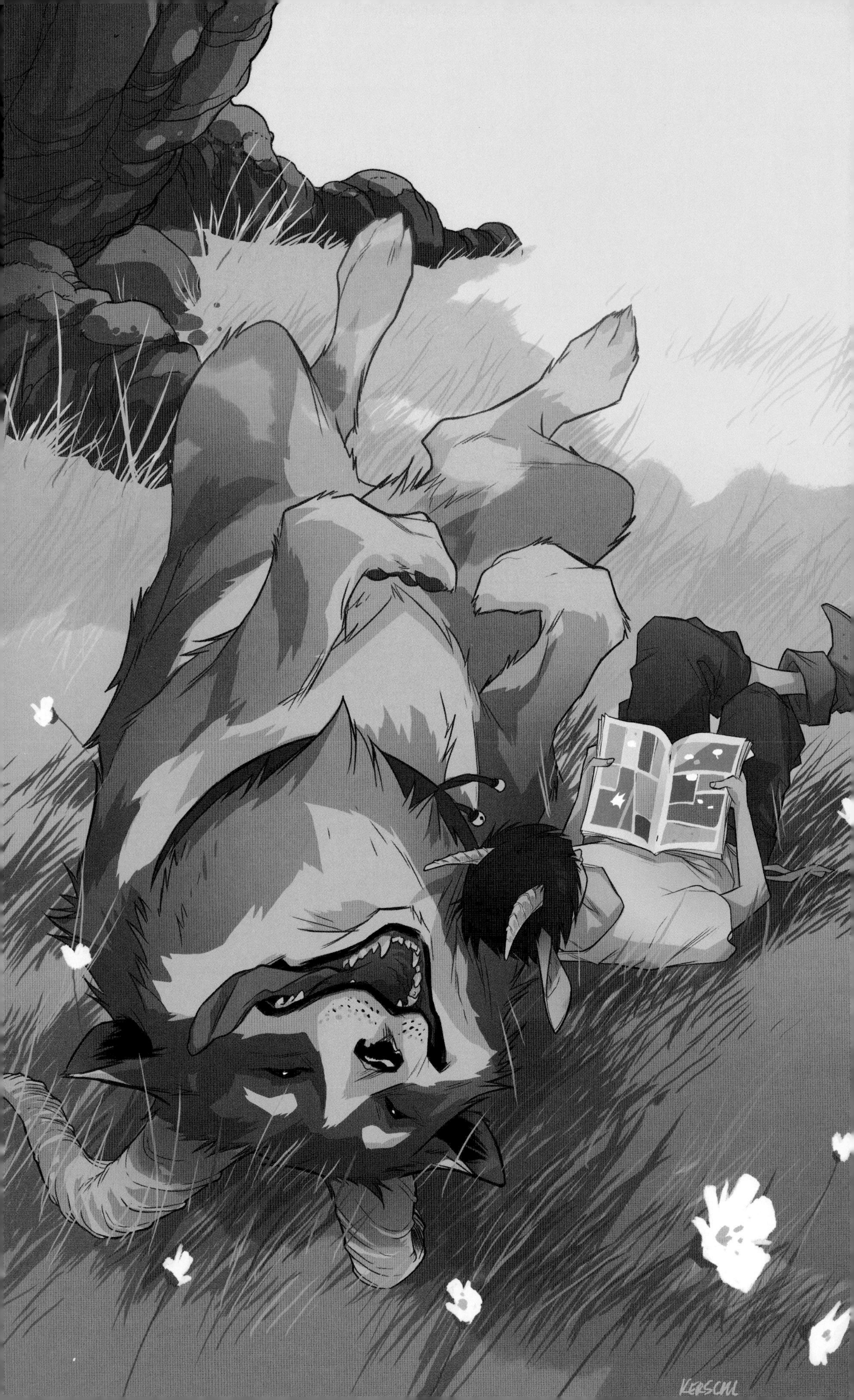
KERSCHL

KARL KERSCHL

I'm so glad we have an abundance of cute creatures for Karl, the master of this stuff, to choose from. Whether he's pencilling or painting, he's able to create entire lush, living fantasy worlds, often with a touch of darkness.

After I drew some *Gotham Academy* covers and burned through Karl's whole run for "research," I couldn't resist seeing what the *Saga* universe might look like in his animation-inspired style. – FS

Thanks so much for being part of this *Saga* gallery! May we ask, why did you choose the character(s) you did?

Any excuse to draw an animal! I wish I had a dog like Rumfer and I thought he'd be fun to draw; Marko was kind of incidental to the piece, actually. :)

If you were a sentient slice of pizza, what kind of pizza would you be?

One with pineapples on it.

Which work of yours—past, present and/or future—do you think readers of *Saga* might dig?

I'm currently working on *Isola*, which features a girl and a tiger who's her queen, which I hope people will like. And I'm also very proud of my webcomic, *The Abominable Charles Christopher*, which you can read for free at *www.abominable.cc*.

What is the definition of a good parent?

For me, I think it's someone who can admit when they are (frequently) wrong and change course to adapt.

Just curious, is there a particular genre you haven't really drawn yet that you'd still love to tackle someday?

Horror. I think there's often an element of horror in my work, but it would be fun to go all the way with it.

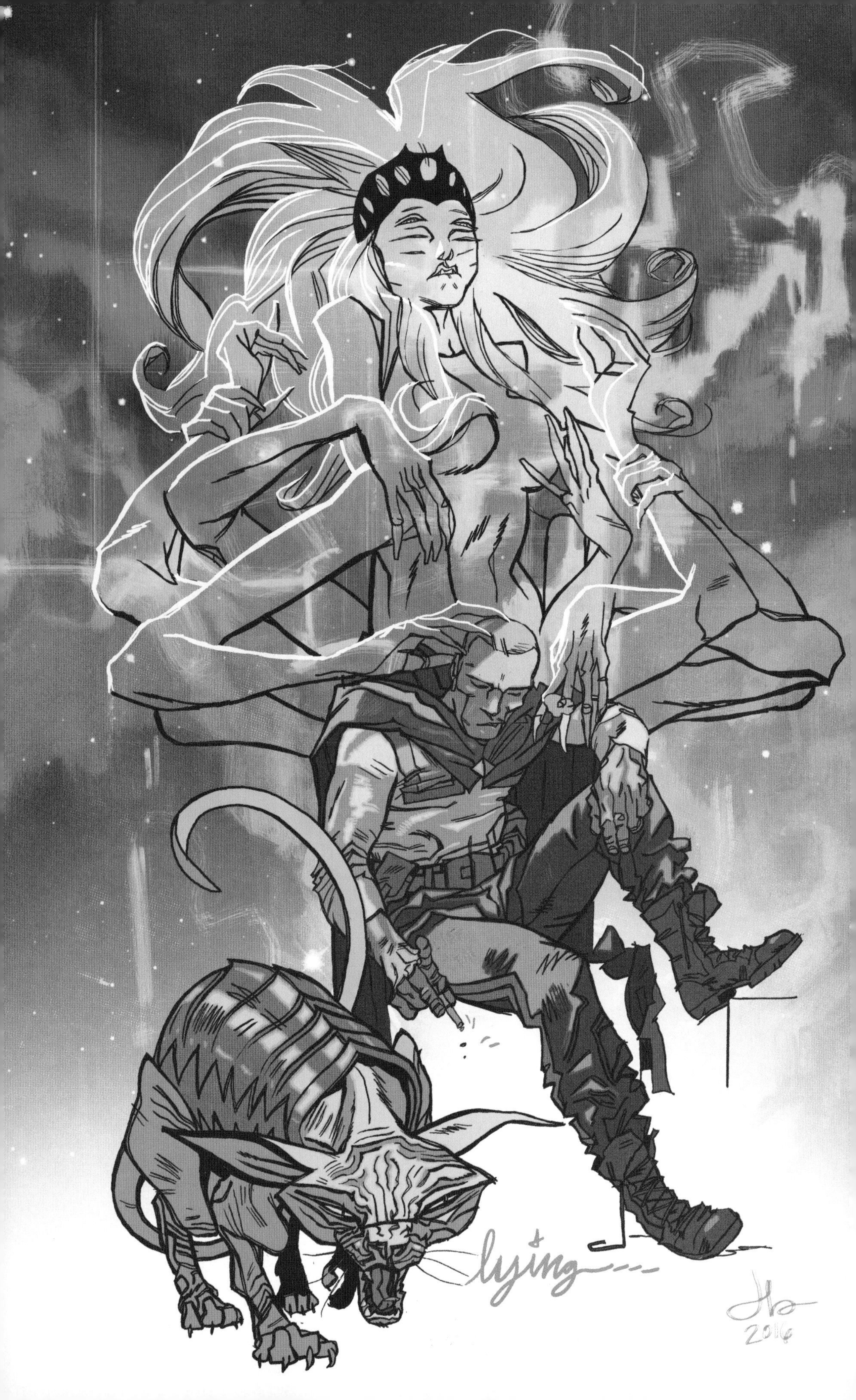
lying
2016

JASON LATOUR

I don't know Jason very well, but I feel like I do because of how much of himself he clearly pours into his work, especially *Southern Bastards*, the exceptional series from Image Comics he co-created with everybody's favorite writer Jason Aaron. Mr. Latour's art is angry, complex and gorgeous, so it was especially cool to see him illustrate our most tragic duo. – BKV

Thanks so much for being part of this *Saga* gallery! May we ask, why did you choose the character(s) you did?

I'm a sucker for a doomed romance. It's probably hubris, but it's scary how much I can identify with feeling like something has tragically slipped through your fingers. It's that sort of sad, angry country song way that The Will pines for The Stalk that really made me love the character.

If you were a sentient slice of pizza, what kind of pizza would you be?

The last slice from a pizza delivery truck that's been abducted by aliens. After all the rest of the pie is devoured, they'd fight a crazed civil war for the honor of eating me, only to eventually worship my rarity after their warp drive is destroyed in the conflict. No more Earth Pizza for those dummies! Eventually they'd rebuild and retool their society so that everything is pizza slice shaped. Even the wheels on cars. All Hail, King Slice.

Which work of yours—past, present and/or future—do you think readers of *Saga* might dig?

Well that's tricky, 'cause *Southern Bastards* is my best work and I think people would find it a lot more like *Saga* than they might expect in terms of pushing conventions and expectations. But *Loose Ends* is another crime fiction series I did, now being published at Image, about a similarly "doomed" romance. Would-be, should-be lovers on the run. But with the backdrop of the American South in early 2000s, and the shadow of the Iraq War. There's some similar themes in terms of trying to escape the machinations of a world you didn't choose to be born into.

What is the definition of a good parent?

I actually have a pair of amazing parents myself. Married 44 years and still cuddling on the couch. I'm the only artist in the family, so we often have very, very different views of the world, but its never become a real wedge between us. They demanded a lot of us, but they were always supportive and selfless and taught us how to love and respect ourselves. I think that's really all you can ask of a parent, is to give as much love as they can even when they don't understand. I think kids who are loved tend to find their way... eventually.

Just curious, is there a particular genre you haven't really drawn yet that you'd still love to tackle someday?

I grew up on *Teen Wolf* and *The Incredible Hulk* so I'm into people being cursed. So I guess "werewolves" count as a genre? The catch is, I think werewolves are really awesome and also really damn stupid. So the name of my hypothetical werewolf book is *Werewolves Are Stupid*.

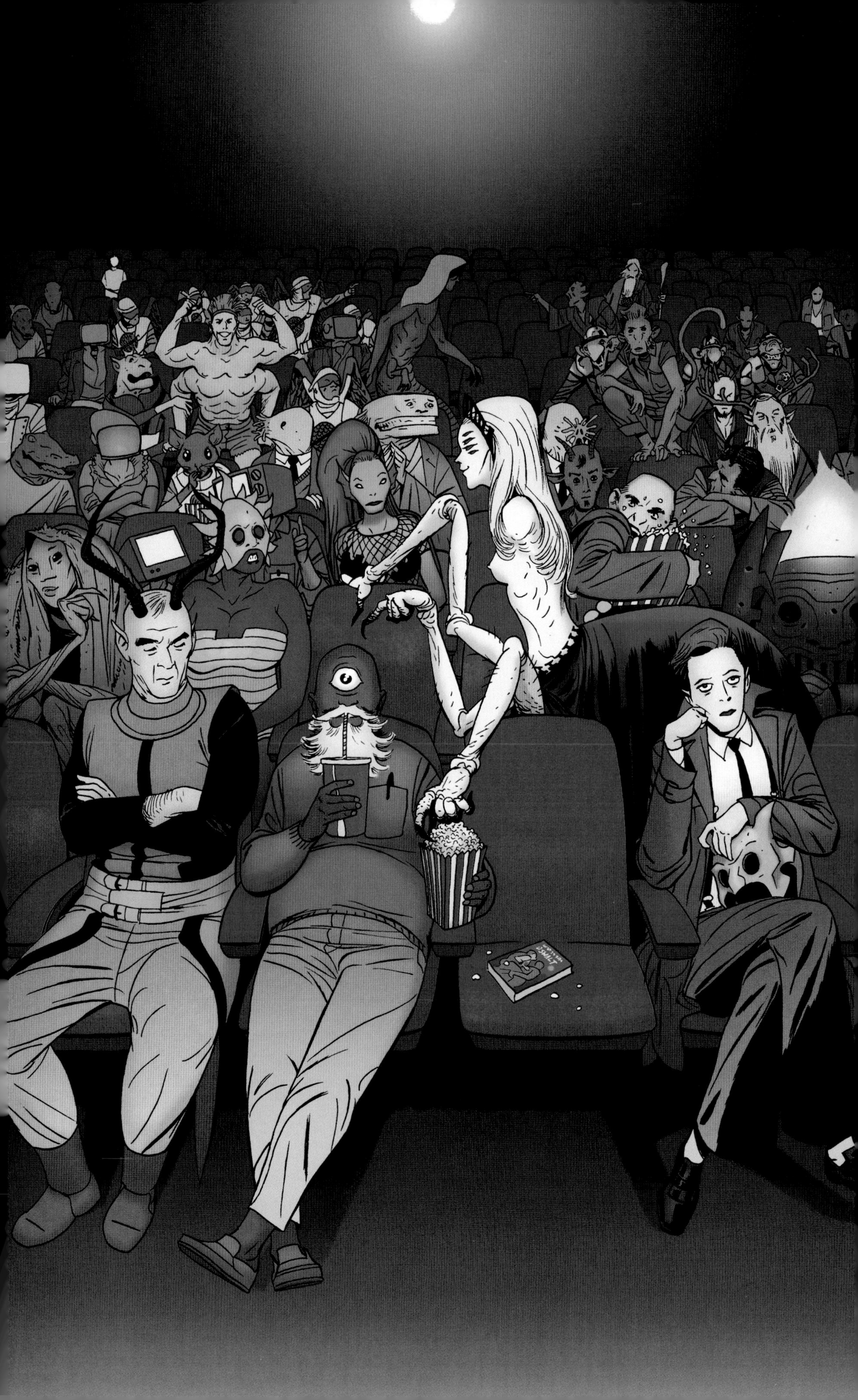

MARCOS MARTIN

Marcos Martin is a no-good bastard, but I once helped him bury the body of a meddlesome editor in the dense forests of Monte Perdido, so he owed me this pinup. Marcos explained to me that its absurdly complete lineup of Saga's death toll was intended "as a tribute to both Fiona's genius and to your ruthlessness and complete lack of compassion."

I can't stand the guy, but goddamn I love his precisely detailed artwork, most recently in The Alien, our canonical The Walking Dead one-shot, which you can read exclusively over at the "pay what you want" digital comics site that mad genius Marcos created: PanelSyndicate.com – BKV

Thanks so much for being part of this Saga gallery! May we ask, why did you choose the character(s) you did?

Because none of those beautifully designed characters deserved the cruel fate that heartless Lex Luthor of a writer schemed. Also, I couldn't make up my mind.

If you were a sentient slice of pizza, what kind of pizza would you be?

The kind that leaves a sad, bitter taste in your mouth. So pineapple, I guess.

Which work of yours—past, present and/or future—do you think readers of Saga might dig?

Although I'm very proud of all the work I did at Marvel and DC, I can only point towards my latest collaborations at Panel Syndicate with Saga's weak link, BKV. So The Private Eye and Barrier (both series currently available at PanelSyndicate.com for whatever price you think is fair!).

What is the definition of a good parent?

The Opposite of Me seems to be the general consensus.

Just curious, is there a particular genre you haven't really drawn yet that you'd still love to tackle someday?

Hmmm... I think I'd enjoy some sort of sword and sorcery, Conan-like type of story if only because it's so out of my comfort zone. Get on it, Vaughan!

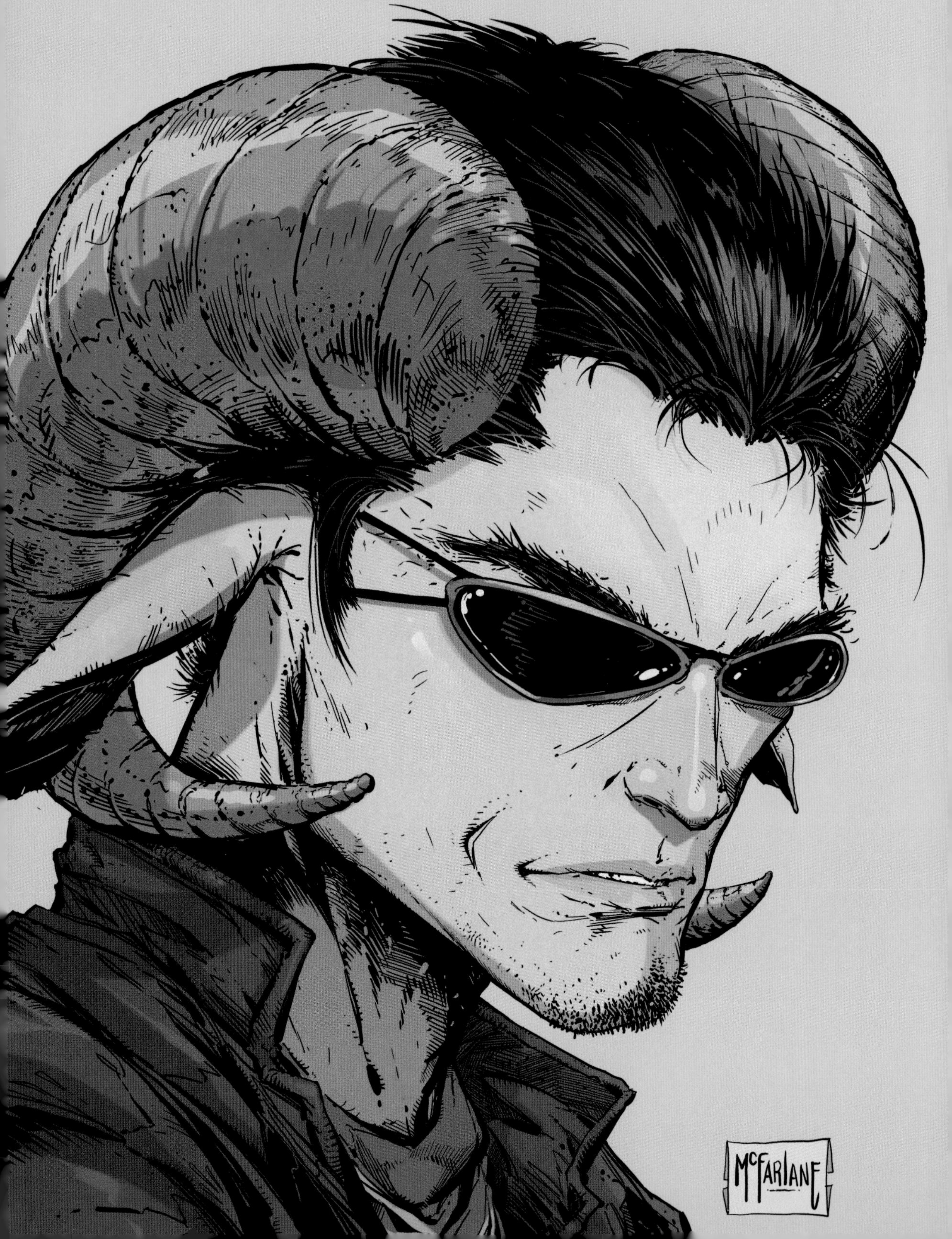
McFARLANE

TODD McFARLANE

The incomparable Todd McFarlane has been one of my all-time favorite comics artists ever since his run on Marvel's *Incredible Hulk*. When I was 12 years old, I'd obsessively trace Todd's issues of *Amazing Spider-Man* to try to figure out why his drawings made me feel so much more than other comics. But Todd's biggest influence on me came when he helped found Image Comics, and paved the way for a new generation of comic creators to truly own and control their creations.

It's fair to say there'd probably be no *Saga* without Todd, so special thanks to our champion coordinator Eric Stephenson for somehow tricking his friend into contributing this fantastic piece (lovingly colored by Fiona!). – BKV

Thanks so much for being part of this *Saga* gallery! May we ask, why did you choose the character(s) you did?

Because he's one of the most popular characters.

If you were a sentient slice of pizza, what kind of pizza would you be?

I'd be vegetable pizza with extra artichokes.

Which work of yours—past, present and/or future—do you think readers of *Saga* might dig?

My future work in three years! 2020 is gonna rock!

What is the definition of a good parent?

Someone whose kid is a good neighbor and a decent human being regardless of their status, job or finances.

Just curious, is there a particular genre you haven't really drawn yet that you'd still love to tackle someday?

More comedy; fun stuff instead of the serious superhero stuff I've done and am still doing.

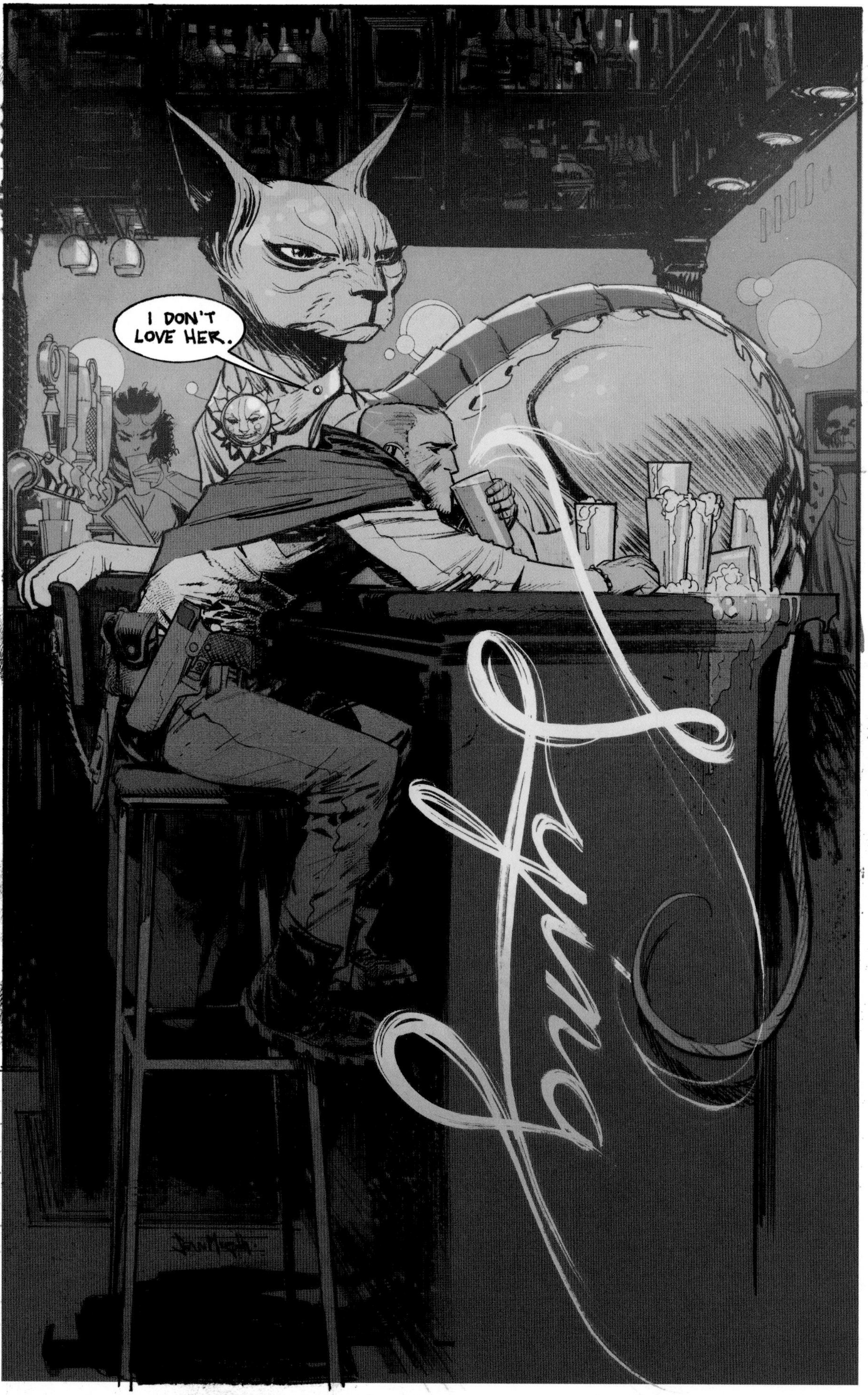
I DON'T LOVE HER.

SEAN GORDON MURPHY

Sean had to do this pin-up for me because I drew a variant cover for *Chrononauts*, his Image miniseries with Mark Millar. And let me tell you, it feels good to be able to call in a favour from one of the most admired artists in the industry. It's rare to see someone so technically adept that they make the most intricate scenes look effortless, but Sean pulls it off it every time, whether he's drawing the Batcave or The Will's space pub here.

Fairly regularly one of us will say, "we should collaborate on a piece!" and since I've coloured this one, now we finally have! – FS

Thanks so much for being part of this *Saga* gallery! May we ask, why did you choose the character(s) you did?

I'm not great at drawing women, so I went with The Will because I'm better at drawing beefcakes. Especially tortured ones.

If you were a sentient slice of pizza, what kind of pizza would you be?

A diarrhea pizza. So no one would eat me.

Which work of yours—past, present and/or future—do you think readers of *Saga* might dig?

Probably *The Wake*. It has strong female characters and a big fantasy element.

What is the definition of a good parent?

One that will drive you to the comic shop. Also, feed you.

Just curious, is there a particular genre you haven't really drawn yet that you'd still love to tackle someday?

Maybe something erotic. That way I could write off my porn collection.

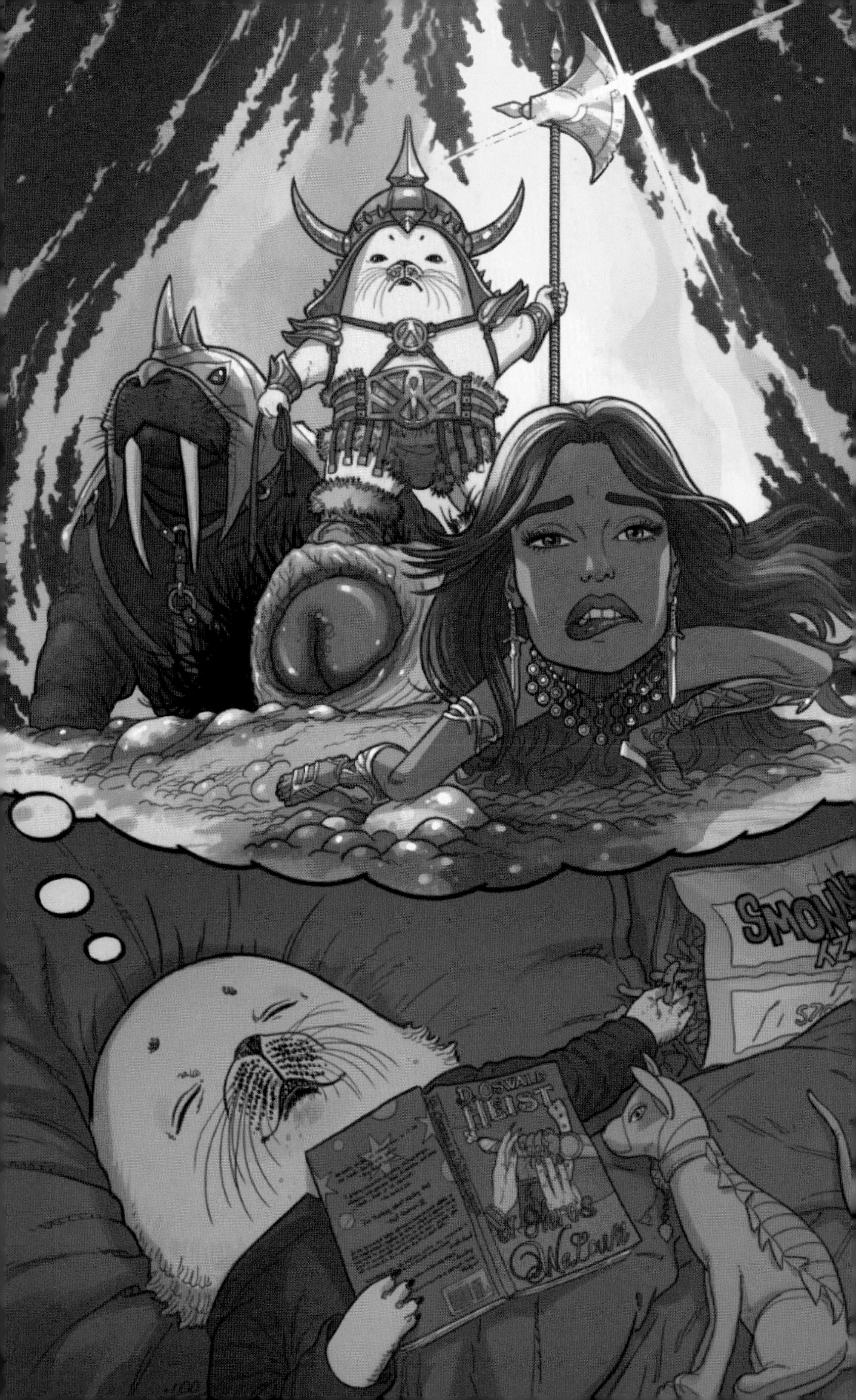
D. OSWALD
HEIST

STEVE
SKROCE

Yeah yeah, he's the superstar storyboard artist of nearly every cool movie from *The Matrix* on, but Steve Skroce's veins run black with inky comic-book ink.

Do comic artists even use ink anymore? I don't know, but along with being the nicest, funniest creator in the history of this medium, Steve is somehow both an amazing visual artist AND writer, as you'll see in his upcoming Image series *Maestros*. I've only read the first issue, but I'm already 100% confident that it will be every *Saga* reader's favorite new series. For now, please enjoy the absurd amount of detail in Steve's contribution, which Fiona generously offered to color after Steve and his wife gave birth to their perfect kid. Congrats, fam! – BKV

Thanks so much for being part of this *Saga* gallery! May we ask, why did you choose the character(s) you did?

I love all the *Saga* characters but Ghüs is special. He's fierce, pure of heart and so goddamn cute it makes you want to pull your hair out! I wanted an image that allowed me to pull in *Saga* elements from all over the place but didn't necessarily fit together. *Saga* is emotional, philosophical, hilarious and gross and I tried to capture that in my drawing.

If you were a sentient slice of pizza, what kind of pizza would you be?

I always have trouble with deep, existential questions but I like to think I'd be a pizza slice that was kind and lactose tolerant, a slice that was active in its community and maybe left behind a topping combo that made Pizza World a better place in some small way. I'd definitely have cheese in the crust though, I've got cholesterol issues.

Which work of yours—past, present and/or future—do you think readers of *Saga* might dig?

Doc Frankenstein was a book that I started in 2005 that may finally see print this year, and *We Stand On Guard* with BKV was a great time, but I'm digging my current project. It's called *Maestros*. The most powerful wizard king in existence is murdered and his kingdom goes to his banished human son from Earth, a millennial from the USA who thinks he's got it all figured out. Coming from Image in 2017!

What is the definition of a good parent?

My wife and I just had our first child so I had to take a minute and figure this out for myself just last week. I think providing a stable and nurturing home, being an active, positive presence and setting limits and consequences for their behavior is key. Also, get your kids into Esperanto immersion early, it's the language of the future.

Just curious, is there a particular genre you haven't really drawn yet that you'd still love to tackle someday?

I'd love to do a cool horror story one day.

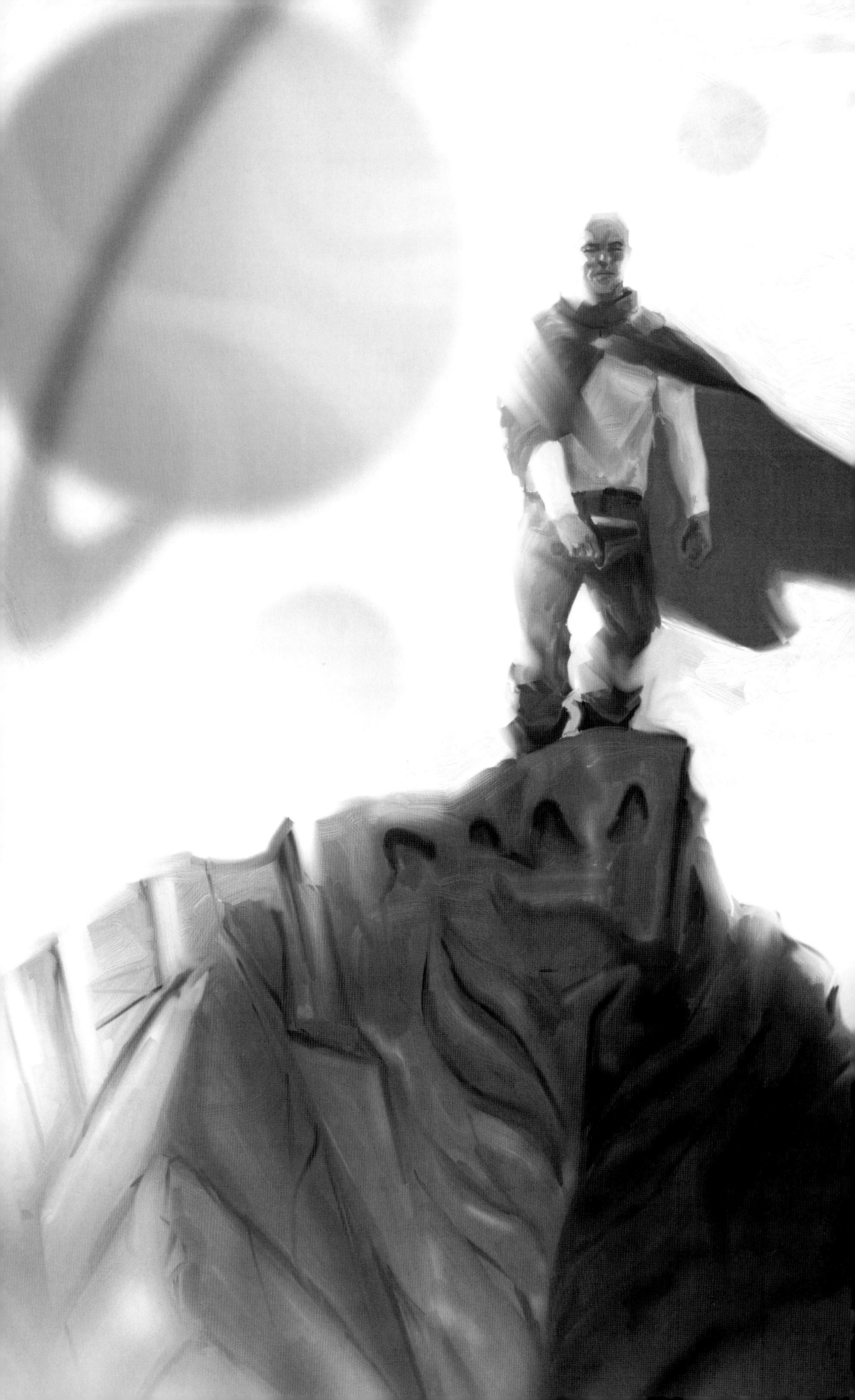

CHIP ZDARSKY

I had to draw a filthy XXX variant cover for *Sex Criminals* in exchange for this piece by Zdarsky, compromising all my morals and values, but it was worth it. Their book is now slightly more tacky, whereas ours is graced by a dignified, elegantly rendered portrait of The Will. – FS

Thanks so much for being part of this *Saga* gallery! May we ask, why did you choose the character(s) you did?

I LOVE The Will's design. I'd say he's a modern Han Solo, but I think he's better than Han Solo. Like, could Han Solo get away with a cape? No. Could Han Solo gain a bunch of weight and still be sexy? Maybe.

If you were a sentient slice of pizza, what kind of pizza would you be?

I would probably be HAWAIIAN pizza. Because it was conceived in Canada, weirdly enough, and I hate pineapple on pizza. Fruit on pizza is an abomination. Also, I hate myself, if that wasn't clear.

Which work of yours—past, present and/or future—do you think readers of *Saga* might dig?

Sex Criminals with Mr. Matt Fraction. It's like *Saga* but on Earth and we tend to keep people alive because we aren't MONSTERS.

What is the definition of a good parent?

I just cried for five minutes trying to think of the answer, so probably not me.

Just curious, is there a particular genre you haven't really drawn yet that you'd still love to tackle someday?

YOU CAN'T FENCE ME IN WITH GENRES, MAN.

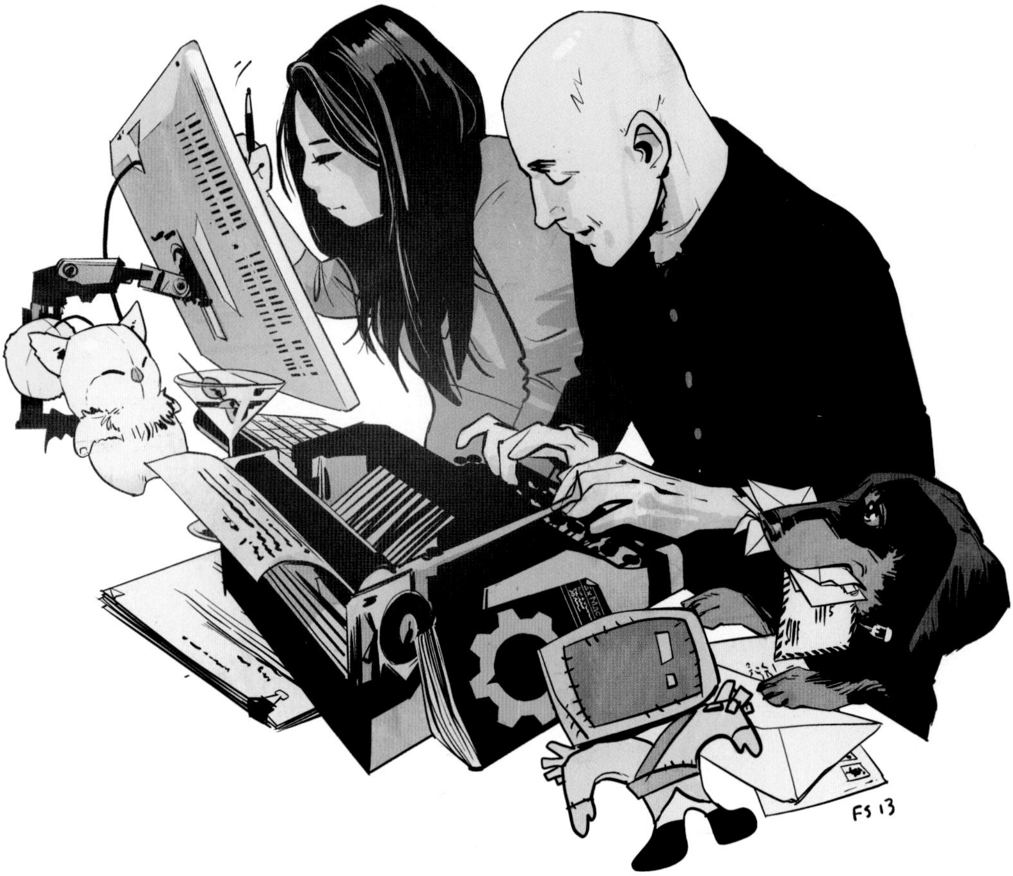
FS 13

BRIAN K. VAUGHAN Along with *Saga*, BKV is the writer and co-creator of *Paper Girls, Y: The Last Man, Runaways, Ex Machina, Pride of Baghdad, We Stand On Guard, The Private Eye*, and most recently *Barrier*, a digital comic about immigration at *PanelSyndicate.com*. His work has been recognized at the Eisner, Harvey, Hugo, Shuster, Eagle, and British Fantasy Awards. Brian sometimes works in film and television in Los Angeles, where he lives with his family and their dogs Hamburger and Milkshake.

FIONA STAPLES *Saga* artist Fiona Staples has been drawing and colouring comics for ten years and has contributed to titles such as *North 40, Mystery Society*, and *Archie*. Her work has been recognized with multiple Eisner and Harvey awards. Fiona lives in Calgary, Alberta and has spent 187 hours playing *The Witcher 3*.

FONOGRAFIKS The banner name for the comics work of British designer Steven Finch, 'Fonografiks' has contributed lettering and graphic design to a number of other Image Comics titles, most notably the Eisner-nominated *Nowhere Men* and the multi-award winning anthology series *Popgun*. In addition to his work on *Saga*, he currently also letters and designs the Image series *Injection, They're Not Like Us*, and *Redlands*.

ERIC STEPHENSON As Publisher for Image Comics, Eric has helped foster the creator-owned projects of numerous bestselling writers and artists, including Robert Kirkman, Ed Brubaker, Matt Fraction, Jonathan Hickman, Nick Dragotta, Kieron Gillen, Jamie McKelvie, Kelly Sue DeConnick, Rick Remender, and Brandon Graham, as well as a well-known pair of award magnets whose names rhyme with Frian and Biona. He is also the Eisner-nominated writer and co-creator of *Nowhere Men* and *They're Not Like Us*. Eric lives, loves, and works in Portland, OR.